MW01246065

Historical Adventures: 3

Historical Adventures: 3

Montezuma's Daughter
★
The Lady of Blossholme

H. Rider Haggard

LEONAUR

Historical Adventures: 3
Montezuma's Daughter & The Lady of Blossholme
by H. Rider Haggard

Leonaur is an imprint of Oakpast Ltd

Material original to this edition and
presentation of text in this form
copyright © 2009 Oakpast Ltd

ISBN: 978-1-84677-998-5 (hardcover)
ISBN: 978-1-84677-997-8 (softcover)

http://www.leonaur.com

Publisher's Notes

The views expressed in this book are not necessarily
those of the publisher.

Contents

Montezuma's
Daughter

Dedication

My dear Jebb,

Strange as were the adventures and escapes of Thomas Wingfield, once of this parish, whereof these pages tell, your own can almost equal them in these latter days, and, since a fellow feeling makes us kind, you at least they may move to a sigh of sympathy. Among many a distant land you know that in which he loved and fought, following vengeance and his fate, and by your side I saw its relics and its peoples, its volcanos and its valleys. You know even where lies the treasure which, three centuries and more ago, he helped to bury, the countless treasure that an evil fortune held us back from seeking. Now the Indians have taken back their secret, and though many may search, none will lift the graven stone that seals it, nor shall the light of day shine again upon the golden head of Montezuma. So be it! The wealth which Cortes wept over, and his Spaniards sinned and died for, is for ever hidden yonder by the shores of the bitter lake whose waters gave up to you that ancient horror, the veritable and sleepless god of Sacrifice, of whom I would not rob you— and, for my part, I do not regret the loss.

What cannot be lost, what to me seem of more worth than the dead hero Guatemoc's gems and jars of gold, are the memories of true friendship shown to us far away beneath the shadow of the Slumbering Woman,[1] and it is in gratitude for these that I ask permission to set your name within a book which were it not for you would never have been written.

I am, my dear Jebb,
Always sincerely yours,
H. Rider Haggard
Ditchingham
Norfolk
October 5, 1892
To J. Gladwyn Jebb, Esq.

---

1. The volcano Izticcihuatl in Mexico.

Note

Worn out prematurely by a life of hardship and extraordinary adventure, Mr. Jebb passed away on March 18, 1893, taking with him the respect and affection of all who had the honour of his friendship. The author has learned with pleasure that the reading of this tale in proof and the fact of its dedication to himself afforded him some amusement and satisfaction in the intervals of his sufferings.

H. R. H.
March 22, 1893

Author's Note

The more unpronounceable of the Aztec names are shortened in many instances out of consideration for the patience of the reader; thus 'Popocatapetl' becomes 'Popo,' 'Huitzelcoatl' becomes 'Huitzel,' &c. The prayer in Chapter 26. is freely rendered from Jourdanet's French translation of Fray Bernardino de Sahagun's *History of New Spain*, written shortly after the conquest of Mexico (Book VI, chap. v.), to which monumental work and to Prescott's admirable history the author of this romance is much indebted. The portents described as heralding the fall of the Aztec Empire, and many of the incidents and events written of in this story, such as the annual personation of the god Tezcatlipoca by a captive distinguished for his personal beauty, and destined to sacrifice, are in the main historical. The noble speech of the Emperor Guatemoc to the Prince of Tacuba uttered while they both were suffering beneath the hands of the Spaniards is also authentic.

CHAPTER 1

Why Thomas Wingfield
Tells His Tale

Now glory be to God who has given us the victory! It is true, the strength of Spain is shattered, her ships are sunk or fled, the sea has swallowed her soldiers and her sailors by hundreds and by thousands, and England breathes again. They came to conquer, to bring us to the torture and the stake—to do to us free Englishmen as Cortes did by the Indians of Anahuac. Our manhood to the slave bench, our daughters to dishonour, our souls to the loving-kindness of the priest, our wealth to the Emperor and the Pope! God has answered them with his winds, Drake has answered them with his guns. They are gone, and with them the glory of Spain.

I, Thomas Wingfield, heard the news to-day on this very Thursday in the Bungay market-place, whither I went to gossip and to sell the apples which these dreadful gales have left me, as they hang upon my trees.

Before there had been rumours of this and of that, but here in Bungay was a man named Young, of the Youngs of Yarmouth, who had served in one of the Yarmouth ships in the fight at Gravelines, aye and sailed north after the Spaniards till they were lost in the Scottish seas.

Little things lead to great, men say, but here great things lead to little, for because of these tidings it comes about that I, Thomas Wingfield, of the Lodge and the parish of Ditchingham in the county of Norfolk, being now of a great age and having only a short time to live, turn to pen and ink. Ten years ago, namely, in the year 1578, it pleased her Majesty, our gracious Queen Elizabeth, who at that date visited this county, that I should be brought before her at Norwich. There and then, saying that the fame of it had reached her, she commanded me to give her some particulars of the story of my life, or rather of those twenty years, more or less, which I spent among the Indians at that time when Cortes conquered their country of Anahuac, which is now known as Mexico. But almost before I could begin my tale, it was time for her to start for Cossey to hunt the deer, and she said it was her wish that I should write the story down that she might read it, and moreover that if it were but half as wonderful as it promised to be, I should end my days as Sir Thomas Wingfield. To this I answered her Majesty that pen and ink were tools I had no skill in, yet I would bear her command in mind. Then I made bold to give her a great emerald that once had hung upon the breast of Montezuma's daughter, and of many a princess before her, and at the sight of it her eyes glistened brightly as the gem, for this Queen of ours loves such costly playthings. Indeed, had I so desired, I think that I might then and there have struck a bargain, and set the stone against a title; but I, who for many years had been the prince of a great tribe, had no wish to be a knight. So I kissed the royal hand, and so tightly did it grip the gem within that the knuckle joints shone white, and I went my ways, coming back home to this my house by the Waveney on that same day.

Now the Queen's wish that I should set down the story of my life remained in my mind, and for long I have desired to do it before life and story end together. The labour, indeed, is great to one unused to such tasks; but why should I fear labour who am so near to the holiday of death? I have seen things that no other Englishman has seen, which are worthy to be recorded; my life has been most strange, many a time it has pleased God to preserve it when all seemed lost, and this perchance He has done that the lesson of it might become known to others. For there is a lesson in it and in the things that I have seen, and it is that no wrong can ever bring about a right, that wrong will breed wrong at last, and be it in man or people, will fall upon the brain that thought it and the hand that wrought it.

Look now at the fate of Cortes—that great man whom I have known clothed with power like a god. Nearly forty years ago, so I have heard, he died poor and disgraced in Spain; he, the conqueror—yes, and I have learned also that his son Don Martin has been put to the torture in that city which the father won with so great cruelties for Spain. Malinche, she whom the Spaniards named Marina, the chief and best beloved of all the women of this same Cortes, foretold it to him in her anguish when after all that had been, after she had so many times preserved him and his soldiers to look upon the sun, at the last he deserted her, giving her in marriage to Don Juan Xaramillo. Look again at the fate of Marina herself. Because she loved this man Cortes, or Malinche, as the Indians named him after her, she brought evil on her native land; for without her aid Tenoctitlan, or Mexico, as they call it now, had never bowed beneath the yoke of Spain—yes, she forgot her honour in her passion. And what was her reward, what right came to her of her wrongdoing? This was her reward at last: to be given away in marriage to another and a lesser man when her beauty waned, as a worn-out beast is sold to a poorer master.

Consider also the fate of those great peoples of the land of Anahuac. They did evil that good might come. They sacrificed the lives of thousands to their false gods, that their wealth might increase, and peace and prosperity be theirs throughout the generations. And now the true God has answered them. For wealth He has given them desolation, for peace the sword of the Spaniard, for prosperity the rack and the torment and the day of slavery. For this it was that they did sacrifice, offering their own children on the altars of Huitzel and of Tezcat.

And the Spaniards themselves, who in the name of mercy have wrought cruelties greater than any that were done by the benighted Aztecs, who in the name of Christ daily violate His law to the uttermost extreme, say shall they prosper, shall their evil-doing bring them welfare? I am old and cannot live to see the question answered, though even now it is in the way of answering. Yet I know that their wickedness shall fall upon their own heads, and I seem to see them, the proudest of the peoples of the earth, bereft of fame and wealth and honour, a starveling remnant happy in nothing save their past. What Drake began at Gravelines God will finish in many another place and time, till at last Spain is of no more account and lies as low as the empire of Montezuma lies to-day.

Thus it is in these great instances of which all the world may know, and thus it is even in the life of so humble a man as I, Thomas Wingfield. Heaven indeed has been merciful to me, giving me time to repent my sins; yet my sins have been visited on my head, on me who took His prerogative of vengeance from the hand of the Most High. It is just, and because it is so I wish to set out the matter of my life's history that others may learn from it. For many years this has been in my mind, as I have said, though to speak truth it was her Majesty the Queen who first set the seed. But only on this day, when I have heard for certain of the fate of the Armada, does it begin to grow, and who can say if ever it will come to flower? For this tidings has stirred me strangely, bringing back my youth and the deeds of love and war and wild adventure which I have been mingled in, fighting for my own hand and for Guatemoc and the people of the Otomie against these same Spaniards, as they have not been brought back for many years. Indeed, it seems to me, and this is no rare thing with the aged, as though there in the far past my true life lay, and all the rest were nothing but a dream.

From the window of the room wherein I write I can see the peaceful valley of the Waveney. Beyond its stream are the common lands golden with gorse, the ruined castle, and the red roofs of Bungay town gathered about the tower of St. Mary's Church. Yonder far away are the king's forests of Stowe and the fields of Flixton Abbey; to the right the steep bank is green with the Earsham oaks, to the left the fast marsh lands spotted with cattle stretch on to Beccles and Lowestoft, while behind me my gardens and orchards rise in terraces up the turfy hill that in old days was known as the Earl's Vineyard. All these are about me, and yet in this hour they are as though they were not. For the valley of the Waveney I see the vale of Tenoctitlan, for the slopes of Stowe the snowy shapes of the volcanoes Popo and Iztac, for the spire of Earsham and the towers of Ditchingham, of Bungay, and of Beccles, the soaring pyramids of sacrifice gleaming with the sacred fires, and for the cattle in the meadows the horsemen of Cortes sweeping to war.

It comes back to me; that was life, the rest is but a dream. Once more I feel young, and, should I be spared so long, I will set down the story of my youth before I am laid in yonder churchyard and lost in the world of dreams. Long ago I had begun it, but it was only on last Christmas Day that my dear wife died, and while she lived I knew that this task was better left undone. Indeed, to be frank, it was thus with my wife: She loved me, I believe, as few men have the fortune to be loved, and there is much in my past that jarred upon this love of hers, moving her to a jealousy of the dead that was not the less deep because it was so gentle and so closely coupled with forgiveness. For she had a secret sorrow that ate her heart away, although she never spoke of it. But one child was born to us, and this child died in infancy, nor for all her prayers did it please God to give her another, and indeed remembering the words of Otomie I did not expect that it would be so. Now she knew well that yonder across the seas I had children whom I loved by another wife, and though they were long dead, must always love unalterably, and this thought wrung her heart. That I had been the husband of another woman she could forgive, but that this woman should have borne me children whose memory was still so dear, she could not forget if she forgave it, she who was childless. Why it was so, being but a man, I cannot say; for who can know all the mystery of a loving woman's heart? But so it was. Once, indeed, we quarrelled on the matter; it was our only quarrel.

16

It chanced that when we had been married but two years, and our babe was some few days buried in the churchyard of this parish of Ditchingham, I dreamed a very vivid dream as I slept one night at my wife's side. I dreamed that my dead children, the four of them, for the tallest lad bore in his arms my firstborn, that infant who died in the great siege, came to me as they had often come when I ruled the people of the Otomie in the City of Pines, and talked with me, giving me flowers and kissing my hands. I looked upon their strength and beauty, and was proud at heart, and, in my dream, it seemed as though some great sorrow had been lifted from my mind; as though these dear ones had been lost and now were found again. Ah! what misery is there like to this misery of dreams, that can thus give us back our dead in mockery, and then departing, leave us with a keener woe?

Well, I dreamed on, talking with my children in my sleep and naming them by their beloved names, till at length I woke to look on emptiness, and knowing all my sorrow I sobbed aloud. Now it was early morning, and the light of the August sun streamed through the window, but I, deeming that my wife slept, still lay in the shadow of my dream as it were, and groaned, murmuring the names of those whom I might never see again. It chanced, however, that she was awake, and had overheard those words which I spoke with the dead, while I was yet asleep and after; and though some of this talk was in the tongue of the Otomie, the most was English, and knowing the names of my children she guessed the purport of it all. Suddenly she sprang from the bed and stood over me, and there was such anger in her eyes as I had never seen before nor have seen since, nor did it last long then, for presently indeed it was quenched in tears.

'What is it, wife?' I asked astonished.

'It is hard,' she answered, 'that I must bear to listen to such talk from your lips, husband. Was it not enough that, when all men thought you dead, I wore my youth away faithful to your memory? though how faithful you were to mine you know best. Did I ever reproach you because you had forgotten me, and wedded a savage woman in a distant land?'

'Never, dear wife, nor had I forgotten you as you know well; but what I wonder at is that you should grow jealous now when all cause is done with.'

'Cannot we be jealous of the dead? With the living we may cope, but who can fight against the love which death has completed, sealing it for ever and making it immortal! Still, *that* I forgive you, for against this woman I can hold my own, seeing that you were mine before you became hers, and are mine after it. But with the children it is otherwise.

17

They are hers and yours alone. I have no part nor lot in them, and whether they be dead or living I know well you love them always, and will love them beyond the grave if you may find them there. Already I grow old, who waited twenty years and more before I was your wife, and I shall give you no other children. One I gave you, and God took it back lest I should be too happy; yet its name was not on your lips with those strange names. My dead babe is little to you, husband!'

Here she choked, bursting into tears; nor did I think it well to answer her that there was this difference in the matter, that whereas, with the exception of one infant, those sons whom I had lost were almost adolescent, the babe she bore lived but sixty days.

Now when the Queen first put it in my mind to write down the history of my life, I remembered this outbreak of my beloved wife; and seeing that I could write no true tale and leave out of it the story of her who was also my wife, Montezuma's daughter, Otomie, Princess of the Otomie, and of the children that she gave me, I let the matter lie. For I knew well, that though we spoke very rarely on the subject during all the many years we passed together, still it was always in Lily's mind; nor did her jealousy, being of the finer sort, abate at all with age, but rather gathered with the gathering days. That I should execute the task without the knowledge of my wife would not have been possible, for till the very last she watched over my every act, and, as I verily believe, divined the most of my thoughts.

And so we grew old together, peacefully, and side by side, speaking seldom of that great gap in my life when we were lost to each other and of all that then befell. At length the end came. My wife died suddenly in her sleep in the eighty-seventh year of her age. I buried her on the south side of the church here, with sorrow indeed, but not with sorrow inconsolable, for I know that I must soon rejoin her, and those others whom I have loved.

There in that wide heaven are my mother and my sister and my sons; there are great Guatemoc my friend, last of the emperors, and many other companions in war who have preceded me to peace; there, too, though she doubted of it, is Otomie the beautiful and proud. In the heaven which I trust to reach, all the sins of my youth and the errors of my age notwithstanding, it is told us there is no marrying and giving in marriage; and this is well, for I do not know how my wives, Montezuma's daughter and the sweet English gentlewoman, would agree together were it otherwise.

And now to my task.

CHAPTER 2

Of the Parentage of
Thomas Wingfield

I, Thomas Wingfield, was born here at Ditchingham, and in this very room where I write to-day. The house of my birth was built or added to early in the reign of the seventh Henry, but long before his time some kind of tenement stood here, which was lived in by the keeper of the vineyards, and known as Gardener's Lodge. Whether it chanced that the climate was more kindly in old times, or the skill of those who tended the fields was greater, I do not know, but this at the least is true, that the hillside beneath which the house nestles, and which once was the bank of an arm of the sea or of a great broad, was a vineyard in Earl Bigod's days. Long since it has ceased to grow grapes, though the name of the 'Earl's Vineyard' still clings to all that slope of land which lies between this house and a certain health-giving spring that bubbles from the bank the half of a mile away, in the waters of which sick folks come to bathe even from Norwich and Lowestoft. But sheltered as it is from the east winds, to this hour the place has the advantage that gardens planted here are earlier by fourteen days than any others in the country side, and that a man may sit in them coatless in the bitter month of May, when on the top of the hill, not two hundred paces hence, he must shiver in a jacket of otter skins.

The Lodge, for so it has always been named, in its beginnings having been but a farmhouse, faces to the south-west, and is built so low that it might well be thought that the damp from the river Waveney, which runs through the marshes close by, would rise in it. But this is not so, for though in autumn the roke, as here in Norfolk we name ground fog, hangs about the house at nightfall, and in seasons of great flood the water has been known to pour into the stables at the back of it, yet being built on sand and gravel there is no healthier habitation in the parish. For the rest the building is of stud-work and red brick, quaint and mellow looking, with many corners and gables that in summer are half hidden in roses and other creeping plants, and with its outlook on the marshes and the common where the lights vary continually with the seasons and even with the hours of the day, on the red roofs of Bungay town, and on the wooded bank that stretches round the Earsham lands; though there are many larger, to my mind there is none pleasanter in these parts. Here in this house I was born, and here doubtless I shall die, and having spoken of it at some length, as we are wont to do of spots which long custom has endeared to us, I will go on to tell of my parentage.

First, then, I would set out with a certain pride—for who of us does not love an ancient name when we happen to be born to it?—that I am sprung from the family of the Wingfields of Wingfield Castle in Suffolk, that lies some two hours on horseback from this place. Long ago the heiress of the Wingfields married a De la Pole, a family famous in our history, the last of whom, Edmund, Earl of Suffolk, lost his head for treason when I was young, and the castle passed to the De la Poles with her. But some offshoots of the old Wingfield stock lingered in the neighbourhood, perchance there was a bar sinister on their coat of arms, I know not and do not care to know; at the least my fathers and I are of this blood. My grandfather was a shrewd man, more of a yeoman than a squire, though his birth was gentle. He it was who bought this place with the lands round it, and gathered up some fortune, mostly by careful marrying and living, for though he had but one son he was twice married, and also by trading in cattle.

Now my grandfather was godly-minded even to superstition, and strange as it may seem, having only one son, nothing would satisfy him but that the boy should be made a priest. But my father had little leaning towards the priesthood and life in a monastery, though at all seasons my grandfather strove to reason it into him, sometimes with words and examples, at others with his thick cudgel of holly, that still hangs over the ingle in the smaller sitting-room. The end of it was that the lad was sent to the priory here in Bungay, where his conduct was of such nature that within a year the prior prayed his parents to take him back and set him in some way of secular life. Not only, so said the prior, did my father cause scandal by his actions, breaking out of the priory at night and visiting drinking houses and other places; but, such was the sum of his wickedness, he did not scruple to question and make mock of the very doctrines of the Church, alleging even that there was nothing sacred in the image of the Virgin Mary which stood in the chancel, and shut its eyes in prayer before all the congregation when the priest elevated the Host. 'Therefore,' said the prior, 'I pray you take back your son, and let him find some other road to the stake than that which runs through the gates of Bungay Priory.'

Now at this story my grandfather was so enraged that he almost fell into a fit; then recovering, he bethought him of his cudgel of holly, and would have used it. But my father, who was now nineteen years of age and very stout and strong, twisted it from his hand and flung it full fifty yards, saying that no man should touch him more were he a hundred times his father. Then he walked away, leaving the prior and my grandfather staring at each other.

Now to shorten a long tale, the end of the matter was this. It was believed both by my grandfather and the prior that the true cause of my father's contumacy was a passion which he had conceived for a girl of humble birth, a miller's fair daughter who dwelt at Waingford Mills. Perhaps there was truth in this belief, or perhaps there was none. What does it matter, seeing that the maid married a butcher at Beccles and died years since at the good age of ninety and five? But true or false, my grandfather believed the tale, and knowing well that absence is the surest cure for love, he entered into a plan with the prior that my father should be sent to a monastery at Seville in Spain, of which the prior's brother was abbot, and there learn to forget the miller's daughter and all other worldly things.

When this was told to my father he fell into it readily enough, being a young man of spirit and having a great desire to see the world, otherwise, however, than through the gratings of a monastery window. So the end of it was that he went to foreign parts in the care of a party of Spanish monks, who had journeyed here to Norfolk on a pilgrimage to the shrine of our Lady of Walsingham.

It is said that my grandfather wept when he parted with his son, feeling that he should see him no more; yet so strong was his religion, or rather his superstition, that he did not hesitate to send him away, though for no reason save that he would mortify his own love and flesh, offering his son for a sacrifice as Abraham would have offered Isaac. But though my father appeared to consent to the sacrifice, as did Isaac, yet his mind was not altogether set on altars and faggots; in short, as he himself told me in after years, his plans were already laid.

Thus it chanced that when he had sailed from Yarmouth a year and six months, there came a letter from the abbot of the monastery in Seville to his brother, the prior of St. Mary's at Bungay, saying that my father had fled from the monastery, leaving no trace of where he had gone. My grandfather was grieved at this tidings, but said little about it.

Two more years passed away, and there came other news, namely, that my father had been captured, that he had been handed over to the power of the Holy Office, as the accursed Inquisition was then named, and tortured to death at Seville. When my grandfather heard this he wept, and bemoaned himself that his folly in forcing one into the Church who had no liking for that path, had brought about the shameful end of his only son. After that date also he broke his friendship with the prior of St. Mary's at Bungay, and ceased his offerings to the priory. Still he did not believe that my father was dead in truth, since on the last day of his own life, that ended two years later, he spoke of him as a living man, and left messages to him as to the management of the lands which now were his.

And in the end it became clear that this belief was not ill-founded, for one day three years after the old man's death, there landed at the port of Yarmouth none other than my father, who had been absent some eight years in all. Nor did he come alone, for with him he brought a wife, a young and very lovely lady, who afterwards was my mother. She was a Spaniard of noble family, having been born at Seville, and her maiden name was Donna Luisa de Garcia.

Now of all that befell my father during his eight years of wandering I cannot speak certainly, for he was very silent on the matter, though I may have need to touch on some of his adventures. But I know it is true that he fell under the power of the Holy Office, for once when as a little lad I bathed with him in the Elbow Pool, where the river Waveney bends some three hundred yards above this house, I saw that his breast and arms were scored with long white scars, and asked him what had caused them. I remember well how his face changed as I spoke, from kindliness to the hue of blackest hate, and how he answered speaking to himself rather than to me.

'Devils,' he said, 'devils set on their work by the chief of all devils that live upon the earth and shall reign in hell. Hark you, my son Thomas, there is a country called Spain where your mother was born, and there these devils abide who torture men and women, aye, and burn them living in the name of Christ. I was betrayed into their hands by him whom I name the chief of the devils, though he is younger than I am by three years, and their pincers and hot irons left these marks upon me. Aye, and they would have burnt me alive also, only I escaped, thanks to your mother—but such tales are not for a little lad's hearing; and see you never speak of them, Thomas, for the Holy Office has a long arm. You are half a Spaniard, Thomas, your skin and eyes tell their own tale, but whatever skin and eyes may tell, let your heart give them the lie. Keep your heart English, Thomas; let no foreign devilments enter there. Hate all Spaniards except your mother, and be watchful lest her blood should master mine within you.'

I was a child then, and scarcely understood his words or what he meant by them. Afterwards I learned to understand them but too well. As for my father's counsel, that I should conquer my Spanish blood, would that I could always have followed it, for I know that from this blood springs the most of such evil as is in me. Hence come my fixedness of purpose or rather obstinacy, and my powers of unchristian hatred that are not small towards those who have wronged me. Well, I have done what I might to overcome these and other faults, but strive as we may, that which is bred in the bone will out in the flesh, as I have seen in many signal instances.

There were three of us children, Geoffrey my elder brother, myself, and my sister Mary, who was one year my junior, the sweetest child and the most beautiful that I have ever known. We were very happy children, and our beauty was the pride of our father and mother, and the envy of other parents. I was the darkest of the three, dark indeed to swarthiness, but in Mary the Spanish blood showed only in her rich eyes of velvet hue, and in the glow upon her cheek that was like the blush on a ripe fruit. My mother used to call me her little Spaniard, because of my swarthiness, that is when my father was not near, for such names angered him. She never learned to speak English very well, but he would suffer her to talk in no other tongue before him. Still, when he was not there she spoke in Spanish, of which language, however, I alone of the family became a master—and that more because of certain volumes of old Spanish romances which she had by her, than for any other reason. From my earliest childhood I was fond of such tales, and it was by bribing me with the promise that I should read them that she persuaded me to learn Spanish. For my mother's heart still yearned towards her old sunny home, and often she would talk of it with us children, more especially in the winter season, which she hated as I do. Once I asked her if she wished to go back to Spain. She shivered and answered no, for there dwelt one who was her enemy and would kill her; also her heart was with us children and our father. I wondered if this man who sought to kill my mother was the same as he of whom my father had spoken as 'the chief of the devils,' but I only answered that no man could wish to kill one so good and beautiful.

'Ah! my boy,' she said, 'it is just because I am, or rather have been, beautiful that he hates me. Others would have wedded me besides your dear father, Thomas.' And her face grew troubled as though with fear.

Now when I was eighteen and a half years old, on a certain evening in the month of May it happened that a friend of my father's, Squire Bozard, late of the Hall in this parish, called at the Lodge on his road from Yarmouth, and in the course of his talk let it fall that a Spanish ship was at anchor in the Roads, laden with merchandise. My father pricked up his ears at this, and asked who her captain might be. Squire Bozard answered that he did not know his name, but that he had seen him in the market-place, a tall and stately man, richly dressed, with a handsome face and a scar upon his temple.

At this news my mother turned pale beneath her olive skin, and muttered in Spanish:

'Holy Mother! grant that it be not he.'

My father also looked frightened, and questioned the squire closely as to the man's appearance, but without learning anything more. Then he bade him *adieu* with little ceremony, and taking horse rode away for Yarmouth.

That night my mother never slept, but sat all through it in her nursing chair, brooding over I know not what. As I left her when I went to my bed, so I found her when I came from it at dawn. I can remember well pushing the door ajar to see her face glimmering white in the twilight of the May morning, as she sat, her large eyes fixed upon the lattice.

'You have risen early, mother,' I said.

'I have never lain down, Thomas,' she answered.

'Why not? What do you fear?'

'I fear the past and the future, my son. Would that your father were back.'

About ten o'clock of that morning, as I was making ready to walk into Bungay to the house of that physician under whom I was learning the art of healing, my father rode up. My mother, who was watching at the lattice, ran out to meet him.

Springing from his horse he embraced her, saying, 'Be of good cheer, sweet, it cannot be he. This man has another name.'

'But did you see him?' she asked.

'No, he was out at his ship for the night, and I hurried home to tell you, knowing your fears.'

'It were surer if you had seen him, husband. He may well have taken another name.'

'I never thought of that, sweet,' my father answered; 'but have no fear. Should it be he, and should he dare to set foot in the parish of Ditchingham, there are those who will know how to deal with him. But I am sure that it is not he.'

'Thanks be to Jesu then!' she said, and they began talking in a low voice.

Now, seeing that I was not wanted, I took my cudgel and started down the bridle-path towards the common footbridge, when suddenly my mother called me back.

'Kiss me before you go, Thomas,' she said. 'You must wonder what all this may mean. One day your father will tell you. It has to do with a shadow which has hung over my life for many years, but that is, I trust, gone for ever.'

'If it be a man who flings it, he had best keep out of reach of this,' I said, laughing, and shaking my thick stick.

'It is a man,' she answered, 'but one to be dealt with otherwise than by blows, Thomas, should you ever chance to meet him.'

'May be, mother, but might is the best argument at the last, for the most cunning have a life to lose.'

'You are too ready to use your strength, son,' she said, smiling and kissing me. 'Remember the old Spanish proverb: "He strikes hardest who strikes last."'

'And remember the other proverb, mother: "Strike before thou art stricken,"' I answered, and went.

When I had gone some ten paces something prompted me to look back, I know not what. My mother was standing by the open door, her stately shape framed as it were in the flowers of a white creeping shrub that grew upon the wall of the old house. As was her custom, she wore a mantilla of white lace upon her head, the ends of which were wound beneath her chin, and the arrangement of it was such that at this distance for one moment it put me in mind of the wrappings which are placed about the dead. I started at the thought and looked at her face. She was watching me with sad and earnest eyes that seemed to be filled with the spirit of farewell.

I never saw her again till she was dead.

CHAPTER 3

The Coming of the Spaniard

And now I must go back and speak of my own matters. As I have told, it was my father's wish that I should be a physician, and since I came back from my schooling at Norwich, that was when I had entered on my sixteenth year, I had studied medicine under the doctor who practised his art in the neighbourhood of Bungay. He was a very learned man and an honest, Grimstone by name, and as I had some liking for the business I made good progress under him. Indeed I had learned almost all that he could teach me, and my father purposed to send me to London, there to push on my studies, so soon as I should attain my twentieth year, that is within some five months of the date of the coming of the Spaniard.

But it was not fated that I should go to London.

Medicine was not the only thing that I studied in those days, however. Squire Bozard of Ditchingham, the same who told my father of the coming of the Spanish ship, had two living children, a son and a daughter, though his wife had borne him many more who died in infancy. The daughter was named Lily and of my own age, having been born three weeks after me in the same year. Now the Bozards are gone from these parts, for my great-niece, the granddaughter and sole heiress of this son, has married and has issue of another name. But this is by the way.

From our earliest days we children, Bozards and Wingfields, lived almost as brothers and sisters, for day by day we met and played together in the snow or in the flowers. Thus it would be hard for me to say when I began to love Lily or when she began to love me; but I know that when first I went to school at Norwich I grieved more at losing sight of her than because I must part from my mother and the rest. In all our games she was ever my partner, and I would search the country round for days to find such flowers as she chanced to love.

When I came back from school it was the same, though by degrees Lily grew shyer, and I also grew suddenly shy, perceiving that from a child she had become a woman. Still we met often, and though neither said anything of it, it was sweet to us to meet.

Thus things went on till this day of my mother's death. But before I go further I must tell that Squire Bozard looked with no favour on the friendship between his daughter and myself—and this, not because he disliked me, but rather because he would have seen Lily wedded to my elder brother Geoffrey, my father's heir, and not to a younger son. So hard did he grow about the matter at last that we two might scarcely meet except by seeming accident, whereas my brother was ever welcome at the Hall. And on this account some bitterness arose between us two brothers, as is apt to be the case when a woman comes between friends however close. For it must be known that my brother Geoffrey also loved Lily, as all men would have loved her, and with a better right perhaps than I had—for he was my elder by three years and born to possessions. It may seem indeed that I was somewhat hasty to fall into this state, seeing that at the time of which I write I was not yet of age; but young blood is nimble, and moreover mine was half Spanish, and made a man of me when many a pure-bred Englishman is still nothing but a boy. For the blood and the sun that ripens it have much to do with such matters, as I have seen often enough among the Indian peoples of Anahuac, who at the age of fifteen will take to themselves a bride of twelve. At the least it is certain that when I was eighteen years of age I was old enough to fall in love after such fashion that I never fell out of it again altogether, although the history of my life may seem to give me the lie when I say so. But I take it that a man may love several women and yet love one of them the best of all, being true in the spirit to the law which he breaks in the letter.

Now when I had attained nineteen years I was a man full grown, and writing as I do in extreme old age, I may say it without false shame, a very handsome youth to boot. I was not over tall, indeed, measuring but five feet nine inches and a half in height, but my limbs were well made, and I was both deep and broad in the chest. In colour I was, and my white hair notwithstanding, am still extraordinarily dark hued, my eyes also were large and dark, and my hair, which was wavy, was coal black. In my deportment I was reserved and grave to sadness, in speech I was slow and temperate, and more apt at listening than in talking. I weighed matters well before I made up my mind upon them, but being made up, nothing could turn me from that mind short of death itself, whether it were set on good or evil, on folly or wisdom. In

27

those days also I had little religion, since, partly because of my father's secret teaching and partly through the workings of my own reason, I had learned to doubt the doctrines of the Church as they used to be set out. Youth is prone to reason by large leaps as it were, and to hold that all things are false because some are proved false; and thus at times in those days I thought that there was no God, because the priest said that the image of the Virgin at Bungay wept and did other things which I knew that it did not do. Now I know well that there is a God, for my own story proves it to my heart. In truth, what man can look back across a long life and say that there is no God, when he can see the shadow of His hand lying deep upon his tale of years?

On this sad day of which I write I knew that Lily, whom I loved, would be walking alone beneath the great pollard oaks in the park of Ditchingham Hall. Here, in Grubswell as the spot is called, grew, and indeed still grow, certain hawthorn trees that are the earliest to blow of any in these parts, and when we had met at the church door on the Sunday, Lily said that there would be bloom upon them by the Wednesday, and on that afternoon she should go to cut it. It may well be that she spoke thus with design, for love will breed cunning in the heart of the most guileless and truthful maid. Moreover, I noticed that though she said it before her father and the rest of us, yet she waited to speak till my brother Geoffrey was out of hearing, for she did not wish to go maying with him, and also that as she spoke she shot a glance of her grey eyes at me. Then and there I vowed to myself that I also would be gathering hawthorn bloom in this same place and on that Wednesday afternoon, yes, even if I must play truant and leave all the sick of Bungay to Nature's nursing. Moreover, I was determined on one thing, that if I could find Lily alone I would delay no longer, but tell her all that was in my heart; no great secret indeed, for though no word of love had ever passed between us as yet, each knew the other's hidden thoughts. Not that I was in the way to become affianced to a maid, who had my path to cut in the world, but I feared that if I delayed to make sure of her affection my brother would be before me with her father, and Lily might yield to that to which she would not yield if once we had plighted troth.

Now it chanced that on this afternoon I was hard put to it to escape to my tryst, for my master, the physician, was ailing, and sent me to visit the sick for him, carrying them their medicines. At the last, however, between four and five o'clock, I fled, asking no leave. Taking the Norwich road I ran for a mile and more till I had passed the Manor House and the church turn, and drew near to Ditchingham Park.

Then I dropped my pace to a walk, for I did not wish to come before Lily heated and disordered, but rather looking my best, to which end I had put on my Sunday garments. Now as I went down the little hill in the road that runs past the park, I saw a man on horseback who looked first at the bridle-path, that at this spot turns off to the right, then back across the common lands towards the Vineyard Hills and the Waveney, and then along the road as though he did not know which way to turn. I was quick to notice things—though at this moment my mind was not at its swiftest, being set on other matters, and chiefly as to how I should tell my tale to Lily—and I saw at once that this man was not of our country.

He was very tall and noble-looking, dressed in rich garments of velvet adorned by a gold chain that hung about his neck, and as I judged about forty years of age. But it was his face which chiefly caught my eye, for at that moment there was something terrible about it. It was long, thin, and deeply carved; the eyes were large, and gleamed like gold in sunlight; the mouth was small and well shaped, but it wore a devilish and cruel sneer; the forehead lofty, indicating a man of mind, and marked with a slight scar. For the rest the cavalier was dark and southern-looking, his curling hair, like my own, was black, and he wore a peaked chestnut-coloured beard.

By the time that I had finished these observations my feet had brought me almost to the stranger's side, and for the first time he caught sight of me. Instantly his face changed, the sneer left it, and it became kindly and pleasant looking. Lifting his bonnet with much courtesy he stammered something in broken English, of which all that I could catch was the word Yarmouth; then perceiving that I did not understand him, he cursed the English tongue and all those who spoke it, aloud and in good Castilian.

'If the senor will graciously express his wish in Spanish,' I said, speaking in that language, 'it may be in my power to help him.'

'What! you speak Spanish, young sir,' he said, starting, 'and yet you are not a Spaniard, though by your face you well might be. *Caramba!* but it is strange!' and he eyed me curiously.

'It may be strange, sir,' I answered, 'but I am in haste. Be pleased to ask your question and let me go.'

'Ah!' he said, 'perhaps I can guess the reason of your hurry. I saw a white robe down by the streamlet yonder,' and he nodded towards the park. 'Take the advice of an older man, young sir, and be careful. Make what sport you will with such, but never believe them and never marry them—lest you should live to desire to kill them!'

Here I made as though I would pass on, but he spoke again.

'Pardon my words, they were well meant, and perhaps you may come to learn their truth. I will detain you no more. Will you graciously direct me on my road to Yarmouth, for I am not sure of it, having ridden by another way, and your English country is so full of trees that a man cannot see a mile?'

I walked a dozen paces down the bridle-path that joined the road at this place, and pointed out the way that he should go, past Ditchingham church. As I did so I noticed that while I spoke the stranger was watching my face keenly and, as it seemed to me, with an inward fear which he strove to master and could not. When I had finished again he raised his bonnet and thanked me, saying,

'Will you be so gracious as to tell me your name, young Sir?'

'What is my name to you?' I answered roughly, for I disliked this man. 'You have not told me yours.'

'No, indeed, I am travelling incognito. Perhaps I also have met a lady in these parts,' and he smiled strangely. 'I only wished to know the name of one who had done me a courtesy, but who it seems is not so courteous as I deemed.' And he shook his horse's reins.

'I am not ashamed of my name,' I said. 'It has been an honest one so far, and if you wish to know it, it is Thomas Wingfield.'

'I thought it,' he cried, and as he spoke his face grew like the face of a fiend. Then before I could find time even to wonder, he had sprung from his horse and stood within three paces of me.

'A lucky day! Now we will see what truth there is in prophecies,' he said, drawing his silver-mounted sword. 'A name for a name; Juan de Garcia gives you greeting, Thomas Wingfield.'

Now, strange as it may seem, it was at this moment only that there flashed across my mind the thought of all that I had heard about the Spanish stranger, the report of whose coming to Yarmouth had stirred my father and mother so deeply. At any other time I should have remembered it soon enough, but on this day I was so set upon my tryst with Lily and what I should say to her, that nothing else could hold a place in my thoughts.

'This must be the man,' I said to myself, and then I said no more, for he was on me, sword up. I saw the keen point flash towards me, and sprang to one side having a desire to fly, as, being unarmed except for my stick, I might have done without shame. But spring as I would I could not avoid the thrust altogether. It was aimed at my heart and it pierced the sleeve of my left arm, passing through the flesh—no more. Yet at the pain of that cut all thought of flight left me, and instead of it a cold anger filled me, causing me to wish to kill this man who had attacked me thus and unprovoked. In my hand was my stout oaken staff which I had cut myself on the banks of Hollow Hill, and if I would fight I must make such play with this as I might. It seems a poor weapon indeed to match against a Toledo blade in the hands of one who could handle it well, and yet there are virtues in a cudgel, for when a man sees himself threatened with it, he is likely to forget that he holds in his hand a more deadly weapon, and to take to the guarding of his own head in place of running his adversary through the body.

And that was what chanced in this case, though how it came about exactly I cannot tell. The Spaniard was a fine swordsman, and had I been armed as he was would doubtless have overmatched me, who at that age had no practice in the art, which was almost unknown in England. But when he saw the big stick flourished over him he forgot his own advantage, and raised his arm to ward away the blow. Down it came upon the back of his hand, and lo! his sword fell from it to the grass. But I did not spare him because of that, for my blood was up. The next stroke took him on the lips, knocking out a tooth and sending him backwards. Then I caught him by the leg and beat him most unmercifully, not upon the head indeed, for now that I was victor I did not wish to kill one whom I thought a madman as I would that I had done, but on every other part of him.

Indeed I thrashed him till my arms were weary and then I fell to kicking him, and all the while he writhed like a wounded snake and cursed horribly, though he never cried out or asked for mercy. At last I ceased and looked at him, and he was no pretty sight to see—indeed, what with his cuts and bruises and the mire of the roadway, it would have been hard to know him for the gallant cavalier whom I had met not five minutes before. But uglier than all his hurts was the look in his wicked eyes as he lay there on his back in the pathway and glared up at me.

'Now, friend Spaniard,' I said, 'you have learned a lesson; and what is there to hinder me from treating you as you would have dealt with me who had never harmed you?' and I took up his sword and held it to his throat.

'Strike home, you accursed whelp!' he answered in a broken voice; 'it is better to die than to live to remember such shame as this.'

'No,' I said, 'I am no foreign murderer to kill a defenceless man. You shall away to the justice to answer for yourself. The hangman has a rope for such as you.'

'Then you must drag me thither,' he groaned, and shut his eyes as though with faintness, and doubtless he was somewhat faint.

Now as I pondered on what should be done with the villain, it chanced that I looked up through a gap in the fence, and there, among the Grubswell Oaks three hundred yards or more away, I caught sight of the flutter of a white robe that I knew well, and it seemed to me that the wearer of that robe was moving towards the bridge of the 'watering' as though she were weary of waiting for one who did not come.

Then I thought to myself that if I stayed to drag this man to the village stocks or some other safe place, there would be an end of meeting with my love that day, and I did not know when I might find another chance. Now I would not have missed that hour's talk with Lily to bring a score of murderous-minded foreigners to their deserts, and, moreover, this one had earned good payment for his behaviour. Surely thought I, he might wait a while till I had done my love-making, and if he would not wait I could find a means to make him do so. Not twenty paces from us the horse stood cropping the grass. I went to him and undid his bridle rein, and with it fastened the Spaniard to a small wayside tree as best I was able.

'Now, here you stay,' I said, 'till I am ready to fetch you;' and I turned to go.

But as I went a great doubt took me, and once more I remembered my mother's fear, and how my father had ridden in haste to Yarmouth on business about a Spaniard. Now to-day a Spaniard had wandered to Ditchingham, and when he learned my name had fallen upon me madly trying to kill me. Was not this the man whom my mother feared, and was it right that I should leave him thus that I might go maying with my dear? I knew in my breast that it was not right, but I was so set upon my desire and so strongly did my heartstrings pull me towards her whose white robe now fluttered on the slope of the Park Hill, that I never heeded the warning.

Well had it been for me if I had done so, and well for some who were yet unborn. Then they had never known death, nor I the land of exile, the taste of slavery, and the altar of sacrifice.

CHAPTER 4

Thomas Tells His Love

Having made the Spaniard as fast as I could, his arms being bound to the tree behind him, and taking his sword with me, I began to run hard after Lily and caught her not too soon, for in one more minute she would have turned along the road that runs to the watering and over the bridge by the Park Hill path to the Hall.

Hearing my footsteps, she faced about to greet me, or rather as though to see who it was that followed her. There she stood in the evening light, a bough of hawthorn bloom in her hand, and my heart beat yet more wildly at the sight of her. Never had she seemed fairer than as she stood thus in her white robe, a look of amaze upon her face and in her grey eyes, that was half real half feigned, and with the sunlight shifting on her auburn hair that showed beneath her little bonnet. Lily was no round-cheeked country maid with few beauties save those of health and youth, but a tall and shapely lady who had ripened early to her full grace and sweetness, and so it came about that though we were almost of an age, yet in her presence I felt always as though I were the younger. Thus in my love for her was mingled some touch of reverence.

'Oh! it is you, Thomas,' she said, blushing as she spoke. 'I thought you were not—I mean that I am going home as it grows late. But say, why do you run so fast, and what has happened to you, Thomas, that your arm is bloody and you carry a sword in your hand?'

'I have no breath to speak yet,' I answered. 'Come back to the haw-thorns and I will tell you.'

'No, I must be wending homewards. I have been among the trees for more than an hour, and there is little bloom upon them.'

'I could not come before, Lily. I was kept, and in a strange manner. Also I saw bloom as I ran.'

'Indeed, I never thought that you would come, Thomas,' she answered, looking down, 'who have other things to do than to go out maying like a girl. But I wish to hear your story, if it is short, and I will walk a little way with you.'

So we turned and walked side by side towards the great pollard oaks, and by the time that we reached them, I had told her the tale of the Spaniard, and how he strove to kill me, and how I had beaten him with my staff. Now Lily listened eagerly enough, and sighed with fear when she learned how close I had been to death.

'But you are wounded, Thomas,' she broke in; 'see, the blood runs fast from your arm. Is the thrust deep?'

'I have not looked to see. I have had no time to look.'

'Take off your coat, Thomas, that I may dress the wound. Nay, I will have it so.'

So I drew off the garment, not without pain, and rolled up the shirt beneath, and there was the hurt, a clean thrust through the fleshy part of the lower arm. Lily washed it with water from the brook, and bound it with her kerchief, murmuring words of pity all the while. To say truth, I would have suffered a worse harm gladly, if only I could find her to tend it. Indeed, her gentle care broke down the fence of my doubts and gave me a courage that otherwise might have failed me in her presence. At first, indeed, I could find no words, but as she bound my wound, I bent down and kissed her ministering hand. She flushed red as the evening sky, the flood of crimson losing itself at last beneath her auburn hair, but it burned deepest upon the white hand which I had kissed.

'Why did you do that, Thomas?' she said, in a low voice.

Then I spoke. 'I did it because I love you, Lily, and do not know how to begin the telling of my love. I love you, dear, and have always loved as I always shall love you.'

'Are you so sure of that, Thomas?' she said, again.

'There is nothing else in the world of which I am so sure, Lily. What I wish to be as sure of is that you love me as I love you.'

For a moment she stood quiet, her head sunk almost to her breast, then she lifted it and her eyes shone as I had never seen them shine before.

'Can you doubt it, Thomas?' she said.

And now I took her in my arms and kissed her on the lips, and the memory of that kiss has gone with me through my long life, and is with me yet, when, old and withered, I stand upon the borders of the grave. It was the greatest joy that has been given to me in all my days. Too soon, alas! it was done, that first pure kiss of youthful love—and I spoke again somewhat aimlessly.

'It seems then that you do love me who love you so well.'

'If you doubted it before, can you doubt it NOW?' she answered very softly. 'But listen, Thomas. It is well that we should love each other, for we were born to it, and have no help in the matter, even if we wished to find it. Still, though love be sweet and holy, it is not all, for there is duty to be thought of, and what will my father say to this, Thomas?'

'I do not know, Lily, and yet I can guess. I am sure, sweet, that he wishes you to take my brother Geoffrey, and leave me on one side.'

'Then his wishes are not mine, Thomas. Also, though duty be strong, it is not strong enough to force a woman to a marriage for which she has no liking. Yet it may prove strong enough to keep a woman from a marriage for which her heart pleads—perhaps, also, it should have been strong enough to hold me back from the telling of my love.'

'No, Lily, the love itself is much, and though it should bring no fruit, still it is something to have won it for ever and a day.'

'You are very young to talk thus, Thomas. I am also young, I know, but we women ripen quicker. Perhaps all this is but a boy's fancy, to pass with boyhood.'

'It will never pass, Lily. They say that our first loves are the longest, and that which is sown in youth will flourish in our age. Listen, Lily; I have my place to make in the world, and it may take a time in the making, and I ask one promise of you, though perhaps it is a selfish thing to seek. I ask of you that you will be faithful to me, and come fair weather or foul, will wed no other man till you know me dead.'

'It is something to promise, Thomas, for with time come changes. Still I am so sure of myself that I promise—nay I swear it. Of you I cannot be sure, but things are so with us women that we must risk all upon a throw, and if we lose, good-bye to happiness.'

Then we talked on, and I cannot remember what we said, though these words that I have written down remain in my mind, partly because of their own weight, and in part because of all that came about in the after years.

And at last I knew that I must go, though we were sad enough at parting. So I took her in my arms and kissed her so closely that some blood from my wound ran down her white attire. But as we embraced I chanced to look up, and saw a sight that frightened me enough. For there, not five paces from us, stood Squire Bozard, Lily's father, watching all, and his face wore no smile.

He had been riding by a bridle-path to the watering ford, and seeing a couple trespassing beneath the oaks, dismounted from his horse to hunt them away. Not till he was quite near did he know whom he came to hunt, and then he stood still in astonishment. Lily and I drew slowly apart and looked at him. He was a short stout man, with a red face and stern grey eyes, that seemed to be starting from his head with anger. For a while he could not speak, but when he began at length the words came fast enough. All that he said I forget, but the upshot of it was that he desired to know what my business was with his daughter. I waited till he was out of breath, then answered him that Lily and I loved each other well, and were plighting our troth.

'Is this so, daughter?' he asked.

'It is so, my father,' she answered boldly.

Then he broke out swearing. 'You light minx,' he said, 'you shall be whipped and kept cool on bread and water in your chamber. And for you, my half-bred Spanish cockerel, know once and for all that this maid is for your betters. How dare you come wooing my daughter, you empty pill-box, who have not two silver pennies to rattle in your pouch! Go win fortune and a name before you dare to look up to such as she.'

'That is my desire, and I will do it, sir,' I answered.

'So, you apothecary's drudge, you will win name and place, will you! Well, long before that deed is done the maid shall be safely wedded to one who has them and who is not unknown to you. Daughter, say now that you have finished with him.'

'I cannot say that, father,' she replied, plucking at her robe. 'If it is not your will that I should marry Thomas here, my duty is plain and I may not wed him. But I am my own and no duty can make me marry where I will not. While Thomas lives I am sworn to him and to no other man.'

'At the least you have courage, hussey,' said her father. 'But listen now, either you will marry where and when I wish, or tramp it for your bread. Ungrateful girl, did I breed you to flaunt me to my face? Now for you, pill-box. I will teach you to come kissing honest men's daughters without their leave,' and with a curse he rushed at me, stick aloft, to thrash me.

Then for the second time that day my quick blood boiled in me, and snatching up the Spaniard's sword that lay upon the grass beside me, I held it at the point, for the game was changed, and I who had fought with cudgel against sword, must now fight with sword against cudgel. And had it not been that Lily with a quick cry of fear struck my arm from beneath, causing the point of the sword to pass over his shoulder, I believe truly that I should then and there have pierced her father through, and ended my days early with a noose about my neck.

'Are you mad?' she cried. 'And do you think to win me by slaying my father? Throw down that sword, Thomas.'

'As for winning you, it seems that there is small chance of it;' I answered hotly, 'but I tell you this, not for the sake of all the maids upon the earth will I stand to be beaten with a stick like a scullion.'

'And there I do not blame you, lad,' said her father, more kindly. 'I see that you also have courage which may serve you in good stead, and it was unworthy of me to call you "pill-box" in my anger. Still, as I have said, the girl is not for you, so be gone and forget her as best you may, and if you value your life, never let me find you two kissing again. And know that to-morrow I will have a word with your father on this matter.'

'I will go since I must go,' I answered, 'but, sir, I still hope to live to call your daughter wife. Lily, farewell till these storms are overpast.'

'Farewell, Thomas,' she said weeping. 'Forget me not and I will never forget my oath to you.'

Then taking Lily by the arm her father led her away.

I also went away—sad, but not altogether ill-pleased. For now I knew that if I had won the father's anger, I had also won the daughter's unalterable love, and love lasts longer than wrath, and here or hereafter will win its way at length. When I had gone a little distance I remembered the Spaniard, who had been clean forgotten by me in all this love and war, and I turned to seek him and drag him to the stocks, the which I should have done with joy, and been glad to find some one on whom to wreak my wrongs. But when I came to the spot where I had left him, I found that fate had befriended him by the hand of a fool, for there was no Spaniard but only the village idiot, Billy Minns by name, who stood staring first at the tree to which the foreigner had been made fast, and then at a piece of silver in his hand.

'Where is the man who was tied here, Billy?' I asked.

'I know not, Master Thomas,' he answered in his Norfolk talk which I will not set down. 'Half-way to wheresoever he was going I should say, measured by the pace at which he left when once I had set him upon his horse.'

'You set him on his horse, fool? How long was that ago?'

'How long! Well, it might be one hour, and it might be two. I'm no reckoner of time, that keeps its own score like an innkeeper, without my help. Lawks! how he did gallop off, working those long spurs he wore right into the ribs of the horse. And little wonder, poor man, and he daft, not being able to speak, but only to bleat sheeplike, and fallen upon by robbers on the king's roads, and in broad daylight. But Billy cut him loose and caught his horse and set him on it, and got this piece for his good charity. Lawks! but he was glad to be gone. How he did gallop!'

'Now you are a bigger fool even than I thought you, Billy Minns,'
I said in anger. 'That man would have murdered me, I overcame him
and made him fast, and you have let him go.'

'He would have murdered you, Master, and you made him fast!
Then why did you not stop to keep him till I came along, and we
would have haled him to the stocks? That would have been sport and
all. You call me fool—but if you found a man covered with blood and
hurts tied to a tree, and he daft and not able to speak, had you not cut
him loose? Well, he's gone, and this alone is left of him,' and he spun
the piece into the air.

Now, seeing that there was reason in Billy's talk, for the fault was
mine, I turned away without more words, not straight homewards, for
I wished to think alone awhile on all that had come about between
me and Lily and her father, but down the way which runs across the
lane to the crest of the Vineyard Hills. These hills are clothed with
underwood, in which large oaks grow to within some two hundred
yards of this house where I write, and this underwood is pierced by
paths that my mother laid out, for she loved to walk here. One of these
paths runs along the bottom of the hill by the edge of the pleasant
river Waveney, and the other a hundred feet or more above and near
the crest of the slope, or to speak more plainly, there is but one path
shaped like the letter O, placed thus [symbol of O laying on its side
omitted], the curved ends of the letter marking how the path turns
upon the hill-side.

Now I struck the path at the end that is furthest from this house,
and followed that half of it which runs down by the river bank, having
the water on one side of it and the brushwood upon the other. Along
this lower path I wandered, my eyes fixed upon the ground, thinking
deeply as I went, now of the joy of Lily's love, and now of the sorrow
of our parting and of her father's wrath. As I went, thus wrapped in
meditation, I saw something white lying upon the grass, and pushed
it aside with the point of the Spaniard's sword, not heeding it. Still,
its shape and fashioning remained in my mind, and when I had left
it some three hundred paces behind me, and was drawing near to the
house, the sight of it came back to me as it lay soft and white upon
the grass, and I knew that it was familiar to my eyes. From the thing,
whatever it might be, my mind passed to the Spaniard's sword with
which I had tossed it aside, and from the sword to the man himself.
What had been his business in this parish?—an ill one surely—and
why had he looked as though he feared me and fallen upon me when
he learned my name?

I stood still, looking downward, and my eyes fell upon footprints stamped in the wet sand of the path. One of them was my mother's. I could have sworn to it among a thousand, for no other woman in these parts had so delicate a foot. Close to it, as though following after, was another that at first I thought must also have been made by a woman, it was so narrow. But presently I saw that this could scarcely be, because of its length, and moreover, that the boot which left it was like none that I knew, being cut very high at the instep and very pointed at the toe. Then, of a sudden, it came upon me that the Spanish stranger wore such boots, for I had noted them while I talked with him, and that his feet were following those of my mother, for they had trodden on her track, and in some places, his alone had stamped their impress on the sand blotting out her footprints. Then, too, I knew what the white rag was that I had thrown aside. It was my mother's mantilla which I knew, and yet did not know, because I always saw it set daintily upon her head. In a moment it had come home to me, and with the knowledge a keen and sickening dread. Why had this man followed my mother, and why did her mantilla lie thus upon the ground?

I turned and sped like a deer back to where I had seen the lace. All the way the footprints went before me. Now I was there. Yes, the wrapping was hers, and it had been rent as though by a rude hand; but where was she?

With a beating heart once more I bent to read the writing of the footsteps. Here they were mixed one with another, as though the two had stood close together, moving now this way and now that in struggle. I looked up the path, but there were none. Then I cast round about like a beagle, first along the river side, then up the bank. Here they were again, and made by feet that flew and feet that followed. Up the bank they went fifty yards and more, now lost where the turf was sound, now seen in sand or loam, till they led to the bole of a big oak, and were once more mixed together, for here the pursuer had come up with the pursued.

Despairingly as one who dreams, for now I guessed all and grew mad with fear, I looked this way and that, till at length I found more footsteps, those of the Spaniard. These were deep marked, as of a man who carried some heavy burden. I followed them; first they went down the hill towards the river, then turned aside to a spot where the brushwood was thick. In the deepest of the clump the boughs, now bursting into leaf, were bent downwards as though to hide something beneath. I wrenched them aside, and there, gleaming whitely in the gathering twilight was the dead face of my mother.

CHAPTER 5

Thomas Swears an Oath

For a while I stood amazed with horror, staring down at the dead face of my beloved mother. Then I stooped to lift her and saw that she had been stabbed, and through the breast, stabbed with the sword which I carried in my hand.

Now I understood. This was the work of that Spanish stranger whom I had met as he hurried from the place of murder, who, because of the wickedness of his heart or for some secret reason, had striven to slay me also when he learned that I was my mother's son. And I had held this devil in my power, and that I might meet my May, I had suffered him to escape my vengeance, who, had I known the truth, would have dealt with him as the priests of Anahuac deal with the victims of their gods. I understood and shed tears of pity, rage, and shame. Then I turned and fled homewards like one mad.

At the doorway I met my father and my brother Geoffrey riding up from Bungay market, and there was that written on my face which caused them to ask as with one voice:

'What evil thing has happened?'

Thrice I looked at my father before I could speak, for I feared lest the blow should kill him. But speak I must at last, though I chose that it should be to Geoffrey my brother. 'Our mother lies murdered yonder on the Vineyard Hill. A Spanish man has done the deed, Juan de Garcia by name.' When my father heard these words his face became livid as though with pain of the heart, his jaw fell and a low moan issued from his open mouth. Presently he rested his hand upon the pommel of the saddle, and lifting his ghastly face he said:

'Where is this Spaniard? Have you killed him?'

'No, father. He chanced upon me in Grubswell, and when he learned my name he would have murdered me. But I played quarter staff with him and beat him to a pulp, taking his sword.'

'Ay, and then?'

'And then I let him go, knowing nothing of the deed he had already wrought upon our mother. Afterwards I will tell you all.'

'You let him go, son! You let Juan de Garcia go! Then, Thomas, may the curse of God rest upon you till you find him and finish that which you began to-day.'

'Spare to curse me, father, who am accursed by my own conscience. Turn your horses rather and ride for Yarmouth, for there his ship lies and thither he has gone with two hours' start. Perhaps you may still trap him before he sets sail.'

Without another word my father and brother wheeled their horses round and departed at full gallop into the gloom of the gathering night.

They rode so fiercely that, their horses being good, they came to the gates of Yarmouth in little more than an hour and a half, and that is fast riding. But the bird was flown. They tracked him to the quay and found that he had shipped a while before in a boat which was in waiting for him, and passed to his vessel that lay in the Roads at anchor but with the most of her canvas set. Instantly she sailed, and now was lost in the night. Then my father caused notice to be given that he would pay reward of two hundred pieces in gold to any ship that should capture the Spaniard, and two started on the quest, but they did not find her that before morning was far on her way across the sea.

So soon as they had galloped away I called together the grooms and other serving men and told them what had chanced. Then we went with lanterns, for by now it was dark, and came to the thick brushwood where lay the body of my mother. I drew near the first, for the men were afraid, and so indeed was I, though why I should fear her lying dead who living had loved me tenderly, I do not know. Yet I know this, that when I came to the spot and saw two eyes glowering at me and heard the crash of bushes as something broke them, I could almost have fallen with fear, although I knew well that it was but a fox or wandering hound haunting the place of death.

Still I went on, calling the others to follow, and the end of it was that we laid my mother's body upon a door which had been lifted from its hinges, and bore her home for the last time. And to me that path is still a haunted place. It is seventy years and more since my mother died by the hand of Juan de Garcia her cousin, yet old as I am and hardened to such sad scenes, I do not love to walk that path alone at night.

Doubtless it was fancy which plays us strange tricks, still but a year ago, having gone to set a springe for a woodcock, I chanced to pass by yonder big oak upon a November eve, and I could have sworn that I saw it all again. I saw myself a lad, my wounded arm still bound with Lily's kerchief, climbing slowly down the hill-side, while behind me, groaning beneath their burden, were the forms of the four serving men. I heard the murmur of the river and the wind that seventy years ago whispered in the reeds. I saw the clouded sky flawed here and there with blue, and the broken light that gleamed on the white burden stretched upon the door, and the red stain at its breast. Ay, I heard myself talk as I went forward with the lantern, bidding the men pass to the right of some steep and rotten ground, and it was strange to me to listen to my own voice as it had been in youth. Well, well, it was but a dream, yet such slaves are we to the fears of fancy, that because of the dead, I, who am almost of their number, do not love to pass that path at night.

At length we came home with our burden, and the women took it weeping and set about their task with it. And now I must not only fight my own sorrows but must strive to soothe those of my sister Mary, who as I feared would go mad with grief and horror. At last she sobbed herself into a torpor, and I went and questioned the men who sat round the fire in the kitchen, for none sought their beds that night. From them I learned that an hour or more before I met the Spaniard, a richly-dressed stranger had been seen walking along the church-path, and that he had tied his horse among some gorse and brambles on the top of the hill, where he stood as though in doubt, till my mother came out, when he descended and followed her. Also I learned that one of the men at work in the garden, which is not more than three hundred paces from where the deed was done, heard cries, but had taken no note of them, thinking forsooth that it was but the play of some lover from Bungay and his lass chasing each other through the woods, as to this hour it is their fashion to do. Truly it seemed to me that day as though this parish of Ditchingham were the very nursery of fools, of whom I was the first and biggest, and indeed this same thought has struck me since concerning other matters.

At length the morning came, and with it my father and brother, who returned from Yarmouth on hired horses, for their own were spent. In the afternoon also news followed them that the ships which had put to sea on the track of the Spaniard had been driven back by bad weather, having seen nothing of him.

Now I told all the story of my dealings with the murderer of my mother, keeping nothing back, and I must bear my father's bitter anger because knowing that my mother was in dread of a Spaniard, I had suffered my reason to be led astray by my desire to win speech with my love. Nor did I meet with any comfort from my brother Geoffrey, who was fierce against me because he learned that I had not pleaded in vain with the maid whom he desired for himself. But he said nothing of this reason. Also that no drop might be lacking in my cup, Squire Bozard, who came with many other neighbours to view the corpse and offer sympathy with my father in his loss, told him at the same time that he took it ill that I should woo his daughter against his wish, and that if I continued in this course it would strain their ancient friendship. Thus I was hit on every side; by sorrow for my mother whom I had loved tenderly, by longing for my dear whom I might not see, by self-reproach because I had let the Spaniard go when I held him fast, and by the anger of my father and my brother. Indeed those days were so dark and bitter, for I was at the age when shame and sorrow sting their sharpest, that I wished that I were dead beside my mother. One comfort reached me indeed, a message from Lily sent by a servant girl whom she trusted, giving me her dear love and bidding me to be of good cheer.

At length came the day of burial, and my mother, wrapped in fair white robes, was laid to her rest in the chancel of the church at Ditchingham, where my father has long been set beside her, hard by the brass effigies that mark the burying place of Lily's forefather, his wife, and many of their children. This funeral was the saddest of sights, for the bitterness of my father's grief broke from him in sobs and my sister Mary swooned away in my arms. Indeed there were few dry eyes in all that church, for my mother, notwithstanding her foreign birth, was much loved because of her gentle ways and the goodness of her heart. But it came to an end, and the noble Spanish lady and English wife was left to her long sleep in the ancient church, where she shall rest on when her tragic story and her very name are forgotten among men. Indeed this is likely to be soon, for I am the last of the Wingfields alive in these parts, though my sister Mary has left descendants of another name to whom my lands and fortune go except for certain gifts to the poor of Bungay and of Ditchingham.

When it was over I went back home. My father was sitting in the front room well nigh beside himself with grief, and by him was my brother. Presently he began to assail me with bitter words because I had let the murderer go when God gave him into my hand.

'You forget, father,' sneered Geoffrey, 'Thomas woos a maid, and it was more to him to hold her in his arms than to keep his mother's murderer safely. But by this it seems he has killed two birds with one stone, he has suffered the Spanish devil to escape when he knew that our mother feared the coming of a Spaniard, and he has made enmity between us and Squire Bozard, our good neighbour, who strangely enough does not favour his wooing.'

'It is so,' said my father. 'Thomas, your mother's blood is on your hands.'

I listened and could bear this goading injustice no longer.

'It is false,' I said, 'I say it even to my father. The man had killed my mother before I met him riding back to seek his ship at Yarmouth and having lost his way; how then is her blood upon my hands? As for my wooing of Lily Bozard, that is my matter, brother, and not yours, though perhaps you wish that it was yours and not mine. Why, father, did you not tell me what you feared of this Spaniard? I heard some loose talk only and gave little thought to it, my mind being full of other things. And now I will say something. You called down God's curse upon me, father, till such time as I should find this murderer and finish what I had begun. So be it! Let God's curse rest upon me till I do find him. I am young, but I am quick and strong, and so soon as may be I start for Spain to hunt him there till I shall run him down or know him to be dead. If you will give me money to help me on my quest, so be it—if not I go without. I swear before God and by my mother's spirit that I will neither rest nor stay till with the very sword that slew her, I have avenged her blood upon her murderer or know him dead, and if I suffer myself to be led astray from the purpose of this oath by aught that is, then may a worse end than hers overtake me, may my soul be rejected in heaven, and my name be shameful for ever upon the earth!'

Thus I swore in my rage and anguish, holding up my hand to heaven that I called upon to witness the oath.

My father looked at me keenly. 'If that is your mind, son Thomas, you shall not lack for money. I would go myself, for blood must be wiped out with blood, but I am too broken in my health; also I am known in Spain and the Holy Office would claim me there. Go, and my blessing go with you. It is right that you should go, for it is through your folly that our enemy has escaped us.'

'Yes, it is right that he should go,' said Geoffrey.

'You say that because you wish to be rid of me, Geoffrey,' I answered hotly, 'and you would be rid of me because you desire to take my place at the side of a certain maid. Follow your nature and do as you will, but if you would outwit an absent man no good shall come to you of it.'

'The girl is to him who can win her,' he said.

'The girl's heart is won already, Geoffrey. You may buy her from her father but you can never win her heart, and without a heart she will be but a poor prize.'

'Peace! now is no time for such talk of love and maids,' said my father, 'and listen. This is the tale of the Spanish murderer and your mother. I have said nothing of it heretofore, but now it must out. When I was a lad it happened that I also went to Spain because my father willed it. I went to a monastery at Seville, but I had no liking for monks and their ways, and I broke out from the monastery. For a year or more I made my living as I best might, for I feared to return to England as a runaway. Still I made a living and not a bad one, now in this way and now in that, but though I am ashamed to say it, mostly by gaming, at which I had great luck. One night I met this man Juan de Garcia—for in his hate he gave you his true name when he would have stabbed you—at play. Even then he had an evil fame, though he was scarcely more than a lad, but he was handsome in person, set high in birth, and of a pleasing manner. It chanced that he won of me at the dice, and being in a good humour, he took me to visit at the house of his aunt, his uncle's widow, a lady of Seville. This aunt had one child, a daughter, and that daughter was your mother. Now your mother, Luisa de Garcia, was affianced to her cousin Juan de Garcia, not with her own will indeed, for the contract had been signed when she was only eight years old. Still it was binding, more binding indeed than in this country, being a marriage in all except in fact. But those women who are thus bound for the most part bear no wife's love in their hearts, and so it was with your mother. Indeed she both hated and feared her cousin Juan, though I think that he loved her more than anything on earth, and by one pretext and another she contrived to bring him to an agreement that no marriage should be celebrated till she was full twenty years of age. But the colder she was to him, the more was he inflamed with desire to win her and also her possessions, which were not small, for like all Spaniards he was passionate, and like most gamesters and men of evil life, much in want of money.

'Now to be brief, from the first moment that your mother and I set eyes on each other we loved one another, and it was our one desire to meet as often as might be; and in this we had no great difficulty, for her mother also feared and hated Juan de Garcia, her nephew by marriage, and would have seen her daughter clear of him if possible. The end of it was that I told my love, and a plot was made between us that we should fly to England. But all this had not escaped the ears of Juan, who had spies in the household, and was jealous and revengeful as only a Spaniard can be. First he tried to be rid of me by challenging me to a duel, but we were parted before we could draw swords. Then he hired bravos to murder me as I walked the streets at night, but I wore a chain shirt beneath my doublet and their daggers broke upon it, and in place of being slain I slew one of them. Twice baffled, de Garcia was not defeated. Fight and murder had failed, but another and surer means remained. I know not how, but he had won some clue to the history of my life, and of how I had broken out from the monastery. It was left to him, therefore, to denounce me to the Holy Office as a renegade and an infidel, and this he did one night; it was the night before the day when we should have taken ship. I was sitting with your mother and her mother in their house at Seville, when six cowled men entered and seized me without a word. When I prayed to know their purpose they gave no other answer than to hold a crucifix before my eyes. Then I knew why I was taken, and the women ceased clinging to me and fell back sobbing. Secretly and silently I was hurried away to the dungeons of the Holy Office, but of all that befell me there I will not stop to tell.

'Twice I was racked, once I was seared with hot irons, thrice I was flogged with wire whips, and all this while I was fed on food such as we should scarcely offer to a dog here in England. At length my offence of having escaped from a monastery and sundry blasphemies, so-called, being proved against me, I was condemned to death by fire.

'Then at last, when after a long year of torment and of horror, I had abandoned hope and resigned myself to die, help came. On the eve of the day upon which I was to be consumed by flame, the chief of my tormentors entered the dungeon where I lay on straw, and embracing me bade me be of good cheer, for the church had taken pity on my youth and given me my freedom. At first I laughed wildly, for I thought that this was but another torment, and not till I was freed of my fetters, clothed in decent garments, and set at midnight without the prison gates, would I believe that so good a thing had befallen me through the hand of God. I stood weak and wondering outside the gates, not knowing where to fly, and as I stood a woman glided up to me wrapped in a dark cloak, who whispered "Come." That woman was your mother. She had learned of my fate from the boasting of de Garcia and set herself to save me. Thrice her plans failed, but at length through the help of some cunning agent, gold won what was denied to justice and to mercy, and my life and liberty were bought with a very great sum.

'That same night we were married and fled for Cadiz, your mother and I, but not her mother, who was bedridden with a sickness. For my sake your beloved mother abandoned her people, what remained to her of her fortune after paying the price of my life, and her country, so strong is the love of woman. All had been made ready, for at Cadiz lay an English ship, the "*Mary*" of Bristol, in which passage was taken for us. But the "*Mary*" was delayed in port by a contrary wind which blew so strongly that notwithstanding his desire to save us, her master dared not take the sea. Two days and a night we lay in the harbour, fearing all things not without cause, and yet most happy in each other's love. Now those who had charge of me in the dungeon had given out that I had escaped by the help of my master the Devil, and I was searched for throughout the country side. De Garcia also, finding that his cousin and affianced wife was missing, guessed that we two were not far apart. It was his cunning, sharpened by jealousy and hate, that dogged us down step by step till at length he found us.

'On the morning of the third day, the gale having abated, the anchor of the "*Mary*" was got home and she swung out into the tideway. As she came round and while the seamen were making ready to hoist the sails, a boat carrying some twenty soldiers, and followed by two others, shot alongside and summoned the captain to heave to, that his ship might be boarded and searched under warrant from the Holy Office. It chanced that I was on deck at the time, and suddenly, as I prepared to hide myself below, a man, in whom I knew de Garcia himself, stood up and called out that I was the escaped heretic whom they sought. Fearing lest his ship should be boarded and he himself thrown into prison with the rest of his crew, the captain would then have surrendered me. But I, desperate with fear, tore my clothes from my body and showed the cruel scars that marked it.

'"You are Englishmen," I cried to the sailors, "and will you deliver me to these foreign devils, who am of your blood? Look at their handiwork," and I pointed to the half-healed scars left by the red-hot pincers; "if you give me up, you send me back to more of this torment and to death by burning. Pity my wife if you will not pity me, or if you will pity neither, then lend me a sword that by death I may save myself from torture."

'Then one of the seamen, a Southwold man who had known my father, called out:"By God! I for one will stand by you,Thomas Wingfield. If they want you and your sweet lady they must kill me first," and seizing a bow from the rack he drew it out of its case and strung it, and setting an arrow on the string he pointed it at the Spaniards in the boat.

'Then the others broke into shouts of:

"'If you want any man from among us, come aboard and take him, you torturing devils," and the like.

'Seeing where the heart of the crew lay, the captain found courage in his turn. He made no answer to the Spaniards, but bade half of the men hoist the sails with all speed, and the rest make ready to keep off the soldiers should they seek to board us.

'By now the other two boats had come up and fastened on to us with their hooks. One man climbed into the chains and thence to the deck, and I knew him for a priest of the Holy Office, one of those who had stood by while I was tormented. Then I grew mad at the thought of all that I had suffered, while that devil watched, bidding them lay on for the love of God. Snatching the bow from the hand of the Southwold seaman, I drew the arrow to its head and loosed. It did not miss its mark, for like you,Thomas, I was skilled with the bow, and he dived back into the sea with an English yard shaft in his heart.

'After that they tried to board us no more, though they shot at us with arrows, wounding one man.The captain called to us to lay down our bows and take cover behind the bulwarks, for by now the sails began to draw. Then de Garcia stood up in the boat and cursed me and my wife.

"'I will find you yet," he screamed, with many Spanish oaths and foul words."If I must wait for twenty years I will be avenged upon you and all you love. Be assured of this, Luisa de Garcia, hide where you will, I shall find you, and when we meet, you shall come with me for so long as I will keep you or that shall be the hour of your death."

'Then we sailed away for England, and the boats fell astern.

'My sons, this is the story of my youth, and of how I came to wed your mother whom I have buried to-day. Juan de Garcia has kept his word.'

'Yet it seems strange,' said my brother, 'that after all these years he should have murdered her thus, whom you say he loved. Surely even the evilest of men had shrunk from such a deed!'

'There is little that is strange about it,' answered my father. 'How can we know what words were spoken between them before he stabbed her? Doubtless he told of some of them when he cried to Thomas that now they would see what truth there was in prophecies.

What did de Garcia swear years since?—that she should come with him or he would kill her. Your mother was still beautiful, Geoffrey, and he may have given her choice between flight and death. Seek to know no more, son'—and suddenly my father hid his face in his hands and broke into sobs that were dreadful to hear.

'Would that you had told us this tale before, father,' I said so soon as I could speak. 'Then there would have lived a devil the less in the world to-day, and I should have been spared a long journey.'

Little did I know how long that journey would be!

CHAPTER 6

Goodbye, Sweetheart

Within twelve days of the burial of my mother and the telling of the story of his marriage to her by my father, I was ready to start upon my search. As it chanced a vessel was about to sail from Yarmouth to Cadiz. She was named the '*Adventuress*,' of one hundred tons burden, and carried wool and other goods outwards, purposing to return with a cargo of wine and yew staves for bows. In this vessel my father bought me a passage. Moreover, he gave me fifty pounds in gold, which was as much as I would risk upon my person, and obtained letters from the Yarmouth firm of merchants to their agents in Cadiz, in which they were advised to advance me such sums as I might need up to a total of one hundred and fifty English pounds, and further to assist me in any way that was possible.

Now the ship '*Adventuress*' was to sail on the third day of June. Already it was the first of that month, and that evening I must ride to Yarmouth, whither my baggage had gone already. Except one my farewells were made, and yet that was the one I most wished to make. Since the day when we had sworn our troth I had gained no sight of Lily except once at my mother's burial, and then we had not spoken. Now it seemed that I must go without any parting word, for her father had sent me notice that if I came near the Hall his serving men had orders to thrust me from the door, and this was a shame that I would not risk. Yet it was hard that I must go upon so long a journey, whence it well might chance I should not return, and bid her no goodbye. In my grief and perplexity I spoke to my father, telling him how the matter stood and asking his help.

'I go hence,' I said, 'to avenge our common loss, and if need be to give my life for the honour of our name. Aid me then in this.'

'My neighbour Bozard means his daughter for your brother Geoffrey, and not for you, Thomas,' he answered; 'and a man may do what he wills with his own. Still I will help you if I can, at the least he cannot drive me from his door. Bid them bring horses, and we will ride to the Hall.'

Within the half of an hour we were there, and my father asked for speech with its master. The serving man looked at me askance, remembering his orders, still he ushered us into the justice room where the Squire sat drinking ale.

'Good morrow to you, neighbour,' said the Squire; 'you are welcome here, but you bring one with you who is not welcome, though he be your son.'

'I bring him for the last time, friend Bozard. Listen to his request, then grant it or refuse it as you will; but if you refuse it, it will not bind us closer. The lad rides to-night to take ship for Spain to seek that man who murdered his mother. He goes of his own free will because after the doing of the deed it was he who unwittingly suffered the murderer to escape, and it is well that he should go.'

'He is a young hound to run such a quarry to earth, and in a strange country,' said the Squire. 'Still I like his spirit and wish him well. What would he of me?'

'Leave to bid farewell to your daughter. I know that his suit does not please you and cannot wonder at it, and for my own part I think it too early for him to set his fancy in the way of marriage. But if he would see the maid it can do no harm, for such harm as there is has been done already. Now for your answer.'

Squire Bozard thought a while, then said:

'The lad is a brave lad though he shall be no son-in-law of mine. He is going far, and mayhap will return no more, and I do not wish that he should think unkindly of me when I am dead. Go without, Thomas Wingfield, and stand under yonder beech—Lily shall join you there and you may speak with her for the half of an hour—no more. See to it that you keep within sight of the window. Nay, no thanks; go before I change my mind.'

So I went and waited under the beech with a beating heart, and presently Lily glided up to me, a more welcome sight to my eyes than any angel out of heaven. And, indeed, I doubt if an angel could have been more fair than she, or more good and gentle.

'Oh! Thomas,' she whispered, when I had greeted her, 'is this true that you sail overseas to seek the Spaniard?'

'I sail to seek the Spaniard, and to find him and to kill him when he is found. It was to come to you, Lily, that I let him go, now I must let you go to come to him. Nay, do not weep, I have sworn to do it, and were I to break my oath I should be dishonoured.'

'And because of this oath of yours I must be widowed, Thomas, before I am a wife? You go and I shall never see you more.'

'Who can say, my sweet? My father went over seas and came back safe, having passed through many perils.'

'Yes, he came back and—not alone. You are young, Thomas, and in far countries there are ladies great and fair, and how shall I hold my own in your heart against them, I being so far away?'

'I swear to you, Lily—'

'Nay, Thomas, swear no oaths lest you should add to your sins by breaking them. Yet, love, forget me not, who shall forget you never. Perhaps—oh! it wrings my heart to say it—this is our last meeting on the earth. If so, then we must hope to meet in heaven. At the least be sure of this, while I live I will be true to you, and father or no father, I will die before I break my troth. I am young to speak so largely, but it shall be as I say. Oh! this parting is more cruel than death. Would that we were asleep and forgotten among men. Yet it is best that you should go, for if you stayed what could we be to each other while my father lives, and may he live long!'

'Sleep and forgetfulness will come soon enough, Lily; none must await them for very long. Meanwhile we have our lives to live. Let us pray that we may live them to each other. I go to seek fortune as well as foes, and I will win it for your sake that we may marry.'

She shook her head sadly. 'It were too much happiness, Thomas. Men and women may seldom wed their true loves, or if they do, it is but to lose them. At the least we love, and let us be thankful that we have learned what love can be, for having loved here, perchance at the worst we may love otherwhere when there are none to say us nay.'

Then we talked on awhile, babbling broken words of love and hope and sorrow, as young folks so placed are wont to do, till at length Lily looked up with a sad sweet smile and said:

'It is time to go, sweetheart. My father beckons me from the lattice. All is finished.'

'Let us go then,' I answered huskily, and drew her behind the trunk of the old beech. And there I caught her in my arms and kissed her again and yet again, nor was she ashamed to kiss me back.

After this I remember little of what happened, except that as we rode away I saw her beloved face, wan and wistful, watching me departing out of her life. For twenty years that sad and beautiful face haunted me, and it haunts me yet athwart life and death. Other women have loved me and I have known other partings, some of them more terrible, but the memory of this woman as she was then, and of her farewell look, overruns them all. Whenever I gaze down the past I see this picture framed in it and I know that it is one which cannot fade. Are there any sorrows like these sorrows of our youth? Can any bitterness equal the bitterness of such good-byes? I know but one of which I was fated to taste in after years, and that shall be told of in its place. It is a common jest to mock at early love, but if it be real, if it be something more than the mere arising of the passions, early love is late love also; it is love for ever, the best and worst event which can befall a man or woman. I say it who am old and who have done with everything, and it is true.

One thing I have forgotten. As we kissed and clung in our despair behind the bole of the great beech, Lily drew a ring from her finger and pressed it into my hand saying, 'Look on this each morning when you wake, and think of me.' It had been her mother's, and to-day it still is set upon my withered hand, gleaming in the winter sunlight as I trace these words. Through the long years of wild adventure, through all the time of after peace, in love and war, in the shine of the camp fire, in the glare of the sacrificial flame, in the light of lonely stars illumining the lonely wilderness, that ring has shone upon my hand, reminding me always of her who gave it, and on this hand it shall go down into the grave. It is a plain circlet of thick gold, somewhat worn now, a posy-ring, and on its inner surface is cut this quaint couplet:

Heart to heart, Though far apart.

A fitting motto for us indeed, and one that has its meaning to this hour.

That same day of our farewell I rode with my father to Yarmouth. My brother Geoffrey did not come with us, but we parted with kindly words, and of this I am glad, for we never saw each other again. No more was said between us as to Lily Bozard and our wooing of her, though I knew well enough that so soon as my back was turned he would try to take my place at her side, as indeed happened. I forgive it to him; in truth I cannot blame him much, for what man is there that would not have desired to wed Lily who knew her? Once we were dear friends, Geoffrey and I, but when we ripened towards manhood, our love of Lily came between us, and we grew more and more apart. It is a common case enough. Well, as it chanced he failed, so why should I think unkindly of him? Let me rather remember the affection of our childhood and forget the rest. God rest his soul.

Mary, my sister, who after Lily Bozard was now the fairest maiden in the country side, wept much at my going. There was but a year between us, and we loved each other dearly, for no such shadow of jealousy had fallen on our affection. I comforted her as well as I was able, and telling her all that had passed between me and Lily, I prayed her to stand my friend and Lily's, should it ever be in her power to do so. This Mary promised to do readily enough, and though she did not give the reason, I could see that she thought it possible that she might be able to help us. As I have said, Lily had a brother, a young man of some promise, who at this time was away at college, and he and my sister Mary had a strong fancy for each other, that might or might not ripen into something closer. So we kissed and bade farewell with tears.

And after that my father and I rode away. But when we had passed down Pirnhow Street, and mounted the little hill beyond Waingford Mills to the left of Bungay town, I halted my horse, and looked back upon the pleasant valley of the Waveney where I was born, and my heart grew full to bursting. Had I known all that must befall me, before my eyes beheld that scene again, I think indeed that it would have burst. But God, who in his wisdom has laid many a burden upon the backs of men, has saved them from this; for had we foreknowledge of the future, I think that of our own will but few of us would live to see it. So I cast one long last look towards the distant mass of oaks that marked the spot where Lily lived, and rode on.

On the following day I embarked on board the 'Adventuress' and we sailed. Before I left, my father's heart softened much towards me, for he remembered that I was my mother's best beloved, and feared also lest we should meet no more. So much did it soften indeed, that at the last hour he changed his mind and wished to hold me back from going. But having put my hand to the plough and suffered all the bitterness of farewell, I would not return to be mocked by my brother and my neighbours. 'You speak too late, father,' I said. 'You desired me to go to work this vengeance and stirred me to it with many bitter words, and now I would go if I knew that I must die within a week, for such oaths cannot be lightly broken, and till mine is fulfilled the curse rests on me.'

'So be it, son,' he answered with a sigh. 'Your mother's cruel death maddened me and I said what I may live to be sorry for, though at the best I shall not live long, for my heart is broken. Perhaps I should have remembered that vengeance is in the hand of the Lord, who wreaks it at His own time and without our help. Do not think unkindly of me, my boy, if we should chance to meet no more, for I love you, and it was but the deeper love that I bore to your mother which made me deal harshly with you.'

'I know it, father, and bear no grudge. But if you think that you owe me anything, pay it by holding back my brother from working wrong to me and Lily Bozard while I am absent.'

'I will do my best, son, though were it not that you and she have grown so dear to each other, the match would have pleased me well. But as I have said, I shall not be long here to watch your welfare in this or any other matter, and when I am gone things must follow their own fate. Do not forget your God or your home wherever you chance to wander, Thomas: keep yourself from brawling, beware of women that are the snare of youth, and set a watch upon your tongue and your temper which is not of the best. Moreover, wherever you may be do not speak ill of the religion of the land, or make a mock of it by your way of life, lest you should learn how cruel men can be when they think that it is pleasing to their gods, as I have learnt already.'

I said that I would bear his counsel in mind, and indeed it saved me from many a sorrow. Then he embraced me and called on the Almighty to take me in His care, and we parted.

I never saw him more, for though he was but middle-aged, within a year of my going my father died suddenly of a distemper of the heart in the nave of Ditchingham church, as he stood there, near the rood screen, musing by my mother's grave one Sunday after mass, and my brother took his lands and place. God rest him also! He was a true-hearted man, but more wrapped up in his love for my mother than it is well for any man to be who would look at life largely and do right by all. For such love, though natural to women, is apt to turn to something that partakes of selfishness, and to cause him who bears it to think all else of small account. His children were nothing to my father when compared to my mother, and he would have been content to lose them every one if thereby he might have purchased back her life. But after all it was a noble infirmity, for he thought little of himself and had gone through much to win her.

Of my voyage to Cadiz, to which port I had learned that de Garcia's ship was bound, there is little to be told. We met with contrary winds in the Bay of Biscay and were driven into the harbour of Lisbon, where we refitted. But at last we came safely to Cadiz, having been forty days at sea.

CHAPTER 7

Andres de Fonseca

Now I shall dwell but briefly on all the adventures which befell me during the year or so that I remained in Spain, for were I to set out everything at length, this history would have no end, or at least mine would find me before I came to it.

Many travellers have told of the glories of Seville, to which ancient Moorish city I journeyed with all speed, sailing there up the Guadalquiver, and I have to tell of lands from which no other wanderer has returned to England, and must press on to them. To be short then; foreseeing that it might be necessary for me to stop some time in Seville, and being desirous to escape notice and to be at the smallest expense possible, I bethought me that it would be well if I could find means of continuing my studies of medicine, and to this end I obtained certain introductions from the firm of merchants to whose care I had been recommended, addressed to doctors of medicine in Seville. These letters at my request were made out not in my own name but in that of 'Diego d'Aila,' for I did not wish it to be known that I was an Englishman. Nor, indeed, was this likely, except my speech should betray me, for, as I have said, in appearance I was very Spanish, and the hindrance of the language was one that lessened every day, since having already learned it from my mother, and taking every opportunity to read and speak it, within six months I could talk Castilian except for some slight accent, like a native of the land. Also I have a gift for the acquiring of languages.

When I was come to Seville, and had placed my baggage in an inn, not one of the most frequented, I set out to deliver a letter of recommendation to a famous physician of the town whose name I have long forgotten. This physician had a fine house in the street of Las Palmas, a great avenue planted with graceful trees, that has other little streets running into it. Down one of these I came from my inn, a quiet narrow place having houses with patios or courtyards on either side of it. As I walked down this street I noticed a man sitting in the shade on a stool in the doorway of his patio. He was small and withered, with keen black eyes and a wonderful air of wisdom, and he watched me as I went by. Now the house of the famous physician whom I sought was so placed that the man sitting at this doorway could command it with his eyes and take note of all who went in and came out. When I had found the house I returned again into the quiet street and walked to and fro there for a while, thinking of what tale I should tell to the physician, and all the time the little man watched me with his keen eyes. At last I had made up my story and went to the house, only to find that the physician was from home. Having inquired when I might find him I left, and once more took to the narrow street, walking slowly till I came to where the little man sat. As I passed him, his broad hat with which he was fanning himself slipped to the ground before my feet. I stooped down, lifted it from the pavement, and restored it to him.

'A thousand thanks, young sir,' he said in a full and gentle voice. 'You are courteous for a foreigner.'

'How do you know me to be a foreigner, senor?' I asked, surprised out of my caution.

'If I had not guessed it before, I should know it now,' he answered, smiling gravely. 'Your Castilian tells its own tale.'

I bowed, and was about to pass on, when he addressed me again.

'What is your hurry, young sir? Step in and take a cup of wine with me; it is good.'

I was about to say him nay, when it came into my mind that I had nothing to do, and that perhaps I might learn something from this gossip.

'The day is hot, senor, and I accept.'

He spoke no more, but rising, led me into a courtyard paved with marble in the centre of which was a basin of water, having vines trained around it. Here were chairs and a little table placed in the shade of the vines. When he had closed the door of the patio and we were seated, he rang a silver bell that stood upon the table, and a girl, young and fair, appeared from the house, dressed in a quaint Spanish dress.

'Bring wine,' said my host.

The wine was brought, white wine of Oporto such as I had never tasted before.

'Your health, senor?' And my host stopped, his glass in his hand, and looked at me inquiringly.

'Diego d'Aila,' I answered.

'Humph,' he said. 'A Spanish name, or perhaps an imitation Spanish name, for I do not know it, and I have a good head for names.'

'That is my name, to take or to leave, senor?'—And I looked at him in turn.

'Andres de Fonseca,' he replied bowing, 'a physician of this city, well known enough, especially among the fair. Well, Senor Diego, I take your name, for names are nothing, and at times it is convenient to change them, which is nobody's business except their owners'. I see that you are a stranger in this city—no need to look surprised, senor, one who is familiar with a town does not gaze and stare and ask the path of passers-by, nor does a native of Seville walk on the sunny side of the street in summer. And now, if you will not think me impertinent, I will ask you what can be the business of so healthy a young man with my rival yonder?' And he nodded towards the house of the famous physician.

'A man's business, like his name, is his own affair, senor,' I answered, setting my host down in my mind as one of those who disgrace our art by plying openly for patients that they may capture their fees. 'Still, I will tell you. I am also a physician, though not yet fully qualified, and I seek a place where I may help some doctor of repute in his daily practice, and thus gain experience and my living with it.'

'Ah is it so? Well, senor, then you will look in vain yonder,' and again he nodded towards the physician's house. 'Such as he will take no apprentice without the fee be large indeed; it is not the custom of this city.'

'Then I must seek a livelihood elsewhere, or otherwise.'

'I did not say so. Now, senor, let us see what you know of medicine, and what is more important, of human nature, for of the first none of us can ever know much, but he who knows the latter will be a leader of men—or of women—who lead the men.'

And without more ado he put me many questions, each of them so shrewd and going so directly to the heart of the matter in hand, that I marvelled at his sagacity. Some of these questions were medical, dealing chiefly with the ailments of women, others were general and dealt more with their characters. At length he finished.

'You will do, senor,' he said; 'you are a young man of parts and promise, though, as was to be expected from one of your years, you lack experience. There is stuff in you, senor, and you have a heart, which is a good thing, for the blunders of a man with a heart often carry him further than the cunning of the cynic; also you have a will and know how to direct it.'

I bowed, and did my best to hold back my satisfaction at his words from showing in my face.

'Still,' he went on, 'all this would not cause me to submit to you the offer that I am about to make, for many a prettier fellow than yourself is after all unlucky, or a fool at the bottom, or bad tempered and destined to the dogs, as for aught I know you may be also. But I take my chance of that because you suit me in another way. Perhaps you may scarcely know it yourself, but you have beauty, senor, beauty of a very rare and singular type, which half the ladies of Seville will praise when they come to know you.'

'I am much flattered,' I said, 'but might I ask what all these compliments may mean? To be brief, what is your offer?'

'To be brief then, it is this. I am in need of an assistant who must possess all the qualities that I see in you, but most of all one which I can only guess you to possess—discretion. That assistant would not be ill-paid; this house would be at his disposal, and he would have opportunities of learning the world such as are given to few. What say you?'

'I say this, senor, that I should wish to know more of the business in which I am expected to assist. Your offers sound too liberal, and I fear that I must earn your bounty by the doing of work that honest men might shrink from.'

'A fair argument, but, as it happens, not quite a correct one. Listen: you have been told that yonder physician, to whose house you went but now, and these'—here he repeated four or five names— 'are the greatest of their tribe in Seville. It is not so. I am the greatest and the richest, and I do more business than any two of them. Do you know what my earnings have been this day alone? I will tell you; just over twenty-five gold *pesos*,[1] more than all the rest of the profession have taken together, I will wager. You want to know how I earn so much; you want to know also, why, if I have earned so much, I am not content to rest from my labours. Good, I will tell you. I earn it by ministering to the vanities of women and sheltering them from the results of their own folly. Has a lady a sore heart, she comes to me for comfort and advice. Has she pimples on her face, she flies to me to cure them. Has she a secret love affair, it is I who hide her indiscretion; I consult the future for her, I help her to atone the past, I doctor her for imaginary ailments, and often enough I cure her of real ones. Half the secrets of Seville are in my hands; did I choose to speak I could set a score of noble houses to broil and bloodshed. But I do not speak, I am paid to keep silent; and when I am not paid, still

1. About sixty-three pounds sterling.

I keep silent for my credit's sake. Hundreds of women think me their saviour, I know them for my dupes. But mark you, I do not push this game too far. A love philtre—of coloured water—I may give at a price, but not a poisoned rose. These they must seek elsewhere. For the rest, in my way I am honest. I take the world as it comes, that is all, and, as women will be fools, I profit by their folly and have grown rich upon it.

'Yes, I have grown rich, and yet I cannot stop. I love the money that is power; but more than all, I love the way of life. Talk of romances and adventure! What romance or adventure is half so wonderful as those that come daily to my notice? And I play a part in every one of them, and none the less a leading part because I do not shout and strut upon the boards.'

'If all this is so, why do you seek the help of an unknown lad, a stranger of whom you know nothing?' I asked bluntly.

'Truly, you lack experience,' the old man answered with a laugh. 'Do you then suppose that I should choose one who was NOT a stranger—one who might have ties within this city with which I was unacquainted. And as for knowing nothing of you, young man, do you think that I have followed this strange trade of mine for forty years without learning to judge at sight? Perhaps I know you better than you know yourself. By the way, the fact that you are deeply enamoured of that maid whom you have left in England is a recommendation to me, for whatever follies you may commit, you will scarcely embarrass me and yourself by suffering your affections to be seriously entangled. Ah! have I astonished you?'

'How do you know?' I began—then ceased.

'How do I know? Why, easily enough. Those boots you wear were made in England. I have seen many such when I travelled there; your accent also though faint is English, and twice you have spoken English words when your Castilian failed you. Then for the maid, is not that a betrothal ring upon your hand? And when I spoke to you of the ladies of this country, my talk did not interest you overmuch as at your age it had done were you heart-whole. Surely also the lady is fair and tall? Ah! I thought so. I have noticed that men and women love their opposite in colour, no invariable rule indeed, but good for a guess.'

'You are very clever, senor.'

'No, not clever, but trained, as you will be when you have been a year in my hands, though perchance you do not intend to stop so long in Seville. Perhaps you came here with an object, and wish to pass the time profitably till it is fulfilled. A good guess again, I think.

Well, so be it, I will risk that; object and attainment are often far apart. Do you take my offer?'

'I incline to do so.'

'Then you will take it. Now I have something more to say before we come to terms. I do not want you to play the part of an apothecary's drudge. You will figure before the world as my nephew, come from abroad to learn my trade. You will help me in it indeed, but that is not all your duty. Your part will be to mix in the life of Seville, and to watch those whom I bid you watch, to drop a word here and a hint there, and in a hundred ways that I shall show you to draw grist to my mill—and to your own. You must be brilliant and witty, or sad and learned, as I wish; you must make the most of your person and your talents, for these go far with my customers. To the hidalgo you must talk of arms, to the lady, of love; but you must never commit yourself beyond redemption. And above all, young man'—and here his manner changed and his face grew stern and almost fierce—'you must never violate my confidence or the confidence of my clients. On this point I will be quite open within you, and I pray you for your own sake to believe what I say, however much you may mistrust the rest. If you break faith with me, *you die*. You die, not by my hand, but you die. That is my price; take it or leave it. Should you leave it and go hence to tell what you have heard this day, even then misfortune may overtake you suddenly. Do you understand?'

'I understand. For my own sake I will respect your confidence.'

'Young sir, I like you better than ever. Had you said that you would respect it because it was a confidence, I should have mistrusted you, for doubtless you feel that secrets communicated so readily have no claim to be held sacred. Nor have they, but when their violation involves the sad and accidental end of the violator, it is another matter. Well now, do you accept?'

'I accept.'

'Good. Your baggage I suppose is at the inn. I will send porters to discharge your score and bring it here. No need for you to go, nephew, let us stop and drink another glass of wine; the sooner we grow intimate the better, nephew.'

It was thus that first I became acquainted with Senor Andres de Fonseca, my benefactor, the strangest man whom I have ever known. Doubtless any person reading this history would think that I, the narrator, was sowing a plentiful crop of troubles for myself in having to deal with him, setting him down as a rogue of the deepest, such as sometimes, for their own wicked purposes, decoy young men to crime and ruin. But it was not so, and this is the strangest part of the strange story. All that Andres de Fonseca told me was true to the very letter.

He was a gentleman of great talent who had been rendered a little mad by misfortunes in his early life. As a physician I have never met his master, if indeed he has one in these times, and as a man versed in the world and more especially in the world of women, I have known none to compare with him. He had travelled far, and seen much, and he forgot nothing. In part he was a quack, but his quackery always had a meaning in it. He fleeced the foolish, indeed, and even juggled with astronomy, making money out of their superstition; but on the other hand he did many a kind act without reward. He would make a rich lady pay ten gold *pesos* for the dyeing of her hair, but often he would nurse some poor girl through her trouble and ask no charge; yes, and find her honest employment after it. He who knew all the secrets of Seville never made money out of them by threat of exposure, as he said because it would not pay to do so, but really because though he affected to be a selfish knave, at bottom his heart was honest.

For my own part I found life with him both easy and happy, so far as mine could be quite happy. Soon I learned my role and played it well. It was given out that I was the nephew of the rich old physician Fonseca, whom he was training to take his place; and this, together with my own appearance and manners, ensured me a welcome in the best houses of Seville. Here I took that share of our business which my master could not take, for now he never mixed among the fashion of the city. Money I was supplied with in abundance so that I could ruffle it with the best, but soon it became known that I looked to business as well as to pleasure. Often and often during some gay ball or carnival, a lady would glide up to me and ask beneath her breath if Don Andres de Fonseca would consent to see her privately on a matter of some importance, and I would fix an hour then and there. Had it not been for me such patients would have been lost to us, since, for the most part, their timidity had kept them away.

In the same fashion when the festival was ended and I prepared to wend homewards, now and again a gallant would slip his arm in mine and ask my master's help in some affair of love or honour, or even of the purse. Then I would lead him straight to the old Moorish house where Don Andres sat writing in his velvet robe like some spider in his web, for the most of our business was done at night; and straightway the matter would be attended to, to my master's profit and the satisfaction of all. By degrees it became known that though I was so young yet I had discretion, and that nothing which went in at my ears came out of my lips; that I neither brawled nor drank nor gambled to any length, and that though I was friendly with many fair ladies, there were none who were entitled to know my secrets. Also it became known that I had some skill in my art of healing, and it was said among the ladies of Seville that there lived no man in that city so deft at clearing the skin of blemishes or changing the colour of the hair as old Fonseca's nephew, and as any one may know this reputation alone was worth a fortune. Thus it came about that I was more and more consulted on my own account. In short, things went so well with us that in the first six months of my service I added by one third to the receipts of my master's practice, large as they had been before, besides lightening his labours not a little.

It was a strange life, and of the things that I saw and learned, could they be written, I might make a tale indeed, but they have no part in this history. For it was as though the smiles and silence with which men and women hide their thoughts were done away, and their hearts spoke to us in the accents of truth. Now some fair young maid or wife would come to us with confessions of wickedness that would be thought impossible, did not her story prove itself; the secret murder perchance of a spouse, or a lover, or a rival; now some aged dame who would win a husband in his teens, now some wealthy low-born man or woman, who desired to buy an alliance with one lacking money, but of noble blood. Such I did not care to help indeed, but to the love-sick or the love-deluded I listened with a ready ear, for I had a fellow-feeling with them. Indeed so deep and earnest was my sympathy that more than once I found the unhappy fair ready to transfer their affections to my unworthy self, and in fact once things came about so that, had I willed it, I could have married one of the loveliest and wealthiest noble ladies of Seville.

But I would none of it, who thought of my English Lily by day and night.

CHAPTER 8

The Second Meeting

It may be thought that while I was employed thus I had forgotten the object of my coming to Spain, namely to avenge my mother's murder on the person of Juan de Garcia. But this was not so. So soon as I was settled in the house of Andres de Fonseca I set myself to make inquiries as to de Garcia's whereabouts with all possible diligence, but without result.

Indeed, when I came to consider the matter coolly it seemed that I had but a slender chance of finding him in this city. He had, indeed, given it out in Yarmouth that he was bound for Seville, but no ship bearing the same name as his had put in at Cadiz or sailed up the Guadalquivir, nor was it likely, having committed murder in England, that he would speak the truth as to his destination. Still I searched on. The house where my mother and grandmother had lived was burned down, and as their mode of life had been retired, after more than twenty years of change few even remembered their existence. Indeed I only discovered one, an old woman whom I found living in extreme poverty, and who once had been my grandmother's servant and knew my mother well, although she was not in the house at the time of her flight to England. From this woman I gathered some information, though, needless to say, I did not tell her that I was the grandson of her old mistress.

It seemed that after my mother fled to England with my father, de Garcia persecuted my grandmother and his aunt with lawsuits and by other means, till at last she was reduced to beggary, in which condition the villain left her to die. So poor was she indeed, that she was buried in a public grave. After that the old woman, my informant, said she had heard that de Garcia had committed some crime and been forced to flee the country. What the crime was she could not remember, but it had happened about fifteen years ago.

All this I learned when I had been about three months in Seville, and though it was of interest it did not advance me in my search.

Some four or five nights afterwards, as I entered my employer's house I met a young woman coming out of the doorway of the patio; she was thickly veiled and my notice was drawn to her by her tall and beautiful figure and because she was weeping so violently that her body shook with her sobs. I was already well accustomed to such sights, for many of those who sought my master's counsel had good cause to weep, and I passed her without remark. But when I was come into the room where he received his patients, I mentioned that I had met such a person and asked if it was any one whom I knew.

'Ah! nephew,' said Fonseca, who always called me thus by now, and indeed began to treat me with as much affection as though I were really of his blood, 'a sad case, but you do not know her and she is no paying patient. A poor girl of noble birth who had entered religion and taken her vows, when a gallant appears, meets her secretly in the convent garden, promises to marry her if she will fly with him, indeed does go through some mummery of marriage with her—so she says—and the rest of it. Now he has deserted her and she is in trouble, and what is more, should the priests catch her, likely to learn what it feels like to die by inches in a convent wall. She came to me for counsel and brought some silver ornaments as the fee. Here they are.'

'You took them!'

'Yes, I took them—I always take a fee, but I gave her back their weight in gold. What is more, I told her where she might hide from the priests till the hunt is done with. What I did not like to tell her is that her lover is the greatest villain who ever trod the streets of Seville. What was the good? She will see little more of him. *Hist!* here comes the duchess—an astrological case this. Where are the horoscope and the wand, yes, and the crystal ball? There, shade the lamps, give me the book, and vanish.'

I obeyed, and presently met the great lady, a stout woman attended by a *duenna*, gliding fearfully through the darkened archways to learn the answer of the stars and pay many good *pesos* for it, and the sight of her made me laugh so much that I forgot quickly about the other lady and her woes.

And now I must tell how I met my cousin and my enemy de Garcia for the second time. Two days after my meeting with the veiled lady it chanced that I was wandering towards midnight through a lonely part of the old city little frequented by passers-by. It was scarcely safe to be thus alone in such a place and hour, but the business with which

I had been charged by my master was one that must be carried out unattended. Also I had no enemies whom I knew of, and was armed with the very sword that I had taken from de Garcia in the lane at Ditchingham, the sword that had slain my mother, and which I bore in the hope that it might serve to avenge her. In the use of this weapon I had grown expert enough by now, for every morning I took lessons in the art of fence.

My business being done I was walking slowly homeward, and as I went I fell to thinking of the strangeness of my present life and of how far it differed from my boyhood in the valley of the Waveney, and of many other things. And then I thought of Lily and wondered how her days passed, and if my brother Geoffrey persecuted her to marry him, and whether or no she would resist his importunities and her father's. And so as I walked musing I came to a water-gate that opened on to the Guadalquivir, and leaning upon the coping of a low wall I rested there idly to consider the beauty of the night. In truth it was a lovely night, for across all these years I remember it. Let those who have seen it say if they know any prospect more beautiful than the sight of the August moon shining on the broad waters of the Guadalquivir and the clustering habitations of the ancient city.

Now as I leaned upon the wall and looked, I saw a man pass up the steps beside me and go on into the shadow of the street. I took no note of him till presently I heard a murmur of distant voices, and turning my head I discovered that the man was in conversation with a woman whom he had met at the head of the path that ran down to the water-gate. Doubtless it was a lovers' meeting, and since such sights are of interest to all, and more especially to the young, I watched the pair. Soon I learned that there was little of tenderness in this tryst, at least on the part of the gallant, who drew continually backwards toward me as though he would seek the boat by which doubtless he had come, and I marvelled at this, for the moonlight shone upon the woman's face, and even at that distance I could see that it was very fair. The man's face I could not see however, since his back was towards me for the most part, moreover he wore a large sombrero that shaded it. Now they came nearer to me, the man always drawing backward and the woman always following, till at length they were within ear-shot. The woman was pleading with the man.

'Surely you will not desert me,' she said, 'after marrying me and all that you have sworn; you will not have the heart to desert me. I abandoned everything for you. I am in great danger. I——' and here her voice fell so that I could not catch her words.

Then he spoke. 'Fairest, now as always I adore you. But we must part awhile. You owe me much, Isabella. I have rescued you from the grave, I have taught you what it is to live and love. Doubtless with your advantages and charms, your great charms, you will profit by the lesson. Money I cannot give you, for I have none to spare, but I have endowed you with experience that is more valuable by far. This is our farewell for awhile and I am broken-hearted. Yet

"'Neath fairer skies Shine other eyes," and I—' and again he spoke so low that I could not catch his words.

As he talked on, all my body began to tremble. The scene was moving indeed, but it was not that which stirred me so deeply, it was the man's voice and bearing that reminded me—no, it could scarcely be!

'Oh! you will not be so cruel,' said the lady, 'to leave me, your wife, thus alone and in such sore trouble and danger. Take me with you, Juan, I beseech you!' and she caught him by the arm and clung to him.

He shook her from him somewhat roughly, and as he did so his wide hat fell to the ground so that the moonlight shone upon his face. By Heaven! it was he—Juan de Garcia and no other! I could not be mistaken. There was the deeply carved, cruel face, the high forehead with the scar on it, the thin sneering mouth, the peaked beard and curling hair. Chance had given him into my hand, and I would kill him or he should kill me. I took three paces and stood before him, drawing my sword as I came.

'What, my dove, have you a bully at hand?' he said stepping back astonished. 'Your business, senor? Are you here to champion beauty in distress?'

'I am here, Juan de Garcia, to avenge a murdered woman. Do you remember a certain river bank away in England, where you chanced to meet a lady you had known, and to leave her dead? Or if you have forgotten, perhaps at least you will remember this, which I carry that it may kill you,' and I flashed the sword that had been his before his eyes.

'Mother of God! It is the English boy who—' and he stopped.

'It is Thomas Wingfield who beat and bound you, and who now purposes to finish what he began yonder as he has sworn. Draw, or, Juan de Garcia, I will stab you where you stand.'

De Garcia heard this speech, that to-day seems to me to smack of the theatre, though it was spoken in grimmest earnest, and his face grew like the face of a trapped wolf. Yet I saw that he had no mind to fight, not because of cowardice, for to do him justice he was no coward, but because of superstition. He feared to fight with me since, as I learned afterwards, he believed that he would meet his end at my hand, and it was for this reason chiefly that he strove to kill me when first we met.

'The duello has its laws, senor,' he said courteously. 'It is not usual to fight thus unseconded and in the presence of a woman. If you believe that you have any grievance against me—though I know not of what you rave, or the name by which you call me—I will meet you where and when you will.' And all the while he looked over his shoulder seeking some way of escape.

'You will meet me now,' I answered. 'Draw or I strike!'

Then he drew, and we fell to it desperately enough, till the sparks flew, indeed, and the rattle of steel upon steel rang down the quiet street. At first he had somewhat the better of me, for my hate made me wild in my play, but soon I settled to the work and grew cooler. I meant to kill him—more, I knew that I should kill him if none came between us. He was still a better swordsman than I, who, till I fought with him in the lane at Ditchingham, had never even seen one of these Spanish rapiers, but I had the youth and the right on my side, as also I had an eye like a hawk's and a wrist of steel.

Slowly I pressed him back, and ever my play grew closer and better and his became wilder. Now I had touched him twice, once in the face, and I held him with his back against the wall of the way that led down to the water-gate, and it had come to this, that he scarcely strove to thrust at me at all, but stood on his defence waiting till I should tire. Then, when victory was in my hand disaster overtook me, for the woman, who had been watching bewildered, saw that her faithless lover was in danger of death and straightway seized me from behind, at the same time sending up shriek after shriek for help. I shook her from me quickly enough, but not before de Garcia, seeing his advantage, had dealt me a coward's thrust that took me in the right shoulder and half crippled me, so that in my turn I must stand on my defence if I would keep my life in me. Meanwhile the shrieks had been heard, and of a sudden the watch came running round the corner whistling for help. De Garcia saw them, and disengaging suddenly, turned and ran for the water-gate, the lady also vanishing, whither I do not know.

Now the watch was on me, and their leader came at me to seize me, holding a lantern in his hand. I struck it with the handle of the sword, so that it fell upon the roadway, where it blazed up like a bonfire. Then I turned also and fled, for I did not wish to be dragged before the magistrates of the city as a brawler, and in my desire to escape I forgot that de Garcia was escaping also. Away I went and three of the watch after me, but they were stout and scant of breath, and by the time that I had run three furlongs I distanced them. I halted to get my breath and remembered that I had lost de Garcia and did not know when I should find him again. At first I was minded to return and seek him, but reflection told me that by now it would be useless, also that the end of it might be that I should fall into the hands of the watch, who would know me by my wound, which began to pain me. So I went homeward cursing my fortune, and the woman who had clasped me from behind just as I was about to send the death-thrust home, and also my lack of skill which had delayed that thrust so long. Twice I might have made it and twice I had waited, being overcautious and over-anxious to be sure, and now I had lost my chance, and might bide many a day before it came again.

How should I find him in this great city? Doubtless, though I had not thought of it, de Garcia passed under some feigned name as he had done at Yarmouth. It was bitter indeed to have been so near to vengeance and to have missed it.

By now I was at home and bethought me that I should do well to go to Fonseca, my master, and ask his help. Hitherto I had said nothing of this matter to him, for I have always loved to keep my own counsel, and as yet I had not spoken of my past even to him. Going to the room where he was accustomed to receive patients, I found he had retired to rest, leaving orders that I was not to awake him this night as he was weary. So I bound up my hurt after a fashion and sought my bed also, very ill-satisfied with my fortune.

On the morrow I went to my master's chamber where he still lay abed, having been seized by a sudden weakness that was the beginning of the illness which ended in his death. As I mixed a draught for him he noticed that my shoulder was hurt and asked me what had happened. This gave me my opportunity, which I was not slow to take.

'Have you patience to listen to a story?' I said, 'for I would seek your help.'

'Ah!' he answered, 'it is the old case, the physician cannot heal himself. Speak on, nephew.'

Then I sat down by the bed and told him all, keeping nothing back. I told him the history of my mother and my father's courtship, of my own childhood, of the murder of my mother by de Garcia, and of the oath that I had sworn to be avenged upon him. Lastly I told him of what had happened upon the previous night and how my enemy had evaded me. All the while that I was speaking Fonseca, wrapped in a rich Moorish robe, sat up in the bed holding his knees beneath his chin, and watching my face with his keen eyes. But he spoke no word and made no sign till I had finished the tale.

'You are strangely foolish, nephew,' he said at length. 'For the most part youth fails through rashness, but you err by over-caution. By over-caution in your fence you lost your chance last night, and so by over-caution in hiding this tale from me you have lost a far greater opportunity. What, have you not seen me give counsel in many such matters, and have you ever known me to betray the confidence even of the veriest stranger? Why then did you fear for yours?'

'I do not know,' I answered, 'but I thought that first I would search for myself.'

'Pride goeth before a fall, nephew. Now listen: had I known this history a month ago, by now de Garcia had perished miserably, and not by your hand, but by that of the law. I have been acquainted with the man from his childhood, and know enough to hang him twice over did I choose to speak. More, I knew your mother, boy, and now I see that it was the likeness in your face to hers that haunted me, for from the first it was familiar. It was I also who bribed the keepers of the Holy Office to let your father loose, though, as it chanced, I never saw him, and arranged his flight. Since then, I have had de Garcia through my hands some four or five times, now under this name and now under that. Once even he came to me as a client, but the villainy that he would have worked was too black for me to touch. This man is the wickedest whom I have known in Seville, and that is saying much, also he is the cleverest and the most revengeful. He lives by vice for vice, and there are many deaths upon his hands. But he has never prospered in his evil-doing, and to-day he is but an adventurer without a name, who lives by blackmail, and by ruining women that he may rob them at his leisure. Give me those books from the strong box yonder, and I will tell you of this de Garcia.'

I did as he bade me, bringing the heavy parchment volumes, each bound in vellum and written in cipher.

'These are my records,' he said, 'though none can read them except myself. Now for the index. Ah! here it is. Give me volume three, and open it at page two hundred and one.'

I obeyed, laying the book on the bed before him, and he began to read the crabbed marks as easily as though they were good black-letter.

'De Garcia—Juan. Height, appearance, family, false names, and so on. This is it—history. Now listen.'

Then came some two pages of closely written matter, expressed in secret signs that Fonseca translated as he read. It was brief enough, but such a record as it contained I have never heard before nor since. Here, set out against this one man's name, was well nigh every wickedness of which a human being could be capable, carried through by him to gratify his appetites and revengeful hate, and to provide himself with gold.

In that black list were two murders: one of a rival by the knife, and one of a mistress by poison. And there were other things even worse, too shameful, indeed, to be written.

'Doubtless there is more that has not come beneath my notice,' said Fonseca coolly, 'but these things I know for truth, and one of the murders could be proved against him were he captured. Stay, give me ink, I must add to the record.'

And he wrote in his cipher: 'In May, 1517, the said de Garcia sailed to England on a trading voyage, and there, in the parish of Ditchingham, in the county of Norfolk, he murdered Luisa Wingfield, spoken of above as Luisa de Garcia, his cousin, to whom he was once betrothed. In September of the same year, or previously, under cover of a false marriage, he decoyed and deserted one Donna Isabella of the noble family of Siguenza, a nun in a religious house in this city.'

'What!' I exclaimed, 'is the girl who came to seek your help two nights since the same that de Garcia deserted?'

'The very same, nephew. It was she whom you heard pleading with him last night. Had I known two days ago what I know to-day, by now this villain had been safe in prison. But perhaps it is not yet too late. I am ill, but I will rise and see to it. Leave it to me, nephew. Go, nurse yourself, and leave it to me; if anything may be done I can do it. Stay, bid a messenger be ready. This evening I shall know whatever there is to be known.'

That night Fonseca sent for me again.

'I have made inquiries,' he said. 'I have even warned the officers of justice for the first time for many years, and they are hunting de Garcia as bloodhounds hunt a slave. But nothing can be heard of him. He has vanished and left no trace. To-night I write to Cadiz, for he may have fled there down the river. One thing I have discovered, however. The Senora Isabella was caught by the watch, and being recognised as having escaped from a convent, she was handed over to the executories of the Holy Office, that her case may be investigated, or in other words, should her fault be proved, to death.'

'Can she be rescued?'

'Impossible. Had she followed my counsel she would never have been taken.'

'Can she be communicated with?'

'No. Twenty years ago it might have been managed, now the Office is stricter and purer. Gold has no power there. We shall never see or hear of her again, unless, indeed, it is at the hour of her death, when, should she choose to speak with me, the indulgence may possibly be granted to her, though I doubt it. But it is not likely that she will wish to do so. Should she succeed in hiding her disgrace, she may escape; but it is not probable. Do not look so sad, nephew, religion must have its sacrifices. Perchance it is better for her to die thus than to live for many years dead in life. She can die but once. May her blood lie heavy on de Garcia's head!'

'Amen!' I answered.

CHAPTER 9

Thomas Becomes Rich

For many months we heard no more of de Garcia or of Isabella de Siguenza. Both had vanished leaving no sign, and we searched for them in vain. As for me I fell back into my former way of life of assistant to Fonseca, posing before the world as his nephew. But it came about that from the night of my duel with the murderer, my master's health declined steadily through the action of a wasting disease of the liver which baffled all skill, so that within eight months of that time he lay almost bedridden and at the point of death. His mind indeed remained quite clear, and on occasions he would even receive those who came to consult him, reclining on a chair and wrapped in his embroidered robe. But the hand of death lay on him, and he knew that it was so. As the weeks went by he grew more and more attached to me, till at length, had I been his son, he could not have treated me with a greater affection, while for my part I did what lay in my power to lessen his sufferings, for he would let no other physician near him.

At length when he had grown very feeble he expressed a desire to see a notary. The man he named was sent for and remained closeted with him for an hour or more, when he left for a while to return with several of his clerks, who accompanied him to my master's room, from which I was excluded. Presently they all went away, bearing some parchments with them.

That evening Fonseca sent for me. I found him very weak, but cheerful and full of talk.

'Come here, nephew,' he said, 'I have had a busy day. I have been busy all my life through, and it would not be well to grow idle at the last. Do you know what I have been doing this day?'

I shook my head.

'I will tell you. I have been making my will—there is something to leave; not so very much, but still something.'

73

'Do not talk of wills,' I said; 'I trust that you may live for many years.'

He laughed. 'You must think badly of my case, nephew, when you think that I can be deceived thus. I am about to die as you know well, and I do not fear death. My life has been prosperous but not happy, for it was blighted in its spring—no matter how. The story is an old one and not worth telling; moreover, whichever way it had read, it had all been one now in the hour of death. We must travel our journey each of us; what does it matter if the road has been good or bad when we have reached the goal? For my part religion neither comforts nor frightens me now at the last. I will stand or fall upon the record of my life. I have done evil in it and I have done good; the evil I have done because nature and temptation have been too strong for me at times, the good also because my heart prompted me to it. Well, it is finished, and after all death cannot be so terrible, seeing that every human being is born to undergo it, together with all living things. Whatever else is false, I hold this to be true, that God exists and is more merciful than those who preach Him would have us to believe.' And he ceased exhausted.

Often since then I have thought of his words, and I still think of them now that my own hour is so near. As will be seen Fonseca was a fatalist, a belief which I do not altogether share, holding as I do that within certain limits we are allowed to shape our own characters and destinies. But his last sayings I believe to be true. God is and is merciful, and death is not terrible either in its act or in its consequence.

Presently Fonseca spoke again. 'Why do you lead me to talk of such things? They weary me and I have little time. I was telling of my will. Nephew, listen. Except certain sums that I have given to be spent in charities—not in masses, mind you—I have left you all I possess.'

'You have left it to *me*!' I said astonished.

'Yes, nephew, to you. Why not? I have no relations living and I have learned to love you, I who thought that I could never care again for any man or woman or child. I am grateful to you, who have proved to me that my heart is not dead, take what I give you as a mark of my gratitude.'

Now I began to stammer my thanks, but he stopped me. 'The sum that you will inherit, nephew, amounts in all to about five thousand gold *pesos*, or perhaps twelve thousand of your English pounds, enough for a young man to begin life on, even with a wife. Indeed there in England it may well be held a great fortune, and I think that your betrothed's father will make no more objection to you as a son-in-law. Also there is this house and all that it contains; the library and

74

the silver are valuable, and you will do well to keep them. All is left to you with the fullest formality, so that no question can arise as to your right to take it; indeed, foreseeing my end, I have of late called in my moneys, and for the most part the gold lies in strong boxes in the secret cupboard in the wall yonder that you know of. It would have been more had I known you some years ago, for then, thinking that I grew too rich who was without an heir, I gave away as much as what remains in acts of mercy and in providing refuge for the homeless and the suffering. Thomas Wingfield, for the most part this money has come to me as the fruit of human folly and human wretchedness, frailty and sin. Use it for the purposes of wisdom and the advancing of right and liberty. May it prosper you, and remind you of me, your old master, the Spanish quack, till at last you pass it on to your children or the poor. And now one word more. If your conscience will let you, abandon the pursuit of de Garcia. Take your fortune and go with it to England; wed that maid whom you desire, and follow after happiness in whatever way seems best to you. Who are you that you should meet out vengeance on this knave de Garcia? Let him be, and he will avenge himself upon himself. Otherwise you may undergo much toil and danger, and in the end lose love, and life, and fortune at a blow.'

'But I have sworn to kill him,' I answered, 'and how can I break so solemn an oath? How could I sit at home in peace beneath the burden of such shame?'

'I do not know; it is not for me to judge. You must do as you wish, but in the doing of it, it may happen that you will fall into greater shames than this. You have fought the man and he has escaped you. Let him go if you are wise. Now bend down and kiss me, and bid me farewell. I do not desire that you should see me die, and my death is near. I cannot tell if we shall meet again when in your turn you have lain as I lie now, or if we shape our course for different stars. If so, farewell for ever.'

Then I leant down and kissed him on the forehead, and as I did so I wept, for not till this hour did I learn how truly I had come to love him, so truly that it seemed to me as though my father lay there dying.

'Weep not,' he said, 'for all our life is but a parting. Once I had a son like you, and ours was the bitterest of farewells. Now I go to seek for him again who could not come back to me, so weep not because I die. Good-bye, Thomas Wingfield. May God prosper and protect you! Now go!'

So I went weeping, and that night, before the dawn, all was over with Andres de Fonseca. They told me that he was conscious to the end and died murmuring the name of that son of whom he spoke in his last words to me.

What was the history of this son, or of Fonseca himself, I never learned, for like an Indian he hid his trail as step by step he wandered down the path of life. He never spoke of his past, and in all the books and documents that he left behind him there is no allusion to it. Once, some years ago, I read through the cipher volumes of records that I have spoken of, and of which he gave me the key before he died. They stand before me on the shelf as I write, and in them are many histories of shame, sorrow, and evil, of faith deluded and innocence betrayed, of the cruelty of priests, of avarice triumphant over love, and of love triumphant over death—enough, indeed, to furnish half a hundred of true romances. But among these chronicles of a generation now past and forgotten, there is no mention of Fonseca's own name and no hint of his own story. It is lost for ever, and perhaps this is well. So died my benefactor and best friend.

When he was made ready for burial I went in to see him and he looked calm and beautiful in his death sleep. Then it was that she who had arrayed him for the grave handed to me two portraits most delicately painted on ivory and set in gold, which had been found about his neck. I have them yet. One is of the head of a lady with a sweet and wistful countenance, and the other the face of a dead youth also beautiful, but very sad. Doubtless they were mother and son, but I know no more about them.

On the morrow I buried Andres de Fonseca, but with no pomp, for he had said that he wished as little money as possible spent upon his dead body, and returned to the house to meet the notaries. Then the seals were broken and the parchments read and I was put in full possession of the dead man's wealth, and having deducted such sums as were payable for dues, legacies, and fees, the notaries left me bowing humbly, for was I not rich? Yes, I was rich, wealth had come to me without effort, and I had reason to desire it, yet this was the saddest night that I had passed since I set foot in Spain, for my mind was filled with doubts and sorrow, and moreover my loneliness got a hold of me. But sad as it might be, it was destined to seem yet more sorrowful before the morning. For as I sat making pretence to eat, a servant came to me saying that a woman waited in the outer room who had asked to see his late master. Guessing that this was some client who had not heard of Fonseca's death I was about to order that she should be dismissed, then bethought me that I might be of service to her or at the least forget some of my own trouble in listening to hers. So I bade him bring her in. Presently she came, a tall woman wrapped in a dark cloak that hid her face. I bowed and motioned to her to be seated, when suddenly she started and spoke.

'I asked to see Don Andres de Fonseca,' she said in a low quick voice. 'You are not he, senor.'

'Andres de Fonseca was buried to-day,' I answered. 'I was his assistant in his business and am his heir. If I can serve you in any way I am at your disposal.'

'You are young—very young,' she murmured confusedly, 'and the matter is terrible and urgent. How can I trust you?'

'It is for you to judge, senora.'

She thought a while, then drew off her cloak, displaying the robes of a nun.

'Listen,' she said. 'I must do many a penance for this night's work, and very hardly have I won leave to come hither upon an errand of mercy. Now I cannot go back empty-handed, so I must trust you. But first swear by thine blessed Mother of God that you will not betray me.'

'I give you my word,' I answered; 'if that is not enough, let us end this talk.'

'Do not be angry with me,' she pleaded; 'I have not left my convent walls for many years and I am distraught with grief. I seek a poison of the deadliest. I will pay well for it.'

'I am not the tool of murderers,' I answered. 'For what purpose do you wish the poison?'

'Oh! I must tell you—yet how can I? In our convent there dies to-night a woman young and fair, almost a girl indeed, who has broken the vows she took. She dies to-night with her babe—thus, oh God, thus! by being built alive into the foundations of the house she has disgraced. It is the judgment that has been passed upon her, judgment without forgiveness or reprieve. I am the abbess of this convent—ask not its name or mine—and I love this sinner as though she were my daughter. I have obtained this much of mercy for her because of my faithful services to the church and by secret influence, that when I give her the cup of water before the work is done, I may mix poison with it and touch the lips of the babe with poison, so that their end is swift. I may do this and yet have no sin upon my soul. I have my pardon under seal. Help me then to be an innocent murderess, and to save this sinner from her last agonies on earth.'

I cannot set down the feelings with which I listened to this tale of horror, for words could not carry them. I stood aghast seeking an answer, and a dreadful thought entered my mind.

'Is this woman named Isabella de Siguenza?' I asked.

'That name was hers in the world,' she answered, 'though how you know it I cannot guess.'

'We know many things in this house, mother. Say now, can this Isabella be saved by money or by interest?'

'It is impossible; her sentence has been confirmed by the Tribunal of Mercy. She must die and within two hours. Will you not give the poison?'

'I cannot give it unless I know its purpose, mother. This may be a barren tale, and the medicine might be used in such a fashion that I should fall beneath the law. At one price only can I give it, and it is that I am there to see it used.'

She thought a while and answered: 'It may be done, for as it chances the wording of my absolution will cover it. But you must come cowled as a priest, that those who carry out the sentence may know nothing. Still others will know and I warn you that should you speak of the matter you yourself will meet with misfortune. The Church avenges itself on those who betray its secrets, senor.'

'As one day its secrets will avenge themselves upon the Church,' I answered bitterly. 'And now let me seek a fitting drug—one that is swift, yet not too swift, lest your hounds should see themselves baffled of the prey before all their devilry is done. Here is something that will do the work,' and I held up a phial that I drew from a case of such medicines. 'Come, veil yourself, mother, and let us be gone upon this "errand of mercy."'

She obeyed, and presently we left the house and walked away swiftly through the crowded streets till we came to the ancient part of the city along the river's edge. Here the woman led me to a wharf where a boat was in waiting for her. We entered it, and were rowed for a mile or more up the stream till the boat halted at a landing-place beneath a high wall. Leaving it, we came to a door in the wall on which my companion knocked thrice. Presently a shutter in the woodwork was drawn, and a white face peeped through the grating and spoke. My companion answered in a low voice, and after some delay the door was opened, and I found myself in a large walled garden planted with orange trees. Then the abbess spoke to me.

'I have led you to our house,' she said. 'If you know where you are, and what its name may be, for your own sake I pray you forget it when you leave these doors.'

I made no answer, but looked round the dim and dewy garden. Here it was doubtless that de Garcia had met that unfortunate who must die this night. A walk of a hundred paces brought us to another door in the wall of a long low building of Moorish style. Here the knocking and the questioning were repeated at more length. Then the door was opened, and I found myself in a passage, ill lighted, long and narrow, in the depths of which I could see the figures of nuns flitting to and fro like bats in a tomb. The abbess walked down the passage till she came to a door on the right which she opened. It led into a cell, and here she left me in the dark. For ten minutes or more I stayed there, a prey to thoughts that I had rather forget. At length the door opened again, and she came in, followed by a tall priest whose face I could not see, for he was dressed in the white robe and hood of the Dominicans that left nothing visible except his eyes.

'Greeting, my son,' he said, when he had scanned me for a while. 'The abbess mother has told me of your errand. You are full young for such a task.'

'Were I old I should not love it better, father. You know the case. I am asked to provide a deadly drug for a certain merciful purpose. I have provided that drug, but I must be there to see that it is put to proper use.'

'You are very cautious, my son. The Church is no murderess. This woman must die because her sin is flagrant, and of late such wickedness has become common. Therefore, after much thought and prayer, and many searchings to find a means of mercy, she is condemned to death by those whose names are too high to be spoken. I, alas, am here to see the sentence carried out with a certain mitigation which has been allowed by the mercy of her chief judge. It seems that your presence is needful to this act of love, therefore I suffer it. The mother abbess has warned you that evil dogs the feet of those who reveal the secrets of the Church. For your own sake I pray you to lay that warning to heart.'

'I am no babbler, father, so the caution is not needed. One word more. This visit should be well feed, the medicine is costly.'

'Fear not, physician,' the monk answered with a note of scorn in his voice; 'name your sum, it shall be paid to you.'

'I ask no money, father. Indeed I would pay much to be far away to-night. I ask only that I may be allowed to speak with this girl before she dies.'

'What!' he said, starting, 'surely you are not that wicked man? If so, you are bold indeed to risk the sharing of her fate.'

'No, father, I am not that man. I never saw Isabella de Siguenza except once, and I have never spoken to her. I am not the man who tricked her but I know him; he is named Juan de Garcia.'

'Ah!' he said quickly, 'she would never tell his real name, even under threat of torture. Poor erring soul, she could be faithful in her unfaith. Of what would you speak to her?'

'I wish to ask her whither this man has gone. He is my enemy, and I would follow him as I have already followed him far. He has done worse by me and mine than by this poor girl even. Grant my request, father, that I may be able to work my vengeance on him, and with mine the Church's also.'

'"Vengeance is mine," saith the Lord; "I will repay." Yet it may be, son, that the Lord will choose you as the instrument of his wrath. An opportunity shall be given you to speak with her. Now put on this dress'—and he handed me a white Dominican hood and robe—'and follow me.'

'First,' I said, 'let me give this medicine to the abbess, for I will have no hand in its administering. Take it, mother, and when the time comes, pour the contents of the phial into a cup of water. Then, having touched the mouth and tongue of the babe with the fluid, give it to the mother to drink and be sure that she does drink it. Before the bricks are built up about them both will sleep sound, never to wake again.'

'I will do it,' murmured the abbess; 'having absolution I will be bold, and do it for love and mercy's sake!'

'Your heart is too soft, sister. Justice is mercy,' said the monk with a sigh. 'Alas for the frailty of the flesh that wars against the spirit!'

Then I clothed myself in the ghastly looking dress, and they took lamps and motioned to me to follow them.

CHAPTER 10

The Passing of
Isabella de Siguenza

Silently we went down the long passage, and as we went I saw the eyes of the dwellers in this living tomb watch us pass through the gratings of their cell doors. Little wonder that the woman about to die had striven to escape from such a home back to the world of life and love! Yet for that crime she must perish. Surely God will remember the doings of such men as these priests, and the nation that fosters them. And, in deed, He does remember, for where is the splendour of Spain to-day, and where are the cruel rites she gloried in? Here in England their fetters are broken for ever, and in striving to bind them fast upon us free Englishmen she is broken also—never to be whole again.

At the far end of the passage we found a stair down which we passed. At its foot was an iron-bound door that the monk unlocked and locked again upon the further side. Then came another passage hollowed in the thickness of the wall, and a second door, and we were in the place of death.

It was a vault low and damp, and the waters of the river washed its outer wall, for I could hear their murmuring in the silence. Perhaps the place may have measured ten paces in length by eight broad. For the rest its roof was supported by massive columns, and on one side there was a second door that led to a prison cell. At the further end of this gloomy den, that was dimly lighted by torches and lamps, two men with hooded heads, and draped in coarse black gowns, were at work, silently mixing lime that sent up a hot steam upon the stagnant air. By their sides were squares of dressed stone ranged neatly against the end of the vault, and before them was a niche cut in the thickness of the wall itself, shaped like a large coffin set upon its smaller end. In front of this niche was placed a massive chair of chestnut wood. I noticed also that two other such coffin-shaped niches had been cut in this same wall, and filled in with similar blocks of whitish stone. On the face of each was a date graved in deep letters. One had been sealed up some thirty years before, and one hard upon a hundred.

These two men were the only occupants of the vault when we entered it, but presently a sound of soft and solemn singing stole down the second passage. Then the door was opened, the mason monks ceased labouring at the heap of lime, and the sound of singing grew louder so that I could catch the refrain. It was that of a Latin hymn for the dying. Next through the open door came the choir, eight veiled nuns walking two by two, and ranging themselves on either side of the vault they ceased their singing. After them followed the doomed woman, guarded by two more nuns, and last of all a priest bearing a crucifix. This man wore a black robe, and his thin half-frenzied face was uncovered. All these and other things I noticed and remembered, yet at the time it seemed to me that I saw nothing except the figure of the victim. I knew her again, although I had seen her but once in the moonlight. She was changed indeed, her lovely face was fuller and the great tormented eyes shone like stars against its waxen pallor, relieved by the carmine of her lips alone. Still it was the same face that some eight months before I had seen lifted in entreaty to her false lover. Now her tall shape was wrapped about with grave clothes over which her black hair streamed, and in her arms she bore a sleeping babe that from time to time she pressed convulsively to her breast.

On the threshold of her tomb Isabella de Siguenza paused and looked round wildly as though for help, scanning each of the silent watchers to find a friend among them. Then her eye fell upon the niche and the heap of smoking lime and the men who guarded it, and she shuddered and would have fallen had not those who attended her led her to the chair and placed her in it—a living corpse.

Now the dreadful rites began. The Dominican father stood before her and recited her offence, and the sentence that had been passed upon her, which doomed her, 'to be left alone with God and the child of your sin, that He may deal with you as He sees fit.'[1] To all of this

---

1. Lest such cruelty should seem impossible and unprecedented, the writer may mention that in the museum of the city of Mexico, he has seen the desiccated body of a young woman, which was found immured in the walls of a religious building. With it is the body of an infant. Although the exact cause of her execution remains a matter of conjecture, there can be no doubt as to the manner of her death, for in addition to other evidences, the marks of the rope with which her limbs were bound in life are still distinctly visible. Such in those days were the mercies of religion!

she seemed to pay no heed, nor to the exhortation that followed. At length he ceased with a sigh, and turning to me said:

'Draw near to this sinner, brother, and speak with her before it is too late.'

Then he bade all present gather themselves at the far end of the vault that our talk might not be overheard, and they did so without wonder, thinking doubtless that I was a monk sent to confess the doomed woman.

So I drew near with a beating heart, and bending over her I spoke in her ear.

'Listen to me, Isabella de Siguenza!' I said; and as I uttered the name she started wildly. 'Where is that de Garcia who deceived and deserted you?'

'How have you learnt his true name?' she answered. 'Not even torture would have wrung it from me as you know.'

'I am no monk and I know nothing. I am that man who fought with de Garcia on the night when you were taken, and who would have killed him had you not seized me.'

'At the least I saved him, that is my comfort now.'

'Isabella de Siguenza,' I said, 'I am your friend, the best you ever had and the last, as you shall learn presently. Tell me where this man is, for there is that between us which must be settled.'

'If you are my friend, weary me no more. I do not know where he is. Months ago he went whither you will scarcely follow, to the furthest Indies; but you will never find him there.'

'It may still be that I shall, and if it should so chance, say have you any message for this man?'

'None—yes, this. Tell him how we died, his child and his wife— tell him that I did my best to hide his name from the priests lest some like fate should befall him.'

'Is that all?'

'Yes. No, it is not all. Tell him that I passed away loving and forgiving.'

'My time is short,' I said; 'awake and listen!' for having spoken thus she seemed to be sinking into a lethargy. 'I was the assistant of that Andres de Fonseca whose counsel you put aside to your ruin, and I have given a certain drug to the abbess yonder. When she offers you the cup of water, see that you drink and deep, you and the child. If so none shall ever die more happily. Do you understand?'

'Yes—yes,' she gasped, 'and may blessings rest upon you for the gift. Now I am no more afraid—for I have long desired to die—it was the way I feared.'

'Then farewell, and God be with you, unhappy woman.'

'Farewell,' she answered softly, 'but call me not unhappy who am about to die thus easily with that I love.' And she glanced at the sleeping babe.

Then I drew back and stood with bent head, speaking no word. Now the Dominican motioned to all to take the places where they had stood before and asked her:

'Erring sister, have you aught to say before you are silent for ever?'

'Yes,' she answered in a clear, sweet voice, that never even quavered, so bold had she become since she learned that her death would be swift and easy. 'Yes, I have this to say, that I go to my end with a clean heart, for if I have sinned it is against custom and not against God. I broke the vows indeed, but I was forced to take those vows, and, therefore, they did not bind. I was a woman born for light and love, and yet I was thrust into the darkness of this cloister, there to wither dead in life. And so I broke the vows, and I am glad that I have broken them, though it has brought me to this. If I was deceived and my marriage is no marriage before the law as they tell me now, I knew nothing of it, therefore to me it is still valid and holy and on my soul there rests no stain. At the least I have lived, and for some few hours I have been wife and mother, and it is as well to die swiftly in this cell that your mercy has prepared, as more slowly in those above. And now for you—I tell you that your wickedness shall find you out, you who dare to say to God's children—"Ye shall not love," and to work murder on them because they will not listen. It shall find you out I say, and not only you but the Church you serve. Both priest and Church shall be broken together and shall be a scorn in the mouths of men to come.'

'She is distraught,' said the Dominican as a sigh of fear and wonder went round the vault, 'and blasphemes in her madness. Forget her words. Shrive her, brother, swiftly ere she adds to them.'

Then the black-robed, keen-eyed priest came to her, and holding the cross before her face, began to mutter I know not what. But she rose from the chair and thrust the crucifix aside.

'Peace!' she said, 'I will not be shriven by such as you. I take my sins to God and not to you—you who do murder in the name of Christ.'

The fanatic heard and a fury took him.

'Then go unshriven down to hell, you—' and he named her by ill names and struck her in the face with the ivory crucifix.

The Dominican bade him cease his revilings angrily enough, but Isabella de Siguenza wiped her bruised brow and laughed aloud a dreadful laugh to hear.

'Now I see that you are a coward also,' she said. 'Priest, this is my last prayer, that you also may perish at the hands of fanatics, and more terribly than I die to-night.'

Then they hurried her into the place prepared for her and she spoke again:

'Give me to drink, for we thirst, my babe and I!'

Now I saw the abbess enter that passage whence the victim had been led. Presently she came back bearing a cup of water in her hand and with it a loaf of bread, and I knew by her mien that my draught was in the water. But of what befell afterwards I cannot say certainly, for I prayed the Dominican to open the door by which we had entered the vault, and passing through it I stood dazed with horror at some distance. A while went by, I do not know how long, till at length I saw the abbess standing before me, a lantern in her hand, and she was sobbing bitterly.

'All is done,' she said. 'Nay, have no fear, the draught worked well. Before ever a stone was laid mother and child slept sound. Alas for her soul who died unrepentant and unshriven!'

'Alas for the souls of all who have shared in this night's work,' I answered. 'Now, mother, let me hence, and may we never meet again!'

Then she led me back to the cell, where I tore off that accursed monk's robe, and thence to the door in the garden wall and to the boat which still waited on the river, and I rejoiced to feel the sweet air upon my face as one rejoices who awakes from some foul dream. But I won little sleep that night, nor indeed for some days to come. For whenever I closed my eyes there rose before me the vision of that beauteous woman as I saw her last by the murky torchlight, wrapped in grave clothes and standing in the coffin-shaped niche, proud and defiant to the end, her child clasped to her with one arm while the other was outstretched to take the draught of death. Few have seen such a sight, for the Holy Office and its helpers do not seek witnesses to their dark deeds, and none would wish to see it twice. If I have described it ill, it is not that I have forgotten, but because even now, after the lapse of some seventy years, I can scarcely bear to write of it or to set out its horrors fully. But of all that was wonderful about it perhaps the most wonderful was that even to the last this unfortunate lady should still have clung to her love for the villain who, having deceived her by a false marriage, deserted her, leaving her to such a doom. To what end can so holy a gift as this great love of hers have been bestowed on such a man? None can say, but so it was. Yet now that I think of it, there is one thing even stranger than her faithfulness.

It will be remembered that when the fanatic priest struck her she prayed that he also might die at such hands and more terribly than she must do. So it came about. In after years that very man, Father Pedro by name, was sent to convert the heathen of Anahuac, among whom, because of his cruelty, he was known as the 'Christian Devil.' But it chanced that venturing too far among a clan of the Otomie before they were finally subdued, he fell into the hands of some priests of the war god Huitzel, and by them was sacrificed after their dreadful fashion. I saw him as he went to his death, and without telling that I had been present when it was uttered, I called to his mind the dying curse of Isabella de Siguenza. Then for a moment his courage gave way, for seeing in me nothing but an Indian chief, he believed that the devil had put the words into my lips to torment him, causing me to speak of what I knew nothing. But enough of this now; if it is necessary I will tell of it in its proper place. At least, whether it was by chance, or because she had a gift of vision in her last hours, or that Providence was avenged on him after this fashion, so it came about, and I do not sorrow for it, though the death of this priest brought much misfortune on me.

This then was the end of Isabella de Siguenza who was murdered by priests because she had dared to break their rule.

So soon as I could clear my mind somewhat of all that I had seen and heard in that dreadful vault, I began to consider the circumstances in which I found myself. In the first place I was now a rich man, and if it pleased me to go back to Norfolk with my wealth, as Fonseca had pointed out, my prospects were fair indeed. But the oath that I had taken hung like lead about my neck. I had sworn to be avenged upon de Garcia, and I had prayed that the curse of heaven might rest upon me till I was so avenged, but in England living in peace and plenty I could scarcely come by vengeance. Moreover, now I knew where he was, or at least in what portion of the world I might seek him, and there where white men are few he could not hide from me as in Spain. This tidings I had gained from the doomed lady, and I have told her story at some length because it was through it and her that I came to journey to Hispaniola, as it was because of the sacrifice of her tormentor, Father Pedro, by the priests of the Otomie that I am here in England this day, since had it not been for that sacrifice the Spaniards would never have stormed the City of Pines, where, alive or dead, I should doubtless have been to this hour; for thus do seeming accidents build up the fates of men. Had those words never passed Isabella's lips, doubtless in time I should have wearied of a useless search and sailed for home and happiness. But having heard them it seemed to me, to my undoing, that this would be to play the part of a sorry coward. Moreover, strange as it may look, now I felt as though I had two wrongs to avenge, that of my mother and that of Isabella de Siguenza. Indeed none could have seen that young and lovely lady die thus terribly and not desire to wreak her death on him who had betrayed and deserted her.

So the end of it was that being of a stubborn temper, I determined to do violence to my own desires and the dying counsels of my benefactor, and to follow de Garcia to the ends of the earth and there to kill him as I had sworn to do.

First, however, I inquired secretly and diligently as to the truth of the statement that de Garcia had sailed for the Indies, and to be brief, having the clue, I discovered that two days after the date of the duel I had fought with him, a man answering to de Garcia's description, though bearing a different name, had shipped from Seville in a *carak* bound for the Canary Islands, which *carak* was there to await the arrival of the fleet sailing for Hispaniola. Indeed from various circumstances I had little doubt that the man was none other than de Garcia himself, which, although I had not thought of it before, was not strange, seeing that then as now the Indies were the refuge of half the desperadoes and villains who could no longer live in Spain. Thither then I made up my mind to follow him, consoling myself a little by the thought that at least I should see new and wonderful countries, though how new and wonderful they were I did not guess.

Now it remained for me to dispose of the wealth which had come to me suddenly. While I was wondering how I could place it in safety till my return, I heard by chance that the '*Adventuress*' of Yarmouth, the same ship in which I had come to Spain a year before, was again in the port of Cadiz, and I bethought me that the best thing I could do with the gold and other articles of value would be to ship them to England, there to be held in trust for me. So having despatched a message to my friend the captain of the '*Adventuress*,' that I had freight of value for him, I made my preparations to depart from Seville with such speed as I might, and to this end I sold my benefactor's house, with many of the effects, at a price much below their worth. The most of the books and plate, together with some other articles, I kept, and packing them in cases, I caused them to be transported down the river to Cadiz, to the care of those same agents to whom I had received letters from the Yarmouth merchants.

This being done I followed thither myself, taking the bulk of my fortune with me in gold, which I hid artfully in numerous packages. And so it came to pass that after a stay of a year in Seville, I turned my back on it for ever. My sojourn there had been fortunate, for I came to it poor and left it a rich man, to say nothing of what I had gained in experience, which was much. Yet I was glad to be gone, for here Juan de Garcia had escaped me, here I had lost my best friend and seen Isabella de Siguenza die.

I came to Cadiz in safety and without loss of any of my goods or gold, and taking boat proceeded on board the '*Adventuress*,' where I found her captain, whose name was Bell, in good health and very glad to see me. What pleased me more, however, was that he had three letters for me, one from my father, one from my sister Mary, and one from my betrothed, Lily Bozard, the only letter I ever received from her. The contents of these writings were not altogether pleasing however, for I learned from them that my father was in broken health and almost bedridden, and indeed, though I did not know it for many years after, he died in Ditchingham Church upon the very day that I received his letter. It was short and sad, and in it he said that he sorrowed much that he had allowed me to go upon my mission, since he should see me no more and could only commend me to the care of the Almighty, and pray Him for my safe return. As for Lily's letter, which, hearing that the 'Adventuress' was to sail for Cadiz, she had found means to despatch secretly, though it was not short it was sad also, and told me that so soon as my back was turned on home, my brother Geoffrey had asked her in marriage from her father, and that they pushed the matter strongly, so that her life was made a misery to her, for my brother waylaid her everywhere, and her father did not cease to revile her as an obstinate jade who would fling away her fortune for the sake of a penniless wanderer.

'But,' it went on, 'be assured, sweetheart, that unless they marry me by force, as they have threatened to do, I will not budge from my promise. And, Thomas, should I be wedded thus against my will, I shall not be a wife for long, for though I am strong I believe that I shall die of shame and sorrow. It is hard that I should be thus tormented, and for one reason only, that you are not rich. Still I have good hope that things may better themselves, for I see that my brother Wilfred is much inclined towards your sister Mary, and though he also urges this marriage on me to-day, she is a friend to both of us and may be in the way to make terms with him before she accepts his suit.' Then the writing ended with many tender words and prayers for my safe return.

As for the letter from my sister Mary it was to the same purpose. As yet, she said, she could do nothing for me with Lily Bozard, for my brother Geoffrey was mad with love for her, my father was too ill to meddle in the matter, and Squire Bozard was fiercely set upon the marriage because of the lands that were at stake. Still, she hinted, things might not always be so, as a time might come when she could speak up for me and not in vain.

Now all this news gave me much cause for thought. More indeed, it awoke in me a longing for home which was so strong that it grew almost to a sickness. Her loving words and the perfume that hung about the letter of my betrothed brought Lily back to me in such sort that my heart ached with a desire to be with her. Moreover I knew that I should be welcome now, for my fortune was far greater than my brother's would ever be, and parents do not show the door to suitors who bring more than twelve thousand golden pieces in their baggage. Also I wished to see my father again before he passed beyond my reach. But still between me and my desire lay the shadow of de Garcia and my oath. I had brooded on vengeance for so long that I felt even in the midst of this strong temptation that I should have no pleasure in my life if I forsook my quest. To be happy I must first kill de Garcia. Moreover I had come to believe that did I so forsake it the curse which I had invoked would surely fall upon me.

Meanwhile I did this. Going to a notary I caused him to prepare a deed which I translated into English. By this deed I vested all my fortune except two hundred pesos that I kept for my own use, in three persons to hold the same on my behalf till I came to claim it. Those three persons were my old master, Doctor Grimstone of Bungay, whom I knew for the honestest of men, my sister Mary Wingfield, and my betrothed, Lily Bozard. I directed them by this deed, which for greater validity I signed upon the ship and caused to be witnessed by Captain Bell and two other Englishmen, to deal with the property according to their discretion, investing not less than half of it in the purchase of lands and putting the rest out to interest, which interest with the rent of the lands was to be paid to the said Lily Bozard for her own use for so long as she remained unmarried.

Also with the deed I executed a will by which I devised the most of my property to Lily Bozard should she be unmarried at the date of my death, and the residue to my sister Mary. In the event of the marriage or death of Lily, then the whole was to pass to Mary and her heirs.

These two documents being signed and sealed, I delivered them, together with all my treasure and other goods, into the keeping of

Captain Bell, charging him solemnly to hand them and my possessions to Dr. Grimstone of Bungay, by whom he would be liberally rewarded. This he promised to do, though not until he had urged me almost with tears to accompany them myself.

With the gold and the deeds I sent several letters; to my father, my sister, my brother, Dr. Grimstone, Squire Bozard, and lastly to Lily herself. In these letters I gave an account of my life and fortunes since I had come to Spain, for I gathered that others which I had sent had never reached England, and told them of my resolution to follow de Garcia to the ends of the earth.

'Others,' I wrote to Lily, 'may think me a madman thus to postpone, or perchance to lose, a happiness which I desire above anything on earth, but you who understand my heart will not blame me, however much you may grieve for my decision. You will know that when once I have set my mind upon an object, nothing except death itself can turn me from it, and that in this matter I am bound by an oath which my conscience will not suffer me to break. I could never be happy even at your side if I abandoned my search now. First must come the toil and then the rest, first the sorrow and then the joy. Do not fear for me, I feel that I shall live to return again, and if I do not return, at least I am able to provide for you in such fashion that you need never be married against your will. While de Garcia lives I must follow him.'

To my brother Geoffrey I wrote very shortly, telling him what I thought of his conduct in persecuting an undefended maiden and striving to do wrong to an absent brother. I have heard that my letter pleased him very ill.

And here I may state that those letters and everything else that I sent came safely to Yarmouth. There the gold and goods were taken to Lowestoft and put aboard a wherry, and when he had discharged his ship, Captain Bell sailed up the Waveney with them till he brought them to Bungay Staithe and thence to the house of Dr. Grimstone in Nethergate Street. Here were gathered my sister and brother, for my father was then two months buried—and also Squire Bozard and his son and daughter, for Captain Bell had advised them of his coming by messenger, and when all the tale was told there was wonder and to spare. Still greater did it grow when the chests were opened and the weight of bullion compared with that set out in my letters, for there had never been so much gold at once in Bungay within the memory of man.

And now Lily wept, first for joy because of my good fortune, and then for sorrow because I had not come with my treasure, and when he had seen all and heard the deeds read by virtue of which Lily was a rich woman whether I lived or died, the Squire her father swore aloud and said that he had always thought well of me, and kissed his daughter, wishing her joy of her luck. In short all were pleased except my brother, who left the house without a word and straightway took to evil courses. For now the cup was dashed from his lips, seeing that having come into my father's lands, he had brought it about that Lily was to be married to him by might if no other means would serve. For even now a man can force his daughter into marriage while she is under age, and Squire Bozard was not one to shrink from such a deed, holding as he did that a woman's fancies were of no account. But on this day, so great is the power of gold, there was no more talk of her marrying any man except myself, indeed her father would have held her back from such a thing had she shown a mind to it, seeing that then Lily would have lost the wealth which I had settled on her. But all talked loudly of my madness because I would not abandon the chase of my enemy but chose to follow him to the far Indies, though Squire Bozard took comfort from the thought that whether I lived or died the money was still his daughter's. Only Lily spoke up for me, saying 'Thomas has sworn an oath and he does well to keep it, for his honour is at stake. Now I go to wait until he comes to me in this world or the next.'

But all this is out of place, for many a year passed away before I heard of these doings.

CHAPTER 11

The Loss of the Carak

On the day after I had given my fortune and letters into the charge of Captain Bell, I watched the '*Adventuress*' drop slowly round the mole of Cadiz, and so sad was I at heart, that I am not ashamed to confess I wept. I would gladly have lost the wealth she carried if she had but carried me. But my purpose was indomitable, and it must be some other ship that would bear me home to the shores of England.

As it chanced, a large Spanish *carak* named '*Las Cinque Llagas*,' or '*The Five Wounds*,' was about to sail for Hispaniola, and having obtained a licence to trade, I took passage in her under my assumed name of d'Aila, passing myself off as a merchant. To further this deception I purchased goods the value of one hundred and five pesos, and of such nature as I was informed were most readily saleable in the Indies, which merchandise I shipped with me. The vessel was full of Spanish adventurers, mostly ruffians of varied career and strange history, but none the less good companions enough when not in drink. By this time I could speak Castilian so perfectly, and was so Spanish in appearance, that it was not difficult for me to pass myself off as one of their nation and this I did, inventing a feigned tale of my parentage, and of the reasons that led me to tempt the seas. For the rest, now as ever I kept my own counsel, and notwithstanding my reserve, for I would not mingle in their orgies, I soon became well liked by my comrades, chiefly because of my skill in ministering to their sicknesses.

Of our voyage there is little to tell except of its sad end. At the Canary Isles we stayed a month, and then sailed away for Hispaniola, meeting with fine weather but light winds. When, as our captain reckoned, we were within a week's sail of the port of San Domingo for which we were bound, the weather changed, and presently gathered to a furious tempest from the north that grew more terrible every hour. For three days and nights our cumbrous vessel groaned and laboured beneath the stress of the gale, that drove us on rapidly we knew not whither, till at length it became clear that, unless the weather moderated, we must founder. Our ship leaked at every seam, one of our masts was carried away, and another broken in two, at a height of twenty feet from the deck. But all these misfortunes were small compared to what was to come, for on the fourth morning a great wave swept off our rudder, and we drifted helpless before the waves. An hour later a green sea came aboard of us, washing away the captain, so that we filled and settled down to founder.

Then began a most horrid scene. For several days both the crew and passengers had been drinking heavily to allay their terror, and now that they saw their end at hand, they rushed to and fro screaming, praying, and blaspheming. Such of them as remained sober began to get out the two boats, into which I and another man, a worthy priest, strove to place the women and children, of whom we had several on board. But this was no easy task, for the drunken sailors pushed them aside and tried to spring into the boats, the first of which overturned, so that all were lost. Just then the *carak* gave a lurch before she sank, and, seeing that everything was over, I called to the priest to follow me, and springing into the sea I swam for the second boat, which, laden with some shrieking women, had drifted loose in the confusion. As it chanced I reached it safely, being a strong swimmer, and was able to rescue the priest before he sank. Then the vessel reared herself up on her stern and floated thus for a minute or more, which gave us time to get out the oars and row some fathoms further away from her. Scarcely had we done so, when, with one wild and fearful scream from those on board of her, she rushed down into the depths below, nearly taking us with her. For a while we sat silent, for our horror overwhelmed us, but when the whirlpool which she made had ceased to boil, we rowed back to where the *carak* had been. Now all the sea was strewn with wreckage, but among it we found only one child living that had clung to an oar. The rest, some two hundred souls, had been sucked down with the ship and perished miserably, or if there were any still living, we could not find them in that weltering sea over which the darkness was falling.

Indeed, it was well for our own safety that we failed in so doing, for the little boat had ten souls on board in all, which was as many as she could carry—the priest and I being the only men among them. I have said that the darkness was falling, and as it chanced happily for us, so was the sea, or assuredly we must have been swamped. All that we could do was to keep the boat's head straight to the waves, and this we did through the long night. It was a strange thing to see, or rather to hear, that good man the priest my companion, confessing the women one by one as he laboured at his oar, and when all were shriven sending up prayers to God for the salvation of our souls, for of the safety of our bodies we despaired. What I felt may well be imagined, but I forbear to describe it, seeing that, bad as was my case, there were worse ones before me of which I shall have to tell in their season.

At length the night wore away, and the dawn broke upon the desolate sea. Presently the sun came up, for which at first we were thankful, for we were chilled to the bone, but soon its heat grew intolerable, since we had neither food nor water in the boat, and already we were parched with thirst. But now the wind had fallen to a steady breeze, and with the help of the oars and a blanket, we contrived to fashion a sail that drew us through the water at a good speed. But the ocean was vast, and we did not know whither we were sailing, and every hour the agony of thirst pressed us more closely. Towards mid-day a child died suddenly and was thrown into the sea, and some three hours later the mother filled a bailing bowl and drank deep of the bitter water. For a while it seemed to assuage her thirst, then suddenly a madness took her, and springing up she cast herself overboard and sank. Before the sun, glowing like a red-hot ball, had sunk beneath the horizon, the priest and I were the only ones in that company who could sit upright—the rest lay upon the bottom of the boat heaped one on another like dying fish groaning in their misery. Night fell at last and brought us some relief from our sufferings, for the air grew cooler. But the rain we prayed for did not fall, and so great was the heat that, when the sun rose again in a cloudless sky, we knew, if no help reached us, that it must be the last which we should see.

An hour after dawn another child died, and as we were in the act of casting the body into the sea, I looked up and saw a vessel far away, that seemed to be sailing in such fashion that she would pass within two miles of where we were. Returning thanks to God for this most blessed sight, we took to the oars, for the wind was now so light that our clumsy sail would no longer draw us through the water, and rowed feebly so as to cut the path of the ship. When we had laboured for more than an hour the wind fell altogether and the vessel lay becalmed at a distance of about three miles. So the priest and I rowed on till I thought that we must die in the boat, for the heat of the sun was like that of a flame and there came no wind to temper it; by now, too, our lips were cracked with thirst. Still we struggled on till the shadow of the ship's masts fell athwart us and we saw her sailors watching us from the deck. Now we were alongside and they let down a ladder of rope, speaking to us in Spanish.

How we reached the deck I cannot say, but I remember falling beneath the shade of an awning and drinking cup after cup of the water that was brought to me. At last even my thirst was satisfied, and for a while I grew faint and dizzy, and had no stomach for the meat which was thrust into my hand. Indeed, I think that I must have fainted, for when I came to myself the sun was straight overhead, and it seemed to me that I had dreamed I heard a familiar and hateful voice. At the time I was alone beneath the awning, for the crew of the ship were gathered on the foredeck clustering round what appeared to be the body of a man. By my side was a large plate of victuals and a flask of spirits, and feeling stronger I ate and drank of them heartily. I had scarcely finished my meal when the men on the foredeck lifted the body of the man, which I saw was black in colour, and cast it overboard. Then three of them, whom from their port I took to be officers, came towards me and I rose to my feet to meet them.

'Senor,' said the tallest of them in a soft and gentle voice, 'suffer me to offer you our felicitations on your wonderful—' and he stopped suddenly.

Did I still dream, or did I know the voice? Now for the first time I could see the man's face—it was that of *Juan de Garcia*! But if I knew him he also knew me.

'*Caramba!*' he said, 'whom have we here? Senor Thomas Wingfield I salute you. Look, my comrades, you see this young man whom the sea has brought to us. He is no Spaniard but an English spy. The last time that I saw him was in the streets of Seville, and there he tried to murder me because I threatened to reveal his trade to the authorities. Now he is here, upon what errand he knows best.'

'It is false,' I answered; 'I am no spy, and I am come to these seas for one purpose only—to find you.'

'Then you have succeeded well, too well for your own comfort, perhaps. Say now, do you deny that you are Thomas Wingfield and an Englishman?'

'I do not deny it. I—'

'Your pardon. How comes it then that, as your companion the priest tells me, you sailed in *Las Cinque Llagas* under the name of *D'Aila*?'

'For my own reasons, Juan de Garcia.'

'You are confused, senor. My name is Sarceda, as these gentlemen can bear me witness. Once I knew a cavalier of the name of de Garcia, but he is dead.'

'You lie,' I answered; whereon one of De Garcia's companions struck me across the mouth.

'Gently, friend,' said de Garcia; 'do not defile your hand by striking such rats as this, or if you must strike, use a stick. You have heard that he confesses to passing under a false name and to being an Englishman, and therefore one of our country's foes. To this I add upon my word of honour that to my knowledge he is a spy and a would-be murderer. Now, gentlemen, under the commission of his majesty's representative, we are judges here, but since you may think that, having been called a liar openly by this English dog, I might be minded to deal unjustly with him, I prefer to leave the matter in your hands.'

Now I tried to speak once more, but the Spaniard who had struck me, a ferocious-looking villain, drew his sword and swore that he would run me through if I dared to open my lips. So I thought it well to keep silent.

'This Englishman would grace a yardarm very well,' he said.

De Garcia, who had begun to hum a tune indifferently, smiled, looking first at the yard and then at my neck, and the hate in his eyes seemed to burn me.

'I have a better thought than that,' said the third officer. 'If we hung him questions might be asked, and at the least, it would be a waste of good money. He is a finely built young man and would last some years in the mines. Let him be sold with the rest of the cargo, or I will take him myself at a valuation. I am in want of a few such on my estate.'

At these words I saw de Garcia's face fall a little, for he wished to be rid of me for ever. Still he did not think it politic to interfere beyond saying with a slight yawn:

'So far as I am concerned, take him, comrade, and free of cost. Only I warn you, watch him well or you will find a stiletto in your back.'

The officer laughed and said: 'Our friend will scarcely get a chance at me, for I do not go a hundred paces underground, where he will find his quarters. And now, Englishman, there is room for you below I think;' and he called to a sailor bidding him bring the irons of the man who had died.

This was done, and after I had been searched and a small sum in gold that I had upon my person taken from me—it was all that remained to me of my possessions—fetters were placed upon my ankles and round my neck, and I was dragged into the hold. Before I reached it I knew from various signs what was the cargo of this ship. She was laden with slaves captured in Fernandina, as the Spaniards name the island of Cuba, that were to be sold in Hispaniola. Among these slaves I was now numbered.

How to tell the horrors of that hold I know not. The place was low, not more than seven feet in height, and the slaves lay ironed in the bilge water on the bottom of the vessel. They were crowded as thick as they could lie, being chained to rings fixed in the sides of the ship. Altogether there may have been two hundred of them, men, women and children, or rather there had been two hundred when the ship sailed a week before. Now some twenty were dead, which was a small number, since the Spaniards reckon to lose from a third to half of their cargo in this devilish traffic. When I entered the place a deadly sickness seized me, weak as I was, brought on by the horrible sounds and smells, and the sights that I saw in the flare of the lanterns which my conductors carried, for the hold was shut off from light and air. But they dragged me along and presently I found myself chained in the midst of a line of black men and women, many feet resting in the bilge water. There the Spaniards left me with a jeer, saying that this was too good a bed for an Englishman to lie on. For a while I endured, then sleep or insensibility came to my succour, and I sank into oblivion, and so I must have remained for a day and a night.

When I awoke it was to find the Spaniard to whom I had been sold or given, standing near me with a lantern and directing the removal of the fetters from a woman who was chained next to me. She was dead, and in the light of the lantern I could see that she had been carried off by some horrible disease that was new to me, but which I afterwards learned to know by the name of the Black Vomit. Nor was she the only one, for I counted twenty dead who were dragged out in succession, and I could see that many more were sick. Also I saw that the Spaniards were not a little frightened, for they could make nothing of this sickness, and strove to lessen it by cleansing the hold and letting air into it by the removal of some planks in the deck above. Had they not done this I believe that every soul of us must have perished, and I set down my own escape from the sickness to the fact that the largest opening in the deck was made directly above my head, so that by standing up, which my chains allowed me to do, I could breathe air that was almost pure.

Having distributed water and meal cakes, the Spaniards went away. I drank greedily of the water, but the cakes I could not eat, for they were mouldy. The sights and sounds around me were so awful that I will not try to write of them.

And all the while we sweltered in the terrible heat, for the sun pierced through the deck planking of the vessel, and I could feel by her lack of motion that we were becalmed and drifting. I stood up, and by resting my heels upon a rib of the ship and my back against her side, I found myself in a position whence I could see the feet of the passers-by on the deck above.

Presently I saw that one of these wore a priest's robe, and guessing that he must be my companion with whom I had escaped, I strove to attract his notice, and at length succeeded. So soon as he knew who it was beneath him, the priest lay down on the deck as though to rest himself, and we spoke together. He told me, as I had guessed, that we were becalmed and that a great sickness had taken hold of the ship, already laying low a third of the crew, adding that it was a judgment from heaven because of their cruelty and wickedness.

To this I answered that the judgment was working on the captives as well as on the captors, and asked him where was Sarceda, as they named de Garcia. Then I learned that he had been taken sick that morning, and I rejoiced at the news, for if I had hated him before, it may be judged how deeply I hated him now. Presently the priest left me and returned with water mixed with the juice of limes, that tasted to me like nectar from the gods, and some good meat and fruit. These he gave me through the hole in the planks, and I made shift to seize them in my manacled hands and devoured them. After this he went away, to my great chagrin; why, I did not discover till the following morning.

That day passed and the long night passed, and when at length the Spaniards visited the hold once more, there were forty bodies to be dragged out of it, and many others were sick. After they had gone I stood up, watching for my friend the priest, but he did not come then, nor ever again.

CHAPTER 12

Thomas Comes to Shore

For an hour or more I stood thus craning my neck upwards to seek for the priest. At length when I was about to sink back into the hold, for I could stand no longer in that cramped posture, I saw a woman's dress pass by the hole in the deck, and knew it for one that was worn by a lady who had escaped with me in the boat.

'Senora,' I whispered, 'for the love of God listen to me. It is I, d'Aila, who am chained down here among the slaves.'

She started, then as the priest had done, she sat herself down upon the deck, and I told her of my dreadful plight, not knowing that she was acquainted with it, and of the horrors below.

'Alas! senor,' she answered, 'they can be little worse than those above. A dreadful sickness is raging among the crew, six are already dead and many more are raving in their last madness. I would that the sea had swallowed us with the rest, for we have been rescued from it only to fall into hell. Already my mother is dead and my little brother is dying.'

'Where is the priest?' I asked.

'He died this morning and has just been cast into the sea. Before he died he spoke of you, and prayed me to help you if I could. But his words were wild and I thought that he might be distraught. And indeed how can I help you?'

'Perhaps you can find me food and drink,' I answered 'and for our friend, God rest his soul. What of the Captain Sarceda? Is he also dead?'

'No, senor, he alone is recovering of all whom the scourge has smitten. And now I must go to my brother, but first I will seek food for you.'

She went and presently returned with meat and a flask of wine which she had hidden beneath her dress, and I ate and blessed her.

For two days she fed me thus, bringing me food at night. On the second night she told me that her brother was dead and of all the crew only fifteen men and one officer remained untouched by the sickness, and that she herself grew ill. Also she said that the water was almost finished, and there was little food left for the slaves. After this she came no more, and I suppose that she died also.

It was within twenty hours of her last visit that I left this accursed ship. For a day none had come to feed or tend the slaves, and indeed many needed no tending, for they were dead. Some still lived however, though so far as I could see the most of them were smitten with the plague. I myself had escaped the sickness, perhaps because of the strength and natural healthiness of my body, which has always saved me from fevers and diseases, fortified as it was by the good food that I had obtained. But now I knew that I could not live long, indeed chained in this dreadful charnel-house I prayed for death to release me from the horrors of such existence. The day passed as before in sweltering heat, unbroken by any air or motion, and night came at last, made hideous by the barbarous ravings of the dying. But even there and then I slept and dreamed that I was walking with my love in the vale of Waveney.

Towards the morning I was awakened by a sound of clanking iron, and opening my eyes, I saw that men were at work, by the light of lanterns, knocking the fetters from the dead and the living together. As the fetters were loosed a rope was put round the body of the slave, and dead or quick, he was hauled through the hatchway. Presently a heavy splash in the water without told the rest of the tale. Now I understood that all the slaves were being thrown overboard because of the want of water, and in the hope that it might avail to save from the pestilence those of the Spaniards who still remained alive.

I watched them at their work for a while till there were but two slaves between me and the workers, of whom one was living and the other dead. Then I bethought me that this would be my fate also, to be cast quick into the sea, and took counsel with myself as to whether I should declare that I was whole from the plague and pray them to spare me, or whether I should suffer myself to be drowned. The desire for life was strong, but perhaps it may serve to show how great were the torments from which I was suffering, and how broken was my spirit by misfortunes and the horrors around me, when I say that I determined to make no further effort to live, but rather to accept death as a merciful release. And, indeed, I knew that there was little likelihood of such attempts being of avail, for I saw that the Spanish sailors were mad with fear and had but one desire, to be rid of the slaves who consumed the water, and as they believed, had bred the pestilence. So I said such prayers as came into my head, and although with a great shivering of fear, for the poor flesh shrinks from its end and the unknown beyond it, however high may be the spirit, I prepared myself to die.

Now, having dragged away my neighbour in misery, the living savage, the men turned to me. They were naked to the middle, and worked furiously to be done with their hateful task, sweating with the heat, and keeping themselves from fainting by draughts of spirit.

'This one is alive also and does not seem so sick,' said a man as he struck the fetters from me.

'Alive or dead, away with the dog!' answered another hoarsely, and I saw that it was the same officer to whom I had been given as a slave. 'It is that Englishman, and he it is who brought us ill luck. Cast the Jonah overboard and let him try his evil eye upon the sharks.'

'So be it,' answered the other man, and finished striking off my fetters. 'Those who have come to a cup of water each a day, do not press their guests to share it. They show them the door. Say your prayers, Englishman, and may they do you more good than they have done for most on this accursed ship. Here, this is the stuff to make drowning easy, and there is more of it on board than of water,' and he handed me the flask of spirit. I took it and drank deep, and it comforted me a little. Then they put the rope round me and at a signal those on the deck above began to haul till I swung loose beneath the hatchway. As I passed that Spaniard to whom I had been given in slavery, and who but now had counselled my casting away, I saw his face well in the light of the lantern, and there were signs on it that a physician could read clearly.

'Farewell,' I said to him, 'we may soon meet again. Fool, why do you labour? Take your rest, for the plague is on you. In six hours you will be dead!'

His jaw dropped with terror at my words, and for a moment he stood speechless. Then he uttered a fearful oath and aimed a blow at me with the hammer he held, which would swiftly have put an end to my sufferings had I not at that moment been lifted from his reach by those who pulled above.

In another second I had fallen on the deck as they slacked the rope. Near me stood two black men whose office it was to cast us poor wretches into the sea, and behind them, seated in a chair, his face haggard from recent illness, sat de Garcia fanning himself with his sombrero, for the night was very hot.

He recognised me at once in the moonlight, which was brilliant, and said, 'What! are you here and still alive, Cousin? You are tough indeed; I thought that you must be dead or dying. Indeed had it not been for this accursed plague, I would have seen to it myself. Well, it has come right at last, and here is the only lucky thing in all this voyage, that I shall have the pleasure of sending you to the sharks. It consoles me for much, friend Wingfield. So you came across the seas to seek vengeance on me? Well, I hope that your stay has been pleasant. The accommodation was a little poor, but at least the welcome was hearty. And now it is time to speed the parting guest. Good night, Thomas Wingfield; if you should chance to meet your mother presently, tell her from me that I was grieved to have to kill her, for she is the one being whom I have loved. I did not come to murder her as you may have thought, but she forced me to it to save myself, since had I not done so, I should never have lived to return to Spain. She had too much of my own blood to suffer me to escape, and it seems that it runs strong in your veins also, else you would scarcely hold so fast by vengeance. Well, it has not prospered you!' And he dropped back into the chair and fell to fanning himself again with the broad hat.

Even then, as I stood upon the eve of death, I felt my blood run hot within me at the sting of his coarse taunts. Truly de Garcia's triumph was complete. I had come to hunt him down, and what was the end of it? He was about to hurl me to the sharks. Still I answered him with such dignity as I could command.

'You have me at some disadvantage,' I said. 'Now if there is any manhood left in you, give me a sword and let us settle our quarrel once and for all. You are weak from sickness I know, but what am I who have spent certain days and nights in this hell of yours. We should be well matched, de Garcia.'

'Perhaps so, Cousin, but where is the need? To be frank, things have not gone over well with me when we stood face to face before, and it is odd, but do you know, I have been troubled with a foreboding that you would be the end of me. That is one of the reasons why I sought a change of air to these warmer regions. But see the folly of forebodings, my friend. I am still alive, though I have been ill, and I mean to go on living, but you are—forgive me for mentioning it—you are already dead. Indeed those gentlemen,' and he pointed to the two black men who were taking advantage of our talk to throw into the sea the slave who followed me up the hatchway, 'are waiting to put a stop to our conversation. Have you any message that I can deliver for you? If so, out with it, for time is short and that hold must be cleared by daybreak.'

'I have no message to give you from myself, though I have a message for you, de Garcia,' I answered. 'But before I tell it, let me say a word. You seem to have won, wicked murderer as you are, but perhaps the game is not yet played. Your fears may still come true. I am dead, but my vengeance may yet live on, for I leave it to the Hand in which I should have left it at first. You may live some years longer, but do you think that you shall escape? One day you will die as surely as I must die to-night, and what then, de Garcia?'

'A truce, I pray you,' he said with a sneer. 'Surely you have not been consecrated priest. You had a message, you said. Pray deliver it quickly. Time presses, Cousin Wingfield. Who sends messages to an exile like myself?'

'Isabella de Siguenza, whom you cheated with a false marriage and abandoned,' I said.

He started from his chair and stood over me.

'What of her?' he whispered fiercely.

'Only this, the monks walled her up alive with her babe.'

'Walled her up alive! Mother of God! how do you know that?'

'I chanced to see it done, that is all. She prayed me to tell you of her end and the child's, and that she died hiding your name, loving and forgiving. This was all her message, but I will add to it. May she haunt you for ever, she and my mother; may they haunt you through life and death, through earth and hell.'

He covered his face with his hands for a moment, then dropping them sank back into the chair and called to the black sailors.

'Away with this slave. Why are you so slow?'

The men advanced upon me, but I was not minded to be handled by them if I could help it, and I was minded to cause de Garcia to share my fate. Suddenly I bounded at him, and gripping him round the middle, I dragged him from his chair. Such was the strength that rage and despair gave to me that I succeeded in swinging him up to the level of the bulwarks. But there the matter ended, for at that moment the two black sailors sprang upon us both, and tore him from my grip. Then seeing that all was lost, for they were about to cut me down with their swords, I placed my hand upon the bulwark and leaped into the sea.

My reason told me that I should do well to drown as quickly as possible, and I thought to myself that I would not try to swim, but would sink at once. Yet love of life was too strong for me, and so soon as I touched the water, I struck out and began to swim along the side of the ship, keeping myself in her shadow, for I feared lest de Garcia should cause me to be shot at with arrows and musket balls. Presently as I went I heard him say with an oath:

'He has gone, and for good this time, but my foreboding went near to coming true after all. Bah! how the sight of that man frightens me.'

Now I knew in my heart that I was doing a mad thing, for though if no shark took me, I might float for six or eight hours in this warm water yet I must sink at last, and what would my struggle have profited me? Still I swam on slowly, and after the filth and stench of the slave hold, the touch of the clean water and the breath of the pure air were like food and wine to me, and I felt strength enter into me as I went. By this time I was a hundred yards or more from the ship, and though those on board could scarcely have seen me, I could still hear the splash of the bodies, as the slaves were flung from her, and the drowning cries of such among them as still lived.

I lifted my head and looked round the waste of water, and seeing something floating on it at a distance, I swam towards it, expecting that every moment would be my last, because of the sharks which abound in these seas. Soon I was near it, and to my joy I perceived that it was a large barrel, which had been thrown from the ship, and was floating upright in the water. I reached it, and pushing at it from below, contrived to tilt it so that I caught its upper edge with my hand. Then I saw that it was half full of meal cakes, and that it had been cast away because the meal was stinking. It was the weight of these rotten cakes acting as ballast, that caused the tub to float upright in the water. Now I bethought me, that if I could get into this barrel I should be safe from the sharks for a while, but how to do it I did not know.

While I wondered, chancing to glance behind me, I saw the fin of a shark standing above the water not twenty paces away, and advancing rapidly towards me. Then terror seized me and gave me strength and the wit of despair. Pulling down the edge of the barrel till the water began to pour into it, I seized it on either side with my hands, and lifting my weight upon them, I doubled my knees. To this hour I cannot tell how I accomplished it, but the next second I was in the cask, with no other hurt than a scraped shin. But though I had found a boat, the boat itself was like to sink, for what with my weight and that of the rotten meal, and of the water which had poured over the rim, the edge of the barrel was not now an inch above the level of the sea, and I knew that did another bucketful come aboard, it would no longer bear me. At that moment also I saw the fin of the shark within four yards, and then felt the barrel shake as the fish struck it with his nose.

Now I began to bail furiously with my hands, and as I bailed, the edge of the cask lifted itself above the water. When it had risen some two inches, the shark, enraged at my escape, came to the surface, and turning on its side, bit at the tub so that I heard its teeth grate on the wood and iron bands, causing it to heel over and to spin round, shipping more water as it heeled. Now I must bail afresh, and had the fish renewed its onset, I should have been lost. But not finding wood and iron to its taste, it went away for a while, although I saw its fin from time to time for the space of some hours. I bailed with my hands till I could lift the water no longer, then making shift to take off my boot, I bailed with that. Soon the edge of the cask stood twelve inches above the water, and I did not lighten it further, fearing lest it should overturn. Now I had time to rest and to remember that all this was of no avail, since I must die at last either by the sea or because of thirst, and I lamented that my cowardice had only sufficed to prolong my sufferings.

Then I prayed to God to succour me, and never did I pray more heartily than in that hour, and when I had finished praying some sort of peace and hope fell upon me. I thought it marvellous that I should thus have escaped thrice from great perils within the space of a few days, first from the sinking *carak*, then from pestilence and starvation in the bold of the slave-ship, and now, if only for a while, from the cruel jaws of the sharks. It seemed to me that I had not been preserved from dangers which proved fatal to so many, only that I might perish miserably at last, and even in my despair I began to hope when hope was folly; though whether this relief was sent to me from above, or whether it was simply that being so much alive at the moment I could not believe that I should soon be dead, is not for me to say.

At the least my courage rose again, and I could even find heart to note the beauty of the night. The sea was smooth as a pond, there was no breath of wind, and now that the moon began to sink, thousands of stars of a marvellous brightness, such as we do not see in England, gemmed the heavens everywhere. At last these grew pale, and dawn began to flush the east, and after it came the first rays of sunlight. But now I could not see fifty yards around me, because of a dense mist that gathered on the face of the quiet water, and hung there for an hour or more. When the sun was well up and at length the mist cleared away, I perceived that I had drifted far from the ship, of which I could only see the masts that grew ever fainter till they vanished. Now the surface of the sea was clear of fog except in one direction, where it hung in a thick bank of vapour, though why it should rest there and nowhere else, I could not understand.

Then the sun grew hot, and my sufferings commenced, for except the draught of spirits that had been given me in the hold of the slave-ship, I had touched no drink for a day and a night. I will not tell them all in particular detail, it is enough to say that those can scarcely imagine them who have never stood for hour after hour in a barrel, bare-headed and parched with thirst, while the fierce heat of a tropical sun beat down on them from above, and was reflected upward from the glassy surface of the water. In time, indeed, I grew faint and dizzy, and could hardly save myself from falling into the sea, and at last I sank into a sort of sleep or insensibility, from which I was awakened by a sound of screaming birds and of falling water. I looked and saw to my wonder and delight, that what I had taken to be a bank of mist was really low-lying land, and that I was drifting rapidly with the tide towards the bar of a large river. The sound of birds came from great flocks of sea-gulls that were preying on the shoals of fish, which fed at the meeting of the fresh and salt water. Presently, as I watched, a gull seized a fish that could not have weighed less than three pounds, and strove to lift it from the sea. Failing in this, it beat the fish on the head with its beak till it died, and had begun to devour it, when I drifted down upon the spot and made haste to seize the fish. In another moment, dreadful as it may seem, I was devouring the food raw, and never have I eaten with better appetite, or found more refreshment in a meal.

When I had swallowed all that I was able, without drinking water, I put the rest of the fish into the pocket of my coat, and turned my thoughts to the breakers on the bar. Soon it was evident to me that I could not pass them standing in my barrel, so I hastened to upset myself into the water and to climb astride of it. Presently we were in the surf, and I had much ado to cling on, but the tide bore me forward bravely, and in half an hour more the breakers were past, and I was in the mouth of the great river. Now fortune favoured me still further, for I found a piece of wood floating on the stream which served me for a paddle, and by its help I was enabled to steer my craft towards the shore, that as I went I perceived to be clothed with thick reeds, in which tall and lovely trees grew in groups, bearing clusters of large nuts in their crowns. Hither to this shore I came without further ac-cident, having spent some ten hours in my tub, though it was but a chance that I did so, because of the horrible reptiles called crocodiles, or, by some, alligators, with which this river swarmed. But of them I knew nothing as yet.

I reached land but just in time, for before I was ashore the tide turned, and tide and current began to carry me out to sea again, whence assuredly I had never come back. Indeed, for the last ten minutes, it took all the strength that I had to force the barrel along towards the bank. At length, however, I perceived that it floated in not more than four feet of water, and sliding from it, I waded to the bank and cast myself at length there to rest and thank God who thus far had preserved me miraculously. But my thirst, which now returned upon me more fiercely than ever, would not suffer me to lie thus for long, so I staggered to my feet and walked along the bank of the river till I came to a pool of rain water, which on the tasting, proved to be sweet and good. Then I drank, weeping for joy at the taste of the water, drank till I could drink no more, and let those who have stood in such a plight remember what water was to them, for no words of mine can tell it. After I had drunk and washed the brine from my face and body, I drew out the remainder of my fish and ate it thankfully, and thus refreshed, cast myself down to sleep in the shade of a bush bearing white flowers, for I was utterly outworn.

When I opened my eyes again it was night, and doubtless I should have slept on through many hours more had it not been for a dreadful itch and pain that took me in every part, till at length I sprang up and cursed in my agony. At first I was at a loss to know what occasioned this torment, till I perceived that the air was alive with gnat-like insects which made a singing noise, and then settling on my flesh, sucked blood and spat poison into the wound at one and the same time. These dreadful insects the Spaniards name mosquitoes. Nor were they the only flies, for hundreds of other creatures, no bigger than a pin's head, had fastened on to me like bulldogs to a baited bear, boring their heads into the flesh, where in the end they cause festers. They are named *garrapatas* by the Spanish, and I take them to be the young of the tic. Others there were, also, too numerous to mention, and of every shape and size, though they had this in common, all bit and all were venomous. Before the morning these plagues had driven me almost to madness, for in no way could I obtain relief from them. Towards dawn I went and lay in the water, thinking to lessen my sufferings, but before I had been there ten minutes I saw a huge crocodile rise up from the mud beside me. I sprang away to the bank horribly afraid, for never before had I beheld so monstrous and evil-looking a brute, to fall again into the clutches of the creatures, winged and crawling, that were waiting for me there by myriads.

But enough of these damnable insects!

CHAPTER 13

The Stone of Sacrifice

At length the morning broke and found me in a sorry plight, for my face was swollen to the size of a pumpkin by the venom of the mosquitoes, and the rest of my body was in little better case. Moreover I could not keep myself still because of the itching, but must run and jump like a madman. And where was I to run to through this huge swamp, in which I could see no shelter or sign of man? I could not guess, so since I must keep moving I followed the bank of the river, as I walked disturbing many crocodiles and loathsome snakes. Now I knew that I could not live long in such suffering, and determined to struggle forward till I fell down insensible and death put an end to my torments.

For an hour or more I went on thus till I came to a place that was clear of bush and reeds. Across this I skipped and danced, striking with my swollen hands at the gnats which buzzed about my head. Now the end was not far off, for I was exhausted and near to falling, when suddenly I came upon a party of men, brown in colour and clothed with white garments, who had been fishing in the river. By them on the water were several canoes in which were loads of merchandise, and they were now engaged in eating. So soon as these men caught sight of me they uttered exclamations in an unknown tongue and seizing weapons that lay by them, bows and arrows and wooden clubs set on either side with spikes of flinty glass, they made towards me as though to kill me. Now I lifted up my hands praying for mercy, and seeing that I was unarmed and helpless the men laid down their arms and addressed me. I shook my head to show that I could not understand, and pointed first to the sea and then to my swollen features. They nodded, and going to one of the canoes a man brought from it a paste of a brown colour and aromatic smell. Then by signs he directed me to remove such garments as remained on me, the fashion of which seemed to puzzle them greatly. This being done, they proceeded to anoint my body with the paste, the touch of which gave me a most blessed relief from my intolerable itching and burning, and moreover rendered my flesh distasteful to the insects, for after that they plagued me little.

When I was anointed they offered me food, fried fish and cakes of meal, together with a most delicious hot drink covered with a brown and foaming froth that I learned to know afterwards as chocolate. When I had finished eating, having talked a while together in low tones, they motioned me to enter one of the canoes, giving me mats to lie on. I obeyed, and three other men came with me, for the canoe was large. One of these, a very grave man with a gentle face and manner whom I took to be the chief of the party, sat down opposite to me, the other two placing themselves in the bow and stern of the boat which they drove along by means of paddles. Then we started, followed by three other canoes, and before we had gone a mile utter weariness overpowered me and I fell asleep.

I awoke much refreshed, having slept many hours, for now the sun was setting, and was astonished to find the grave-looking man my companion in the canoe, keeping watch over my sleep and warding the gnats from me with a leafy branch. His kindness seemed to show that I was in no danger of ill-treatment, and my fears on that point being set at rest, I began to wonder as to what strange land I had come and who its people might be. Soon, however, I gave over, having nothing to build on, and observed the scenery instead. Now we were paddling up a smaller river than the one on the banks of which I had been cast away, and were no longer in the midst of marshes. On either side of us was open land, or rather land that would have been open had it not been for the great trees, larger than the largest oak, which grew upon it, some of them of surpassing beauty. Up these trees climbed creepers that hung like ropes even from the topmost boughs, and among them were many strange and gorgeous flowering plants that seemed to cling to the bark as moss clings to a wall. In their branches also sat harsh-voiced birds of brilliant colours, and apes that barked and chattered at us as we went.

Just as the sun set over all this strange new scene the canoes came to a landing place built of timber, and we disembarked. Now it grew dark suddenly, and all I could discover was that I was being led along a good road. Presently we reached a gate, which, from the barking of dogs and the numbers of people who thronged about it, I judged to be the entrance to a town, and passing it, we advanced down a long street with houses on either side. At the doorway of the last house my companion halted, and taking me by the hand, led me into a long low

109

room lit with lamps of earthenware. Here some women came forward and kissed him, while others whom I took to be servants, saluted him by touching the floor with one hand. Soon, however, all eyes were turned on me and many eager questions were asked of the chief, of which I could only guess the purport.

When all had gazed their fill supper was served, a rich meal of many strange meats, and of this I was invited to partake, which I did, seated on a mat and eating of the dishes that were placed upon the ground by the women. Among these I noticed one girl who far surpassed all the others in grace, though none were unpleasing to the eye. She was dark, indeed, but her features were regular and her eyes fine. Her figure was tall and straight, and the sweetness of her face added to the charm of her beauty. I mention this girl here for two reasons, first because she saved me once from sacrifice and once from torture, and secondly because she was none other than that woman who afterwards became known as Marina, the mistress of Cortes, without whose aid he had never conquered Mexico. But at this time she did not guess that it was her destiny to bring her country of Anahuac beneath the cruel yoke of the Spaniard.

From the moment of my entry I saw that Marina, as I will call her, for her Indian name is too long to be written, took pity on my forlorn state, and did what lay in her power to protect me from vulgar curiosity and to minister to my wants. It was she who brought me water to wash in, and a clean robe of linen to replace my foul and tattered garments, and a cloak fashioned of bright feathers for my shoulders.

When supper was done a mat was given me to sleep on in a little room apart, and here I lay down, thinking that though I might be lost for ever to my own world, at least I had fallen among a people who were gentle and kindly, and moreover, as I saw from many tokens, no savages. One thing, however, disturbed me; I discovered that though I was well treated, also I was a prisoner, for a man armed with a copper spear slept across the doorway of my little room. Before I lay down I looked through the wooden bars which served as a protection to the window place, and saw that the house stood upon the border of a large open space, in the midst of which a great pyramid towered a hundred feet or more into the air. On the top of this pyramid was a building of stone that I took to be a temple, and rightly, in front of which a fire burned. Marvelling what the purpose of this great work might be, and in honour of what faith it was erected, I went to sleep.

On the morrow I was to learn.

Here it may be convenient for me to state, what I did not discover till afterwards, that I was in the city of Tobasco, the capital of one of the southern provinces of Anahuac, which is situated at a distance of some hundreds of miles from the central city of Tenoctitlan, or Mexico. The river where I had been cast away was the Rio de Tobasco, where Cortes landed in the following year, and my host, or rather my captor, was the *cacique* or chief of Tobasco, the same man who subsequently presented Marina to Cortes. Thus it came about that, with the exception of a certain Aguilar, who with some companions was wrecked on the coast of Yucatan six years before, I was the first white man who ever dwelt among the Indians. This Aguilar was rescued by Cortes, though his companions were all sacrificed to Huitzel, the horrible war-god of the country. But the name of the Spaniards was already known to the Indians, who looked on them with superstitious fear, for in the year previous to my being cast away, the hidalgo Hernandez de Cordova had visited the coast of Yucatan and fought several battles with the natives, and earlier in the same year of my arrival, Juan de Grigalva had come to this very river of Tobasco. Thus it came about that I was set down as one of this strange new nation of Teules, as the Indians named the Spaniards, and therefore as an enemy for whose blood the gods were thirsting.

I awoke at dawn much refreshed with sleep, and having washed and clothed myself in the linen robes that were provided for me, I came into the large room, where food was given me. Scarcely had I finished my meal when my captor, the *cacique*, entered, accompanied by two men whose appearance struck terror to my heart. In countenance they were fierce and horrible; they wore black robes embroidered with mystic characters in red, and their long and tangled hair was matted together with some strange substance. These men, whom all present, including the chief or cacique, seemed to look on with the utmost reverence, glared at me with a fierce glee that made my blood run cold. One of them, indeed, tore open my white robe and placed his filthy hand upon my heart, which beat quickly enough, counting its throbs aloud while the other nodded at his words. Afterwards I learned that he was saying that I was very strong.

Glancing round to find the interpretation of this act upon the faces of those about me, my eyes caught those of the girl Marina, and there was that in them which left me in little doubt. Horror and pity were written there, and I knew that some dreadful death overshadowed me. Before I could do anything, before I could even think, I was seized by the priests, or *pabas* as the Indians name them, and dragged from the room, all the household following us except Marina and the cacique.

111

Now I found myself in a great square or market place bordered by many fine houses of stone and lime, and some of mud, which was filling rapidly with a vast number of people, men women and children, who all stared at me as I went towards the pyramid on the top of which the fire burned. At the foot of this pyramid I was led into a little chamber hollowed in its thickness, and here my dress was torn from me by more priests, leaving me naked except for a cloth about my loins and a chaplet of bright flowers which was set upon my head. In this chamber were three other men, Indians, who from the horror on their faces I judged to be also doomed to death.

Presently a drum began to beat high above us, and we were taken from the chamber and placed in a procession of many priests, I being the first among the victims. Then the priests set up a chant and we began the ascent of the pyramid, following a road that wound round and round its bulk till it ended on a platform at its summit, which may have measured forty paces in the square. Hence the view of the surrounding country was very fine, but in that hour I scarcely noticed it, having no care for prospects, however pleasing. On the further side of the platform were two wooden towers fifty feet or so in height. These were the temples of the gods, Huitzel God of War and Quetzal God of the Air, whose hideous effigies carved in stone grinned at us through the open doorways. In the chambers of these temples stood small altars, and on the altars were large dishes of gold, containing the hearts of those who had been sacrificed on the yesterday. These chambers, moreover, were encrusted with every sort of filth. In front of the temples stood the altar whereon the fire burned eternally, and before it were a hog-backed block of black marble of the size of an inn drinking table, and a great carven stone shaped like a wheel, measuring some ten feet across with a copper ring in its centre.

All these things I remembered afterwards, though at the time I scarcely seemed to see them, for hardly were we arrived on the platform when I was seized and dragged to the wheel-shaped stone. Here a hide girdle was put round my waist and secured to the ring by a rope long enough to enable me to run to the edge of the stone and no further. Then a flint-pointed spear was given to me and spears were given also to the two captives who accompanied me, and it was made clear to me by signs that I must fight with them, it being their part to leap upon the stone and mine to defend it. Now I thought that if I could kill these two poor creatures, perhaps I myself should be allowed to go free, and so to save my life I prepared to take theirs if I could. Presently the head priest gave a signal commanding the two men to attack me, but they were so lost in fear that they did not even stir. Then the priests began to flog them with leather girdles till at length crying out with pain, they ran at me. One reached the stone and leapt upon it a little before the other, and I struck the spear through his arm. Instantly he dropped his weapon and fled, and the other man fled also, for there was no fight in them, nor would any flogging bring them to face me again.

Seeing that they could not make them brave, the priests determined to have done with them. Amidst a great noise of music and chanting, he whom I had smitten was seized and dragged to the hog-backed block of marble, which in truth was a stone of sacrifice. On this he was cast down, breast upwards, and held so by five priests, two gripping his hands, two his legs, and one his head. Then, having donned a scarlet cloak, the head priest, that same who had felt my heart, uttered some kind of prayer, and, raising a curved knife of the flint-like glass or *itztli*, struck open the poor wretch's breast at a single blow, and made the ancient offering to the sun.

As he did this all the multitude in the place below, in full view of whom this bloody game was played, prostrated themselves, remaining on their knees till the offering had been thrown into the golden censer before the statue of the god Huitzel. Thereon the horrible priests, casting themselves on the body, carried it with shouts to the edge of the pyramid or *teocalli*, and rolled it down the steep sides. At the foot of the slope it was lifted and borne away by certain men who were waiting, for what purpose I did not know at that time.

Scarcely was the first victim dead when the second was seized and treated in a like fashion, the multitude prostrating themselves as before. And then last of all came my turn. I felt myself seized and my senses swam, nor did I recover them till I found myself lying on the accursed stone, the priests dragging at my limbs and head, my breast strained upwards till the skin was stretched tight as that of a drum, while over me stood the human devil in his red mantle, the glass knife in his hand. Never shall I forget his wicked face maddened with the lust for blood, or the glare in his eyes as he tossed back his matted locks. But he did not strike at once, he gloated over me, pricking me with the point of the knife. It seemed to me that I lay there for years while the *paba* aimed and pointed with the knife, but at last through a mist that gathered before my eyes, I saw it flash upward. Then when I thought that my hour had come, a hand caught his arm in mid-air and held it and I heard a voice whispering.

What was said did not please the priest, for suddenly he howled aloud and made a dash towards me to kill me, but again his arm was caught before the knife fell. Then he withdrew into the temple of the god Quetzal, and for a long while I lay upon the stone suffering the agonies of a hundred deaths, for I believed that it was determined to torture me before I died, and that my slaughter had been stayed for this purpose.

There I lay upon the stone, the fierce sunlight beating on my breast, while from below came the faint murmur of the thousands of the wondering people. All my life seemed to pass before me as I was stretched upon that awful bed, a hundred little things which I had forgotten came back to me, and with them memories of childhood, of my oath to my father, of Lily's farewell kiss and words, of de Garcia's face as I was hurled into the sea, of the death of Isabella de Siguenza, and lastly a vague wonder as to why all priests were so cruel!

At length I heard footsteps and shut my eyes, for I could bear the sight of that dreadful knife no longer. But behold! no knife fell. Suddenly my hands were loosed and I was lifted to my feet, on which I never hoped to stand again. Then I was borne to the edge of the *teocalli*, for I could not walk, and here my would-be murderer, the priest, having first shouted some words to the spectators below, that caused them to murmur like a forest when the wind stirs it, clasped me in his blood-stained arms and kissed me on the forehead. Now it was for the first time that I noticed my captor, the *cacique*, standing at my side, grave, courteous, and smiling. As he had smiled when he handed me to the *pabas*, so he smiled when he took me back from them. Then having been cleansed and clothed, I was led into the sanctuary of the god Quetzal and stood face to face with the hideous image there, staring at the golden censer that was to have received my heart while the priests uttered prayers. Thence I was supported down the winding road of the pyramid till I came to its foot, where my captor the cacique took me by the hand and led me through the people who, it seemed, now regarded me with some strange veneration. The first person that I saw when we reached the house was Marina, who looked at me and murmured some soft words that I could not understand. Then I was suffered to go to my chamber, and there I passed the rest of the day prostrated by all that I had undergone. Truly I had come to a land of devils!

And now I will tell how it was that I came to be saved from the knife. Marina having taken some liking to me, pitied my sad fate, and being very quick-witted, she found a way to rescue me. For when I had been led off to sacrifice, she spoke to the *cacique*, her lord, bringing it to his mind that, by common report Montezuma, the Emperor of Anahuac, was disturbed as to the Teules or Spaniards, and desired much to see one. Now, she said, I was evidently a Teule, and Montezuma would be angered, indeed, if I were sacrificed in a far-off town, instead of being sent to him to sacrifice if he saw fit. To this the *cacique* answered that the words were wise, but that she should have spoken them before, for now the priests had got hold of me, and it was hopeless to save me from their grip.

'Nay,' answered Marina, 'there is this to be said. Quetzal, the god to whom this Teule is to be offered, was a white man,[1] and it may well happen that this man is one of his children. Will it please the god that his child should be offered to him? At the least, if the god is not angered, Montezuma will certainly be wroth, and wreak a vengeance on you and on the priests.'

Now when the *cacique* heard this he saw that Marina spoke truth, and hurrying up the *teocalli*, he caught the knife as it was in the act of falling upon me. At first the head priest was angered and called out that this was sacrilege, but when the *cacique* had told him his mind, he understood that he would do wisely not to run a risk of the wrath of Montezuma. So I was loosed and led into the sanctuary, and when I came out the *paba* announced to the people that the god had declared me to be one of his children, and it was for this reason that then and thereafter they treated me with reverence.

---

1. Quetzal, or more properly Quetzalcoatl, was the divinity who is fabled to have taught the natives of Anahuac all the useful arts, including those of government and policy, he was white-skinned and dark-haired. Finally he sailed from the shores of Anahuac for the fabulous country of Tlapallan in a bark of serpents' skins. But before he sailed he promised that he would return again with a numerous progeny. This promise was remembered by the Aztecs, and it was largely on account of it that the Spaniards were enabled to conquer the country, for they were supposed to be his descendants. Perhaps Quetzalcoatl was a Norseman! Vide Sagas of Eric the Red and of Thorfinn Karlsefne.—*Author.*

CHAPTER 14

The Saving of Guatemoc

Now after this dreadful day I was kindly dealt with by the people of Tobasco, who gave me the name of Teule or Spaniard, and no longer sought to put me to sacrifice. Far from it indeed, I was well clothed and fed, and suffered to wander where I would, though always under the care of guards who, had I escaped, would have paid for it with their lives. I learned that on the morrow of my rescue from the priests, messengers were despatched to Montezuma, the great king, acquainting him with the history of my capture, and seeking to know his pleasure concerning me. But the way to Tenoctitlan was far, and many weeks passed before the messengers returned again. Meanwhile I filled the days in learning the Maya language, and also something of that of the Aztecs, which I practised with Marina and others. For Marina was not a Tobascan, having been born at Painalla, on the south-eastern borders of the empire. But her mother sold her to merchants in order that Marina's inheritance might come to another child of hers by a second marriage, and thus in the end the girl fell into the hands of the cacique of Tobasco.

Also I learned something of the history and customs, and of the picture writing of the land, and how to read it, and moreover I obtained great repute among the Tobascans by my skill in medicine, so that in time they grew to believe that I was indeed a child of Quetzal, the good god. And the more I studied this people the less I could understand of them. In most ways they were equal to any nation of our own world of which I had knowledge. None are more skilled in the arts, few are better architects or boast purer laws. Moreover, they were brave and had patience. But their faith was the canker at the root of the tree. In precept it was noble and had much in common with our own, such as the rite of baptism, but I have told what it was in practice. And yet, when all is said, is it more cruel to offer up victims

116

to the gods than to torture them in the vaults of the Holy Office or to immure them in the walls of nunneries?

When I had lived a month in Tobasco I had learned enough of the language to talk with Marina, with whom I grew friendly, though no more, and it was from her that I gathered the most of my knowledge, and also many hints as to the conduct necessary to my safety. In return I taught her something of my own faith, and of the customs of the Europeans, and it was the knowledge that she gained from me which afterwards made her so useful to the Spaniards, and prepared her to accept their religion, giving her insight into the ways of white people.

So I abode for four months and more in the house of the *cacique* of Tobasco, who carried his kindness towards me to the length of offering me his sister in marriage. To this proposal I said no as gently as I might, and he marvelled at it, for the girl was fair. Indeed, so well was I treated, that had it not been that my heart was far away, and because of the horrible rites of their religion which I was forced to witness almost daily, I could have learned to love this gentle, skilled, and industrious people.

At length, when full four months had passed away, the messengers returned from the court of Montezuma, having been much delayed by swollen rivers and other accidents of travel. So great was the importance that the Emperor attached to the fact of my capture, and so desirous was he to see me at his capital, that he had sent his own nephew, the Prince Guatemoc, to fetch me and a great escort of warriors with him.

Never shall I forget my first meeting with this prince who afterwards became my dear companion and brother in arms. When the escort arrived I was away from the town shooting deer with the bow and arrow, a weapon in the use of which I had such skill that all the Indians wondered at me, not knowing that twice I had won the prize at the butts on Bungay Common. Our party being summoned by a messenger, we returned bearing our deer with us. On reaching the courtyard of the *cacique's* house, I found it filled with warriors most gorgeously attired, and among them one more splendid than the rest. He was young, very tall and broad, most handsome in face, and having eyes like those of an eagle, while his whole aspect breathed majesty and command. His body was encased in a cuirass of gold, over which hung a mantle made of the most gorgeous feathers, exquisitely set in bands of different colours. On his head he wore a helmet of gold surmounted by the royal crest, an eagle, standing on a snake fashioned in gold and gems. On his arms, and beneath his knees, he wore circlets of gold and gems, and in his hand was a copper-bladed spear. Round this man were many nobles dressed in a somewhat similar fashion, except that the most of them wore a vest of quilted cotton in place of the gold *cuirass*, and a jewelled panache of the plumes of birds instead of the royal symbol.

This was Guatemoc, Montezuma's nephew, and afterwards the last emperor of Anahuac. So soon as I saw him I saluted him in the Indian fashion by touching the earth with my right hand, which I then raised to my head. But Guatemoc, having scanned me with his eye as I stood, bow in hand, attired in my simple hunter's dress, smiled frankly and said:

'Surely, Teule, if I know anything of the looks of men, we are too equal in our birth, as in our age, for you to salute me as a slave greets his master.' And he held his hand to me.

I took it, answering with the help of Marina, who was watching this great lord with eager eyes.

'It may be so, prince, but though in my own country I am a man of repute and wealth, here I am nothing but a slave snatched from the sacrifice.'

'I know it,' he said frowning. 'It is well for all here that you were so snatched before the breath of life had left you, else Montezuma's wrath had fallen on this city.' And he looked at the *cacique* who trembled, such in those days was the terror of Montezuma's name.

Then he asked me if I was a Teule or Spaniard. I told him that I was no Spaniard but one of another white race who had Spanish blood in his veins. This saying seemed to puzzle him, for he had never so much as heard of any other white race, so I told him something of my story, at least so much of it as had to do with my being cast away.

When I had finished, he said, 'If I have understood aright, Teule, you say that you are no Spaniard, yet that you have Spanish blood in you, and came hither in a Spanish ship, and I find this story strange. Well, it is for Montezuma to judge of these matters, so let us talk of them no more. Come and show me how you handle that great bow of yours. Did you bring it with you or did you fashion it here? They tell me, Teule, that there is no such archer in the land.'

So I came up and showed him the bow which was of my own make, and would shoot an arrow some sixty paces further than any that I saw in Anahuac, and we fell into talk on matters of sport and war, Marina helping out my want of language, and before that day was done we had grown friendly.

For a week the prince Guatemoc and his company rested in the town of Tobasco, and all this time we three talked much together.

Soon I saw that Marina looked with eyes of longing on the great lord, partly because of his beauty rank and might, and partly because she wearied of her captivity in the house of the *cacique*, and would share Guatemoc's power, for Marina was ambitious. She tried to win his heart in many ways, but he seemed not to notice her, so that at last she spoke more plainly and in my hearing.

'You go hence to-morrow, prince,' she said softly, 'and I have a favour to ask of you, if you will listen to your handmaid.'

'Speak on, maiden,' he answered.

'I would ask this, that if it pleases you, you will buy me of the cacique my master, or command him to give me up to you, and take me with you to Tenoctitlan.'

Guatemoc laughed aloud. 'You put things plainly, maiden,' he said, 'but know that in the city of Tenoctitlan, my wife and royal cousin, Tecuichpo, awaits me, and with her three other ladies, who as it chances are somewhat jealous.'

Now Marina flushed beneath her brown skin, and for the first and last time I saw her gentle eyes grow hard with anger as she answered:

'I asked you to take me with you, prince; I did not ask to be your wife or love.'

'But perchance you meant it,' he said dryly.

'Whatever I may have meant, prince, it is now forgotten. I wished to see the great city and the great king, because I weary of my life here and would myself grow great. You have refused me, but perhaps a time will come when I shall grow great in spite of you, and then I may remember the shame that has been put upon me against you, prince, and all your royal house.'

Again Guatemoc laughed, then of a sudden grew stern.

'You are over-bold, girl,' he said; 'for less words than these many a one might find herself stretched upon the stone of sacrifice. But I will forget them, for your woman's pride is stung, and you know not what you say. Do you forget them also, Teule, if you have understood.'

Then Marina turned and went, her bosom heaving with anger and outraged love or pride, and as she passed me I heard her mutter, 'Yes, prince, you may forget, but I shall not.'

Often since that day I have wondered if some vision of the future entered into the girl's breast in that hour, or if in her wrath she spoke at random. I have wondered also whether this scene between her and Guatemoc had anything to do with the history of her after life; or did Marina, as she avowed to me in days to come, bring shame and ruin on her country for the love of Cortes alone? It is hard to say, and perhaps these things had nothing to do with what followed, for when great events have happened, we are apt to search out causes for them in the past that were no cause. This may have been but a passing mood of hers and one soon put out of mind, for it is certain that few build up the temples of their lives upon some firm foundation of hope or hate, of desire or despair, though it has happened to me to do so, but rather take chance for their architect—and indeed whether they take him or no, he is still the master builder. Still that Marina did not forget this talk I know, for in after times I heard her remind this very prince of the words that had passed between them, ay, and heard his noble answer to her.

Now I have but one more thing to tell of my stay in Tobasco, and then let me on to Mexico, and to the tale of how Montezuma's daughter became my wife, and of my further dealings with de Garcia.

On the day of our departure a great sacrifice of slaves was held upon the *teocalli* to propitiate the gods, so that they might give us a safe journey, and also in honour of some festival, for to the festivals of the Indians there was no end. Thither we went up the sides of the steep pyramid, since I must look upon these horrors daily. When all was prepared, and we stood around the stone of sacrifice while the multitude watched below, that fierce *paba* who once had felt the beatings of my heart, came forth from the sanctuary of the god Quetzal and signed to his companions to stretch the first of the victims on the stone. Then of a sudden the prince Guatemoc stepped forward, and addressing the priests, pointed to their chief, and said:

'Seize that man!'

They hesitated, for though he who commanded was a prince of the blood royal, to lay hands upon a high priest was sacrilege. Then with a smile Guatemoc drew forth a ring having a dull blue stone set in its bezel, on which was engraved a strange device. With the ring he drew out also a scroll of picture-writing, and held them both before the eyes of the *pabas*. Now the ring was the ring of Montezuma, and the scroll was signed by the great high priest of Tenoctitlan, and those who looked on the ring and the scroll knew well that to disobey the mandate of him who bore them was death and dishonour in one. So without more ado they seized their chief and held him. Then Guatemoc spoke again and shortly:

'Lay him on the stone and sacrifice him to the god Quetzal.'

Now he who had taken such fierce joy in the death of others on this same stone, began to tremble and weep, for he did not desire to drink of his own medicine.

'Why must I be offered up, O prince?' he cried, 'I who have been a faithful servant to the gods and to the Emperor.'

'Because you dared to try to offer up this Teule,' answered Guatemoc, pointing to me, 'without leave from your master Montezuma, and because of the other evils that you have done, all of which are written in this scroll. The Teule is a son of Quetzal, as you have yourself declared, and Quetzal will be avenged because of his son. Away with him, here is your warrant.'

Then the priests, who till this moment had been his servants, dragged their chief to the stone, and there, notwithstanding his prayers and bellowings, one who had donned his mantle practised his own art upon him, and presently his body was cast down the side of the pyramid. For my part I am not sufficient of a Christian to pretend that I was sorry to see him die in that same fashion by which he had caused the death of so many better men.

When it was done Guatemoc turned to me and said, 'So perish all your enemies, my friend Teule.'

Within an hour of this event, which revealed to me how great was the power of Montezuma, seeing that the sight of a ring from his finger could bring about the instant death of a high priest at the hands of his disciples, we started on our long journey. But before I went I bid a warm farewell to my friend the *cacique*, and also to Marina, who wept at my going. The *cacique* I never saw again, but Marina I did see.

For a whole month we travelled, for the way was far and the road rough, and sometimes we must cut our path through forests and sometimes we must wait upon the banks of rivers. Many were the strange sights that I saw upon that journey, and many the cities in which we sojourned in much state and honour, but I cannot stop to tell of all these.

One thing I will relate, however, though briefly, because it changed the regard that the prince Guatemoc and I felt one to the other into a friendship which lasted till his death, and indeed endures in my heart to this hour.

One day we were delayed by the banks of a swollen river, and in pastime went out to hunt for deer. When we had hunted a while and killed three deer, it chanced that Guatemoc perceived a buck standing on a hillock, and we set out to stalk it, five of us in all. But the buck was in the open, and the trees and bush ceased a full hundred yards away from where he stood, so that there was no way by which we might draw near to him. Then Guatemoc began to mock me, saying, 'Now, Teule, they tell tales of your archery, and this deer is thrice as far as we Aztecs can make sure of killing. Let us see your skill.'

'I will try,' I answered, 'though the shot is long.'

So we drew beneath the cover of a *ceiba* tree, of which the lowest branches drooped to within fifteen feet of the ground, and having set an arrow on the string of the great bow that I had fashioned after the shape of those we use in merry England, I aimed and drew it. Straight sped the arrow and struck the buck fair, passing through its heart, and a low murmur of wonderment went up from those who saw the feat.

Then, just as we prepared to go to the fallen deer, a male puma, which is nothing but a cat, though fifty times as big, that had been watching the buck from above, dropped down from the boughs of the *ceiba* tree full on to the shoulders of the prince Guatemoc, felling him to the ground, where he lay face downwards while the fierce brute clawed and bit at his back. Indeed had it not been for his golden cuirass and helm Guatemoc would never have lived to be emperor of Anahuac, and perhaps it might have been better so.

Now when they saw the puma snarling and tearing at the person of their prince, though brave men enough, the three nobles who were with us were seized by sudden panic and ran, thinking him dead. But I did not run, though I should have been glad enough to do so. At my side hung one of the Indian weapons that serve them instead of swords, a club of wood set on both sides with spikes of obsidian, like the teeth in the bill of a swordfish. Snatching it from its loop I gave the puma battle, striking a blow upon his head that rolled him over and caused the blood to pour. In a moment he was up and at me roaring with rage. Whirling the wooden sword with both hands I smote him in mid air, the blow passing between his open paws and catching him full on the snout and head. So hard was this stroke that my weapon was shattered, still it did not stop the puma. In a second I was cast to the earth with a great shock, and the brute was on me tearing and biting at my chest and neck. It was well for me at that moment that I wore a garment of quilted cotton, otherwise I must have been ripped open, and even with this covering I was sadly torn, and to this day I bear the marks of the beast's claws upon my body. But now when I seemed to be lost the great blow that I had struck took effect on him, for one of the points of glass had pierced to his brain. He lifted his head, his claws contracted themselves in my flesh, then he howled like a dog in pain and fell dead upon my body. So I lay upon the ground unable to stir, for I was much hurt, until my companions, having taken heart, came back and pulled the puma off me. By this time Guatemoc, who saw all, but till now was unable to move from lack of breath, had found his feet again.

'Teule,' he gasped, 'you are a brave man indeed, and if you live I swear that I will always stand your friend to the death as you have stood mine.'

Thus he spoke to me; but to the others he said nothing, casting no reproaches at them.

Then I fainted away.

CHAPTER 15

The Court of Montezuma

Now for a week I was so ill from my wounds that I was unable to be moved, and then I must be carried in a litter till we came to within three days' journey of the city of Tenoctitlan or Mexico. After that, as the roads were now better made and cared for than any I have seen in England, I was able to take to my feet again. Of this I was glad, for I have no love of being borne on the shoulders of other men after the womanish Indian fashion, and, moreover, as we had now come to a cold country, the road running through vast table-lands and across the tops of mountains, it was no longer necessary as it had been in the hot lands. Never did I see anything more dreary than these immense lengths of desolate plains covered with aloes and other thorny and succulent shrubs of fantastic aspect, which alone could live on the sandy and waterless soil. This is a strange land, that can boast three separate climates within its borders, and is able to show all the glories of the tropics side by side with deserts of measureless expanse.

One night we camped in a rest house, of which there were many built along the roads for the use of travellers, that was placed almost on the top of the sierra or mountain range which surrounds the valley of Tenoctitlan. Next morning we took the road again before dawn, for the cold was so sharp at this great height that we, who had travelled from the hot land, could sleep very little, and also Guatemoc desired if it were possible to reach the city that night.

When we had gone a few hundred paces the path came to the crest of the mountain range, and I halted suddenly in wonder and admiration. Below me lay a vast bowl of land and water, of which, however, I could see nothing, for the shadows of the night still filled it. But before me, piercing the very clouds, towered the crests of two snow-clad mountains, and on these the light of the unrisen sun played, already changing their whiteness to the stain of blood. Popo, or the Hill that

124

Smokes, is the name of the one, and Ixtac, or the Sleeping Woman, that of the other, and no grander sight was ever offered to the eyes of man than they furnished in that hour before the dawn. From the lofty summit of Popo went up great columns of smoke which, what with the fire in their heart and the crimson of the sunrise, looked like rolling pillars of flame. And for the glory of the glittering slopes below, that changed continually from the mystery of white to dull red, from red to crimson, and from crimson to every dazzling hue that the rainbow holds, who can tell it, who can even imagine it? None, indeed, except those that have seen the sun rise over the volcanoes of Tenoctitlan.

When I had feasted my eyes on Popo I turned to Ixtac. She is not so lofty as her 'husband,' for so the Aztecs name the volcano Popo, and when first I looked I could see nothing but the gigantic shape of a woman fashioned in snow, and lying like a corpse upon her lofty bier, whose hair streamed down the mountain side. But now the sunbeams caught her also, and she seemed to start out in majesty from a veil of rosy mist, a wonderful and thrilling sight. But beautiful as she was then, still I love the Sleeping Woman best at eve. Then she lies a shape of glory on the blackness beneath, and is slowly swallowed up into the solemn night as the dark draws its veil across her.

Now as I gazed the light began to creep down the sides of the volcanoes, revealing the forests on their flanks. But still the vast valley was filled with mist that lay in dense billows resembling those of the sea, through which hills and temple tops started up like islands. By slow degrees as we passed upon our downward road the vapours cleared away, and the lakes of Tezcuco, Chalco, and Xochicalco shone in the sunlight like giant mirrors. On their banks stood many cities, indeed the greatest of these, Mexico, seemed to float upon the waters; beyond them and about them were green fields of corn and aloe, and groves of forest trees, while far away towered the black wall of rock that hedges in the valley.

All day we journeyed swiftly through this fairy land. We passed through the cities of Amaquem and Ajotzinco, which I will not stay to describe, and many a lovely village that nestled upon the borders of Lake Chalco. Then we entered on the great causeway of stone built like a road resting on the waters, and with the afternoon we came to the town of Cuitlahuac. Thence we passed on to Iztapalapan, and here Guatemoc would have rested for the night in the royal house of his uncle Cuitlahua. But when we reached the town we found that Montezuma, who had been advised of our approach by runners, had sent orders that we were to push on to Tenoctitlan, and that palanquins had been made ready to bear us. So we entered the palanquins, and leaving that lovely city of gardens, were borne swiftly along the southern causeway. On we went past towns built upon piles fixed in the bottom of the lake, past gardens that were laid out on reeds and floated over the waters like a boat, past *teocallis* and glistening temples without number, through fleets of light canoes and thousands of Indians going to and fro about their business, till at length towards sunset we reached the battlemented fort that is called Xoloc which stands upon the dyke. I say stands, but alas! it stands no more. Cortes has destroyed it, and with it all those glorious cities which my eyes beheld that day.

At Xoloc we began to enter the city of Tenoctitlan or Mexico, the mightiest city that ever I had seen. The houses on the outskirts, indeed, were built of mud or adobe, but those in the richer parts were constructed of red stone. Each house surrounded a courtyard and was in turn surrounded by a garden, while between them ran canals, having footpaths on either side. Then there were squares, and in the squares pyramids, palaces, and temples without end. I gazed on them till I was bewildered, but all seemed as nothing when at length I saw the great temple with its stone gateways opening to the north and the south, the east and the west, its wall carven everywhere with serpents, its polished pavements, its *teocallis* decked with human skulls, thousands upon thousands of them, and its vast surrounding *tianquez*, or market place. I caught but a glimpse of it then, for the darkness was falling, and afterwards we were borne on through the darkness, I did not know whither.

A while went by and I saw that we had left the city, and were passing up a steep hill beneath the shadow of mighty cedar trees. Presently we halted in a courtyard and here I was bidden to alight. Then the prince Guatemoc led me into a wondrous house, of which all the rooms were roofed with cedar wood, and its walls hung with richly-coloured cloths, and in that house gold seemed as plentiful as bricks and oak are with us in England. Led by domestics who bore cedar wands in their hands, we went through many passages and rooms, till at length we came to a chamber where other domestics were awaiting us, who washed us with scented waters and clothed us in gorgeous apparel. Thence they conducted us to a door where we were bidden to remove our shoes, and a coarse coloured robe was given to each of us to hide our splendid dress. The robes having been put on, we were suffered to pass the door, and found ourselves in a vast chamber in which were many noble men and some women, all standing and clad in coarse robes. At the far end of this chamber was a gilded screen, and from behind it floated sounds of sweet music.

Now as we stood in the great chamber that was lighted with sweet-smelling torches, many men advanced and greeted Guatemoc the prince, and I noticed that all of them looked upon me curiously. Presently a woman came and I saw that her beauty was great. She was tall and stately, and beneath her rough outer robe splendidly attired in worked and jewelled garments. Weary and bewildered as I was, her loveliness seized me as it were in a vice, never before had I seen such loveliness. For her eye was proud and full like the eye of a buck, her curling hair fell upon her shoulders, and her features were very noble, yet tender almost to sadness, though at times she could seem fierce enough. This lady was yet in her first youth, perchance she may have seen some eighteen years, but her shape was that of a full-grown woman and most royal.

'Greeting, Guatemoc my cousin,' she said in a sweet voice; 'so you are come at last. My royal father has awaited you for long and will ask questions as to your delay. My sister your wife has wondered also why you tarried.'

Now as she spoke I felt rather than saw that this lady was searching me with her eyes.

'Greeting, Otomie my cousin,' answered the prince. 'I have been delayed by the accidents of travel. Tobasco is far away, also my charge and companion, Teule,' and he nodded towards me, 'met with an accident on the road.'

'What was the accident?' she asked.

'Only this, that he saved me from the jaws of a puma at the risk of his life when all the others fled from me, and was somewhat hurt in the deed. He saved me thus—' and in few words he told the story.

She listened and I saw that her eyes sparkled at the tale. When it was done she spoke again, and this time to me.

'Welcome, Teule,' she said smiling. 'You are not of our people, yet my heart goes out to such a man.' And still smiling she left us.

'Who is that great lady?' I asked of Guatemoc.

'That is my cousin Otomie, the princess of the Otomie, my uncle Montezuma's favourite daughter,' he answered. 'She likes you, Teule, and that is well for you for many reasons. Hush!'

As he spoke the screen at the far end of the chamber was drawn aside. Beyond it a man sat upon a broidered cushion, who was inhaling the fumes of the tobacco weed from a gilded pipe of wood after the Indian fashion. This man, who was no other than the monarch Montezuma, was of a tall build and melancholy countenance, having a very pale face for one of his nation, and thin black hair. He was dressed in a white robe of the purest cotton, and wore a golden belt and sandals set with pearls, and on his head a plume of feathers of the royal green. Behind him were a band of beautiful girls somewhat slightly clothed, some of whom played on lutes and other instruments of music, and on either side stood four ancient counsellors, all of them barefooted and clad in the coarsest garments.

So soon as the screen was drawn all the company in the chamber prostrated themselves upon their knees, an example that I hastened to follow, and thus they remained till the emperor made a sign with the gilded bowl of his pipe, when they rose to their feet again and stood with folded hands and eyes fixed abjectly upon the floor. Presently Montezuma made another signal, and three aged men whom I understood to be ambassadors, advanced and asked some prayer of him. He answered them with a nod of the head and they retreated from his presence, making obeisance and stepping backward till they mingled with the crowd. Then the emperor spoke a word to one of the counsellors, who bowed and came slowly down the hall looking to the right and to the left. Presently his eye fell upon Guatemoc, and, indeed, he was easy to see, for he stood a head taller than any there.

'Hail, prince,' he said. 'The royal Montezuma desires to speak with you, and with the Teule, your companion.'

'Do as I do, Teule,' said Guatemoc, and led the way up the chamber, till we reached the place where the wooden screen had been, which, as we passed it, was drawn behind us, shutting us off from the hall.

Here we stood a while, with folded hands and downcast eyes, till a signal was made to us to advance.

'Your report, nephew,' said Montezuma in a low voice of command.

'I went to the city of Tobasco, O glorious Montezuma. I found the Teule and brought him hither. Also I caused the high priest to be sacrificed according to the royal command, and now I hand back the imperial signet,' and he gave the ring to a counsellor.

'Why did you delay so long upon the road, nephew?'

'Because of the chances of the journey; while saving my life, royal Montezuma, the Teule my prisoner was bitten by a puma. Its skin is brought to you as an offering.'

Now Montezuma looked at me for the first time, then opened a picture scroll that one of the counsellors handed to him, and read in it, glancing at me from time to time.

'The description is good,' he said at length, 'in all save one thing— it does not say that this prisoner is the handsomest man in Anahuac.

Say, Teule, why have your countrymen landed on my dominions and slain my people?'

'I know nothing of it, O king,' I answered as well as I might with the help of Guatemoc, 'and they are not my countrymen.'

'The report says that you confess to having the blood of these Teules in your veins, and that you came to these shores, or near them, in one of their great canoes.'

'That is so, O king, yet I am not of their people, and I came to the shore floating on a barrel.'

'I hold that you lie,' answered Montezuma frowning, 'for the sharks and crocodiles would devour one who swam thus.' Then he added anxiously, 'Say, are you of the descendants of Quetzal?'

'I do not know, O king. I am of a white race, and our forefather was named Adam.'

'Perchance that is another name for Quetzal,' he said. 'It has long been prophesied that his children would return, and now it seems that the hour of their coming is at hand,' and he sighed heavily, then added: 'Go now. To-morrow you shall tell me of these Teules, and the council of the priests shall decide your fate.'

Now when I heard the name of the priests I trembled in all my bones and cried, clasping my hands in supplication:

'Slay me if you will, O king, but I beseech you deliver me not again into the hands of the priests.'

'We are all in the hands of the priests, who are the mouth of God,' he answered coldly. 'Besides, I hold that you have lied to me.'

Then I went foreboding evil, and Guatemoc also looked downcast. Bitterly did I curse the hour when I had said that I was of the Spanish blood and yet no Spaniard. Had I known even what I knew that day, torture would not have wrung those words from me. But now it was too late.

Now Guatemoc led me to certain apartments of this palace of Chapoltepec, where his wife, the royal princess Tecuichpo, was waiting him, a very lovely lady, and with her other ladies, among them the princess Otomie, Montezuma's daughter, and some nobles. Here a rich repast was served to us, and I was seated next to the princess Otomie, who spoke to me most graciously, asking me many things concerning my land and the people of the Teules. It was from her that I learned first that the emperor was much disturbed at heart because of these Teules or Spaniards, for he was superstitious, and held them to be the children of the god Quetzal, who according to ancient prophecy would come to take the land. Indeed, so gracious was she, and so royally lovely, that for the first time I felt my heart stirred by any other woman than my betrothed whom I had left far away in England, and whom, as I thought, I should never see again. And as I learned in after days mine was not the only heart that was stirred that night.

Near to us sat another royal lady, Papantzin, the sister of Montezuma, but she was neither young nor lovely, and yet most sweet faced and sad as though with the presage of death. Indeed she died not many weeks after but could not rest quiet in her grave, as shall be told.

When the feast was done and we had drunk of the cocoa or chocolate, and smoked tobacco in pipes, a strange but most soothing custom that I learned in Tobasco and of which I have never been able to break myself, though the weed is still hard to come by here in England, I was led to my sleeping place, a small chamber panelled with cedar boards. For a while I could not sleep, for I was overcome by the memory of all the strange sights that I had seen in this wonderful new land which was so civilised and yet so barbarous. I thought of that sad-faced king, the absolute lord of millions, surrounded by all that the heart of man can desire, by vast wealth, by hundreds of lovely wives, by loving children, by countless armies, by all the glory of the arts, ruling over the fairest empire on the earth, with every pleasure to his hand, a god in all things save his mortality, and worshipped as a god, and yet a victim to fear and superstition, and more heavy hearted than the meanest slave about his palaces. Here was a lesson such as Solomon would have loved to show, for with Solomon this Montezuma might cry:

'I gathered me also silver and gold, and the peculiar treasure of kings and of the provinces: I gat me men singers and women singers, and the delights of the sons of men, and musical instruments, and that of all sorts. And whatsoever my eyes desired I kept not from them, I withheld not my heart from any joy. And behold, all was vanity and vexation of spirit, and there was no profit under the sun.'

So he might have cried, so, indeed, he did cry in other words, for, as the painting of the skeletons and the three monarchs that is upon the north wall of the aisle of Ditchingham Church shows forth so aptly, kings have their fates and happiness is not to them more than to any other of the sons of men. Indeed, it is not at all, as my benefactor Fonseca once said to me; true happiness is but a dream from which we awake continually to the sorrows of our short laborious day.

Then my thoughts flew to the vision of that most lovely maid, the princess Otomie, who, as I believed, had looked on me so kindly, and I found that vision sweet, for I was young, and the English Lily, my own love, was far away and lost to me for ever. Was it then wonderful that I should find this Indian poppy fair? Indeed, where is the man who would not have been overcome by her sweetness, her beauty, and that stamp of royal grace which comes with kingly blood and the daily exercise of power? Like the rich wonders of the robe she wore, her very barbarism, of which now I saw but the better side, drew and dazzled my mind's eye, giving her woman's tenderness some new quality, sombre and strange, an eastern richness which is lacking in our well schooled English women, that at one and the same stroke touched both the imagination and the senses, and through them enthralled the heart.

For Otomie seemed such woman as men dream of but very rarely win, seeing that the world has few such natures and fewer nurseries where they can be reared. At once pure and passionate, of royal blood and heart, rich natured and most womanly, yet brave as a man and beautiful as the night, with a mind athirst for knowledge and a spirit that no sorrows could avail to quell, ever changing in her outer moods, and yet most faithful and with the honour of a man, such was Otomie, Montezuma's daughter, princess of the Otomie. Was it wonderful then that I found her fair, or, when fate gave me her love, that at last I loved her in turn? And yet there was that in her nature which should have held me back had I but known of it, for with all her charm, her beauty and her virtues, at heart she was still a savage, and strive as she would to hide it, at times her blood would master her.

But as I lay in the chamber of the palace of Chapoltepec, the tramp of the guards without my door reminded me that I had little now to do with love and other delights, I whose life hung from day to day upon a hair. To-morrow the priests would decide my fate, and when the priests were judges, the prisoner might know the sentence before it was spoken. I was a stranger and a white man, surely such a one would prove an offering more acceptable to the gods than that furnished by a thousand Indian hearts. I had been snatched from the altars of Tobasco that I might grace the higher altars of Tenoctitlan, and that was all. My fate would be to perish miserably far from my home, and in this world never to be heard of more.

Musing thus sadly at last I slept. When I woke the sun was up. Rising from my mat I went to the wood-barred window place and looked through. The palace whence I gazed was placed on the crest of a rocky hill. On one side this hill was bathed by the blue waters of Tezcuco, on the other, a mile or more away, rose the temple towers of Mexico. Along the slopes of the hill, and in some directions for a mile from its base, grew huge cedar trees from the boughs of which hung a grey and ghostly-looking moss. These trees are so large that the smallest of them is bigger than the best oak in this parish of Ditchingham, while the greatest measures twenty-two paces round the base. Beyond and between these marvellous and ancient trees were the gardens of Montezuma, that with their strange and gorgeous flowers, their marble baths, their aviaries and wild beast dens, were, as I believe, the most wonderful in the whole world.[1]

'At the least,' I thought to myself, 'even if I must die, it is something to have seen this country of Anahuac, its king, its customs, and its people.'

---

1. The gardens of Montezuma have been long destroyed, but some of the cedars still flourish at Chapoltepec, though the Spaniards cut down many. One of them, which tradition says was a favourite tree of the great emperor's, measures (according to a rough calculation the author of this book made upon the spot) about sixty feet round the bole. It is strange to think that a few ancient conifers should alone survive of all the glories of Montezuma's wealth and state.—*Author.*

CHAPTER 16

Thomas Becomes a God

Little did I, plain Thomas Wingfield, gentleman, know, when I rose that morning, that before sunset I should be a god, and after Montezuma the Emperor, the most honoured man, or rather god, in the city of Mexico.

It came about thus. When I had breakfasted with the household of the prince Guatemoc, I was led to the hall of justice, which was named the 'tribunal of god.' Here on a golden throne sat Montezuma, administering justice in such pomp as I cannot describe. About him were his counsellors and great lords, and before him was placed a human skull crowned with emeralds so large that a blaze of light went up from them. In his hand also he held an arrow for a sceptre. Certain chiefs or caciques were on their trial for treason, nor were they left long in doubt as to their fate. For when some evidence had been heard they were asked what they had to say in their defence. Each of them told his tale in few words and short. Then Montezuma, who till now had said and done nothing, took the painted scroll of their indictments and pricked it with the arrow in his hand where the picture of each prisoner appeared upon the scroll. Then they were led away to death, but how they died I do not know.

When this trial was finished certain priests entered the hall clothed in sable robes, their matted hair hanging down their backs. They were fierce, wild-eyed men of great dignity, and I shivered when I saw them. I noticed also that they alone made small reverence to the majesty of Montezuma. The counsellors and nobles having fallen back, these priests entered into talk with the emperor, and presently two of them came forward and taking me from the custody of the guards, led me forward before the throne. Then of a sudden I was commanded to strip myself of my garments, and this I did with no little shame, till I stood naked before them all. Now the priests came forward and examined every part of me closely. On my arms were the scars left by de Garcia's sword, and on my breast the scarcely healed marks of the puma's teeth and claws. These wounds they scanned, asking how I had come by them. I told them, and thereupon they carried on a discussion among themselves, and out of my hearing, which grew so warm that at length they appealed to the emperor to decide the point. He thought a while, and I heard him say:

'The blemishes do not come from within the body, nor were they upon it at birth, but have been inflicted by the violence of man and beast.'

Then the priests consulted together again, and presently their leader spoke some words into the ear of Montezuma. He nodded, and rising from his throne, came towards me who stood naked and shivering before him, for the air of Mexico is keen. As he advanced he loosed a chain of emeralds and gold that hung about his neck, and unclasped the royal cloak from his shoulders. Then with his own hand, he put the chain about my throat, and the cloak upon my shoulders, and having humbly bent the knee before me as though in adoration, he cast his arms about me and embraced me.

'Hail! most blessed,' he said, 'divine son of Quetzal, holder of the spirit of Tezcat, Soul of the World, Creator of the World. What have we done that you should honour us thus with your presence for a season? What can we do to pay the honour back? You created us and all this country; behold! while you tarry with us, it is yours and we are nothing but your servants. Order and your commands shall be obeyed, think and your thought shall be executed before it can pass your lips. O Tezcat, I, Montezuma your servant, offer you my adoration, and through me the adoration of all my people,' and again he bowed the knee.

'We adore you, O Tezcat!' chimed in the priests.

Now I remained silent and bewildered, for of all this foolery I could understand nothing, and while I stood thus Montezuma clapped his hands and women entered bearing beautiful clothing with them, and a wreath of flowers. The clothing they put upon my body and the wreath of flowers on my head, worshipping me the while and saying, 'Tezcat who died yesterday is come again. Be joyful, Tezcat has come again in the body of the captive Teule.'

Then I understood that I was now a god and the greatest of gods, though at that moment within myself I felt more of a fool than I had ever been before.

And now men appeared, grave and reverend in appearance, bearing lutes in their hands. I was told that these were my tutors, and with them a train of royal pages who were to be my servants. They led me forth from the hall making music as they went, and before me marched a herald, calling out that this was the god Tezcat, Soul of the World, Creator of the World, who had come again to visit his people. They led me through all the courts and endless chambers of the palace, and wherever I went, man woman and child bowed themselves to the earth before me, and worshipped me, Thomas Wingfield of Ditchingham, in the county of Norfolk, till I thought that I must be mad.

Then they placed me in a litter and carried me down the hill Chapoltepec, and along causeways and through streets, till we came to the great square of the temple. Before me went heralds and priests, after me followed pages and nobles, and ever as we passed the multitudes prostrated themselves till I began to understand how wearisome a thing it is to be a god. Next they carried me through the wall of serpents and up the winding paths of the mighty *teocalli* till we reached the summit, where the temples and idols stood, and here a great drum beat, and the priests sacrificed victim after victim in my honour and I grew sick with the sight of wickedness and blood. Presently they invited me to descend from the litter, laying rich carpets and flowers for my feet to tread on, and I was much afraid, for I thought that they were about to sacrifice me to myself or some other divinity. But this was not so. They led me to the edge of the pyramid, or as near as I would go, for I shrank back lest they should seize me suddenly and cast me over the edge. And there the high priest called out my dignity to the thousands who were assembled beneath, and every one of them bent the knee in adoration of me, the priests above and the multitudes below. And so it went on till I grew dizzy with the worship, and the shouting, and the sounds of music, and the sights of death, and very thankful was I, when at last they carried me back to Chapoltepec.

Here new honours awaited me, for I was conducted to a splendid range of apartments, next to those of the emperor himself, and I was told that all Montezuma's household were at my command and that he who refused to do my bidding should die.

So at last I spoke and said it was my bidding that I should be suffered to rest a while, till a feast was prepared for me in the apartments of Guatemoc the prince, for there I hoped to meet Otomie.

My tutors and the nobles who attended me answered that Montezuma my servant had trusted that I would feast with him that night. Still my command should be done. Then they left me, saying that they would come again in an hour to lead me to the banquet. Now I threw off the emblems of my godhead and cast myself down on cushions to rest and think, and a certain exultation took possession of me, for was I not a god, and had I not power almost absolute? Still being of a cautious mind I wondered why I was a god, and how long my power would last.

Before the hour had gone by, pages and nobles entered, bearing new robes which were put upon my body and fresh flowers to crown my head, and I was led away to the apartments of Guatemoc, fair women going before me who played upon instruments of music.

Here Guatemoc the prince waited to receive me, which he did as though I, his captive and companion, was the first of kings. And yet I thought that I saw merriment in his eye, mingled with sorrow. Bending forward I spoke to him in a whisper:

'What does all this mean, prince?' I said. 'Am I befooled, or am I indeed a god?'

'Hush!' he answered, bowing low and speaking beneath his breath. 'It means both good and ill for you, my friend Teule. Another time I will tell you.' Then he added aloud, 'Does it please you, O Tezcat, god of gods, that we should sit at meat with you, or will you eat alone?'

'The gods like good company, prince,' I said.

Now during this talk I had discovered that among those gathered in the hall was the princess Otomie. So when we passed to the low table around which we were to sit on cushions, I hung back watching where she would place herself, and then at once seated myself beside her. This caused some little confusion among the company, for the place of honour had been prepared for me at the head of the table, the seat of Guatemoc being to my right and that of his wife, the royal Tecuichpo, to my left.

'Your seat is yonder, O Tezcat,' she said, blushing beneath her olive skin as she spoke.

'Surely a god may sit where he chooses, royal Otomie,' I answered; 'besides,' I added in a low voice, 'what better place can he find than by the side of the most lovely goddess on the earth.'

Again she blushed and answered, 'Alas! I no goddess, but only a mortal maid. Listen, if you desire that I should be your companion at our feasts, you must issue it as a command; none will dare to disobey you, not even Montezuma my father.'

So I rose and said in very halting Aztec to the nobles who waited on me, 'It is my will that my place shall always be set by the side of the princess Otomie.'

At these words Otomie blushed even more, and a murmur went round among the guests, while Guatemoc first looked angry and then laughed. But the nobles, my attendants, bowed, and their spokesman answered:

'The words of Tezcat shall be obeyed. Let the seat of Otomie, the royal princess, the favoured of Tezcat, be placed by the side of the god.'

Afterwards this was always done, except when I ate with Montezuma himself. Moreover the princess Otomie became known throughout the city as 'the blessed princess, the favoured of Tezcat.' For so strong a hold had custom and superstition upon this people that they thought it the greatest of honours to her, who was among the first ladies in the land, that he who for a little space was supposed to hold the spirit of the soul of the world, should deign to desire her companionship when he ate. Now the feast went on, and presently I made shift to ask Otomie what all this might mean.

'Alas!' she whispered, 'you do not know, nor dare I tell you now. But I will say this: though you who are a god may sit where you will to-day, an hour shall come when you must lie where you would not. Listen: when we have finished eating, say that it is your wish to walk in the gardens of the palace and that I should accompany you. Then I may find a chance to speak.'

Accordingly, when the feast was over I said that I desired to walk in the gardens with the princess Otomie, and we went out and wandered under the solemn trees, that are draped in a winding-sheet of grey moss which, hanging from every bough as though the forest had been decked with the white beards of an army of aged men, waved and rustled sadly in the keen night air. But alas! we might not be alone, for after us at a distance of twenty paces followed all my crowd of attendant nobles, together with fair dancing girls and minstrels armed with their accursed flutes, on which they blew in season and out of it, dancing as they blew. In vain did I command them to be silent, telling them that it was written of old that there is a time to play and dance and a time to cease from dancing, for in this alone they would not obey me. Never could I be at peace because of them then or thereafter, and not till now did I learn how great a treasure is solitude.

Still we were allowed to walk together under the trees, and though the clamour of music pursued us wherever we went, we were soon deep in talk. Then it was that I learned how dreadful was the fate which overshadowed me.

'Know, O Teule,' said Otomie, for she would call me by the old name when there were none to hear; 'this is the custom of our land, that every year a young captive should be chosen to be the earthly image of the god Tezcat, who created the world. Only two things are necessary to this captive, namely, that his blood should be noble, and that his person should be beautiful and without flaw or blemish. The day that you came hither, Teule, chanced to be the day of choosing a new captive to personate the god, and you have been chosen because you are both noble and more beautiful than any man in Anahuac, and also because being of the people of the Teules, the children of Quetzal of whom so many rumours have reached us, and whose coming my father Montezuma dreads more than anything in the world, it was thought by the priests that you may avert their anger from us, and the anger of the gods.'

Now Otomie paused as one who has something to say that she can scarcely find words to fit, but I, remembering only what had been said, swelled inwardly with the sense of my own greatness, and because this lovely princess had declared that I was the most beautiful man in Anahuac, I who though I was well-looking enough, had never before been called 'beautiful' by man, woman, or child. But in this case as in many another, pride went before a fall.

'It must be spoken, Teule,' Otomie continued. 'Alas! that it should be I who am fated to tell you. For a year you will rule as a god in this city of Tenoctitlan, and except for certain ceremonies that you must undergo, and certain arts which you must learn, none will trouble you. Your slightest wish will be a law, and when you smile on any, it shall be an omen of good to them and they will bless you; even my father Montezuma will treat you with reverence as an equal or more. Every delight shall be yours except that of marriage, and this will be withheld till the twelfth month of the year. Then the four most beautiful maidens in the land will be given to you as brides.'

'And who will choose them?' I asked.

'Nay, I know not, Teule, who do not meddle in such mysteries,' she answered hurriedly. 'Sometimes the god is judge and sometimes the priests judge for him. It is as it may chance. Listen now to the end of my tale and you will surely forget the rest. For one month you will live with your wives, and this month you will pass in feasting at all the noblest houses in the city. On the last day of the month, however, you will be placed in a royal barge and together with your wives, paddled across the lake to a place that is named "Melting of Metals." Thence you will be led to the *teocalli* named "House of Weapons," where your wives will bid farewell to you for ever, and there, Teule, alas! that I must say it, you are doomed to be offered as a sacrifice to the god whose spirit you hold, the great god Tezcat, for your heart will be torn from your body, and your head will be struck from your shoulders and set upon the stake that is known as "post of heads."'

Now when I heard this dreadful doom I groaned aloud and my knees trembled so that I almost fell to the ground. Then a great fury seized me and, forgetting my father's counsel, I blasphemed the gods of that country and the people who worshipped them, first in the Aztec and Maya languages, then when my knowledge of these tongues failed me, in Spanish and good English. But Otomie, who heard some of my words and guessed more, was seized with fear and lifted her hands, saying:

'Curse not the awful gods, I beseech you, lest some terrible thing befall you at once. If you are overheard it will be thought that you have an evil spirit and not a good one, and then you must die now and by torment. At the least the gods, who are everywhere, will hear you.'

'Let them hear,' I answered. 'They are false gods and that country is accursed which worships them. They are doomed I say, and all their worshippers are doomed. Nay, I care not if I am heard—as well die now by torment as live a year in the torment of approaching death. But I shall not die alone, all the sea of blood that your priests have shed cries out for vengeance to the true God, and He will avenge.'

Thus I raved on, being mad with fear and impotent anger, while the princess Otomie stood terrified and amazed at my blasphemies, and the flutes piped and the dancers danced behind us. And as I raved I saw that the mind of Otomie wandered from my words, for she was staring towards the east like one who sees a vision. Then I looked also towards the east and saw that the sky was alight there. For from the edge of the horizon to the highest parts of heaven spread a fan of pale and fearful light powdered over with sparks of fire, the handle of the fan resting on the earth as it were, while its wings covered the eastern sky. Now I ceased my cursing and stood transfixed, and as I stood, a cry of terror arose from all the precincts of the palace and people poured from every door to gaze upon the portent that flared and blazed in the east. Presently Montezuma himself came out, attended by his great lords, and in that ghastly light I saw that his lips worked and his hands writhed over each other. Nor was the miracle done with, for anon from the clear sky that hung over the city, descended a ball of fire, which seemed to rest upon the points of the lofty temple in the great square, lighting up the *teocalli* as with the glare of day. It vanished, but where it had been another light now burned, for the temple of Quetzal was afire.

Now cries of fear and lamentation arose from all who beheld these wonders on the hill of Chapoltepec and also from the city below. Even I was frightened, I do not know why, for it may well be that the blaze of light which we saw on that and after nights was nothing but the brightness of a comet, and that the fire in the temple was caused by a thunderbolt. But to these people, and more especially to Montezuma, whose mind was filled already with rumours of the coming of a strange white race, which, as it was truly prophesied, would bring his empire to nothingness, the omens seemed very evil. Indeed, if they had any doubt as to their meaning, it was soon to be dispelled, in their minds at least. For as we stood wonder-struck, a messenger, panting and soiled with travel, arrived among us and prostrating himself before the majesty of the emperor, he drew a painted scroll from his robe and handed it to an attendant noble. So desirous was Montezuma to know its contents, that contrary to all custom he snatched the roll from the hands of the counsellor, and unrolling it, he began to read the picture writing by the baleful light of the blazing sky and temple. Presently, as we watched and he read, Montezuma groaned aloud, and casting down the writing he covered his face with his hands. As it chanced it fell near to where I stood, and I saw painted over it rude pictures of ships of the Spanish rig, and of men in the Spanish armour. Then I understood why Montezuma groaned. The Spaniards had landed on his shores!

Now some of his counsellors approached him to console him, but he thrust them aside, saying:

'Let me mourn—the doom that was foretold is fallen upon the children of Anahuac. The children of Quetzal muster on our shores and slay my people. Let me mourn, I say.'

At that moment another messenger came from the palace, having grief written on his face.

'Speak,' said Montezuma.

'O king, forgive the tongue that must tell such tidings. Your royal sister Papantzin was seized with terror at yonder dreadful sight,' and he pointed to the heavens; 'she lies dying in the palace!'

Now when the emperor heard that his sister whom he loved was dying, he said nothing, but covering his face with his royal mantle, he passed slowly back to the palace.

And all the while the crimson light gleamed and sparkled in the east like some monstrous and unnatural dawn, while the temple of Quetzal burned fiercely in the city beneath.

Now, I turned to the princess Otomie, who had stood by my side throughout, overcome with wonder and trembling.

'Did I not say that this country was accursed, princess of the Otomie?'

'You said it, Teule,' she answered, 'and it is accursed.'

Then we went into the palace, and even in this hour of fear, after me came the minstrels as before.

CHAPTER 17

The Arising of Papantzin

On the morrow Papantzin died, and was buried with great pomp that same evening in the burial-ground at Chapoltepec, by the side of the emperor's royal ancestors. But, as will be seen, she was not content with their company. On that day also, I learned that to be a god is not all pleasure, since it was expected of me that I must master various arts, and chiefly the horrid art of music, to which I never had any desire. Still my own wishes were not allowed to weigh in the matter, for there came to me tutors, aged men who might have found better employment, to instruct me in the use of the lute, and on this instrument I must learn to strum. Others there were also, who taught me letters, poetry, and art, as they were understood among the Aztecs, and all this knowledge I was glad of. Still I remembered the words of the preacher which tell us that he who increaseth knowledge increaseth sorrow, and moreover I could see little use in acquiring learning that was to be lost shortly on the stone of sacrifice.

As to this matter of my sacrifice I was at first desperate. But reflection told me that I had already passed many dangers and come out unscathed, and therefore it was possible that I might escape this one also. At least death was still a long way off, and for the present I was a god. So I determined that whether I died or lived, while I lived I would live like a god and take such pleasures as came to my hand, and I acted on this resolve. No man ever had greater or more strange opportunities, and no man can have used them better. Indeed, had it not been for the sorrowful thoughts of my lost love and home which would force themselves upon me, I should have been almost happy, because of the power that I wielded and the strangeness of all around me. But I must to my tale.

During the days that followed the death of Papantzin the palace and the city also were plunged in ferment. The minds of men were

141

shaken strangely because of the rumours that filled the air. Every night the fiery portent blazed in the east, every day a new wonder or omen was reported, and with it some wild tale of the doings of the Spaniards, who by most were held to be white gods, the children of Quetzal, come back to take the land which their forefather ruled.

But of all that were troubled, none were in such bad case as the emperor himself, who, during these weeks scarcely ate or drank or slept, so heavy were his fears upon him. In this strait he sent messengers to his ancient rival, that wise and severe man Neza, the king of the allied state of Tezcuco, begging that he would visit him. This king came, an old man with a fierce and gleaming eye, and I was witness to the interview that followed, for in my quality of god I had full liberty of the palace, and even to be present at the councils of the emperor and his nobles. When the two monarchs had feasted together, Montezuma spoke to Neza of the matter of the omens and of the coming of the Teules, asking him to lighten the darkness by his wisdom. Then Neza pulled his long grey beard and answered that heavy as the heart of Montezuma might be, it must grow still heavier before the end.

'See, Lord,' he said, 'I am so sure that the days of our empire are numbered, that I will play you at dice for my kingdoms which you and your forefathers have ever desired to win.'

'For what wager?' asked Montezuma.

'I will play you thus,' answered Neza. 'You shall stake three fighting cocks, of which, should I win, I ask the spurs only. I set against them all the wide empire of Tezcuco.'

'A small stake,' said Montezuma; 'cocks are many and kingdoms few.'

'Still, it shall serve our turn,' answered the aged king, 'for know that we play against fate. As the game goes, so shall the issue be. If you win my kingdoms all is well; if I win the cocks, then good-bye to the glory of Anahuac, for its people will cease to be a people, and strangers shall possess the land.'

'Let us play and see,' said Montezuma, and they went down to the place that is called *tlachco*, where the games are set. Here they began the match with dice and at first all went well for Montezuma, so that he called aloud that already he was lord of Tezcuco.

'May it be so!' answered the aged Neza, and from that moment the chance changed. For strive as he would, Montezuma could not win another point, and presently the set was finished, and Neza had won the cocks. Now the music played, and courtiers came forward to give the king homage on his success. But he rose sighing, and said:

'I had far sooner lose my kingdoms than have won these fowls, for if I had lost my kingdoms they would still have passed into the hands of one of my own race. Now alas! my possessions and his must come under the hand of strangers, who shall cast down our gods and bring our names to nothing.'

And having spoken thus, he rose, and taking farewell of the emperor, he departed for his own land, where, as it chanced, he died very shortly, without living to see the fulfilment of his fears.

On the morrow of his departure came further accounts of the doings of the Spaniards that plunged Montezuma into still greater alarm. In his terror he sent for an astronomer, noted throughout the land for the truth of his divinations. The astronomer came, and was received by the emperor privately. What he told him I do not know, but at least it was nothing pleasant, for that very night men were commanded to pull down the house of this sage, who was buried in its ruins.

Two days after the death of the astronomer, Montezuma bethought him that, as he believed, I also was a Teule, and could give him information. So at the hour of sunset he sent for me, bidding me walk with him in the gardens. I went thither, followed by my musicians and attendants, who would never leave me in peace, but he commanded that all should stand aside, as he wished to speak with me alone. Then he began to walk beneath the mighty cedar trees, and I with him, but keeping one pace behind.

'Teule,' he said at length, 'tell me of your countrymen, and why they have come to these shores. See that you speak truth.'

'They are no countrymen of mine, O Montezuma,' I answered, 'though my mother was one of them.'

'Did I not bid you speak the truth, Teule? If your mother was one of them, must you not also be of them; for are you not of your mother's bone and blood?'

'As the king pleases,' I answered bowing. Then I began and told him of the Spaniards—of their country, their greatness, their cruelty and their greed of gold, and he listened eagerly, though I think that he believed little of what I said, for his fear had made him very suspicious. When I had done, he spoke and said:

'Why do they come here to Anahuac?'

'I fear, O king, that they come to take the land, or at the least to rob it of all its treasure, and to destroy its faiths.'

'What then is your counsel, Teule? How can I defend myself against these mighty men, who are clothed in metal, and ride upon fierce wild beasts, who have instruments that make a noise like thunder, at the sound of which their adversaries fall dead by hundreds, and who bear weapons of shining silver in their hands? Alas! there is no defence possible, for they are the children of Quetzal come back to take the land. From my childhood I have known that this evil overshadowed me, and now it is at my door.'

'If I, who am only a god, may venture to speak to the lord of the earth,' I answered, 'I say that the reply is easy. Meet force by force. The Teules are few and you can muster a thousand soldiers for every one of theirs. Fall on them at once, do not hesitate till their prowess finds them friends, but crush them.'

'Such is the counsel of one whose mother was a Teule;' the emperor answered, with sarcasm and bitter meaning. 'Tell me now, counsellor, how am I to know that in fighting against them I shall not be fighting against the gods; how even am I to learn the true wishes and purposes of men or gods who cannot speak my tongue and whose tongue I cannot speak?'

'It is easy, O Montezuma,' I answered. 'I can speak their tongue; send me to discover for you.'

Now as I spoke thus my heart bounded with hope, for if once I could come among the Spaniards, perhaps I might escape the altar of sacrifice. Also they seemed a link between me and home. They had sailed hither in ships, and ships can retrace their path. For though at present my lot was not all sorrow, it will be guessed that I should have been glad indeed to find myself once more among Christian men.

Montezuma looked at me a while and answered:

'You must think me very foolish, Teule. What! shall I send you to tell my fears and weakness to your countrymen, and to show them the joints in my harness? Do you then suppose that I do not know you for a spy sent to this land by these same Teules to gather knowledge of the land? Fool, I knew it from the first, and by Huitzel! were you not vowed to Tezcat, your heart should smoke to-morrow on the altar of Huitzel. Be warned, and give me no more false counsels lest your end prove swifter than you think. Learn that I have asked these questions of you to a purpose, and by the command of the gods, as it was written on the hearts of those sacrificed this day. This was the purpose and this was the command, that I might discover your secret mind, and that I should shun whatever advice you chanced to give. You counsel me to fight the Teules, therefore I will not fight them, but meet them with gifts and fair words, for I know well that you would have me to do that which should bring me to my doom.'

Thus he spoke very fiercely and in a low voice, his head held low and his arms crossed upon his breast, and I saw that he shook with passion. Even then, though I was very much afraid, for god as I was, a nod from this mighty king would have sent me to death by torment, I wondered at the folly of one who in everything else was so wise. Why should he doubt me thus and allow superstition to drag him down to ruin? To-day I see the answer. Montezuma did not these things of himself, but because the hand of destiny worked with his hand, and the voice of destiny spoke in his voice. The gods of the Aztecs were false gods indeed, but I for one believe that they had life and intelligence, for those hideous shapes of stone were the habitations of devils, and the priests spoke truth when they said that the sacrifice of men was pleasing to their gods.

To these devils the king went for counsel through the priests, and now this doom was on them, that they must give false counsel to their own destruction, and to the destruction of those who worshipped them, as was decreed by One more powerful than they.

Now while we were talking the sun had sunk swiftly, so that all the world was dark. But the light still lingered on the snowy crests of the volcanoes Popo and Ixtac, staining them an awful red. Never before to my sight had the shape of the dead woman whose everlasting bier is Ixtac's bulk, seemed so clear and wonderful as on that night, for either it was so or my fancy gave it the very shape and colour of a woman's corpse steeped in blood and laid out for burial. Nor was it my fantasy alone, for when Montezuma had finished upbraiding me he chanced to look up, and his eyes falling on the mountain remained fixed there.

'Look now, Teule!' he said, presently, with a solemn laugh; 'yonder lies the corpse of the nations of Anahuac washed in a water of blood and made ready for burial. Is she not terrible in death?'

As he spoke the words and turned to go, a sound of doleful wailing came from the direction of the mountain, a very wild and unearthly sound that caused the blood in my veins to stand still. Now Montezuma caught my arm in his fear, and we gazed together on Ixtac, and it seemed to us that this wonder happened. For in that red and fearful light the red figure of the sleeping woman arose, or appeared to rise, from its bier of stone. It arose slowly like one who awakes from sleep, and presently it stood upright upon the mountain's brow, towering high into the air. There it stood a giant and awakened corpse, its white wrappings stained with blood, and we trembled to see it.

For a while the wraith remained thus gazing towards the city of Tenoctitlan, then suddenly it threw its vast arms upward as though in grief, and at that moment the night rushed in upon it and covered it, while the sound of wailing died slowly away.

'Say, Teule,' gasped the emperor, 'do I not well to be afraid when such portents as these meet my eyes day by day? Hearken to the lamentations in the city; we have not seen this sight alone. Listen how the people cry aloud with fear and the priests beat their drums to avert the omen. Weep on, ye people, and ye priests pray and do sacrifice; it is very fitting, for the day of your doom is upon you. O Tenoctitlan, queen of cities, I see you ruined and desolate, your palaces blackened with fire, your temples desecrated, your pleasant gardens a wilderness. I see your highborn women the wantons of stranger lords, and your princes their servants; the canals run red with the blood of your children, your gateways are blocked with their bones. Death is about you everywhere, dishonour is your daily bread, desolation is your portion. Farewell to you, queen of the cities, cradle of my forefathers in which I was nursed!'

Thus Montezuma lamented in the darkness, and as he cried aloud the great moon rose over the edge of the world and poured its level light through the boughs of the cedars clothed in their ghostly robe of moss. It struck upon Montezuma's tall shape, on his distraught countenance and thin hands as he waved them to and fro in his prophetic agony, on my glittering garments, and the terror-stricken band of courtiers, and the musicians who had ceased from their music. A little wind sprang up also, moaning sadly in the mighty trees above and against the rocks of Chapoltepec. Never did I witness a scene more strange or more pregnant with mystery and the promise of unborn horror, than that of this great monarch mourning over the downfall of his race and power. As yet no misfortune had befallen the one or the other, and still he knew that both were doomed, and these words of lamentation burst from a heart broken by a grief of which the shadow only lay upon it.

But the wonders of that night were not yet done with.

When Montezuma had made an end of crying his prophecies, I asked him humbly if I should summon to him the lords who were in attendance on him, but who stood at some distance.

'Nay,' he answered, 'I will not have them see me thus with grief and terror upon my face. Whoever fears, at least I must seem brave. Walk with me a while, Teule, and if it is in your mind to murder me I shall not grieve.'

I made no answer, but followed him as he led the way down the darkest of the winding paths that run between the cedar trees, where it would have been easy for me to kill him if I wished, but I could not see how I should be advantaged by the deed; also though I knew

146

that Montezuma was my enemy, my heart shrank from the thought of murder. For a mile or more he walked on without speaking, now beneath the shadow of the trees, and now through open spaces of garden planted with lovely flowers, till at last we came to the gates of the place where the royal dead are laid to rest. Now in front of these gates was an open space of turf on which the moonlight shone brightly, and in the centre of this space lay something white, shaped like a woman. Here Montezuma halted and looked at the gates, then said:

'These gates opened four days since for Papantzin, my sister; how long, I wonder, will pass before they open for me?'

As he spoke, the white shape upon the grass which I had seen and he had not seen, stirred like an awakening sleeper. As the snow shape upon the mountain had stirred, so this shape stirred; as it had arisen, so this one arose; as it threw its arms upwards, so this one threw up her arms. Now Montezuma saw and stood still trembling, and I trembled also.

Then the woman—for it was a woman—advanced slowly towards us, and as she came we saw that she was draped in grave-clothes. Presently she lifted her head and the moonlight fell full upon her face. Now Montezuma groaned aloud and I groaned, for we saw that the face was the thin pale face of the princess Papantzin—Papantzin who had lain four days in the grave. On she came toward us, gliding like one who walks in her sleep, till she stopped before the bush in the shadow of which we stood. Now Papantzin, or the ghost of Papantzin, looked at us with blind eyes, that is with eyes that were open and yet did not seem to see.

'Are you there, Montezuma, my brother?' she said in the voice of Papantzin; 'surely I feel your presence though I cannot see you.'

Now Montezuma stepped from the shadow and stood face to face with the dead.

'Who are you?' he said, 'who wear the shape of one dead and are dressed in the garments of the dead?'

'I am Papantzin,' she answered, 'and I am risen out of death to bring you a message, Montezuma, my brother.'

'What message do you bring me?' he asked hoarsely.

'I bring you a message of doom, my brother. Your empire shall fall and soon you shall be accompanied to death by tens of thousands of your people. For four days I have lived among the dead, and there I have seen your false gods which are devils. There also I have seen the priests that served them, and many of those who worshipped them plunged into torment unutterable. Because of the worship of these demon gods the people of Anahuac is destined to destruction.'

147

'Have you no word of comfort for me, Papantzin, my sister?' he asked.

'None,' she answered. 'Perchance if you abandon the worship of the false gods you may save your soul; your life you cannot save, nor the lives of your people.'

Then she turned and passed away into the shadow of the trees; I heard her grave-clothes sweep upon the grass.

Now a fury seized Montezuma and he raved aloud, saying:

'Curses on you, Papantzin, my sister! Why then do you come back from the dead to bring me such evil tidings? Had you brought hope with you, had you shown a way of escape, then I would have welcomed you. May you go back into darkness and may the earth lie heavy on your heart for ever. As for my gods, my fathers worshipped them and I will worship them till the end; ay, if they desert me, at least I will never desert them. The gods are angry because the sacrifices are few upon their altars, henceforth they shall be doubled; ay, the priests of the gods shall themselves be sacrificed because they neglect their worship.'

Thus he raved on, after the fashion of a weak man maddened with terror, while his nobles and attendants who had followed him at a distance, clustered about him, fearful and wondering. At length there came an end, for tearing with his thin hands at his royal robes and at his hair and beard, Montezuma fell and writhed in a fit upon the ground.

Then they carried him into the palace and none saw him for three days and nights. But he made no idle threat as to the sacrifices, for from that night forward they were doubled throughout the land. Already the shadow of the Cross lay deep upon the altars of Anahuac, but still the smoke of their offerings went up to heaven and the cry of the captives rang round the *teocallis*. The hour of the demon gods was upon them indeed, but now they reaped their last red harvest, and it was rich.

Now I, Thomas Wingfield, saw these portents with my own eyes, but I cannot say whether they were indeed warnings sent from heaven or illusions springing from the accidents of nature. The land was terror-struck, and it may happen that the minds of men thus smitten can find a dismal meaning in omens which otherwise had passed unnoticed. That Papantzin rose from the dead is true, though perhaps she only swooned and never really died. At the least she did not go back there for a while, for though I never saw her again, it is said that she lived to become a Christian and told strange tales of what she had seen in the land of Death.[1]

1. For the history of the resurrection of Papantzin, see note to Jourdanet's translation of Sahagun, page 870.—*Author.*

CHAPTER 18

The Naming of the Brides

Now some months passed between the date of my naming as the god Tezcat and the entry of the Spaniards into Mexico, and during all this space the city was in a state of ferment. Again and again Montezuma sent embassies to Cortes, bearing with them vast treasures of gold and gems as presents, and at the same time praying him to withdraw, for this foolish prince did not understand that by displaying so much wealth he flew a lure which must surely bring the falcon on himself. To these ambassadors Cortes returned courteous answers together with presents of small value, and that was all.

Then the advance began and the emperor learned with dismay of the conquest of the warlike tribe of the Tlascalans, who, though they were Montezuma's bitter and hereditary foes, yet made a stand against the white man. Next came the tidings that from enemies the conquered Tlascalans had become the allies and servants of the Spaniard, and that thousands of their fiercest warriors were advancing with him upon the sacred city of Cholula. A while passed and it was known that Cholula also had been given to massacre, and that the holy, or rather the unholy gods, had been torn from their shrines. Marvellous tales were told of the Spaniards, of their courage and their might, of the armour that they wore, the thunder that their weapons made in battle, and the fierce beasts which they bestrode. Once two heads of white men taken in a skirmish were sent to Montezuma, fierce-looking heads, great and hairy, and with them the head of a horse. When Montezuma saw these ghastly relics he almost fainted with fear, still he caused them to be set up on pinnacles of the great temple and proclamation to be made that this fate awaited every invader of the land.

Meanwhile all was confusion in his policies. Day by day councils were held of the nobles, of high priests, and of neighbouring and friendly kings. Some advised one thing, some another, and the end

149

of it was hesitation and folly. Ah! had Montezuma but listened to the voice of that great man Guatemoc, Anahuac would not have been a Spanish fief to-day. For Guatemoc prayed him again and yet again to put away his fears and declare open war upon the Teules before it was too late; to cease from making gifts and sending embassies, to gather his countless armies and smite the foe in the mountain passes.

But Montezuma would answer, 'To what end, nephew? How can I struggle against these men when the gods themselves have declared for them? Surely the gods can take their own parts if they wish it, and if they will not, for myself and my own fate I do not care, but alas! for my people, alas! for the women and the children, the aged and the weak.'

Then he would cover his face and moan and weep like a child, and Guatemoc would pass from his presence dumb with fury at the folly of so great a king, but helpless to remedy it. For like myself, Guatemoc believed that Montezuma had been smitten with a madness sent from heaven to bring the land to ruin.

Now it must be understood that though my place as a god gave me opportunities of knowing all that passed, yet I Thomas Wingfield, was but a bubble on that great wave of events which swept over the world of Anahuac two generations since. I was a bubble on the crest of the wave indeed, but at that time I had no more power than the foam has over the wave. Montezuma distrusted me as a spy, the priests looked on me as a god and future victim and no more, only Guatemoc my friend, and Otomie who loved me secretly, had any faith in me, and with these two I often talked, showing them the true meaning of those things that were happening before our eyes. But they also were strengthless, for though his reason was no longer captain, still the unchecked power of Montezuma guided the ship of state first this way and then that, just as a rudder directs a vessel to its ruin when the helmsman has left it, and it swings at the mercy of the wind and tide.

The people were distraught with fear of the future, but not the less on that account, or perhaps because of it, they plunged with fervour into pleasures, alternating them with religious ceremonies. In those days no feast was neglected and no altar lacked its victim. Like a river that quickens its flow as it draws near the precipice over which it must fall, so the people of Mexico, foreseeing ruin, awoke as it were and lived as they had never lived before. All day long the cries of victims came from a hundred temple tops, and all night the sounds of revelry were heard among the streets. 'Let us eat and drink,' they said, 'for the gods of the sea are upon us and to-morrow we die.' Now women who had been held virtuous proved themselves wantons, and men whose names were honest showed themselves knaves, and none cried fie upon them; ay, even children were seen drunken in the streets, which is an abomination among the Aztecs.

The emperor had moved his household from Chapoltepec to the palace in the great square facing the temple, and this palace was a town in itself, for every night more than a thousand human beings slept beneath its roof, not to speak of the dwarfs and monsters, and the hundreds of wild birds and beasts in cages. Here every day I feasted with whom I would, and when I was weary of feasting it was my custom to sally out into the streets playing on the lute, for by now I had in some degree mastered that hateful instrument, dressed in shining apparel and attended by a crowd of nobles and royal pages. Then the people would rush from their houses shouting and doing me reverence, the children pelted me with flowers, and the maidens danced before me, kissing my hands and feet, till at length I was attended by a mob a thousand strong. And I also danced and shouted like any village fool, for I think that a kind of mad humour, or perhaps it was the drunkenness of worship, entered into me in those days. Also I sought to forget my griefs, I desired to forget that I was doomed to the sacrifice, and that every day brought me nearer to the red knife of the priest.

I desired to forget, but alas! I could not. The fumes of the *mescal* and the *pulque* that I had drunk at feasts would pass from my brain, the perfume of flowers, the sights of beauty and the adoration of the people would cease to move me, and I could only brood heavily upon my doom and think with longing of my distant love and home. In those days, had it not been for the tender kindness of Otomie, I think that my heart would have broken or I should have slain myself. But this great and beauteous lady was ever at hand to cheer me in a thousand ways, and now and again she would let fall some vague words of hope that set my pulses bounding. It will be remembered that when first I came to the court of Montezuma, I had found Otomie fair and my fancy turned towards her. Now I still found her fair, but my heart was so full of terror that there was no room in it for tender thoughts of her or of any other woman. Indeed when I was not drunk with wine or adoration, I turned my mind to the making of my peace with heaven, of which I had some need.

Still I talked much with Otomie, instructing her in the matters of my faith and many other things, as I had done by Marina, who we now heard was the mistress and interpreter of Cortes, the Spanish leader. She for her part listened gravely, watching me the while with her tender eyes, but no more, for of all women Otomie was the most modest, as she was the proudest and most beautiful.

So matters went on until the Spaniards had left Cholula on their road to Mexico. It was then that I chanced one morning to be sitting in the gardens, my lute in hand, and having my attendant nobles and tutors gathered at a respectful distance behind me. From where I sat I could see the entrance to the court in which the emperor met his council daily, and I noted that when the princes had gone the priests began to come, and after them a number of very lovely girls attended by women of middle age. Presently Guatemoc the prince, who now smiled but rarely, came up to me smiling, and asked me if I knew what was doing yonder. I replied that I knew nothing and cared less, but I supposed that Montezuma was gathering a peculiar treasure to send to his masters the Spaniards.

'Beware how you speak, Teule,' answered the prince haughtily. 'Your words may be true, and yet did I not love you, you should rue them even though you hold the spirit of Tezcat. Alas!' he added, stamping on the ground, 'alas! that my uncle's madness should make it possible that such words can be spoken. Oh! were I emperor of Anahuac, in a single week the head of every Teule in Cholula should deck a pinnacle of yonder temple.'

'Beware how you speak, prince,' I answered mocking him, 'for there are those who did they hear, might cause *you* to rue *your* words. Still one day you may be emperor, and then we shall see how you will deal with the Teules, at least others will see though I shall not. But what is it now? Does Montezuma choose new wives?'

'He chooses wives, but not for himself. You know, Teule, that your time grows short. Montezuma and the priests name those who must be given to you to wife.'

'Given me to wife!' I said starting to my feet; 'to me whose bride is death! What have I to do with love or marriage? I who in some few short weeks must grace an altar? Ah! Guatemoc, you say you love me, and once I saved you. Did you love me, surely you would save me now as you swore to do.'

'I swore that I would give my life for yours, Teule, if it lay in my power, and that oath I would keep, for all do not set so high a store on life as you, my friend. But I cannot help you; you are dedicated to the gods, and did I die a hundred times, it would not save you from your fate. Nothing can save you except the hand of heaven if it wills. Therefore, Teule, make merry while you may, and die bravely when you must. Your case is no worse than mine and that of many others, for death awaits us all. Farewell.'

When he had gone I rose, and leaving the gardens I passed into the chamber where it was my custom to give audience to those who wished to look upon the god Tezcat as they called me. Here I sat upon my golden couch, inhaling the fumes of tobacco, and as it chanced I was alone, for none dared to enter that room unless I gave them leave. Presently the chief of my pages announced that one would speak with me, and I bent my head, signifying that the person should enter, for I was weary of my thoughts. The page withdrew, and presently a veiled woman stood before me. I looked at her wondering, and bade her draw her veil and speak. She obeyed, and I saw that my visitor was the princess Otomie. Now I rose amazed, for it was not usual that she should visit me thus alone. I guessed therefore that she had tidings, or was following some custom of which I was ignorant.

'I pray you be seated,' she said confusedly; 'it is not fitting that you should stand before me.'

'Why not, princess?' I answered. 'If I had no respect for rank, surely beauty must claim it.'

'A truce to words,' she replied with a wave of her slim hand. 'I come here, O Tezcat, according to the ancient custom, because I am charged with a message to you. Those whom you shall wed are chosen. I am the bearer of their names.'

'Speak on, princess of the Otomie.'

'They are'—and she named three ladies whom I knew to be among the loveliest in the land.

'I thought that there were four,' I said with a bitter laugh. 'Am I to be defrauded of the fourth?'

'There is a fourth,' she answered, and was silent.

'Give me her name,' I cried. 'What other slut has been found to marry a felon doomed to sacrifice?'

'One has been found, O Tezcat, who has borne other titles than this you give her.'

Now I looked at her questioningly, and she spoke again in a low voice.

'I, Otomie, princess of the Otomie, Montezuma's daughter, am the fourth and the first.'

'You!' I said, sinking back upon my cushions. '*You!*'

'Yes, I. Listen: I was chosen by the priests as the most lovely in the land, however unworthily. My father, the emperor, was angry and said that whatever befell, I should never be the wife of a captive

153

who must die upon the altar of sacrifice. But the priests answered that this was no time for him to claim exception for his blood, now when the gods were wroth. Was the first lady in the land to be withheld from the god? they asked. Then my father sighed and said that it should be as I willed. And I said with the priests, that now in our sore distress the proud must humble themselves to the dust, even to the marrying of a captive slave who is named a god and doomed to sacrifice. So I, princess of the Otomie, have consented to become your wife, O Tezcat, though perchance had I known all that I read in your eyes this hour, I should not have consented. It may happen that in this shame I hoped to find love if only for one short hour, and that I purposed to vary the custom of our people, and to complete my marriage by the side of the victim on the altar, as, if I will, I have the right to do. But I see well that I am not welcome, and though it is too late to go back upon my word, have no fear. There are others, and I shall not trouble you. I have given my message, is it your pleasure that I should go? The solemn ceremony of wedlock will be on the twelfth day from now, O Tezcat.'

Now I rose from my seat and took her hand, saying:

'I thank you, Otomie, for your nobleness of mind. Had it not been for the comfort and friendship which you and Guatemoc your cousin have given me, I think that ere now I should be dead. So you desire to comfort me to the last; it seems that you even purposed to die with me. How am I to interpret this, Otomie? In our land a woman would need to love a man after no common fashion before she consented to share such a bed as awaits me on yonder pyramid. And yet I may scarcely think that you whom kings have sued for can place your heart so low. How am I to read the writing of your words, princess of the Otomie?'

'Read it with your heart,' she whispered low, and I felt her hand tremble in my own.

I looked at her beauty, it was great; I thought of her devotion, a devotion that did not shrink from the most horrible of deaths, and a wind of feeling which was akin to love swept through my soul. But even as I looked and thought, I remembered the English garden and the English maid from whom I had parted beneath the beech at Ditchingham, and the words that we had spoken then. Doubtless she still lived and was true to me; while I lived should I not keep true at heart to her? If I must wed these Indian girls, I must wed them, but if once I told Otomie that I loved her, then I broke my troth, and with nothing less would she be satisfied. As yet, though I was deeply moved and the temptation was great, I had not come to this.

'Be seated, Otomie,' I said, 'and listen to me. You see this golden token,' and I drew Lily's posy ring from my hand, 'and you see the writing within it.'

She bent her head but did not speak, and I saw that there was fear in her eyes.

'I will read you the words, Otomie,' and I translated into the Aztec tongue the quaint couplet:

Heart to heart, Though far apart.

Then at last she spoke. 'What does the writing mean?' she said. 'I can only read in pictures, Teule.'

'It means, Otomie, that in the far land whence I come, there is a woman who loves me, and who is my love.'

'Is she your wife then?'

'She is not my wife, Otomie, but she is vowed to me in marriage.'

'She is vowed to you in marriage,' she answered bitterly: 'why, then we are equal, for so am I, Teule. But there is this difference between us; you love her, and me you do not love. That is what you would make clear to me. Spare me more words, I understand all. Still it seems that if I have lost, she is also in the path of loss. Great seas roll between you and this love of yours, Teule, seas of water, and the altar of sacrifice, and the nothingness of death. Now let me go. Your wife I must be, for there is no escape, but I shall not trouble you over much, and it will soon be done with. Then you may seek your desire in the Houses of the Stars whither you must wander, and it is my prayer that you shall win it. All these months I have been planning to find hope for you, and I thought that I had found it. But it was built upon a false belief, and it is ended. Had you been able to say from your heart that you loved me, it might have been well for both of us; should you be able to say it before the end, it may still be well. But I do not ask you to say it, and beware how you tell me a lie. I leave you, Teule, but before I go I will say that I honour you more in this hour than I have honoured you before, because you have dared to speak the truth to me, Montezuma's daughter, when a lie had been so easy and so safe. That woman beyond the seas should be grateful to you, but though I bear her no ill will, between me and her there is a struggle to the death. We are strangers to each other, and strangers we shall remain, but she has touched your hand as I touch it now; you link us together and are our bond of enmity. Farewell my husband that is to be. We shall meet no more till that sorry day when a "slut" shall be given to a "felon" in marriage. I use your own words, Teule!'

Then rising, Otomie cast her veil about her face and passed slowly from the chamber, leaving me much disturbed. It was a bold deed to have rejected the proffered love of this queen among women, and now that I had done so I was not altogether glad. Would Lily, I wondered, have offered to descend from such state, to cast off the purple of her royal rank that she might lie at my side on the red stone of sacrifice? Perhaps not, for this fierce fidelity is only to be found in women of another breed. These daughters of the Sun love wholly when they love at all, and as they love they hate. They ask no priest to consecrate their vows, nor if these become hateful, will they be bound by them for duty's sake. Their own desire is their law, but while it rules them they follow it unflinchingly, and if need be, they seek its consummation in the gates of death, or failing that, forgetfulness.

CHAPTER 19

The Four Goddesses

Some weary time went by, and at last came the day of the entry into Mexico of Cortes and his conquerors. Now of all the doings of the Spaniards after they occupied the city, I do not propose to speak at length, for these are matters of history, and I have my own story to tell. So I shall only write of those of them with which I was concerned myself. I did not see the meeting between Montezuma and Cortes, though I saw the emperor set out to it clad like Solomon in his glory and surrounded by his nobles. But I am sure of this, that no slave being led to sacrifice carried a heavier heart in his breast than that of Montezuma on this unlucky day. For now his folly had ruined him, and I think he knew that he was going to his doom.

Afterwards, towards evening, I saw the emperor come back in his golden litter, and pass over to the palace built by Axa his father, that stood opposite to and some five hundred paces from his own, facing the western gate of the temple. Presently I heard the sound of a multitude shouting, and amidst it the tramp of horses and armed soldiers, and from a seat in my chamber I saw the Spaniards advance down the great street, and my heart beat at the sight of Christian men. In front, clad in rich armour, rode their leader Cortes, a man of middle size but noble bearing, with thoughtful eyes that noted everything, and after him, some few on horseback but the most of them on foot, marched his little army of conquerors, staring about them with bold wondering eyes and jesting to each other in Castilian. They were but a handful, bronzed with the sun and scarred by battle, some of them ill-armed and almost in rags, and looking on them I could not but marvel at the indomitable courage that had enabled them to pierce their way through hostile thousands, sickness, and war, even to the home of Montezuma's power.

By the side of Cortes, holding his stirrup in her hand, walked a beautiful Indian woman dressed in white robes and crowned with flowers. As she passed the palace she turned her face. I knew her at once; it was my friend Marina, who now had attained to the greatness which she desired, and who, notwithstanding all the evil that she had brought upon her country, looked most happy in it and in her master's love.

As the Spaniards went by I searched their faces one by one, with the vague hope of hate. For though it might well chance that death had put us out of each other's reach, I half thought to see de Garcia among the number of the conquerors. Such a quest as theirs, with its promise of blood, and gold, and rapine, would certainly commend itself to his evil heart should it be in his power to join it, and a strange instinct told me that he was NOT dead. But neither dead nor living was he among those men who entered Mexico that day.

That night I saw Guatemoc and asked him how things went.

'Well for the kite that roosts in the dove's nest,' he answered with a bitter laugh, 'but very ill for the dove. Montezuma, my uncle, has been cooing yonder,' and he pointed to the palace of Axa, 'and the captain of the Teules has cooed in answer, but though he tried to hide it, I could hear the hawk's shriek in his pigeon's note. Ere long there will be merry doings in Tenoctitlan.'

He was right. Within a week Montezuma was treacherously seized by the Spaniards and kept a prisoner in their quarters, watched day and night by their soldiers. Then came event upon event. Certain lords in the coast lands having killed some Spaniards, were summoned to Mexico by the instigation of Cortes. They came and were burned alive in the courtyard of the palace. Nor was this all, for Montezuma, their monarch, was forced to witness the execution with fetters on his ankles. So low had the emperor of the Aztecs fallen, that he must bear chains like a common felon. After this insult he swore allegiance to the King of Spain, and even contrived to capture Cacama, the lord of Tezcuco, by treachery and to deliver him into the hands of the Spaniards on whom he would have made war. To them also he gave up all the hoarded gold and treasure of the empire, to the value of hundreds of thousands of English pounds. All this the nation bore, for it was stupefied and still obeyed the commands of its captive king. But when he suffered the Spaniards to worship the true God in one of the sanctuaries of the great temple, a murmur of discontent and sullen fury rose among the thousands of the Aztecs. It filled the air, it could be heard wherever men were gathered, and its sound was like that of a distant angry sea. The hour of the breaking of the tempest was at hand.

Now all this while my life went on as before, save that I was not allowed to go outside the walls of the palace, for it was feared lest I should find some means of intercourse with the Spaniards, who did not know that a man of white blood was confined there and doomed to sacrifice. Also in these days I saw little of the princess Otomie, the chief of my destined brides, who since our strange love scene had avoided me, and when we met at feasts or in the gardens spoke to me only on indifferent matters, or of the affairs of state. At length came the day of my marriage. It was, I remember, the night before the massacre of the six hundred Aztec nobles on the occasion of the festival of Huitzel.

On this my wedding day I was treated with great circumstance and worshipped like a god by the highest in the city, who came in to do me reverence and burned incense before me, till I was weary of the smell of it, for though such sorrow was on the land, the priests would abate no jot of their ceremonies or cruelties, and great hopes were held that I being of the race of Teules, my sacrifice would avert the anger of the gods. At sunset I was entertained with a splendid feast that lasted two hours or more, and at its end all the company rose and shouted as with one voice:

'Glory to thee, O Tezcat! Happy art thou here on earth, happy mayst thou be in the Houses of the Sun. When thou comest thither, remember that we dealt well by thee, giving thee of our best, and intercede for us that our sins may be forgiven. Glory to thee, O Tezcat!'

Then two of the chief nobles came forward, and taking torches led me to a magnificent chamber that I had never seen before. Here they changed my apparel, investing me in robes which were still more splendid than any that I had worn hitherto, being made of the finest embroidered cotton and of the glittering feathers of the humming bird. On my head they set wreaths of flowers, and about my neck and wrists emeralds of vast size and value, and a sorry popinjay I looked in this attire, that seemed more suited to a woman's beauty than to me.

When I was arrayed, suddenly the torches were extinguished and for a while there was silence. Then in the distance I heard women's voices singing a bridal song that was beautiful enough after its fashion, though I forbear to write it down. The singing ceased and there came a sound of rustling robes and of low whispering. Then a man's voice spoke, saying:

'Are ye there, ye chosen of heaven?'

And a woman's voice, I thought it was that of Otomie, answered: 'We are here.'

'O maidens of Anahuac,' said the man speaking from the darkness, 'and you, O Tezcat, god among the gods, listen to my words. Maidens, a great honour has been done to you, for by the very choice of heaven, you have been endowed with the names, the lovelinesses, and the virtues of the four great goddesses, and chosen to abide a while at the side of this god, your maker and your master, who has been pleased to visit us for a space before he seeks his home in the habitations of the Sun. See that you show yourselves worthy of this honour. Comfort him and cherish him, that he may forget his glory in your kindness, and when he returns to his own place may take with him grateful memories and a good report of your people. You have but a little while to live at his side in this life, for already, like those of a caged bird, the wings of his spirit beat against the bars of the flesh, and soon he will shake himself free from us and you. Yet if you will, it is allowed to one of you to accompany him to his home, sharing his flight to the Houses of the Sun. But to all of you, whether you go also, or whether you stay to mourn him during your life days, I say love and cherish him, be tender and gentle towards him, for otherwise ruin shall overtake you here and hereafter, and you and all of us will be ill spoken of in heaven. And you, O Tezcat, we pray of you to accept these maidens, who bear the names and wear the charms of your celestial consorts, for there are none more beautiful or better born in the realms of Anahuac, and among them is numbered the daughter of our king. They are not perfect indeed, for perfection is known to you in the heavenly kingdoms only, since these ladies are but shadows and symbols of the divine goddesses your true wives, and here there are no perfect women. Alas, we have none better to offer you, and it is our hope that when it pleases you to pass hence you will think kindly of the women of this land, and from on high bless them with your blessing, because your memory of these who were called your wives on earth is pleasant.'

The voice paused, then spoke again:

'Women, in your own divine names of Xochi, Xilo, Atla, and Clixto, and in the name of all the gods, I wed you to Tezcat, the creator, to sojourn with him during his stay on earth. The god incarnate takes you in marriage whom he himself created, that the symbol may be perfect and the mystery fulfilled. Yet lest your joy should be too full— look now on that which shall be.'

As the voice spoke these words, many torches sprang into flame at the far end of the great chamber, revealing a dreadful sight. For there, stretched upon a stone of sacrifice, was the body of a man, but whether the man lived or was modelled in wax I do not know to this hour, though unless he was painted, I think that he must have been fashioned in wax, since his skin shone white like mine. At the least his limbs and head were held by five priests, and a sixth stood over him clasping a knife of obsidian in his two hands. It flashed on high, and as it gleamed the torches were extinguished. Then came the dull echo of a blow and a sound of groans, and all was still, till once more the brides broke out into their marriage song, a strange chant and a wild and sweet, though after what I had seen and heard it had little power to move me.

They sang on in the darkness ever more loudly, till presently a single torch was lit at the end of the chamber, then another and another, though I could not see who lit them, and the room was a flare of light. Now the altar, the victim, and the priests were all gone, there was no one left in the place except myself and the four brides. They were tall and lovely women all of them, clad in white bridal robes starred over with gems and flowers, and wearing on their brows the emblems of the four goddesses, but Otomie was the stateliest and most beautiful of the four, and seemed in truth a goddess. One by one they drew near to me, smiling and sighing, and kneeling before me kissed my hand, saying:

'I have been chosen to be your wife for a space, Tezcat, happy maid that I am. May the good gods grant that I become pleasing to your sight, so that you may love me as I worship you.'

Then she who had spoken would draw back again out of earshot, and the next would take her place.

Last of all came Otomie. She knelt and said the words, then added in a low voice,

'Having spoken to you as the bride and goddess to the husband and the god Tezcat, now, O Teule, I speak as the woman to the man. You do not love me, Teule, therefore, if it is your will, let us be divorced of our own act who were wed by the command of others, for so I shall be spared some shame. These are friends to me and will not betray us;' and she nodded towards her companion brides.

'As you will, Otomie,' I answered briefly.

'I thank you for your kindness, Teule,' she said smiling sadly, and withdrew making obeisance, looking so stately and so sweet as she went, that again my heart was shaken as though with love. Now from that night till the dreadful hour of sacrifice, no kiss or tender word passed between me and the princess of the Otomie. And yet our friendship and affection grew daily, for we talked much together, and I sought to turn her heart to the true King of Heaven. But this was not easy, for like her father Montezuma, Otomie clung to the gods of her people, though she hated the priests, and save when the victims were the foes of her country, shrank from the rites of human sacrifice, which she said were instituted by the *pabas*, since in the early days there were no men offered on the altars of the gods, but flowers only. Daily it grew and ripened till, although I scarcely knew it, at length in my heart, after Lily, I loved her better than anyone on earth. As for the other women, though they were gentle and beautiful, I soon learned to hate them. Still I feasted and revelled with them, partly since I must, or bring them to a miserable death because they failed to please me, and partly that I might drown my terrors in drink and pleasure, for let it be remembered that the days left to me on earth were few, and the awful end drew near.

The day following the celebration of my marriage was that of the shameless massacre of six hundred of the Aztec nobles by the order of the hidalgo Alvarado, whom Cortes had left in command of the Span-iards. For at this time Cortes was absent in the coast lands, whither he had gone to make war on Narvaez, who had been sent to subdue him by his enemy Velasquez, the governor of Cuba.

On this day was celebrated the feast of Huitzel, that was held with sacrifice, songs, and dances in the great court of the temple, that court which was surrounded by a wall carved over with the writhing shapes of snakes. It chanced that on this morning before he went to join in the festival, Guatemoc, the prince, came to see me on a visit of ceremony.

I asked him if he intended to take part in the feast, as the splendour of his apparel brought me to believe.

'Yes,' he answered, 'but why do you ask?'

'Because, were I you, Guatemoc, I would not go. Say now, will the dancers be armed?'

'No, it is not usual.'

'They will be unarmed, Guatemoc, and they are the flower of the land. Unarmed they will dance in yonder enclosed space, and the Teules will watch them armed. Now, how would it be if these chanced to pick a quarrel with the nobles?'

'I do not know why you should speak thus, Teule, for surely these white men are not cowardly murderers, still I take your words as an omen, and though the feast must be held, for see already the nobles gather, I will not share in it.'

'You are wise, Guatemoc,' I said. 'I am sure that you are wise.'

Afterwards Otomie, Guatemoc, and I went into the garden of the palace and sat upon the crest of a small pyramid, a *teocalli* in miniature that Montezuma had built for a place of outlook on the market and the courts of the temple. From this spot we saw the dancing of the Aztec nobles, and heard the song of the musicians. It was a gay sight, for in the bright sunlight their feather dresses flashed like coats of gems, and none would have guessed how it was to end. Mingling with the dancers were groups of Spaniards clad in mail and armed with swords and matchlocks, but I noted that, as the time went on, these men separated themselves from the Indians and began to cluster like bees about the gates and at various points under the shadow of the Wall of Serpents.

'Now what may this mean?' I said to Guatemoc, and as I spoke, I saw a Spaniard wave a white cloth in the air. Then, in an instant, before the cloth had ceased to flutter, a smoke arose from every side, and with it came the sound of the firing of matchlocks. Everywhere among the dancers men fell dead or wounded, but the mass of them, unharmed as yet, huddled themselves together like frightened sheep, and stood silent and terror-stricken. Then the Spaniards, shouting the name of their patron saint, as it is their custom to do when they have some such wickedness in hand, drew their swords, and rushing on the unarmed Aztec nobles began to kill them. Now some shrieked and fled, and some stood still till they were cut down, but whether they stayed or ran the end was the same, for the gates were guarded and the wall was too high to climb. There they were slaughtered every man of them, and may God, who sees all, reward their murderers! It was soon over; within ten minutes of the waving of the cloth, those six hundred men were stretched upon the pavement dead or dying, and with shouts of victory the Spaniards were despoiling their corpses of the rich ornaments they had worn.

Then I turned to Guatemoc and said, 'It seems that you did well not to join in yonder revel.'

But Guatemoc made no answer. He stared at the dead and those who had murdered them, and said nothing. Only Otomie spoke: 'You Christians are a gentle people,' she said with a bitter laugh; 'it is thus that you repay our hospitality. Now I trust that Montezuma, my father, is pleased with his guests. Ah! were I he, every man of them should lie on the stone of sacrifice. If our gods are devils as you say, what are those who worship yours?'

Then at length Guatemoc said, 'Only one thing remains to us, and that is vengeance. Montezuma has become a woman, and I heed him no more, nay, if it were needful, I would kill him with my own hand. But two men are still left in the land, Cuitlahua, my uncle, and myself. Now I go to summon our armies.' And he went.

All that night the city murmured like a swarm of wasps, and next day at dawn, so far as the eye could reach, the streets and market place were filled with tens of thousands of armed warriors. They threw themselves like a wave upon the walls of the palace of Axa, and like a wave from a rock they were driven back again by the fire of the guns. Thrice they attacked, and thrice they were repulsed. Then Montezuma, the woman king, appeared upon the walls, praying them to desist because, forsooth, did they succeed, he himself might perish. Even then they obeyed him, so great was their reverence for his sacred royalty, and for a while attacked the Spaniards no more. But further than this they would not go. If Montezuma forbade them to kill the Spaniards, at least they determined to starve them out, and from that hour a strait blockade was kept up against the palace. Hundreds of the Aztec soldiers had been slain already, but the loss was not all upon their side, for some of the Spaniards and many of the Tlascalans had fallen into their hands. As for these unlucky prisoners, their end was swift, for they were taken at once to the temples of the great *teocalli*, and sacrificed there to the gods in the sight of their comrades.

Now it was that Cortes returned with many more men, for he had conquered Narvaez, whose followers joined the standard of Cortes, and with them others, one of whom I had good reason to know. Cortes was suffered to rejoin his comrades in the palace of Axa without attack, I do not know why, and on the following day Cuitlahua, Montezuma's brother, king of Palapan, was released by him that he might soothe the people. But Cuitlahua was no coward. Once safe outside his prison walls, he called the council together, of whom the chief was Guatemoc.

There they resolved on war to the end, giving it out that Montezuma had forfeited his kingdom by his cowardice, and on that resolve they acted. Had it been taken but two short months before, by this date no Spaniard would have been left alive in Tenoctitlan. For after Marina, the love of Cortes, whose subtle wit brought about his triumph, it was Montezuma who was the chief cause of his own fall, and of that of the kingdom of Anahuac.

CHAPTER 20

Otomie's Counsel

On the day after the return of Cortes to Mexico, before the hour of dawn I was awakened from my uneasy slumbers by the whistling cries of thousands of warriors and the sound of *atabals* and drums.

Hurrying to my post of outlook on the little pyramid, where Otomie joined me, I saw that the whole people were gathered for war. So far as the eye could reach, in square, market place, and street, they were massed in thousands and tens of thousands. Some were armed with slings, some with bows and arrows, others with javelins tipped with copper, and the club set with spikes of obsidian that is called *maqua*, and yet others, citizens of the poorer sort, with stakes hardened in the fire. The bodies of some were covered with golden coats of mail and mantles of feather-work, and their skulls protected by painted wooden helms, crested with hair, and fashioned like the heads of pumas, snakes, or wolves—others wore *escaupils*, or coats of quilted cotton, but the most of them were naked except for a cloth about the loins. On the flat *azoteas*, or roofs of houses also, and even on the top of the *teocalli* of sacrifice, were bands of men whose part it was to rain missiles into the Spanish quarters. It was a strange sight to see in that red sunrise, and one never to be forgotten, as the light flashed from temples and palace walls, on to the glittering feather garments and gay banners, the points of countless spears and the armour of the Spaniards, who hurried to and fro behind their battlements making ready their defence.

So soon as the sun was up, a priest blew a shrill note upon a shell, which was answered by a trumpet call from the Spanish quarters. Then with a shriek of rage the thousands of the Aztecs rushed to the attack, and the air grew dark with missiles. Instantly a wavering line of fire and smoke, followed by a sound as of thunder, broke from the walls of the palace of Axa, and the charging warriors fell like autumn leaves beneath the cannon and arquebuss balls of the Christians.

For a moment they wavered and a great groan went up to heaven, but I saw Guatemoc spring forward, a banner in his hand, and forming up again they rushed after him. Now they were beneath the wall of the palace, and the assault began. The Aztecs fought furiously. Time upon time they strove to climb the wall, piling up the bodies of the dead to serve them as ladders, and time upon time they were repulsed with cruel loss. Failing in this, they set themselves to battering it down with heavy beams, but when the breach was made and they clustered in it like herded sheep, the cannon opened fire on them, tearing long lanes through their mass and leaving them dead by scores. Then they took to the shooting of flaming arrows, and by this means fired the outworks, but the palace was of stone and would not burn. Thus for twelve long hours the struggle raged unceasingly, till the sudden fall of darkness put an end to it, and the only sight to be seen was the flare of countless torches carried by those who sought out the dead, and the only sounds to be heard were the voice of women lamenting, and the groans of the dying.

On the morrow the fight broke out again at dawn, when Cortes sallied forth with the greater part of his soldiers, and some thousands of his Tlascalan allies. At first I thought that he aimed his attack at Montezuma's palace, and a breath of hope went through me, since then it might become possible for me to escape in the confusion. But this was not so, his object being to set fire to the houses, from the flat roofs of which numberless missiles were hailed hourly upon his followers. The charge was desperate and it succeeded, for the Indians could not withstand the shock of horsemen any more than their naked skins could turn the Spaniards' steel. Presently scores of houses were in flames, and thick columns of smoke rolled up like those that float from the mouth of Popo. But many of those who rode and ran from the gates of Axa did not come back thither, for the Aztecs clung to the legs of the horses and dragged their riders away living. That very day these captives were sacrificed on the altar of Huitzel, and in the sight of their comrades, and with them a horse was offered up, which had been taken alive, and was borne and dragged with infinite labour up the steep sides of the pyramid. Indeed never had the sacrifices been so many as during these days of combat. All day long the altars ran red, and all day long the cries of the victims rang in my ears, as the maddened priests went about their work. For thus they thought to please the gods who should give them victory over the Teules.

Even at night the sacrifices continued by the light of the sacred fires, that from below gave those who wrought them the appearance of devils flitting through the flames of hell, and inflicting its torments on the damned, much as they are depicted in the 'Doom' painting of the resurrection of the dead that is over the chancel arch in this church of Ditchingham. And hour by hour through the darkness, a voice called out threats and warnings to the Spaniards, saying, 'Huitzel is hungry for your blood, ye Teules, ye shall surely follow where ye have seen your fellows go: the cages are ready, the knives are sharp, and the irons are hot for the torture. Prepare, ye Teules, for though ye slay many, ye cannot escape.'

Thus the struggle went on day after day, till thousands of the Aztecs were dead, and the Spaniards were well nigh worn out with hunger, war, and wounds, for they could not rest a single hour. At length one morning, when the assault was at its hottest, Montezuma himself appeared upon the central tower of the palace, clad in splendid robes and wearing the diadem. Before him stood heralds bearing golden wands, and about him were the nobles who attended him in his captivity, and a guard of Spaniards. He stretched out his hand, and suddenly the fighting was stayed and a silence fell upon the place, even the wounded ceased from their groaning. Then he addressed the multitude. What he said I was too far off to hear, though I learned its purport afterwards. He prayed his people to cease from war, for the Spaniards were his friends and guests and would presently leave the city of Tenoctitlan. When these cowardly words had passed his lips, a fury took his subjects, who for long years had worshipped him as a god, and a shriek rent the air that seemed to say two words only:

'Woman! Traitor!'

Then I saw an arrow rush upwards and strike the emperor, and after the arrow a shower of stones, so that he fell down there upon the tower roof.

Now a voice cried, 'We have slain our king. Montezuma is dead,' and instantly with a dreadful wailing the multitude fled this way and that, so that presently no living man could be seen where there had been thousands.

I turned to comfort Otomie, who was watching at my side, and had seen her royal father fall, and led her weeping into the palace. Here we met Guatemoc, the prince, and his mien was fierce and wild. He was fully armed and carried a bow in his hand.

'Is Montezuma dead?' I asked.

'I neither know nor care,' he answered with a savage laugh, then added:

'Now curse me, Otomie my cousin, for it was my arrow that smote him down, this king who has become a woman and a traitor, false to his manhood and his country.'

Then Otomie ceased weeping and answered:

'I cannot curse you, Guatemoc, for the gods have smitten my father with a madness as you smote him with your arrow, and it is best that he should die, both for his own sake and for that of his people. Still, Guatemoc, I am sure of this, that your crime will not go unpunished, and that in payment for this sacrilege, you shall yourself come to a shameful death.'

'It may be so,' said Guatemoc, 'but at least I shall not die betraying my trust;' and he went.

Now I must tell that, as I believed, this was my last day on earth, for on the morrow my year of godhead expired, and I, Thomas Wingfield, should be led out to sacrifice. Notwithstanding all the tumult in the city, the mourning for the dead and the fear that hung over it like a cloud, the ceremonies of religion and its feasts were still celebrated strictly, more strictly indeed than ever before. Thus on this night a festival was held in my honour, and I must sit at the feast crowned with flowers and surrounded by my wives, while those nobles who remained alive in the city did me homage, and with them Cuitlahua, who, if Montezuma were dead, would now be emperor. It was a dreary meal enough, for I could scarcely be gay though I strove to drown my woes in drink, and as for the guests, they had little jollity left in them. Hundreds of their relatives were dead and with them thousands of the people; the Spaniards still held their own in the fortress, and that day they had seen their emperor, who to them was a god, smitten down by one of their own number, and above all they felt that doom was upon themselves. What wonder that they were not merry? Indeed no funeral feast could have been more sad, for flowers and wine and fair women do not make pleasure, and after all it was a funeral feast—for me.

At length it came to an end and I fled to my own apartments, whither my three wives followed me, for Otomie did not come, calling me most happy and blessed who to-morrow should be with myself, that is with my own godhead, in heaven. But I did not call them blessed, for, rising in wrath, I drove them away, saying that I had but one comfort left, and it was that wherever I might go I should leave them behind.

Then I cast myself upon the cushions of my bed and mourned in my fear and bitterness of heart. This was the end of the vengeance which I had sworn to wreak on de Garcia, that I myself must have my heart torn from my breast and offered to a devil. Truly Fonseca, my benefactor, had spoken words of wisdom when he counselled me to take my fortune and forget my oath. Had I done so, to-day I might have been my betrothed's husband and happy in her love at home in peaceful England, instead of what I was, a lost soul in the power of fiends and about to be offered to a fiend. In the bitterness of the thought and the extremity of my anguish I wept aloud and prayed to my Maker that I might be delivered from this cruel death, or at the least that my sins should be forgiven me, so that to-morrow night I might rest at peace in heaven.

Thus weeping and praying I sank into a half sleep, and dreamed that I walked on the hillside near the church path that runs through the garden of the Lodge at Ditchingham. The whispers of the wind were in the trees which clothe the bank of the Vineyard Hills, the scent of the sweet English flowers was in my nostrils and the balmy air of June blew on my brow. It was night in this dream of mine, and I thought that the moon shone sweetly on the meadows and the river, while from every side came the music of the nightingale. But I was not thinking of these delightful sights and sounds, though they were present in my mind, for my eyes watched the church path which goes up the hill at the back of the house, and my heart listened for a footstep that I longed to hear. Then there came a sound of singing from beyond the hill, and the words of the song were sad, for they told of one who had sailed away and returned no more, and presently between the apple trees I saw a white figure on its crest. Slowly it came towards me and I knew that it was she for whom I waited, Lily my beloved. Now she ceased to sing, but drew on gently and her face seemed very sad. Moreover it was the face of a woman in middle life, but still most beautiful, more beautiful indeed than it had been in the bloom of youth. She had reached the foot of the hill and was turning towards the little garden gate, when I came forward from the shadow of the trees, and stood before her. Back she started with a cry of fear, then grew silent and gazed into my face.

'So changed,' she murmured; 'can it be the same? Thomas, is it you come back to me from the dead, or is this but a vision?' and slowly and doubtingly the dream wraith stretched out her arms as though to clasp me.

Then I awoke. I awoke and lo! before me stood a fair woman clothed in white, on whom the moonlight shone as in my dream, and her arms were stretched towards me lovingly.

'It is I, beloved, and no vision,' I cried, springing from my bed and clasping her to my breast to kiss her. But before my lips touched hers I saw my error, for she whom I embraced was not Lily Bozard, my betrothed, but Otomie, princess of the Otomie, who was called my wife. Then I knew that this was the saddest and the most bitter of dreams that had been sent to mock me, for all the truth rushed into my mind. Losing my hold of Otomie, I fell back upon the bed and groaned aloud, and as I fell I saw the flush of shame upon her brow and breast. For this woman loved me, and thus my act and words were an insult to her, who could guess well what prompted them. Still she spoke gently.

'Pardon me, Teule, I came but to watch and not to waken you. I came also that I may see you alone before the daybreak, hoping that I might be of service, or at the least, of comfort to you, for the end draws near. Say then, in your sleep did you mistake me for some other woman dearer and fairer than I am, that you would have embraced me?'

'I dreamed that you were my betrothed whom I love, and who is far away across the sea,' I answered heavily. 'But enough of love and such matters. What have I to do with them who go down into darkness?'

'In truth I cannot tell, Teule, still I have heard wise men say that if love is to be found anywhere, it is in this same darkness of death, that is light indeed. Grieve not, for if there is truth in the faith of which you have told me or in our own, either on this earth or beyond it, with the eyes of the spirit you will see your dear before another sun is set, and I pray that you may find her faithful to you. Tell me now, how much does she love you? Would SHE have lain by your side on the bed of sacrifice as, had things gone otherwise between us, Teule, it was my hope to do?'

'No,' I answered, 'it is not the custom of our women to kill themselves because their husbands chance to die.'

'Perhaps they think it better to live and wed again,' answered Otomie very quietly, but I saw her eyes flash and her breast heave in the moonlight as she spoke.

'Enough of this foolish talk,' I said. 'Listen, Otomie; if you had cared for me truly, surely you would have saved me from this dreadful doom, or prevailed on Guatemoc to save me. You are Montezuma's daughter, could you not have brought it about during all these months that he issued his royal mandate, commanding that I should be spared?'

'Do you, then, take me for so poor a friend, Teule?' she answered hotly. 'Know that for all these months, by day and by night, I have worked and striven to find a means to rescue you. Before he became a prisoner I importuned my father the emperor, till he ordered me from his presence. I have sought to bribe the priests, I have plotted ways of escape, ay, and Guatemoc has helped, for he loves you. Had it not been for the coming of these accursed Teules, and the war that they have levied in the city, I had surely saved you, for a woman's thought leaps far, and can find a path where none seems possible. But this war has changed everything, and moreover the star-readers and diviners of auguries have given a prophecy which seals your fate. For they have prophesied that if your blood flows, and your heart is offered at the hour of noon to-morrow on the altar of Tezcat, our people shall be victorious over the Teules, and utterly destroy them. But if the sacrifice is celebrated one moment before or after that propitious hour, then the doom of Tenoctitlan is sealed. Also they have declared that you must die, not, according to custom, at the Temple of Arms across the lake, but on the great pyramid before the chief statue of the god. All this is known throughout the land; thousands of priests are now offering up prayers that the sacrifice may be fortunate, and a golden ring has been hung over the stone of slaughter in such a fashion that the light of the sun must strike upon the centre of your breast at the very moment of mid-day. For weeks you have been watched as a jaguar watches its prey, for it was feared that you would escape to the Teules, and we, your wives, have been watched also. At this moment there is a triple ring of guards about the palace, and priests are set without your doors and beneath the window places. Judge, then, what chance there is of escape, Teule.'

'Little indeed,' I said, 'and yet I know a road. If I kill myself, they cannot kill me.'

'Nay,' she answered hastily, 'what shall that avail you? While you live you may hope, but once dead, you are dead for ever. Also if you must die, it is best that you should die by the hand of the priest. Believe me, though the end is horrible,' and she shuddered, 'it is almost painless, so they say, and very swift. They will not torture you, that we have saved you, Guatemoc and I, though at first they wished thus to honour the god more particularly on this great day.'

'O Teule,' Otomie went on, seating herself by me on the bed, and taking my hand, 'think no more of these brief terrors, but look beyond them. Is it so hard a thing to die, and swiftly? We all must die, to-day, or to-night, or the next day, it matters little when—and your faith, like ours, teaches that beyond the grave is endless blessedness. Think then, my friend, to-morrow you will have passed far from this strife and turmoil; the struggle and the sorrows and the daily fears for the future that make the soul sick will be over for you, you will be taken to your peace, where no one shall disturb you for ever. There you will find that mother whom you have told me of, and who loved you, and there perhaps one will join you who loves you better than your mother, mayhap even I may meet you there, friend,' and she looked up at me strangely. 'The road that you are doomed to walk is dark indeed, but surely it must be well-trodden, and there is light shining beyond it. So be a man, my friend, and do not grieve; rejoice rather that at so early an age you have done with woes and doubts, and come to the gates of joy, that you have passed the thorny, unwatered wilderness and see the smiling lakes and gardens, and among them the temples of your eternal city.

'And now farewell. We meet no more till the hour of sacrifice, for we women who masquerade as wives must accompany you to the first platforms of the temple. Farewell, dear friend, and think upon my words; whether they are acceptable to you or no, I am sure of this, that both for the sake of your own honour and because I ask it of you, you will die bravely as though the eyes of your own people were watching all.' And bending suddenly, Otomie kissed me on the forehead gently as a sister might, and was gone.

The curtains swung behind her, but the echoes of her noble words still dwelt in my heart. Nothing can make man look on death lovingly, and that awaiting me was one from which the bravest would shrink, yet I felt that Otomie had spoken truth, and that, terrible as it seemed, it might prove less terrible than life had shown itself to be. An unnatural calm fell upon my soul like some dense mist upon the face of the ocean. Beneath that mist the waters might foam, above it the sun might shine, yet around was one grey peace. In this hour I seemed to stand outside of my earthly self, and to look on all things with a new sense. The tide of life was ebbing away from me, the shore of death loomed very near, and I understood then, as in extreme old age I understand to-day, how much more part we mortals have in death than in this short accident of life. I could consider all my past, I could wonder on the future of my spirit, and even marvel at the gentleness and wisdom of the Indian woman, who was able to think such thoughts and utter them.

Well, whatever befell, in one thing I would not disappoint her, I would die bravely as an Englishman should do, leaving the rest to God. These barbarians should never say of me that the foreigner was a coward. Who was I that I should complain? Did not hundreds of men as good as I was perish daily in yonder square, and without a murmur?

Had not my mother died also at the hand of a murderer? Was not that unhappy lady, Isabella de Siguenza, walled up alive because she had been mad enough to love a villain who betrayed her? The world is full of terrors and sorrows such as mine, who was I that I should complain?

So I mused on till at length the day dawned, and with the rising sun rose the clamour of men making ready for battle. For now the fight raged from day to day, and this was to be one of the most terrible. But I thought little then of the war between the Aztecs and the Spaniards, who must prepare myself for the struggle of my own death that was now at hand.

CHAPTER 21

The Kiss of Love

Presently there was a sound of music, and, accompanied by certain artists, my pages entered, bearing with them apparel more gorgeous than any that I had worn hitherto. First, these pages having stripped me of my robes, the artists painted all my body in hideous designs of red, and white, and blue, till I resembled a flag, not even sparing my face and lips, which they coloured with carmine hues. Over my heart also they drew a scarlet ring with much care and measurement. Then they did up my hair that now hung upon my shoulders, after the fashion in which it was worn by generals among the Indians, tying it on the top of my head with an embroidered ribbon red in colour, and placed a plume of cock's feathers above it. Next, having arrayed my body in gorgeous vestments not unlike those used by popish priests at the celebration of the mass, they set golden earrings in my ears, golden bracelets on my wrists and ankles, and round my neck a collar of priceless emeralds. On my breast also they hung a great gem that gleamed like moonlit water, and beneath my chin a false beard made from pink sea shells. Then having twined me round with wreaths of flowers till I thought of the maypole on Bungay Common, they rested from their labours, filled with admiration at their handiwork.

Now the music sounded again and they gave me two lutes, one of which I must hold in either hand, and conducted me to the great hall of the palace. Here a number of people of rank were gathered, all dressed in festal attire, and here also on a dais to which I was led, stood my four wives clad in the rich dresses of the four goddesses Xochi, Xilo, Atla, and Clixto, after whom they were named for the days of their wifehood, Atla being the princess Otomie. When I had taken my place upon the dais, my wives came forward one by one, and kissing me on the brow, offered me sweetmeats and meal cakes in golden platters, and cocoa and *mescal* in golden cups. Of the *mescal* I drank, for it is a spirit and I needed inward comfort, but the other dainties I could not touch. These ceremonies being finished, there was silence for a while, till presently a band of filthy priests entered at the far end of the chamber, clad in their scarlet sacrificial robes. Blood was on them everywhere, their long locks were matted with it, their hands were red with it, even their fierce eyes seemed full of it. They advanced up the chamber till they stood before the dais, then suddenly the head priest lifted up his hands, crying aloud:

'Adore the immortal god, ye people,' and all those gathered there prostrated themselves shouting:

'We adore the god.'

Thrice the priest cried aloud, and thrice they answered him thus, prostrating themselves at every answer. Then they rose again, and the priest addressed me, saying:

'Forgive us, O Tezcat, that we cannot honour you as it is meet, for our sovereign should have been here to worship you with us. But you know, O Tezcat, how sore is the strait of your servants, who must wage war in their own city against those who blaspheme you and your brother gods. You know that our beloved emperor lies wounded, a prisoner in their unholy hands. When we have gratified your longing to pass beyond the skies, O Tezcat, and when in your earthly person you have taught us the lesson that human prosperity is but a shadow which flees away; in memory of our love for you intercede for us, we beseech you, that we may smite these wicked ones and honour you and them by the rite of their own sacrifice. O Tezcat, you have dwelt with us but a little while, and now you will not suffer that we hold you longer from your glory, for your eyes have longed to see this happy day, and it is come at last. We have loved you, Tezcat, and ministered to you, grant in return that we may see you in your splendour, we who are your little children, and till we come, watch well over our earthly welfare, and that of the people among whom you have deigned to sojourn.'

Having spoken some such words as these, that at times could scarcely be heard because of the sobbing of the people, and of my wives who wept loudly, except Otomie alone, this villainous priest made a sign and once more the music sounded. Then he and his band placed themselves about me, my wives the goddesses going before and after, and led me down the hall and on to the gateways of the palace, which were thrown wide for us to pass. Looking round me with a stony wonder, for in this my last hour nothing seemed to escape my notice, I saw that a strange play was being played about us. Some hundreds of paces away the attack on the palace of Axa, where the Spaniards were entrenched, raged with fury. Bands of warriors were attempting to scale the walls and being driven back by the deadly fire of the Spaniards and the pikes and clubs of their Tlascalan allies, while from the roofs of such of the neighbouring houses as remained un-burned, and more especially from the platform of the great *teocalli*, on which I must presently give up the ghost, arrows, javelins, and stones were poured by thousands into the courtyards and outer works of the Spanish quarters.

Five hundred yards away or so, raged this struggle to the death, but about me, around the gates of Montezuma's palace on the hither side of the square, was a different scene. Here were gathered a vast crowd, among them many women and children, waiting to see me die. They came with flowers in their hands, with the sound of music and joyous cries, and when they saw me they set up such a shout of welcome that it almost drowned the thunder of the guns and the angry roar of bat-tle. Now and again an ill-aimed cannon ball would plough through them, killing some and wounding others, but the rest took no heed, only crying the more, 'Welcome, Tezcat, and farewell. Blessings on you, our deliverer, welcome and farewell!'

We went slowly through the press, treading on a path of flowers, till we came across the courtyard to the base of the pyramid. Here at the outer gate there was a halt because of the multitude of the people, and while we waited a warrior thrust his way through the crowd and bowed before me. Glancing up I saw that it was Guatemoc.

'Teule,' he whispered to me, 'I leave my charge yonder,' and he nodded towards the force who strove to break a way into the palace of Axa, 'to bid you farewell. Doubtless we shall meet again ere long. Believe me, Teule, I would have helped you if I could, but it cannot be. I wish that I might change places with you. My friend, farewell. Twice you have saved my life, but yours I cannot save.'

'Farewell, Guatemoc,' I answered 'heaven prosper you, for you are a true man.'

Then we passed on.

At the foot of the pyramid the procession was formed, and here one of my wives bade me *adieu* after weeping on my neck, though I did not weep on hers. Now the road to the summit of the *teocalli* winds round and round the pyramid, ever mounting higher as it winds, and along this road we went in solemn state. At each turn we halted and another wife bade me a last good-bye, or one of my instruments of music, which I did not grieve to see the last of, or some article of my strange attire, was taken from me. At length after an hour's march, for our progress was slow, we reached the flat top of the pyramid that is approached by a great stair, a space larger than the area of the churchyard here at Ditchingham, and unfenced at its lofty edge. Here on this dizzy place stood the temples of Huitzel and of Tezcat, soaring structures of stone and wood, within which were placed the horrid effigies of the gods, and dreadful chambers stained with sacrifice. Here, too, were the holy fires that burned eternally, the sacrificial stones, the implements of torment, and the huge drum of snakes' skin, but for the rest the spot was bare. It was bare but not empty, for on that side of it which looked towards the Spanish quarters were stationed some hundreds of men who hurled missiles into their camp without ceasing. On the other side also were gathered a concourse of priests awaiting the ceremony of my death. Below the great square, fringed round with burnt-out houses, was crowded with thousands of people, some of them engaged in combat with the Spaniards, but the larger part collected there to witness my murder.

Now we reached the top of the pyramid, two hours before midday, for there were still many rites to be carried out ere the moment of sacrifice. First I was led into the sanctuary of Tezcat, the god whose name I bore. Here was his statue or idol, fashioned in black marble and covered with golden ornaments. In the hand of this idol was a shield of burnished gold on which its jewelled eyes were fixed, reading there, as his priests fabled, all that passed upon the earth he had created. Before him also was a plate of gold, which with muttered invocations the head priest cleansed as I watched, rubbing it with his long and matted locks. This done he held it to my lips that I might breathe on it, and I turned faint and sick, for I knew that it was being made ready to receive the heart which I felt beating in my breast.

Now what further ceremonies were to be carried out in this unholy place I do not know, for at that moment a great tumult arose in the square beneath, and I was hurried from the sanctuary by the priests. Then I perceived this: galled to madness by the storm of missiles rained upon them from its crest, the Spaniards were attacking the *teocalli*. Already they were pouring across the courtyard in large companies, led by Cortes himself, and with them came many hundreds of their allies the Tlascalans. On the other hand some thousands of the Aztecs were rushing to the foot of the first stairway to give the white men battle there. Five minutes passed and the fight grew fierce. Again and again, covered by the fire of the arquebusiers, the Spaniards charged the Aztecs, but their horses slipping upon the stone pavement, at length they dismounted and continued the fray on foot. Slowly and with great slaughter the Indians were pushed back and the Spaniards gained a footing on the first stairway. But hundreds of warriors still crowded the lofty winding road, and hundreds more held the top, and it was plain that if the Spaniards won through at all, the task would be a hard one. Still a fierce hope smote me like a blow when I saw what was toward. If the Spaniards took the temple there would be no sacrifice. No sacrifice could be offered till midday, so Otomie had told me, and that was not for hard upon two hours. It came to this then, if the Spaniards were victorious within two hours, there was a chance of life for me, if not I must die.

Now when I was led out of the sanctuary of Tezcat, I wondered because the princess Otomie, or rather the goddess Atla as she was then called, was standing among the chief priests and disputing with them, for I had seen her bow her head at the door of the holy place, and thought that it was in token of farewell, seeing that she was the last of the four women to leave me. Of what she disputed I could not hear because of the din of battle, but the argument was keen and it seemed to me that the priests were somewhat dismayed at her words, and yet had a fierce joy in them. It appeared also that she won her cause, for presently they bowed in obeisance to her, and turning slowly she swept to my side with a peculiar majesty of gait that even then I noted. Glancing up at her face also, I saw that it was alight as though with a great and holy purpose, and moreover that she looked like some happy bride passing to her husband's arms.

'Why are you not gone, Otomie?' I said. 'Now it is too late. The Spaniards surround the *teocalli* and you will be killed or taken prisoner.'

'I await the end whatever it may be,' she answered briefly, and we spoke no more for a while, but watched the progress of the fray, which was fierce indeed. Grimly the Aztec warriors fought before the symbols of their gods, and in the sight of the vast concourse of the people who crowded the square beneath and stared at the struggle in silence. They hurled themselves upon the Spanish swords, they gripped the Spaniards with their hands and screaming with rage dragged them to the steep sides of the roadway, purposing to cast them over. Sometimes they succeeded, and a ball of men clinging together would roll down the slope and be dashed to pieces on the stone flooring of the courtyard, a Spaniard being in the centre of the ball. But do what they would, like some vast and writhing snake, still the long array of Teules clad in their glittering mail ploughed its way upward through the storm of spears and arrows. Minute by minute and step by step they crept on, fighting as men fight who know the fate that awaits the desecrators of the gods of Anahuac, fighting for life, and honour, and safety from the stone of sacrifice. Thus an hour went by, and the Spaniards were half way up the pyramid. Louder and louder grew the fearful sounds of battle, the Spaniards cheered and called on their patron saints to aid them, the Aztecs yelled like wild beasts, the priests screamed invocations to their gods and cries of encouragement to the warriors, while above all rose the rattle of the arquebusses, the roar of the cannon, and the fearful note of the great drum of snake's skin on which a half-naked priest beat madly. Only the multitudes below never moved, nor shouted. They stood silent gazing upward, and I could see the sunlight flash on the thousands of their staring eyes.

Now all this while I was standing near the stone of sacrifice with Otomie at my side. Round me were a ring of priests, and over the stone was fixed a square of black cloth supported upon four poles, which were set in sockets in the pavement. In the centre of this black cloth was sewn a golden funnel measuring six inches or so across at its mouth, and the sunbeams passing through this funnel fell in a bright patch, the size of an apple, upon the space of pavement that was shaded by the cloth. As the sun moved in the heavens, so did this ring of light creep across the shadow till at length it climbed the stone of sacrifice and lay upon its edge.

Then at a sign from the head priest, his ministers laid hold of me and plucked what were left of my fine clothes from me as cruel boys pluck a living bird, till I stood naked except for the paint upon my body and a cloth about my loins. Now I knew that my hour had come, and strange to tell, for the first time this day courage entered into me, and I rejoiced to think that soon I should have done with my tormentors. Turning to Otomie I began to bid her farewell in a clear voice, when to my amaze I saw that as I had been served so she was being served, for her splendid robes were torn off her and she stood before me arrayed in nothing except her beauty, her flowing hair, and a broidered cotton smock.

'Do not wonder, Teule,' she said in a low voice, answering the question my tongue refused to frame, 'I am your wife and yonder is our marriage bed, the first and last. Though you do not love me, to-day I die your death and at your side, as I have the right to do. I could not save you, Teule, but at least I can die with you.'

At the moment I made no answer, for I was stricken silent by my wonder, and before I could find my tongue the priests had cast me down, and for the second time I lay upon the stone of doom. As they held me a yell fiercer and longer than any which had gone before, told that the Spaniards had got foot upon the last stair of the ascent. Scarcely had my body been set upon the centre of the great stone, when that of Otomie was laid beside it, so close that our sides touched, for I must lie in the middle of the stone and there was no great place for her. Then the moment of sacrifice not being come, the priests made us fast with cords which they knotted to copper rings in the pavement, and turned to watch the progress of the fray.

For some minutes we lay thus side by side, and as we lay a great wonder and gratitude grew in my heart, wonder that a woman could be so brave, gratitude for the love she gave me, sealing it with her life-blood. Because Otomie loved me she had chosen this fearful death, because she loved me so well that she desired to die thus at my side rather than to live on in greatness and honour without me. Of a sudden, in a moment while I thought of this marvel, a new light shone upon my heart and it was changed towards her. I felt that no woman could ever be so dear to me as this glorious woman, no, not even my betrothed. I felt—nay, who can say what I did feel? But I know this, that the tears rushed to my eyes and ran down my painted face, and I turned my head to look at her. She was lying as much upon her left side as her hands would allow, her long hair fell from the stone to the paving where it lay in masses, and her face was towards me. So close was it indeed that there was not an inch between our lips.

'Otomie,' I whispered, 'listen to me. I love you, Otomie.' Now I saw her breast heave beneath the bands and the colour come upon her brow.

'Then I am repaid,' she answered, and our lips clung together in a kiss, the first, and as we thought the last. Yes, there we kissed, on the stone of sacrifice, beneath the knife of the priest and the shadow of death, and if there has been a stranger love scene in the world, I have never heard its story.

'Oh! I am repaid,' she said again; 'I would gladly die a score of deaths to win this moment, indeed I pray that I may die before you take back your words. For, Teule, I know well that there is one who is dearer to you than I am, but now your heart is softened by the faithfulness of an Indian girl, and you think that you love her. Let me die then believing that the dream is true.'

'Talk not so,' I answered heavily, for even at that moment the memory of Lily came into my mind. 'You give your life for me and I love you for it.'

'My life is nothing and your love is much,' she answered smiling. 'Ah! Teule, what magic have you that you can bring me, Montezuma's daughter, to the altar of the gods and of my own free will? Well, I desire no softer bed, and for the why and wherefore it will soon be known by both of us, and with it many other things.'

CHAPTER 22

The Triumph of the Cross

'Otomie,' I said presently, 'when will they kill us?'

'When the point of light lies within the ring that is painted over your heart,' she answered.

Now I turned my head from her, and looked at the sunbeam which pierced the shadow above us like a golden pencil. It rested at my side about six inches from me, and I reckoned that it would lie in the scarlet ring painted upon my breast within some fifteen minutes. Meanwhile the clamour of battle grew louder and nearer. Shifting myself so far as the cords would allow, I strained my head upwards and saw that the Spaniards had gained the crest of the pyramid, since the battle now raged upon its edge, and I have rarely seen so terrible a fight, for the Aztecs fought with the fury of despair, thinking little of their own lives if they could only bring a Spaniard to his death. But for the most part their rude weapons would not pierce the coats of mail, so that there remained only one way to compass their desire, namely, by casting the white men over the edge of the *teocalli* to be crushed like eggshells upon the pavement two hundred feet below. Thus the fray broke itself up into groups of foes who rent and tore at each other upon the brink of the pyramid, now and again to vanish down its side, ten or twelve of them together. Some of the priests also joined in the fight, thinking less of their own deaths than of the desecration of their temples, for I saw one of them, a man of huge strength and stature, seize a Spanish soldier round the middle and leap with him into space. Still, though very slowly, the Spaniards and Tlascalans forced their way towards the centre of the platform, and as they came the danger of this dreadful end grew less, for the Aztecs must drag them further.

Now the fight drew near to the stone of sacrifice, and all who remained alive of the Aztecs, perhaps some two hundred and fifty of them, besides the priests, ringed themselves round us and it in a circle.

Also the outer rim of the sunbeam that fell through the golden funnel, creeping on remorselessly, touched my painted side which it seemed to burn as hot iron might, for alas, I could not command the sun to stand still while the battle raged, as did Joshua in the valley of Ajalon. When it touched me, five priests seized my limbs and head, and the father of them, he who had conducted me from the palace, clasped his flint knife in both hands. Now a deathly sickness took me and I shut my eyes dreaming that all was done, but at that moment I heard a wild-eyed man, the chief of the astronomers whom I had noted standing by, call out to the minister of death:

'Not yet, O priest of Tezeat! If you smite before the sunbeam lies upon the victim's heart, your gods are doomed and doomed are the people of Anahuac.'

The priest gnashed his teeth with rage, and glared first at the creeping point of light and then over his shoulder at the advancing battle. Slowly the ring of warriors closed in upon us, slowly the golden ray crept up my breast till its outer rim touched the red circle painted upon my heart. Again the priest heaved up his awful knife, again I shut my eyes, and again I heard the shrill scream of the astronomer, 'Not yet, not yet, or your gods are doomed!'

Then I heard another sound. It was the voice of Otomie crying for help.

'Save us, Teules; they murder us!' she shrieked in so piercing a note that it reached the ears of the Spaniards, for one shouted in answer and in the Castilian tongue, 'On, my comrades, on! The dogs do murder on their altars!'

Then there was a mighty rush and the defending Aztecs were swept in upon the altar, lifting the priest of sacrifice from his feet and throwing him across my body. Thrice that rush came like a rush of the sea, and each time the stand of the Aztecs weakened. Now their circle was broken and the swords of the Spaniards flashed up on every side, and now the red ray lay within the ring upon my heart.

'Smite, priest of Tezcat,' screamed the voice of the astronomer; 'smite home for the glory of your gods!'

With a fearful yell the priest lifted the knife; I saw the golden sunbeam that rested full upon my heart shine on it. Then as it was descending I saw the same sunbeam shine upon a yard of steel that flashed across me and lost itself in the breast of the murderer priest. Down came the great flint knife, but its aim was lost. It struck indeed, but not upon my bosom, though I did not escape it altogether. Full upon the altar of sacrifice it fell and was shattered there, piercing between my side and that of Otomie, and gashing the flesh of both so that our blood was mingled upon the stone, making us one indeed. Down too came the priest across our bodies for the second time, but to rise no more, for he writhed dying on those whom he would have slain.

Then as in a dream I heard the wail of the astronomer singing the dirge of the gods of Anahuac.

'The priest is dead and his gods are fallen,' he cried. 'Tezcat has rejected his victim and is fallen; doomed are the gods of Anahuac! Victory is to the Cross of the Christians!'

Thus he wailed, then came the sound of sword blows and I knew that this prophet was dead also.

Now a strong arm pulled the dying priest from off us, and he staggered back till he fell over the altar where the eternal fire burned, quenching it with his blood and body after it had flared for many generations, and a knife cut the rope that bound us.

I sat up staring round me wildly, and a voice spoke above me in Castilian, not to me indeed but to some comrade.

'These two went near to it, poor devils,' said the voice. 'Had my cut been one second later, that savage would have drilled a hole in him as big as my head. By all the saints! the girl is lovely, or would be if she were washed. I shall beg her of Cortes as my prize.'

The voice spoke and I knew the voice. None other ever had that hard clear ring. I knew it even then and looked up, slipping off the death-stone as I looked. Now I saw. Before me fully clad in mail was my enemy, de Garcia. It was HIS sword that by the good providence of God had pierced the breast of the priest. He had saved me who, had he known, would as soon have turned his steel against his own heart as on that of my destroyer.

I gazed at him, wondering if I dreamed, then my lips spoke, without my will as it were:

'De Garcia!'

He staggered back at the sound of my voice, like a man struck by a shot, then stared at me, rubbed his eyes with his hand, and stared again. Now at length he knew me through my paint.

'Mother of God!' he gasped, 'it is that knave Thomas Wingfield, *and i have saved his life!*'

By this time my senses had come back to me, and knowing all my folly, I turned seeking escape. But de Garcia had no mind to suffer this. Lifting his sword, he sprang at me with a beastlike scream of rage and hate. Swiftly as thought I slipped round the stone of sacrifice and after me came the uplifted sword of my enemy. It would have overtaken me soon enough, for I was weak with fear and fasting, and my limbs were cramped with bonds, but at that moment a cavalier whom by his dress and port I guessed to be none other than Cortes himself, struck up de Garcia's sword, saying:

'How now, Sarceda? Are you mad with the lust of blood that you would take to sacrificing victims like an Indian priest? Let the poor devil go.'

'He is no Indian, he is an English spy,' cried de Garcia, and once more struggled to get at me.

'Decidedly our friend is mad,' said Cortes, scanning me; 'he says that this wretched creature is an Englishman. Come, be off both of you, or somebody else may make the same mistake,' and he waved his sword in token to us to go, deeming that I could not understand his words; then added angrily, as de Garcia, speechless with rage, made a new attempt to get at me:

'No, by heaven! I will not suffer it. We are Christians and come to save victims, not to slay them. Here, comrades, hold this fool who would stain his soul with murder.'

Now the Spaniards clutched de Garcia by the arms, and he cursed and raved at them, for as I have said, his rage was that of a beast rather than of a man. But I stood bewildered, not knowing whither to fly. Fortunate it was for me indeed that one was by who though she understood no Spanish, yet had a quicker wit. For while I stood thus, Otomie clasped my hand, and whispering, 'Fly, fly swiftly!' led me away from the stone of sacrifice.

'Whither shall we go?' I said at length. 'Were it not better to trust to the mercy of the Spaniards?'

'To the mercy of that man-devil with the sword?' she answered. 'Peace, Teule, and follow me.'

Now she led me on, and the Spaniards let us by unharmed, ay, and even spoke words of pity as we passed, for they knew that we were victims snatched from sacrifice. Indeed, when a certain brute, a Tlascalan Indian, rushed at us, purposing to slay us with a club, one of the Spaniards ran him through the shoulder so that he fell wounded to the pavement.

So we went on, and at the edge of the pyramid we glanced back and saw that de Garcia had broken from those who held him, or perhaps he found his tongue and had explained the truth to them. At the least he was bounding from the altar of sacrifice nearly fifty yards away, and coming towards us with uplifted sword. Then fear gave us strength, and we fled like the wind. Along the steep path we rushed side by side, leaping down the steps and over the hundreds of dead and dying, only pausing now and again to save ourselves from being smitten into space by the bodies of the priests whom the Spaniards were hurling from the crest of the *teocalli*. Once looking up, I caught sight of de Garcia pursuing far above us, but after that we saw him no more; doubtless he wearied of the chase, or feared to fall into the hands of such of the Aztec warriors as still clustered round the foot of the pyramid.

We had lived through many dangers that day, the princess Otomie and I, but one more awaited us before ever we found shelter for awhile. After we had reached the foot of the pyramid and turned to mingle with the terrified rabble that surged and flowed through the courtyard of the temple, bearing away the dead and wounded as the sea at flood reclaims its waste and wreckage, a noise like thunder caught my ear. I looked up, for the sound came from above, and saw a huge mass bounding down the steep side of the pyramid. Even then I knew it again; it was the idol of the god Tezcat that the Spaniards had torn from its shrine, and like an avenging demon it rushed straight on to me. Already it was upon us, there was no retreat from instant death, we had but escaped sacrifice to the spirit of the god to be crushed to powder beneath the bulk of his marble emblem. On he came while on high the Spaniards shouted in triumph. His base had struck the stone side of the pyramid fifty feet above us, now he whirled round and round in the air to strike again within three paces of where we stood. I felt the solid mountain shake beneath the blow, and next instant the air was filled with huge fragments of marble, that whizzed over us and past us as though a mine of powder had been fired beneath our feet, tearing the rocks from their base. The god Tezcat had burst into a score of pieces, and these fell round us like a flight of arrows, and yet we were not touched. My head was grazed by his head, his feet dug a pit before my feet, but I stood there unhurt, the false god had no power over the victim who had escaped him!

After that I remember nothing till I found myself once more in my apartments in Montezuma's palace, which I never hoped to see again. Otomie was by me, and she brought me water to wash the paint from my body and the blood from my wound, which, leaving her own untended, she dressed skilfully, for the cut of the priest's knife was deep and I had bled much. Also she clothed herself afresh in a white robe and brought me raiment to wear, with food and drink, and I partook of them. Then I bade her eat something herself, and when she had done so I gathered my wits together and spoke to her.

'What next?' I said. 'Presently the priests will be on us, and we shall be dragged back to sacrifice. There is no hope for me here, I must fly to the Spaniards and trust to their mercy.'

'To the mercy of that man with the sword? Say, Teule, who is he?'

'He is that Spaniard of whom I have spoken to you, Otomie; he is my mortal enemy whom I have followed across the seas.'

'And now you would put yourself into his power. Truly, you are foolish, Teule.'

'It is better to fall into the hands of Christian men than into those of your priests,' I answered.

'Have no fear,' she said; 'the priests are harmless for you. You have escaped them and there's an end. Few have ever come alive from their clutches before, and he who does so is a wizard indeed. For the rest I think that your God is stronger than our gods, for surely He must have cast His mantle over us when we lay yonder on the stone. Ah! Teule, to what have you brought me that I should live to doubt my gods, ay, and to call upon the foes of my country for succour in your need. Believe me, I had not done it for my own sake, since I would have died with your kiss upon my lips and your word of love echoing in my ears, who now must live knowing that these joys have passed from me.'

'How so?' I answered. 'What I have said, I have said. Otomie, you would have died with me, and you saved my life by your wit in calling on the Spaniards. Henceforth it is yours, for there is no other woman in the world so tender and so brave, and I say it again, Otomie, my wife, I love you. Our blood has mingled on the stone of sacrifice and there we kissed; let these be our marriage rites. Perhaps I have not long to live, but till I die I am yours, Otomie my wife.'

Thus I spoke from the fullness of my heart, for my strength and courage were shattered, horror and loneliness had taken hold of me. But two things were left to me in the world, my trust in Providence and the love of this woman, who had dared so much for me. Therefore I forgot my troth and clung to her as a child clings to its mother. Doubtless it was wrong, but I will be bold to say that few men so placed would have acted otherwise. Moreover, I could not take back the fateful words that I had spoken on the stone of sacrifice. When I said them I was expecting death indeed, but to renounce them now that its shadow was lifted from me, if only for a little while, would have been the act of a coward. For good or evil I had given myself to Montezuma's daughter, and I must abide by it or be shamed. Still such was the nobleness of this Indian lady that even then she would not take me at my word. For a little while she stood smiling sadly and drawing a lock of her long hair through the hollow of her hand. Then she spoke:

'You are not yourself, Teule, and I should be base indeed if I made so solemn a compact with one who does not know what he sells. Yonder on the altar and in a moment of death you said that you loved me, and doubtless it was true. But now you have come back to life, and say, lord, who set that golden ring upon your hand and what is written in its circle? Yet even if the words are true that you have spoken and you love me a little, there is one across the sea whom you love better. That I could bear, for my heart is fixed on you alone among men, and at the least you would be kind to me, and I should move in the sunlight of your presence. But having known the light, I cannot live to wander in the darkness. You do not understand. I will tell you what I fear. I fear that if—if we were wed, you would weary of me as men do, and that memory would grow too strong for you. Then by and by it might be possible for you to find your way back across the waters to your own land and your own love, and so you would desert me, Teule. This is what I could not bear, Teule. I can forego you now, ay, and remain your friend. But I cannot be put aside like a dancing girl, the companion of a month, I, Montezuma's daughter, a lady of my own land. Should you wed me, it must be for my life, Teule, and that is perhaps more than you would wish to promise, though you could kiss me on yonder stone and there is blood fellowship between us,' and she glanced at the red stain in the linen robe that covered the wound upon her side.

'And now, Teule, I leave you a while, that I may find Guatemoc, if he still lives, and others who, now that the strength of the priests is shattered, have power to protect you and advance you to honour. Think then on all that I have said, and do not be hasty to decide. Or would you make an end at once and fly to the white men if I can find a means of escape?'

'I am too weary to fly anywhere,' I answered, 'even if I could. Moreover, I forget. My enemy is among the Spaniards, he whom I have sworn to kill, therefore his friends are my foes and his foes my friends. I will not fly, Otomie.'

'There you are wise,' she said, 'for if you come among the Teules that man will murder you; by fair means or foul he will murder you within a day, I saw it in his eyes. Now rest while I seek your safety, if there is any safety in this blood-stained land.'

CHAPTER 23

Thomas is Married

Otomie turned and went. I watched the golden curtains close behind her; then I sank back upon the couch and instantly was lost in sleep, for I was faint and weak, and so dazed with weariness, that at the time I scarcely knew what had happened, or the purpose of our talk. Afterwards, however, it came back to me. I must have slept for many hours, for when I awoke it was far on into the night. It was night but not dark, for through the barred window places came the sound of tumult and fighting, and red rays of light cast by the flames of burning houses. One of these windows was above my couch, and standing on the bed I seized the sill with my hands. With much pain, because of the flesh wound in my side, I drew myself up till I could look through the bars. Then I saw that the Spaniards, not content with the capture of the *teocalli*, had made a night attack and set fire to hundreds of houses in the city. The glare of the flames was that of a lurid day, and by it I could see the white men retreating to their quarters, pursued by thousands of Aztecs, who hung upon their flanks, shooting at them with stones and arrows.

Now I dropped down from the window place and began to think as to what I should do, for again my mind was wavering. Should I desert Otomie and escape to the Spaniards if that were possible, taking my chance of death at the hands of de Garcia? Or should I stay among the Aztecs if they would give me shelter, and wed Otomie? There was a third choice, indeed, to stay with them and leave Otomie alone, though it would be difficult to do this and keep my honour. One thing I understood, if I married Otomie it must be at her own price, for then I must become an Indian and give over all hope of returning to England and to my betrothed. Of this, indeed, there was little chance, still, while my life remained to me, it might come about if I was free. But once my hands were tied by this marriage it could never be during Otomie's lifetime, and so far as Lily Bozard was concerned I should be dead. How could I be thus faithless to her memory and my troth, and on the other hand, how could I discard the woman who had risked all for me, and who, to speak truth, had grown so dear to me, though there was one yet dearer? A hero or an angel might find a path out of this tangle, but alas! I was neither the one nor the other, only a man afflicted as other men are with human weakness, and Otomie was at hand, and very sweet and fair. Still, almost I determined that I would avail myself of her nobleness, that I would go back upon my words, and beg her to despise me and see me no more, in order that I might not be forced to break the troth that I had pledged beneath the beech at Ditchingham. For I greatly dreaded this oath of life-long fidelity which I should be forced to swear if I chose any other path.

Thus I thought on in pitiable confusion of mind, not knowing that all these matters were beyond my ordering, since a path was already made ready to my feet, which I must follow or die. And let this be a proof of the honesty of my words, since, had I been desirous of glozing the truth, I need have written nothing of these struggles of conscience, and of my own weakness. For soon it was to come to this, though not by her will, that I must either wed Otomie or die at once, and few would blame me for doing the first and not the last. Indeed, though I did wed her, I might still have declared myself to my affianced and to all the world as a slave of events from which there was no escape. But it is not all the truth, since my mind was divided, and had it not been settled for me, I cannot say how the struggle would have ended.

Now, looking back on the distant past, and weighing my actions and character as a judge might do, I can see, however, that had I found time to consider, there was another matter which would surely have turned the scale in favour of Otomie. De Garcia was among the Spaniards, and my hatred of de Garcia was the ruling passion of my life, a stronger passion even than my love for the two dear women who have been its joy. Indeed, though he is dead these many years I still hate him, and evil though the desire be, even in my age I long that my vengeance was still to wreak. While I remained among the Aztecs de Garcia would be their enemy and mine, and I might meet him in war and kill him there. But if I succeeded in reaching the Spanish camp, then it was almost sure that he would bring about my instant death. Doubtless he had told such a tale of me already, that within an hour I should be hung as a spy, or otherwise made away with.

But I will cease from these unprofitable wonderings which have but one value, that of setting out my strange necessity of choice between an absent and a present love, and go on with the story of an event in which there was no room to balance scruples.

While I sat musing on the couch the curtain was drawn, and a man entered bearing a torch. It was Guatemoc as he had come from the fray, which, except for its harvest of burning houses, was finished for that night. The plumes were shorn from his head, his golden armour was hacked by the Spanish swords, and he bled from a shot wound in the neck.

'Greeting, Teule,' he said. 'Certainly I never thought to see you alive to-night, or myself either for that matter. But it is a strange world, and now, if never before in Tenoctitlan, those things happen for which we look the least. But I have no time for words. I came to summon you before the council.'

'What is to be my fate?' I asked. 'To be dragged back to the stone of sacrifice?'

'Nay, have no fear of that. But for the rest I cannot say. In an hour you may be dead or great among us, if any of us can be called great in these days of shame. Otomie has worked well for you among the princes and the counsellors, so she says, and if you have a heart, you should be grateful to her, for it seems to me that few women have loved a man so much. As for me, I have been employed elsewhere,' and he glanced at his rent armour, 'but I will lift up my voice for you. Now come, friend, for the torch burns low. By this time you must be well seasoned in dangers; one more or less will matter as little to you as to me.'

Then I rose and followed him into the great cedar-panelled hall, where that very morning I had received adoration as a god. Now I was a god no longer, but a prisoner on trial for his life. Upon the dais where I had stood in the hour of my godhead were gathered those of the princes and counsellors who were left alive. Some of them, like Guatemoc, were clad in rent and bloody mail, others in their customary dress, and one in a priest's robe. They had only two things in common among them, the sternness of their faces and the greatness of their rank, and they sat there this night not to decide my fate, which was but a little thing, but to take counsel as to how they might expel the Spaniards before the city was destroyed.

When I entered, a man in mail, who sat in the centre of the half circle, and in whom I knew Cuitlahua, who would be emperor should Montezuma die, looked up quickly and said:

'Who is this, Guatemoc, that you bring with you? Ah! I remember; the Teule that was the god Tezcat, and who escaped the sacrifice today. Listen, nobles. What is to be done with this man? Say, is it lawful that he be led back to sacrifice?'

Then the priest answered: 'I grieve to say that it is not lawful most noble prince. This man has lain on the altar of the god, he has even been wounded by the holy knife. But the god rejected him in a fateful hour, and he must lie there no more. Slay him if you will, but not upon the stone of sacrifice.'

'What then shall be done with him?' said the prince again.

'He is of the blood of the Teules, and therefore an enemy. One thing is certain; he must not be suffered to join the white devils and give them tidings of our distresses. Is it not best that he be put away forthwith?'

Now several of the council nodded their heads, but others sat silent, making no sign.

'Come,' said Cuitlahua, 'we have no time to waste over this man when the lives of thousands are hourly at stake. The question is, Shall the Teule be slain?'

Then Guatemoc rose and spoke, saying: 'Your pardon, noble kinsman, but I hold that we may put this prisoner to better use than to kill him. I know him well; he is brave and loyal, as I have proved, moreover, he is not all a Teule, but half of another race that hates them as he hates them. Also he has knowledge of their customs and mode of warfare, which we lack, and I think that he may be able to give us good counsel in our strait.'

'The counsel of the wolf to the deer perhaps,' said Cuitlahua, coldly; 'counsel that shall lead us to the fangs of the Teules. Who shall answer for this foreign devil, that he will not betray us if we trust him?'

'I will answer with my life,' answered Guatemoc.

'Your life is of too great worth to be set on such a stake, nephew. Men of this white breed are liars, and his own word is of no value even if he gives it. I think that it will be best to kill him and have done with doubts.'

'This man is wed to Otomie, princess of the Otomie, Montezuma's daughter, your niece,' said Guatemoc again, 'and she loves him so well that she offered herself upon the stone of sacrifice with him. Unless I mistake she will answer for him also. Shall she be summoned before you?'

'If you wish, nephew; but a woman in love is a blind woman, and doubtless he has deceived her also. Moreover, she was his wife according to the rule of religion only. Is it your desire that the princess should be summoned before you, comrades?'

Now some said nay, but the most, those whose interest Otomie had gained, said yea, and the end of it was that one of their number was sent to summon her.

Presently she came, looking very weary, but proud in mien and royally attired, and bowed before the council.

'This is the question, princess,' said Cuitlahua. 'Whether this Teule shall be slain forthwith, or whether he shall be sworn as one of us, should he be willing to take the oath? The prince Guatemoc here vouches for him, and he says, moreover, that you will vouch for him also. A woman can do this in one way only, by taking him she vouches as her husband. You are already wed to this foreigner by the rule of religion. Are you willing to marry him according to the custom of our land, and to answer for his faith with your own life?'

'I am willing,' Otomie answered quietly, 'if he is willing.'

'In truth it is a great honour that you would do this white dog,' said Cuitlahua. 'Bethink you, you are princess of the Otomie and one of our master's daughters, it is to you that we look to bring back the mountain clans of the Otomie, of whom you are chieftainess, from their unholy alliance with the accursed Tlascalans, the slaves of the Teules. Is not your life too precious to be set on such a stake as this foreigner's faith? for learn, Otomie, if he proves false your rank shall not help you.'

'I know it all,' she replied quietly. 'Foreigner or not, I love this man and I will answer for him with my blood. Moreover, I look to him to assist me to win back the people of the Otomie to their allegiance. But let him speak for himself, my lord. It may happen that he has no desire to take me in marriage.'

Cuitlahua smiled grimly and said, 'When the choice lies between the breast of death and those fair arms of yours, niece, it is easy to guess his answer. Still, speak, Teule, and swiftly.'

'I have little to say, lord. If the princess Otomie is willing to wed me, I am willing to wed her,' I answered, and thus in the moment of my danger all my doubts and scruples vanished. As Cuitlahua had said, it was easy to guess the choice of one set between death and Otomie.

She heard and looked at me warningly, saying in a low voice: 'Remember our words, Teule. In such a marriage you renounce your past and give me your future.'

'I remember,' I answered, and while I spoke, there came before my eyes a vision of Lily's face as it had been when I bade her farewell. This then was the end of the vows that I had sworn. Cuitlahua looked at me with a glance which seemed to search my heart and said:

'I hear your words, Teule. You, a white wanderer, are graciously willing to take this princess to wife, and by her to be lifted high among the great lords of this land. But say, how can we trust you? If you fail us your wife dies indeed, but that may be naught to you.'

'I am ready to swear allegiance,' I answered. 'I hate the Spaniards, and among them is my bitterest enemy whom I followed across the sea to kill—the man who strove to murder me this very day. I can say no more, if you doubt my words it were best to make an end of me. Already I have suffered much at the hands of your people; it matters little if I die or live.'

'Boldly spoken, Teule. Now, lords, I ask your judgment. Shall this man be given to Otomie as husband and be sworn as one of us, or shall he be killed instantly? You know the matter. If he can be trusted, as Guatemoc and Otomie believe, he will be worth an army to us, for he is acquainted with the language, the customs, the weapons, and the modes of warfare of these white devils whom the gods have let loose upon us. If on the other hand he is not to be trusted, and it is hard for us to put faith in one of his blood, he may do us much injury, for in the end he will escape to the Teules, and betray our counsels and our strength, or the lack of it. It is for you to judge, lords.'

Now the councillors consulted together, and some said one thing and some another, for they were not by any means of a mind in the matter. At length growing weary, Cuitlahua called on them to put the question to the vote, and this they did by a lifting of hands. First those who were in favour of my death held up their hands, then those who thought that it would be wise to spare me. There were twenty-six councillors present, not counting Cuitlahua, and of these thirteen voted for my execution and thirteen were for saving me alive.

'Now it seems that I must give a casting vote,' said Cuitlahua when the tale had been rendered, and my blood turned cold at his words, for I had seen that his mind was set against me. Then it was that Otomie broke in, saying:

'Your pardon, my uncle, but before you speak I have a word to say. You need my services, do you not? for if the people of the Otomie will listen to any and suffer themselves to be led from their evil path, it is to me. My mother was by birth their chieftainess, the last of a long line, and I am her only child, moreover my father is their emperor. Therefore my life is of no small worth now in this time of trouble, for though I am nothing in myself, yet it may chance that I can bring thirty thousand warriors to your standard. The priests knew this on yonder pyramid, and when I claimed my right to lie at the side of the

Teule, they gainsayed me, nor would they suffer it, though they hungered for the royal blood, till I called down the vengeance of the gods upon them. Now my uncle, and you, lords, I tell you this: Slay yonder man if you will, but know that then you must find another than me to lure the Otomie from their rebellion, for then I complete what I began to-day, and follow him to the grave.'

She ceased and a murmur of amazement went round the chamber, for none had looked to find such love and courage in this lady's heart. Only Cuitlahua grew angry.

'Disloyal girl,' he said; 'do you dare to set your lover before your country? Shame upon you, shameless daughter of our king. Why, it is in the blood—as the father is so is the daughter. Did not Montezuma forsake his people and choose to lie among these Teules, the false children of Quetzal? And now this Otomie follows in his path. Tell us how is it, woman, that you and your lover alone escaped from the *teocalli* yonder when all the rest were killed. Are you then in league with these Teules? I say to you, niece, that if things were otherwise and I had my way, you should win your desire indeed, for you should be slain at this man's side and within the hour.' And he ceased for lack of breath, and looked upon her fiercely.

But Otomie never quailed; she stood before him pale and quiet, with folded hands and downcast eyes, and answered:

'Forbear to reproach me because my love is strong, or reproach me if you will, I have spoken my last word. Condemn this man to die and Prince you must seek some other envoy to win back the Otomie to the cause of Anahuac.'

Now Cuitlahua pondered, staring into the gloom above him and pulling at his beard, and the silence was great, for none knew what his judgment would be. At last he spoke:

'So be it. We have need of Otomie, my niece, and it is of no avail to fight against a woman's love. Teule, we give you life, and with the life honour and wealth, and the greatest of our women in marriage, and a place in our councils. Take these gifts and her, but I say to you both, beware how you use them. If you betray us, nay, if you do but think on treachery, I swear to you that you shall die a death so slow and horrible that the very name of it would turn your heart to water; you and your wife, your children and your servants. Come, let him be sworn!'

I heard and my head swam, and a mist gathered before my eyes. Once again I was saved from instant death.

Presently it cleared, and looking up my eyes met those of the woman who had saved me, Otomie my wife, who smiled upon me somewhat sadly. Then the priest came forward bearing a wooden bowl, carved about with strange signs, and a flint knife, and bade me bare my arm. He cut my flesh with the knife, so that blood ran from it into the bowl. Some drops of this blood he emptied on to the ground, muttering invocations the while. Then he turned and looked at Cuitlahua as though in question, and Cuitlahua answered with a bitter laugh:

'Let him be baptized with the blood of the princess Otomie my niece, for she is bail for him.'

'Nay, lord,' said Guatemoc, 'these two have mingled bloods already upon the stone of sacrifice, and they are man and wife. But I also have vouched for him, and I offer mine in earnest of my faith.'

'This Teule has good friends,' said Cuitlahua; 'you honour him overmuch. But so be it.'

Then Guatemoc came forward, and when the priest would have cut him with the knife, he laughed and said, pointing to the bullet wound upon his neck:

'No need for that, priest. Blood runs here that was shed by the Teules. None can be fitter for this purpose.'

So the priest drew away the bandage and suffered the blood of Guatemoc to drop into a second smaller bowl. Then he came to me and dipping his finger into the blood, he drew the sign of a cross upon my forehead as a Christian priest draws it upon the forehead of an infant, and said:

'In the presence and the name of god our lord, who is everywhere and sees all things, I sign you with this blood and make you of this blood. In the presence and the name of god our lord, who is everywhere and sees all things, I pour forth your blood upon the earth!' (here he poured as he spoke). 'As this blood of yours sinks into the earth, so may the memory of your past life sink and be forgotten, for you are born again of the people of Anahuac. In the presence and the name of god our lord, who is everywhere and sees all things, I mingle these bloods' (here he poured from one bowl into the other), 'and with them I touch your tongue' (here dipping his finger into the bowl he touched the tip of my tongue with it) 'and bid you swear thus:

'"May every evil to which the flesh of man is subject enter into my flesh, may I live in misery and die in torment by the dreadful death, may my soul be rejected from the Houses of the Sun, may it wander homeless for ever in the darkness that is behind the Stars, if I depart from this my oath. I, Teule, swear to be faithful to the people of Anahuac and to their lawful governors. I swear to wage war upon their foes and to compass their destruction, and more especially upon the

Teules till they are driven into the sea. I swear to offer no affront to the gods of Anahuac. I swear myself in marriage to Otomie, princess of the Otomie, the daughter of Montezuma my lord, for so long as her life shall endure. I swear to attempt no escape from these shores. I swear to renounce my father and my mother, and the land where I was born, and to cling to this land of my new birth; and this my oath shall endure till the volcano Popo ceases to vomit smoke and fire, till there is no king in Tenoctitlan, till no priest serves the altars of the gods, and the people of Anahuac are no more a people."

'Do you swear these things, one and all?'

'One and all I swear them,' I answered because I must, though there was much in the oath that I liked little enough. And yet mark how strangely things came to pass. Within fifteen years from that night the volcano Popo had ceased to vomit smoke and fire, the kings had ceased to reign in Tenoctitlan, the priests had ceased to serve the altars of the gods, the people of Anahuac were no more a people, and my vow was null and void. Yet the priests who framed this form chose these things as examples of what was immortal!

When I had sworn Guatemoc came forward and embraced me, saying: 'Welcome, Teule, my brother in blood and heart. Now you are one of us, and we look to you for help and counsel. Come, be seated by me.'

I looked towards Cuitlahua doubtfully, but he smiled graciously, and said: 'Teule, your trial is over. We have accepted you, and you have sworn the solemn oath of brotherhood, to break which is to die horribly in this world, and to be tortured through eternity by demons in the next. Forget all that may have been said in the hour of your weighing, for the balance is in your favour, and be sure that if you give us no cause to doubt you, you shall find none to doubt us. Now as the husband of Otomie, you are a lord among the lords, having honour and great possessions, and as such be seated by your brother Guatemoc, and join our council.'

I did as he bade me, and Otomie withdrew from our presence. Then Cuitlahua spoke again, no longer of me and my matters, but of the urgent affairs of state. He spoke in slow words and weighty, and more than once his voice broke in his sorrow. He told of the grievous misfortunes that had overcome the country, of the death of hundreds of its bravest warriors, of the slaughter of the priests and soldiers that day on the *teocalli*, and the desecration of his nation's gods. What was to be done in this extremity? he asked. Montezuma lay dying, a prisoner in the camp of the Teules, and the fire that he had nursed with

197

his breath devoured the land. No efforts of theirs could break the iron strength of these white devils, armed as they were with strange and terrible weapons. Day by day disaster overtook the arms of the Aztecs. What wisdom had they now that the protecting gods were shattered in their very shrines, when the altars ran red with the blood of their ministering priests, when the oracles were dumb or answered only in the accents of despair?

Then one by one princes and generals arose and gave counsel according to their lights. At length all had spoken, and Cuitlahua said, looking towards me:

'We have a new counsellor among us, who is skilled in the warfare and customs of the white men, who till an hour ago was himself a white man. Has he no word of comfort for us?'

'Speak, my brother?' said Guatemoc.

Then I spoke. 'Most noble Cuitlahua, and you lords and princes. You honour me by asking my counsel, and it is this in few words and brief. You waste your strength by hurling your armies continually against stone walls and the weapons of the Teules. So you shall not prevail against them. Your devices must be changed if you would win victory. The Spaniards are like other men; they are no gods as the ignorant imagine, and the creatures on which they ride are not demons but beasts of burden, such as are used for many purposes in the land where I was born. The Spaniards are men I say, and do not men hunger and thirst? Cannot men be worn out by want of sleep, and be killed in many ways? Are not these Teules already weary to the death? This then is my word of comfort to you. Cease to attack the Spaniards and invest their camp so closely that no food can reach them and their allies the Tlascalans. If this is done, within ten days from now, either they will surrender or they will strive to break their way back to the coast. But to do this, first they must win out of the city, and if dykes are cut through the causeways, that will be no easy matter. Then when they strive to escape cumbered with the gold they covet and came here to seek, then I say will be the hour to attack them and to destroy them utterly.'

I ceased, and a murmur of applause went round the council.

'It seems that we came to a wise judgment when we determined to spare this man's life,' said Cuitlahua, 'for all that he tells us is true, and I would that we had followed this policy from the first. Now, lords, I give my voice for acting as our brother points the way. What say you?'

'We say with you that our brother's words are good,' answered Guatemoc presently, 'and now let us follow them to the end.'

Then, after some further talk, the council broke up and I sought my chamber well nigh blind with weariness and crushed by the weight of all that I had suffered on that eventful day. The dawn was flaring in the eastern sky, and by its glimmer I found my path down the empty corridors, till at length I came to the curtains of my sleeping place. I drew them and passed through. There, far up the room, the faint light gleaming on her snowy dress, her raven hair and ornaments of gold, stood Otomie my bride.

I went towards her, and as I came she glided to meet me with outstretched arms. Presently they were about my neck and her kiss was on my brow.

'Now all is done, my love and lord,' she whispered, 'and come good or ill, or both, we are one till death, for such vows as ours cannot be broken.'

'All is done indeed, Otomie, and our oaths are lifelong, though other oaths have been broken that they might be sworn,' I answered.

Thus then I, Thomas Wingfield, was wed to Otomie, princess of the Otomie, Montezuma's daughter.

CHAPTER 24

The Night of Fear

Long before I awoke that day the commands of the council had been carried out, and the bridges in the great causeways were broken down wherever dykes crossed the raised roads that ran through the waters of the lake. That afternoon also I went dressed as an Indian warrior with Guatemoc and the other generals, to a parley which was held with Cortes, who took his stand on the same tower of the palace that Montezuma had stood on when the arrow of Guatemoc struck him down. There is little to be said of this parley, and I remember it chiefly because it was then for the first time since I had left the Tobascans that I saw Marina close, and heard her sweet and gentle voice. For now as ever she was by the side of Cortes, translating his proposals of peace to the Aztecs. Among those proposals was one which showed me that de Garcia had not been idle. It asked that the false white man who had been rescued from the altars of the gods upon the *teocalli* should be given in exchange for certain Aztec prisoners, in order that he might be hung according to his merits as a spy and deserter, a traitor to the emperor of Spain. I wondered as I heard, if Marina knew when she spoke the words, that 'the false white man' was none other than the friend of her Tobascan days.

'You see that you are fortunate in having found place among us Aztecs, Teule,' said Guatemoc with a laugh, 'for your own people would greet you with a rope.'

Then he answered Cortes, saying nothing of me, but bidding him and all the Spaniards prepare for death:

'Many of us have perished,' he said; 'you also must perish, Teules. You shall perish of hunger and thirst, you shall perish on the altars of the gods. There is no escape for you Teules; the bridges are broken.'

And all the multitude took up the words and thundered out, 'There is no escape for you Teules; the bridges are broken!'

Then the shooting of arrows began, and I sought the palace to tell Otomie my wife what I had gathered of the state of her father Montezuma, who the Spaniards said still lay dying, and of her two sisters who were hostages in their quarters. Also I told her how my surrender had been sought, and she kissed me, and said smiling, that though my life was now burdened with her, still it was better so than that I should fall into the hands of the Spaniards.

Two days later came the news that Montezuma was dead, and shortly after it his body, which the Spaniards handed over to the Aztecs for burial, attired in the gorgeous robes of royalty. They laid it in the hall of the palace, whence it was hurried secretly and at night to Chapoltepec, and there hidden away with small ceremony, for it was feared that the people might rend it limb from limb in their rage. With Otomie weeping at my side, I looked for the last time on the face of that most unhappy king, whose reign so glorious in its beginning had ended thus. And while I looked I wondered what suffering could have equalled his, as fallen from his estate and hated by the subjects whom he had betrayed, he lay dying, a prisoner in the power of the foreign wolves who were tearing out his country's heart. It is little wonder indeed that Montezuma rent the bandages from his wounds and would not suffer them to tend his hurts. For the real hurt was in his soul; there the iron had entered deeply, and no leech could cure it except one called Death. And yet the fault was not all his, the devils whom he worshipped as gods were revenged upon him, for they had filled him with the superstitions of their wicked faith, and because of these the gods and their high priest must sink into a common ruin. Were it not for these unsubstantial terrors that haunted him, the Spaniards had never won a foothold in Tenoctitlan, and the Aztecs would have remained free for many a year to come. But Providence willed it otherwise, and this dead and disgraced monarch was but its instrument.

Such were the thoughts that passed through my mind as I gazed upon the body of the great Montezuma. But Otomie, ceasing from her tears, kissed his clay and cried aloud:

'O my father, it is well that you are dead, for none who loved you could desire to see you live on in shame and servitude. May the gods you worshipped give me strength to avenge you, or if they be no gods, then may I find it in myself. I swear this, my father, that while a man is left to me I will not cease from seeking to avenge you.'

Then taking my hand, without another word she turned and passed thence. As will be seen, she kept her oath.

On that day and on the morrow there was fighting with the Spaniards, who sallied out to fill up the gaps in the dykes of the causeway, a task in which they succeeded, though with some loss. But it availed them nothing, for so soon as their backs were turned we opened the dykes again. It was on these days that for the first time I had experience of war, and armed with my bow made after the English pattern, I did good service. As it chanced, the very first arrow that I drew was on my hated foe de Garcia, but here my common fortune pursued me, for being out of practice, or over-anxious, I aimed too high, though the mark was an easy one, and the shaft pierced the iron of his *casque*, causing him to reel in his saddle, but doing him no further hurt. Still this marksmanship, poor as it was, gained me great renown among the Aztecs, who were but feeble archers, for they had never before seen an arrow pierce through the Spanish mail. Nor would mine have done so had I not collected the iron barbs off the crossbow bolts of the Spaniards, and fitted them to my own shafts. I seldom found the mail that would withstand arrows made thus, when the range was short and the aim good.

After the first day's fight I was appointed general over a body of three thousand archers, and was given a banner to be borne before me and a gorgeous captain's dress to wear. But what pleased me better was a chain shirt which came from the body of a Spanish cavalier. For many years I always wore this shirt beneath my cotton mail, and it saved my life more than once, for even bullets would not pierce the two of them.

I had taken over the command of my archers but forty-eight hours, a scant time in which to teach them discipline whereof they had little, though they were brave enough, when the occasion came to use them in good earnest, and with it the night of disaster that is still known among the Spaniards as the *noche triste*. On the afternoon before that night a council was held in the palace at which I spoke, saying, I was certain that the Teules thought of retreat from the city, and in the dark, for otherwise they would not have been so eager to fill up the canals in the causeway. To this Cuitlahua, who now that Montezuma was dead would be emperor, though he was not yet chosen and crowned, answered that it might well be that the Teules meditated flight, but that they could never attempt it in the darkness, since in so doing they must become entangled in the streets and dykes.

I replied that though it was not the Aztec habit to march and fight at night, such things were common enough among white men as they had seen already, and that because the Spaniards knew it was not their habit, they would be the more likely to attempt escape under cover of the darkness, when they thought their enemies asleep. Therefore I counselled that sentries should be set at all the entrances to every causeway. To this Cuitlahua assented, and assigned the causeway of Tlacopan to Guatemoc and myself, making us the guardians of its safety. That night Guatemoc and I, with some soldiers, went out towards midnight to visit the guard that we had placed upon the causeway. It was very dark and a fine rain fell, so that a man could see no further before his eyes than he can at evening through a Norfolk roke in autumn. We found and relieved the guard, which reported that all was quiet, and we were returning towards the great square when of a sudden I heard a dull sound as of thousands of men tramping.

'Listen,' I said.

'It is the Teules who escape,' whispered Guatemoc.

Quickly we ran to where the street from the great square opens on to the causeway, and there even through the darkness and rain we caught the gleam of armour. Then I cried aloud in a great voice, 'To arms! To arms! The Teules escape by the causeway of Tlacopan.'

Instantly my words were caught up by the sentries and passed from post to post till the city rang with them. They were cried in every street and canal, they echoed from the roofs of houses, and among the summits of a hundred temples. The city awoke with a murmur, from the lake came the sound of water beaten by ten thousand oars, as though myriads of wild-fowl had sprung suddenly from their reedy beds. Here, there, and everywhere torches flashed out like falling stars, wild notes were blown on horns and shells, and above all arose the booming of the snakeskin drum which the priests upon the *teocalli* beat furiously.

Presently the murmur grew to a roar, and from this direction and from that, armed men poured towards the causeway of Tlacopan. Some came on foot, but the most of them were in canoes which covered the waters of the lake further than the ear could hear. Now the Spaniards to the number of fifteen hundred or so, accompanied by some six or eight thousand Tlascalans, were emerging on the causeway in a long thin line. Guatemoc and I rushed before them, collecting men as we went, till we came to the first canal, where canoes were already gathering by scores. The head of the Spanish column reached the canal and the fight began, which so far as the Aztecs were concerned was a fray without plan or order, for in that darkness and confusion the captains could not see their men or the men hear their captains. But they were there in countless numbers and had only one desire in their breasts, to kill the Teules. A cannon roared, sending a storm of bullets through us, and by its flash we saw that the Spaniards carried a timber bridge with them, which they were placing across the canal. Then we fell on them, every man fighting for himself. Guatemoc and I were swept over that bridge by the first rush of the enemy, as leaves are swept in a gale, and though both of us won through safely we saw each other no more that night. With us and after us came the long array of Spaniards and Tlascalans, and from every side the Aztecs poured upon them, clinging to their struggling line as ants cling to a wounded worm.

How can I tell all that came to pass that night? I cannot, for I saw but little of it. All I know is that for two hours I was fighting like a madman. The foe crossed the first canal, but when all were over the bridge was sunk so deep in the mud that it could not be stirred, and three furlongs on ran a second canal deeper and wider than the first. Over this they could not cross till it was bridged with the dead. It seemed as though all hell had broken loose upon that narrow ridge of ground. The sound of cannons and of arquebusses, the shrieks of agony and fear, the shouts of the Spanish soldiers, the war-cries of the Aztecs, the screams of wounded horses, the wail of women, the hiss of hurtling darts and arrows, and the dull noise of falling blows went up to heaven in one hideous hurly-burly. Like a frightened mob of cattle the long Spanish array swayed this way and that, bellowing as it swayed. Many rolled down the sides of the causeway to be slaughtered in the water of the lake, or borne away to sacrifice in the canoes, many were drowned in the canals, and yet more were trampled to death in the mud. Hundreds of the Aztecs perished also, for the most part beneath the weapons of their own friends, who struck and shot not knowing on whom the blow should fall or in whose breast the arrow would find its home.

For my part I fought on with a little band of men who had gathered about me, till at last the dawn broke and showed an awful sight. The most of those who were left alive of the Spaniards and their allies had crossed the second canal upon a bridge made of the dead bodies of their fellows mixed up with a wreck of baggage, cannon, and packages of treasure. Now the fight was raging beyond it. A mob of Spaniards and Tlascalans were still crossing the second breach, and on these I fell with such men as were with me. I plunged right into the heart of them, and suddenly before me I saw the face of de Garcia. With a shout I rushed at him. He heard my voice and knew me. With an oath he struck at my head. The heavy sword came down upon my helmet of painted wood, shearing away one side of it and felling me, but ere I fell I smote him on the breast with the club I carried, tumbling him to the earth. Now half stunned and blinded I crept towards him through the press. All that I could see was a gleam of armour in the mud. I threw myself upon it, gripping at the wearer's throat, and together we rolled down the side of the causeway into the shallow water at the edge of the lake. I was uppermost, and with a fierce joy I dashed the blood from my eyes that I might see to kill my enemy caught at last. His body was in the lake but his head lay upon the sloping bank, and my plan was to hold him beneath the water till he was drowned, for I had lost my club.

'At length, de Garcia!' I cried in Spanish as I shifted my grip.

'For the love of God let me go!' gasped a rough voice beneath me. 'Fool, I am no Indian dog.'

Now I peered into the man's face bewildered. I had seized de Garcia, but the voice was not his voice, nor was the face his face, but that of a rough Spanish soldier.

'Who are you?' I asked, slackening my hold. 'Where is de Garcia—he whom you name Sarceda?'

'Sarceda? I don't know. A minute ago he was on his back on the causeway. The fellow pulled me down and rolled behind me. Let me be I say. I am not Sarceda, and if I were, is this a time to settle private quarrels? I am your comrade, Bernal Diaz. Holy Mother! who are you? An Aztec who speaks Castilian?'

'I am no Aztec,' I answered. 'I am an Englishman and I fight with the Aztecs that I may slay him whom you name Sarceda. But with you I have no quarrel, Bernal Diaz. Begone and escape if you can. No, I will keep the sword with your leave.'

'Englishman, Spaniard, Aztec, or devil,' grunted the man as he drew himself from his bed of ooze, 'you are a good fellow, and I promise you that if I live through this, and it should ever come about that I get *you* by the throat, I will remember the turn you did me. Farewell;' and without more ado he rushed up the bank and plunged into a knot of his flying countrymen, leaving his good sword in my hand. I strove to follow him that I might find my enemy, who once more had escaped me by craft, but my strength failed me, for de Garcia's sword had bitten deep and I bled much. So I must sit where I was till a canoe came and bore me back to Otomie to be nursed, and ten days went by before I could walk again.

This was my share in the victory of the *noche triste*. Alas! it was a

205

barren triumph, though more than five hundred of the Spaniards were slain and thousands of their allies. For there was no warlike skill or discipline among the Aztecs, and instead of following the Spaniards till not one of them remained alive, they stayed to plunder the dead and drag away the living to sacrifice. Also this day of revenge was a sad one to Otomie, seeing that two of her brothers, Montezuma's sons whom the Spaniards held in hostage, perished with them in the fray.

As for de Garcia I could not learn what had become of him, nor whether he was dead or living.

CHAPTER 25

The Burying of
Montezuma's Treasure

Cuitlahua was crowned Emperor of the Aztecs in succession to his brother Montezuma, while I lay sick with the wound given me by the sword of de Garcia, and also with that which I had received on the altar of sacrifice. This hurt had found no time to heal, and in the fierce fighting on the Night of Fear it burst open and bled much. Indeed it gave me trouble for years, and to this hour I feel it in the autumn season. Otomie, who nursed me tenderly, and so strange is the heart of woman, even seemed to be consoled in her sorrow at the loss of her father and nearest kin, because I had escaped the slaughter and won fame, told me of the ceremony of the crowning, which was splendid enough. Indeed the Aztecs were almost mad with rejoicing because the Teules had gone at last. They forgot, or seemed to forget, the loss of thousands of their bravest warriors and of the flower of their rank, and as yet, at any rate, they did not look forward to the future. From house to house and street to street ran troops of young men and maidens garlanded with flowers, crying, 'The Teules are gone, rejoice with us; the Teules are fled!' and woe to them who were not merry, ay, even though their houses were desolate with death. Also the statues of the gods were set up again on the great pyramid and their temples rebuilt, the holy crucifix that the Spaniards had placed there being served as the idols Huitzel and Tezcat had been served, and tumbled down the sides of the *teocalli*, and that after sacrifice of some Spanish prisoners had been offered in its presence. It was Guatemoc himself who told me of this sacrilege, but not with any exultation, for I had taught him something of our faith, and though he was too sturdy a heathen to change his creed, in secret he believed that the God of the Christians was a true and mighty God. Moreover, though he was obliged to countenance

207

them, because of the power of the priests, like Otomie, Guatemoc never loved the horrid rites of human sacrifice.

Now when I heard this tale my anger overcame my reason, and I spoke fiercely, saying:

'I am sworn to your cause, Guatemoc, my brother, and I am married to your blood, but I tell you that from this hour it is an accursed cause; because of your bloodstained idols and your priests, it is accursed. That God whom you have desecrated, and those who serve Him shall come back in power, and He shall sit where your idols sat and none shall stir Him for ever.'

Thus I spoke, and my words were true, though I do not know what put them into my heart, since I spoke at random in my wrath. For to-day Christ's Church stands upon the site of the place of sacrifice in Mexico, a sign and a token of His triumph over devils, and there it shall stand while the world endures.

'You speak rashly, my brother,' Guatemoc answered, proudly enough, though I saw him quail at the evil omen of my words. 'I say you speak rashly, and were you overheard there are those, notwithstanding the rank we have given you, the honour which you have won in war and council, and that you have passed the stone of sacrifice, who might force you to look again upon the faces of the beings you blaspheme. What worse thing has been done to your Christian God than has been done again and again to our gods by your white kindred? But let us talk no more of this matter, and I pray you, my brother, do not utter such ill-omened words to me again, lest it should strain our love. Do you then believe that the Teules will return?'

'Ay, Guatemoc, so surely as to-morrow's sun shall rise. When you held Cortes in your hand you let him go, and since then he has won a victory at Otompan. Is he a man, think you, to sheathe the sword that he has once drawn, and go down into darkness and dishonour? Before a year is past the Spaniards will be back at the gates of Tenoctitlan.'

'You are no comforter to-night, my brother,' said Guatemoc, 'and yet I fear that your words are true. Well, if we must fight, let us strive to win. Now, at least, there is no Montezuma to take the viper to his breast and nurse it till it stings him.' Then he rose and went in silence, and I saw that his heart was heavy.

On the morrow of this talk I could leave my bed, and within a week I was almost well. Now it was that Guatemoc came to me again, saying that he had been bidden by Cuitlahua the emperor, to command me to accompany him, Guatemoc, on a service of trust and secrecy. And indeed the nature of the service showed how great a confidence the leaders of the Aztecs now placed in me, for it was none other than the hiding away of the treasure that had been recaptured from the Spaniards on the Night of Fear, and with it much more from the secret stores of the empire.

At the fall of darkness we started, some of the great lords, Guatemoc and I, and coming to the water's edge, we found ten large canoes, each laden with something that was hidden by cotton cloths. Into these canoes we entered secretly, thinking that none saw us, three to a canoe, for there were thirty of us in all, and led by Guatemoc, we paddled for two hours or more across the Lake Tezcuco, till we reached the further shore at a spot where this prince had a fair estate. Here we landed, and the cloths were withdrawn from the cargoes of the canoes, which were great jars and sacks of gold and jewels, besides many other precious objects, among them a likeness of the head of Montezuma, fashioned in solid gold, which was so heavy that it was as much as Guatemoc and I could do to lift it between us. As for the jars, of which, if my memory serves me, there were seventeen, six men must carry each of them by the help of paddles lashed on either side, and then the task was not light. All this priceless stuff we bore in several journeys to the crest of a rise some six hundred paces distant from the water, setting it down by the mouth of a shaft behind the shelter of a mound of earth. When everything was brought up from the boats, Guatemoc touched me and another man, a great Aztec noble, born of a Tlascalan mother, on the shoulder, asking us if we were willing to descend with him into the hole, and there to dispose of the treasure.

'Gladly,' I answered, for I was curious to see the place, but the noble hesitated awhile, though in the end he came with us, to his ill-fortune.

Then Guatemoc took torches in his hand, and was lowered into the shaft by a rope. Next came my turn, and down I went, hanging to the cord like a spider to its thread, and the hole was very deep. At length I found myself standing by the side of Guatemoc at the foot of the shaft, round which, as I saw by the light of the torch he carried, an edging of dried bricks was built up to the height of a man above our heads. Resting on this edging and against the wall of the shaft, was a massive block of stone sculptured with the picture writing of the Aztecs. I glanced at the writing, which I could now read well, and saw that it recorded the burying of the treasure in the first year of Cuitlahua, Emperor of Mexico, and also a most fearful curse on him who should dare to steal it. Beyond us and at right angles to the shaft ran another passage, ten paces in length and high enough for a man to walk in, which led to a chamber hollowed in the earth, as large as that wherein I write to-day at Ditchingham. By the mouth of this chamber were placed piles of adobe bricks and mortar, much as the blocks of hewn stone had been placed in that underground vault at Seville where Isabella de Siguenza was bricked up living.

'Who dug this place?' I asked.

'Those who knew not what they dug,' answered Guatemoc. 'But see, here is our companion. Now, my brother, I charge you be surprised at nothing which comes to pass, and be assured I have good reason for anything that I may do.'

Before I could speak again the Aztec noble was at our side. Then those above began to lower the jars and sacks of treasure, and as they reached us one by one, Guatemoc loosed the ropes and checked them, while the Aztec and I rolled them down the passage into the chamber, as here in England men roll a cask of ale. For two hours and more we worked, till at length all were down and the tale was complete. The last parcel to be lowered was a sack of jewels that burst open as it came, and descended upon us in a glittering rain of gems. As it chanced, a great necklace of emeralds of surpassing size and beauty fell over my head and hung upon my shoulders.

'Keep it, brother,' laughed Guatemoc, 'in memory of this night,' and nothing loth, I hid the bauble in my breast. That necklace I have yet, and it was a stone of it—the smallest save one—that I gave to our gracious Queen Elizabeth. Otomie wore it for many years, and for this reason it shall be buried with me, though its value is priceless, so say those who are skilled in gems. But priceless or no, it is doomed to lie in the mould of Ditchingham churchyard, and may that same curse which is graved upon the stone that hides the treasure of the Aztecs fall upon him who steals it from my bones.

Now, leaving the chamber, we three entered the tunnel and began the work of building the adobe wall. When it was of a height of between two and three feet, Guatemoc paused from his labour and bade me hold a torch aloft. I obeyed wondering what he wished to see. Then he drew back some three paces into the tunnel and spoke to the Aztec noble, our companion, by name.

'What is the fate of discovered traitors, friend?' he said in a voice that, quiet though it was, sounded very terrible; and, as he spoke, he loosed from his side the war club set with spikes of glass that hung there by a thong.

Now the Aztec turned grey beneath his dusky skin and trembled in his fear.

'What mean you, lord?' he gasped.

'You know well what I mean,' answered Guatemoc in the same terrible voice, and lifted the club.

Then the doomed man fell upon his knees crying for mercy, and his wailing sounded so awful in that deep and lonely place that in my horror I went near to letting the torch fall.

'To a foe I can give mercy—to a traitor, none,' answered Guatemoc, and whirling the club aloft, he rushed upon the noble and killed him with a blow. Then, seizing the body in his strong embrace, he cast it into the chamber with the treasure, and there it lay still and dreadful among the gems and gold, the arms, as it chanced, being wound about two of the great jars as though the dead man would clasp them to his heart.

Now I looked at Guatemoc who had slain him, wondering if my hour was at hand also, for I knew well that when princes bury their wealth they hold that few should share the secret.

'Fear not, my brother,' said Guatemoc. 'Listen: this man was a thief, a dastard, and a traitor. As we know now, he strove twice to betray us to the Teules. More, it was his plan to show this nest of wealth to them, should they return again, and to share the spoil. All this we learned from a woman whom he thought his love, but who was in truth a spy set to worm herself into the secrets of his wicked heart. Now let him take his fill of gold; look how he grips it even in death, a white man could not hug the stuff more closely to his breast. Ah! Teule, would that the soil of Anahuac bore naught but corn for bread and flint and copper for the points of spears and arrows, then had her sons been free for ever. Curses on yonder dross, for it is the bait that sets these sea sharks tearing at our throats. Curses on it, I say; may it never glitter more in the sunshine, may it be lost for ever!' And he fell fiercely to the work of building up the wall.

Soon it was almost done; but before we set the last bricks, which were shaped in squares like the clay lump that we use for the building of farmeries and hinds' houses in Norfolk, I thrust a torch through the opening and looked for the last time at the treasure chamber that was also a dead-house. There lay the glittering gems; there, stood upon a jar, gleamed the golden head of Montezuma, of which the emerald eyes seemed to glare at me, and there, his back resting against this same jar, and his arms encircling two others to the right and left, was the dead man. But he was no longer dead, or so it seemed to me; at the least his eyes that were shut had opened, and they stared at me like the emerald eyes of the golden statue above him, only more fearfully.

211

Very hastily I withdrew the torch, and we finished in silence. When it was done we withdrew to the end of the passage and looked up the shaft, and I for one was glad to see the stars shining in heaven above me. Then we made a double loop in the rope, and at a signal were hauled up till we hung over the ledge where the black mass of marble rested, the tombstone of Montezuma's treasure, and of him who sleeps among it.

This stone, that was nicely balanced, we pushed with our hands and feet till presently it fell forward with a heavy sound, and catching on the ridge of brick which had been prepared to receive it, shut the treasure shaft in such a fashion that those who would enter it again must take powder with them.

Then we were dragged up, and came to the surface of the earth in safety.

Now one asked of the Aztec noble who had gone down with us and returned no more.

'He has chosen to stay and watch the treasure, like a good and loyal man, till such time as his king needs it,' answered Guatemoc grimly, and the listeners nodded, understanding all.

Then they fell to and filled up the narrow shaft with the earth that lay ready, working without cease, and the dawn broke before the task was finished. When at length the hole was full, one of our companions took seeds from a bag and scattered them on the naked earth, also he set two young trees that he had brought with him in the soil of the shaft, though why he did this I do not know, unless it was to mark the spot. All being done we gathered up the ropes and tools, and embarking in the canoes, came back to Mexico in the morning, leaving the canoes at a landing-place outside the city, and finding our way to our homes by ones and twos, as we thought unnoticed of any.

Thus it was that I helped in the burying of Montezuma's treasure, for the sake of which I was destined to suffer torture in days to come. Whether any will help to unbury it I do not know, but till I left the land of Anahuac the secret had been kept, and I think that then, except myself, all those were dead who laboured with me at this task. It chanced that I passed the spot as I came down to Mexico for the last time, and knew it again by the two trees that were growing tall and strong, and as I went by with Spaniards at my side, I swore in my heart that they should never finger the gold by my help. It is for this reason that even now I do not write of the exact bearings of the place where it lies buried with the bones of the traitor, though I know them well enough, seeing that in days to come what I set down here might fall into the hands of one of their nation.

And now, before I go on to speak of the siege of Mexico, I must tell of one more matter, namely of how I and Otomie my wife went up among the people of the Otomie, and won a great number of them back to their allegiance to the Aztec crown. It must be known, if my tale has not made this clear already, that the Aztec power was not of one people, but built up of several, and that surrounding it were many other tribes, some of whom were in alliance with it or subject to it, and some of whom were its deadly enemies. Such for instance were the Tlascalans, a small but warlike people living between Mexico and the coast, by whose help Cortes overcame Montezuma and Guatemoc. Beyond the Tlascalans and to the west, the great Otomie race lived or lives among its mountains. They are a braver nation than the Aztecs, speaking another language, of a different blood, and made up of many clans. Sometimes they were subject to the great Aztec empire, sometimes in alliance, and sometimes at open war with it and in close friendship with the Tlascalans. It was to draw the tie closer between the Aztecs and the Otomies, who were to the inhabitants of Anahuac much what the Scottish clans are to the people of England, that Montezuma took to wife the daughter and sole legitimate issue of their great chief or king. This lady died in childbirth, and her child was Otomie my wife, hereditary princess of the Otomie. But though her rank was so great among her mother's people, as yet Otomie had visited them but twice, and then as a child. Still, she was well skilled in their language and customs, having been brought up by nurses and tutors of the tribes, from which she drew a great revenue every year and over whom she exercised many rights of royalty that were rendered to her far more freely than they had been to Montezuma her father.

Now as has been said, some of these Otomie clans had joined the Tlascalans, and as their allies had taken part in the war on the side of the Spaniards, therefore it was decided at a solemn council that Otomie and I her husband should go on an embassy to the chief town of the nation, that was known as the City of Pines, and strive to win it back to the Aztec standard.

Accordingly, heralds having been sent before us, we started upon our journey, not knowing how we should be received at the end of it. For eight days we travelled in great pomp and with an ever-increasing escort, for when the tribes of the Otomie learned that their princess was come to visit them in person, bringing with her her husband, a man of the Teules who had espoused the Aztec cause, they flocked in vast numbers to swell her retinue, so that it came to pass that before we reached the City of Pines we were accompanied by an army of at least ten thousand mountaineers, great men and wild, who made a savage music as we marched. But with them and with their chiefs as yet we held no converse except by way of formal greeting, though every morning when we started on our journey, Otomie in a litter and I on a horse that had been captured from the Spaniards, they set up shouts of salutation and made the mountains ring. Ever as we went the land like its people grew wilder and more beautiful, for now we were passing through forests clad with oak and pine and with many a lovely plant and fern. Sometimes we crossed great and sparkling rivers and sometimes we wended through gorges and passes of the mountains, but every hour we mounted higher, till at length the climate became like that of England, only far more bright. At last on the eighth day we passed through a gorge riven in the red rock, which was so narrow in places that three horsemen could scarcely have ridden there abreast. This gorge, that is five miles long, is the high road to the City of Pines, to which there was no other access except by secret paths across the mountains, and on either side of it are sheer and towering cliffs that rise to heights of between one and two thousand feet.

'Here is a place where a hundred men might hold an army at bay,' I said to Otomie, little knowing that it would be my task to do so in a day to come.

Presently the gorge took a turn and I reined up amazed, for before me was the City of Pines in all its beauty. The city lay in a wheel shaped plain that may measure twelve miles across, and all around this plain are mountains clad to their summits with forests of oak and cedar trees. At the back of the city and in the centre of the ring of mountains is one, however, that is not green with foliage but black with lava, and above the lava white with snow, over which again hangs a pillar of smoke by day and a pillar of fire by night. This was the volcano Xaca, or the Queen, and though it is not so lofty as its sisters Orizaba, Popo, and Ixtac, to my mind it is the loveliest of them all, both because of its perfect shape, and of the colours, purple and blue, of the fires that it sends forth at night or when its heart is troubled. The Otomies worshipped this mountain as a god, offering human sacrifice to it, which was not wonderful, for once the lava pouring from its bowels cut a path through the City of Pines. Also they think it holy and haunted, so that none dare set foot upon its loftier snows. Nevertheless I was destined to climb them—I and one other.

Now in the lap of this ring of mountains and watched over by the mighty Xaca, clad in its robe of snow, its cap of smoke, and its crown of fire, lies, or rather lay the City of Pines, for now it is a ruin, or so I left it. As to the city itself, it was not so large as some others that I have seen in Anahuac, having only a population of some five and thirty thousand souls, since the Otomie, being a race of mountaineers, did not desire to dwell in cities. But if it was not great, it was the most beautiful of Indian towns, being laid out in straight streets that met at the square in its centre. All along these streets were houses each standing in a garden, and for the most part built of blocks of lava and roofed with a cement of white lime. In the midst of the square stood the *teocalli* or pyramid of worship, crowned with temples that were garnished with ropes of skulls, while beyond the pyramid and facing it, was the palace, the home of Otomie's forefathers, a long, low, and very ancient building having many courts, and sculptured everywhere with snakes and grinning gods. Both the palace and the pyramid were cased with a fine white stone that shone like silver in the sunlight, and contrasted strangely with the dark-hued houses that were built of lava.

Such was the City of Pines when I saw it first. When I saw it last it was but a smoking ruin, and now doubtless it is the home of bats and jackals; now it is 'a court for owls,' now 'the line of confusion is stretched out upon it and the stones of emptiness fill its streets.'

Passing from the mouth of the gorge we travelled some miles across the plain, every foot of which was cultivated with corn, maguey or aloe, and other crops, till we came to one of the four gates of the city. Entering it we found the flat roofs on either side of the wide street crowded with hundreds of women and children who threw flowers on us as we passed, and cried, 'Welcome, princess! Welcome, Otomie, princess of the Otomie!' And when at length we reached the great square, it seemed as though all the men in Anahuac were gathered there, and they too took up the cry of 'Welcome, Otomie, princess of the Otomie!' till the earth shook with the sound. Me also they saluted as I passed, by touching the earth with their right hands and then holding the hand above the head, but I think that the horse I rode caused them more wonder than I did, for the most of them had never seen a horse and looked on it as a monster or a demon. So we went on through the shouting mass, followed and preceded by thousands of warriors, many of them decked in glittering feather mail and bearing broidered banners, till we had passed the pyramid, where I saw the priests at their cruel work above us, and were come to the palace gates. And here in a strange chamber sculptured with grinning demons we found rest for a while.

On the morrow in the great hall of the palace was held a council of the chiefs and head men of the Otomie clans, to the number of a hundred or more. When all were gathered, dressed as an Aztec noble of the first rank, I came out with Otomie, who wore royal robes and looked most beautiful in them, and the council rose to greet us. Otomie bade them be seated and addressed them thus:

'Hear me, you chiefs and captains of my mother's race, who am your princess by right of blood, the last of your ancient rulers, and who am moreover the daughter of Montezuma, Emperor of Anahuac, now dead to us but living evermore in the Mansions of the Sun. First I present to you this my husband, the lord Teule, to whom I was given in marriage when he held the spirit of the god Tezcat, and whom, when he had passed the altar of the god, being chosen by heaven to aid us in our war, I wedded anew after the fashion of the earth, and by the will of my royal brethren. Know, chiefs and captains, that this lord, my husband, is not of our Indian blood, nor is he altogether of the blood of the Teules with whom we are at war, but rather of that of the true children of Quetzal, the dwellers in a far off northern sea who are foes to the Teules. And as they are foes, so this my lord is their foe, and as doubtless you have heard, of all the deeds of arms that were wrought upon the night of the slaying of the Teules, none were greater than his, and it was he who first discovered their retreat.

'Chiefs and captains of the great and ancient people of the Otomie, I your princess have been sent to you by Cuitlahua, my king and yours, together with my lord, to plead with you on a certain matter. Our king has heard, and I also have heard with shame, that many of the warriors of our blood have joined the Tlascalans, who were ever foes to the Aztecs, in their unholy alliance with the Teules. Now for a while the white men are beaten back, but they have touched the gold they covet, and they will return again like bees to a half-drained flower. They will return, yet of themselves they can do nothing against the glory of Tenoctitlan. But how shall it go if with them come thousands and tens of thousands of the Indian peoples? I know well that now in this time of trouble, when kingdoms crumble, when the air is full of portents, and the very gods seem impotent, there are many who would seize the moment and turn it to their profit. There are many men and tribes who remember ancient wars and wrongs, and who cry, "Now is the hour of vengeance, now we will think on the widows that the Aztec spears have made, on the tribute which they have wrung from our poverty to swell their wealth, and on the captives who have decked the altars of their sacrifice!"

'Is it not so? Ay, it is so, and I cannot wonder at it. Yet I ask you to remember this, that the yoke you would help to set upon the neck of the queen of cities will fit your neck also. O foolish men, do you think that you shall be spared when by your aid Tenoctitlan is a ruin and the Aztecs are no more a people? I say to you never. The sticks that the Teules use to beat out the life of Tenoctitlan shall by them be broken one by one and cast into the fire to burn. If the Aztecs fall, then early or late every tribe within this wide land shall fall. They shall be slain, their cities shall be stamped flat, their wealth shall be wrung from them, and their children shall eat the bread of slavery and drink the water of affliction. Choose, ye people of the Otomie. Will you stand by the men of your own customs and country, though they have been your foes at times, or will you throw in your lot with the stranger? Choose, ye people of the Otomie, and know this, that on your choice and that of the other men of Anahuac, depends the fate of Anahuac. I am your princess, and you should obey me, but to-day I issue no command. I say choose between the alliance of the Aztec and the yoke of the Teule, and may the god above the gods, the almighty, the invisible god, direct your choice.'

Otomie ceased and a murmur of applause went round the hall. Alas, I can do no justice to the fire of her words, any more than I can describe the dignity and loveliness of her person as it seemed in that hour. But they went to the hearts of the rude chieftains who listened. Many of them despised the Aztecs as a womanish people of the plains and the lakes, a people of commerce. Many had blood feuds against them dating back for generations. But still they knew that their princess spoke truth, and that the triumph of the Teule in Tenoctitlan would mean his triumph over every city throughout the land. So then and there they chose, though in after days, in the stress of defeat and trouble, many went back upon their choice as is the fashion of men.

'Otomie,' cried their spokesman, after they had taken counsel together, 'we have chosen. Princess, your words have conquered us. We throw in our lot with the Aztecs and will fight to the last for freedom from the Teule.'

'Now I see that you are indeed my people, and I am indeed your ruler,' answered Otomie. 'So the great lords who are gone, my forefathers, your chieftains, would have spoken in a like case. May you never regret this choice, my brethren, Men of the Otomie.'

And so it came to pass that when we left the City of Pines we took from it to Cuitlahua the emperor, a promise of an army of twenty thousand men vowed to serve him to the death in his war against the Spaniard.

217

The Crowning of Guatemoc

Our business with the people of the Otomie being ended for a while, we returned to the city of Tenoctitlan, which we reached safely, having been absent a month and a day. It was but a little time, and yet long enough for fresh sorrows to have fallen on that most unhappy town. For now the Almighty had added to the burdens which were laid upon her. She had tasted of death by the sword of the white man, now death was with her in another shape. For the Spaniard had brought the foul sicknesses of Europe with him, and small-pox raged throughout the land. Day by day thousands perished of it, for these ignorant people treated the plague by pouring cold water upon the bodies of those smitten, driving the fever inwards to the vitals, so that within two days the most of them died.[1] It was pitiful to see them maddened with suffering, as they wandered to and fro about the streets, spreading the distemper far and wide. They were dying in the houses, they lay dead by companies in the market places awaiting burial, for the sickness took its toll of every family, the very priests were smitten by it at the altar as they sacrificed children to appease the anger of the gods. But the worst is still to tell; Cuitlahua, the emperor, was struck down by the illness, and when we reached the city he lay dying. Still, he desired to see us, and sent commands that we should be brought to his bedside. In vain did I pray Otomie not to obey; she, who was without fear, laughed at me, saying, 'What, my husband, shall I shrink from that which you must face? Come, let us go and make report of our mission. If the sickness takes me and I die, it will be because my hour has come.'

So we went and were ushered into a chamber where Cuitlahua lay covered by a sheet, as though he were already dead, and with

---

1. This treatment is followed among the Indians of Mexico to this day, but if the writer may believe what he heard in that country, the patient is frequently cured by it.

incense burning round him in golden censers. When we entered he was in a stupor, but presently he awoke, and it was announced to him that we waited.

'Welcome, niece,' he said, speaking through the sheet and in a thick voice; 'you find me in an evil case, for my days are numbered, the pestilence of the Teules slays those whom their swords spared. Soon another monarch must take my throne, as I took your father's, and I do not altogether grieve, for on him will rest the glory and the burden of the last fight of the Aztecs. Your report, niece; let me hear it swiftly. What say the clans of the Otomie, your vassals?'

'My lord,' Otomie answered, speaking humbly and with bowed head, 'may this distemper leave you, and may you live to reign over us for many years! My lord, my husband Teule and I have won back the most part of the people of the Otomie to our cause and standard. An army of twenty thousand mountain men waits upon your word, and when those are spent there are more to follow.'

'Well done, daughter of Montezuma, and you, white man,' gasped the dying king. 'The gods were wise when they refused you both upon the stone of sacrifice, and I was foolish when I would have slain you, Teule. To you and all I say be of a steadfast heart, and if you must die, then die with honour. The fray draws on, but I shall not share it, and who knows its end?'

Now he lay silent for a while, then of a sudden, as though an inspiration had seized him, he cast the sheet from his face and sat upon his couch, no pleasant sight to see, for the pestilence had done its worst with him.

'Alas!' he wailed, 'and alas! I see the streets of Tenoctitlan red with blood and fire, I see her dead piled up in heaps, and the horses of the Teules trample them. I see the Spirit of my people, and her voice is sighing and her neck is heavy with chains. The children are visited because of the evil of the fathers. Ye are doomed, people of Anahuac, whom I would have nurtured as an eagle nurtures her young. Hell yawns for you and Earth refuses you because of your sins, and the remnant that remains shall be slaves from generation to generation, till the vengeance is accomplished!'

Having cried thus with a great voice, Cuitlahua fell back upon the cushions, and before the frightened leech who tended him could lift his head, he had passed beyond the troubles of this earth. But the words which he had spoken remained fixed in the hearts of those who heard them, though they were told to none except to Guatemoc.

Thus then in my presence and in that of Otomie died Cuitlahua, emperor of the Aztecs, when he had reigned but fifteen weeks. Once more the nation mourned its king, the chief of many a thousand of its children whom the pestilence swept with him to the 'Mansions of the Sun,' or perchance to the 'darkness behind the Stars.'

But the mourning was not for long, for in the urgency of the times it was necessary that a new emperor should be crowned to take command of the armies and rule the nation. Therefore on the morrow of the burial of Cuitlahua the council of the four electors was convened, and with them lesser nobles and princes to the number of three hundred, and I among them in the right of my rank as general, and as husband of the princess Otomie. There was no great need of deliberation, indeed, for though the names of several were mentioned, the princes knew that there was but one man who by birth, by courage, and nobility of mind, was fitted to cope with the troubles of the nation. That man was Guatemoc, my friend and blood brother, the nephew of the two last emperors and the husband of my wife's sister, Montezuma's daughter, Tecuichpo. All knew it, I say, except, strangely enough, Guatemoc himself, for as we passed into the council he named two other princes, saying that without doubt the choice lay between them.

It was a splendid and a solemn sight, that gathering of the four great lords, the electors, dressed in their magnificent robes, and of the lesser council of confirmation of three hundred lords and princes, who sat without the circle but in hearing of all that passed. Very solemn also was the prayer of the high priest, who, clad in his robes of sable, seemed like a blot of ink dropped on a glitter of gold. Thus he prayed:

'O god, thou who art everywhere and seest all, knowest that Cuitlahua our king is gathered to thee. Thou hast set him beneath thy footstool and there he rests in his rest. He has travelled that road which we must travel every one, he has reached the royal inhabitations of our dead, the home of everlasting shadows. There where none shall trouble him he is sunk in sleep. His brief labours are accomplished, and soiled with sin and sorrow, he has gone to thee. Thou gavest him joys to taste but not to drink; the glory of empire passed before his eyes like the madness of a dream. With tears and with prayers to thee he took up his load, with happiness he laid it down. Where his forefathers went, thither he has followed, nor can he return to us. Our fire is an ash and our lamp is darkness. Those who wore his purple before him bequeathed to him the intolerable weight of rule, and he in his turn bequeaths it to another. Truly, he should give thee praise, thou king of kings, master of the stars, that standest alone, who hast lifted from his shoulders so great a burden, and from his brow this crown of woes, paying him peace for war and rest for labour.

'O god our hope, choose now a servant to succeed him, a man after thine own heart, who shall not fear nor falter, who shall toil and not be weary, who shall lead thy people as a mother leads her children. Lord of lords, give grace to Guatemoc thy creature, who is our choice. Seal him to thy service, and as thy priest let him sit upon thy earthly throne for his life days. Let thy foes become his footstool, let him exalt thy glory, proclaim thy worship, and protect thy kingdom. Thus have I prayed to thee in the name of the nation. O god, thy will be done!'

When the high priest had made an end of his prayer, the first of the four great electors rose, saying:

'Guatemoc, in the name of god and with the voice of the people of Anahuac, we summon you to the throne of Anahuac. Long may you live and justly may you rule, and may the glory be yours of beating back into the sea those foes who would destroy us. Hail to you, Guatemoc, Emperor of the Aztecs and of their vassal tribes.' And all the three hundred of the council of confirmation repeated in a voice of thunder, 'Hail to you, Guatemoc, Emperor!'

Now the prince himself stood forward and spoke:

'You lords of election, and you, princes, generals, nobles and captains of the council of confirmation, hear me. May the gods be my witness that when I entered this place I had no thought or knowledge that I was destined to so high an honour as that which you would thrust upon me. And may the gods be my witness again that were my life my own, and not a trust in the hands of this people, I would say to you, "Seek on and find one worthier to fill the throne." But my life is not my own. Anahuac calls her son and I obey the call. War to the death threatens her, and shall I hang back while my arm has strength to smite and my brain has power to plan? Not so. Now and henceforth I vow myself to the service of my country and to war against the Teules. I will make no peace with them, I will take no rest till they are driven back whence they came, or till I am dead beneath their swords. None can say what the gods have in store for us, it may be victory or it may be destruction, but be it triumph or death, let us swear a great oath together, my people and my brethren. Let us swear to fight the Teules and the traitors who abet them, for our cities, our hearths and our altars; till the cities are a smoking ruin, till the hearths are cumbered with their dead, and the altars run red with the blood of their worshippers. So, if we are destined to conquer, our triumph shall be made sure, and if we are doomed to fail, at least there will be a story to be told of us. Do you swear, my people and my brethren?'

'We swear,' they answered with a shout.

'It is well,' said Guatemoc. 'And now may everlasting shame overtake him who breaks this oath.'

Thus then was Guatemoc, the last and greatest of the Aztec emperors, elected to the throne of his forefathers. It was happy for him that he could not foresee that dreadful day when he, the noblest of men, must meet a felon's doom at the hand of these very Teules. Yet so it came about, for the destiny that lay upon the land smote all alike, indeed the greater the man the more certain was his fate.

When all was done I hurried to the palace to tell Otomie what had come to pass, and found her in our sleeping chamber lying on her bed.

'What ails you, Otomie?' I asked.

'Alas! my husband,' she answered, 'the pestilence has stricken me. Come not near, I pray you, come not near. Let me be nursed by the women. You shall not risk your life for me, beloved.'

'Peace,' I said and came to her. It was too true, I who am a physician knew the symptoms well. Indeed had it not been for my skill, Otomie would have died. For three long weeks I fought with death at her bedside, and in the end I conquered. The fever left her, and thanks to my treatment, there was no single scar upon her lovely face. During eight days her mind wandered without ceasing, and it was then I learned how deep and perfect was her love for me. For all this while she did nothing but rave of me, and the secret terror of her heart was disclosed—that I should cease to care for her, that her beauty and love might pall upon me so that I should leave her, that 'the flower maid,' for so she named Lily, who dwelt across the sea should draw me back to her by magic; this was the burden of her madness. At length her senses returned and she spoke, saying:

'How long have I lain ill, husband?'

I told her and she said, 'And have you nursed me all this while, and through so foul a sickness?'

'Yes, Otomie, I have tended you.'

'What have I done that you should be so good to me?' she murmured. Then some dreadful thought seemed to strike her, for she moaned as though in pain, and said, 'A mirror! Swift, bring me a mirror!'

I gave her one, and rising on her arm, eagerly she scanned her face in the dim light of the shadowed room, then let the plate of burnished gold fall, and sank back with a faint and happy cry:

'I feared,' she said, 'I feared that I had become hideous as those are whom the pestilence has smitten, and that you would cease to love me, than which it had been better to die.'

'For shame,' I said. 'Do you then think that love can be frightened away by some few scars?'

'Yes,' Otomie answered, 'that is the love of a man; not such love as mine, husband. Had I been thus—ah! I shudder to think of it—within a year you would have hated me. Perhaps it had not been so with another, the fair maid of far away, but me you would have hated. Nay, I know it, though I know this also, that I should not have lived to feel your hate. Oh! I am thankful, thankful.'

Then I left her for a while, marvelling at the great love which she had given me, and wondering also if there was any truth in her words, and if the heart of man could be so ungrateful and so vile. Supposing that Otomie was now as many were who walked the streets of Tenoctitlan that day, a mass of dreadful scars, hairless, and with blind and whitened eyeballs, should I then have shrunk from her? I do not know, and I thank heaven that no such trial was put upon my constancy. But I am sure of this; had I become a leper even, Otomie would not have shrunk from me.

So Otomie recovered from her great sickness, and shortly afterwards the pestilence passed away from Tenoctitlan. And now I had many other things to think of, for the choosing of Guatemoc—my friend and blood brother—as emperor meant much advancement to me, who was made a general of the highest class, and a principal adviser in his councils. Nor did I spare myself in his service, but laboured by day and night in the work of preparing the city for siege, and in the marshalling of the troops, and more especially of that army of Otomies, who came, as they had promised, to the number of twenty thousand. The work was hard indeed, for these Indian tribes lacked discipline and powers of unity, without which their thousands were of little avail in a war with white men. Also there were great jealousies between their leaders which must be overcome, and I was myself an object of jealousy. Moreover, many tribes took this occasion of the trouble of the Aztecs to throw off their allegiance or vassalage, and even if they did not join the Spaniards, to remain neutral watching for the event of the war. Still we laboured on, dividing the armies into regiments after the fashion of Europe, and stationing each in its own quarter drilling them to the better use of arms, provisioning the city for a siege, and weeding out as many useless mouths as we might; and there was but one man in Tenoctitlan who toiled at these tasks more heavily than I, and that was Guatemoc the emperor, who did not rest day or night. I tried even to make powder with sulphur which was brought from the throat of the volcano Popo, but, having no knowledge of that art, I failed. Indeed, it would have availed us little had I succeeded, for having neither arquebusses nor cannons, and no skill to cast them, we could only have used it in mining roads and gateways, and, perhaps, in grenades to be thrown with the hand.

And so the months went on, till at length spies came in with the tidings that the Spaniards were advancing in numbers, and with them countless hosts of allies.

Now I would have sent Otomie to seek safety among her own people, but she laughed me to scorn, and said:

'Where you are, there I will be, husband. What, shall it be suffered that you face death, perhaps to find him, when I am not at your side to die with you? If that is the fashion of white women, I leave it to them, beloved, and here with you I stay.'

CHAPTER 27

The Fall of Tenoctitlan

Now shortly after Christmas, having marched from the coast with a great array of Spaniards, for many had joined his banner from over sea, and tens of thousands of native allies, Cortes took up his head quarters at Tezcuco in the valley of Mexico. This town is situated near the borders of the lake, at a distance of several leagues from Tenoctitlan, and being on the edge of the territory of the Tlascalans his allies, it was most suitable to Cortes as a base of action. And then began one of the most terrible wars that the world has seen. For eight months it raged, and when it ceased at length, Tenoctitlan, and with it many other beautiful and populous towns, were blackened ruins, the most of the Aztecs were dead by sword and famine, and their nation was crushed for ever. Of all the details of this war I do not purpose to write, for were I to do so, there would be no end to this book, and I have my own tale to tell. These, therefore, I leave to the maker of histories. Let it be enough to say that the plan of Cortes was to destroy all her vassal and allied cities and peoples before he grappled with Mexico, queen of the valley, and this he set himself to do with a skill, a valour, and a straightness of purpose, such as have scarcely been shown by a general since the days of Caesar.

Iztapalapan was the first to fall, and here ten thousand men, women, and children were put to the sword or burned alive. Then came the turn of the others; one by one Cortes reduced the cities till the whole girdle of them was in his hand, and Tenoctitlan alone remained untouched. Many indeed surrendered, for the nations of Anahuac being of various blood were but as a bundle of reeds and not as a tree. Thus when the power of Spain cut the band of empire that bound them together, they fell this way and that, having no unity. So it came about that as the power of Guatemoc weakened that of Cortes increased, for he garnered these loosened reeds into his basket. And, indeed, now that the people saw that Mexico had met her match, many an ancient hate and smouldering rivalry broke into flame, and they fell upon her and tore her, like half-tamed wolves upon their master when his scourge is broken. It was this that brought about the fall of Anahuac. Had she remained true to herself, had she forgotten her feuds and jealousies and stood against the Spaniards as one man, then Tenoctitlan would never have fallen, and Cortes with every Teule in his company had been stretched upon the stone of sacrifice.

Did I not say when I took up my pen to write this book that every wrong revenges itself at last upon the man or the people that wrought it? So it was now. Mexico was destroyed because of the abomination of the worship of her gods. These feuds between the allied peoples had their root in the horrible rites of human sacrifice. At some time in the past, from all these cities captives have been dragged to the altars of the gods of Mexico, there to be slaughtered and devoured by the cannibal worshippers. Now these outrages were remembered, now when the arm of the queen of the valley was withered, the children of those whom she had slain rose up to slay her and to drag *her* children to their altars.

By the month of May, strive as we would, and never was a more gallant fight made, all our allies were crushed or had deserted us, and the siege of the city began. It began by land and by water, for with incredible resource Cortes caused thirteen brigantines of war to be constructed in Tlascala, and conveyed in pieces for twenty leagues across the mountains to his camp, whence they were floated into the lake through a canal, which was hollowed out by the labour of ten thousand Indians, who worked at it without cease for two months. The bearers of these brigantines were escorted by an army of twenty thousand Tlascalans, and if I could have had my way that army should have been attacked in the mountain passes. So thought Guatemoc also, but there were few troops to spare, for the most of our force had been despatched to threaten a city named Chalco, that, though its people were of the Aztec blood, had not been ashamed to desert the Aztec cause. Still I offered to lead the twenty thousand Otomies whom I commanded against the Tlascalan convoy, and the matter was debated hotly at a council of war. But the most of the council were against the risking of an engagement with the Spaniards and their allies so far from the city, and thus the opportunity went by to return no more. It was an evil fortune like the rest, for in the end these brigantines brought about the fall of Tenoctitlan by cutting off the supply of food, which was carried in canoes across the lake. Alas! the bravest can do nothing against the power of famine. Hunger is a very great man, as the Indians say.

Now the Aztecs fighting alone were face to face with their foes and the last struggle began. First the Spaniards cut the aqueduct which supplied the city with water from the springs at the royal house of Chapoltepec, whither I was taken on being brought to Mexico. Henceforth till the end of the siege, the only water that we found to drink was the brackish and muddy fluid furnished by the lake and wells sunk in the soil. Although it might be drunk after boiling to free it of the salt, it was unwholesome and filthy to the taste, breeding various painful sicknesses and fevers. It was on this day of the cutting of the aqueduct that Otomie bore me a son, our first-born. Already the hardships of the siege were so great and nourishing food so scarce, that had she been less strong, or had I possessed less skill in medicine, I think that she would have died. Still she recovered to my great thankfulness and joy, and though I am no clerk I baptized the boy into the Christian Church with my own hand, naming him Thomas after me.

Now day by day and week by week the fighting went on with varying success, sometimes in the suburbs of the city, sometimes on the lake, and sometimes in the very streets. Time on time the Spaniards were driven back with loss, time on time they advanced again from their different camps. Once we captured sixty of them and more than a thousand of their allies. All these were sacrificed on the altar of Huitzel, and given over to be devoured by the Aztecs according to the beastlike custom which in Anahuac enjoined the eating of the bodies of those who were offered to the gods, not because the Indians love such meat but for a secret religious reason.

In vain did I pray Guatemoc to forego this horror.

'Is this a time for gentleness?' he answered fiercely. 'I cannot save them from the altar, and I would not if I could. Let the dogs die according to the custom of the land, and to you, Teule my brother, I say presume not too far.'

Alas! the heart of Guatemoc grew ever fiercer as the struggle wore on, and indeed it was little to be wondered at.

This was the dreadful plan of Cortes: to destroy the city piecemeal as he advanced towards its heart, and it was carried out without mercy. So soon as the Spaniards got footing in a quarter, thousands of the Tlascalans were set to work to fire the houses and burn all in them alive. Before the siege was done Tenoctitlan, queen of the valley, was but a heap of blackened ruins. Cortes might have cried over Mexico with Isaiah the prophet: 'Thy pomp is brought down to the grave, and the noise of thy viols: the worm is spread under thee and the worms cover thee. How art thou fallen from heaven, O Lucifer, son of the morning! how art thou cut down to the ground which didst weaken the nations!'

In all these fights I took my part, though it does not become me to boast my prowess. Still the Spaniards knew me well and they had good reason. Whenever they saw me they would greet me with revilings, calling me 'traitor and renegade,' and 'Guatemoc's white dog,' and moreover, Cortes set a price upon my head, for he knew through his spies that some of Guatemoc's most successful attacks and stratagems had been of my devising. But I took no heed even when their insults pierced me like arrows, for though many of the Aztecs were my friends and I hated the Spaniards, it was a shameful thing that a Christian man should be warring on the side of cannibals who made human sacrifice. I took no heed, since always I was seeking for my foe de Garcia. He was there I knew, for I saw him many times, but I could never come at him. Indeed, if I watched for him he also watched for me, but with another purpose, to avoid me. For now as of old de Garcia feared me, now as of old he believed that I should bring his death upon him.

It was the custom of warriors in the opposing armies to send challenges to single combat, one to another, and many such duels were fought in the sight of all, safe conduct being given to the combatants and their seconds. Upon a day, despairing of meeting him face to face in battle, I sent a challenge to de Garcia by a herald, under his false name of Sarceda. In an hour the herald returned with this message written on paper in Spanish:

'Christian men do not fight duels with renegade heathen dogs, white worshippers of devils and eaters of human flesh. There is but one weapon which such cannot defile, a rope, and it waits for you, Thomas Wingfield.'

I tore the writing to pieces and stamped upon it in my rage, for now, to all his other crimes against me, de Garcia had added the blackest insult. But wrath availed me nothing, for I could never come near him, though once, with ten of my Otomies, I charged into the heart of the Spanish column after him.

From that rush I alone escaped alive, the ten Otomies were sacrificed to my hate.

How shall I paint the horrors that day by day were heaped upon the doomed city? Soon all the food was gone, and men, ay, and worse still, tender women and children, must eat such meat as swine would have turned from, striving to keep life in them for a little longer. Grass, the bark of trees, slugs and insects, washed down with brackish water from the lake, these were their best food, these and the flesh of captives offered in sacrifice. Now they began to die by hundreds and by thousands, they died so fast that none could bury them. Where they perished, there they lay, till at length their bodies bred a plague, a black and horrible fever that swept off thousands more, who in turn became the root of pestilence. For one who was killed by the Spaniards and their allies, two were swept off by hunger and plague. Think then what was the number of dead when not less than seventy thousand perished beneath the sword and by fire alone. Indeed, it is said that forty thousand died in this manner in a single day, the day before the last of the siege.

One night I came back to the lodging where Otomie dwelt with her royal sister Tecuichpo, the wife of Guatemoc, for now all the palaces had been burnt down. I was starving, for I had scarcely tasted food for forty hours, but all that my wife could set before me were three little meal cakes, or tortillas, mixed with bark. She kissed me and bade me eat them, but I discovered that she herself had touched no food that day, so I would not till she shared them. Then I noted that she could scarcely swallow the bitter morsels, and also that she strove to hide tears which ran down her face.

'What is it, wife?' I asked.

Then Otomie broke out into a great and bitter crying and said:

'This, my beloved: for two days the milk has been dry in my breast— hunger has dried it—and our babe is dead! Look, he lies dead!' and she drew aside a cloth and showed me the tiny body.

'Hush,' I said, 'he is spared much. Can we then desire that a child should live to see such days as we have seen, and after all, to die at last?'

'He was our son, our first-born,' she cried again. 'Oh! why must we suffer thus?'

'We must suffer, Otomie, because we are born to it. Just so much happiness is given to us as shall save us from madness and no more. Ask me not why, for I cannot answer you! There is no answer in my faith or in any other.'

And then, looking on that dead babe, I wept also. Every hour in those terrible months it was my lot to see a thousand sights more awful, and yet this sight of a dead infant moved me the most of all of them. The child was mine, my firstborn, its mother wept beside me, and its stiff and tiny fingers seemed to drag at my heart strings. Seek not the cause, for the Almighty Who gave the heart its infinite power of pain alone can answer, and to our ears He is dumb.

Then I took a mattock and dug a hole outside the house till I came to water, which in Tenoctitlan is found at a depth of two feet or so. And, having muttered a prayer over him, there in the water I laid the body of our child, burying it out of sight. At the least he was not left for the *zapilotes*, as the Aztecs call the vultures, like the rest of them.

After that we wept ourselves to sleep in each other's arms, Otomie murmuring from time to time, 'Oh! my husband, I would that we were asleep and forgotten, we and the babe together.'

'Rest now,' I answered, 'for death is very near to us.'

The morrow came, and with it a deadlier fray than any that had gone before, and after it more morrows and more deaths, but still we lived on, for Guatemoc gave us of his food. Then Cortes sent his heralds demanding our surrender, and now three-fourths of the city was a ruin, and three-fourths of its defenders were dead. The dead were heaped in the houses like bees stifled in a hive, and in the streets they lay so thick that we walked upon them.

The council was summoned—fierce men, haggard with hunger and with war, and they considered the offer of Cortes.

'What is your word, Guatemoc?' said their spokesman at last.

'Am I Montezuma, that you ask me? I swore to defend this city to the last,' he answered hoarsely, 'and, for my part, I will defend it. Better that we should all die, than that we should fall living into the hands of the Teules.'

'So say we,' they replied, and the war went on.

At length there came a day when the Spaniards made a new attack and gained another portion of the city. There the people were huddled together like sheep in a pen. We strove to defend them, but our arms were weak with famine. They fired into us with their pieces, mowing us down like corn before the sickle. Then the Tlascalans were loosed upon us, like fierce hounds upon a defenceless buck, and on this day it is said that there died forty thousand people, for none were spared. On the morrow, it was the last day of the siege, came a fresh embassy from Cortes, asking that Guatemoc should meet him. The answer was the same, for nothing could conquer that noble spirit.

'Tell him,' said Guatemoc, 'that I will die where I am, but that I will hold no parley with him. We are helpless, let Cortes work his pleasure on us.'

By now all the city was destroyed, and we who remained alive within its bounds were gathered on the causeways and behind the ruins of walls; men, women, and children together.

Here they attacked us again. The great drum on the *teocalli* beat for the last time, and for the last time the wild scream of the Aztec warriors went up to heaven. We fought our best; I killed four men that day with my arrows which Otomie, who was at my side, handed me as I shot. But the most of us had not the strength of a child, and what could we do? They came among us like seamen among a flock of seals, and slaughtered us by hundreds. They drove us into the canals and trod us to death there, till bridges were made of our bodies. How we escaped I do not know.

At length a party of us, among whom was Guatemoc with his wife Tecuichpo, were driven to the shores of the lake where lay canoes, and into these we entered, scarcely knowing what we did, but thinking that we might escape, for now all the city was taken. The brigantines saw us and sailed after us with a favouring wind—the wind always favoured the foe in that war—and row as we would, one of them came up with us and began to fire into us. Then Guatemoc stood up and spoke, saying:

'I am Guatemoc. Bring me to Malinche. But spare those of my people who remain alive.'

'Now,' I said to Otomie at my side, 'my hour has come, for the Spaniards will surely hang me, and it is in my mind, wife, that I should do well to kill myself, so that I may be saved from a death of shame.'

'Nay, husband,' she answered sadly, 'as I said in bygone days, while you live there is hope, but the dead come back no more. Fortune may favour us yet; still, if you think otherwise, I am ready to die.'

'That I will not suffer, Otomie.'

'Then you must hold your hand, husband, for now as always, where you go, I follow.'

'Listen,' I whispered; 'do not let it be known that you are my wife; pass yourself as one of the ladies of Tecuichpo, the queen, your sister. If we are separated, and if by any chance I escape, I will try to make my way to the City of Pines. There, among your own people, we may find refuge.'

'So be it, beloved,' she answered, smiling sadly. 'But I do not know how the Otomie will receive me, who have led twenty thousand of their bravest men to a dreadful death.'

Now we were on the deck of the brigantine and must stop talking, and thence, after the Spaniards had quarrelled over us a while, we were taken ashore and led to the top of a house which still stood, where Cortes had made ready hurriedly to receive his royal prisoner. Surrounded by his escort, the Spanish general stood, cap in hand, and by his side was Marina, grown more lovely than before, whom I now met for the first time since we had parted in Tobasco.

Our eyes met and she started, thereby showing that she knew me again, though it must have been hard for Marina to recognise her friend Teule in the blood-stained, starving, and tattered wretch who could scarcely find strength to climb the *azotea*. But at that time no words passed between us, for all eyes were bent on the meeting between Cortes and Guatemoc, between the conqueror and the conquered.

Still proud and defiant, though he seemed but a living skeleton, Guatemoc walked straight to where the Spaniard stood, and spoke, Marina translating his words.

'I am Guatemoc, the emperor, Malinche,' he said. 'What a man might do to defend his people, I have done. Look on the fruits of my labour,' and he pointed to the blackened ruins of Tenoctitlan that stretched on every side far as the eye could reach. 'Now I have come to this pass, for the gods themselves have been against me. Deal with me as you will, but it will be best that you kill me now,' and he touched the dagger of Cortes with his hand, 'and thus rid me swiftly of the misery of life.'

'Fear not, Guatemoc,' answered Cortes. 'You have fought like a brave man, and such I honour. With me you are safe, for we Spaniards love a gallant foe. See, here is food,' and he pointed to a table spread with such viands as we had not seen for many a week; 'eat, you and your companions together, for you must need it. Afterwards we will talk.'

So we ate, and heartily, I for my part thinking that it would be well to die upon a full stomach, having faced death so long upon an empty one, and while we devoured the meat the Spaniards stood on one side scanning us, not without pity. Presently, Tecuichpo was brought before Cortes, and with her Otomie and some six other ladies. He greeted her graciously, and they also were given to eat. Now, one of the Spaniards who had been watching me whispered something into the ear of Cortes, and I saw his face darken.

'Say,' he said to me in Castilian, 'are you that renegade, that traitor who has aided these Aztecs against us?'

'I am no renegade and no traitor, general,' I answered boldly, for the food and wine had put new life into me. 'I am an Englishman, and I have fought with the Aztecs because I have good cause to hate you Spaniards.'

'You shall soon have better, traitor,' he said furiously. 'Here, lead this man away and hang him on the mast of yonder ship.'

Now I saw that it was finished, and made ready to go to my death, when Marina spoke into the ear of Cortes. All she said I could not catch, but I heard the words 'hidden gold.' He listened, then hesitated, and spoke aloud: 'Do not hang this man to-day. Let him be safely guarded. Tomorrow I will inquire into his case.'

CHAPTER 28

Thomas is Doomed

At the words of Cortes two Spaniards came forward, and seizing me one by either arm, they led me across the roof of the house towards the stairway. Otomie had heard also, and though she did not understand the words, she read the face of Cortes, and knew well that I was being taken to imprisonment or death. As I passed her, she started forward, a terror shining in her eyes. Fearing that she was about to throw herself upon my breast, and thus to reveal herself as my wife, and bring my fate upon her, I glanced at her warningly, then making pretence to stumble, as though with fear and exhaustion, I fell at her feet. The soldiers who led me laughed brutally, and one of them kicked me with his heavy boot. But Otomie stooped down and held her hand to me to help me rise, and as I did so, we spoke low and swiftly.

'Farewell, wife,' I said; 'whatever happens, keep silent.'

'Farewell,' she answered; 'if you must die, await me in the gates of death, for I will join you there.'

'Nay, live on. Time shall bring comfort.'

'You are my life, beloved. With you time ends for me.' Now I was on my feet again, and I think that none noted our whispered words, for all were listening to Cortes, who rated the man that had kicked me.

'I bade you guard this traitor, not to kick him,' he said angrily in Castilian. 'Will you put us to open shame before these savages? Do so once more, and you shall pay for it smartly. Learn a lesson in gentleness from that woman; she is starving, yet she leaves her food to help your prisoner to his feet. Now take him away to the camp, and see that he comes to no harm, for he can tell me much.'

Then the soldiers led me away, grumbling as they went, and the last thing that I saw was the despairing face of Otomie my wife, as she gazed after me, faint with the secret agony of our parting. But when

I came to the head of the stairway, Guatemoc, who stood near, took my hand and shook it.

'Farewell, my brother,' he said with a heavy smile; 'the game we played together is finished, and now it is time for us to rest. I thank you for your valour and your aid.'

'Farewell, Guatemoc,' I answered. 'You are fallen, but let this comfort you, in your fall you have found immortal fame.'

'On, on!' growled the soldiers, and I went, little thinking how Guatemoc and I should meet again.

They took me to a canoe, and we were paddled across the lake by Tlascalans, till at length we came to the Spanish camp. All the journey through, my guards, though they laid no hand on me, fearing the anger of Cortes, mocked and taunted me, asking me how I liked the ways of the heathen, and whether I ate the flesh of the sacrifices raw or cooked; and many another such brutal jest they made at my expense. For a while I bore it, for I had learned to be patient from the Indians, but at last I answered them in few words and bitter.

'Peace, cowards,' I said; 'remember that I am helpless, and that were I before you strong and armed, either I should not live to listen to such words, or you would not live to repeat them.'

Then they were silent, and I also was silent.

When we reached their camp I was led through it, followed by a throng of fierce Tlascalans and others, who would have torn me limb from limb had they not feared to do so. I saw some Spaniards also, but the most of these were so drunk with *mescal*, and with joy at the tidings that Tenoctitlan had fallen, and their labours were ended at last, that they took no heed of me. Never did I see such madness as possessed them, for these poor fools believed that henceforth they should eat their very bread off plates of gold. It was for gold that they had followed Cortes; for gold they had braved the altar of sacrifice and fought in a hundred fights, and now, as they thought, they had won it.

The room of the stone house where they prisoned me had a window secured by bars of wood, and through these bars I could see and hear the revellings of the soldiers during the time of my confinement. All day long, when they were not on duty, and most of the night also, they gambled and drank, staking tens of pesos on a single throw, which the loser must pay out of his share of the countless treasures of the Aztecs. Little did they care if they won or lost, they were so sure of plunder, but played on till drink overpowered them, and they rolled senseless beneath the tables, or till they sprang up and danced wildly to and fro, catching at the sunbeams and screaming 'Gold! gold! gold!'

Listening at this window also I gathered some of the tidings of the camp. I learned that Cortes had come back, bringing Guatemoc and several of the princes with him, together with many of the noble Aztec ladies. Indeed I saw and heard the soldiers gambling for these women when they were weary of their play for money, a description of each of them being written on a piece of paper. One of these ladies answered well to Otomie, my wife, and she was put up to auction by the brute who won her in the gamble, and sold to a common soldier for a hundred pesos. For these men never doubted but that the women and the gold would be handed over to them.

Thus things went for several days, during which I sat and slept in my prison untroubled by any, except the native woman who waited on me and brought me food in plenty. During those days I ate as I have never eaten before or since, and I slept much, for my sorrows could not rid my body of its appetites and commanding need for food and rest. Indeed I verily believe that at the end of a week, I had increased in weight by a full half; also my weariness was conquered at length, and I was strong again.

But when I was neither sleeping nor eating I watched at my window, hoping, though in vain, to catch some sight of Otomie or of Guatemoc. If I might not see my friends, however, at least I saw my foe, for one evening de Garcia came and stared at my prison. He could not see me, but I saw him, and the devilish smile that flickered on his face as he went away like a wolf, made me shiver with a presage of woes to come. For ten minutes or more he stood gazing at my window hungrily, as a cat gazes at a caged bird, and I felt that he was waiting for the door to be opened, and *knew* that it would soon be opened.

This happened on the eve of the day upon which I was put to torture.

Meanwhile, as time went on, I noticed that a change came over the temper of the camp. The soldiers ceased to gamble for untold wealth, they even ceased from drinking to excess and from their riotous joy, but took to hanging together in knots discussing fiercely I could not learn of what. On the day when de Garcia came to look at my prison there was a great gathering in the square opposite my prison, to which I saw Cortes ride up on a white horse and richly dressed. The meeting was too far away for me to overhear what passed, but I noted that several officers addressed Cortes angrily, and that their speeches were loudly cheered by the soldiers. At length the great captain answered them at some length, and they broke up in silence. Next morning after I had breakfasted, four soldiers came into my prison and ordered me to accompany them.

'Whither?' I asked.

'To the captain, traitor,' their leader answered.

'It has come at last,' I thought to myself, but I said only:

'It is well. Any change from this hole is one for the better.'

'Certainly,' he replied; 'and it is your last shift.'

Then I knew that the man believed that I was going to my death. In five minutes I was standing before Cortes in his private house. At his side was Marina and around him were several of his companions in arms. The great man looked at me for a while, then spoke.

'Your name is Wingfield; you are of mixed blood, half English and half Spanish. You were cast away in the Tobasco River and taken to Tenoctitlan. There you were doomed to personate the Aztec god Tezcat, and were rescued by us when we captured the great *teocalli*. Subsequently you joined the Aztecs and took part in the attack and slaughter of the *noche triste*. You were afterwards the friend and counsellor of Guatemoc, and assisted him in his defence of Tenoctitlan. Is this true, prisoner?'

'It is all true, general,' I answered.

'Good. You are now our prisoner, and had you a thousand lives, you have forfeited them all because of your treachery to your race and blood. Into the circumstances that led you to commit this horrible treason I cannot enter; the fact remains. You have slain many of the Spaniards and their allies; that is, being in a state of treason you have murdered them. Wingfield, your life is forfeit and I condemn you to die by hanging as a traitor and an apostate.'

'Then there is nothing more to be said,' I answered quietly, though a cold fear froze my blood.

'There is something,' answered Cortes. 'Though your crimes have been so many, I am ready to give you your life and freedom upon a condition. I am ready to do more, to find you a passage to Europe on the first occasion, where you may perchance escape the echoes of your infamy if God is good to you. The condition is this. We have reason to believe that you are acquainted with the hiding place of the gold of Montezuma, which was unlawfully stolen from us on the night of the *noche triste*. Nay, we know that this is so, for you were seen to go with the canoes that were laden with it. Choose now, apostate, between a shameful death and the revealing to us of the secret of this treasure.'

For a moment I wavered. On the one hand was the loss of honour with life and liberty and the hope of home, on the other a dreadful end. Then I remembered my oath and Otomie, and what she would think of me living or dead, if I did this thing, and I wavered no more.

'I know nothing of the treasure, general,' I answered coldly. 'Send me to my death.'

'You mean that you will say nothing of it, traitor. Think again. If you have sworn any oaths they are broken by God. The empire of the Aztecs is at an end, their king is my prisoner, their great city is a ruin. The true God has triumphed over these devils by my hand. Their wealth is my lawful spoil, and I must have it to pay my gallant comrades who cannot grow rich on desolation. Think again.'

'I know nothing of this treasure, general.'

'Yet memory sometimes wakens, traitor. I have said that you shall die if yours should fail you, and so you shall to be sure. But death is not always swift. There are means, doubtless you who have lived in Spain have heard of them,' and he arched his brows and glared at me meaningly, 'by which a man may die and yet live for many weeks. Now, loth as I am to do it, it seems that if your memory still sleeps, I must find some such means to rouse it—before you die.'

'I am in your power, general,' I answered. 'You call me traitor again and again. I am no traitor. I am a subject of the King of England, not of the King of Spain. I came hither following a villain who has wrought me and mine bitter wrong, one of your company named de Garcia or Sarceda. To find him and for other reasons I joined the Aztecs. They are conquered and I am your prisoner. At the least deal with me as a brave man deals with a fallen enemy. I know nothing of the treasure; kill me and make an end.'

'As a man I might wish to do this, Wingfield, but I am more than a man, I am the hand of the Church here in Anahuac. You have partaken with the worshippers of idols, you have seen your fellow Christians sacrificed and devoured by your brute comrades. For this alone you deserve to be tortured eternally, and doubtless that will be so after we have done with you. As for the hidalgo Don Sarceda, I know him only as a brave companion in arms, and certainly I shall not listen to tales told against him by a wandering apostate. It is, however, unlucky for you,' and here a gleam of light shot across the face of Cortes, 'that there should be any old feud between you, seeing that it is to his charge that I am about to confide you. Now for the last time I say choose. Will you reveal the hiding place of the treasure and go free, or will you be handed over to the care of Don Sarceda till such time as he shall find means to make you speak?'

Now a great faintness seized me, for I knew that I was condemned to be tortured, and that de Garcia was to be the torturer. What mercy had I to expect from his cruel heart when I, his deadliest foe, lay in his power to wreak his vengeance on? But still my will and my honour prevailed against my terrors, and I answered:

'I have told you, general, that I know nothing of this treasure. Do your worst, and may God forgive you for your cruelty.'

'Dare not to speak that holy Name, apostate and worshipper of idols, eater of human flesh. Let Sarceda be summoned.'

A messenger went out, and for a while there was silence. I caught Marina's glance and saw pity in her gentle eyes. But she could not help me here, for Cortes was mad because no gold had been found, and the clamour of the soldiers for reward had worn him out and brought him to this shameful remedy, he who was not cruel by nature. Still she strove to plead for me with him, whispering earnestly in his ear. For a while Cortes listened, then he pushed her from him roughly.

'Peace, Marina,' he said. 'What, shall I spare this English dog some pangs, when my command, and perchance my very life, hangs upon the finding of the gold? Nay, he knows well where it lies hid; you said it yourself when I would have hung him for a traitor, and certainly he was one of those whom the spy saw go out with it upon the lake. Our friend was with them also, but he came back no more; doubtless they murdered him. What is this man to you that you should plead for him? Cease to trouble me, Marina, am I not troubled enough already?' and Cortes put his hands to his face and remained lost in thought. As for Marina, she looked at me sadly and sighed as though to say, 'I have done my best,' and I thanked her with my eyes.

Presently there was a sound of footsteps and I looked up to see de Garcia standing before me. Time and hardship had touched him lightly, and the lines of silver in his curling hair and peaked beard did but add dignity to his noble presence. Indeed, when I looked at him in his dark Spanish beauty, his rich garments decked with chains of gold, as he bowed before Cortes hat in hand, I was fain to confess that I had never seen a more gallant cavalier, or one whose aspect gave the lie so wholly to the black heart within. But knowing him for what he was, my very blood quivered with hate at the sight of him, and when I thought of my own impotence and of the errand on which he had come, I ground my teeth and cursed the day that I was born. As for de Garcia, he greeted me with a little cruel smile, then spoke to Cortes.

'Your pleasure, general?'

'Greeting to you, comrade,' answered Cortes. 'You know this renegade?'

'But too well, general. Three times he has striven to murder me.'

'Well, you have escaped and it is your hour now, Sarceda. He says that he has a quarrel with you; what is it?'

De Garcia hesitated, stroking his peaked beard, then answered: 'I am loth to tell it because it is a tale of error for which I have often sorrowed and done penance. Yet I will speak for fear you should think worse of me than I deserve. This man has some cause to dislike me, since to be frank, when I was younger than I am to-day and given to the follies of youth, it chanced that in England I met his mother, a beautiful Spanish lady who by ill fortune was wedded to an Englishman, this man's father and a clown of clowns, who maltreated her. I will be short; the lady learned to love me and I worsted her husband in a duel. Hence this traitor's hate of me.'

I heard and thought that my heart must burst with fury. To all his wickedness and offences against me, de Garcia now had added slander of my dead mother's honour.

'You lie, murderer,' I gasped, tearing at the ropes that bound me.

'I must ask you to protect me from such insult, general,' de Garcia answered coldly. 'Were the prisoner worthy of my sword, I would ask further that his bonds should be loosed for a little space, but my honour would be tarnished for ever were I to fight with such as he.'

'Dare to speak thus once more to a gentleman of Spain,' said Cortes coldly, 'and, you heathen dog, your tongue shall be dragged from you with red-hot pincers. For you, Sarceda, I thank you for your confidence. If you have no worse crime than a love affair upon your soul, I think that our good chaplain Olmedo will frank you through the purgatorial fires. But we waste words and time. This man has the secret of the treasure of Guatemoc and of Montezuma. If Guatemoc and his nobles will not tell it, he at least may be forced to speak, for the torments that an Indian can endure without a groan will soon bring truth bubbling from the lips of this white heathen. Take him, Sarceda, and hearken, let him be your especial care. First let him suffer with the others, and afterwards, should he prove obdurate, alone. The method I leave to you. Should he confess, summon me.'

'Pardon me, general, but this is no task for an hidalgo of Spain. I have been more wont to pierce my enemies with the sword than to tear them with pincers,' said de Garcia, but as he spoke I saw a gleam of triumph shine in his black eyes, and heard the ring of triumph through the mock anger of his voice.

'I know it, comrade. But this must be done; though I hate it, it must be done, there is no other way. The gold is necessary to me— by the Mother of God! the knaves say that I have stolen it!—and I doubt these stubborn Indian dogs will ever speak, however great their agony. This man knows and I give him over to you because you are acquainted with his wickedness, and that knowledge will steel your heart against all pity. Spare not, comrade; remember that he must be forced to speak.'

'It is your command, Cortes, and I will obey it, though I love the task little; with one proviso, however, that you give me your warrant in writing.'

'It shall be made out at once,' answered the general. 'And now away with him.'

'Where to?'

'To the prison that he has left. All is ready and there he will find his comrades.'

Then a guard was summoned and I was dragged back to my own place, de Garcia saying as I went that he would be with me presently.

CHAPTER 29

De Garcia Speaks His Mind

At first I was not taken into the chamber that I had left, but placed in a little room opening out of it where the guard slept. Here I waited a while, bound hand and foot and watched by two soldiers with drawn swords. As I waited, torn by rage and fear, I heard the noise of hammering through the wall, followed by a sound of groans. At length the suspense came to an end; a door was opened, and two fierce Tlascalan Indians came through it and seized me by the hair and ears, dragging me thus into my own chamber.

'Poor devil!' I heard one of the Spanish soldiers say as I went. 'Apostate or no, I am sorry for him; this is bloody work.'

Then the door closed and I was in the place of torment. The room was darkened, for a cloth had been hung in front of the window bars, but its gloom was relieved by certain fires that burned in braziers. It was by the light of these fires chiefly that I saw the sight. On the floor of the chamber were placed three solid chairs, one of them empty. The other two were filled by none other than Guatemoc, Emperor of the Aztecs, and by his friend and mine the cacique of Tacuba. They were bound in the chairs, the burning braziers were placed at their feet, behind them stood a clerk with paper and an inkhorn, and around them Indians were busy at some dreadful task, directed to it by two Spanish soldiers. Near the third chair stood another Spaniard who as yet took no part in the play; it was de Garcia. As I looked, an Indian lifted one of the braziers and seizing the naked foot of the Tacuban prince, thrust it down upon the glowing coals. For a while there was silence, then the Tacuban broke into groans. Guatemoc turned his head towards him and spoke, and as he spoke I saw that his foot also was resting in the flames of a brazier. 'Why do you complain, friend,' he said, in a steady voice, 'when I keep silence? Am I then taking my pleasure in a bed? Follow me now as always, friend, and be silent beneath your sufferings.'

The clerk wrote down his words, for I heard the quill scratching on the paper, and as he wrote, Guatemoc turned his head and saw me. His face was grey with pain, still he spoke as a hundred times I had heard him speak at council, slowly and clearly. 'Alas! are you also here, my friend Teule?' he said; 'I hoped that they had spared you. See how these Spaniards keep faith. Malinche swore to treat me with all honour; behold how he honours me, with hot coals for my feet and pincers for my flesh. They think that we have buried treasure, Teule, and would wring its secret from us. You know that it is a lie. If we had treasure would we not give it gladly to our conquerors, the god-born sons of Quetzal? You know that there is nothing left except the ruins of our cities and the bones of our dead.'

Here he ceased suddenly, for the demon who tormented him struck him across the mouth saying, 'Silence, dog.'

But I understood, and I swore in my heart that I would die ere I revealed my brother's secret. This was the last triumph that Guatemoc could win, to keep his gold from the grasp of the greedy Spaniard, and that victory at least he should not lose through me. So I swore, and very soon my oath must be put to the test, for at a motion from de Garcia the Tlascalans seized me and bound me to the third chair.

Then he spoke into my ear in Castilian: 'Strange are the ways of Providence, Cousin Wingfield. You have hunted me across the world, and several times we have met, always to your sorrow. I thought I had you in the slave ship, I thought that the sharks had you in the water, but somehow you escaped me whom you came to hunt. When I knew it I grieved, but now I grieve no more, for I see that you were reserved for this moment. Cousin Wingfield, it shall go hard if you escape me this time, and yet I think that we shall spend some days together before we part. Now I will be courteous with you. You may have a choice of evils. How shall we begin? The resources at my command are not all that we could wish, alas! the Holy Office is not yet here with its unholy armoury, but still I have done my best. These fellows do not understand their art: hot coals are their only inspiration. I, you see, have several,' and he pointed to various instruments of torture. 'Which will you select?'

I made no answer, for I had determined that I would speak no word and utter no cry, do what they might with me.

'Let me think, let me think,' went on de Garcia, smoothing his beard. 'Ah, I have it. Here, slaves.'

Now I will not renew my own agonies, or awake the horror of any who may chance to read what I have written by describing what befell me after this. Suffice it to say that for two hours and more this devil, helped in his task by the Tlascalans, worked his wicked will upon me. One by one torments were administered to me with a skill and ingenuity that cannot often have been surpassed, and when at times I fainted I was recovered by cold water being dashed upon me and spirits poured down my throat. And yet, I say it with some pride, during those two dreadful hours I uttered no groan however great my sufferings, and spoke no word good or bad.

Nor was it only bodily pain that I must bear, for all this while my enemy mocked me with bitter words, which tormented my soul as his instruments and hot coals tormented my body. At length he paused exhausted, and cursed me for an obstinate pig of an Englishman, and at that moment Cortes entered the shambles and with him Marina.

'How goes it?' he said lightly, though his face turned pale at the sight of horror.

'The *cacique* of Tacuba has confessed that gold is buried in his garden, the other two have said nothing, general,' the clerk answered, glancing down his paper.

'Brave men, indeed!' I heard Cortes mutter to himself; then said aloud, 'Let the *cacique* be carried to-morrow to the garden of which he speaks, that he may point out the gold. As for the other two, cease tormenting them for this day. Perhaps they may find another mind before to-morrow. I trust so, for their own sakes I trust so!'

Then he drew to the corner of the room and consulted with Sarceda and the other torturers, leaving Marina face to face with Guatemoc and with me. For a while she stared at the prince as though in horror, then a strange light came into her beautiful eyes, and she spoke to him in a low voice, saying in the Aztec tongue:

'Do you remember how once you rejected me down yonder in Tobasco, Guatemoc, and what I told you then?—that I should grow great in spite of you? You see it has all come true and more than true, and you are brought to this. Are you not sorry, Guatemoc? I am sorry, though were I as some women are, perchance I might rejoice to see you thus.'

'Woman,' the prince answered in a thick voice, 'you have betrayed your country and you have brought me to shame and torment. Yes, had it not been for you, these things had never been. I am sorry, indeed I am sorry—that I did not kill you. For the rest, may your name be shameful for ever in the ears of honest men and your soul be everlastingly accursed, and may you yourself, even before you die, know the bitterness of dishonour and betrayal! Your words were fulfilled, and so shall mine be also.'

She heard and turned away trembling, and for a while was silent. Then her glance fell upon me and she began to weep.

'Alas! poor man,' she said; 'alas! my friend.'

'Weep not over me, Marina,' I answered, speaking in Aztec, 'for our tears are of no worth, but help me if you may.'

'Ah that I could!' she sobbed, and turning fled from the place, followed presently by Cortes.

Now the Spaniards came in again and removed Guatemoc and the *cacique* of Tacuba, carrying them in their arms, for they could not walk, and indeed the cacique was in a swoon.

'Farewell, Teule,' said Guatemoc as he passed me; 'you are indeed a true son of Quetzal and a gallant man. May the gods reward you in times to come for all that you have suffered for me and mine, since I cannot.'

Then he was borne out and these were the last words that I ever heard him utter.

Now I was left alone with the Tlascalans and de Garcia, who mocked me as before.

'A little tired, eh, friend Wingfield?' he said sneering. 'Well, the play is rough till you get used to it. A night's sleep will refresh you, and tomorrow you will be a new man. Perhaps you believe that I have done my worst. Fool, this is but a beginning. Also you think doubtless that your obstinacy angers me? Wrong again, my friend, I only pray that you may keep your lips sealed to the last. Gladly would I give my share of this hidden gold in payment for two more such days with you. I have still much to pay you back, and look you, I have found a way to do it. There are more ways of hurting a man than through his own flesh—for instance, when I wished to be revenged upon your father, I struck him through her whom he loved. Now I have touched you and you wonder what I mean. Well, I will tell you. Perhaps you may know an Aztec lady of royal blood who is named Otomie?'

'Otomie, what of her?' I cried, speaking for the first time, since fear for her stirred me more than all the torments I had borne.

'A triumph indeed; I have found a way to make you speak at last; why, then, to-morrow you will be full of words. Only this, Cousin Wingfield; Otomie, Montezuma's daughter, a very lovely woman by the way, is your wife according to the Indian customs. Well, I know all the story and—she is in my power. I will prove it to you, for she shall be brought here presently and then you can console each other. For listen, dog, to-morrow she will sit where you are sitting, and before your eyes she shall be dealt with as you have been dealt with. Ah! then you will talk fast enough, but perhaps it will be too late.'

And now for the first time I broke down and prayed for mercy even of my foe.

'Spare her,' I groaned; 'do what you will with me, but spare her! Surely you must have a heart, even you, for you are human. You can never do this thing, and Cortes would not suffer it.'

'As for Cortes,' he answered, 'he will know nothing of it—till it is done. I have my warrant that charges me to use every means in my power to force the truth from you. Torture has failed; this alone is left. And for the rest, you must read me ill. You know what it is to hate, for you hate me; multiply your hate by ten and you may find the sum of mine for you. I hate you for your blood, I hate you because you have your mother's eyes, but much more do I hate you for yourself, for did you not beat me, a gentleman of Spain, with a stick as though I were a hound? Shall I then shrink from such a deed when I can satisfy my hate by it? Also perhaps, though you are a brave man, at this moment you know what it is to fear, and are tasting of its agony. Now I will be open with you; Thomas Wingfield, I fear you. When first I saw you I feared you as I had reason to do, and that is why I tried to kill you, and as time has gone by I have feared you more and more, so much indeed, that at times I cannot rest because of a nameless terror that dogs me and which has to do with you. Because of you I fled from Spain, because of you I have played the coward in more frays than one. The luck has always been mine in this duel between us, and yet I tell you that even as you are, I fear you still. If I dared I would kill you at once, only then you would haunt me as your mother haunts me, and also I must answer for it to Cortes. Fear, Cousin Wingfield, is the father of cruelty, and mine makes me cruel to you. Living or dead, I know that you will triumph over me at the last, but it is my turn now, and while you breathe, or while one breathes who is dear to you, I will spend my life to bring you and them to shame and misery and death, as I brought your mother, my cousin, though she forced me to it to save myself. Why not? There is no forgiveness for me, I cannot undo the past. You came to take vengeance on me, and soon or late by you, or through you, it will be glutted, but till then I triumph, ay, even when I must sink to this butcher's work to do it,' and suddenly he turned and left the place.

Then weakness and suffering overcame me and I swooned away. When I awoke it was to find that my bonds had been loosed and that I lay on some sort of bed, while a woman bent over me, tending me with murmured words of pity and love. The night had fallen, but there was light in the chamber, and by it I saw that the woman was none

245

other than Otomie, no longer starved and wretched, but almost as lovely as before the days of siege and hunger.

'Otomie! you here!' I gasped through my wounded lips, for with my senses came the memory of de Garcia's threats.

'Yes, beloved, it is I,' she murmured; 'they have suffered that I nurse you, devils though they are. Oh! that I must see you thus and yet be helpless to avenge you,' and she burst into weeping.

'Hush,' I said, 'hush. Have we food?'

'In plenty. A woman brought it from Marina.'

'Give me to eat, Otomie.'

Now for a while she fed me and the deadly sickness passed from me, though my poor flesh burned with a hundred agonies.

'Listen, Otomie: have you seen de Garcia?'

'No, husband. Two days since I was separated from my sister Tecuichpo and the other ladies, but I have been well treated and have seen no Spaniard except the soldiers who led me here, telling me that you were sick. Alas! I knew not from what cause,' and again she began to weep.

'Still some have seen you and it is reported that you are my wife.'

'It is likely enough,' she answered, 'for it was known throughout the Aztec hosts, and such secrets cannot be kept. But why have they treated you thus? Because you fought against them?'

'Are we alone?' I asked.

'The guard is without, but there are none else in the chamber.'

'Then bend down your head and I will tell you,' and I told her all.

When I had done so she sprang up with flashing eyes and her hand pressed upon her breast, and said:

'Oh! if I loved you before, now I love you more if that is possible, who could suffer thus horribly and yet be faithful to the fallen and your oath. Blessed be the day when first I looked upon your face, O my husband, most true of men. But they who could do this—what of them? Still it is done with and I will nurse you back to health. Surely it is done with, or they had not suffered me to come to you?'

'Alas! Otomie, I must tell all—it is NOT done with,' and with faltering voice I went on with the tale, yes, and since I must, I told her for what purpose she had been brought here. She listened without a word, though her lips turned pale.

'Truly,' she said when I had done, 'these Teules far surpass the *pabas* of our people, for if the priests torture and sacrifice, it is to the gods and not for gold and secret hate. Now, husband, what is your counsel? Surely you have some counsel.'

'I have none that I dare offer, wife,' I groaned.

'You are timid as a girl who will not utter the love she burns to tell,' Otomie answered with a proud and bitter laugh. 'Well, I will speak it for you. It is in your mind that we must die to-night.'

'It is,' I said; 'death now, or shame and agony to-morrow and then death at last, that is our choice. Since God will not protect us, we must protect ourselves if we can find the means.'

'God! there is no God. At times I have doubted the gods of my people and turned to yours; now I renounce and reject Him. If there were a God of mercy such as you cling to, could He suffer that such things be? You are my god, husband, to you and for you I pray, and you alone. Let us have done now with pleading to those who are not, or who, if they live, are deaf to our cries and blind to our misery, and befriend ourselves. Yonder lies rope, that window has bars, very soon we can be beyond the sun and the cruelty of Teules, or sound asleep. But there is time yet; let us talk a while, they will scarcely begin their torments before the dawn, and ere dawn we shall be far.'

So we talked as well as my sufferings would allow. We talked of how we first had met, of how Otomie had been vowed to me as the wife of Tezcat, Soul of the World, of that day when we had lain side by side upon the stone of sacrifice, of our true marriage thereafter, of the siege of Tenoctitlan and the death of our first-born. Thus we talked till midnight was two hours gone. Then there came a silence.

'Husband,' said Otomie at last in a hushed and solemn voice, 'you are worn with suffering, and I am weary. It is time to do that which must be done. Sad is our fate, but at least rest is before us. I thank you, husband, for your gentleness, I thank you more for your faithfulness to my house and people. Shall I make ready for our last journey?'

'Make ready!' I answered.

Then she rose and soon was busy with the ropes. At length all was prepared and the moment of death was at hand.

'You must aid me, Otomie,' I said; 'I cannot walk by myself.'

She came and lifted me with her strong and tender arms, till I stood upon a stool beneath the window bars. There she placed the rope about my throat, then taking her stand by me she fitted the second rope upon her own. Now we kissed in solemn silence, for there was nothing more to say. Yet Otomie said something, asking:

'Of whom do you think in this moment, husband? Of me and of my dead child, or of that lady who lives far across the sea? Nay, I will not ask. I have been happy in my love, it is enough. Now love and life must end together, and it is well for me, but for you I grieve. Say, shall I thrust away the stool?'

'Yes, Otomie, since there is no hope but death. I cannot break my faith with Guatemoc, nor can I live to see you shamed and tortured.'

'Then kiss me first and for the last time.'

We kissed again and then, as she was in the very act of pushing the stool from beneath us, the door opened and shut, and a veiled woman stood before us, bearing a torch in one hand and a bundle in the other. She looked, and seeing us and our dreadful purpose, ran to us.

'What do you?' she cried, and I knew the voice for that of Marina. 'Are you then mad, Teule?'

'Who is this who knows you so well, husband, and will not even suffer that we die in peace?' asked Otomie.

'I am Marina,' answered the veiled woman, 'and I come to save you if I can.'

CHAPTER 30

The Escape

Now Otomie put the rope off her neck, and descending from the stool, stood before Marina.

'You are Marina,' she said coldly and proudly, 'and you come to save us, you who have brought ruin on the land that bore you, and have given thousands of her children to death, and shame, and torment. Now, if I had my way, I would have none of your salvation, nay, I would rather save myself as I was about to do.'

Thus Otomie spoke, and never had she looked more royal than in this moment, when she risked her last chance of life that she might pour out her scorn upon one whom she deemed a traitress, no, one who was a traitress, for had it not been for Marina's wit and aid, Cortes would never have conquered Anahuac. I trembled as I heard her angry words, for, all I suffered notwithstanding, life still seemed sweet to me, who, ten seconds ago, had stood upon the verge of death. Surely Marina would depart and leave us to our doom. But it was not so. Indeed, she shrank and trembled before Otomie's contempt. They were a strange contrast in their different loveliness as they stood face to face in the torture den, and it was strange also to see the spirit of the lady of royal blood, threatened as she was with a shameful death, or still more shameful life, triumph over the Indian girl whom to-day fortune had set as far above her as the stars.

'Say, royal lady,' asked Marina in her gentle voice, 'for what cause did you, if tales are true, lie by the side of yonder white man upon the stone of sacrifice?'

'Because I love him, Marina.'

'And for this same cause have I, Marina, laid my honour upon a different altar, for this same cause I have striven against the children of my people, because I love another such as he. It is for love of Cortes that I have aided Cortes, therefore despise me not, but let your love plead for mine, seeing that, to us women, love is all. I have sinned, I know, but doubtless in its season my sin shall find a fitting punishment.'

'It had need be sharp,' answered Otomie. 'My love has harmed none, see before you but one grain of the countless harvest of your own. In yonder chair Guatemoc your king was this day tortured by your master Cortes, who swore to treat him with all honour. By his side sat Teule, my husband and your friend; him Cortes gave over to has private enemy, de Garcia, whom you name Sarceda. See how he has left him. Nay, do not shudder, gentle lady; look now at his wounds! Consider to what a pass we are driven when you find us about to die thus like dogs, he, my husband, that he may not live to see me handled as he has been, and I with him, because a princess of the Otomie and of Montezuma's blood cannot submit to such a shame while death has one door through which to creep. It is but a single grain of your harvest, outcast and traitress, the harvest of misery and death that is stored yonder in the ruins of Tenoctitlan. Had I my will, I tell you that I had sooner die a score of times than take help from a hand so stained with the blood of my people and of yours—I—'

'Oh! cease, lady, cease,' groaned Marina, covering her eyes with her hand, as though the sight of Otomie were dreadful to her. 'What is done is done; do not add to my remorse. What did you say, that you, the lady Otomie, were brought here to be tortured?'

'Even so, and before my husband's eyes. Why should Montezuma's daughter and the princess of the Otomie escape the fate of the emperor of the Aztecs? If her womanhood does not protect her, has she anything to hope of her lost rank?'

'Cortes knows nothing of this, I swear it,' said Marina. 'To the rest he has been driven by the clamour of the soldiers, who taunt him with stealing treasure that he has never found. But of this last wickedness he is innocent.'

'Then let him ask his tool Sarceda of it.'

'As for Sarceda, I promise you, princess, that if I can I will avenge this threat upon him. But time is short, I am come here with the knowledge of Cortes, to see if I can win the secret of the treasure from Teule, your husband, and for my friendship's sake I am about to betray my trust and help him and you to fly. Do you refuse my aid?'

Otomie said nothing, but I spoke for the first time.

'Nay, Marina, I have no love for this thief's fate if I can escape it, but how is it to be done?'

'The chance is poor enough, Teule, but I bethought me that once out of this prison you might slip away disguised. Few will be stirring at dawn, and of them the most will not be keen to notice men or things. See, I have brought you the dress of a Spanish soldier; your skin is dark, and in the half light you might pass as one; and for the princess your wife, I have brought another dress, indeed I am ashamed to offer it, but it is the only one that will not be noted at this hour; also, Teule, I bring you a sword, that which was taken from you, though I think that once it had another owner.'

Now while she spoke Marina undid her bundle, and there in it were the dresses and the sword, the same that I had taken from the Spaniard Diaz in the massacre of the *noche triste*. First she drew out the woman's robe and handed it to Otomie, and I saw that it was such a robe as among the Indians is worn by the women who follow camps, a robe with red and yellow in it. Otomie saw it also and drew back.

'Surely, girl, you have brought a garment of your own in error,' she said quietly, but in such a fashion as showed more of the savage heart that is native to her race than she often suffered to be seen; 'at the least I cannot wear such robes.'

'It seems that I must bear too much,' answered Marina, growing wroth at last, and striving to keep back the tears that started to her eyes. 'I will away and leave you;' and she began to roll up her bundle.

'Forgive her, Marina,' I said hastily, for the desire to escape grew on me every minute; 'sorrow has set an edge upon her tongue.' Then turning to Otomie I added, 'I pray you be more gentle, wife, for my sake if not for your own. Marina is our only hope.'

'Would that she had left us to die in peace, husband. Well, so be it, for your sake I will put on these garments of a drab. But how shall we escape out of this place and the camp? Will the door be opened to us, and the guards removed, and if we pass them, can you walk, husband?'

'The doors will not be opened, lady,' said Marina, 'for those wait without, who will see that they are locked when I have passed them. But there will be nothing to fear from the guard, trust to me for it. See, the bars of this window are but of wood, that sword will soon sever them, and if you are seen you must play the part of a drunken soldier being guided to his quarters by a woman. For the rest I know nothing, save that I run great risk for your sakes, since if it is discovered that I have aided you, then I shall find it hard to soften the rage of Cortes, who, the war being won,' and she sighed, 'does not need me now so much as once he did.'

'I can make shift to hop on my right foot,' I said, 'and for the rest we must trust to fortune. It can give us no worse gifts than those we have already.'

'So be it, Teule, and now farewell, for I dare stay no longer. I can do nothing more. May your good star shine on you and lead you hence in safety; and Teule, if we never meet again, I pray you think of me kindly, for there are many in the world who will do otherwise in the days to come.'

'Farewell, Marina,' I said, and she was gone.

We heard the doors close behind her, and the distant voices of those who bore her litter, then all was silence. Otomie listened at the window for a while, but the guards seemed to be gone, where or why I do not know to this hour, and the only sound was that of distant revelry from the camp.

'And now to the work,' I said to Otomie.

'As you wish, husband, but I fear it will be profitless. I do not trust that woman. Faithless in all, without doubt she betrays us. Still at the worst you have the sword, and can use it.'

'It matters little,' I answered. 'Our plight cannot be worse than it is now; life has no greater evils than torment and death, and they are with us already.'

Then I sat upon the stool, and my arms being left sound and strong, I hacked with the sharp sword at the wooden bars of the window, severing them one by one till there was a space big enough for us to creep through. This being done and no one having appeared to disturb us, Otomie clad me in the clothes of a Spanish soldier which Marina had brought, for I could not dress myself. What I suffered in the donning of those garments, and more especially in the pulling of the long boot on to my burnt foot, can never be told, but more than once I stopped, pondering whether it would not be better to die rather than to endure such agonies. At last it was done, and Otomie must put on the red and yellow robe, a garb of shame such as many honest Indian women would die sooner than be seen in, and I think that as she did this, her agony was greater than mine, though of another sort, for to her proud heart, that dress was a very shirt of Nessus. Presently she was clad, and minced before me with savage mockery, saying:

'Prithee, soldier, do I look my part?'

'A peace to such fooling,' I answered; 'our lives are at stake, what does it matter how we disguise ourselves?'

'It matters much, husband, but how can you understand, who are a man and a foreigner? Now I will clamber through the window, and you must follow me if you can, if not I will return to you and we will end this masquerade.'

Then she passed through the hole swiftly, for Otomie was agile and strong as an ocelot, and mounting the stool I made shift to follow her as well as my hurts would allow. In the end I was able to throw myself upon the sill of the window, and there I was stretched out like a dead cat till she drew me across it, and I fell with her to the ground on the further side, and lay groaning. She lifted me to my feet, or rather to my foot, for I could use but one of them, and we stared round us. No one was to be seen, and the sound of revelry had died away, for the crest of Popo was already red with the sunlight and the dawn grew in the valley.

'Where to?' I said.

Now Otomie had been allowed to walk in the camp with her sister, the wife of Guatemoc, and other Aztec ladies, and she had this gift in common with most Indians, that where she had once passed there she could pass again, even in the darkest night.

'To the south gate,' she whispered; 'perhaps it is unguarded now that the war is done, at the least I know the road thither.'

So we started, I leaning on her shoulder and hopping on my right foot, and thus very painfully we traversed some three hundred yards meeting nobody. But now our good luck failed us, for passing round the corner of some buildings, we came face to face with three soldiers returning to their huts from a midnight revel, and with them some native servants.

'Whom have we here?' said the first of these. 'Your name, comrade?'

'Good-night, brother, good-night,' I answered in Spanish, speaking with the thick voice of drunkenness.

'Good morning, you mean,' he said, for the dawn was breaking. 'Your name. I don't know your face, though it seems that you have been in the wars,' and he laughed.

'You mustn't ask a comrade his name,' I said solemnly and swinging to and fro. 'The captain might send for me and he's a temperate man. Your arm, girl; it is time to go to sleep, the sun sets.'

They laughed, but one of them addressed Otomie, saying:

'Leave the sot, my pretty, and come and walk with us,' and he caught her by the arm. But she turned on him with so fierce a look that he let her go again astonished, and we staggered on till the corner of another house hid us from their view. Here I sank to the ground overcome with pain, for while the soldiers were in sight, I was obliged to use my wounded foot lest they should suspect. But Otomie pulled me up, saying:

'Alas! beloved, we must pass on or perish.'

253

I rose groaning, and by what efforts I reached the south gate I cannot describe, though I thought that I must die before I came there. At last it was before us, and as chance would have it, the Spanish guard were asleep in the guardhouse. Three Tlascalans only were crouched over a little fire, their *zerapes* or blankets about their heads, for the dawn was chilly.

'Open the gates, dogs!' I said in a proud voice.

Seeing a Spanish soldier one of them rose to obey, then paused and said:

'Why, and by whose orders?'

I could not see the man's face because of the blanket, but his voice sounded familiar to me and I grew afraid. Still I must speak.

'Why?—because I am drunk and wish to lie without till I grow sober. By whose orders? By mine, I am an officer of the day, and if you disobey I'll have you flogged till you never ask another question.'

'Shall I call the Teules within?' said the man sulkily to his companion.

'No,' he answered; 'the lord Sarceda is weary and gave orders that he should not be awakened without good cause. Keep them in or let them through as you will, but do not wake him.'

I trembled in every limb; de Garcia was in the guardhouse! What if he awoke, what if he came out and saw me? More—now I guessed whose voice it was that I knew again; it was that of one of those Tlascalans who had aided in tormenting me. What if he should see my face? He could scarcely fail to know that on which he had left his mark so recently. I was dumb with fear and could say nothing, and had it not been for the wit of Otomie, there my story would have ended. But now she played her part and played it well, plying the man with the coarse raillery of the camp, till at length she put him in a good humour, and he opened the gate, bidding her begone and me with her. Already we had passed the gate when a sudden faintness seized me, and I stumbled and fell, rolling over on to my back as I touched the earth.

'Up, friend, up!' said Otomie, with a harsh laugh. 'If you must sleep, wait till you find some friendly bush,' and she dragged at me to lift me. The Tlascalan, still laughing, came forward to help her, and between them I gained my feet again, but as I rose, my cap, which fitted me but ill, fell off. He picked it up and gave it to me and our eyes met, my face being somewhat in the shadow. Next instant I was hobbling on, but looking back, I saw the Tlascalan staring after us with a puzzled air, like that of a man who is not sure of the witness of his senses.

'He knows me,' I said to Otomie, 'and presently when he has found his wits, he will follow us.'

'On, on!' answered Otomie; 'round yonder corner are aloe bushes where we may hide.'

'I am spent, I can no more;' and again I began to fall.

Then Otomie caught me as I fell, and of a sudden she put out her strength, and lifting me from the ground, as a mother lifts her child, staggered forward holding me to her breast. For fifty paces or more she carried me thus, love and despair giving her strength, till at last we reached the edge of the aloe plants and there we sank together to the earth. I cast my eyes back over the path which we had travelled. Round the corner came the Tlascalan, a spiked club in his hand, seeking us to solve his doubts.

'It is finished,' I gasped; 'the man comes.'

For answer Otomie drew my sword from its scabbard and hid it in the grass. 'Now feign sleep,' she said; 'it is our last chance.'

I cast my arm over my face and pretended to be asleep. Presently I heard the sound of a man passing through the bushes, and the Tlascalan stood over me.

'What would you?' asked Otomie. 'Can you not see that he sleeps? Let him sleep.'

'I must look on his face first, woman,' he answered, dragging aside my arm. 'By the gods, I thought so! This is that Teule whom we dealt with yesterday and who escapes.'

'You are mad,' she said laughing. 'He has escaped from nowhere, save from a brawl and a drinking bout.'

'You lie, woman, or if you do not lie, you know nothing. This man has the secret of Montezuma's treasure, and is worth a king's ransom,' and he lifted his club.

'And yet you wish to slay him! Well, I know nothing of him. Take him back whence he came. He is but a drunken sot and I shall be well rid of him.'

'Well said. It would be foolish to kill him, but by bearing him alive to the lord Sarceda, I shall win honour and reward. Come, help me.'

'Help yourself,' she answered sullenly. 'But first search his pouch; there may be some trifle there which we can divide.'

'Well said, again,' he answered, and kneeling down he bent over me and began to fumble at the fastenings of the pouch.

Otomie was behind him. I saw her face change and a terrible light came into her eyes, such a light as shines in the eyes of the priest at sacrifice. Quick as thought she drew the sword from the grass and smote with all her strength upon the man's bent neck. Down he fell, making no sound, and she also fell beside him. In a moment she was on her feet again, staring at him wildly—the naked sword in her hand.

'Up,' she said, 'before others come to seek him. Nay, you must.'

Now, again we were struggling forward through the bushes, my mind filled with a great wonder that grew slowly to a whirling nothingness. For a while it seemed to me as though I were lost in an evil dream and walking on red hot irons in my dream. Then came a vision of armed men with lifted spears, and of Otomie running towards them with outstretched arms.

I knew no more.

CHAPTER 31

Otomie Pleads With Her People

When I awoke it was to find myself in a cave, where the light shone very dimly. Otomie leant over me, and not far away a man was cooking a pot over a fire made of dry aloe leaves.

'Where am I and what has happened?' I asked.

'You are safe, beloved,' she answered, 'at least for awhile. When you have eaten I will tell you more.'

She brought me broth and food and I ate eagerly, and when I was satisfied she spoke.

'You remember how the Tlascalan followed us and how—I was rid of him?'

'I remember, Otomie, though how you found strength to kill him I do not understand.'

'Love and despair gave it to me, and I pray that I may never have such another need. Do not speak of it, husband, for this is more horrible to me than all that has been before. One thing comforts me, however; I did not kill him, the sword twisted in my hand and I believe that he was but stunned. Then we fled a little way, and looking back I saw that two other Tlascalans, companions of the senseless man, were following us and him. Presently, they came up to where he lay and stared at him. Then they started on our tracks, running hard, and very soon they must have caught us, for now you could scarcely stir, your mind was gone, and I had no more strength to carry you. Still we stumbled on till presently, when the pursuers were within fifty paces of us, I saw armed men, eight of them, rushing at us from the bushes. They were of my own people, the Otomies, soldiers that had served under you, who watched the Spanish camp, and seeing a Spaniard alone they came to slay him. They very nearly did so indeed, for at first I was so breathless that I could scarcely speak, but at last in few words I made shift to declare my name and rank, and your sad plight. By now the two Tlascalans were upon us, and I called to the men of the Otomie to protect us, and falling on the Tlascalans before they knew that enemies were there, they killed one of them and took the other prisoner. Then they made a litter, and placing you on it, bore you without rest twenty leagues into the mountains, till they reached this secret hiding place, and here you have lain three days and nights. The Teules have searched for you far and wide, but they have searched in vain. Only yesterday two of them with ten Tlascalans, passed within a hundred paces of this cave and I had much ado to prevent our people from attacking them. Now they are gone whence they came, and I think that we are safe for a time. Soon you will be better and we can go hence.'

'Where can we go to, Otomie? We are birds without a nest.'

'We must seek shelter in the City of Pines, or fly across the water; there is no other choice, husband.'

'We cannot try the sea, Otomie, for all the ships that come here are Spanish, and I do not know how they will greet us in the City of Pines now that our cause is lost, and with it so many thousands of their warriors.'

'We must take the risk, husband. There are still true hearts in Ana-huac, who will stand by us in our sorrow and their own. At the least we have escaped from greater dangers. Now let me dress your wounds and rest awhile.'

So for three more days I lay in the cave of the mountains and Otomie tended me, and at the end of that time my state was such that I could travel in a litter, though for some weeks I was unable to set foot to the ground. On the fourth day we started by night, and I was carried on men's shoulders till at length we passed up the gorge that leads to the City of Pines. Here we were stopped by sentries to whom Otomie told our tale, bidding some of them go forward and repeat it to the captains of the city. We followed the messengers slowly, for my bearers were weary, and came to the gates of the beautiful town just as the red rays of sunset struck upon the snowy pinnacle of Xaca that towers behind it, turning her cap of smoke to a sullen red, like that of molten iron.

The news of our coming had spread about, and here and there knots of people were gathered to watch us pass. For the most part they stood silent, but now and again some woman whose husband or son had perished in the siege, would hiss a curse at us.

Alas! how different was our state this day to what it had been when not a year before we entered the City of Pines for the first time.

Then we were escorted by an army ten thousand strong, then musicians had sung before us and our path was strewn with flowers. And now! Now we came two fugitives from the vengeance of the Teules, I borne in a litter by four tired soldiers, while Otomie, the princess of this people, still clad in her wanton's robe, at which the women mocked, for she had been able to come by no other, tramped at my side, since there were none to carry her, and the inhabitants of the place cursed us as the authors of their woes. Nor did we know if they would stop at words.

At length we crossed the square beneath the shadow of the *teocalli*, and reached the ancient and sculptured palace as the light failed, and the smoke on Xaca, the holy hill, began to glow with the fire in its heart. Here small preparation had been made to receive us, and that night we supped by the light of a torch upon tortillas or meal cakes and water, like the humblest in the land. Then we crept to our rest, and as I lay awake because of the pain of my hurts, I heard Otomie, who thought that I slept, break into low sobbing at my side. Her proud spirit was humbled at last, and she, whom I had never known to weep except once, when our firstborn died in the siege, wept bitterly.

'Why do you sorrow thus, Otomie?' I asked at length.

'I did not know that you were awake, husband,' she sobbed in answer, 'or I would have checked my grief. Husband, I sorrow over all that has befallen us and my people—also, though these are but little things, because you are brought low and treated as a man of no estate, and of the cold comfort that we find here.'

'You have cause, wife,' I answered. 'Say, what will these Otomies do with us—kill us, or give us up to the Teules?'

'I do not know; to-morrow we shall learn, but for my part I will not be surrendered living.'

'Nor I, wife. Death is better than the tender mercies of Cortes and his minister, de Garcia. Is there any hope?'

'Yes, there is hope, beloved. Now the Otomie are cast down and they remember that we led the flower of their land to death. But they are brave and generous at heart, and if I can touch them there, all may yet be well. Weariness, pain and memory make us weak, who should be full of courage, having escaped so many ills. Sleep, my husband, and leave me to think. All shall yet go well, for even misfortune has an end.'

So I slept, and woke in the morning somewhat refreshed and with a happier mind, for who is there that is not bolder when the light shines on him and he is renewed by rest?

259

When I opened my eyes the sun was already high, but Otomie had risen with the dawn and she had not been idle during those three hours. For one thing she had contrived to obtain food and fresh raiment more befitting to our rank than the rags in which we were clothed. Also she had brought together certain men of condition who were friendly and loyal to her in misfortune, and these she sent about the city, letting it be known that she would address the people at mid-day from the steps of the palace, for as Otomie knew well, the heartstrings of a crowd are touched more easily than those of cold and ancient counsellors.

'Will they come to listen?' I asked.

'Have no fear,' she answered. 'The desire to look upon us who have survived the siege, and to know the truth of what has happened, will bring them. Moreover, some will be there seeking vengeance on us.'

Otomie was right, for as the morning drew on towards mid-day, I saw the dwellers in the City of Pines gathering in thousands, till the space between the steps of the palace and the face of the pyramid was black with them. Now Otomie combed her curling hair and placed flowers in it, and set a gleaming feather cloak about her shoulders, so that it hung down over her white robes, and on her breast that splendid necklace of emeralds which Guatemoc had given to me in the treasure chamber, and which she had preserved safely through all our evil fortune, and a golden girdle about her waist. In her hand also she took a little sceptre of ebony tipped with gold, that was in the palace, with other ornaments and emblems of rank, and thus attired, though she was worn with travel and suffering, and grief had dimmed her beauty for a while, she seemed the queenliest woman that my eyes have seen. Next she caused me to be laid upon my rude litter, and when the hour of noon was come, she commanded those soldiers who had borne me across the mountains to carry me by her side. Thus we issued from the wide doorway of the palace and took our stand upon the platform at the head of the steps. As we came a great cry rose from the thousands of the people, a fierce cry like that of wild beasts howling for their prey. Higher and higher it rose, a sound to strike terror into the bravest heart, and by degrees I caught its purport.

'Kill them!' said the cry. 'Give the liars to the Teules.'

Otomie stepped forward to the edge of the platform, and lifting the ebony sceptre she stood silent, the sunlight beating on her lovely face and form. But the multitude screamed a thousand taunts and threats at us, and still the tumult grew. Once they rushed towards her as though to tear her to pieces, but fell back at the last stair, as a wave falls from a rock, and once a spear was thrown that passed between her neck and shoulder.

Now the soldiers who had carried me, making certain that our death was at hand, and having no wish to share it, set my litter down upon the stones and slipped back into the palace, but all this while Otomie never so much as moved, no, not even when the spear hissed past her. She stood before them stately and scornful, a very queen among women, and little by little the majesty of her presence and the greatness of her courage hushed them to silence. When there was quiet at length, she spoke in a clear voice that carried far.

'Am I among my own people of the Otomie?' she asked bitterly, 'or have we lost our path and wandered perchance among some savage Tlascalan tribe? Listen, people of the Otomie. I have but one voice and none can reason with a multitude. Choose you a tongue to speak for you, and let him set out the desire of your hearts.'

Now the tumult began again, for some shouted one name and some another, but in the end a priest and noble named Maxtla stepped forward, a man of great power among the Otomie, who, above all had favoured an alliance with the Spaniards and opposed the sending of an army to aid Guatemoc in the defence of Tenoctitlan. Nor did he come alone, for with him were four chiefs, whom by their dress I knew to be Tlascalans and envoys from Cortes. Then my heart sank, for it was not difficult to guess the object of their coming.

'Speak on, Maxtla,' said Otomie, 'for we must hear what there is for us to answer, and you, people of the Otomie, I pray you keep silence, that you may judge between us when there is an end of talking.'

Now a great silence fell upon the multitude, who pressed together like sheep in a pen, and strained their ears to catch the words of Maxtla.

'My speech with you, princess, and the Teule your outlawed husband, shall be short and sharp,' he began roughly. 'A while hence you came hither to seek an army to aid Cuitlahua, Emperor of the Aztecs, in his struggle with the Teules, the sons of Quetzal. That army was given you, against the wishes of many of us, for you won over the council by the honey of your words, and we who urged caution, or even an alliance with the white men, the children of god, were overruled. You went hence, and twenty thousand men, the flower of our people, followed you to Tenoctitlan. Where are they now? I will tell you. Some two hundred of them have crept back home, the rest fly to and fro through the air in the gizzards of the *zaphilotes*, or crouch on the earth in the bellies of jackals. Death has them all, and you led them to their deaths. Is it then much that we should seek the lives of you two in payment for those of twenty thousand of our sons, our husbands, and our fathers? But we do not even ask this. Here beside me stand ambassadors from Malinche, the captain of the Teules, who reached our city but an hour ago. This is the demand that they bring from Malinche, and in his own words:

"'Deliver back to me Otomie, the daughter of Montezuma, and the renegade her paramour, who is known as Teule, and who has fled from the justice due to his crimes, and it shall be well with you, people of the Otomie. Hide them or refuse to deliver them, and the fate of the City of Pines shall be as the fate of Tenoctitlan, queen of the valley. Choose then between my love and my wrath, people of the Otomie. If you obey, the past shall be forgiven and my yoke will be light upon you; if you refuse, your city shall be stamped flat and your very name wiped out of the records of the world.'"

'Say, messengers of Malinche, are not these the words of Malinche?'

'They are his very words, Maxtla,' said the spokesman of the embassy.

Now again there was a tumult among the people, and voices cried, 'Give them up, give them to Malinche as a peace offering.' Otomie stood forward to speak and it died away, for all desired to hear her words. Then she spoke:

'It seems, people of the Otomie, that I am on my trial before my own vassals, and my husband with me. Well, I will plead our cause as well as a woman may, and having the power, you shall judge between us and Maxtla and his allies, Malinche and the Tlascalans. What is our offence? It is that we came hither by the command of Cuitlahua to seek your aid in his war with the Teules. What did I tell you then? I told you that if the people of Anahuac would not stand together against the white men, they must be broken one by one like the sticks of an unbound faggot, and cast into the flames. Did I speak lies? Nay, I spoke truth, for through the treason of her tribes, and chiefly through the treason of the Tlascalans, Anahuac is fallen, and Tenoctitlan is a ruin sown with dead like a field with corn.'

'It is true,' cried a voice.

'Yes, people of the Otomie, it is true, but I say that had all the warriors of the nations of Anahuac played the part that your sons played, the tale had run otherwise. They are dead, and because of their death you would deliver us to our foes and yours, but I for one do not mourn them, though among their number are many of my kin. Nay, be not wroth, but listen. It is better that they should lie dead in honour, having earned for themselves a wreath of fame, and an immortal dwelling in the Houses of the Sun, than that they should live to be slaves, which it seems is your desire, people of the Otomie. There is no false word in what I said to you. Now the sticks that Malinche has used to beat out the brains of Guatemoc shall be broken and burnt to cook the pot of the Teules. Already these false children are his slaves. Have you not heard his command, that the tribes his allies shall labour in the quarries and the streets till the glorious city which he has burned rises afresh upon the face of the waters? Will you not hasten to take your share in the work, people of the Otomie, the work that knows no rest and no reward except the lash of the overseer and the curse of the Teule? Surely you will hasten, people of the mountains! Your hands are shaped to the spade and the trowel, not to the bow and the spear, and it will be sweeter to toil to do the will and swell the wealth of Malinche in the sun of the valley or the shadow of the mine, than to bide here free upon your hills where as yet no foe has set his foot!'

Again she paused, and a murmur of doubt and unrest went through the thousands who listened. Maxtla stepped forward and would have spoken, but the people shouted him down, crying: 'Otomie, Otomie! Let us hear the words of Otomie.'

'I thank you, my people,' she said, 'for I have still much to tell you. Our crime is then, that we drew an army after us to fight against the Teules. And how did we draw this army? Did I command you to muster your array? Nay, I set out my case and I said "Now choose." You chose, and of your own free will you despatched those glorious companies that now are dead. My crime is therefore that you chose wrongly as you say, but as I still hold, most rightly, and because of this crime I and my husband are to be given as a peace offering to the Teules. Listen: let me tell you something of those wars in which we have fought before you give us to the Teules and our mouths are silent for ever. Where shall I begin? I know not. Stay, I bore a child—had he lived he would have been your prince to-day. That child I saw starve to death before my eyes, inch by inch and day by day I saw him starve. But it is nothing; who am I that I should complain because I have lost my son, when so many of your sons are dead and their blood is required at my hands? Listen again:' and she went on to tell in burning words of the horrors of the siege, of the cruelties of the Spaniards, and of the bravery of the men of the Otomie whom I had commanded. For a full hour she spoke thus, while all that vast audience hung upon her words. Also she told of the part that I played in the struggle, and of the deeds which I had done, and now and again some soldier in the crowd who served under me, and who had escaped the famine and the massacre, cried out:

'It is true; we saw it with our eyes.'

'And so,' she said, 'at last it was finished, at last Tenoctitlan was a ruin and my cousin and my king, the glorious Guatemoc, lay a prisoner in the hands of Malinche, and with him my husband Teule, my sister, I myself, and many another. Malinche swore that he would treat Guatemoc and his following with all honour. Do you know how he treated him? Within a few days Guatemoc our king was seated in the chair of torment, while slaves burned him with hot irons to cause him to declare the hiding place of the treasure of Montezuma! Ay, you may well cry "Shame upon him," you shall cry it yet more loudly before I have done, for know that Guatemoc did not suffer alone, one lies there who suffered with him and spoke no word, and I also, your princess, was doomed to torment. We escaped when death was at our door, for I told my husband that the people of the Otomie had true hearts, and would shelter us in our sorrow, and for his sake I, Otomie, disguised myself in the robe of a wanton and fled with him hither. Could I have known what I should live to see and hear, could I have dreamed that you would receive us thus, I had died a hundred deaths before I came to stand and plead for pity at your hands.

'Oh! my people, my people, I beseech of you, make no terms with the false Teule, but remain bold and free. Your necks are not fitted to the yoke of the slave, your sons and daughters are of too high a blood to serve the foreigner in his needs and pleasures. Defy Malinche. Some of our race are dead, but many thousands remain. Here in your mountain nest you can beat back every Teule in Anahuac, as in bygone years the false Tlascalans beat back the Aztecs. Then the Tlascalans were free, now they are a race of serfs. Say, will you share their serfdom? My people, my people, think not that I plead for myself, or even for the husband who is more dear to me than aught save honour. Do you indeed dream that we will suffer you to hand us living to these dogs of Tlascalans, whom Malinche insults you by sending as his messengers? Look,' and she walked to where the spear that had been hurled at her lay upon the pavement and lifted it, 'here is a means of death that some friend has sent us, and if you will not listen to my pleading you shall see it used before your eyes. Then, if you will, you may send our bodies to Malinche as a peace offering. But for your own sakes I plead with you. Defy Malinche, and if you must die at last, die as free men and not as the slaves of the Teule. Behold now his tender mercies, and see the lot that shall be yours if you take another counsel, the counsel of Maxtla;' and coming to the litter on which I lay, swiftly Otomie rent my robes from me leaving me almost naked to the waist, and unwound the bandages from my wounded limb, then lifted me up so that I rested upon my sound foot.

'Look!' she cried in a piercing voice, and pointing to the scars and unhealed wounds upon my face and leg; 'look on the work of the Teule and the Tlascalan, see how the foe is dealt with who surrenders to them. Yield if you will, desert us if you will, but I say that then your own bodies shall be marked in a like fashion, till not an ounce of gold is left that can minister to the greed of the Teule, or a man or a maiden who can labour to satisfy his indolence.'

Then she ceased, and letting me sink gently to the ground, for I could not stand alone, she stood over me, the spear in her hand, as though waiting to plunge it to my heart should the people still demand our surrender to the messengers of Cortes.

For one instant there was silence, then of a sudden the clamour and the tumult broke out again ten times more furiously than at first. But it was no longer aimed at us. Otomie had conquered. Her noble words, her beauty, the tale of our sorrows and the sight of my torments, had done their work, and the heart of the people was filled with fury against the Teules who had destroyed their army, and the Tlascalans that had aided them. Never did the wit and eloquence of a woman cause a swifter change. They screamed and tore their robes and shook their weapons in the air. Maxtla strove to speak, but they pulled him down and presently he was flying for his life. Then they turned upon the Tlascalan envoys and beat them with sticks, crying:

'This is our answer to Malinche. Run, you dogs, and take it!' till they were driven from the town.

Now at length the turmoil ceased, and some of the great chiefs came forward and, kissing the hand of Otomie, said:

'Princess, we your children will guard you to the death, for you have put another heart into us. You are right; it is better to die free than to live as slaves.'

'See, my husband,' said Otomie, 'I was not mistaken when I told you that my people were loyal and true. But now we must make ready for war, for they have gone too far to turn back, and when this tidings comes to the ears of Malinche he will be like a puma robbed of her young. Now, let us rest, I am very weary.'

'Otomie,' I answered, 'there has lived no greater woman than you upon this earth.'

'I cannot tell, husband,' she said, smiling; 'if I have won your praise and safety, it is enough for me.'

CHAPTER 32

The End of Guatemoc

Now for a while we dwelt in quiet at the City of Pines, and by slow degrees and with much suffering I recovered from the wounds that the cruel hand of de Garcia had inflicted upon me. But we knew that this peace could not last, and the people of the Otomie knew it also, for had they not scourged the envoys of Malinche out of the gates of their city? Many of them were now sorry that this had been done, but it was done, and they must reap as they had sown.

So they made ready for war, and Otomie was the president of their councils, in which I shared. At length came news that a force of fifty Spaniards with five thousand Tlascalan allies were advancing on the city to destroy us. Then I took command of the tribesmen of the Otomie—there were ten thousand or more of them, all well-armed after their own fashion—and advanced out of the city till I was two-thirds of the way down the gorge which leads to it. But I did not bring all my army down this gorge, since there was no room for them to fight there, and I had another plan. I sent some seven thousand men round the mountains, of which the secret paths were well known to them, bidding them climb to the crest of the precipices that bordered either side of the gorge, and there, at certain places where the cliff is sheer and more than one thousand feet in height, to make a great provision of stones.

The rest of my army, excepting five hundred whom I kept with me, I armed with bows and throwing spears, and stationed them in ambush in convenient places where the sides of the cliff were broken, and in such fashion that rocks from above could not be rolled on them. Then I sent trusty men as spies to warn me of the approach of the Spaniards, and others whose mission it was to offer themselves to them as guides.

Now I thought my plan good, and everything looked well, and yet it missed failure but by a very little. For Maxtla, our enemy and the friend of the Spaniards, was in my camp—indeed, I had brought him with me that I might watch him—and he had not been idle.

For when the Spaniards were half a day's march from the mouth of the defile, one of those men whom I had told off to watch their advance, came to me and made it known that Maxtla had bribed him to go to the leader of the Spaniards and disclose to him the plan of the ambuscade. This man had taken the bribe and started on his errand of treachery, but his heart failed him and, returning, he told me all. Then I caused Maxtla to be seized, and before nightfall he had paid the price of his wickedness.

On the morning after his death the Spanish array entered the pass. Half-way down it I met them with my five hundred men and engaged them, but suffered them to drive us back with some loss. As they followed they grew bolder and we fled faster, till at length we flew down the defile followed by the Spanish horse. Now, some three furlongs from its mouth that leads to the City of Pines, this pass turns and narrows, and here the cliffs are so sheer and high that a twilight reigns at the foot of them.

Down the narrow way we ran in seeming rout, and after us came the Spaniards shouting on their saints and flushed with victory. But scarcely had we turned the corner when they sang another song, for those who were watching a thousand feet above us gave the signal, and down from on high came a rain of stones and boulders that darkened the air and crashed among them, crushing many of them. On they struggled, seeing a wider way in front where the cliffs sloped, and perhaps half of them won through. But here the archers were waiting, and now, in the place of stones, arrows were hailed upon them, till at length, utterly bewildered and unable to strike a blow in their own defence, they turned to fly towards the open country. This finished the fight, for now we assailed their flank, and once more the rocks thundered on them from above, and the end of it was that those who remained of the Spaniards and their Indian allies were driven in utter rout back to the plain beyond the Pass of Pines.

After this battle the Spaniards troubled us no more for many years except by threats, and my name grew great among the people of the Otomie.

One Spaniard I rescued from death and afterwards I gave him his liberty. From him I inquired of the doings of de Garcia or Sarceda, and learned that he was still in the service of Cortes, but that Marina had been true to her word, and had brought disgrace upon him because he had threatened to put Otomie to the torture. Moreover Cortes was angry with him because of our escape, the burden of which Marina had laid upon his shoulders, hinting that he had taken a bribe to suffer us to pass the gate.

Of the fourteen years of my life which followed the defeat of the Spaniards I can speak briefly, for compared to the time that had gone before they were years of quiet. In them children were born to me and Otomie, three sons, and these children were my great joy, for I loved them dearly and they loved me. Indeed, except for the strain of their mother's blood, they were English boys and not Indian, for I christened them all, and taught them our English tongue and faith, and their mien and eyes were more English than Indian, though their skins were dark. But I had no luck with these dear children of mine, any more than I have had with that which Lily bore me. Two of them died—one from a fever that all my skill would not avail to cure, and another by a fall from a lofty cedar tree, which he climbed searching for a kite's nest. Thus of the three of them—since I do not speak now of that infant, my firstborn, who perished in the siege—there remained to me only the eldest and best beloved of whom I must tell hereafter.

For the rest, jointly with Otomie I was named *cacique* of the City of Pines at a great council that was held after I had destroyed the Spaniards and their allies, and as such we had wide though not absolute power. By the exercise of this power, in the end I succeeded in abolishing the horrible rites of human sacrifice, though, because of this, a large number of the outlying tribes fell away from our rule, and the enmity of the priests was excited against me. The last sacrifice, except one only, the most terrible of them all, of which I will tell afterwards, that was ever celebrated on the *teocalli* in front of the palace, took place after the defeat of the Spaniards in the pass.

When I had dwelt three years in the City of Pines and two sons had been born to me there, secret messengers arrived that were sent by the friends of Guatemoc, who had survived the torture and was still a prisoner in the hands of Cortes. From these messengers we learned that Cortes was about to start upon an expedition to the Gulf of Honduras, across the country that is now known as Yucatan, taking Guatemoc and other Aztec nobles with him for he feared to leave them behind. We heard also that there was much murmuring among the conquered tribes of Anahuac because of the cruelties and extortions of the Spaniards, and many thought that the hour had come when a rising against them might be carried to a successful issue.

This was the prayer of those who sent the envoys, that I should raise a force of Otomies and travel with it across the country to Yucatan, and there with others who would be gathered, wait a favourable opportunity to throw myself upon the Spaniards when they were entangled in the forests and swamps, putting them to the sword and releasing Guatemoc. Such was the first purpose of the plot, though it had many others of which it is useless to speak, seeing that they came to nothing.

When the message had been delivered I shook my head sadly, for I could see no hope in such a scheme, but the chief of the messengers rose and led me aside, saying that he had a word for my ear.

'Guatemoc sends these words,' he said; 'I hear that you, my brother, are free and safe with my cousin Otomie in the mountains of the Otomie. I, alas! linger in the prisons of the Teules like a crippled eagle in a cage. My brother, if it is in your power to help me, do so I conjure you by the memory of our ancient friendship, and of all that we have suffered together. Then a time may still come when I shall rule again in Anahuac, and you shall sit at my side.'

I heard and my heart was stirred, for then, as to this hour, I loved Guatemoc as a brother.

'Go back,' I said, 'and find means to tell Guatemoc that if I can save him I will, though I have small hopes that way. Still, let him look for me in the forests of Yucatan.'

Now when Otomie heard of this promise of mine she was vexed, for she said that it was foolish and would only end in my losing my life. Still, having given it she held with me that it must be carried out, and the end of it was that I raised five hundred men, and with them set out upon my long and toilsome march, which I timed so as to meet Cortes in the passes of Yucatan. At the last moment Otomie wished to accompany me, but I forbade it, pointing out that she could leave neither her children nor her people, and we parted with bitter grief for the first time.

Of all the hardships that I underwent I will not write. For two and a half months we struggled on across mountains and rivers and through swamps and forests, till at last we reached a mighty deserted city, that is called Palenque by the Indians of those parts, which has been uninhabited for many generations. This city is the most marvellous place that I have seen in all my travels, though much of it is hidden in bush, for wherever the traveller wanders there he finds vast palaces of marble, carven within and without, and sculptured *teocallis* and the huge images of grinning gods. Often have I wondered what nation was strong enough to build such a capital, and who were the kings that dwelt in it. But these are secrets belonging to the past, and they cannot be answered till some learned man has found the key to the stone symbols and writings with which the walls of the buildings are covered over.

In this city I hid with my men, though it was no easy task to persuade them to take up their habitation among so many ghosts of the departed, not to speak of the noisome fevers and the wild beasts and snakes that haunted it, for I had information that the Spaniards would pass through the swamp that lies between the ruins and the river, and there I hoped to ambush them. But on the eighth day of my hiding I learned from spies that Cortes had crossed the great river higher up, and was cutting his way through the forest, for of swamps he had passed more than enough. So I hurried also to the river intending to cross it. But all that day and all that night it rained as it can rain nowhere else in the world that I have seen, till at last we waded on our road knee deep in water, and when we came to the ford of the river it was to find a wide roaring flood, that no man could pass in anything less frail than a Yarmouth herring boat. So there on the bank we must stay in misery, suffering many ills from fever, lack of food, and plenitude of water, till at length the stream ran down.

Three days and nights we waited there, and on the fourth morning I made shift to cross, losing four men by drowning in the passage. Once over, I hid my force in the bush and reeds, and crept forward with six men only, to see if I could discover anything of the whereabouts of the Spaniards. Within an hour I struck the trail that they had cut through the forest, and followed it cautiously. Presently we came to a spot where the forest was thin, and here Cortes had camped, for there was heat left in the ashes of his fires, and among them lay the body of an Indian who had died from sickness. Not fifty yards from this camp stood a huge *ceiba*, a tree that has a habit of growth not unlike that of our English oak, though it is soft wooded and white barked, and will increase more in bulk in twenty years than any oak may in a hundred. Indeed I never yet saw an oak tree so large as this *ceiba* of which I write, either in girth or in its spread of top, unless it be the Kirby oak or the tree that is called the 'King of Scoto' which grows at Broome, that is the next parish to this of Ditchingham in Norfolk. On this *ceiba* tree many *zaphilotes* or vultures were perched, and as we crept towards it I saw what it was they came to seek, for from the lowest branches of the *ceiba* three corpses swung in the breeze. 'Here are the Spaniard's footprints,' I said. 'Let us look at them,' and we passed beneath the shadow of the tree.

As I came, a *zaphilote* alighted on the head of the body that hung nearest to me, and its weight, or the wafting of the fowl's wing, caused the dead man to turn round so that he came face to face with me. I looked, started back, then looked again and sank to the earth groaning. For here was he whom I had come to seek and save, my friend, my brother, Guatemoc the last emperor of Anahuac. Here he hung in the dim and desolate forest, dead by the death of a thief, while the vulture shrieked upon his head. I sat bewildered and horror-stricken, and as I sat I remembered the proud sign of Aztec royalty, a bird of prey clasping an adder in its claw. There before me was the last of the stock, and behold! a bird of prey gripped his hair in its talons, a fitting emblem indeed of the fall of Anahuac and the kings of Anahuac.

I sprang to my feet with an oath, and lifting the bow I held I sent an arrow through the vulture and it fell to the earth fluttering and screaming. Then I bade those with me to cut down the corpses of Guatemoc and of the prince of Tacuba and another noble who hung with him, and hollow a deep grave beneath the tree. There I laid them, and there I left them to sleep for ever in its melancholy shadow, and thus for the last time I saw Guatemoc my brother, whom I came from far to save and found made ready for burial by the Spaniard.

Then I turned my face homewards, for now Anahuac had no king to rescue, but it chanced that before I went I caught a Tlascalan who could speak Spanish, and who had deserted from the army of Cortes because of the hardships that he suffered in their toilsome march. This man was present at the murder of Guatemoc and his companions, and heard the Emperor's last words. It seems that some knave had betrayed to Cortes that an attempt would be made to rescue the prince, and that thereon Cortes commanded that he should be hung. It seems also that Guatemoc met his death as he had met the misfortunes of his life, proudly and without fear. These were his last words: 'I did ill, Malinche, when I held my hand from taking my own life before I surrendered myself to you. Then my heart told me that all your promises were false, and it has not lied to me. I welcome my death, for I have lived to know shame and defeat and torture, and to see my people the slaves of the Teule, but still I say that God will reward you for this deed.'

Then they murdered him in the midst of a great silence.

And so farewell to Guatemoc, the most brave, the best and the noblest Indian that ever breathed, and may the shadow of his tormentings and shameful end lie deep upon the fame of Cortes for so long as the names of both of them are remembered among men!

For two more months I journeyed homeward and at length I reached the City of Pines, well though wearied, and having lost only forty men by various misadventures of travel, to find Otomie in good health, and overjoyed to know me safe whom she thought never to see again. But when I told her what was the end of her cousin Guatemoc she grieved bitterly, both for his sake and because the last hope of the Aztec was gone, and she would not be comforted for many days.

CHAPTER 33

Isabella de Siguenza is Avenged

For many years after the death of Guatemoc I lived with Otomie at peace in the City of Pines. Our country was poor and rugged, and though we defied the Spaniards and paid them no tribute, now that Cortes had gone back to Spain, they had no heart to attempt our conquest. Save some few tribes that lived in difficult places like ourselves, all Anahuac was in their power, and there was little to gain except hard blows in the bringing of a remnant of the people of the Otomie beneath their yoke, so they let us be till a more convenient season. I say of a remnant of the Otomie, for as time went on many clans submitted to the Spaniards, till at length we ruled over the City of Pines alone and some leagues of territory about it. Indeed it was only love for Otomie and respect for the shadow of her ancient race and name, together with some reverence for me as one of the unconquerable white men, and for my skill as a general, that kept our following together.

And now it may be asked was I happy in those years? I had much to make me happy—no man could have been blessed with a wife more beautiful and loving, nor one who had exampled her affection by more signal deeds of sacrifice. This woman of her own free will had lain by my side on the stone of slaughter; overriding the instincts of her sex she had not shrunk from dipping her hands in blood to secure my safety, her wit had rescued me in many a trouble, her love had consoled me in many a sorrow: surely therefore if gratitude can conquer the heart of man, mine should have been at her feet for ever and a day, and so indeed it was, and in a sense is still. But can gratitude, can love itself, or any passion that rules our souls, make a man forget the house where he was born? Could I, an Indian chief struggling with a fallen people against an inevitable destiny, forget my youth and all its hopes and fears, could I forget the valley of the Waveney and that Flower who dwelt therein, and forsworn though I might be, could I forget the oath that I once had sworn? Chance had been against me, circumstances overpowered me, and I think that there are few who, could they read this story, would not find in it excuse for all that I had done. Certainly there are very few who, standing where I stood, surrounded as I was by doubts, difficulties, and dangers, would not have acted as I did.

And yet memory would rise up against me, and time upon time I would lie awake at night, even by the side of Otomie, and remember and repent, if a man may repent of that over which he has no control. For I was a stranger in a strange land, and though my home was there and my children were about me, the longing for my other home was yet with me, and I could not put away the memory of that Lily whom I had lost. Her ring was still upon my hand, but nothing else of her remained to me. I did not know if she were married or single, living or dead. The gulf between us widened with the widening years, but still the thought of her went with me like my shadow; it shone across the stormy love of Otomie, I remembered it even in my children's kiss. And worst of all I despised myself for these regrets. Nay, if the worst can have a worse, there was one here, for though she never spoke of it, I feared that Otomie had read my mind.

Heart to heart, Though far apart,

so ran the writing upon Lily's betrothal ring, and so it was with me. Far apart we were indeed, so far that no bridge that I might imagine could join that distance, and yet I could not say that we had ceased from being 'heart to heart.' Her heart might throb no more, but mine beat still toward it. Across the land, across the sea, across the gulf of death—if she were dead—still in secret must I desire the love that I had forsworn.

And so the years rolled on, bringing little of change with them, till I grew sure that here in this far place I should live and die. But that was not to be my fate.

If any should read this, the story of my early life, he will remember that the tale of the death of a certain Isabella de Siguenza is pieced into its motley. He will remember how this Isabella, in the last moments of her life, called down a curse upon that holy father who added outrage and insult to her torment, praying that he might also die by the hands of fanatics and in a worse fashion. If my memory does not play me false, I have said that this indeed came to pass, and very strangely. For after the conquest of Anahuac by Cortes, among others this same fiery priest came from Spain to turn the Indians to the love of God by torment and by sword. Indeed, of all of those who

274

entered on this mission of peace, he was the most zealous. The Indian *pabas* wrought cruelties enough when, tearing out the victim's heart, they offered it like incense to Huitzel or to Quetzal, but they at least dismissed his soul to the Mansions of the Sun. With the Christian priests the thumb-screw and the stake took the place of the stone of sacrifice, but the soul which they delivered from its earthly bondage they consigned to the House of Hell.

Of these priests a certain Father Pedro was the boldest and the most cruel. To and fro he passed, marking his path with the corpses of idolaters, until he earned the name of the 'Christian Devil.' At length he ventured too far in his holy fervour, and was seized by a clan of the Otomie that had broken from our rule upon this very question of human sacrifice, but which was not yet subjugated by the Spaniards. One day, it was when we had ruled for some fourteen years in the City of Pines, it came to my knowledge that the *pabas* of this clan had captured a Christian priest, and designed to offer him to the god Tezcat.

Attended by a small guard only, I passed rapidly across the mountains, purposing to visit the cacique of this clan with whom, although he had cast off his allegiance to us, I still kept up a show of friendship, and if I could, to persuade him to release the priest. But swiftly as I travelled the vengeance of the *pabas* had been more swift, and I arrived at the village only to find the 'Christian Devil' in the act of being led to sacrifice before the image of a hideous idol that was set upon a stake and surrounded with piles of skulls. Naked to the waist, his hands bound behind him, his grizzled locks hanging about his breast, his keen eyes fixed upon the faces of his heathen foes in menace rather than in supplication, his thin lips muttering prayers, Father Pedro passed on to the place of his doom, now and again shaking his head fiercely to free himself from the torment of the insects which buzzed about it.

I looked upon him and wondered. I looked again and knew. Suddenly there rose before my mind a vision of that gloomy vault in Seville, of a woman, young and lovely, draped in cerements, and of a thin-faced black-robed friar who smote her upon the lips with his ivory crucifix and cursed her for a blaspheming heretic. There before me was the man. Isabella de Siguenza had prayed that a fate like to her own fate should befall him, and it was upon him now. Nor indeed, remembering all that had been, was I minded to avert it, even if it had been in my power to do so. I stood by and let the victim pass, but as he passed I spoke to him in Spanish, saying:

'Remember that which it may well be you have forgotten, holy father, remember now the dying prayer of Isabella de Siguenza whom many years ago you did to death in Seville.'

The man heard me; he turned livid beneath his bronzed skin and staggered until I thought that he would have fallen. He stared upon me, with terror in his eye, to see as he believed a common sight enough, that of an Indian chief rejoicing at the death of one of his oppressors.

'What devil are you,' he said hoarsely, 'sent from hell to torment me at the last?'

'Remember the dying prayer of Isabella de Siguenza, whom you struck and cursed,' I answered mocking. 'Seek not to know whence I am, but remember this only, now and for ever.'

For a moment he stood still, heedless of the urgings of his tormentors. Then his courage came to him again, and he cried with a great voice: 'Get thee behind me, Satan, what have I to fear from thee? I remember that dead sinner well—may her soul have peace—and her curse has fallen upon me. I rejoice that it should be so, for on the further side of yonder stone the gates of heaven open to my sight. Get thee behind me, Satan, what have I to fear from thee?'

Crying thus he staggered forward saying, 'O God, into Thy hand I commend my spirit!' May his soul have peace also, for if he was cruel, at least he was brave, and did not shrink beneath those torments which he had inflicted on many others.

Now this was a little matter, but its results were large. Had I saved Father Pedro from the hands of the *pabas* of the Otomie, it is likely enough that I should not to-day be writing this history here in the valley of the Waveney. I do not know if I could have saved him, I only know that I did not try, and that because of his death great sorrows came upon me. Whether I was right or wrong, who can say? Those who judge my story may think that in this as in other matters I was wrong; had they seen Isabella de Siguenza die within her living tomb, certainly they would hold that I was right. But for good or ill, matters came about as I have written.

And it came about also, that the new viceroy sent from Spain was stirred to anger at the murder of the friar by the rebellious and heathen people of the Otomie, and set himself to take vengeance on the tribe that wrought the deed.

Soon tidings reached me that a great force of Tlascalan and other Indians were being collected to put an end to us, root and branch, and that with them marched more than a hundred Spaniards, the expedition being under the command of none other than the Captain Bernal Diaz, that same soldier whom I had spared in the slaughter of the *noche triste*, and whose sword to this day hung at my side.

Now we must needs prepare our defence, for our only hope lay in boldness. Once before the Spaniards had attacked us with thousands of their allies, and of their number but few had lived to look again on the camp of Cortes. What had been done could be done a second time— so said Otomie in the pride of her unconquerable heart. But alas! in fourteen years things had changed much with us. Fourteen years ago we held sway over a great district of mountains, whose rude clans would send up their warriors in hundreds at our call. Now these clans had broken from our yoke, which was acknowledged by the people of the City of Pines alone and those of some adjacent villages. When the Spaniards came down on me the first time, I was able to muster an army of ten thousand soldiers to oppose them, now with much toil I could collect no more than between two and three thousand men, and of these some slipped away as the hour of danger drew nigh.

Still I must put a bold face on my necessities, and make what play I might with such forces as lay at my command, although in my heart I feared much for the issue. But of my fears I said nothing to Otomie, and if she felt any she, on her part, buried them in her breast. In truth I do believe her faith in me was so great, that she thought my single wit enough to over-match all the armies of the Spaniards.

Now at length the enemy drew near, and I set my battle as I had done fourteen years before, advancing down the pass by which alone they could approach us with a small portion of my force, and stationing the remainder in two equal companies upon either brow of the beetling cliffs that overhung the road, having command to overwhelm the Spaniards with rocks, hurled upon them from above, so soon as I should give the signal by flying before them down the pass. Other measures I took also, for seeing that do what I would it well might happen that we should be driven back upon the city, I caused its walls and gates to be set in order, and garrisoned them. As a last resource too, I stored the lofty summit of the *teocalli*, which now that sacrifices were no longer offered there was used as an arsenal for the material of war, with water and provisions, and fortified its sides by walls studded with volcanic glass and by other devices, till it seemed well nigh impossible that any should be able to force them while a score of men still lived to offer a defence.

It was on one night in the early summer, having bid farewell to Otomie and taking my son with me, for he was now of an age when, according to the Indian customs, lads are brought face to face with the dangers of battle, that I despatched the appointed companies to their stations on the brow of the precipice, and sallied into the darksome mouth of the pass with the few hundred men who were left to me. I knew by my spies that the Spaniards who were encamped on the further side would attempt its passage an hour before the daylight, trusting to finding me asleep. And sure enough, on the following morning, so early that the first rays of the sun had not yet stained the lofty snows of the volcano Xaca that towered behind us, a distant murmuring which echoed through the silence of the night told me that the enemy had begun his march. I moved down the pass to meet him easily enough; there was no stone in it that was not known to me and my men. But with the Spaniards it was otherwise, for many of them were mounted, and moreover they dragged with them two carronades. Time upon time these heavy guns remained fast in the boulder-strewn roadway, for in the darkness the slaves who drew them could find no places for the wheels to run on, till in the end the captains of the army, unwilling to risk a fight at so great a disadvantage, ordered them to halt until the day broke.

At length the dawn came, and the light fell dimly down the depths of the vast gulf, revealing the long ranks of the Spaniards clad in their bright armour, and the yet more brilliant thousands of their native allies, gorgeous in their painted helms and their glittering coats of feathers. They saw us also, and mocking at our poor array, their column twisted forward like some huge snake in the crack of a rock, till they came to within a hundred paces of us. Then the Spaniards raised their battle cry of Saint Peter, and lance at rest, they charged us with their horse. We met them with a rain of arrows that checked them a little, but not for long. Soon they were among us, driving us back at the point of their lances, and slaying many, for our Indian weapons could work little harm to men and horses clad in armour. Therefore we must fly, and indeed, flight was my plan, for by it I hoped to lead the foe to that part of the defile where the road was narrow and the cliffs sheer, and they might be crushed by the stones which should hail on them from above. All went well; we fled, the Spaniards followed flushed with victory, till they were fairly in the trap. Now a single boulder came rushing from on high, and falling on a horse, killed him, then rebounding, carried dismay and wounds to those behind. Another followed, and yet another, and I grew glad at heart, for it seemed to me that the danger was over, and that for the second time my strategy had succeeded.

But suddenly from above there came a sound other than that of the rushing rocks, the sound of men joining in battle, that grew and grew till the air was full of its tumult, then something whirled down from on high. I looked; it was no stone, but a man, one of my own men. Indeed he was but as the first rain-drop of a shower.

Alas! I saw the truth; I had been outwitted. The Spaniards, old in war, could not be caught twice by such a trick; they advanced down the pass with the carronades indeed because they must, but first they sent great bodies of men to climb the mountain under shelter of the night, by secret paths which had been discovered to them, and there on its summit to deal with those who would stay their passage by hurling rocks upon them. And in truth they dealt with them but too well, for my men of the Otomie, lying on the verge of the cliff among the scrub of aloes and other prickly plants that grew there, watching the advance of the foe beneath, and never for one moment dreaming that foes might be upon their flank, were utterly surprised. Scarcely had they time to seize their weapons, which were laid at their sides that they might have the greater freedom in the rolling of heavy masses of rock, when the enemy, who outnumbered them by far, were upon them with a yell. Then came a fight, short but decisive.

Too late I saw it all, and cursed the folly that had not provided against such chances, for, indeed, I never thought it possible that the forces of the Spaniards could find the secret trails upon the further side of the mountain, forgetting that treason makes most things possible.

CHAPTER 34

The Siege of the City of Pines

The battle was already lost. From a thousand feet above us swelled the shouts of victory. The battle was lost, and yet I must fight on. As swiftly as I could I withdrew those who were left to me to a certain angle in the path, where a score of desperate men might, for a while, hold back the advance of an army. Here I called for some to stand at my side, and many answered to my call. Out of them I chose fifty men or more, bidding the rest run hard for the City of Pines, there to warn those who were left in garrison that the hour of danger was upon them, and, should I fall, to conjure Otomie my wife to make the best resistance in her power, till, if it were possible, she could wring from the Spaniards a promise of safety for herself, her child, and her people. Meanwhile I would hold the pass so that time might be given to shut the gates and man the walls. With the main body of those who were left to me I sent back my son, though he prayed hard to be allowed to stay with me. But, seeing nothing before me except death, I refused him.

Presently all were gone, and fearing a snare the Spaniards came slowly and cautiously round the angle of the rock, and seeing so few men mustered to meet them halted, for now they were certain that we had set a trap for them, since they did not think it possible that such a little band would venture to oppose their array. Here the ground lay so that only a few of them could come against us at one time, nor could they bring their heavy pieces to bear on us, and even their arquebusses helped them but little. Also the roughness of the road forced them to dismount from their horses, so that if they would attack at all, it must be on foot. This in the end they chose to do. Many fell upon either side, though I myself received no wound, but in the end they drove us back. Inch by inch they drove us back, or rather those who were left of us, at the point of their long lances, till at length they forced us into the mouth of the pass, that is some five furlongs distant from what was once the wall of the City of Pines.

To fight further was of no avail, here we must choose between death and flight, and as may be guessed, for wives' and children's sake if not for our own, we chose to fly. Across the plain we fled like deer, and after us came the Spaniards and their allies like hounds. Happily the ground was rough with stones so that their horses could not gallop freely, and thus it happened that some of us, perhaps twenty, gained the gates in safety. Of my army not more than five hundred in all lived to enter them again, and perchance there were as many left within the city.

The heavy gates swung to, and scarcely were they barred with the massive beams of oak, when the foremost of the Spaniards rode up to them. My bow was still in my hand and there was one arrow left in my quiver. I set it on the string, and drawing the bow with my full strength, I loosed the shaft through the bars of the gate at a young and gallant looking cavalier who rode the first of all. It struck him truly between the joint of his helm and neck piece, and stretching his arms out wide he fell backward over the crupper of his horse, to move no more. Then they withdrew, but presently one of their number came forward bearing a flag of truce. He was a knightly looking man, clad in rich armour, and watching him, it seemed to me that there was something in his bearing, and in the careless grace with which he sat his horse, that was familiar to me. Reining up in front of the gates he raised his visor and began to speak.

I knew him at once; before me was de Garcia, my ancient enemy, of whom I had neither heard nor seen anything for hard upon twelve years. Time had touched him indeed, which was scarcely to be wondered at, for now he was a man of sixty or more. His peaked chestnut-coloured beard was streaked with grey, his cheeks were hollow, and at that distance his lips seemed like two thin red lines, but the eyes were as they had always been, bright and piercing, and the same cold smile played about his mouth. Without a doubt it was de Garcia, who now, as at every crisis of my life, appeared to shape my fortunes to some evil end, and I felt as I looked upon him that the last and greatest struggle between us was at hand, and that before many days were sped, the ancient and accumulated hate of one or of both of us would be buried for ever in the silence of death. How ill had fate dealt with me, now as always. But a few minutes before, when I set that arrow on the string, I had wavered for a moment, doubting whether to loose it at the young cavalier who lay dead, or at the knight who rode next to him; and see! I had slain one with whom I had no quarrel and left my enemy unharmed.

'Ho there!' cried de Garcia in Spanish. 'I desire to speak with the leader of the rebel Otomie on behalf of the Captain Bernal Diaz, who commands this army.'

Now I mounted on the wall by means of a ladder which was at hand, and answered, 'Speak on, I am the man you seek.'

'You know Spanish well, friend,' said de Garcia, starting and looking at me keenly beneath his bent brows. 'Say now, where did you learn it? And what is your name and lineage?'

'I learned it, Juan de Garcia, from a certain Donna Luisa, whom you knew in your days of youth. And my name is Thomas Wingfield.'

Now de Garcia reeled in his saddle and swore a great oath.

'Mother of God!' he said, 'years ago I was told that you had taken up your abode among some savage tribe, but since then I have been far, to Spain and back indeed, and I deemed that you were dead, Thomas Wingfield. My luck is good in truth, for it has been one of the great sorrows of my life that you have so often escaped me, renegade. Be sure that this time there shall be no escape.'

'I know well that there will be no escape for one or other of us, Juan de Garcia,' I answered. 'Now we play the last round of the game, but do not boast, for God alone knows to whom the victory shall be given. You have prospered long, but a day may be at hand when your prosperity shall cease with your breath. To your errand, Juan de Garcia.'

For a moment he sat silent, pulling at his pointed beard, and watching him I thought that I could see the shadow of a half-forgotten fear creep into his eyes. If so, it was soon gone, for lifting his head, he spoke boldly and clearly.

'This is my message to you, Thomas Wingfield, and to such of the Otomie dogs with whom you herd as we have left alive to-day. The Captain Bernal Diaz offers you terms on behalf of his Excellency the viceroy.'

'What are his terms?' I asked.

'Merciful enough to such pestilent rebels and heathens,' he answered sneering. 'Surrender your city without condition, and the viceroy, in his clemency, will accept the surrender. Nevertheless, lest you should say afterwards that faith has been broken with you, be it known to you, that you shall not go unpunished for your many crimes. This is the punishment that shall be inflicted on you. All those who had part or parcel in the devilish murder of that holy saint Father Pedro, shall be burned at the stake, and the eyes of all those who beheld it shall be put out. Such of the leaders of the Otomie as the judges may select shall be hanged publicly, among them yourself, Cousin Wingfield, and more particularly the woman Otomie, daughter of Montezuma the late king. For the rest, the dwellers in the City of Pines must surrender their wealth into the treasury of the viceroy, and they themselves, men, women and children, shall be led from the city and be distributed according to the viceroy's pleasure upon the estates of such of the Spanish settlers as he may select, there to learn the useful arts of husbandry and mining. These are the conditions of surrender, and I am commanded to say that an hour is given you in which to decide whether you accept or reject them.'

'And if we reject them?'

'Then the Captain Bernal Diaz has orders to sack and destroy this city, and having given it over for twelve hours to the mercy of the Tlascalans and other faithful Indian allies, to collect those who may be left living within it, and bring them to the city of Mexico, there to be sold as slaves.'

'Good,' I said; 'you shall have your answer in an hour.' Now, leaving the gate guarded, I hurried to the palace, sending messengers as I went to summon such of the council of the city as remained alive. At the door of the palace I met Otomie, who greeted me fondly, for after hearing of our disaster she had hardly looked to see me again.

'Come with me to the Hall of Assembly,' I said; 'there I will speak to you.'

We went to the hall, where the members of the council were already gathering. So soon as the most of them were assembled, there were but eight in all, I repeated to them the words of de Garcia without comment. Then Otomie spoke, as being the first in rank she had a right to do. Twice before I had heard her address the people of the Otomie upon these questions of defence against the Spaniards. The first time, it may be remembered, was when we came as envoys from Cuitlahua, Montezuma her father's successor, to pray the aid of the children of the mountain against Cortes and the Teules. The second time was when, some fourteen years ago, we had returned to the City of Pines as fugitives after the fall of Tenoctitlan, and the populace, moved to fury by the destruction of nearly twenty thousand of their soldiers, would have delivered us as a peace offering into the hands of the Spaniards.

On each of these occasions Otomie had triumphed by her eloquence, by the greatness of her name and the majesty of her presence. Now things were far otherwise, and even had she not scorned to use

283

them, such arts would have availed us nothing in this extremity. Now her great name was but a shadow, one of many waning shadows cast by an empire whose glory had gone for ever; now she used no passionate appeal to the pride and traditions of a doomed race, now she was no longer young and the first splendour of her womanhood had departed from her. And yet, as with her son and mine at her side, she rose to address those seven councillors, who, haggard with fear and hopeless in the grasp of fate, crouched in silence before her, their faces buried in their hands, I thought that Otomie had never seemed more beautiful, and that her words, simple as they were, had never been more eloquent.

'Friends,' she said, 'you know the disaster that has overtaken us. My husband has given you the message of the Teules. Our case is desperate. We have but a thousand men at most to defend this city, the home of our forefathers, and we alone of all the peoples of Anahuac still dare to stand in arms against the white men. Years ago I said to you, Choose between death with honour and life with shame! To-day again I say to you, Choose! For me and mine there is no choice left, since whatever you decide, death must be our portion. But with you it is otherwise. Will you die fighting, or will you and your children serve your remaining years as slaves?'

For a while the seven consulted together, then their spokesman answered.

'Otomie, and you, Teule, we have followed your counsels for many years and they have brought us but little luck. We do not blame you, for the gods of Anahuac have deserted us as we have deserted them, and the gods alone stand between men and their evil destiny. Whatever misfortunes we may have borne, you have shared in them, and so it is now at the end. Nor will we go back upon our words in this the last hour of the people of the Otomie. We have chosen; we have lived free with you, and still free, we will die with you. For like you we hold that it is better for us and ours to perish as free men than to drag out our days beneath the yoke of the Teule.'

'It is well,' said Otomie; 'now nothing remains for us except to seek a death so glorious that it shall be sung of in after days. Husband, you have heard the answer of the council. Let the Spaniards hear it also.'

So I went back to the wall, a white flag in my hand, and presently an envoy advanced from the Spanish camp to speak with me—not de Garcia, but another. I told him in few words that those who remained alive of the people of the Otomie would die beneath the ruins of their city like the children of Tenoctitlan before them, but that while they had a spear to throw and an arm to throw it, they would never yield to the tender mercies of the Spaniard.

The envoy returned to the camp, and within an hour the attack began. Bringing up their pieces of ordnance, the Spaniards set them within little more than an hundred paces of the gates, and began to batter us with iron shot at their leisure, for our spears and arrows could scarcely harm them at such a distance. Still we were not idle, for seeing that the wooden gates must soon be down, we demolished houses on either side of them and filled up the roadway with stones and rubbish. At the rear of the heap thus formed I caused a great trench to be dug, which could not be passed by horsemen and ordnance till it was filled in again. All along the main street leading to the great square of the *teocalli* I threw up other barricades, protected in the front and rear by dykes cut through the roadway, and in case the Spaniards should try to turn our flank and force a passage through the narrow and tortuous lanes to the right and left, I also barricaded the four entrances to the great square or market place.

Till nightfall the Spaniards bombarded the shattered remains of the gates and the earthworks behind them, doing no great damage beyond the killing of about a score of people by cannon shot and arquebuss balls. But they attempted no assault that day. At length the darkness fell and their fire ceased, but not so our labours. Most of the men must guard the gates and the weak spots in the walls, and therefore the building of the barricades was left chiefly to the women, working under my command and that of my captains. Otomie herself took a share in the toil, an example that was followed by every lady and indeed by every woman in the city, and there were many of them, for the women outnumbered the men among the Otomie, and moreover not a few of them had been made widows on that same day.

It was a strange sight to see them in the glare of hundreds of torches split from the resin pine that gave its name to the city, as all night long they moved to and fro in lines, each of them staggering beneath the weight of a basket of earth or a heavy stone, or dug with wooden spades at the hard soil, or laboured at the pulling down of houses. They never complained, but worked on sullenly and despairingly; no groan or tear broke from them, no, not even from those whose husbands and sons had been hurled that morning from the precipices of the pass. They knew that resistance would be useless and that their doom was at hand, but no cry arose among them of surrender to the Spaniards. Those of them who spoke of the matter at all said with Otomie, that it was better to die free than to live as slaves, but the most did not speak;

the old and the young, mother, wife, widow, and maid, they laboured in silence and the children laboured at their sides.

Looking at them it came into my mind that these silent patient women were inspired by some common and desperate purpose, that all knew of, but which none of them chose to tell.

'Will you work so hard for your masters the Teules?' cried a man in bitter mockery, as a file of them toiled past beneath their loads of stone.

'Fool!' answered their leader, a young and lovely lady of rank; 'do the dead labour?'

'Nay,' said this ill jester, 'but such as you are too fair for the Teules to kill, and your years of slavery will be many. Say, how shall you escape them?'

'Fool!' answered the lady again, 'does fire die from lack of fuel only, and must every man live till age takes him? We shall escape them thus,' and casting down the torch she carried, she trod it into the earth with her sandal, and went on with her load. Then I was sure that they had some purpose, though I did not guess how desperate it was, and Otomie would tell me nothing of this woman's secret.

'Otomie,' I said to her that night, when we met by chance, 'I have ill news for you.'

'It must be bad indeed, husband, to be so named in such an hour,' she answered.

'De Garcia is among our foes.'

'I knew it, husband.'

'How did you know it?'

'By the hate written in your eyes,' she answered.

'It seems that his hour of triumph is at hand,' I said.

'Nay, beloved, not HIS but YOURS. You shall triumph over de Garcia, but victory will cost you dear. I know it in my heart; ask me not how or why. See, the Queen puts on her crown,' and she pointed to the volcano Xaca, whose snows grew rosy with the dawn, 'and you must go to the gate, for the Spaniards will soon be stirring.'

As Otomie spoke I heard a trumpet blare without the walls. Hurrying to the gates by the first light of day, I could see that the Spaniards were mustering their forces for attack. They did not come at once, however, but delayed till the sun was well up. Then they began to pour a furious fire upon our defences, that reduced the shattered beams of the gates to powder, and even shook down the crest of the earthwork beyond them. Suddenly the firing ceased and again a trumpet called. Now they charged us in column, a thousand or more Tlascalans leading the van, followed by the Spanish force. In two minutes I, who awaited them beyond it together with some three hundred warriors of the Otomie, saw their heads appear over the crest of the earthwork, and the fight began. Thrice we drove them back with our spears and arrows, but at the fourth charge the wave of men swept over our defence, and poured into the dry ditch beyond.

Now we were forced to fly to the next earthwork, for we could not hope to fight so many in the open street, whither, so soon as a passage had been made for their horse and ordnance, the enemy followed us. Here the fight was renewed, and this barricade being very strong, we held it for hard upon two hours with much loss to ourselves and to the Spanish force. Again we retreated and again we were assailed, and so the struggle went on throughout the live-long day. Every hour our numbers grew fewer and our arms fainter, but still we fought on desperately. At the two last barricades, hundreds of the women of the Otomie fought by the sides of their husbands and their brothers.

The last earthwork was captured by the Spaniards just as the sun sank, and under the shadow of approaching darkness those of us that remained alive fled to the refuge which we had prepared upon the *teocalli*, nor was there any further fighting during that night.

CHAPTER 35

The Last Sacrifice of the
Women of the Otomie

Here in the courtyard of the *teocalli*, by the light of burning houses, for as they advanced the Spaniards fired the town, we mustered
our array to find that there were left to us in all some four hundred
fighting men, together with a crowd of nearly two thousand women
and many children. Now although this *teocalli* was not quite so lofty
as that of the great temple of Mexico, its sides were steeper and
everywhere faced with dressed stone, and the open space upon its
summit was almost as great, measuring indeed more than a hundred
paces every way. This area was paved with blocks of marble, and in
its centre stood the temple of the war-god, where his statue still sat,
although no worship had been offered to him for many years; the
stone of sacrifice, the altar of fire, and the storehouses of the priests.
Moreover in front of the temple, and between it and the stone of
sacrifice, was a deep cemented hole the size of a large room, which
once had been used as a place for the safe keeping of grain in times
of famine. This pit I had caused to be filled with water borne with
great toil to the top of the pyramid, and in the temple itself I stored a
great quantity of food, so that we had no cause to fear present death
from thirst or famine.

But now we were face to face with a new trouble. Large as was
the summit of the pyramid, it would not give shelter to a half of our
numbers, and if we desired to defend it some of the multitude herded
round its base must seek refuge elsewhere. Calling the leaders of the
people together, I put the matter before them in few words, leaving
them to decide what must be done. They in turn consulted among
themselves, and at length gave me this answer: that it was agreed that
all the wounded and aged there, together with most of the children,
and with them any others who wished to go, should leave the *teocalli*

that night, to find their way out of the city if they could, or if not, to trust to the mercy of the Spaniards.

I said that it was well, for death was on every side, and it mattered little which way men turned to meet it. So they were sorted out, fifteen hundred or more of them, and at midnight the gates of the courtyard were thrown open, and they left. Oh! it was dreadful to see the farewells that took place in that hour. Here a daughter clung to the neck of her aged father, here husbands and wives bade each other a last farewell, here mothers kissed their little children, and on every side rose up the sounds of bitter agony, the agony of those who parted for ever. I buried my face in my hands, wondering as I had often wondered before, how a God whose name is Mercy can bear to look upon sights that break the hearts of sinful men to witness.

Presently I raised my eyes and spoke to Otomie, who was at my side, asking her if she would not send our son away with the others, passing him off as the child of common people.

'Nay, husband,' she answered, 'it is better for him to die with us, than to live as a slave of the Spaniards.'

At length it was over and the gates had shut behind the last of them. Soon we heard the distant challenge of the Spanish sentries as they perceived them, and the sounds of some shots followed by cries.

'Doubtless the Tlascalans are massacring them,' I said. But it was not so. When a few had been killed the leaders of the Spaniards found that they waged war upon an unarmed mob, made up for the most part of aged people, women and children, and their commander, Bernal Diaz, a merciful man if a rough one, ordered that the onslaught should cease. Indeed he did more, for when all the able-bodied men, together with such children as were sufficiently strong to bear the fatigues of travel, had been sorted out to be sold as slaves, he suffered the rest of that melancholy company to depart whither they would. And so they went, though what became of them I do not know.

That night we spent in the courtyard of the *teocalli*, but before it was light I caused the women and children who remained with us, perhaps some six hundred in all, for very few of the former who were unmarried, or who being married were still young and comely, had chosen to desert our refuge, to ascend the pyramid, guessing that the Spaniards would attack us at dawn. I stayed, however, with the three hundred fighting men that were left to me, a hundred or more having thrown themselves upon the mercy of the Spaniards, with the refugees, to await the Spanish onset under shelter of the walls of the courtyard. At dawn it began, and by midday, do what we could to

289

stay it, the wall was stormed, and leaving nearly a hundred dead and wounded behind me, I was driven to the winding way that led to the summit of the pyramid. Here they assaulted us again, but the road was steep and narrow, and their numbers gave them no great advantage on it, so that the end of it was that we beat them back with loss, and there was no more fighting that day.

The night which followed we spent upon the summit of the pyramid, and for my part I was so weary that after I had eaten I never slept more soundly. Next morning the struggle began anew; and this time with better success to the Spaniards. Inch by inch under cover of the heavy fire from their arquebusses and pieces, they forced us upward and backward. All day long the fight continued upon the narrow road that wound from stage to stage of the pyramid. At length, as the sun sank, a company of our foes, their advance guard, with shouts of victory, emerged upon the flat summit, and rushed towards the temple in its centre. All this while the women had been watching, but now one of them sprang up, crying with a loud voice:

'Seize them; they are but few.'

Then with a fearful scream of rage, the mob of women cast themselves upon the weary Spaniards and Tlascalans, bearing them down by the weight of their numbers. Many of them were slain indeed, but in the end the women conquered, ay, and made their victims captive, fastening them with cords to the rings of copper that were let into the stones of the pavement, to which in former days those doomed to sacrifice had been secured, when their numbers were so great that the priests feared lest they should escape. I and the soldiers with me watched this sight wondering, then I cried out:

'What! men of the Otomie, shall it be said that our women outdid us in courage?' and without further ado, followed by a hundred or more of my companions, I rushed desperately down the steep and narrow path.

At the first corner we met the main array of Spaniards and their allies, coming up slowly, for now they were sure of victory, and so great was the shock of our encounter that many of them were hurled over the edge of the path, to roll down the steep sides of the pyramid. Seeing the fate of their comrades, those behind them halted, then began to retreat. Presently the weight of our rush struck them also, and they in turn pushed upon those below, till at length panic seized them, and with a great crying the long line of men that wound round and round the pyramid from its base almost to its summit, sought their safety in flight. But some of them found none, for the rush of those above pressing with ever increasing force upon their friends below, drove many to their death, since here on the pyramid there was nothing to cling to, and if once a man lost his foothold on the path, his fall was broken only when his body reached the court beneath. Thus in fifteen short minutes all that the Spaniards had won this day was lost again, for except the prisoners at its summit, none of them remained alive upon the *teocalli*; indeed so great a terror took them, that bearing with them their dead and wounded, they retreated under cover of the night to their camp without the walls of the courtyard.

Now, weary but triumphant, we wended back towards the crest of the pyramid, but as I turned the corner of the second angle that was perhaps nearly one hundred feet above the level of the ground, a thought struck me and I set those with me at a task. Loosening the blocks of stone that formed the edge of the roadway, we rolled them down the sides of the pyramid, and so laboured on removing layer upon layer of stones and of the earth beneath, till where the path had been, was nothing but a yawning gap thirty feet or more in width.

'Now,' I said, surveying our handiwork by the light of the rising moon, 'that Spaniard who would win our nest must find wings to fly with.'

'Ay, Teule,' answered one at my side, 'but say what wings shall *we* find?'

'The wings of Death,' I said grimly, and went on my upward way.

It was near midnight when I reached the temple, for the labour of levelling the road took many hours and food had been sent to us from above. As I drew nigh I was amazed to hear the sound of solemn chanting, and still more was I amazed when I saw that the doors of the temple of Huitzel were open, and that the sacred fire which had not shone there for many years once more flared fiercely upon his altar. I stood still listening. Did my ears trick me, or did I hear the dreadful song of sacrifice? Nay, again its wild refrain rang out upon the silence:

To Thee we sacrifice! Save us, O Huitzel, Huitzel, lord god!

I rushed forward, and turning the angle of the temple I found myself face to face with the past, for there as in bygone years were the *pabas* clad in their black robes, their long hair hanging about their shoulders, the dreadful knife of glass fixed in their girdles; there to the right of the stone of sacrifice were those destined to the god, and there being led towards it was the first victim, a Tlascalan prisoner, his limbs held by men clad in the dress of priests. Near him, arrayed in the scarlet robe of sacrifice, stood one of my own captains, who I remembered had once served as a priest of Tezcat before idolatry was forbidden in the City of Pines, and around were a wide circle of women that watched, and from whose lips swelled the awful chant.

Now I understood it all. In their last despair, maddened by the loss of fathers, husbands, and children, by their cruel fate, and standing face to face with certain death, the fire of the old faith had burnt up in their savage hearts. There was the temple, there were the stone and implements of sacrifice, and there to their hands were the victims taken in war. They would glut a last revenge, they would sacrifice to their fathers' gods as their fathers had done before them, and the victims should be taken from their own victorious foes. Ay, they must die, but at the least they would seek the Mansions of the Sun made holy by the blood of the accursed Teule.

I have said that it was the women who sang this chant and glared so fiercely upon the victims, but I have not yet told all the horror of what I saw, for in the fore-front of their circle, clad in white robes, the necklet of great emeralds, Guatemoc's gift, flashing upon her breast, the plumes of royal green set in her hair, giving the time of the death chant with a little wand, stood Montezuma's daughter, Otomie my wife. Never had I seen her look so beautiful or so dreadful. It was not Otomie whom I saw, for where was the tender smile and where the gentle eyes? Here before me was a living Vengeance wearing the shape of woman. In an instant I guessed the truth, though I did not know it all. Otomie, who although she was not of it, had ever favoured the Christian faith, Otomie, who for years had never spoken of these dreadful rites except with anger, whose every act was love and whose every word was kindness, was still in her soul an idolater and a savage. She had hidden this side of her heart from me well through all these years, perchance she herself had scarcely known its secret, for but twice had I seen anything of the buried fierceness of her blood. The first time was when Marina had brought her a certain robe in which she might escape from the camp of Cortes, and she had spoken to Marina of that robe; and the second when on this same day she had played her part to the Tlascalan, and had struck him down with her own hand as he bent over me.

All this and much more passed through my mind in that brief moment, while Otomie marked the time of the death chant, and the *pabas* dragged the Tlascalan to his doom.

The next I was at her side.

'What passes here?' I asked sternly.

Otomie looked on me with a cold wonder, and empty eyes as though she did not know me.

'Go back, white man,' she answered; 'it is not lawful for strangers to mingle in our rites.'

I stood bewildered, not knowing what to do, while the flame burned and the chant went up before the effigy of Huitzel, of the demon Huitzel awakened after many years of sleep.

Again and yet again the solemn chant arose, Otomie beating time with her little rod of ebony, and again and yet again the cry of triumph rose to the silent stars.

Now I awoke from my dream, for as an evil dream it seemed to me, and drawing my sword I rushed towards the priest at the altar to cut him down. But though the men stood still the women were too quick for me. Before I could lift the sword, before I could even speak a word, they had sprung upon me like the jaguars of their own forests, and like jaguars they hissed and growled into my ear:

'Get you gone, Teule,' they said, 'lest we stretch you on the stone with your brethren.' And still hissing they pushed me thence.

I drew back and thought for a while in the shadow of the temple. My eye fell upon the long line of victims awaiting their turn of sacrifice. There were thirty and one of them still alive, and of these five were Spaniards. I noted that the Spaniards were chained the last of all the line. It seemed that the murderers would keep them till the end of the feast, indeed I discovered that they were to be offered up at the rising of the sun. How could I save them, I wondered. My power was gone. The women could not be moved from their work of vengeance; they were mad with their sufferings. As well might a man try to snatch her prey from a puma robbed of her whelps, as to turn them from their purpose. With the men it was otherwise, however. Some of them mingled in the orgy indeed, but more stood aloof watching with a fearful joy the spectacle in which they did not share. Near me was a man, a noble of the Otomie, of something more than my own age. He had always been my friend, and after me he commanded the warriors of the tribe. I went to him and said, 'Friend, for the sake of the honour of your people, help me to end this.'

'I cannot, Teule,' he answered, 'and beware how you meddle in the play, for none will stand by you. Now the women have power, and you see they use it. They are about to die, but before they die they will do as their fathers did, for their strait is sore, and though they have been put aside, the old customs are not forgotten.'

'At the least can we not save these Teules?' I answered.

'Why should you wish to save the Teules? Will they save us some few days hence, when *we* are in their power?'

'Perhaps not,' I said, 'but if we must die, let us die clean from this shame.'

'What then do you wish me to do, Teule?'

'This: I would have you find some three or four men who are not fallen into this madness, and with them aid me to loose the Teules, for we cannot save the others. If this may be done, surely we can lower them with ropes from that point where the road is broken away, down to the path beneath, and thus they may escape to their own people.'

'I will try,' he answered, shrugging his shoulders, 'not from any tenderness towards the accursed Teules, whom I could well bear to see stretched upon the stone, but because it is your wish, and for the sake of the friendship between us.'

Then he went, and presently I saw several men place themselves, as though by chance, between the spot where the last of the line of Indian prisoners, and the first of the Spaniards were made fast, in such a fashion as to hide them from the sight of the maddened women, engrossed as they were in their orgies.

Now I crept up to the Spaniards. They were squatted upon the ground, bound by their hands and feet to the copper rings in the pavement. There they sat silently awaiting the dreadful doom, their faces grey with terror, and their eyes starting from their sockets.

'Hist!' I whispered in Spanish into the ear of the first, an old man whom I knew as one who had taken part in the wars of Cortes. 'Would you be saved?'

He looked up quickly, and said in a hoarse voice:

'Who are you that talk of saving us? Who can save us from these she devils?'

'I am Teule, a man of white blood and a Christian, and alas that I must say it, the captain of this savage people. With the aid of some few men who are faithful to me, I purpose to cut your bonds, and afterwards you shall see. Know, Spaniard, that I do this at great risk, for if we are caught, it is a chance but that I myself shall have to suffer those things from which I hope to rescue you.'

'Be assured, Teule,' answered the Spaniard, 'that if we should get safe away, we shall not forget this service. Save our lives now, and the time may come when we shall pay you back with yours. But even if we are loosed, how can we cross the open space in this moonlight and escape the eyes of those furies?'

'We must trust to chance for that,' I answered, and as I spoke, fortune helped us strangely, for by now the Spaniards in their camp below had perceived what was going forward on the crest of the *teocalli*.

A yell of horror rose from them and instantly they opened fire upon us with their pieces and arquebusses, though, because of the shape of the pyramid and of their position beneath it, the storm of shot swept over us, doing us little or no hurt. Also a great company of them poured across the courtyard, hoping to storm the temple, for they did not know that the road had been broken away.

Now, though the rites of sacrifice never ceased, what with the roar of cannon, the shouts of rage and terror from the Spaniards, the hiss of musket balls, and the crackling of flames from houses which they had fired to give them more light, and the sound of chanting, the turmoil and confusion grew so great as to render the carrying out of my purpose easier than I had hoped. By this time my friend, the captain of the Otomie, was at my side, and with him several men whom he could trust. Stooping down, with a few swift blows of a knife I cut the ropes which bound the Spaniards. Then we gathered ourselves into a knot, twelve of us or more, and in the centre of the knot we set the five Spaniards. This done, I drew my sword and cried:

'The Teules storm the temple!' which was true, for already their long line was rushing up the winding path. 'The Teules storm the temple, I go to stop them,' and straightway we sped across the open space.

None saw us, or if they saw us, none hindered us, for all the company were intent upon the consummation of a fresh sacrifice; moreover, the tumult was such, as I afterwards discovered, that we were scarcely noticed. Two minutes passed, and our feet were set upon the winding way, and now I breathed again, for we were beyond the sight of the women. On we rushed swiftly as the cramped limbs of the Spaniards would carry them, till presently we reached that angle in the path where the breach began. The attacking Spaniards had already come to the further side of the gap, for though we could not see them, we could hear their cries of rage and despair as they halted helplessly and understood that their comrades were beyond their aid.

'Now we are sped,' said the Spaniard with whom I had spoken; 'the road is gone, and it must be certain death to try the side of the pyramid.'

'Not so,' I answered; 'some fifty feet below the path still runs, and one by one we will lower you to it with this rope.'

Then we set to work. Making the cord fast beneath the arms of a soldier we let him down gently, till he came to the path, and was received there by his comrades as a man returned from the dead. The last to be lowered was that Spaniard with whom I had spoken.

'Farewell,' he said, 'and may the blessing of God be on you for this act of mercy, renegade though you are. Say, now, will you not come with me? I set my life and honour in pledge for your safety. You tell me that you are still a Christian man. Is that a place for Christians?' and he pointed upwards.

'No, indeed,' I answered, 'but still I cannot come, for my wife and son are there, and I must return to die with them if need be. If you bear me any gratitude, strive in return to save their lives, since for my own I care but little.'

'That I will,' he said, and then we let him down among his friends, whom he reached in safety.

Now we returned to the temple, giving it out that the Spaniards were in retreat, having failed to cross the breach in the roadway. Here before the temple the orgy still went on. But two Indians remained alive; and the priests of sacrifice grew weary.

'Where are the Teules?' cried a voice. 'Swift! strip them for the altar.'

But the Teules were gone, nor, search where they would, could they find them.

'Their God has taken them beneath His wing,' I said, speaking from the shadow and in a feigned voice. 'Huitzel cannot prevail before the God of the Teules.'

Then I slipped aside, so that none knew that it was I who had spoken, but the cry was caught up and echoed far and wide.

'The God of the Christians has hidden them beneath His wing. Let us make merry with those whom He rejects,' said the cry, and the last of the captives were dragged away.

Now I thought that all was finished, but this was not so. I have spoken of the secret purpose which I read in the sullen eyes of the Indian women as they laboured at the barricades, and I was about to see its execution. Madness still burned in the hearts of these women; they had accomplished their sacrifice, but their festival was still to come. They drew themselves away to the further side of the pyramid, and, heedless of the shots which now and again pierced the breast of one of them—for here they were exposed to the Spanish fire—remained a while in preparation. With them went the priests of sacrifice, but now, as before, the rest of the men stood in sullen groups, watching what befell, but lifting no hand or voice to hinder its hellishness.

One woman did not go with them, and that woman was Otomie my wife.

She stood by the stone of sacrifice, a piteous sight to see, for her frenzy or rather her madness had outworn itself, and she was as she had ever been. There stood Otomie, gazing with wide and horror-stricken eyes now at the tokens of this unholy rite and now at her own hands—as though she thought to see them red, and shuddered at the thought. I drew near to her and touched her on the shoulder. She turned swiftly, gasping,

'Husband! husband!'

'It is I,' I answered, 'but call me husband no more.'

'Oh! what have I done?' she wailed, and fell senseless in my arms.

And here I will add what at the time I knew nothing of, for it was told me in after years by the Rector of this parish, a very learned man, though one of narrow mind. Had I known it indeed, I should have spoken more kindly to Otomie my wife even in that hour, and thought more gently of her wickedness. It seems, so said my friend the Rector, that from the most ancient times, those women who have bent the knee to demon gods, such as were the gods of Anahuac, are subject at any time to become possessed by them, even after they have abandoned their worship, and to be driven in their frenzy to the working of the greatest crimes. Thus, among other instances, he told me that a Greek poet named Theocritus sets out in one of his idylls how a woman called Agave, being engaged in a secret religious orgy in honour of a demon named Dionysus, perceived her own son Pentheus watching the celebration of the mysteries, and thereon becoming possessed by the demon she fell on him and murdered him, being aided by the other women. For this the poet, who was also a worshipper of Dionysus, gave her great honour and not reproach, seeing that she did the deed at the behest of this god, 'a deed not to be blamed.'

Now I write of this for a reason, though it has nothing to do with me, for it seems that as Dionysus possessed Agave, driving her to unnatural murder, so did Huitzel possess Otomie, and indeed she said as much to me afterwards. For I am sure that if the devils whom the Greeks worshipped had such power, a still greater strength was given to those of Anahuac, who among all fiends were the first. If this be so, as I believe, it was not Otomie that I saw at the rites of sacrifice, but rather the demon Huitzel whom she had once worshipped, and who had power, therefore, to enter into her body for awhile in place of her own spirit.

CHAPTER 36

The Surrender

Taking Otomie in my arms, I bore her to one of the storehouses attached to the temple. Here many children had been placed for safety, among them my own son.

'What ails our mother, father?' said the boy. 'And why did she shut me in here with these children when it seems that there is fighting without?'

'Your mother has fainted,' I answered, 'and doubtless she placed you here to keep you safe. Now do you tend her till I return.'

'I will do so,' answered the boy, 'but surely it would be better that I, who am almost a man, should be without, fighting the Spaniards at your side rather than within, nursing sick women.'

'Do as I bid you, son,' I said, 'and I charge you not to leave this place until I come for you again.'

Now I passed out of the storehouse, shutting the door behind me. A minute later I wished that I had stayed where I was, since on the platform my eyes were greeted by a sight more dreadful than any that had gone before. For there, advancing towards us, were the women divided into four great companies, some of them bearing infants in their arms. They came singing and leaping, many of them naked to the middle. Nor was this all, for in front of them ran the *pabas* and such of the women themselves as were persons in authority. These leaders, male and female, ran and leaped and sang, calling upon the names of their demon-gods, and celebrating the wickednesses of their forefathers, while after them poured the howling troops of women.

To and fro they rushed, now making obeisance to the statue of Huitzel, now prostrating themselves before his hideous sister, the goddess of Death, who sat beside him adorned with her carven necklace of men's skulls and hands, now bowing around the stone of sacrifice, and now thrusting their bare arms into the flames of the holy fire. For an hour or more they celebrated this ghastly carnival, of which even I, versed as I was in the Indian customs, could not fully understand the meaning, and then, as though some single impulse had possessed them, they withdrew to the centre of the open space, and, forming themselves into a double circle, within which stood the *pabas*, of a sudden they burst into a chant so wild and shrill that as I listened my blood curdled in my veins.

Even now the burden of that chant with the vision of those who sang it sometimes haunts my sleep at night, but I will not write it here. Let him who reads imagine all that is most cruel in the heart of man, and every terror of the evillest dream, adding to these some horror-ridden tale of murder, ghosts, and inhuman vengeance; then, if he can, let him shape the whole in words and, as in a glass darkly, perchance he may mirror the spirit of that last ancient song of the women of the Otomie, with its sobs, its cries of triumph, and its death wailings.

Ever as they sang, step by step they drew backwards, and with them went the leaders of each company, their eyes fixed upon the statues of their gods. Now they were but a segment of a circle, for they did not advance towards the temple; backward and outward they went with a slow and solemn tramp. There was but one line of them now, for those in the second ring filled the gaps in the first as it widened; still they drew on till at length they stood on the sheer edge of the platform. Then the priests and the women leaders took their place among them and for a moment there was silence, until at a signal one and all they bent them backwards. Standing thus, their long hair waving on the wind, the light of burning houses flaring upon their breasts and in their maddened eyes, they burst into the cry of:

'Save us, Huitzel! Receive us, lord God, our home!'

Thrice they cried it, each time more shrilly than before, then suddenly they were *gone*, the women of the Otomie were no more!

With their own self-slaughter they had consummated the last celebration of the rites of sacrifice that ever shall be held in the City of Pines. The devil gods were dead and their worshippers with them.

A low murmur ran round the lips of the men who watched, then one cried, and his voice rang strangely in the sudden silence: 'May our wives, the women of the Otomie, rest softly in the Houses of the Sun, for of a surety they teach us how to die.'

'Ay,' I answered, 'but not thus. Let women do self-murder, our foes have swords for the hearts of men.'

I turned to go, and before me stood Otomie.

'What has befallen?' she said. 'Where are my sisters? Oh! surely I have dreamed an evil dream. I dreamed that the gods of my forefathers were strong once more, and that once more they drank the blood of men.'

'Your ill dream has a worse awakening, Otomie,' I answered. 'The gods of hell are still strong indeed in this accursed land, and they have taken your sisters into their keeping.'

'Is it so?' she said softly, 'yet in my dream it seemed to me that this was their last strength ere they sink into death unending. Look yonder!' and she pointed toward the snowy crest of the volcano Xaca.

I looked, but whether I saw the sight of which I am about to tell or whether it was but an imagining born of the horrors of that most hideous night, in truth I cannot say. At the least I seemed to see this, and afterwards there were some among the Spaniards who swore that they had witnessed it also.

On Xaca's lofty summit, now as always stood a pillar of fiery smoke, and while I gazed, to my vision the smoke and the fire separated themselves. Out of the fire was fashioned a cross of flame, that shone like lightning and stretched for many a rod across the heavens, its base resting on the mountain top. At its foot rolled the clouds of smoke, and now these too took forms vast and terrifying, such forms indeed as those that sat in stone within the temple behind me, but magnified a hundredfold.

'See,' said Otomie again, 'the cross of your God shines above the shapes of mine, the lost gods whom to-night I worshipped though not of my own will.' Then she turned and went.

For some few moments I stood very much afraid, gazing upon the vision on Xaca's snow, then suddenly the rays of the rising sun smote it and it was gone.

Now for three days more we held out against the Spaniards, for they could not come at us and their shot swept over our heads harmlessly. During these days I had no talk with Otomie, for we shrank from one another. Hour by hour she would sit in the storehouse of the temple a very picture of desolation. Twice I tried to speak with her, my heart being moved to pity by the dumb torment in her eyes, but she turned her head from me and made no answer.

Soon it came to the knowledge of the Spaniards that we had enough food and water upon the *teocalli* to enable us to live there for a month or more, and seeing that there was no hope of capturing the place by force of arms, they called a parley with us.

I went down to the breach in the roadway and spoke with their envoy, who stood upon the path below. At first the terms offered were that we should surrender at discretion. To this I answered that sooner than do so we would die where we were. Their reply was that if we would give over all who had any part in the human sacrifice, the rest of us might go free. To this I said that the sacrifice had been carried out by women and some few men, and that all of these were dead by their own hands. They asked if Otomie was also dead. I told them no, but that I would never surrender unless they swore that neither she nor her son should be harmed, but rather that together with myself they should be given a safe-conduct to go whither we willed. This was refused, but in the end I won the day, and a parchment was thrown up to me on the point of a lance. This parchment, which was signed by the Captain Bernal Diaz, set out that in consideration of the part that I and some men of the Otomie had played in rescuing the Spanish captives from death by sacrifice, a pardon was granted to me, my wife and child, and all upon the *teocalli*, with liberty to go whithersoever we would unharmed, our lands and wealth being however declared forfeit to the viceroy.

With these terms I was well content, indeed I had never hoped to win any that would leave us our lives and liberty.

And yet for my part death had been almost as welcome, for now Otomie had built a wall between us that I could never climb, and I was bound to her, to a woman who, willingly or no, had stained her hands with sacrifice. Well, my son was left to me and with him I must be satisfied; at the least he knew nothing of his mother's shame. Oh! I thought to myself as I climbed the *teocalli*, oh! that I could but escape far from this accursed land and bear him with me to the English shores, ay, and Otomie also, for there she might forget that once she had been a savage. Alas! it could scarcely be!

Coming to the temple, I and those with me told the good tidings to our companions, who received it silently. Men of a white race would have rejoiced thus to escape, for when death is near all other loss seems as nothing. But with these Indian people it is not so, since when fortune frowns upon them they do not cling to life. These men of the Otomie had lost their country, their wives, their wealth, their brethren, and their homes; therefore life, with freedom to wander whither they would, seemed no great thing to them. So they met the boon that I had won from the mercy of our foes, as had matters gone otherwise they would have met the bane, in sullen silence.

I came to Otomie, and to her also I told the news.

'I had hoped to die here where I am,' she answered. 'But so be it; death is always to be found.'

Only my son rejoiced, because he knew that God had saved us all from death by sword or hunger.

'Father,' he said, 'the Spaniards have given us life, but they take our country and drive us out of it. Where then shall we go?'

'I do not know, my son,' I answered.

'Father,' the lad said again, 'let us leave this land of Anahuac where there is nothing but Spaniards and sorrow. Let us find a ship and sail across the seas to England, our own country.'

The boy spoke my very thought and my heart leapt at his words, though I had no plan to bring the matter about. I pondered a moment, looking at Otomie.

'The thought is good, Teule,' she said, answering my unspoken question; 'for you and for our son there is no better, but for myself I will answer in the proverb of my people, "The earth that bears us lies lightest on our bones."'

Then she turned, making ready to quit the storehouse of the temple where we had been lodged during the siege, and no more was said about the matter.

Before the sun set a weary throng of men, with some few women and children, were marching across the courtyard that surrounded the pyramid, for a bridge of timbers taken from the temple had been made over the breach in the roadway that wound about its side. At the gates the Spaniards were waiting to receive us. Some of them cursed us, some mocked, but those of the nobler sort said nothing, for they pitied our plight and respected us for the courage we had shown in the last struggle. Their Indian allies were there also, and these grinned like unfed pumas, snarling and whimpering for our lives, till their masters kicked them to silence. The last act of the fall of Anahuac was as the first had been, dog still ate dog, leaving the goodly spoil to the lion who watched.

At the gates we were sorted out; the men of small condition, together with the children, were taken from the ruined city by an escort and turned loose upon the mountains, while those of note were brought to the Spanish camp, to be questioned there before they were set free. I, with my wife and son, was led to the palace, our old home, there to learn the will of the Captain Diaz.

It is but a little way to go, and yet there was something to be seen in the path. For as we walked I looked up, and before me, standing with folded arms and apart from all men, was de Garcia. I had scarcely thought of him for some days, so full had my mind been of other matters, but at the sight of his evil face I remembered that while this man lived, sorrow and danger must be my bedfellows.

He watched us pass, taking note of all, then he called to me who walked last:

'Farewell, Cousin Wingfield. You have lived through this bout also and won a free pardon, you, your woman and your brat together. If the old war-horse who is set over us as a captain had listened to me you should have been burned at the stake, every one of you, but so it is. Farewell for a while, friend. I am away to Mexico to report these matters to the viceroy, who may have a word to say.'

I made no answer, but asked of our conductor, that same Spaniard whom I had saved from the sacrifice, what the senor meant by his words.

'This, Teule; that there has been a quarrel between our comrade Sarceda and our captain. The former would have granted you no terms, or failing this would have decoyed you from your stronghold with false promises, and then have put you to the sword as infidels with whom no oath is binding. But the captain would not have it so, for he said that faith must be kept even with the heathen, and we whom you had saved cried shame on him. And so words ran high, and in the end the Senor Sarceda, who is third in command among us, declared that he would be no party to this peacemaking, but would be gone to Mexico with his servants, there to report to the viceroy. Then the Captain Diaz bade him begone to hell if he wished and report to the devil, saying that he had always believed that he had escaped thence by mistake, and they parted in wrath who, since the day of *noche triste*, never loved each other much; the end of it being that Sarceda rides for Mexico within an hour, to make what mischief he can at the viceroy's court, and I think that you are well rid of him.'

'Father,' said my son to me, 'who is that Spaniard who looks so cruelly upon us?'

'That is he of whom I have told you, son, de Garcia, who has been the curse of our race for two generations, who betrayed your grandfather to the Holy Office, and murdered your grandmother, who put me to torture, and whose ill deeds are not done with yet. Beware of him, son, now and ever, I beseech you.'

Now we were come to the palace, almost the only house that was left standing in the City of Pines. Here an apartment was given to us at the end of the long building, and presently a command was brought to us that I and my wife should wait upon the Spanish captain Diaz.

So we went, though Otomie desired to stay behind, leaving our son alone in the chamber where food had been brought to him. I remember that I kissed him before I left, though I do not know what moved me to do so, unless it was because I thought that he might be asleep when I returned. The Captain Diaz had his quarters at the other end of the palace, some two hundred paces away. Presently we stood before him. He was a rough-looking, thick-set man well on in years, with bright eyes and an ugly honest face, like the face of a peasant who has toiled a lifetime in all weathers, only the fields that Diaz tilled were fields of war, and his harvest had been the lives of men. Just then he was joking with some common soldiers in a strain scarcely suited to nice ears, but so soon as he saw us he ceased and came forward. I saluted him after the Indian fashion by touching the earth with my hand, for what was I but an Indian captive?

'Your sword,' he said briefly, as he scanned me with his quick eyes.

I unbuckled it from my side and handed it to him, saying in Spanish:

'Take it, Captain, for you have conquered, also it does but come back to its owner.' For this was the same sword that I had captured from one Bernal Diaz in the fray of the *noche triste.*

He looked at it, then swore a great oath and said:

'I thought that it could be no other man. And so we meet again thus after so many years. Well, you gave me my life once, and I am glad that I have lived to pay the debt. Had I not been sure that it was you, you had not won such easy terms, friend. How are you named? Nay, I know what the Indians call you.'

'I am named Wingfield.'

'Friend Wingfield then. For I tell you that I would have sat beneath yonder devil's house,' and he nodded towards the *teocalli,* 'till you starved upon its top. Nay, friend Wingfield, take back the sword. I suited myself with another many years ago, and you have used this one gallantly; never have I seen Indians make a better fight. And so that is Otomie, Montezuma's daughter and your wife, still handsome and royal, I see. Lord! Lord! it is many years ago, and yet it seems but yesterday that I saw her father die, a Christian-hearted man, though no Christian, and one whom we dealt ill with. May God forgive us all! Well, Madam, none can say that *you* have a Christian heart. If a certain tale that I have heard of what passed yonder, some three nights since, is true. But we will speak no more of it, for the savage blood will show, and you are pardoned for your husband's sake who saved my comrades from the sacrifice.'

To all this Otomie listened, standing still like a statue, but she never answered a word. Indeed she had spoken very rarely since that dreadful night of her unspeakable shame.

'And now, friend Wingfield,' went on the Captain Diaz, 'what is your purpose? You are free to go where you will, whither then will you go?'

'I do not know,' I answered. 'Years ago, when the Aztec emperor gave me my life and this princess my wife in marriage, I swore to be faithful to him and his cause, and to fight for them till Popo ceased to vomit smoke, till there was no king in Tenoctitlan, and the people of Anahuac were no more a people.'

'Then you are quit of your oath, friend, for all these things have come about, and there has been no smoke on Popo for these two years. Now, if you will be advised by me, you will turn Christian again and enter the service of Spain. But come, let us to supper, we can talk of these matters afterwards.'

So we sat down to eat by the light of torches in the banqueting hall with Bernal Diaz and some other of the Spaniards. Otomie would have left us, and though the captain bade her stay she ate nothing, and presently slipped away from the chamber.

CHAPTER 37

Vengeance

During that meal Bernal Diaz spoke of our first meeting on the causeway, and of how I had gone near to killing him in error, thinking that he was Sarceda, and then he asked me what was my quarrel with Sarceda.

In as few words as possible I told him the story of my life, of all the evil that de Garcia or Sarceda had worked upon me and mine, and of how it was through him that I was in this land that day. He listened amazed.

'Holy Mother!' he said at length, 'I always knew him for a villain, but that, if you do not lie, friend Wingfield, he could be such a man as this, I did not know. Now by my word, had I heard this tale an hour ago, Sarceda should not have left this camp till he had answered it or cleared himself by combat with you. But I fear it is too late; he was to leave for Mexico at the rising of the moon, to stir up mischief against me because I granted you terms—not that I fear him there, where his repute is small.'

'I do not lie indeed,' I answered. 'Much of this tale I can prove if need be, and I tell you that I would give half the life that is left to me to stand face to face in open fight with him again. Ever he has escaped me, and the score between us is long.'

Now as I spoke thus it seemed to me that a cold and dreadful air played upon my hands and brow and a warning sense of present evil crept into my soul, overcoming me so that I could not stir or speak for a while.

'Let us go and see if he has gone,' said Diaz presently, and summoning a guard, he was about to leave the chamber. It was at this moment that I chanced to look up and see a woman standing in the doorway. Her hand rested on the doorpost; her head, from which the long hair streamed, was thrown back, and on her face was a look of such anguish that at first, so much was she changed, I did not know her for Otomie.

When I knew her, I knew all; one thing only could conjure up the terror and agony that shone in her deep eyes.

'What has chanced to our son?' I asked.

'*Dead, dead*!' she answered in a whisper that seemed to pierce my marrow.

I said nothing, for my heart told me what had happened, but Diaz asked, 'Dead—why, what has killed him?'

'De Garcia! I saw him go,' replied Otomie; then she tossed her arms high, and without another sound fell backwards to the earth.

In that moment I think that my heart broke—at least I know that nothing has had the power to move me greatly since, though this memory moves me day by day and hour by hour, till I die and go to seek my son.

'Say, Bernal Diaz,' I cried, with a hoarse laugh, 'did I lie to you concerning this comrade of yours?'

Then, springing over Otomie's body I left the chamber, followed by Bernal Diaz and the others.

Without the door I turned to the left towards the camp. I had not gone a hundred paces when, in the moonlight, I saw a small troop of horsemen riding towards us. It was de Garcia and his servants, and they headed towards the mountain pass on their road to Mexico. I was not too late.

'Halt!' cried Bernal Diaz.

'Who commands me to halt?' said the voice of de Garcia.

'I, your captain,' roared Diaz. 'Halt, you devil, you murderer, or you shall be cut down.'

I saw him start and turn pale.

'These are strange manners, senor,' he said. 'Of your grace I ask—'

At this moment de Garcia caught sight of me for the first time, for I had broken from the hold of Diaz who clutched my arm, and was moving towards him. I said nothing, but there was something in my face which told him that I knew all, and warned him of his doom. He looked past me, but the narrow road was blocked with men. I drew near, but he did not wait for me. Once he put his hand on the hilt of the sword, then suddenly he wheeled his horse round and fled down the street of Xaca.

De Garcia fled, and I followed after him, running fast and low like a hound. At first he gained on me, but soon the road grew rough, and he could not gallop over it. We were clear of the town now, or rather of its ruins, and travelling along a little path which the Indians used to bring down snow from Xaca in the hot weather. Perhaps there are some five miles of this path before the snow line is reached, beyond which no Indian dared to set his foot, for the ground above was holy. Along this path he went, and I was content to see it, for I knew well that the traveller cannot leave it, since on either side lie water-courses and cliffs. Mile after mile de Garcia followed it, looking now to the left, now to the right, and now ahead at the great dome of snow crowned with fire that towered above him. But he never looked behind him; he knew what was there—death in the shape of a man!

I came on doggedly, saving my strength. I was sure that I must catch him at last, it did not matter when.

At length he reached the snow-line where the path ended, and for the first time he looked back. There I was some two hundred paces behind him. I, his death, was behind him, and in front of him shone the snow. For a moment he hesitated, and I heard the heavy breathing of his horse in the great stillness. Then he turned and faced the slope, driving his spurs into the brute's sides. The snow was hard, for here the frost bit sharply, and for a while, though it was so steep, the horse travelled over it better than he had done along the pathway. Now, as before, there was only one road that he could take, for we passed up the crest of a ridge, a pleat as it were in the garment of the mountain, and on either side were steeps of snow on which neither horse nor man might keep his footing. For two hours or more we followed that ridge, and as we went through the silence of the haunted volcano, and the loneliness of its eternal snows, it seemed to me that my spirit entered into the spirit of my quarry, and that with its eyes I saw all that was passing in his heart. To a man so wronged the dream was pleasant even if it were not true, for I read there such agony, such black despair, such haunting memories, such terror of advancing death and of what lay beyond it, that no revenge of man's could surpass their torment. And it was true—I knew that it was true; he suffered all this and more, for if he had no conscience, at least he had fear and imagination to quicken and multiply the fear.

Now the snow grew steeper, and the horse was almost spent, for he could scarcely breathe at so great a height. In vain did de Garcia drive his spurs into its sides, the gallant beast could do no more. Suddenly it fell down. Surely, I thought, he will await me now. But even I had not fathomed the depth of his terrors, for de Garcia disengaged himself from the fallen horse, looked towards me, then fled forward on his feet, casting away his armour as he went that he might travel more lightly.

By this time we had passed the snow and were come to the edge of the ice cap that is made by the melting of the snow with the heat of the inner fires, or perhaps by that of the sun in hot seasons, I know not, and its freezing in the winter months or in the cold of the nights. At least there is such a cap on Xaca, measuring nearly a mile in depth, which lies between the snow and the black rim of the crater. Up this ice climbed de Garcia, and the task is not of the easiest, even for one of untroubled mind, for a man must step from crack to crack or needle to needle of rough ice, that stand upon the smooth surface like the bristles on a hog's back, and woe to him if one break or if he slip, for then, as he falls, very shortly the flesh will be filed from his bones by the thousands of sword-like points over which he must pass in his descent towards the snow. Indeed, many times I feared greatly lest this should chance to de Garcia, for I did not desire to lose my vengeance thus. Therefore twice when I saw him in danger I shouted to him, telling him where to put his feet, for now I was within twenty paces of him, and, strange to say, he obeyed me without question, forgetting everything in his terror of instant death. But for myself I had no fear, for I knew that I should not fall, though the place was one which I had surely shrunk from climbing at any other time.

All this while we had been travelling towards Xaca's fiery crest by the bright moonlight, but now the dawn broke suddenly on the mountain top, and the flame died away in the heart of the pillar of smoke. It was wonderful to see the red glory that shone upon the ice-cap, and on us two men who crept like flies across it, while the mountain's breast and the world below were plunged in the shadows of night.

'Now we have a better light to climb by, comrade!' I called to de Garcia, and my voice rang strangely among the ice cliffs, where never a man's voice had echoed before.

As I spoke the mountain rumbled and bellowed beneath us, shaking like a wind-tossed tree, as though in wrath at the desecration of its sacred solitudes. With the rumbling came a shower of grey ashes that rained down on us, and for a little while hid de Garcia from my sight. I heard him call out in fear, and was afraid lest he had fallen; but presently the ashes cleared away, and I saw him standing safely on the lava rim that surrounds the crater.

Now, I thought, he will surely make a stand, for could he have found courage it had been easy for him to kill me with his sword, which he still wore, as I climbed from the ice to the hot lava. It seemed that he thought of it, for he turned and glared at me like a devil, then went on again, leaving me wondering where he believed that he would find refuge. Some three hundred paces from the edge of the ice, the smoke and steam of the crater rose into the air, and between the two was lava so hot that in places it was difficult to walk upon it. Across this bed, that trembled as I passed over it, went de Garcia somewhat slowly, for now he was weary, and I followed him at my ease, getting my breath again.

Presently I saw that he had come to the edge of the crater, for he leaned forward and looked over, and I thought that he was about to destroy himself by plunging into it. But if such thoughts had been in his mind, he forgot them when he had seen what sort of nest this was to sleep in, for turning, he came back towards me, sword up, and we met within a dozen paces of the edge. I say met, but in truth we did not meet, for he stopped again, well out of reach of my sword. I sat down upon a block of lava and looked at him; it seemed to me that I could not feast my eyes enough upon his face. And what a face it was; that of a more than murderer about to meet his reward! Would that I could paint to show it, for no words can tell the fearfulness of those red and sunken eyes, those grinning teeth and quivering lips. I think that when the enemy of mankind has cast his last die and won his last soul, he too will look thus as he passes into doom.

'At length, de Garcia!' I said.

'Why do you not kill me and make an end?' he asked hoarsely.

'Where is the hurry, cousin? For hard on twenty years I have sought you, shall we then part so soon? Let us talk a while. Before we part to meet no more, perhaps of your courtesy you will answer me a question, for I am curious. Why have you wrought these evils on me and mine? Surely you must have some reason for what seems to be an empty and foolish wickedness.'

I spoke to him thus calmly and coldly, feeling no passion, feeling nothing. For in that strange hour I was no longer Thomas Wingfield, I was no longer human, I was a force, an instrument; I could think of my dead son without sorrow, he did not seem dead to me, for I partook of the nature that he had put on in this change of death. I could even think of de Garcia without hate, as though he also were nothing but a tool in some other hand. Moreover, I *knew* that he was mine, body and mind, and that he must answer and truly, so surely as he must die when I chose to kill him. He tried to shut his lips, but they opened of themselves and word by word the truth was dragged from his black heart as though he stood already before the judgment seat.

'I loved your mother, my cousin,' he said, speaking slowly and painfully; 'from a child I loved her only in the world, as I love her to this hour, but she hated me because I was wicked and feared me because I was cruel. Then she saw your father and loved him, and brought about his escape from the Holy Office, whither I had delivered him to be tortured and burnt, and fled with him to England. I was jealous and would have been revenged if I might, but there was no way. I led an evil life, and when nearly twenty years had gone by, chance took me to England on a trading journey. By chance I learned that your father and mother lived near Yarmouth, and I determined to see her, though at that time I had no thought of killing her. Fortune favoured me, and we met in the woodland, and I saw that she was still beautiful and knew that I loved her more than ever before. I gave her choice to fly with me or to die, and after a while she died. But as she shrank up the wooded hillside before my sword, of a sudden she stood still and said:

"'Listen before you smite, Juan. I have a death vision. As I have fled from you, so shall you fly before one of my blood in a place of fire and rock and snow, and as you drive me to the gates of heaven, so he shall drive you into the mouth of hell.'"

'In such a place as this, cousin,' I said.

'In such a place as this,' he whispered, glancing round.

'Continue.'

Again he strove to be silent, but again my will mastered him and he spoke.

'It was too late to spare her if I wished to escape myself, so I killed her and fled. But terror entered my heart, terror which has never left it to this hour, for always before my eyes was the vision of him of your mother's blood, before whom I should fly as she fled before me, who shall drive me into the mouth of hell.'

'That must be yonder, cousin,' I said, pointing with the sword toward the pit of the crater.

'It is yonder; I have looked.'

'But only for the body, cousin, not for the spirit.'

'Only for the body, not for the spirit,' he repeated after me.

'Continue,' I said.

'Afterwards on that same day I met you, Thomas Wingfield. Already your dead mother's prophecy had taken hold of me, and seeing one of her blood I strove to kill him lest he should kill me.'

'As he will do presently, cousin.'

'As he will do presently,' he repeated like a talking bird.

'You know what happened and how I escaped. I fled to Spain and strove to forget. But I could not. One night I saw a face in the streets of Seville that reminded me of your face. I did not think that it could

311

be you, yet so strong was my fear that I determined to fly to the far Indies. You met me on the night of my flight when I was bidding farewell to a lady.'

'One Isabella de Siguenza, cousin. I bade farewell to her afterwards and delivered her dying words to you. Now she waits to welcome you again, she and her child.'

He shuddered and went on. 'In the ocean we met again. You rose out of the sea. I did not dare to kill you at once, I thought that you must die in the slave-hold and that none could bear witness against me and hold me guilty of your blood. You did not die, even the sea could not destroy you. But I thought that you were dead. I came to Anahuac in the train of Cortes and again we met; that time you nearly killed me. Afterwards I had my revenge and I tortured you well; I meant to murder you on the morrow, though first I would torture you, for terror can be very cruel, but you escaped me. Long years passed, I wandered hither and thither, to Spain, back to Mexico, and elsewhere, but wherever I went my fear, the ghosts of the dead, and my dreams went with me, and I was never fortunate. Only the other day I joined the company of Diaz as an adventurer. Not till we reached the City of Pines did I learn that you were the captain of the Otomie; it was said that you were long dead. You know the rest.'

'Why did you murder my son, cousin?'

'Was he not of your mother's blood, of the blood that should bring my doom upon me, and did I owe you no reward for all the terrors of these many years? Moreover he is foolish who strives to slay the father and spares the son. He is dead and I am glad that I killed him, though he haunts me now with the others.'

'And shall haunt you eternally. Now let us make an end. You have your sword, use it if you can. It will be easier to die fighting.'

'I cannot,' he groaned; 'my doom is upon me.'

'As you will,' and I came at him, sword up.

He ran from before me, moving backwards and keeping his eyes fixed upon mine, as I have seen a rat do when a snake is about to swallow it. Now we were upon the edge of the crater, and looking over I saw an awful sight. For there, some thirty feet beneath us, the red-hot lava glowing sullenly beneath a shifting pall of smoke, rolled and spouted like a thing alive. Jets of steam flew upwards from it with a screaming sound, lines of noxious vapours, many-coloured, crept and twisted on its surface, and a hot and horrid stench poisoned the heated air. Here indeed was such a gate as I could wish for de Garcia to pass through to his own abode.

I looked, pointed with my sword, and laughed; he looked and shrieked aloud, for now all his manhood had left him, so great was his terror of what lay beyond the end. Yes, this proud and haughty Spaniard screamed and wept and prayed for mercy; he who had done so many villainies beyond forgiveness, prayed for mercy that he might find time to repent. I stood and watched him, and so dreadful was his aspect that horror struck me even through the calm of my frozen heart.

'Come, it is time to finish,' I said, and again I lifted my sword, only to let it fall, for suddenly his brain gave way and de Garcia went mad before my eyes!

Of all that followed I will not write. With his madness courage came back to him, and he began to fight, but not with ME.

He seemed to perceive me no more, but nevertheless he fought, and desperately, thrusting at the empty air. It was terrible to see him thus doing battle with his invisible foes, and to hear his screams and curses, as inch by inch they drove him back to the edge of the crater. Here he stood a while, like one who makes a last stand against over-powering strength, thrusting and striking furiously. Twice he nearly fell, as though beneath a mortal wound, but recovering himself, fought on with Nothingness. Then, with a sharp cry, suddenly he threw his arms wide, as a man does who is pierced through the heart; his sword dropped from his hand, and he fell backwards into the pit.

I turned away my eyes, for I wished to see no more; but often I have wondered *Who* or *What* it was that dealt de Garcia his death wound.

CHAPTER 38

Otomie's Farewell

Thus then did I accomplish the vengeance that I had sworn to my father I would wreak upon de Garcia, or rather, thus did I witness its accomplishment, for in the end he died, terribly enough, not by my hand but by those of his own fears. Since then I have sorrowed for this, for, when the frozen and unnatural calm passed from my mind, I hated him as bitterly as ever, and grieved that I let him die otherwise than by my hand, and to this hour such is my mind towards him. Doubtless, many may think it wicked, since we are taught to forgive our enemies, but here I leave the forgiveness to God, for how can I pardon one who betrayed my father to the priests, who murdered my mother and my son, who chained me in the slave-ship and for many hours tortured me with his own hand? Rather, year by year, do I hate him more. I write of this at some length, since the matter has been a trouble to me. I never could say that I was in charity with all men living and dead, and because of this, some years since, a worthy and learned rector of this parish took upon himself to refuse me the rites of the church. Then I went to the bishop and laid the story before him, and it puzzled him somewhat.

But he was a man of large mind, and in the end he rebuked the rector and commanded him to minister to me, for he thought with me that the Almighty could not ask of an erring man, that he should forgive one who had wrought such evils on him and his, even though that enemy were dead and gone to judgment in another place.

But enough of this question of conscience.

When de Garcia was gone into the pit, I turned my steps homewards, or rather towards the ruined city which I could see beneath me, for I had no home left. Now I must descend the ice cap, and this I found less easy than climbing it had been, for, my vengeance being accomplished, I became as other men are, and a sad and weary one at that, so sad indeed that I should not have sorrowed greatly if I had made a false step upon the ice.

But I made none, and at length I came to the snow where the travelling was easy. My oath was fulfilled and my vengeance was accomplished, but as I went I reckoned up the cost. I had lost my betrothed, the love of my youth; for twenty years I had lived a savage chief among savages and made acquaintance with every hardship, wedded to a woman who, although she loved me dearly, and did not lack nobility of mind, as she had shown the other day, was still at heart a savage or, at the least, a thrall of demon gods.

The tribe that I ruled was conquered, the beautiful city where I dwelt was a ruin, I was homeless and a beggar, and my fortune would be great if in the issue I escaped death or slavery. All this I could have borne, for I had borne the like before, but the cruel end of my last surviving son, the one true joy of my desolate life, I could not bear. The love of those children had become the passion of my middle age, and as I loved them so they had loved me. I had trained them from babyhood till their hearts were English and not Aztec, as were their speech and faith, and thus they were not only my dear children, but companions of my own race, the only ones I had. And now by accident, by sickness, and by the sword, they were dead the three of them, and I was desolate.

Ah! we think much of the sorrows of our youth, and should a sweetheart give us the go by we fill the world with moans and swear that it holds no comfort for us. But when we bend our heads before the shrouded shape of some lost child, then it is that for the first time we learn how terrible grief can be. Time, they tell us, will bring consolation, but it is false, for such sorrows time has no salves—I say it who am old—as they are so they shall be. There is no hope but faith, there is no comfort save in the truth that love which might have withered on the earth grows fastest in the tomb, to flower gloriously in heaven; that no love indeed can be perfect till God sanctifies and completes it with His seal of death.

I threw myself down there upon the desolate snows of Xaca, that none had trod before, and wept such tears as a man may weep but once in his life days.

'O my son Absalom, my son, my son Absalom! would God I had died for thee, O Absalom, my son, my son!' I cried with the ancient king—I whose grief was greater than his, for had I not lost three sons within as many years? Then remembering that as this king had gone to join his son long centuries ago, so I must one day go to join mine, and taking such comfort from the thought as may be found in it, I rose and crept back to the ruined City of Pines.

It was near sunset when I came thither, for the road was long and I grew weak. By the palace I met the Captain Diaz and some of his company, and they lifted their bonnets to me as I went by, for they had respect for my sorrows. Only Diaz spoke, saying:

'Is the murderer dead?'

I nodded and went on. I went on to our chamber, for there I thought that I should find Otomie.

She sat in it alone, cold and beautiful as though she had been fashioned in marble.

'I have buried him with the bones of his brethren and his forefathers,' she said, answering the question that my eyes asked. 'It seemed best that you should see him no more, lest your heart should break.'

'It is well,' I answered; 'but my heart is broken already.'

'Is the murderer dead?' she said presently in the very words of Diaz.

'He is dead.'

'How?'

I told her in few words.

'You should have slain him yourself; our son's blood is not avenged.'

'I should have slain him, but in that hour I did not seek vengeance, I watched it fall from heaven, and was content. Perchance it is best so. The seeking of vengeance has brought all my sorrows upon me; vengeance belongs to God and not to man, as I have learned too late.'

'I do not think so,' said Otomie, and the look upon her face was that look which I had seen when she smote the Tlascalan, when she taunted Marina, and when she danced upon the pyramid, the leader of the sacrifice. 'Had I been in your place, I would have killed him by inches. When I had done with him, then the devils might begin, not before. But it is of no account; everything is done with, all are dead, and my heart with them. Now eat, for you are weary.'

So I ate, and afterwards I cast myself upon the bed and slept.

In the darkness I heard the voice of Otomie that said, 'Awake, I would speak with you,' and there was that about her voice which stirred me from my heavy sleep.

'Speak on,' I said. 'Where are you, Otomie?'

'Seated at your side. I cannot rest, so I am seated here. Listen. Many, many years ago we met, when you were brought by Guatemoc from Tobasco. Ah! well do I remember my first sight of you, the Teule, in the court of my father Montezuma, at Chapoltepec. I loved you then as I have loved you ever since. At least I have never gone astray after strange gods,' and she laughed bitterly.

'Why do you talk of these things, Otomie?' I asked.

'Because it is my fancy to do so. Cannot you spare me one hour from your sleep, who have spared you so many? You remember how you scorned me—oh! I thought I should have died of shame when, after I had caused myself to be given to you as wife, the wife of Tezcat, you told me of the maid across the seas, that Lily maid whose token is still set upon your finger. But I lived through it and I loved you the better for your honesty, and then you know the rest. I won you because I was brave and lay at your side upon the stone of sacrifice, where you kissed me and told me that you loved me. But you never loved me, not truly, all the while you were thinking of the Lily maid. I knew it then, as I know it now, though I tried to deceive myself. I was beautiful in those days and this is something with a man. I was faithful and that is more, and once or twice you thought that you loved me. Now I wish that those Teules had come an hour later, and we had died together there upon the stone, that is I wish it for my own sake, not for yours. Then we escaped and the great struggle came. I told you then that I understood it all. You had kissed me on the stone of sacrifice, but in that moment you were as one dead; when you came back to life, it was otherwise. But fortune took the game out of your hands and you married me, and swore an oath to me, and this oath you have kept faithfully. You married me but you did not know whom you married; you thought me beautiful, and sweet, and true, and all these things I was, but you did not understand that I was far apart from you, that I was still a savage as my forefathers had been. You thought that I had learned your ways, perchance even you thought that I reverenced your God, as for your sake I have striven to do, but all the while I have followed the ways of my own people and I could not quite forget my own gods, or at the least they would not suffer me, their servant, to escape them. For years and years I put them from me, but at last they were avenged and my heart mastered me, or rather they mastered me, for I knew nothing of what I did some few nights since, when I celebrated the sacrifice to Huitzel and you saw me at the ancient rites.

'All these years you had been true to me and I had borne you children whom you loved; but you loved them for their own sake, not for mine, indeed, at heart you hated the Indian blood that was mixed in their veins with yours. Me also you loved in a certain fashion and this half love of yours drove me well nigh mad; such as it was, it died when you saw me distraught and celebrating the rites of my forefathers on the *teocalli* yonder, and you knew me for what I am, a savage. And now the children who linked us together are dead—one by one they died in this way and in that, for the curse which follows my blood descended upon them—and your love for me is dead with them. I alone remain alive, a monument of past days, and I die also.

'Nay, be silent; listen to me, for my time is short. When you bade me call you "husband" no longer, then I knew that it was finished. I obey you, I put you from me, you are no more my husband, and soon I shall cease to be your wife; still, Teule, I pray you listen to me. Now it seems to you in your sorrow, that your days are done and that there is no happiness left for you. This is not so. You are still but a man in the beginning of middle age, and you are yet strong. You will escape from this ruined land, and when you shake the dust of it off your feet its curse shall fall from you; you will return to your own place, and there you will find one who has awaited your coming for many years. There the savage woman whom you mated with, the princess of a fallen house, will become but a fantastic memory to you, and all these strange eventful years will be as a midnight dream. Only your love for the dead children will always remain, these you must always love by day and by night, and the desire of them, that desire for the dead than which there is nothing more terrible, shall follow you to your grave, and I am glad that it should be so, for I was their mother and some thought of me must go with them. This alone the Lily maid has left to me, and there only I shall prevail against her, for, Teule, no child of hers shall live to rob your heart of the memory of those I gave you.

'Oh! I have watched you by day and by night: I have seen the longing in your eyes for a face which you have lost and for the land of your youth. Be happy, you shall gain both, for the struggle is ended and the Lily maid has been too strong for me. I grow weak and I have little more to say. We part, and perhaps for ever, for what is there between us save the souls of those dead sons of ours? Since you desire me no more, that I may make our severance perfect, now in the hour of my death I renounce your gods and I seek my own, though I think that I love yours and hate those of my people. Is there any communion between them? We part, and perchance for ever, yet I pray of you to think of me kindly, for I have loved you and I love you; I was the mother of your children, whom being Christian, you will meet again. I love you now and for always. I am glad to have lived because you kissed me on the stone of sacrifice, and afterwards

I bore you sons. They are yours and not mine; it seems to me now that I only cared for them because they were yours, and they loved you and not me. Take them—take their spirits as you have taken everything. You swore that death alone should sever us, and you have kept your oath in the letter and in the thought. But now I go to the Houses of the Sun to seek my own people, and to you, Teule, with whom I have lived many years and seen much sorrow, but whom I will no longer call husband, since you forbade me so to do, I say, make no mock of me to the Lily maid. Speak of me to her as little as you may—be happy and—farewell!'

Now as she spoke ever more faintly, and I listened bewildered, the light of dawn grew slowly in the chamber. It gathered on the white shape of Otomie seated in a chair hard by the bed, and I saw that her arms hung down and that her head was resting on the back of the chair. Now I sprang up and peered into her face. It was white and cold, and I could feel no breath upon her lips. I seized her hand, that also was cold. I spoke into her ear, I kissed her brow, but she did not move nor answer. The light grew quickly, and now I saw all. Otomie was dead, and by her own act.

This was the manner of her death. She had drunk of a poison of which the Indians have the secret, a poison that works slowly and without pain, leaving the mind unclouded to the end. It was while her life was fading from her that she had spoken to me thus sadly and bitterly. I sat upon the bed and gazed at her. I did not weep, for my tears were done, and as I have said, whatever I might feel nothing could break my calm any more. And as I gazed a great tenderness and sorrow took hold of me, and I loved Otomie better now that she was dead before me than ever I had done in her life days, and this is saying much. I remembered her in the glory of her youth as she was in the court of her royal father, I remembered the look which she had given me when she stepped to my side upon the stone of sacrifice, and that other look when she defied Cuitlahua the emperor, who would have slain me. Once more I seemed to hear her cry of bitter sorrow as she uncovered the body of the dead babe our firstborn, and to see her sword in hand standing over the Tlascalan.

Many things came back to me in that sad hour of dawn while I watched by the corpse of Otomie. There was truth in her words, I had never forgotten my first love and often I desired to see her face. But it was not true to say that I had no love for Otomie. I loved her well and I was faithful in my oath to her, indeed, not until she was dead did I know how dear she had grown to me. It is true that there was a great gulf between us which widened with the years, the gulf of blood and faith, for I knew well that she could not altogether put away her old beliefs, and it is true that when I saw her leading the death chant, a great horror took me and for a while I loathed her. But these things I might have lived to forgive, for they were part of her blood and nature, moreover, the last and worst of them was not done by her own will, and when they were set aside there remained much that I could honour and love in the memory of this most royal and beautiful woman, who for so many years was my faithful wife. So I thought in that hour and so I think to this day. She said that we parted for ever, but I trust and I believe that this is not so. Surely there is forgiveness for us all, and a place where those who were near and dear to each other on the earth may once more renew their fellowship.

At last I rose with a sigh to seek help, and as I rose I felt that there was something set about my neck. It was the collar of great emeralds which Guatemoc had given to me, and that I had given to Otomie. She had set it there while I slept, and with it a lock of her long hair. Both shall be buried with me.

I laid her in the ancient sepulchre amid the bones of her forefathers and by the bodies of her children, and two days later I rode to Mexico in the train of Bernal Diaz. At the mouth of the pass I turned and looked back upon the ruins of the City of Pines, where I had lived so many years and where all I loved were buried. Long and earnestly I gazed, as in his hour of death a man looks back upon his past life, till at length Diaz laid his hand upon my shoulder:

'You are a lonely man now, comrade,' he said; 'what plans have you for the future?'

'None,' I answered, 'except to die.'

'Never talk so,' he said; 'why, you are scarcely forty, and I who am fifty and more do not speak of dying. Listen; you have friends in your own country, England?'

'I had.'

'Folk live long in those quiet lands. Go seek them, I will find you a passage to Spain.'

'I will think of it,' I answered.

In time we came to Mexico, a new and a strange city to me, for Cortes had rebuilt it, and where the *teocalli* had stood, up which I was led to sacrifice, a cathedral was building, whereof the foundations were fitly laid with the hideous idols of the Aztecs. The place was well enough, but it is not so beautiful as the Tenoctitlan of Montezuma, nor ever will be. The people too were changed; then they were warriors and free, now they are slaves.

In Mexico Diaz found me a lodging. None molested me there, for the pardon that I had received was respected. Also I was a ruined man, no longer to be feared, the part that I had played in the *noche triste* and in the defence of the city was forgotten, and the tale of my sorrows won me pity even from the Spaniards. I abode in Mexico ten days, wandering sadly about the city and up to the hill of Chapoltepec, where Montezuma's pleasure-house had been, and where I had met Otomie. Nothing was left of its glories except some of the ancient cedar trees. On the eighth day of my stay an Indian stopped me in the street, saying that an old friend had charged him to say that she wished to see me.

I followed the Indian, wondering who the friend might be, for I had no friends, and he led me to a fine stone house in a new street. Here I was seated in a darkened chamber and waited there a while, till suddenly a sad and sweet voice that seemed familiar to me, addressed me in the Aztec tongue, saying, 'Welcome, Teule.'

I looked and there before me, dressed in the Spanish fashion, stood a lady, an Indian, still beautiful, but very feeble and much worn, as though with sickness and sorrow.

'Do you not know Marina, Teule?' she said again, but before the words had left her lips I knew her. 'Well, I will say this, that I should scarcely have known *you*, Teule. Trouble and time have done their work with both of us.'

I took her hand and kissed it.

'Where then is Cortes?' I asked.

Now a great trembling seized her.

'Cortes is in Spain, pleading his suit. He has wed a new wife there, Teule. Many years ago he put me away, giving me in marriage to Don Juan Xaramillo, who took me because of my possessions, for Cortes dealt liberally with me, his discarded mistress.' And she began to weep.

Then by degrees I learned the story, but I will not write it here, for it is known to the world. When Marina had served his turn and her wit was of no more service to him, the conqueror discarded her, leaving her to wither of a broken heart. She told me all the tale of her anguish when she learned the truth, and of how she had cried to him that thenceforth he would never prosper. Nor indeed did he do so.

For two hours or more we talked, and when I had heard her story

I told her mine, and she wept for me, since with all her faults Marina's heart was ever gentle.

Then we parted never to meet again. Before I went she pressed a gift of money on me, and I was not ashamed to take it who had none.

This then was the history of Marina, who betrayed her country for her love's sake, and this the reward of her treason and her love. But I shall always hold her memory sacred, for she was a good friend to me, and twice she saved my life, nor would she desert me, even when Otomie taunted her so cruelly.

CHAPTER 39

Thomas Comes Back
From the Dead

Now on the morrow of my visit to Marina, the Captain Diaz came to see me and told me that a friend of his was in command of a *carak* which was due to sail from the port of Vera Cruz for Cadiz within ten days, and that this friend was willing to give me a passage if I wished to leave Mexico. I thought for a while and said that I would go, and that very night, having bid farewell to the Captain Diaz, whom may God prosper, for he was a good man among many bad ones, I set out from the city for the last time in the company of some merchants. A week's journey took us safely down the mountains to Vera Cruz, a hot unhealthy town with an indifferent anchorage, much exposed to the fierce northerly winds. Here I presented my letters of recommendation to the commander of the *carak*, who gave me passage without question, I laying in a stock of food for the journey.

Three nights later we set sail with a fair wind, and on the following morning at daybreak all that was left in sight of the land of Anahuac was the snowy crest of the volcano Orizaba. Presently that vanished into the clouds, and thus did I bid farewell to the far country where so many things had happened to me, and which according to my reckoning I had first sighted on this very day eighteen years before.

Of my journey to Spain I have nothing of note to tell. It was more prosperous than such voyages often are, and within ten weeks of the date of our lifting anchor at Vera Cruz, we let it drop in the harbour of Cadiz. Here I sojourned but two days, for as it chanced there was an English ship in the harbour trading to London, and in her I took a passage, though I was obliged to sell the smallest of the emeralds from the necklace to find the means to do so, the money that Marina gave me being spent. This emerald sold for a great sum, however, with part of which I purchased clothing suitable to a person of rank, taking the rest of the gold with me. I grieved to part with the stone indeed, though it was but a pendant to the pendant of the collar, but necessity knows no law. The pendant stone itself, a fine gem though flawed, I gave in after years to her gracious majesty Queen Elizabeth.

On board the English ship they thought me a Spanish adventurer who had made moneys in the Indies, and I did not undeceive them, since I would be left to my own company for a while that I might prepare my mind to return to ways of thought and life that it had long forgotten. Therefore I sat apart like some proud don, saying little but listening much, and learning all I could of what had chanced in England since I left it some twenty years before.

At length our voyage came to an end, and on a certain twelfth of June I found myself in the mighty city of London that I had never yet visited, and kneeling down in the chamber of my inn, I thanked God that after enduring so many dangers and hardships, it had pleased Him to preserve me to set foot again on English soil. Indeed to this hour I count it nothing short of marvellous that this frail body of a man should survive all the sorrows and risks of death by sickness, hunger, battle, murder, drowning, wild beasts, and the cruelty of men, to which mine had been exposed for many years.

In London I bought a good horse, through the kind offices of the host of my inn, and on the morrow at daybreak I set out upon the Ipswich road. That very morning my last adventure befell me, for as I jogged along musing of the beauty of the English landscape and drinking in the sweet air of June, a cowardly thief fired a pistol at me from behind a hedge, purposing to plunder me if I fell. The bullet passed through my hat, grazing the skull, but before I could do anything the rascal fled, seeing that he had missed his mark, and I went on my journey, thinking to myself that it would indeed have been strange, if after passing such great dangers in safety, I had died at last by the hand of a miserable foot-pad within five miles of London town.

I rode hard all that day and the next, and my horse being stout and swift, by half-past seven o'clock of the evening I pulled up upon the little hill whence I had looked my last on Bungay, when I rode thence for Yarmouth with my father. Below me lay the red roofs of the town; there to the right were the oaks of Ditchingham and the beautiful tower of St. Mary's Church, yonder the stream of Waveney wandered, and before me stretched the meadow lands, purple and golden with marsh weeds in bloom. All was as it had been, I could see no change at all, the only change was in myself. I dismounted, and going to a pool of water near the roadway I looked at the reflection of my own face. I was changed indeed, scarcely should I have known it for that of the lad who had ridden up this hill some twenty years ago. Now, alas! the eyes were sunken and very sorrowful, the features were sharp, and there was more grey than black in the beard and hair. I should scarcely have known it myself, would any others know it, I wondered? Would there be any to know it indeed? In twenty years many die and others pass out of sight; should I find a friend at all among the living? Since I read the letters which Captain Bell of the '*Adventuress*' had brought me before I sailed for Hispaniola, I had heard no tidings from my home, and what tidings awaited me now? Above all what of Lily, was she dead or married or gone?

Mounting my horse I pushed on again at a canter, taking the road past Waingford Mills through the fords and Pirnhow town, leaving Bungay upon my left. In ten minutes I was at the gate of the bridle path that runs from the Norwich road for half a mile or more beneath the steep and wooded bank under the shelter of which stands the Lodge at Ditchingham. By the gate a man loitered in the last rays of the sun. I looked at him and knew him; it was Billy Minns, that same fool who had loosed de Garcia when I left him bound that I might run to meet my sweetheart. He was an old man now and his white hair hung about his withered face, moreover he was unclean and dressed in rags, but I could have fallen on his neck and embraced him, so rejoiced was I to look once more on one whom I had known in youth.

Seeing me come he hobbled on his stick to the gate to open it for me, whining a prayer for alms.

'Does Mr. Wingfield live here?' I said, pointing up the path, and my breath came quick as I asked.

'Mr. Wingfield, sir, Mr. Wingfield, which of them?' he answered. 'The old gentleman he's been dead nigh upon twenty years. I helped to dig his grave in the chancel of yonder church I did, we laid him by his wife—her that was murdered. Then there's Mr. Geoffrey.'

'What of him?' I asked.

'He's dead, too, twelve year gone or more; he drank hisself to dead he did. And Mr. Thomas, he's dead, drowned over seas they say, many a winter back; they're all dead, all dead! Ah! he was a rare one, Mr. Thomas was; I mind me well how when I let the furriner go—' and he rambled off into the tale of how he had set de Garcia on his horse after I had beaten him, nor could I bring him back from it.

Casting him a piece of money, I set spurs to my weary horse and cantered up the bridle path, leaving the Mill House on my left, and as I went, the beat of his hoofs seemed to echo the old man's words, 'All dead, all dead!' Doubtless Lily was dead also, or if she was not dead, when the tidings came that I had been drowned at sea, she would have married. Being so fair and sweet she would surely not have lacked for suitors, nor could it be believed that she had worn her life away mourning over the lost love of her youth.

Now the Lodge was before me; it had changed no whit except that the ivy and creepers on its front had grown higher, to the roof indeed, and I could see that people lived in the house, for it was well kept, and smoke hung above the chimneys. The gate was locked, and there were no serving men about, for night fell fast, and all had ceased from their labour. Leaving the house on the right I passed round it to the stables that are at the back near the hillside garden, but here the gate was locked also, and I dismounted not knowing what to do. Indeed I was so unmanned with fear and doubt that for a while I seemed bewildered, and leaving the horse to crop the grass where he stood, I wandered to the foot of the church path and gazed up the hill as though I waited for the coming of one whom I should meet.

'What if they were all dead, what if SHE were dead and gone?' I buried my face in my hands and prayed to the Almighty who had protected me through so many years, to spare me this last bitterness. I was crushed with sorrow, and I felt that I could bear no more. If Lily were lost to me also, then I thought that it would be best that I should die, since there was nothing left for which I cared to live.

Thus I prayed for some while, trembling like a leaf, and when I looked up again, ere I turned to seek tidings from those that dwelt in the house, whoever they might be, the twilight had fallen completely, and lo! nightingales sang both far and near. I listened to their song, and as I listened, some troubled memory came back to me that at first I could not grasp. Then suddenly there rose up in my mind a vision of the splendid chamber in Montezuma's palace in Tenoctitlan, and of myself sleeping on a golden bed, and dreaming on that bed. I knew it now, I was the god Tezcat, and on the morrow I must be sacrificed, and I slept in misery, and as I slept I dreamed. I dreamed that I stood where I stood this night, that the scent of the English flowers was in my nostrils as it was this night, and that the sweet song of the nightingales rang in my ears as at this present hour. I dreamed that as I mused and listened the moon came up over the green ash and oaks, and lo! there she shone. I dreamed that I heard a sound of singing on the hill—

But now I awoke from this vision of the past and of a long lost dream, for as I stood the sweet voice of a woman began to sing yonder on the brow of the slope; I was not mad, I heard it clearly, and the sound grew ever nearer as the singer drew down the steep hillside. It was so near now that I could catch the very words of that sad song which to this day I remember.

Now I could see the woman's shape in the moonlight; it was tall and stately and clad in a white robe. Presently she lifted her head to watch the flitter of a bat and the moonlight lit upon her face. It was the face of Lily Bozard, my lost love, beautiful as of yore, though grown older and stamped with the seal of some great sorrow. I saw, and so deeply was I stirred at the sight, that had it not been for the low paling to which I clung, I must have fallen to the earth, and a deep groan broke from my lips.

She heard the groan and ceased her song, then catching sight of the figure of a man, she stopped and turned as though to fly. I stood quite still, and wonder overcoming her fear, she drew nearer and spoke in the sweet low voice that I remembered well, saying, 'Who wanders here so late? Is it you, John?'

Now when I heard her speak thus a new fear took me. Doubtless she was married and 'John' was her husband. I had found her but to lose her more completely. Of a sudden it came into my mind that I would not discover myself till I knew the truth. I advanced a pace, but not so far as to pass from the shadow of the shrubs which grow here, and taking my stand in such a fashion that the moonlight did not strike upon my face, I bowed low in the courtly Spanish fashion, and disguising my voice spoke as a Spaniard might in broken English which I will spare to write down.

'Madam,' I said, 'have I the honour to speak to one who in bygone years was named the Senora Lily Bozard?'

'That was my name,' she answered. 'What is your errand with me, sir?'

Now I trembled afresh, but spoke on boldly.

'Before I answer, Madam, forgive me if I ask another question. Is this still your name?'

'It is still my name, I am no married woman,' she answered, and for a moment the sky seemed to reel above me and the ground to heave beneath my feet like the lava crust of Xaca. But as yet I did not reveal myself, for I wished to learn if she still loved my memory.

'Senora,' I said, 'I am a Spaniard who served in the Indian wars of Cortes, of which perhaps you have heard.'

She bowed her head and I went on. 'In those wars I met a man who was named Teule, but who had another name in former days, so he told me on his deathbed some two years ago.'

'What name?' she asked in a low voice.

'Thomas Wingfield.'

Now Lily moaned aloud, and in her turn caught at the pales to save herself from falling.

'I deemed him dead these eighteen years,' she gasped; 'drowned in the Indian seas where his vessel foundered.'

'I have heard say that he was shipwrecked in those seas, senora, but he escaped death and fell among the Indians, who made a god of him and gave him the daughter of their king in marriage,' and I paused.

She shivered, then said in a hard voice, 'Continue, sir; I listen to you.'

'My friend Teule took the part of the Indians in the wars, as being the husband of one of their princesses he must do in honour, and fought bravely for them for many years. At length the town that he defended was captured, his one remaining child was murdered, his wife the princess slew herself for sorrow, and he himself was taken into captivity, where he languished and died.'

'A sad tale, sir,' she said with a little laugh—a mournful laugh that was half choked by tears.

'A very sad tale, senora, but one which is not finished. While he lay dying, my friend told me that in his early life he had plighted troth with a certain English maid, named—'

'I know the name—continue.'

'He told me that though he had been wedded, and loved his wife the princess, who was a very royal woman, that many times had risked her life for his, ay, even to lying at his side upon the stone of sacrifice and of her own free will, yet the memory of this maiden to whom he was once betrothed had companioned him through life and was strong upon him now at its close. Therefore he prayed me for our friendship's sake to seek her out when I returned to Europe, should she still live, and to give her a message from him, and to make a prayer to her on his behalf.'

'What message and what prayer?' Lily whispered.

'This: that he loved her at the end of his life as he had loved her at its beginning; that he humbly prayed her forgiveness because he had broken the troth which they two swore beneath the beech at Ditchingham.'

'Sir,' she cried, 'what do you know of that?'

'Only what my friend told me, senora.'

'Your friendship must have been close and your memory must be good,' she murmured.

'Which he had done,' I went on, 'under strange circumstances, so strange indeed that he dared to hope that his broken troth might be renewed in some better world than this. His last prayer was that she should say to me, his messenger, that she forgave him and still loved him, as to his death he loved her.'

'And how can such forgiveness or such an avowal advantage a dead man?' Lily asked, watching me keenly through the shadows. 'Have the dead then eyes to see and ears to hear?'

'How can I know, senora? I do but execute my mission.'

'And how can I know that you are a true messenger. It chanced that I had sure tidings of the drowning of Thomas Wingfield many years ago, and this tale of Indians and princesses is wondrous strange, more like those that happen in romances than in this plain world. Have you no token of your good faith, sir?'

'I have such a token, senora, but the light is too faint for you to see it.'

'Then follow me to the house, there we will get light. Stay,' and once more going to the stable gate, she called 'John.'

An old man answered her, and I knew the voice for that of one of my father's serving men. To him she spoke in low tones, then led the way by the garden path to the front door of the house, which she opened with a key from her girdle, motioning to me to pass in before her. I did so, and thinking little of such matters at the moment, turned by habit into the doorway of the sitting-room which I knew so well, lifting my feet to avoid stumbling on its step, and passing into the room found my way through the gloom to the wide fireplace where I took my stand. Lily watched me enter, then following me, she lit a taper at the fire which smouldered on the hearth, and placed it upon the table in the window in such fashion that though I was now obliged to take off my hat, my face was still in shadow.

'Now, sir, your token if it pleases you.'

Then I drew the posy ring from my finger and gave it to her, and she sat down by the table and examined it in the light of the candle, and as she sat thus, I saw how beautiful she was still, and how little time had touched her, except for the sadness of her face, though now she had seen eight-and-thirty winters. I saw also that though she kept control of her features as she looked upon the ring, her breast heaved quickly and her hand shook.

'The token is a true one,' she said at length. 'I know the ring, though it is somewhat worn since last I saw it, it was my mother's; and many years ago I gave it as a love gage to a youth to whom I promised myself in marriage. Doubtless all your tale is true also, sir, and I thank you for your courtesy in bringing it so far. It is a sad tale, a very sad tale. And now, sir, as I may not ask you to stay in this house where I live alone, and there is no inn near, I propose to send serving men to conduct you to my brother's dwelling that is something more than a mile away, if indeed,' she added slowly, 'you do not already know the path! There you will find entertainment, and there the sister of your dead companion, Mary Bozard, will be glad to learn the story of his strange adventures from your lips.'

I bowed my head and answered, 'First, senora, I would pray your answer to my friend's dying prayer and message.'

'It is childish to send answers to the dead.'

'Still I pray for them as I was charged to do.'

'How reads the writing within this ring, sir?'

'Heart to heart, Though far apart,'

I said glibly, and next instant I could have bitten out my tongue.

'Ah! you know that also, but doubtless you have carried the ring for many months and learned the writing. Well, sir, though we were far apart, and though perchance I cherished the memory of him who wore this ring, and for his sake remained unwed, it seems that his heart went a straying—to the breast indeed of some savage woman whom he married, and who bore him children. That being so, my answer to the prayer of your dead friend is that I forgive him indeed, but I must needs take back the vows which I swore to him for this life and for ever, since he has broken them, and as best I may, strive to cast out the love I bore him since he rejected and dishonoured it,' and standing up Lily made as though she tore at her breast and threw something from her, and at the same time she let fall the ring upon the floor.

I heard and my heart stood still. So this was the end of it. Well, she had the right of me, though now I began to wish that I had been less honest, for sometimes women can forgive a lie sooner than such frankness. I said nothing, my tongue was tied, but a great misery and weariness entered into me. Stooping down I found the ring, and replacing it on my finger, I turned to seek the door with a last glance at the woman who refused me. Halfway thither I paused for one second, wondering if I should do well to declare myself, then bethought me that if she would not abate her anger toward me dead, her pity for me living would be small. Nay, I was dead to her, and dead I would remain.

Now I was at the door and my foot was on its step, when suddenly a voice, Lily's voice, sounded in my ears and it was sweet and kind.

'Thomas,' said the voice, 'Thomas, before you go, will you not take count of the gold and goods and land that you placed in my keeping?'

Now I turned amazed, and lo! Lily came towards me slowly and with outstretched arms.

'Oh! foolish man,' she whispered low, 'did you think to deceive a woman's heart thus clumsily? You who talked of the beech in the Hall garden, you who found your way so well to this dark chamber, and spoke the writing in the ring with the very voice of one who has been dead so long. Listen: I forgive that friend of yours his broken troth, for he was honest in the telling of his fault and it is hard for man to live alone so many years, and in strange countries come strange adventures; moreover, I will say it, I still love him as it seems that he loves me, though in truth I grow somewhat old for love, who have lingered long waiting to find it beyond my grave.'

Thus Lily spoke, sobbing as she spoke, then my arms closed round her and she said no more. And yet as our lips met I thought of Otomie, remembering her words, and remembering also that she had died by her own hand on this very day a year ago.

Let us pray that the dead have no vision of the living!

CHAPTER 40

Amen

And now there is little left for me to tell and my tale draws to its end, for which I am thankful, for I am very old and writing is a weariness to me, so great a weariness indeed that many a time during the past winter I have been near to abandoning the task.

For a while Lily and I sat almost silent in this same room where I write to-day, for our great joy and many another emotion that was mixed with it, clogged our tongues. Then as though moved by one impulse, we knelt down and offered our humble thanks to heaven that had preserved us both to this strange meeting. Scarcely had we risen from our knees when there was a stir without the house, and presently a buxom dame entered, followed by a gallant gentleman, a lad, and a maiden. These were my sister Mary, her husband Wilfred Bozard, Lily's brother, and their two surviving children, Roger and Joan. When she guessed that it was I come home again and no other, Lily had sent them tidings by the servant man John, that one was with her whom she believed they would be glad to see, and they had hurried hither, not knowing whom they should find. Nor were they much the wiser at first, for I was much changed and the light in the room shone dim, but stood perplexed, wondering who this stranger might be.

'Mary,' I said at length, 'Mary, do you not remember me, my sister?'

Then she cried aloud, and throwing herself into my arms, she wept there a while, as would any of us were our beloved dead suddenly to appear before our eyes, alive and well, and her husband clasped me by the hand and swore heartily in his amazement, as is the fashion of some men when they are moved. But the children stood staring blankly till I called the girl to me, who now was much what her mother had been when we parted, and kissing her, told her that I was that uncle of whom perhaps she had heard as dead many years ago.

Then my horse, that all this while had been forgotten, having been caught and stabled, we went to supper and it was a strange meal to me, and after meat I asked for tidings. Now I learned that the fortune which my old master Fonseca had left to me came home in safety, and that it had prospered exceedingly under Lily's care, for she had spent but very little of it for her maintenance, looking on it always as a trust rather than as her own. When my death seemed certain my sister Mary had entered on her share of my possessions, however, and with it had purchased some outlying lands in Earsham and Hedenham, and the wood and manor of Tyndale Hall in Ditchingham and Broome. These lands I made haste to say she might keep as a gift from me, since it seemed that I had greater riches than I could need without them, and this saying of mine pleased her husband Wilfred Bozard not a little, seeing that it is hard for a man to give up what he has held for many years.

Then I heard the rest of the story; of my father's sudden death, of how the coming of the gold had saved Lily from being forced into marriage with my brother Geoffrey, who afterwards had taken to evil courses which ended in his decease at the age of thirty-one; of the end of Squire Bozard, Lily's father and my old enemy, from an apoplexy which took him in a sudden fit of anger. After this it seemed, her brother being married to my sister Mary, Lily had moved down to the Lodge, having paid off the charges that my brother Geoffrey had heaped upon his heritage, and bought out my sister's rights to it. And here at the Lodge she had lived ever since, a sad and lonely woman, and yet not altogether an unhappy one, for she gave much of her time to good works. Indeed she told me that had it not been for the wide lands and moneys which she must manage as my heiress, she would have betaken herself to a sisterhood, there to wear her life away in peace, since I being lost to her, and indeed dead, as she was assured,—for the news of the wreck of the *carak* found its way to Ditchingham,—she no longer thought of marriage, though more than one gentleman of condition had sought her hand. This, with some minor matters, such as the birth and death of children, and the story of the great storm and flood that smote Bungay, and indeed the length of the vale of Waveney in those days, was all the tale that they had to tell who had grown from youth to middle age in quiet. For of the crowning and end of kings and of matters politic, such as the downfall of the power of the Pope of Rome and the sacking of the religious houses which was still in progress, I make no mention here.

But now they called for mine, and I began it at the beginning, and it was strange to see their faces as they listened. All night long, till the thrushes sang down the nightingales, and the dawn shone in the east, I sat at Lily's side telling them my story, and then it was not finished. So we slept in the chambers that had been made ready for us, and on the morrow I took it up again, showing them the sword that had belonged to Bernal Diaz, the great necklace of emeralds which Guatemoc had given to me, and certain scars and wounds in witness of its truth. Never did I see folk so much amazed, and when I came to speak of the last sacrifice of the women of the Otomie, and of the horrid end of de Garcia who died fighting with his own shadow, or rather with the shadows of his own wickedness, they cried aloud with fear, as they wept when I told of the deaths of Isabella de Siguenza and of Guatemoc, and of the loss of my sons.

But I did not tell all the story to this company, for some of it was for Lily's ear alone, and to her I spoke of my dealings with Otomie as a man might speak with a man, for I felt that if I kept anything back now there would never be complete faith between us. Therefore I set out all my doubts and troublings, nor did I hide that I had learned to love Otomie, and that her beauty and sweetness had drawn me from the first moment when I saw her in the court of Montezuma, or that which had passed between us on the stone of sacrifice.

When I had done Lily thanked me for my honesty and said it seemed that in such matters men differed from women, seeing that SHE had never felt the need to be delivered from the temptation of strange loves. Still we were as God and Nature had made us, and therefore had little right to reproach each other, or even to set that down as virtue which was but lack of leaning. Moreover, this Otomie, her sin of heathenism notwithstanding, had been a great-hearted woman and one who might well dazzle the wandering eyes of man, daring more for her love's sake than ever she, Lily, could have dared; and to end with, it was clear that at last I must choose between wedding her and a speedy death, and having sworn so great an oath to her I should have been perjured indeed if I had left her when my dangers were gone by. Therefore she, Lily, was minded to let all this matter rest, nor should she be jealous if I still thought of this dead wife of mine with tenderness.

Thus she spoke most sweetly, looking at me the while with her clear and earnest eyes, that I ever fancied must be such as adorn the shining faces of angels. Ay, and those same eyes of hers were filled with tears when I told her my bitter grief over the death of my firstborn and of my other bereavements. For it was not till some years afterwards, when she had abandoned further hope of children, that Lily grew jealous of those dead sons of mine and of my ever present love for them.

Now the tidings of my return and of my strange adventures among the nations of the Indies were noised abroad far and wide, and people came from miles round, ay, even from Norwich and Yarmouth, to see me and I was pressed to tell my tale till I grew weary of it. Also a service of thanksgiving for my safe deliverance from many dangers by land and sea was held in the church of St. Mary's here in Ditchingham, which service was no longer celebrated after the rites of the Romish faith, for while I had sojourned afar, the saints were fallen like the Aztec gods; the yoke of Rome had been broken from off the neck of England, and though all do not think with me, I for one rejoiced at it heartily who had seen enough of priest-craft and its cruelties.

When that ceremony was over and all people had gone to their homes, I came back again to the empty church from the Hall, where I abode a while as the guest of my sister and her husband, till Lily and I were wed.

And there in the quiet light of the June evening I knelt in the chancel upon the rushes that strewed the grave of my father and my mother, and sent my spirit up towards them in the place of their eternal rest, and to the God who guards them. A great calm came upon me as I knelt thus, and I felt how mad had been that oath of mine that as a lad I had sworn to be avenged upon de Garcia, and I saw how as a tree from a seed, all my sorrows had grown from it. But even then I could not do other than hate de Garcia, no, nor can I to this hour, and after all it was natural that I should desire vengeance on the murderer of my mother though the wreaking of it had best been left in another Hand.

Without the little chancel door I met Lily, who was lingering there knowing me to be within, and we spoke together.

'Lily,' I said, 'I would ask you something. After all that has been, will you still take me for your husband, unworthy as I am?'

'I promised so to do many a year ago, Thomas,' she answered, speaking very low, and blushing like the wild rose that bloomed upon a grave beside her, 'and I have never changed my mind. Indeed for many years I have looked upon you as my husband, though I thought you dead.'

'Perhaps it is more than I deserve,' I said. 'But if it is to be, say when it shall be, for youth has left us and we have little time to lose.'

'When you will, Thomas,' she answered, placing her hand in mine.

Within a week from that evening we were wed.

And now my tale is done. God who gave me so sad and troublous a youth and early manhood, has blessed me beyond measure in my middle age and eld. All these events of which I have written at such length were done with many a day ago: the hornbeam sapling that I set beneath these windows in the year when we were married is now a goodly tree of shade and still I live to look on it. Here in the happy valley of the Waveney, save for my bitter memories and that longing for the dead which no time can so much as dull, year after year has rolled over my silvering hairs in perfect health and peace and rest, and year by year have I rejoiced more deeply in the true love of a wife such as few have known. For it would seem as though the heart-ache and despair of youth had but sweetened that most noble nature till it grew well nigh divine. But one sorrow came to us, the death of our infant child—for it was fated that I should die childless—and in that sorrow, as I have told, Lily showed that she was still a woman. For the rest no shadow lay between us. Hand in hand we passed down the hill of life, till at length in the fullness of her days my wife was taken from me. One Christmas night she lay down to sleep at my side, in the morning she was dead. I grieved indeed and bitterly, but the sorrow was not as the sorrows of my youth had been, since age and use dull the edge of mortal griefs and I knew and know that we are no long space apart. Very soon I shall join Lily where she is, and I do not fear that journey. For the dread of death has left me at length, as it departs from all who live long enough and strive to repent them of their sins, and I am well content to leave my safety at the Gates and my heavenly comfort in the Almighty Hand that saved me from the stone of sacrifice and has guided me through so many perils upon this troubled earth.

And now to God my Father, Who holds me, Thomas Wingfield, and all I have loved and love in His holy keeping, be thanks and glory and praise! *Amen.*

The Lady of
Blossholme

CHAPTER 1

Sir John Foterell

Who that has ever seen them can forget the ruins of Blossholme Abbey, set upon their mount between the great waters of the tidal estuary to the north, the rich lands and grazing marshes that, backed with woods, border it east and south, and to the west by the rolling uplands, merging at last into purple moor, and, far away, the sombre eternal hills! Probably the scene has not changed very much since the days of Henry VIII, when those things happened of which we have to tell, for here no large town has arisen, nor have mines been dug or factories built to affront the earth and defile the air with their hideousness and smoke.

The village of Blossholme we know has scarcely varied in its population, for the old records tell us this, and as there is no railway here its aspect must be much the same. Houses built of the local grey stone do not readily fall down. The folk of that generation walked in and out of the doorways of many of them, although the roofs for the most part are now covered with tiles or rough slates in place of reeds from the dike. The parish wells also, fitted with iron pumps that have superseded the old rollers and buckets, still serve the place with drinking-water as they have done since the days of the first Edward, and perhaps for centuries before.

Although their use, if not their necessity, has passed away, not far from the Abbey gate the stocks and whipping-post, the latter arranged with three sets of iron loops fixed at different heights and of varying diameters to accommodate the wrists of man, woman, and child, may still be found in the middle of the Priests' Green. These stand, it will be remembered, under a quaint old roof supported on rough, oaken pillars, and surmounted by a weathercock which the monkish fancy has fashioned to the shape of the archangel blowing the last trump. His clarion or coach-horn, or whatever instrument of music it was he

339

blew, has vanished. The parish book records that in the time of George I a boy broke it off, melted it down, and was publicly flogged in consequence, the last time, apparently, that the whipping-post was used. But Gabriel still twists about as manfully as he did when old Peter, the famous smith, fashioned and set him up with his own hand in the last year of King Henry VIII, as it is said to commemorate the fact that on this spot stood the stakes to which Cicely Harflete, Lady of Blossholme, and her foster-mother, Emlyn, were chained to be burned as witches.

So it is with everything at Blossholme, a place that Time has touched but lightly. The fields, or many of them, bear the same names and remain identical in their shape and outline. The old farmsteads and the few halls in which reside the gentry of the district, stand where they always stood. The glorious tower of the Abbey still points upwards to the sky, although bells and roof are gone, while half-a-mile away the parish church that was there before it—having been rebuilt indeed upon Saxon foundations in the days of William Rufus—yet lies among its ancient elms. Farther on, situate upon the slope of a vale down which runs a brook through meadows, is the stark ruin of the old Nunnery that was subservient to the proud Abbey on the hill, some of it now roofed in with galvanised iron sheets and used as cow-sheds.

It is of this Abbey and this Nunnery and of those who dwelt around them in a day bygone, and especially of that fair and persecuted woman who came to be known as the Lady of Blossholme, that our story has to tell.

****

It was dead winter in the year 1535—the 31st of December, indeed. Old Sir John Foterell, a white-bearded, red-faced man of about sixty years of age, was seated before the log fire in the dining-hall of his great house at Shefton, spelling through a letter which had just been brought to him from Blossholme Abbey. He mastered it at length, and when it was done any one who had been there to look might have seen a knight and gentleman of large estate in a rage remarkable even for the time of the eighth Henry. He dashed the document to the ground; he drank three cups of strong ale, of which he had already had enough, in quick succession; he swore a number of the best oaths of the period, and finally, in the most expressive language, he consigned the body of the Abbot of Blossholme to the gallows and his soul to hell.

"He claims my lands, does he?" he exclaimed, shaking his fist in the direction of Blossholme. "What does the rogue say? That the abbot who went before him parted with them to my grandfather for no good consideration, but under fear and threats. Now, writes he, this Secretary Cromwell, whom they call Vicar-General, has declared that the said transfer was without the law, and that I must hand over the said lands to the Abbey of Blossholme on or before Candlemas! What was Cromwell paid to sign that order with no inquiry made, I wonder?"

Sir John poured out and drank a fourth cup of ale, then set to walking up and down the hall. Presently he halted in front of the fire and addressed it as though it were his enemy.

"You are a clever fellow, Clement Maldon; they tell me that all Spaniards are, and you were taught your craft at Rome and sent here for a purpose. You began as nothing, and now you are Abbot of Blossholme, and, if the King had not faced the Pope, would be more. But you forget yourself at times, for the Southern blood is hot, and when the wine is in, the truth is out. There were certain words you spoke not a year ago before me and other witnesses of which I will remind you presently. Perhaps when Secretary Cromwell learns them he will cancel his gift of my lands, and mayhap lift that plotting head of yours up higher. I'll go remind you of them."

Sir John strode to the door and shouted; it would not be too much to say that he bellowed like a bull. It opened after a while, and a serving-man appeared, a bow-legged, sturdy-looking fellow with a shock of black hair.

"Why are you not quicker, Jeffrey Stokes?" he asked. "Must I wait your pleasure from noon to night?"

"I came as fast as I could, master. Why, then, do you rate me?"

"Would you argue with me, fellow? Do it again and I will have you tied to a post and lashed."

"Lash yourself, master, and let out the choler and good ale, which you need to do," replied Jeffrey in his gruff voice. "There be some men who never know when they are well served, and such are apt to come to ill and lonely ends. What is your pleasure? I'll do it if I can, and if not, do it yourself."

Sir John lifted his hand as though to strike him, then let it fall again.

"I like one who braves me to my teeth," he said more gently, "and that was ever your nature. Take it not ill, man; I was angered, and have cause to be."

"The anger I see, but not the cause, though, as a monk came from the Abbey but now, perhaps I can hazard a guess."

"Aye, that's it, that's it, Jeffrey. Hark; I ride to yonder crows'-nest, and at once. Saddle me a horse."

"Good, master. I'll saddle two horses."

"Two? I said one. Fool, can I ride a pair at once, like a mountebank?"

"I know not, but you can ride one and I another. When the Abbot of Blossholme visits Sir John Foterell of Shefton he comes with hawk on wrist, with chaplains and pages, and ten stout men-at-arms, of whom he keeps more of late than a priest would seem to need about him. When Sir John Foterell visits the Abbot of Blossholme, at least he should have one serving-man at his back to hold his nag and bear him witness."

Sir John looked at him shrewdly.

"I called you fool," he said, "but you are none except in looks. Do as you will, Jeffrey, but be swift. Stop. Where is my daughter?"

"The Lady Cicely sits in her parlour. I saw her sweet face at the window but now staring out at the snow as though she thought to see a ghost in it."

"Um," grunted Sir John, "the ghost she thinks to see rides a grand grey mare, stands over six feet high, has a jolly face, and a pair of arms well made for sword and shield, or to clip a girl in. Yet that ghost must be laid, Jeffrey."

"Pity if so, master. Moreover, you may find it hard. Ghost-laying is a priest's job, and when maids' waists are willing, men's arms reach far."

"Be off, sirrah," roared Sir John, and Jeffrey went.

Ten minutes later they were riding for the Abbey, three miles away, and within half-an-hour Sir John was knocking, not gently, at its gate, while the monks within ran to and fro like startled ants, for the times were rough, and they were not sure who threatened them. When they knew their visitor at last they set to work to unbar the great doors and let down the drawbridge, that had been hoist up at sunset.

Presently Sir John stood in the Abbot's chamber, warming himself at the great fire, and behind him stood his serving-man, Jeffrey, carrying his long cloak. It was a fine room, with a noble roof of carved chestnut wood and stone walls hung with costly tapestry, whereon were worked scenes from the Scriptures. The floor was hid with rich carpets made of coloured Eastern wools. The furniture also was rich and foreign-looking, being inlaid with ivory and silver, while on the table stood a golden crucifix, a miracle of art, and upon an easel, so that the light from a hanging silver lamp fell on it, a life-sized picture of the Magdalene by some great Italian painter, turning her beauteous eyes to heaven and beating her fair breast.

Sir John looked about him and sniffed.

"Now, Jeffrey, would you think that you were in a monk's cell or in some great dame's bower? Hunt under the table, man; sure, you will find her lute and needlework. Whose portrait is that, think you?" and he pointed to the Magdalene.

"A sinner turning saint, I think, master. Good company for laymen when she was sinner, and good for priests now that she is saint. For the rest, I could snore well here after a cup of yon red wine," and he jerked his thumb towards a long-necked bottle on a sideboard. "Also, the fire burns bright, which is not to be wondered at, seeing that it is made of dry oak from your Sticksley Wood."

"How know you that, Jeffrey?" asked Sir John.

"By the grain of it, master—by the grain of it. I have hewn too many a timber there not to know. There's that in the Sticksley clays which makes the rings grow wavy and darker at the heart. See there."

Sir John looked, and swore an angry oath.

"You are right, man; and now I come to think of it, when I was a little lad my old grandsire bade me note this very thing about the Sticksley oaks. These cursed monks waste my woods beneath my nose. My forester is a rogue. They have scared or bribed him, and he shall hang for it."

"First prove the crime, master, which won't be easy; then talk of hanging, which only kings and abbots, 'with right of gallows,' can do at will. Ah! you speak truth," he added in a changed voice; "it is a lovely chamber, though not good enough for the holy man who dwells in it, since such a saint should have a silver shrine like him before the altar yonder, as doubtless he will do when ere long he is old bones," and, as though by chance, he trod upon his lord's foot, which was somewhat gouty.

Round came Sir John like the Blossholme weathercock on a gusty day.

"Clumsy toad!" he yelled, then paused, for there within the arras, that had been lifted silently, stood a tall, tonsured figure clothed in rich furs, and behind him two other figures, also tonsured, in simple black robes. It was the Abbot with his chaplains.

"Benedicite!" said the Abbot in his soft, foreign voice, lifting the two fingers of his right hand in blessing.

"Good-day," answered Sir John, while his retainer bowed his head and crossed himself. "Why do you steal upon a man like a thief in the night, holy Father?" he added irritably.

"That is how we are told judgment shall come, my son," answered the Abbot, smiling; "and in truth there seems some need of it. We heard loud quarrelling and talk of hanging men. What is your argument?"

"A hard one of oak," answered old Sir John sullenly. "My servant here said those logs upon your fire came from my Sticksley Wood, and I answered him that if so they were stolen, and my reeve should hang for it."

"The worthy man is right, my son, and yet your forester deserves no punishment. I bought our scanty store of firing from him, and, to tell truth, the count has not yet been paid. The money that should have discharged it has gone to London, so I asked him to let it stand until the summer rents come in. Blame him not, Sir John, if, out of friendship, knowing it was naught to you, he has not bared the nakedness of our poor house."

"Is it the nakedness of your poor house"—and he glanced round the sumptuous chamber—"that caused you to send me this letter saying that you have Cromwell's writ to seize my lands?" asked Sir John, rushing at his grievance like a bull, and casting down the document upon the table; "or do you also mean to make payment for them—when your summer rents come in?"

"Nay, son. In that matter duty led me. For twenty years we have disputed of those estates which, as you know, your grandsire took from us in a time of trouble, thus cutting the Abbey lands in twain, against the protest of him who was Abbot in those days. Therefore, at last I laid the matter before the Vicar-General, who, I hear, has been pleased to decide the suit in favour of this Abbey."

"To decide a suit of which the defendant had no notice!" exclaimed Sir John. "My Lord Abbot, this is not justice; it is roguery that I will never bear. Did you decide aught else, pray you?"

"Since you ask it—something, my son. To save costs I laid before him the sundry points at issue between us, and in sum this is the judgment: Your title to all your Blossholme lands and those contiguous, totalling eight thousand acres, is not voided, yet it is held to be tainted and doubtful."

"God's blood! Why?" asked Sir John.

"My son, I will tell you," replied the Abbot gently. "Because within a hundred years they belonged to this Abbey by gift of the Crown, and there is no record that the Crown consented to their alienation."

"No record," exclaimed Sir John, "when I have the indentured deed in my strong-box, signed by my great-grandfather and the Abbot Frank Ingham! No record, when my said forefather gave you other lands in place of them which you now hold? But go on, holy priest."

"My son, I obey you. Your title, though pronounced so doubtful, is not utterly voided; yet it is held that you have all these lands as tenant

344

of this Abbey, to which, should you die without issue, they will relapse. Or should you die with issue under age, such issue will be ward to the Abbot of Blossholme for the time being, and failing him, that is, if there were no Abbot and no Abbey, of the Crown."

Sir John listened, then sank back into a chair, while his face went white as ashes.

"Show me that judgment," he said slowly.

"It is not yet engrossed, my son. Within ten days or so I hope— But you seem faint. The warmth of this room after the cold outer air, perhaps. Drink a cup of our poor wine," and at a motion of his hand one of the chaplains stepped to the sideboard, filled a goblet from the long-necked flask that stood there, and brought it to Sir John.

He took it as one that knows not what he does, then suddenly threw the silver cup and its contents into the fire, whence a chaplain recovered it with the wood-tongs.

"It seems that you priests are my heirs," said Sir John in a new, quiet voice, "or so you say; and, if that is so, my life is likely to be short. I'll not drink your wine, lest it should be poisoned. Hearken now, Sir Abbot. I believe little of this tale, though doubtless by bribes and other means you have done your best to harm me behind my back up yonder in London. Well, to-morrow at the dawn, come fair weather or come foul, I ride through the snows to London, where I too have friends, and we will see, we will see. You are a clever man, Abbot Maldon, and I know that you need money, or its worth, to pay your men-at-arms and satisfy the great costs at which you live—and there are our famous jewels—yes, yes, the old Crusader jewels. Therefore you have sought to rob me, whom you ever hated, and perchance Cromwell has listened to your tale. Perchance, fool priest," he added slowly, "he had it in his mind to fat this Church goose of yours with my meal before he wrings its neck and cooks it."

At these words the Abbot started for the first time, and even the two impassive chaplains glanced at each other.

"Ah! does that touch you?" asked Sir John Foterell. "Well, then, here is what shall make you smart. You think yourself in favour at the Court, do you not? because you took the oath of succession which braver men, like the brethren of the Charterhouse, refused, and died for it. But you forget the words you said to me when the wine you love had a hold of you in my hall—"

"Silence! For your own sake, silence, Sir John Foterell!" broke in the Abbot. "You go too far."

"Not so far as you shall go, my Lord Abbot, ere I have done with you. Not so far as Tower Hill or Tyburn, thither to be hung and quartered as a traitor to his Grace. I tell you, you forget the words you spoke, but I will remind you of them. Did you not say to me when the guests had gone, that King Henry was a heretic, a tyrant, and an infidel whom the Pope would do well to excommunicate and depose? Did you not, when I led you on, ask me if I could not bring about a rising of the common people in these parts, among whom I have great power, and of those gentry who know and love me, to overthrow him, and in his place set up a certain Cardinal Pole, and for the deed promise me the pardon and absolution of the Pope, and much advancement in his name and that of the Spanish Emperor?"

"Never," answered the Abbot.

"And did I not," went on Sir John, taking no note of his denial, "did I not refuse to listen to you and tell you that your words were traitorous, and that had they been spoken otherwhere than in my house, I, as in duty bound by my office, would make report of them? Aye, and have you not from that hour striven to undo me, whom you fear?"

"I deny it all," said the Abbot again. "These be but empty lies bred of your malice, Sir John Foterell."

"Empty words, are they, my Lord Abbot! Well, I tell you that they are all written down and signed in due form. I tell you I had witnesses you knew naught of who heard them with their ears. Here stands one of them behind my chair. Is it not so, Jeffrey?"

"Aye, master," answered the serving-man. "I chanced to be in the little chamber beyond the wainscot with others waiting to escort the Abbot home, and heard them all, and afterward I and they put our marks upon the writing. As I am a Christian man that is so, though, master, this is not the place that I should have chosen to speak of it, however much I might be wronged."

"It will serve my turn," said the enraged knight, "though it is true that I will speak of it louder elsewhere, namely, before the King's Council. To-morrow, my Lord Abbot, this paper and I go to London, and then you shall learn how well it pays you to try to pluck a Foterell of his own."

Now it was the Abbot's turn to be frightened. His smooth, olive-coloured cheeks sank in and went white, as though already he felt the cord about his throat. His jewelled hand shook, and he caught the arm of one of his chaplains and hung to it.

"Man," he hissed, "do you think that you can utter such false threats and go hence to ruin me, a consecrated abbot? I have dungeons here; I have power. It will be said that you attacked me, and that

I did but strive to defend myself. Others can bring witness besides you, Sir John," and he whispered some words in Latin or Spanish into the ear of one of his chaplains, whereon that priest turned to leave the room.

"Now it seems that we are getting to business," said Jeffrey Stokes, as, lying his hand upon the knife at his girdle, he slipped between the monk and the door.

"That's it, Jeffrey," cried Sir John. "Stop the rat's hole. Look you, Spaniard, I have a sword. Show me to your gate, or, by virtue of the King's commission that I hold, I do instant justice on you as a traitor, and afterward answer for it if I win out."

The Abbot considered a moment, taking the measure of the fierce old knight before him. Then he said slowly—

"Go as you came, in peace, O man of wrath and evil, but know that the curse of the Church shall follow you. I say that you stand near to ill."

Sir John looked at him. The anger went out of his face, and, instead, upon it appeared something strange—a breath of foresight, an inspiration, call it what you will.

"By heaven and all its saints! I think you are right, Clement Maldon," he muttered. "Beneath that black dress of yours you are a man like the rest of us, are you not? You have a heart, you have members, you have a brain to think with; you are a fiddle for God to play on, and however much your superstitions mask and alter it, out of those strings now and again will come some squeak of truth. Well, I am another fiddle, of a more honest sort, mayhap, though I do not lift two fingers of my right hand and say, 'Benedicite, my son,' and 'Your sins are forgiven you'; and just now the God of both of us plays His tune in me, and I will tell you what it is. I stand near to death, but you stand not far from the gallows. I'll die an honest man; you will die like a dog, false to everything, and afterwards let your beads and your masses and your saints help you if they can. We'll talk it over when we meet again elsewhere. And now, my Lord Abbot, lead me to your gate, remembering that I follow with my sword. Jeffrey, set those carrion crow in front of you, and watch them well. My Lord Abbot, I am your servant; march!"

CHAPTER 2

The Murder By the Mere

For a while Sir John and his retainer rode in silence. Then he laughed loudly.

"Jeffrey," he called, "that was a near touch. Sir Priest was minded to stick his Spanish pick-tooth between our ribs, and shrive us afterwards, as we lay dying, to salve his conscience."

"Yes, master; only, being reasonable, he remembered that English swords have a longer reach, and that his bullies are in the Ford alehouse seeing the Old Year out, and so put it off. Master, I have always told you that old October of yours is too strong to drink at noon. It should be saved till bed-time."

"What do you mean, man?"

"I mean that ale spoke yonder, not wisdom. You have showed your hand and played the fool."

"Who are you to teach me?" asked Sir John angrily. "I meant that he should hear the truth for once, the slimy traitor."

"Perhaps, perhaps; but these be bad days for Truth and those who court her. Was it needful to tell him that to-morrow you journey to London upon a certain errand?"

"Why not? I'll be there before him."

"Will you ever be there, master? The road runs past the Abbey, and that priest has good ruffians in his pay who can hold their tongues."

"Do you mean that he will waylay me? I say he dare not. Still, to please you, we will take the longer path through the forest."

"A rough one, master; but who goes with you on this business? Most of us are away with the wains, and others make holiday. There are but three serving-men at the hall, and you cannot leave the Lady Cicely without a guard, or take her with you through this cold. Remember there's wealth yonder which some may need more even than your lands," he added meaningly. "Wait a while, then, till your people

348

return or you can call up your tenants, and go to London as one of your quality should, with twenty good men at your back."

"And so give our friend the Abbot time to get Cromwell's ear, and through him that of the King. No, no; I ride to-morrow at the dawn with you, or, if you are afraid, without you, as I have done before and taken no harm."

"None shall say that Jeffrey Stokes is afraid of man or priest or devil," answered the old soldier, colouring. "Your road has been good enough for me this thirty years, and it is good enough now. If I warned you it was not for my own sake, who care little what comes, but for yours and that of your house."

"I know it," said Sir John more kindly. "Take not my words ill, my temper is up to-day. Thank the saints! here is the hall at last. Why! whose horse has passed the gates before us?"

Jeffrey glanced at the tracks which the moonlight showed very clearly in the new-fallen snow.

"Sir Christopher Harflete's grey mare," he said. "I know the shoeing and the round shape of the hoof. Doubtless he is visiting Mistress Cicely."

"Whom I have forbidden to him," grumbled Sir John, swinging himself from the saddle.

"Forbid him not," answered Jeffrey, as he took his horse. "Christopher Harflete may yet be a good friend to a maid in need, and I think that need is nigh."

"Mind your business, knave," shouted Sir John. "Am I to be set at naught in my own house by a chit of a girl and a gallant who would mend his broken fortunes?"

"If you ask me, I think so," replied the imperturbable Jeffrey, as he led away the horses.

Sir John strode into the house by the back way, which opened on to the stable-yard. Taking the lantern that stood by the door, he went along galleries and upstairs to the sitting-chamber above the hall, which, since her mother's death, his daughter had used as her own, for here he guessed that he would find her. Setting down the lantern upon the passage table, he pushed open the door, which was not latched, and entered.

The room was large, and, being lighted only by the great fire that burned upon the hearth and two candles, all this end of it was hid in shadow. Near to the deep window-place the shadow ceased, however, and here, seated in a high-backed oak chair, with the light of the blazing fire falling full upon her, was Cicely Foterell, Sir John's only surviving child. She was a tall and graceful maiden, blue-eyed, brown-haired, fair-skinned, with a round and child-like face which most people thought beautiful to look upon. Just now this face, that generally was so arch and cheerful, seemed somewhat troubled. For this there might be a reason, since, seated upon a stool at her side, was a young man talking to her earnestly.

He was a stalwart young man, very broad about the shoulders, clean-cut in feature, with a long, straight nose, black hair, and merry black eyes. Also, as such a gallant should do, he appeared to be making love with much vigour and directness, for his face was upturned pleading with the girl, who leaned back in her chair answering him nothing. At this moment, indeed, his copious flow of words came to an end, perhaps from exhaustion, perhaps for other reasons, and was succeeded by a more effective method of attack. Suddenly sinking from the stool to his knees, he took the unresisting hand of Cicely and kissed it several times; then, emboldened by his success, threw his long arms about her, and before Sir John, choked with indignation, could find words to stop him, drew her towards him and treated her red lips as he had treated her fingers. This rude proceeding seemed to break the spell that bound her, for she pushed back the chair and, escaping from his grasp, rose, saying in a broken voice—

"Oh! Christopher, dear Christopher, this is most wrong."

"May be," he answered. "So long as you love me I care not what it is."

"That you have known these two years, Christopher. I love you well, but, alas! my father will have none of you. Get you hence now, ere he returns, or we both shall pay for it, and I, perhaps, be sent to a nunnery where no man may come."

"Nay, sweet, I am here to ask his consent to my suit—"

Then at last Sir John broke out.

"To ask my consent to your suit, you dishonest knave!" he roared from the darkness; whereat Cicely sank back into her chair looking as though she would faint, and the strong Christopher staggered like a man pierced by an arrow. "First to take my girl and hug her before my very eyes, and then, when the mischief is done, to ask my consent to your suit!" and he rushed at them like a charging bull.

Cicely rose to fly, then, seeing no escape, took refuge in her lover's arms. Her infuriated father seized the first part of her that came to his hand, which chanced to be one of her long brown plaits of hair, and tugged at it till she cried out with pain, purposing to tear her away, at which sight and sound Christopher lost his temper also.

"Leave go of the maid, sir," he said in a low, fierce voice, "or, by God! I'll make you."

"Leave go of the maid?" gasped Sir John. "Why, who holds her tightest, you or I? Do you leave go of her."

"Yes, yes, Christopher," she whispered, "ere I am pulled in two."

Then he obeyed, lifting her into the chair, but her father still kept his hold of the brown tress.

"Now, Sir Christopher," he said, "I am minded to put my sword through you."

"And pierce your daughter's heart as well as mine. Well, do it if you will, and when we are dead and you are childless, weep yourself and go to the grave."

"Oh! father, father," broke in Cicely, who knew the old man's temper, and feared the worst, "in justice and in pity, listen to me. All my heart is Christopher's, and has been from a child. With him I shall have happiness, without him black despair; and that is his case too, or so he swears. Why, then, should you part us? Is he not a proper man and of good lineage, and name unstained? Until of late did you not ever favour him much and let us be together day by day? And now, when it is too late, you deny him. Oh! why, why?"

"You know why well enough, girl? Because I have chosen another husband for you. The Lord Despard is taken with your baby face, and would marry you. But this morning I had it under his own hand."

"The Lord Despard?" gasped Cicely. "Why, he only buried his second wife last month! Father, he is as old as you are, and drunken, and has grandchildren of well-nigh my age. I would obey you in all things, but never will I go to him alive."

"And never shall he live to take you," muttered Christopher.

"What matter his years, daughter? He is a sound man, and has no son, and should one be born to him, his will be the greatest heritage within three shires. Moreover, I need his friendship, who have bitter enemies. But enough of this. Get you gone, Christopher, before worse befall you."

"So be it, sir, I will go; but first, as an honest man and my father's friend, and, as I thought, my own, answer me one question. Why have you changed your tune to me of late? Am I not the same Christopher Harflete I was a year or two ago? And have I done aught to lower me in the world's eye or in yours?"

"No, lad," answered the old knight bluntly; "but since you will have it, here it is. Within that year or two your uncle whose heir you were has married and bred a son, and now you are but a gentleman of good name, and little to float it on. That big house of yours must go to the hammer, Christopher. You'll never stow a bride in it."

"Ah! I thought as much. Christopher Harflete with the promise of the Lesborough lands was one man; Christopher Harflete without them is another—in your eyes. Yet, sir, I hold you foolish. I love your daughter and she loves me, and those lands and more may come back, or I, who am no fool, will win others. Soon there will be plenty going up there at Court, where I am known. Further, I tell you this: I believe that I shall marry Cicely, and earlier than you think, and I would have had your blessing with her."

"What! Will you steal the girl away?" asked Sir John furiously.

"By no means, sir. But this is a strange world of ours, in which from hour to hour top becomes bottom, and bottom top, and there—I think I shall marry her. At least I am sure that Despard the sot never will, for I'll kill him first, if I hang for it. Sir, sir, surely you will not throw your pearl upon that muckheap. Better crush it beneath your heel at once. Look, and say you cannot do it," and he pointed to the pathetic figure of Cicely, who stood by them with clasped hands, panting breast, and a face of agony.

The old knight glanced at her out of the corners of his eyes, and saw something that moved him to pity, for at bottom his heart was honest, and though he treated her so roughly, as was the fashion of the times, he loved his daughter more than all the world.

"Who are you, that would teach me my duty to my bone and blood?" he grumbled. Then he thought a while, and added, "Hear me, now, Christopher Harflete. To-morrow at the dawn I ride to London with Jeffrey Stokes on a somewhat risky business."

"What business, sir?"

"If you would know—that of a quarrel with yonder Spanish rogue of an Abbot, who claims the best part of my lands, and has poisoned the ear of that upstart, the Vicar-General Cromwell. I go to take the deeds and prove him a liar and a traitor also, which Cromwell does not know. Now, is my nest safe from you while I am away? Give me your word, and I'll believe you, for at least you are an honest gentleman, and if you have poached a kiss or two, that may be forgiven. Others have done the same before you were born. Give me your word, or I must drag the girl through the snows to London at my heels."

"You have it, sir," answered Christopher. "If she needs my company she must come for it to Cranwell Towers, for I'll not seek hers while you are away."

"Good. Then one gift for another. I'll not answer my Lord of Despard's letter till I get back again—not to please you, but because I hate writing. It is a labour to me, and I have no time to spare to-night. Now, have a cup of drink and be off with you. Love-making is thirsty work."

"Aye, gladly, sir, but hear me, hear me. Ride not to London with such slight attendance after a quarrel with Abbot Maldon. Let me wait on you. Although my fortunes be so low I can bring a man or two—six or eight, indeed—while yours are away with the wains."

"Never, Christopher. My own hand has guarded my head these sixty years, and can do so still. Also," he added, with a flash of insight, "as you say, the journey is dangerous, and who knows? If aught went wrong, you might be wanted nearer home. Christopher, you shall never have my girl; she's not for you. Yet, perhaps, if need were, you would strike a blow for her even if it made you excommunicate. Get hence, wench. Why do you stand there gaping on us, like an owl in sunlight? And remember, if I catch you at more such tricks, you'll spend your days mumbling at prayers in a nunnery, and much good may they do you."

"At least I should find peace there, and gentle words," answered Cicely with spirit, for she knew her father, and the worst of her fear had departed. "Only, sir, I did not know that you wished to swell the wealth of the Abbots of Blossholme."

"Swell their wealth!" roared her father. "Nay, I'll stretch their necks. Get you to your chamber, and send up Jeffrey with the liquor."

Then, having no choice, Cicely curtseyed, first to her father and next to Christopher, to whom she sent a message with her eyes that she dared not utter with her lips, and so vanished into the shadows, where presently she was heard stumbling against some article of furniture.

"Show the maid a light, Christopher," said Sir John, who, lost in his own thoughts, was now gazing into the fire.

Seizing one of the two candles, Christopher sprang after her like a hound after a hare, and presently the pair of them passed through the door and down the long passage beyond. At a turn in it they halted, and once more, without word spoken, she found her way into those long arms.

"You will not forget me, even if we must part?" sobbed Cicely.

"Nay, sweet," he answered. "Moreover, keep a brave heart; we do not part for long, for God has given us to each other. Your father does not mean all he says, and his temper, which has been stirred to-day, will soften. If not, we must look to ourselves. I keep a swift horse or two, Cicely. Could you ride one if need were?"

"I have ever loved riding," she said meaningly.

"Good. Then you shall never go to that fat hog's sty, for I'll stick him first. And I have friends both in Scotland and in France. Which like you best?"

"They say the air of France is softer. Now, away from me, or one will come to seek us," and they tore themselves apart.

"Emlyn, your foster-mother, is to be trusted," he said rapidly; "also she loves me well. If there be need, let me hear of you through her."

"Aye," she answered, "without fail," and glided from him like a ghost.

"Have you been waiting to see the moon rise?" asked Sir John, glancing at Christopher from beneath his shaggy eyebrows as he returned.

"Nay, sir, but the passages in this old house of yours are most wondrous long, and I took a wrong turn in threading them."

"Oh!" said Sir John. "Well, you have a talent for wrong turns, and such partings are hard. Now, do you understand that this is the last of them?"

"I understand that you may say so, sir."

"And that I mean it, too, I hope. Listen, Christopher," he added, with earnestness, but in a kindly voice. "Believe me, I like you well, and would not give you pain, or the maid yonder, if I could help it. Yet I have no choice. I am threatened on all sides by priest and king, and you have lost your heritage. She is the only jewel that I can pawn, and for your own safety's sake and her children's sake, must marry well. Yonder Despard will not live long, he drinks too hard; and then your day may come, if you still care for his leavings—perhaps in two years, perhaps in less, for she will soon see him out. Now, let us talk no more of the matter, but if aught befalls me, be a friend to her. Here comes the liquor—drink it up and be off. Though I seem rough with you, my hope is that you may quaff many another cup at Shefton."

****

It was seven o'clock of the next morning, and Sir John, having eaten his breakfast, was girding on his sword—for Jeffrey had already gone to fetch the horses—when the door opened and his daughter entered the great hall, candle in hand, wrapped in a fur cloak, over which her long hair fell. Glancing at her, Sir John noted that her eyes were wide and frightened.

"What is it now, girl?" he asked. "You'll take your death of cold among these draughts."

"Oh! father," she said, kissing him, "I came to bid you farewell, and—and—to pray you not to start."

"Not to start? And why?"

"Because, father, I have dreamed a bad dream. At first last night I could not sleep, and when at length I did I dreamed that dream thrice," and she paused.

"Go on, Cicely; I am not afraid of dreams, which are but foolishness—coming from the stomach."

"Mayhap; yet, father, it was so plain and clear I can scarcely bear to tell it to you. I stood in a dark place amidst black things that I knew to be trees. Then the red dawn broke upon the snow, and I saw a little pool with brown rushes frozen in its ice. And there—there, at the edge of the pool, by a pollard willow with one white limb, you lay, your bare sword in your hand and an arrow in your neck, shot from behind, while in the trunk of the willow were other arrows, and lying near you two slain. Then cloaked men came as though to carry them away, and I awoke. I say I dreamed it thrice."

"A jolly good morrow indeed," said Sir John, turning a shade paler. "And now, daughter, what do you make of this business?"

"I? Oh! I make that you should stop at home and send some one else to do your business. Sir Christopher, for instance."

"Why, then I should baulk your dream, which is either true or false. If true, I have no choice, it must be fulfilled; if false, why should I heed it? Cicely, I am a plain man and take no note of such fancies. Yet I have enemies, and it may well chance that my day is done. If so, use your mother wit, girl; beware of Maldon, look to yourself, and as for your mother's jewels, hide them," and he turned to go.

She clasped him by the arm.

"In that sad case what should I do, father?" she asked eagerly.

He stopped and stared at her up and down.

"I see that you believe in your dream," he said, "and therefore, although it shall not stay a Foterell, I begin to believe in it too. In that case you have a lover whom I have forbid to you. Yet he is a man after my own heart, who would deal well by you. If I die, my game is played. Set your own anew, sweet Cicely, and set it soon, ere that Abbot is at your heels. Rough as I may have been, remember me with kindness, and God's blessing and mine be on you. Hark! Jeffrey calls, and if they stand, the horses will take cold. There, fare you well. Fear not for me, I wear a chain shirt beneath my cloak. Get back to bed and warm you," and he kissed her on the brow, thrust her from him and was gone.

Thus did Cicely and her father part—for ever.

****

All that day Sir John and Jeffrey, his serving-man, trotted forward through the snow—that is, when they were not obliged to walk because of the depth of the drifts. Their plan was to reach a certain farm in a glade of the woodland within two hours of sundown, and sleep there, for they had taken the forest path, leaving again for the Fens and Cambridge at the dawn. This, however, proved not possible because of the exceeding badness of the road. So it came about that when the darkness closed in on them a little before five o'clock, bringing with it a cold, moaning wind and a scurry of snow, they were obliged to shelter in a faggot-built woodman's hut, waiting for the moon to appear among the clouds. Here they fed the horses with corn that they had brought with them, and themselves also from their store of dried meat and barley cakes, which Jeffrey carried on his shoulder in a bag. It was a poor meal eaten thus in the darkness, but served to stay their stomachs and pass away the time.

At length a ray of light pierced the doorway of the hut.

"She's up," said Sir John, "let us be going ere the nags grow stiff."

Making no answer, Jeffrey slipped the bits back into the horses' mouths and led them out. Now the full moon had appeared like a great white eye between two black banks of cloud and turned the world to silver. It was a dreary scene on which she shone; a dazzling plain of snow, broken by patches of hawthorns, and here and there by the gaunt shape of a pollard oak, since this being the outskirt of the forest, folk came hither to lop the tops of the trees for firing. A hundred and fifty yards away or so, at the crest of a slope, was a round-shaped hill, made, not by Nature, but by man. None knew what that hill might be, but tradition said that once, hundreds or thousands of years before, a big battle had been fought around it in which a king was killed, and that his victorious army had raised this mound above his bones to be a memorial for ever.

The story was indeed that, being a sea-king, they had built a boat or dragged it thither from the river shore and set him in it with all the slain for rowers; also that he might be seen at nights seated on his horse in armour, and staring about him, as when he directed the battle. At least it is true that the mount was called King's Grave, and that people feared to pass it after sundown.

As Jeffrey Stokes was holding his master's stirrup for him to mount, he uttered an exclamation and pointed. Following the line of his outstretched hand, in the clear moonlight Sir John saw a man, who sat, still as any statue, upon a horse on the very point of King's Grave. He appeared to be covered with a long cloak, but above it his helmet glittered like silver. Next moment a fringe of black cloud hid the face of the moon, and when it passed away the man and horse were gone.

"What did that fellow there?" asked Sir John.

"Fellow?" answered Jeffrey in a shaken voice, "I saw none. That was the Ghost of the Grave. My grandfather met him ere he came to his end in the forest, none know how, for the wolves, of which there were plenty in his day, picked his bones clean, and so have many others for hundreds of years; always just before their doom. He is an ill fowl, that Ghost of the Grave, and those who clap eyes on him do wisely to turn their horses' heads homewards, as I would to-night if I had my way, master."

"What use, Jeffrey? If the sight of him means death, death will come. Moreover, I believe nothing of the tale. Your ghost was some forest reeve or herdsman."

"A forest reeve or herdsman who wanders about in a steel helm on a fine horse in snow-time when there are no trees to cut or cattle to mind! Well, have it as you will, master; only God save me from such reeves and herdsmen, for I think they hail from hell."

"Then he was a spy watching whither we go," answered Sir John angrily.

"If so, who sent him? The Abbot of Blossholme? In that case I would sooner meet the devil, for this means mischief. I say that we had better ride back to Shefton."

"Then do so, Jeffrey, if you are scared, and I will go on alone, who, being on an honest business, fear not Satan or an abbot, either."

"Nay, master. Many a year ago, when we were younger, I stood by you on Flodden Field when Sir Edward, Christopher Harflete's father, was killed at our side, and those red-bearded Scotch bare-breeks pressed us hard, yet I never itched to turn my back, even after that great fellow with an axe got you down, and we thought that all was lost. Then shall I do so now?—though it is true that I fear yon goblin more than all the Highlanders beyond the Tweed. Ride on; man can die but once, and for my part I care not when it comes, who have little to lose in an ill world."

So without more words they started forward, peering about them as they went. Soon the forest thickened, and the track they followed wound its way round great trunks of primeval oaks, or the edges of bog-holes, or through brakes of thorns. Hard enough it was to find it at times, since the snow made it one with the bordering ground, and the gloom of the oaks was great. But Jeffrey was a woodman born, and from his childhood had known the shape of every tree in that waste, so that they held safely to their road. Well would it have been for them if they had not!

They came to a place where three other tracks crossed that which they rode upon, and here Jeffrey Stokes, who was ahead, held up his hand.

"What is it?" asked Sir John.

"It is the marks of ten or a dozen shod horses passed within two hours, since the last snow fell. And who be they, I wonder?"

"Doubtless travellers like ourselves. Ride on, man; that farm is not a mile ahead."

Then Jeffrey broke out.

"Master, I like it not," he said. "Battle-horses have gone by here, not chapmen's or farmers' nags, and I think I know their breed. I say that we had best turn about if we would not walk into some snare."

"Turn you, then," grumbled Sir John indifferently. "I am cold and weary, and seek my rest."

"Pray God that you may not find it when you are colder," muttered Jeffrey, spurring his horse.

They went on through the dead winter silence, that was broken only by the hoots of a flitting owl hungry for the food that it could not find, and the swish of the feet of a galloping fox as it looped past them through the snow. Presently they came to an open place ringed in by forest, so wet that only marsh-trees would grow there. To their right lay a little ice-covered mere, with sere, brown reeds standing here and there upon its face, and at the end of it a group of stark pollarded willows, whereof the tops had been cut for poles by those who dwelt in the forest farm near by. Sir John looked at the place and shivered a little—perhaps because the frost bit him. Or was it that he remembered his daughter's dream, which told of such a spot? At any rate, he set his teeth, and his right hand sought the hilt of his sword. His weary horse sniffed the air and neighed, and the neigh was answered from close at hand.

"Thank the saints! we are nearer to that farm than I thought," said Sir John.

As he spoke the words a number of men appeared galloping down on them from out of the shelter of a thorn-brake, and the moonlight shone on the bared weapons in their hands.

"Thieves!" shouted Sir John. "At them now, Jeffrey, and win through to the farm."

The man hesitated, for he saw that their foes were many and no common robbers, but his master drew his sword and spurred his beast, so he must do likewise. In twenty seconds they were among them, and some one commanded them to yield. Sir John rushed at the fellow, and, rising in his stirrups, cut him down. He fell all of a heap and lay still in the snow, which grew crimson about him. One came at Jeffrey, who turned his horse so that the blow missed, then took his weight upon the point of his sword, so that this man, too, fell down and lay in the snow, moving feebly.

The rest, thinking this greeting too warm for them, swung round and vanished again among the thorns.

"Now ride for it," said Jeffrey.

"I cannot," answered Sir John. "One of those knaves has hurt my mare," and he pointed to blood that ran from a great gash in the beast's foreleg, which it held up piteously.

"Take mine," said Jeffrey; "I'll dodge them afoot."

"Never, man! To the willows; we will hold our own there;" and, springing from the wounded beast, which tried to hobble after them, but could not, for its sinews were cut, he ran to the shelter of the trees, followed by Jeffrey on his horse.

"Who are these rogues?" he asked.

"The Abbot's men-at-arms," answered Jeffrey. "I saw the face of him I spitted."

Now Sir John's jaw dropped.

"Then we are sped, friend, for they dare not let us go. Cicely dreams well."

As he spoke an arrow whistled by them.

"Jeffrey," he went on, "I have papers on me that should not be lost, for with them might go my girl's heritage. Take them," and he thrust a packet into his hand, "and this purse also. There's plenty in it. Away—anywhere, and lie hid out of reach a while, or they'll still your tongue. Then I charge you on your soul, come back with help and hang that knave Abbot—for your Lady's sake, Jeffrey. She'll reward you, and so will God above."

The man thrust away purse and deeds in some deep pocket.

"How can I leave you to be butchered?" he muttered, grinding his teeth.

As the words left his lips he heard his master utter a gurgling sound, and saw that an arrow, shot from behind, had pierced him through the throat; saw, too, he who was skilled in war, that the wound was mortal. Then he hesitated no longer.

"Christ rest you!" he said. "I'll do your bidding or die;" and, turning his horse, he drove the rowels into its sides, causing it to bound away like a deer.

For a moment the stricken Sir John watched him go. Then he ran out of his cover, shaking his sword above his head—ran into the open moonlight to draw the arrows. They came fast enough, but ere ever he fell, for that steel shirt of his was strong, Jeffrey, lying low on his horse's neck, was safe away, and though the murderers followed hard they never caught him.

Nor, though they searched for days, could they find him at Shefton or elsewhere, for Jeffrey, who knew that all roads were blocked, and who dared not venture home, doubling like a hare across country, had won down to the water, where a ship lay foreign bound, and by dawn was on the sea.

CHAPTER 3

A Wedding

About noon of the day after that upon which Sir John had come to his death, Cicely Foterell sat at her meal in Shefton Hall. Not much of the rough midwinter fare passed her lips, for she was ill at ease. The man she loved had been dismissed from her because his fortunes were on the wane, and her father had gone upon a journey which she felt, rather than knew, to be very dangerous. The great old hall was lonesome, also, for a young girl who had no comrades near. Sitting there in the big room, she bethought her how different it had been in her childhood, before some foul sickness, of which she knew not the name or nature, had swept away her mother, her two brothers, and her sister all in a single week, leaving her untouched. Then there were merry voices about the house where now was silence, and she alone, with naught bout a spaniel dog for company. Also most of the men were away with the wains laden with the year's clip of wool, which her father had held until the price had heightened, nor in this snow would they be back for another week, or perhaps longer.

Oh! her heart was heavy as the winter clouds without, and young and fair as she might be, almost she wished that she had gone when her brothers went, and found her peace.

To cheer her spirits she drank from a cup of spiced ale, that the manservant had placed beside her covered with a napkin, and was glad of its warmth and comfort. Just then the door opened, and her foster-mother, Mrs. Stower, entered. She was still a handsome woman in her prime, for her husband had been carried off by a fever when she was but nineteen, and her baby with him, whereon she had been brought to the Hall to nurse Cicely, whose mother was very ill after her birth. Moreover, she was tall and dark, with black and flashing eyes, for her father had been a Spaniard of gentle birth, and, it was said, gypsy blood ran in her mother's veins.

There were but two people in the world for whom Emlyn Stower cared—Cicely, her foster-child, and a certain playmate of hers, one Thomas Bolle, now a lay-brother at the Abbey who had charge of the cattle. The tale was that in their early youth he had courted her, not against her will, and that when, after her parents' tragic deaths, as a ward of the former Abbot of Blossholme, she was married to her husband, not with her will, this Thomas put on the robe of a monk of the lowest degree, being but a yeoman of good stock though of little learning.

Something in the woman's manner attracted Cicely's attention, and gave a hint of tragedy. She paused at the door, fumbling with its latch, which was not her way, then turned and stood upright against it, like a picture in its frame.

"What is it, Nurse?" asked Cicely in a shaken voice. "From your look you bear tidings."

Emlyn Stower walked forward, rested one hand upon the oak table and answered—

"Aye, evil tidings if they be true. Prepare your heart, my sweet."

"Quick with them, Emlyn," gasped Cicely. "Who is dead? Christopher?"

She shook her head, and Cicely sighed in relief, adding—

"Who, then? Oh! was that dream true?"

"Aye, dear; you are an orphan."

The girl's head fell forward. Then she lifted it, and asked—

"Who told you? Give me all the truth or I shall die."

"A friend of mine who has to do with the Abbey yonder; ask not his name."

"I know it, Emlyn; Thomas Bolle," she whispered back.

"A friend of mine," repeated the tall, dark woman, "told me that Sir John Foterell, your sire, was murdered last night in the forest by a gang of armed men, of whom he slew two."

"From the Abbey?" queried Cicely in the same whisper.

"Who knows? I think it. They say that the arrow in his throat was such as they make there. Jeffrey Stokes was hunted, but escaped on to some ship that had her anchor up."

"I'll have his life for it, the coward!" exclaimed Cicely.

"Blame him not yet. He met another friend of mine, and sent a message. It was that he did but obey his master's last orders, and, as he had seen too much and to linger here was certain death, if he lived, he would return from over-seas with the papers when the times are safer. He prayed that you would not doubt him."

"The papers! What papers, Emlyn?"

She shrugged her broad shoulders.

"How should I know? Doubtless some that your father was taking to London and did not desire to lose. His iron chest stands open in his chamber."

Now poor Cicely remembered that her father had spoken of certain "deeds" which he must take with him, and began to sob.

"Weep not, darling," said her foster-mother, smoothing Cicely's brown hair with her strong hand. "These things are decreed of God, and done with. Now you must look to yourself. Your father is gone, but one remains."

Cicely lifted her tear-stained face.

"Yes, I have you," she said.

"Me!" she answered, with a quick smile. "Nay, of what use am I? Your nursing days are over. What did you tell me your father said to you before he rode—about Sir Christopher? Hush! there's no time to talk; you must away to Cranwell Towers."

"Why?" asked Cicely. "He cannot bring my father back to life, and it would be thought strange indeed that at such a time I should visit a man in his own house. Send and tell him the tidings. I bide here to bury my father, and," she added proudly, "to avenge him."

"If so, sweet, you bide here to be buried yourself in yonder Nunnery. Hark, I have not told you all my news. The Abbot Maldon claims the Blossholme lands under some trick of law. It was as to them that your father quarrelled with him the other night; and with the land goes your wardship, as once mine went under this monk's charter. Before sunset the Abbot rides here with his men-at-arms to take them, and to set you for safe-keeping in the Nunnery, where you will find a husband called Holy Church."

"Name of God! is it so?" said Cicely, springing up; "and the most of the men are away! I cannot hold the Hall against that foreign Abbot and his hirelings, and an orphaned heiress is but a chattel to be sold. Oh! now I understand what my father meant. Order horses. I'll off to Christopher. Yet, stay, Nurse. What will he do with me? It may seem shameless, and will vex him."

"I think he will marry you. I think to-night you will be a wife. If not, I'll know the reason why," she added viciously.

"A wife! To-night!" exclaimed the girl, turning crimson to her hair. "And my father but just dead! How can it be?"

"We'll talk of that with Harflete. Mayhap, like you, he'll wish to wait and ask the banns, or to lay the case before a London lawyer. Meanwhile, I have ordered horses and sent a message to the Abbot to say you come to learn the meaning of these rumours, which will keep him still till nightfall; and another to Cranwell Towers, that we may find food and lodging there. Quick, now, and get your cloak and hood. I have the jewels in their case, for Maldon seeks them more even than your lands, and with them all the money I can find. Also I have bid the sewing-girl make a pack of some garments. Come now, come, for that Abbot is hungry and will be stirring. There is no time for talk."

****

Three hours later in the red glow of the sunset Christopher Harflete, watching at his door, saw two women riding towards him across the snow, and knew them while they were yet far off.

"It is true, then," he said to Father Roger Necton, the old clergyman of Cranwell, whom he had summoned from the vicarage. "I thought that fool of a messenger must be drunk. What can have chanced, Father?"

"Death, I think, my son, for sure naught else would bring the Lady Cicely here unaccompanied save by a waiting-woman. The question is—what will happen now?" and he glanced sideways at him.

"I know well if I can get my way," answered Christopher, with a merry laugh. "Say now, Father, if it should so be that this lady were willing, could you marry us?"

"Without a doubt, my son, with the consent of the parents;" and again he looked at him.

"And if there were no parents?"

"Then with the consent of the guardian, the bride being under age."

"And if no guardian had been declared or admitted?"

"Then such a marriage duly solemnized, being a sacrament of the Church, would hold fast until the crack of doom unless the Pope annulled it, and, as you know, the Pope is out of favour in this realm on this very matter of marriage. Let me explain the law to you, ecclesiastic and civil—"

But Christopher was already running towards the gate, so the old parson's lecture remained undelivered.

The two met in the snow, Emlyn Stower riding on ahead and leaving them together.

"What is it, sweetest?" he asked. "What is it?"

"Oh! Christopher," she answered, weeping, "my poor father is dead—murdered, or so says Emlyn."

"Murdered! By whom?"

"By the Abbot of Blossholme's soldiers—so says Emlyn, yonder in the forest last eve. And the Abbot is coming to Shefton to declare me his ward and thrust me into the Nunnery—that was Emlyn's tale. And so, although it is a strange thing to do, having none to protect me, I have fled to you—because Emlyn said I ought."

"She is a wise woman, Emlyn," broke in Christopher; "I always thought well of her judgment. But did you only come to me because Emlyn told you?"

"Not altogether, Christopher. I came because I am distraught, and you are a better friend than none at all, and—where else should I go? Also my poor father with his last words to me, although he was so angry with you, bade me seek your help if there were need—and—oh! Christopher, I came because you swore you loved me, and, therefore, it seemed right. If I had gone to the Nunnery, although the Prioress, Mother Matilda, is good, and my friend, who knows, she might not have let me out again, for the Abbot is her master, and *not* my friend. It is our lands he loves, and the famous jewels—Emlyn has them with her."

By now they were across the moat and at the steps of the house, so, without answering, Christopher lifted her tenderly from the saddle, pressing her to his breast as he did so, for that seemed his best answer. A groom came to lead away the horses, touching his bonnet, and staring at them curiously; and, leaning on her lover's shoulder, Cicely passed through the arched doorway of Cranwell Towers into the hall, where a great fire burned. Before this fire, warming his thin hands, stood Father Necton, engaged in eager conversation with Emlyn Stower. As the pair advanced this talk ceased, evidently because it was of them.

"Mistress Cicely," said the kindly-faced old man, speaking in a nervous fashion, "I fear that you visit us in sad case," and he paused, not knowing what to add.

"Yes, indeed," she answered, "if all I hear is true. They say that my father is killed by cruel men—I know not for certain why or by whom—and that the Abbot of Blossholme comes to claim me as his ward and immure me in Blossholme Priory, whither I would not go. I have fled here to escape him, having no other refuge, though you may think ill of me for this deed."

"Not I, my child. I should not speak against yonder Abbot, for he is my superior in the Church, though, mind you, I owe him no allegiance, since this benefice is not in his gift, nor am I a Benedictine. Therefore I will tell you the truth. I hold the man not honest. All is provender that comes to his maw; moreover, he is no Englishman, but a Spaniard, one sent here to work against the welfare of this realm; to

365

suck its wealth, stir up rebellion, and make report of all that passes in it, for the benefit of England's enemies."

"Yet he has friends at Court, or so said my father."

"Aye, aye, such folks have ever friends—their money buys them; though mayhap an ill day is at hand for him and his likes. Well, your poor father is gone, God knows how, though I thought for long that would be his end, who ever spoke his mind, or more; and you with your wealth are the morsel that tempts Maldon's appetite. And now what is to be done? This is a hard case. Would you refuge in some other Nunnery?"

"Nay," answered Cicely, glancing sideways at her lover.

"Then what's to be done?"

"Oh! I know not," she said, bursting into a fit of weeping. "How can I tell you, who am mazed with grief and doubt? I had but a single friend—my father, though at times he was a rough one. Yet he loved me in his way, and I have obeyed his last counsel;" and, all her courage gone, she sank into a chair and rocked herself to and fro, her head resting on her hands.

"That is not true," said Emlyn in her bold voice. "Am I who suckled you no friend, and is Father Necton here no friend, and is Sir Christopher no friend? Well, if you have lost your judgment, I have kept mine, and here it is. Yonder, not two bowshots away, stands a church, and before me I see a priest and a pair who would serve for bride and bridegroom. Also we can rake up witnesses and a cup of wine to drink your health; and after that let the Abbot of Blossholme do his worst. What say you, Sir Christopher?"

"You know my mind, Nurse Emlyn; but what says Cicely? Oh! Cicely, what say *you*?" and he bent over her.

She raised herself, still weeping, and, throwing her arms about his neck, laid her head upon his shoulder.

"I think it is the will of God," she whispered, "and why should I fight against it, who am His servant?—and yours, Chris."

"And now, Father, what say you?" asked Emlyn, pointing to the pair.

"I do not think there is much to say," answered the old clergyman, turning his head aside, "save that if it should please you to come to the church in ten minutes' time you will find a candle on the altar, and a priest within the rails, and a clerk to hold the book. More we cannot do at such short notice."

Then he paused for a while, and, hearing no dissent, walked down the hall and out of the door.

Emlyn took Cicely by the hand, led her to a room that was shown to them, and there made her ready for her bridal as best she might. She had no fine dress in which to clothe her, nor, indeed, would there have been time to don it. But she combed out her beautiful brown hair, and, opening that box of Eastern jewels which were the great pride of the Foterells—being the rarest and the most ancient in all the countryside—she decked her with them. On her broad brow she set a circlet from which hung sparkling diamonds that had been brought, the story said, by her mother's ancestor, a Carfax, from the Holy Land, where once they were the peculiar treasure of a *paynim* queen, and upon her bosom a necklet of large pearls. Brooches and rings also she found for her breast and fingers, and for her waist a jewelled girdle with a golden clasp, while to her ears she hung the finest gems of all—two great pearls pink like the hawthorn-bloom when it begins to turn. Lastly she flung over her head a veil of lace most curiously wrought, and stood back with pride to look at her.

Now Cicely, who all this while had been silent and unresisting, spoke for the first time, saying—

"How came this here, Nurse?"

"Your mother wore it at her bridal, and her mother too, so I have been told. Also once before I wrapped it about you—when you were christened, sweet."

"Mayhap; but how came it here?"

"In the bosom of my robe. Not knowing when we should get home again, I brought it, thinking that perhaps one day you might marry, when it would be useful. And now, strangely enough, the marriage has come."

"Emlyn, Emlyn, I believe that you planned all this business, whereof God alone knows the end."

"That is why He makes a beginning, dear, that His end may be fulfilled in due season."

"Aye, but what is that end? Mayhap this is my shroud you wrap about me. In truth, I feel as though death were near."

"He is ever that," replied Emlyn unconcernedly. "But so long as he doesn't touch, what does it matter? Now hark you, sweetest, I've Spanish and gypsy blood in me with which go gifts, and so I'll tell you something for your comfort. However oft he snatches, Death will not lay his bony hand on you for many a long year—not till you are well-nigh as thin with age as he is. Oh! you'll have your troubles like all of us, worse than many, mayhap, but you are Luck's own child, who lived when the rest were taken, and you'll win through and take others on your back, as a whale does barnacles. So snap your fingers at death, as I do," and she suited the action to the word, "and be happy while you may, and when you're not happy, wait till your turn comes round again. Now follow me and, though your father is murdered, smile as you should in such an hour, for what man wants a sad-faced bride?"

They walked down the broad oaken stairs into the hall where Christopher stood waiting for them. Glancing at him shyly, Cicely saw that he was clad in mail beneath his cloak, and that his sword was girded at his side, also that some men with him were armed. For a moment he stared at her glittering beauty confused, then said—

"Fear not this hint of war in love's own hour," and he touched his shining armour. "Cicely, these nuptials are strange as they are happy, and some might try to break in upon them. Come now, my sweet lady;" and bowing before her he took her by the hand and led her from the house, Emlyn walking behind them and the men with torches going before and following after.

Outside it was freezing sharply, so that the snow crunched beneath their feet. In the west the last red glow of sunset still lingered on the steely sky, and over against it the great moon rose above the round edge of the world. In the bushes of the garden, and the tall poplars that bordered the moat, blackbirds and fieldfares chattered their winter evening song, while about the grey tower of the neighbouring church the daws still wheeled.

The picture of that scene whereof at the time she seemed to take no note, always remained fixed in the mind of Cicely: the cold expanse of snow, the inky trees, the hard sky, the lambent beams of the moon, the dull glow of the torches caught and reflected by her jewels and her lover's mail, the midwinter sound of birds, the barking of a distant hound, the black porch of the church that drew nearer, the little oblong mounds which hid the bones of hundreds who in their day had passed it as infants, as bridegrooms and as brides, and at last as cold, white things that had been men and women.

Now they were in the nave of the old fane where the cold struck them like a sword. The dim lights of the torches showed them that, short as had been the time, the news of this marvellous marriage had spread about, for at least a score of people were standing here and there in knots, or a few of them seated on the oak benches near the chancel. All these turned to stare at them eagerly as they walked towards the altar where stood the priest in his robes, and since his sight was dim, behind him the old clerk with a stable-lantern held on high to enable him to read from his book.

They reached the carven rood-screen, and at a sign kneeled down. In a clear voice the clergyman began the service; presently, at another sign, the pair rose, advanced to the altar-rails and again knelt down. The moonlight, flowing through the eastern window, fell full on both of them, turning them to cold, white statues, such as those that knelt in marble upon the tomb at their side.

All through the holy office Cicely watched these statues with fascinated eyes, and it seemed to her that they and the old crusaders, Harfletes of a long-past day who lay near by, were watching her with a wistful and kindly interest. She made certain answers, a ring that was somewhat too small was thrust upon her finger—all the rest of her life that ring hurt her at times, but she would have never it moved, and then some one was kissing her. At first she thought it must be her father, and remembering, nearly wept till she heard Christopher's voice calling her wife, and knew that she was wed.

Father Roger, the old clerk still holding the lantern behind him, writing something in a little vellum book, asking her the date of her birth and her full name, which, as he had been present at her christening, she thought strange. Then her husband signed the book, using the altar as a table, not very easily for he was no great scholar, and she signed also in her maiden name for the last time, and the priest signed, and at his bidding Emlyn Stower, who could write well, signed too. Next, as though by an afterthought, Father Roger called several of the congregation, who rather unwillingly made their marks as witnesses. While they did so he explained to them that, as the circumstances were uncommon, it was well that there should be evidence, and that he intended to send copies of this entry to sundry dignities, not forgetting the holy Father at Rome.

On learning this they appeared to be sorry that they had anything to do with the matter, and one and all of them melted into the darkness of the nave and out of Cicely's mind.

So it was done at last.

Father Necton blew on his little book till the ink was dry, then hid it away in his robe. The old clerk, having pocketed a handsome fee from Christopher, lit the pair down the nave to the porch, where he locked the oaken door behind them, extinguished his lantern and trudged off through the snow to the ale-house, there to discuss these nuptials and hot beer. Escorted by their torch-bearers Cicely and Christopher walked silently arm-in-arm back to the Towers, whither Emlyn, after embracing the bride, had already gone on ahead. So having added one more ceremony to its countless record, perhaps the strangest of them all, the ancient church behind them grew silent as the dead within its graves.

The Towers reached, the new-wed pair, with Father Roger and Emlyn, sat down to the best meal that could be prepared for them at such short notice; a very curious wedding feast. Still, though the company was so small it did not lack for heartiness, since the old clergyman proposed their health in a speech full of Latin words which they did not understand, and every member of the household who had assembled to hear him drank to it in cups of wine. This done, the beautiful bride, now blushing and now pale, was led away to the best chamber, which had been hastily prepared for her. But Emlyn remained behind a while, for she had words to speak.

"Sir Christopher," she said, "you are fast wed to the sweetest lady that ever sun or moon shone on, and in that may hold yourself a lucky man. Yet such deep joys seldom come without their pain, and I think that this is near at hand. There are those who will envy you your fortune, Sir Christopher."

"Yet they cannot change it, Emlyn," he answered anxiously. "The knot that was tied to-night may not be unloosed."

"Never," broke in Father Roger. "Though the suddenness and the circumstances of it may be unusual, this marriage is a sacrament celebrated in the face of the world with the full consent of both parties and of the Holy Church. Moreover, before the dawn I'll send the record of it to the bishop's registry and elsewhere, that it may not be questioned in days to come, giving copies of the same to you and your lady's foster-mother, who is her nearest friend at hand."

"It may not be loosed on earth or in heaven," replied Emlyn solemnly, "yet perchance the sword can cut it. Sir Christopher, I think that we should all do well to travel as soon as may be."

"Not to-night, surely, Nurse!" he exclaimed.

"No, not to-night," she answered, with a faint smile. "Your wife has had a weary day, and could not. Moreover, preparation must be made which is impossible at this hour. But to-morrow, if the roads are open to you, I think we should start for London, where she may make complaint of her father's slaying and claim her heritage and the protection of the law."

"That is good counsel," said the vicar, and Christopher, with whom words seemed to be few, nodded his head.

"Meanwhile," went on Emlyn, "you have six men in this house and others round it. Send out a messenger and summon them all here at dawn, bidding them bring provision with them, and what bows and arms they have. Set a watch also, and after the Father and the messenger have gone, command that the drawbridge be triced."

"What do you fear?" he asked, waking from his dream.

"I fear the Abbot of Blossholme and his hired ruffians, who reck little of the laws, as the soul of dead Sir John knows now, or can use them as a cover to evil deeds. He'll not let such a prize slip between his fingers if he can help it, and the times are turbulent."

"Alas! alas! it is true," said Father Roger, "and that Abbot is a relentless man who sticks at nothing, having much wealth and many friends both here and beyond the seas. Yet surely he would never dare—"

"That we shall learn," interrupted Emlyn. "Meanwhile, Sir Christopher, rouse yourself and give the orders."

So Christopher summoned his men and spoke words to them at which they looked very grave, but being true-hearted fellows who loved him, said they would do his bidding.

A while later, having written out a copy of the marriage lines and witnessed it, Father Roger departed with the messenger. The drawbridge was hoisted above the moat, the doors were barred, and a man set to watch in the gateway tower, while Christopher, forgetful of all else, even of the danger in which they were, sought the company of her who waited for him.

CHAPTER 4

The Abbot's Oath

On the following morning, shortly after it was light, Christopher was called from his chamber by Emlyn, who gave him a letter.

"Whence came this?" he asked, turning it over suspiciously.

"A messenger has brought it from Blossholme Abbey," she answered.

"Wife Cicely," he called through the door, "come hither if you will."

Presently she appeared, looking quaint and lovely in her long fur cloak, and, having embraced her foster-mother, asked what was the matter.

"This, my darling," he answered, handing her the paper. "I never loved book-learnings over-much, and this morn I seem to hate them; read, you who are more scholarly."

"I mistrust me of that great seal; it bodes us no good, Chris," she replied doubtfully, and paling a little.

"The message within is no medlar to soften by keeping," said Emlyn. "Give it me. I was schooled in a nunnery, and can read their scrawls."

So, nothing loth, Cicely handed her the paper, which she took in her strong fingers, broke the seal, snapped the silk, unfolded, and read. It ran thus—

To Sir Christopher Harflete, to Mistress Cicely Foterell, to Emlyn Stower, the waiting-woman, and to all others whom it may concern
I, Clement Maldon, Abbot of Blossholme, having heard of the death of Sir John Foterell, Knt., at the cruel hands of the forest thieves and outlaws, sent last night to serve the declaration of my wardship, according to my prerogative established by law and custom, over the person and property of you, Cicely, his only child surviving. My messengers returned saying that you had fled from your home of Shefton Hall. They said further that it was rumoured that you had ridden with your foster-mother, Emlyn Stower, to Cranwell Towers, the house of Sir Christo-

pher Harflete. If this be so, for the sake of your good name it is needful that you should remove from such company at once, as there is talk about you and the said Sir Christopher Harflete. I purpose, therefore, God permitting me, to ride this day to Cranwell Towers, and if you be there, as your lawful guardian and ghostly father, to command you, being an infant under age, to accompany me thence to the Nunnery of Blossholme. There I have determined, in the exercise of my authority, you shall abide until a fitting husband is found for you, unless, indeed, God should move your heart to remain within its walls as one of the brides of Christ.

Clement
Abbot

Now when the reading of this letter was finished, the three of them stood a little while staring at each other, knowing well that it meant trouble for them all, till Cicely said—

"Bring me ink and paper, Nurse. I will answer this Abbot."

So they were brought, and Cicely wrote in her round, girlish hand—

My Lord Abbot,
In answer to your letter, I would have you know that as my noble father (whose cruel death must be inquired of and avenged) bade me with his last words, I, fearing that a like fate would overtake me at the hands of his murderers, did, as you suppose, seek refuge at this house. Here, yesterday, I was married in the face of God and man in the church of Cranwell, as you may learn from the paper sent herewith. It is not, therefore, needful that you should seek a husband for me, since my dear lord, Sir Christopher Har-flete, and I are one till death do part us. Nor do I admit that now, or at any time, you had or have right of wardship over my person or the lands and goods which I hold and inherit.
Your humble servant,
Cicely Harflete

This letter Cicely copied out fair and sealed, and presently it was given to the Abbot's messenger, who placed it in his pouch and rode off as fast as the snow would let him.

They watched him go from a window.

"Now," said Christopher, turning to his wife, "I think, dear, we shall do well to ride also as soon as may be. Yonder Abbot is sharp-set, and I doubt whether letters will satisfy his appetite."

"I think so also," said Emlyn. "Make ready and eat, both of you. I go to see that the horses are saddled."

An hour later everything was prepared. Three horses stood before the door, and with them an escort of four mounted men, who were all having arms and beasts to ride that Christopher could gather at such short notice, though others of his tenants and servants had already assembled at the Towers in answer to his summons, to the number of twelve, indeed. Without the snow was falling fast, and although she tried to look brave and happy, Cicely shivered a little as she saw it through the open door.

"We go on a strange honeymoon, my sweet," said Christopher uneasily.

"What matter, so long as we go together?" she answered in a gay voice that yet seemed to ring untrue, "although," she added, with a little choke of the throat, "I would that we could have stayed here until I had found and buried my father. It haunts me to think of him lying somewhere in the snows like a perished ox."

"It is his murderers that I wish to bury," exclaimed Christopher; "and, by God's name, I swear I'll do it ere all is done. Think not, dear, that I forget your griefs because I do not speak much of them, but bridals and buryings are strange company. So while we may, let us take what joy we can, since the ill that goes before oft-times follows after also. Come, let us mount and away to London to find friends and justice."

Then, having spoken a few words to his house-people, he lifted Cicely to her horse, and they rode out into the softly-falling snow, thinking that they had seen their last of the Towers for many a day. But this was not to be. For as they passed along the Blossholme highway, purposing to leave the Abbey on their left, when they were about three miles from Cranwell, suddenly a tall fellow, who wore a great sheepskin coat with a monk's hood to it and carried a thick staff in his hand, burst through the fence and stood in front of them.

"Who are you?" asked Christopher, laying his hand upon his sword.

"You'd know me well enough if my hood were back," he answered in a deep voice; "but if you want my name, it's Thomas Bolle, cattle-reeve to the Abbey yonder."

"Your voice proves you," said Christopher, laughing. "And now what is your business, lay-brother Bolle?"

"To get up a bunch of yearling steers that have been running on the forest-edge, living, like the rest of us, on what they can find, as the weather is coming on hard enough to starve them. That's my business, Sir Christopher. But as I see an old friend of mine there," and he nodded towards Emlyn, who was watching him from her horse, "with your leave I'll ask her if she has any confession to make, since she seems to be on a dangerous journey."

Now Christopher made as though he would push on, for he was in no mood to chat with cattle-reeves. But Emlyn, who had been eyeing the man, called out—

"Come here, Thomas, and I will answer you myself, who always have a few sins to spare for a priest's wallet, and need a blessing or two to warm me."

He strode forward, and, taking her horse by the bridle, led it a little way apart, and as soon as they were out of earshot fell into an eager conversation with its rider. A minute or so later Cicely, looking round—for they had ridden forward at a slow pace—saw Thomas Bolle leap through the other fence of the roadway and vanish at a run into the falling snow, while Emlyn spurred her horse after them.

"Stop," she said to Christopher; "I have tidings for you. The Abbot, with all his men-at-arms and servants, to the number of forty or more, waits for us under shelter of Blossholme Grove yonder, purposing to take the Lady Cicely by force. Some spy has told him of this journey."

"I see no one," said Christopher, staring at the Grove, which lay below them about a quarter of a mile away, for they were on the top of a rise. "Still, the matter is not hard to prove," and he called to the two best mounted of his men and bade them ride forward and make report if any lurked behind that wood.

So the men went off, while they remained where they were, silent, but anxious enough. Ten minutes or so later, before they could see them, for the snow was now falling quickly, they heard the sound of many horses galloping. Then the two men appeared, calling out as they came—

"The Abbot and all his folk are after us. Back to Cranwell, ere you be taken!"

Christopher thought for a moment, then, remembering that with but four men and cumbered by two women it was not possible to cut his way through so great a force, and admonished by that sound of advancing hoofs, he gave a sudden order. They turned about, and not too soon, for as they did so, scarce two hundred yards away, the first of the Abbot's horsemen appeared plunging towards them up the slope. Then the race began, and well for them was it that their horses were good and fresh, since before ever they came in sight of Cranwell Towers the pursuers were not ninety yards behind. But here on the flat their beasts, scenting home, answered nobly to whip and spur, and drew ahead a little. Moreover, those who watched within the house saw them, and ran to the drawbridge. When they were within fifty yards of the moat Cicely's horse stumbled, slipped, and fell, throwing her into the snow, then recovered itself and galloped on alone. Christopher reined up alongside of her, and, as she rose, frightened but unharmed, put out his long arm, and, lifting her to the saddle in front of him, plunged forward, while those behind shouted "Yield!"

Under this double burden his horse went but slowly. Still they reached the bridge before any could lay hands upon them, and thundered over it.

"Wind up," shouted Christopher, and all there, even the womenfolk, laid hands upon the cranks. The bridge began to rise, but now five or six of the Abbot's folk, dismounting, sprang at it, catching the end of it with their hands when it was about six feet in the air, and holding on so that it could not be lifted, but remained, moving neither up nor down.

"Leave go, you knaves," shouted Christopher; but by way of answer one of them, with the help of his fellows, scrambled on to the end of the bridge, and stood there, hanging to the chains.

Then Christopher snatched a bow from the hand of a servingman, and the arrow being already on the string, again shouted—

"Get off at your peril!"

In answer the man called out something about the commands of the Lord Abbot.

Christopher, looking past him, saw that others of the company had dismounted and were running towards the bridge. If they reached it he knew well that the game was played. So he hesitated no longer, but, aiming swiftly, drew and loosed the bow. At that distance he could not miss. The arrow struck the man where his steel cap joined the mail beneath, and pierced him through the throat, so that he fell back dead. The others, scared by his fate, loosed their hold, so that now the bridge, relieved of the weight upon it, instantly rose up beyond their reach, and presently came home and was made fast.

As they afterwards discovered, this man, it may here be said, was a captain of the Abbot's guard. Moreover, it was he who had shot the arrow that killed Sir John Foterell some forty hours before, striking him through the throat, as it was fated that he himself should be struck. Thus, then, one of that good knight's murderers reaped his just reward.

Now the men ran back out of range, for they feared more arrows, while Christopher watched them go in silence. Cicely, who stood by his side, her hands held before her face to shut out the sight of death, let them fall suddenly, and, turning to her husband, said, as she pointed to the corpse that lay upon the blood-stained snow of the roadway—

"How many more will follow him, I wonder? I think that is but the first throw of a long game, husband."

"Nay, sweet," he answered, "the second; the first was cast two nights gone by King's Grave Mount in the forest yonder, and blood ever calls for blood."

"Aye," she answered, "blood calls for blood." Then, remembering that she was orphaned and what sort of a honeymoon hers was like to be, she turned and sought her chamber, weeping.

Now, while Christopher still stood irresolute, for he was oppressed by the sense of this man-slaying, and knew not what he should do next, he saw three men separate from the knot of soldiers and ride towards the Towers, one of whom held a white cloth above his head in token of parley. Then Christopher went up into the little gateway turret, followed by Emlyn, who crouched down behind the brick battlement, so that she could see and hear without being seen. Having reached the further side of the moat, he who held the white cloth threw back the hood of his long cape, and they saw that it was the Abbot of Blossholme himself, also that his dark eyes flashed and that his olive-hued face was almost white with rage.

"Why do you hunt me across my own park and come knocking so rudely at my doors, my Lord Abbot?" asked Christopher, leaning on the parapet of the gateway.

"Why do you work murder on my servant, Christopher Harflete?" answered the Abbot, pointing to the dead man in the snow. "Know you not that whoso sheds blood, by man shall his blood be shed, and that under our ancient charters, here I have the right to execute justice on you, as, by God's holy Name, I swear that I will do?" he added in a choked voice.

"Aye," repeated Christopher reflectively, "by man shall his blood be shed. Perhaps that is why this fellow died. Tell me, Abbot, was he not one of those who rode by moonlight round King's Grave lately, and there chanced to meet Sir John Foterell?"

The shot was a random one, yet it seemed that it went home; at least, the Abbot's jaw dropped, and some words that were on his lips never passed them.

"I know naught of the meaning of your talk," he said presently in a quieter voice, "or of how my late friend and neighbour, Sir John— may God rest his soul—came to his end. Yet it is of him, or rather of his, that we must speak. It seems that you have stolen his daughter, a woman under age, and by pretence of a false marriage, as I fear, brought her to shame—a crime even fouler than this murder."

"Nay, by means of a true marriage I have brought her to such small honour as may be the share of Christopher Harflete's lawful wife. If there be any virtue in the rites of Holy Church, then God's own hand has bound us fast as man can be tied to woman, and death is the only pope who can loose that knot."

"Death!" repeated the Abbot in a slow voice, looking up at him very curiously. For a little while he was silent, then went on, "Well, his court is always open, and he has many shrewd and instant messengers, such as this," and he pointed to the arrow in the neck of the slain soldier. "Yet I am a man of peace, and although you have murdered my servant, I would settle our cause more gently if I may. Listen now, Sir Christopher; here is my offer. Yield up to me the person of Cicely Foterell—"

"Of Cicely Harflete," interrupted Christopher.

"Of Cicely Foterell, and I swear to you that no violence shall be done to her, nor shall she be given to a husband till the King or his Vicar-General, or whatever court he may appoint, has passed judgment in this matter and declared this mock marriage of yours null and void."

"What!" broke in Christopher scoffingly; "does the Abbot of Bloss-holme announce that the powers temporal of this realm have right of divorce? Ere now I have heard him argue differently, and so have others, when the case of Queen Catherine was in question."

The Abbot bit his lip, but continued, taking no heed—

"Nor will I lay any complaint against you as to the death of my servant here, for which otherwise you should hang. That I will write down as an accident, and, further, compensate his family. Now you have my offer—answer."

"And what if I refuse this same generous offer to surrender her whom I hold dearer than a thousand lives?"

"Then, by virtue of my rights and authority, I will take her by force, Christopher Harflete, and if harm should happen to come to you, now or hereafter, on your own head be it."

At this Christopher's rage broke out.

"Do you dare to threaten me, a loyal Englishman, you false priest and foreign traitor," he shouted, "whom all men know to be in the pay of Spain, and using the cover of a monk's dress to plot against the land on which you fatten like a horse-leech? Why was John Foterell murdered in the forest two nights gone? You won't answer? Then I will. Because he rode to Court to prove the truth about you and your treachery, and therefore you butchered him. Why do you claim my wife as your ward? Because you wish to steal her lands and goods to feed your plots and luxury. You think you have bought friends at Court, and that for money's sake those in power there will turn a blind eye to your crimes. So it may be for a while; but wait, wait. All eyes are not blind yonder, nor all ears deaf. That head of yours shall yet be lifted higher than you think—so high that it sticks upon the top of Blossholme Towers, a warning to all who would sell England to her enemies. John Foterell lies dead with your knave's arrow in his throat, but Jeffrey Stokes is away with the writings. And now do your worst, Clement Maldon. If you want my wife, come take her."

The Abbot listened, listened intently, drinking in every ominous word. His swarthy face went white with fear, then turned black with rage. The veins upon his forehead gathered into knots; even from that distance Christopher could see them. He looked so evil that his countenance became twisted and ridiculous, and Christopher, noting it, burst into one of his hearty laughs.

The Abbot, who was not accustomed to mockery, whispered something to the two men who were with him, whereon they lifted the crossbows which they carried and pulled trigger. One quarrel went wide and hit the wall of the house behind, where it stuck fast in the joints of the stud-work. But the other, better aimed, smote Christopher above the heart, causing him to stagger, but being shot from below and turned by the mail he wore glanced upwards over his left shoulder. The men, seeing that he was unhurt, pulled their horses round and galloped off, but Christopher, setting another arrow to the string of the bow he carried, drew it to his ear, covering the Abbot.

"Loose, and make an end of him," muttered Emlyn from her shelter behind the parapet. But Christopher thought a moment, then cried—

"Stay a while, Sir Abbot; I have more to say to you."

He took no heed who was also turning about.

"Stay!" thundered Christopher, "or I will kill that fine nag of yours;" then, as the Abbot still dragged upon the reins, he let the arrow fly. The aim was true enough. Right through the arch of the neck it sped, cutting the cord between the bones, so that the poor beast reared straight up and fell in a heap, tumbling its rider off into the snow.

"Now, Clement Maldon," cried Christopher, "will you listen, or will you bide with your horse and servant and hear no more till Judgment Day? If you do not guess it, learn that I have practised archery from my youth. Should you doubt, hold up your hand and I'll send a shaft between your fingers."

The Abbot, who was shaken but unhurt, rose slowly and stood there, the dead horse on one side and the dead man on the other.

"Speak," he said in a muffled voice.

"My Lord Abbot," went on Christopher, "a minute ago you tried to murder me, and, had not my mail been good, would have succeeded. Now your life is in my hand, for, as you have seen, I do not miss. Those servants of yours are coming to your help. Call to them to halt, or—" and he lifted the bow.

The Abbot obeyed, and the men, understanding, stayed where they were, at a distance, but within earshot.

"You have a crucifix upon your breast," continued Christopher. "Take it in your right hand now and swear an oath."

Again the Abbot obeyed.

"Swear thus," he said, Emlyn, who was crouched beneath the parapet, prompting him from time to time; "I, Clement Maldon, Abbot of Blossholme, in the presence of Almighty God in heaven, and of Christopher Harflete and others upon earth," and he jerked his head backwards towards the windows of the house, where all therein were gathered, listening, "make oath upon the symbol of the Rood. I swear that I abandon all claim of wardship over the body of Cicely Harflete, born Cicely Foterell, the lawful wife of Christopher Harflete, and all claim to the lands and goods that she may possess, or that were possessed by her father, John Foterell, Knight, or by her mother, Dame Foterell, deceased. I swear that I will raise no suit in any court, spiritual or temporal, of this or other realms against the said Cicely Harflete or against the said Christopher Harflete, her husband, nor seek to work injury to their bodies or their souls, or to the bodies or the souls of any who cling to them, and that henceforth they may live and die in peace from me or any whom I control. Set your lips to the Rood and swear thus now, Clement Maldon."

The Abbot hearkened, and so great was his rage, for he had no meek heart, that he seemed to swell like an angry toad.

"Who gave you authority to administer oaths to me?" he asked at length. "I'll not swear," and he cast the crucifix down upon the snow.

"Then I'll shoot," answered Christopher. "Come, pick up that cross."

But Maldon stood silent, his arms folded on his breast. Christopher aimed and loosed, and so great was his skill—for there were few archers in England like to him—that the arrow pierced Maldon's fur cap and carried it away without touching the shaven head beneath.

"The next shall be two inches lower," he said, as he set another on the string. "I waste no more good shafts."

Then, very slowly, to save his life, which he loved well enough, Maldon bent down, and, lifting the crucifix from the snow, held it to his lips and kissed it, muttering—

"I swear." But the oath he swore was very different to that which Christopher had repeated to him, for, like a hunted fox, he knew how to meet guile with guile.

"Now that I, a consecrated abbot, deeming it right that I should live on to fulfil my work on earth, have done your bidding, have I leave to go about my business, Christopher Harflete?" he asked, with bitter irony.

"Why not?" asked Christopher. "Only be pleased henceforth not to meddle with me and my business. To-morrow I wish to ride to London with my lady, and we do not seek your company on the road."

Then, having found his cap, the Abbot turned and walked back towards his own men, drawing the arrow from it as he went, and presently all of them rode away over the rise towards Blossholme.

"Now that is well finished, and I have an oath that he will scarcely dare to break," said Christopher presently. "What say you, Nurse?"

"I say that you are even a bigger simpleton than I took you to be," answered Emlyn angrily, as she rose and stretched herself, for her limbs were cramped. "The oath, pshaw! By now he is absolved from it as given under fear. Did you not hear me whisper to you to put an arrow through his heart, instead of playing boy's pranks with his cap?"

"I did not wish to kill an abbot, Nurse."

"Foolish man, what is the difference in such a matter between him and one of his servants? Moreover, he will only say that you tried to slay him, and missed, and produce the cap and arrow in evidence against you. Well, my talk serves nothing to mend a bad matter, and soon you will hear it straighter from himself. Go now and make your house ready for attack, and never dare to set a foot without its doors, for death waits you there."

Emlyn was right. Within three hours an unarmed monk trudged up to Cranwell Towers through the falling snow and cast across the moat a letter that was tied to a stone. Then he nailed a writing to one of the oak posts of the outer gate, and, without a word, departed as he had come. In the presence of Christopher and Cicely, Emlyn opened and read this second letter, as she had read the first. It was short, and ran—

Take notice, Sir Christopher Harflete, and all others whom it may concern, that the oath which I, Clement Maldon, Abbot of Blossholme, swore to you this day, is utterly void and of none effect, having been wrung from me under the threat of instant death. Take notice, further, that a report of the murder which you have done has been forwarded to the King's grace and to the Sheriff and other officers of this county, and that by virtue of my rights and authority, ecclesiastical and civil, I shall proceed to possess myself of the person of Cicely Foterell, my ward, and of the lands and other property held by her father, Sir John Foterell, deceased, upon the former of which I have already entered on her behalf, and by exercise of such force as may be needful to seize you, Christopher Harflete, and to hand you over to justice. Further, by means of notice sent herewith, I warn all that cling to you and abet you in your crimes that they will do so at the peril of their souls and bodies.

Clement Maldon
Abbot of Blossholme

CHAPTER 5

What Passed at Cranwell

A week had gone by. For the first three days of that time little of note had happened at Cranwell Towers; that is, no assault was delivered. Only Christopher and his dozen or so of house-servants and small tenants discovered that they were quite surrounded. Once or twice some of them rode out a little way, to be hunted back again by a much superior force, which emerged from the copses near by or from cottages in the village, and even from the porch of the church. With these men they never came to close quarters, so that no lives were lost. In a fashion this was a disadvantage to them, since they lacked the excitement of actual fighting, the dread of which was ever present, but not its joy.

Meanwhile in other ways things went ill with them. Thus, first of all their beer gave out, and then such other cordials as they had, so that they were reduced to water to drink. Next their fuel became exhausted, for nearly all the stock of it was kept at the farmstead about a quarter of a mile away, and on the second day of the siege this stead was fired and burned with its contents, the cattle and horses being driven off, they knew not where.

So it came about at length they could keep only one fire, in the kitchen, and that but small, which in the end they were obliged to feed with the doors of the outhouses, and even with the floorings torn out of the attics, in order that they might cook their food. Nor was there much of this; only a store of salt meat and some pickled pork and smoked bacon, together with a certain amount of oatmeal and flour, that they made into cakes and bread.

On the fourth day, however, these gave out, so that they were reduced to a scanty diet of hung flesh, with a few apples by way of vegetables, and hot water to drink to warm them. At length, too, there was nothing more to burn, and therefore they must eat their meat raw, and grew sick on it. Moreover, a cold thaw set in, and the house grew

383

icy, so that they moved about it with chattering teeth, and at night, ill-nurtured as they were, could scarce keep the life in them beneath all the coverings which they had.

Ah! how long were those nights, with never a blaze upon the hearth or so much as a candle to light them. At four o'clock the darkness came down, which did not lessen, for the moon grew low and the mists were thick, until day broke about seven on the following morning. And all this time, fearing attack, they must keep watch and ward through the gloom, so that even sleep was denied them.

For a while they bore up bravely, even the tenants, though news was shouted to these that their steads had been harried, and their wives and children hunted off to seek shelter where they might.

Cicely and Emlyn never murmured. Indeed, this new-made wife kept her dreadful honeymoon with a cheerful face, trudging through the black hours around the circle of the moat at her husband's side, or from window-place to window-place in the empty rooms, till at length they cast themselves down upon some bed to sleep a while, giving over the watch to others. Only Emlyn never seemed to sleep. But at length their companions did begin to murmur.

One morning at the dawn, after a very bitter night, they waited upon Christopher and told him that they were willing to fight for his sake and his lady's, but that, as there was no hope of help, they could no longer freeze and starve; in short, that they must either escape from the house or surrender. He listened to them patiently, knowing that what they said was true, and then consulted for a while with Cicely and Emlyn.

"Our case is desperate, dear wife. Now what shall we do, who have no chance of succour, since none know of our plight? Yield, or strive to escape through the darkness?"

"Not yield, I think," answered Cicely, choking back a sob. "If we yield certainly they will separate us, and that merciless Abbot will bring you to your death and me to a nunnery."

"That may happen in any case," muttered Christopher, turning his head aside. "But what say you, Nurse?"

"I say fight for it," answered Emlyn boldly. "It is certain that we cannot stay here, for, to be plain, Sir Christopher, there are some among us whom I do not trust. What wonder? Their stomachs are empty, their hands are blue, their wives and children are they know not where, and the heavy curse of the Church hangs over them, all of which things may be mended if they play you false. Let us take what horses remain and slip away at dead of night if we can; or if we cannot, then let us die, as many better folk have done before."

So they agreed to try their fortune, thinking that it was so bad it could not be worse, and spent the rest of that day in getting ready as best they could. The seven horses still stood in the stable, and although they were stiff from want of exercise, had been hay-fed and watered. On these they proposed to ride, but first they must tell the truth to those who had stood by them. So about three o'clock of the afternoon Christopher called all the men together beneath the gateway and sorrowfully set out his tale. Here, he showed them, they could bide no longer, and to surrender meant that his new-wed wife would soon be made a widow. Therefore they must fly, taking with them as many as there were horses for them to ride, if they cared to risk such a journey. If not, he and the two women would go alone.

Now four of the stoutest-hearted of them, men who had served him and his father for many years, stepped forward, saying that, evil as these seemed to be, they would follow his fortunes to the last. He thanked them shortly, whereon one of the others asked what they were to do, and if he proposed to desert them after leading them into this plight.

"God knows I would rather die," he replied, with a swelling heart; "but, my friends, consider the case. If I bide here, what of my wife? Alas! it has come to this: that you must choose whether you will slip out with us and scatter in the woods, where I think you will not be followed, since yonder Abbot has no quarrel against you; or whether you will wait here, and to-morrow at the dawn, surrender. In either event you can say that I compelled you to stand by us, and that you have shed no man's blood; also I will give you a writing."

So they talked together gloomily, and at last announced that when he and their lady went they would go also and get off as best they could. But there was a man among them, a small farmer named Jonathan Dicksey, who thought otherwise. This Jonathan, who held his land under Christopher, had been forced to this business of the defence of Cranwell Towers somewhat against his will, namely, by the pressure of Christopher's largest tenant, to whose daughter he was affianced. He was a sly young man, and even during the siege, by means that need not be described, he had contrived to convey a message to the Abbot of Blossholme, telling him that had it been in his power he would gladly be in any other place. Therefore, as he knew well, whatever had happened to others, his farm remained unharried. Now he determined to be out of a bad business as soon as he might, for Jonathan was one of those who liked to stand upon the winning side.

Therefore, although he said "Aye, aye," more loudly than his comrades, as soon as the dusk had fallen, while the others were making ready the horses and mounting guard, Jonathan thrust a ladder across the moat at the back of the stable, and clambered along its rungs into the shelter of a cattle-shed in the meadow, and so away.

Half-an-hour later he stood before the Abbot in the cottage where he had taken up his quarters, having contrived to blunder among his people and be captured. To him at first Jonathan would say nothing, but when at length they threatened to take him out and hang him, to save his life, as he said, he found his tongue and told all.

"So, so," said the Abbot when he had finished. "Now God is good to us. We have these birds in our net, and I shall keep St. Hilary's at Blossholme after all. For your services, Master Dicksey, you shall be my reeve at Cranwell Towers when they are in my hands."

But here it may be said that in the end things went otherwise, since, so far from getting the stewardship of Cranwell, when the truth came to be known, Jonathan's maiden would have no more to do with him, and the folk in those parts sacked his farm and hunted him out of the country, so that he was never heard of among them again.

Meanwhile, all being ready, Christopher at the Towers was closeted with Cicely, taking his farewell of her in the dark, for no light was left to them.

"This is a desperate venture," he said to her, "nor can I tell how it will end, or if ever I shall see your sweet face again. Yet, dearest, we have been happy together for some few hours, and if I fall and you live on I am sure that you will always remember me till, as we are taught, we meet again where no enemy has the power to torment us, and cold and hunger and darkness are not. Cicely, if that should be so and any child should come to you, teach it to love the father whom it never saw."

Now she threw her arms about him and wept, and wept, and wept.

"If you die," she sobbed, "surely I will do so also, for although I am but young I find this world a very evil place, and now that my father is gone, without you, husband, it would be a hell."

"Nay, nay," he answered; "live on while you may; for who knows? Often out of the worst comes the best. At least we have had our joy. Swear it now, sweet."

"Aye, if you will swear it also, for I may be taken and you left. In the dark swords do not choose. Let us promise that we will both endure our lives, together or separate, until God calls us."

So they swore there in the icy gloom, and sealed the oath with kisses.

Now the time was come at last, and they crept their way to the courtyard hand in hand, taking some comfort because the night was very favourable to their project. The snow had melted, and a great gale blew from the sou'-west, boisterous but not cold, which caused the tall elms that stood about to screech and groan like things alive. In such a wind as this they were sure that they would not be heard, nor could they be seen beneath that murky, starless sky, while the rain which fell between the gusts would wash out the footprints of their horses.

They mounted silently, and with the four men—for by now all the rest had gone—rode across the drawbridge, which had been lowered in preparation for their flight. Three hundred yards or so away their road ran through an ancient marl-pit worked out generations before, in which self-sown trees grew on either side of the path. As they drew near this place suddenly, in the silence of the night, a horse neighed ahead of them, and one of their beasts answered to the neigh.

"Halt!" whispered Cicely, whose ears were made sharp by fear. "I hear men moving."

They pulled rein and listened. Yes; between the gusts of wind there was a faint sound as of the clanking of armour. They strained their eyes in the darkness, but could see nothing. Again the horse neighed and was answered. One of their servants cursed the beast beneath his breath and struck it savagely with the flat of his sword, whereon, being fresh, it took the bit between its teeth and bolted. Another minute and there arose a great clamour from the marl-pit in front of them—a noise of shoutings, of sword-strokes, and then a heavy groan as from the lips of a dying man.

"An ambush!" exclaimed Christopher.

"Can we get round?" asked Cicely, and there was terror in her voice.

"Nay," he answered, "the stream is in flood; we should be bogged. Hark! they charge us. Back to the Towers—there is no other way."

So they turned and fled, followed by shouts and the thunder of many horses galloping. In two minutes they were there and across the bridge—the women, Christopher, and the three men who were left.

"Up with the bridge!" cried Christopher, and they leapt from their saddles and fumbled for the cranks; too late, for already the Abbot's horsemen pressed it down.

Then a fight began. The horses of the enemy shrank back from the trembling bridge, so their riders, dismounting, rushed forward, to be met by Christopher and his three remaining men, who in that narrow place were as good as a hundred. Wild, random blows were struck in the darkness, and, as it chanced, two of the Abbot's people fell, whereon a deep voice cried—

"Come back and wait for light."

When they had gone, dragging off their wounded with them, Christopher and his servants again strove to wind up the bridge, only to find that it would not stir.

"Some traitor has fouled the chains," he said in the quiet voice of despair. "Cicely and Emlyn, get you into the house. I, and any who will bide with me, stay here to see this business out. When I am down, yield yourself. Afterwards I think that the King will give you justice, if you can come to him."

"I'll not go," she wailed; "I'll die with you."

"Nay, you shall go," he said, stamping his foot, and, as he spoke, an arrow hissed between them. "Emlyn, drag her hence ere she is shot. Swift, I say, swift, or God's curse and mine rest on you. Unclasp your arms, wife; how can I fight while you hang about my neck? What! Must I strike you? Then, there and there!"

She loosed her grasp, and, groaning, fell back upon the breast of Emlyn, who half led, half carried her across the courtyard, where their scared horses galloped loose.

"Whither go we?" sobbed Cicely.

"To the central tower," answered Emlyn; "it seems safest there."

To this tower, whence the place took its name, they groped their way. Unlike the rest of the house, which for the most part was of wood, it was built of stone, being part of an older fabric dating from the Norman days. Slowly they stumbled up the steps till at length they reached the roof, for some instinct prompted them to find a spot whence they could see, should the stars break out. Here, on this lofty perch, they crouched them down and waited the end, whatever it might be—waited in silence.

A while passed—they never knew how long—till at length a sudden flame shot up above the roof of the kitchens at the rear, which the wind caught and blew on to the timbers of the main building, so that presently this began to blaze also. The house had been fired, by whom was never known, though it was said that the traitor, Jonathan Dicksey, had returned and done it, either for a bribe or that his own sin might be forgotten in this great catastrophe.

"The house burns," said Emlyn in her quiet voice. "Now, if you would save your life, follow me. Beneath this tower is a vault where no flame can touch us."

But Cicely would not stir, for by the fierce and ever-growing light she could see what passed beneath, and, as it chanced, the wind blew the smoke away from them. There, beyond the drawbridge, were gathered the Abbey guards, and there in the gateway stood Christopher and his three men with drawn swords, while in the courtyard the horses galloped madly, screaming in their fear. A soldier looked up and saw the two women standing on the top of the tower, then called out something to the Abbot, who sat on horseback near to him. He looked and saw also.

"Yield, Sir Christopher," he shouted; "the Lady Cicely burns. Yield, that we may save her."

Christopher turned and saw also. For a moment he hesitated, then wheeled round to run across the courtyard. Too late, for as he came the flames burst through the main roof of the house, and the timber front of it, blazing furiously, fell outwards, blocking the doorway, so that the place became a furnace into which none might enter and live.

Now a madness seemed to take hold of him. For a moment he stared up at the figures of the two women standing high above the rolling smoke and wrapping flame. Then, with his three men, he charged with a roar into the crowd of soldiers who had followed him into the courtyard, striving, it would seem, to cut his way to the Abbot, who lurked behind. It was a dreadful sight, for he and those with him fought furiously, and many went down. Presently, of the four only Christopher was left upon his feet. Swords and spears smote upon his armour, but he did not fall; it was those in front of him who fell. A great fellow with an axe got behind him and struck with all his might upon his helm. The sword dropped from Harflete's hand; slowly he turned about, looked upward, then stretched out his arms and fell heavily to earth.

The Abbot leapt from his horse and ran to him, kneeling at his side.

"Dead!" he cried, and began to shrive his passing soul, or so it seemed.

"Dead," repeated Emlyn, "and a gallant death!"

"Dead!" wailed Cicely, in so terrible a voice that all below heard it. "Dead, dead!" and sank senseless on Emlyn's breast.

At that moment the rest of the roof fell in, hiding the tower in spouts and veils of flame. Here they might not stay if they would live. Lifting her mistress in her strong arms, as she was wont to do when she was little, Emlyn found the head of the stair, so that when the wind blew the smoke aside for an instant, those below saw that both had vanished, as they thought withered in the fire.

"Now you can enter on the Shefton lands, Abbot," cried a voice from the darkness of the gateway, though in the turmoil none knew who spoke; "but not for all England would I bear that innocent blood!"

The Abbot's face turned ghastly, and though it was hot enough in that courtyard his teeth chattered.

"It is on the head of this woman-thief," he exclaimed with an effort, looking down on Christopher, who lay at his feet. "Take him up, that inquest may be held on him, who died doing murder. Can none enter the house? His pocket full of gold to him who saves the Lady Cicely!"

"Can any enter hell and live?" answered the same voice out of the smoke and gloom. "Seek her sweet soul in heaven, if you may come there, Abbot."

Then, with scared faces, they lifted up Christopher and the other dead and wounded and carried them away, leaving Cranwell Towers to burn itself to ashes, for so fierce was the heat that none could bide there longer.

****

Two hours had gone by. The Abbot sat in the little room of a cottage at Cranwell that he had occupied during the siege of the Towers. It was near midnight, yet, weary as he was, he could not rest; indeed, had the night been less foul and dark he would have spent the time in riding back to Blossholme. His heart was ill at ease. Things had gone well with him, it is true. Sir John Foterell was dead—slain by "outlawed men;" Sir Christopher Harflete was dead—did not his body lie in the neat-house yonder? Cicely, daughter of the one and wife to the other, was dead also, burned in the fire at the Towers, so that doubtless the precious gems and the wide lands he coveted would fall into his lap without further trouble. For, Cromwell being bribed, who would try to snatch them from the powerful Abbot of Blossholme, and had he not a title to them—of a sort?

And yet he was very ill at ease, for, as that voice had said—whose voice was it? he wondered, somehow it seemed familiar—the blood of these people lay on his head; and there came into his mind the text of Holy Writ which he had quoted to Christopher, that he who shed man's blood by man should his blood be shed. Also, although he had paid the Vicar-General to back him, monks were in no great favour at the English Court, and if this story travelled there, as it might, for even the strengthless dead find friends, it was possible that questions would be asked, questions hard to answer. Before Heaven he could justify himself for all that he had done, but before King Henry, who would usurp the powers of the very Pope, if the truth should chance to reach the royal ear—ah! that was another matter.

The room was cold after the heat of that great fire; his Southern

390

blood, which had been warm enough, grew chill; loneliness and depression took hold of him; he began to wonder how far in the eyes of God above the end justifies the means. He opened the door of the place, and holding on to it lest the rough, wintry gale should tear it from its frail hinges, shouted aloud for Brother Martin, one of his chaplains.

Presently Martin arrived, emerging from the cattle shed, a lantern in his hand—a tall, thin man, with perplexed and melancholy eyes, long nose, and a clever face—and, bowing, asked his superior's pleasure.

"My pleasure, Brother," answered the Abbot, "is that you shut the door and keep out the wind, for this accursed climate is killing me. Yes, make up the fire if you can, but the wood is too wet to burn; also it smokes. There, what did I tell you? If this goes on we shall be hams by to-morrow morning. Let it be, for, after all, we have seen enough of fires to-night, and sit down to a cup of wine—nay, I forgot, you drink but water—well, then, to a bite of bread and meat."

"I thank you, my Lord Abbot," answered Martin, "but I may not touch flesh; this is Friday."

"Friday or no we have touched flesh—the flesh of men—up at the Towers yonder this night," answered the Abbot, with an uneasy laugh. "Still, obey your conscience, Brother, and eat bread. Soon it will be midnight, and the meat can follow."

The lean monk bowed, and, taking a hunch of bread, began to bite at it, for he was almost starving.

"Have you come from watching by the body of that bloody and rebellious man who has worked us so much harm and loss?" asked the Abbot presently.

The secretary nodded, then swallowing a crust, said—

"Aye, I have been praying over him and the others. At least he was brave, and it must be hard to see one's new-wed wife burn like a witch. Also, now that I come to study the matter, I know not what his sin was who did but fight bravely when he was attacked. For without doubt the marriage is good, and whether he should have waited to ask your leave to make it is a point that might be debated through every court in Christendom."

The Abbot frowned, not appreciating this open and judicial tone in matters that touched him so nearly.

"You have honoured me of late by choosing me as one of your confessors, though I think you do not tell me everything, my Lord Abbot; therefore I bare my mind to you," continued Brother Martin apologetically.

"Speak on then, man. What do you mean?"

"I mean that I do not like this business," he answered slowly, in the intervals of munching at his bread. "You had a quarrel with Sir John Foterell about those lands which you say belong to the Abbey. God knows the right of it, for I understand no law; but he denied it, for did I not hear it yonder in your chamber at Blossholme? He denied it, and accused you of treason enough to hang all Blossholme, of which again God knows the truth. You threatened him in your anger, but he and his servant were armed and won out, and next day the two of them rode for London with certain papers. Well, that night Sir John Foterell was killed in the forest, though his servant Stokes escaped with the papers. Now, who killed him?"

The Abbot looked at him, then seemed to take a sudden resolution.

"Our people, those men-at-arms whom I have gathered for the defence of our House and the Church. My orders to them were to seize him living, but the old English bull would not yield, and fought so fiercely that it ended otherwise—to my sorrow."

The monk put down his bread, for which he seemed to have no further appetite.

"A dreadful deed," he said, "for which one day you must answer to God and man."

"For which we all must answer," corrected the Abbot, "down to the last lay-brother and soldier—you as much as any of us, Brother, for were you not present at our quarrel?"

"So be it, Abbot. Being innocent, I am ready. But that is not the end of it. The Lady Cicely, on hearing of this murder—nay, be not wrath, I know no other name for it—and learning that you claimed her as your ward, flies to her affianced lover, Sir Christopher Harflete, and that very day is married to him by the parish priest in yonder church."

"It was no marriage. Due notice had not been given. Moreover, how could my ward be wed without my leave?"

"She had not been served with notice of your wardship, if such exists, or so she declared," replied Martin in his quiet, obstinate voice. "I think that there is no court in Europe which would void this open marriage when it learned that the parties lived a while as man and wife, and were so received by those about them—no, not the Pope himself."

"He who says that he is no lawyer still sets out the law," broke in Maldon sarcastically. "Well, what does it matter, seeing that death has voided it? Husband and wife, if such they were, are both dead; it is finished."

"No; for now they lay their appeal in the Court of Heaven, to which every one of us is summoned; and Heaven can stir up its ministers on earth. Oh! I like it not, I like it not; and I mourn for those two, so loving, brave, and young. Their blood and that of many more is on our hands—for what? A stretch of upland and of marsh which the King or others may seize to-morrow."

The Abbot seemed to cower beneath the weight of these sad, earnest words, and for a little while there was silence. Then he plucked up courage, and said—

"I am glad that you remember that their blood is on your hands as well as mine, since now, perhaps, you will keep them hidden."

He rose and walked to the door and the window to see that none were without, then returned and exclaimed fiercely—

"Fool, do you then think that these deeds were done to win a new estate? True it is that those lands are ours by right, and we need their revenues; but there is more behind. The whole Church of this realm is threatened by that accursed son of Belial who sits upon the throne. Why, what is it now, man?"

"Only that I am an Englishman, and love not to hear England's king called a son of Belial. His sins, I know, are many and black, like those of others—still, 'son of Belial!' Let his Highness hear it, and that name alone is enough to hang you!"

"Well, then, angel of grace, if it suits you better. At the least we are threatened. Against the law of God and man our blessed Queen, Catherine of Spain, is thrust away in favour of the slut who fills her place. Even now I have tidings from Kimbolton that she lies dying there of slow poison; so they say and I believe. Also I have other tidings. Fisher and More being murdered, Parliament next month will be moved to strike at the lesser monasteries and steal their goods, and after them our turn will come. But we will not bear it tamely, for ere this new year is out all England shall be ablaze, and I, Clement Maldon, I—I will light the fire. Now you have the truth, Martin. Will you betray me, as that dead knight would have done?"

"Nay, my Lord Abbot, your secrets are safe with me. Am I not your chaplain, and does not this wilful and rebellious King of ours work much mischief against God and His servants? Yet I tell you that I like it not, and cannot see the end. We English are a stiff-necked folk whom you of Spain do not understand and will never break, and Henry is strong and subtle; moreover, his people love him."

"I knew that I could trust you, Martin, and the proof of it is that I have spoken to you so openly," went on Maldon in a gentler voice. "Well, you shall hear all. The great Emperor of Germany and Spain is on our side, as, seeing his blood and faith, he must be. He will avenge the wrongs of the Church and of his royal aunt. I, who know him, am his agent here, and what I do is done at his bidding. But I must have more money than he finds me, and that is why I stirred in this matter of the Shefton lands. Also the Lady Cicely had jewels of vast price, though I fear greatly lest they should have been lost in the fire this night."

"Filthy lucre—the root of all evil," muttered Brother Martin.

"Aye, and of all good. Money, money—I must have more money to bribe men and buy arms, to defend that stronghold of Heaven, the Church. What matters it if lives are lost so that the immortal Church holds her own? Let them go. My friend, you are fearful; these deaths weigh upon your soul—aye, and on mine. I loved that girl, whom as a babe I held in my arms, and even her rough father, I loved him for his honest heart, although he always mistrusted me, the Spaniard—and rightly. The knight Harflete, too, who lies yonder, he was of a brave breed, but not one who would have served our turn. Well, they are gone, and for these blood-sheddings we must find absolution."

"If we can."

"Oh! we can, we can. Already I have it in my pouch, under a seal you know. And for our bodies, fear not. There is such a gale rising in England as will blow out this petty breeze. A question of rights, some arrows shot, a fire and lives lost—what of that when it agitates betwixt powers temporal and spiritual, and which of them shall hold the sceptre in this mighty Britain? Martin, I have a mission for you that may lead you to a bishopric ere all is done, for that's your mind and aim, and if you would put off your doubts and moodiness you've got the brain to rule. That ship, the *Great Yarmouth*, which sailed for Spain some days ago, has been beat back into the river, and should weigh anchor again to-morrow morning. I have letters for the Spanish Court, and you shall take them with my verbal explanations, which I will give you presently, for they would hang us, and may not be trusted to writing. She is bound for Seville, but you will follow the Emperor wherever he may be. You will go, won't you?" and he glanced at him sideways.

"I obey orders," answered Martin, "though I know little of Spaniards or of Spanish."

"In every town the Benedictines have a monastery, and in every monastery interpreters, and you shall be accredited to them all who are of that great Brotherhood. Well, 'tis settled. Go, make ready as best you can; I must write. Stay; the sooner this Harflete is under ground the better. Bid that sturdy fellow, Bolle, find the sexton of the church and help dig his grave, for we will bury him at dawn. Now go, go, I tell you I must write. Come back in an hour, and I will give you money for your faring, also my secret messages."

Brother Martin bowed and went.

"A dangerous man," muttered the Abbot, as the door closed on him; "too honest for our game, and too much an Englishman. That native spirit peeps beneath his cowl; a monk should have no country and no kin. Well, he will learn a trick or two in Spain, and I'll make sure they keep him there a while. Now for my letters," and he sat down at the rude table and began to write.

Half-an-hour later the door opened and Martin entered.

"What is it now?" asked the Abbot testily. "I said, 'Come back in an hour.'"

"Aye, you said that, but I have good news for you that I thought you might like to hear."

"Out with it, then, man. It's scarce now-a-days. Have they found those jewels? No, how could they? the place still flares," and he glanced through the window-place. "What's the news?"

"Better than jewels. Christopher Harflete is not dead. While I was praying over him he turned his head and muttered. I think he is only stunned. You are skilled in medicine; come, look at him."

A minute later and the Abbot knelt over the senseless form of Christopher where it lay on the filthy floor of the neat-house. By the light of the lanterns with deft fingers he felt his wounded head, from which the shattered *casque* had been removed, and afterwards his heart and pulse.

"The skull is cut, but not broken," he said. "My judgment is that though he may lie unsensed for days, if fed and tended this man will live, being so young and strong. But if left alone in this cold place he will be dead by morning, and perhaps he is better dead," and he looked at Martin.

"That would be murder indeed," answered the secretary. "Come, let us bear him to the fire and pour milk down his throat. We may save him yet. Lift you his feet and I will take his head."

The Abbot did so, not very willingly, as it seemed to Martin, but rather as one who has no choice.

Half-an-hour later, when the hurts of Christopher had been dressed with ointment and bound up, and milk poured down his throat, which he swallowed although he was so senseless, the Abbot, looking at him, said to Martin—

"You gave orders for this Harflete's burial, did you not?"

The monk nodded.

"Then have you told any that he needs no grave at present?"

"No one except yourself."

The Abbot thought a while, rubbing his shaven chin.

"I think the funeral should go forward," he said presently. "Look not so frightened; I do not purpose to inter him living. But there is a dead man lying in that shed, Andrew Woods, my servant, the Scotch soldier whom Harflete slew. He has no friends here to claim him, and these two were of much the same height and breadth. Shrouded in a blanket, none would know one body from the other, and it will be thought that Andrew was buried with the rest. Let him be promoted in his death, and fill a knight's grave."

"To what purpose would you play so unholy a trick, which must, moreover, be discovered in a day, seeing that Sir Christopher lives?" asked Martin, staring at him.

"For a very good purpose, my friend. It is well that Sir Christopher Harflete should seem to die, who, if he is known to be alive, has powerful kin in the south who will bring much trouble on us."

"Do you mean—? If so, before God I will have no hand in it."

"I said—seem to die. Where are your wits to-night?" answered the Abbot, with irritation. "Sir Christopher travels with you to Spain as our sick Brother Luiz, who, like myself, is of that country, and desires to return there, as we know, but is too ill to do so. You will nurse him, and on the ship he will die or recover, as God wills. If he recovers our Brotherhood will show him hospitality at Seville, notwithstanding his crimes, and by the time that he reaches England again, which may not be for a long while, men will have forgotten all this fray in a greater that draws on. Nor will he be harmed, seeing that the lady whom he pretends to have married is dead beyond a doubt, as you can tell him should he find his understanding."

"A strange game," muttered Martin.

"Strange or no, it is my game which I must play. Therefore question not, but be obedient, and silent also, on your oath," replied the Abbot in a cold, hard voice. "That covered litter which was brought here for the wounded is in the next chamber. Wrap this man in blankets and a monk's robe, and we will place him in it. Then let him be borne to Blossholme as one of the dead by brethren who will ask no questions, and ere dawn on to the ship *Great Yarmouth*, if he still lives. It lies near the quay not half-a-mile from the Abbey gate. Be swift now, and help me. I will overtake you with the letters, and see that you are furnished with all things needful from our store. Also I must speak with the captain ere he weighs anchor. Waste no more time in talking, but obey and be secret."

"I obey, and I will be secret, as is my duty," answered Brother Martin, bowing his head humbly. "But what will be the end of all this business, God and His angels know alone. I say that I like it not."

"A *very* dangerous man," muttered the Abbot, as he watched Martin go. "He also must bide a while in Spain; a long while. I'll see to it!"

CHAPTER 6

Emlyn's Curse

Just before the wild dawn broke on the morrow of the burning of the Towers, a corpse, roughly shrouded, was borne from the village into the churchyard of Cranwell, where a shallow grave had been dug for its last home.

"Whom do we bury in such haste?" asked the tall Thomas Bolle, who had delved the grave alone in the dark, for his orders were urgent, and the sexton was fled away from these tumults.

"That man of blood, Sir Christopher Harflete, who has caused us so much loss," said the old monk who had been bidden to perform the office, as the clergyman, Father Necton, had gone also, fearing the vengeance of the Abbot for his part in the marriage of Cicely. "A sad story, a very sad story. Wedded by night, and now buried by night, both of them, one in the flame and one in the earth. Truly, O God, Thy judgments are wonderful, and woe to those who lift hands against Thine anointed ministers!"

"Very wonderful," answered Bolle, as, standing in the grave, he took the head of the body and laid it down between his straddled feet; "so wonderful that a plain man wonders what will be the wondrous end of them, also why this noble young knight has grown so wondrously lighter than he used to be. Trouble and hunger in those burnt Towers, I suppose. Why did they not set him in the vault with his ancestors? It would have saved me a lonely job among the ghosts that haunt this place. What do you say, Father? Because the stone is cemented down and the entrance bricked up, and there is no mason to be found? Then why not have waited till one could be fetched? Oh, it is wonderful, all wonderful. But who am I that I should dare to ask questions? When the Lord Abbot orders, the lay-brother obeys, for he also is wonderful—a wonderful abbot.

"There, he is tidy now—straight on his back and his feet pointing to the east, at least I hope so, for I could take no good bearings in the dark; and the whole wonderful story comes to its wonderful end. So give me your hand out of this hole, Father, and say your prayers over the sinful body of this wicked fellow who dared to marry the maid he loved, and to let out the souls of certain holy monks, or rather of their hired rufflers, for monks don't fight, because they wished to separate those whom God—I mean the devil—had joined together, and to add their temporalities to the estate of Mother Church."

Then the old priest, who was shivering with cold, and understood little of this dark talk, began to mumble his ritual, skipping those parts of it which he could not remember. So another grain was planted in the cornfields of death and immortality, though when and where it should grow and what it should bear he neither knew nor cared, who wished to escape from fears and fightings back to his accustomed cell.

It was done, and he and the bearers departed, beating their way against the rough, raw wind, and leaving Thomas Bolle to fill in the grave, which, so long as they were in sight, or rather hearing, he did with much vigour. When they were gone, however, he descended into the hole under pretence of trampling the loose soil, and there, to be out of the wind, sat himself down upon the feet of the corpse and waited, full of reflections.

"Sir Christopher dead," he muttered to himself. "I knew his grand-father when I was a lad, and my grandfather told me that he knew his grandfather's great-grandfather—say three hundred years of them—and now I sit on the cold toes of the last of the lot, butchered like a mad ox in his own yard by a Spanish priest and his hirelings, to win his wife's goods. Oh! yes, it is wonderful, all very wonderful; and the Lady Cicely dead, burnt like a common witch. And Emlyn dead—Emlyn, whom I have hugged many a time in this very churchyard, before they whipped her into marrying that fat old grieve and made a monk of me.

"Well, I had her first kiss, and, by the saints! how she cursed old Stower all the way down yonder path. I stood behind that tree and heard her. She said he would die soon, and he did, and his brat with him. She said she would dance on his grave, and she did; I saw her do it in the moonlight the night after he was buried; dressed in white she danced on his grave! She always kept her promises, did Emlyn. That's her blood. If her mother had not been a gypsy witch, she wouldn't have married a Spaniard when every man in the place was after her for her beautiful eyes. Emlyn is a witch too, or was, for they say she is dead; but I can't think it, she isn't the sort that dies. Still, she must be dead, and that's good for my soul. Oh! miserable man, what are you thinking? Get behind me, Satan, if you can find room. A grave is no place for you, Satan, but I wish you were in it with me, Emlyn. You *must* have been a witch, since, after you, I could never fancy any other woman, which is against nature, for all's fish that comes to a man's net. Evidently a witch of the worst sort, but, my darling, witch or no I wish you weren't dead, and I'll break that Abbot's neck for you yet, if it costs me my soul. Oh! Emlyn, my darling, my darling, do you remember how we kissed in the copse by the river? Never was there a woman who could love like you."

So he moaned on, rocking himself to and fro on the legs of the corpse, till at length a wild ray from the red, risen sun crept into the darksome hole, lighting first of all upon a mouldering skull which Bolle had thrown back among the soil. He rose up and pitched it out with a word that should not have passed the lips of a lay-brother, even as such thoughts should not have passed his mind. Then he set himself to a task which he had planned in the intervals of his amorous meditations—a somewhat grizzly task.

Drawing his knife from its sheath, he cut the rough stitching of the grave-clothes, and, with numb hands, dragged them away from the body's head.

The light went out behind a cloud, but, not to waste time, he began to feel the face.

"Sir Christopher's nose wasn't broken," he muttered to himself, "unless it were in that last fray, and then the bone would be loose, and this is stiff. No, no, he had a very pretty nose."

The light came again, and Thomas peered down at the dead face beneath him; then suddenly burst into a hoarse laugh.

"By all the saints! here's another of our Spaniard's tricks. It is drunken Andrew the Scotchman, turned into a dead English knight. Christopher killed him, and now he is Christopher. But where's Christopher?"

He thought a little while, then, jumping out of the grave, began to fill it in with all his might.

"You're Christopher," he said; "well, stop Christopher until I can prove you're Andrew. Good-bye, Sir Andrew Christopher; I am off to seek your betters. If you are dead, who may not be alive? Emlyn herself, perhaps, after this. Oh, the devil is playing a merry game round old Cranwell Towers to-night, and Thomas Bolle will take a hand in it."

He was right. The devil was playing a merry game. At least, so thought others beside Thomas. For instance, that misguided but honest bigot, Martin, as he contemplated the still senseless form of Christopher, who, re-christened Brother Luiz, had been safely conveyed aboard the *Great Yarmouth*, and now, whether dead or living, which he was not sure, lay in the little cabin that had been allotted to the two of them. Almost did Martin, as he looked at him and shook his bald head, seem to smell brimstone in that close place, which, as he knew well, was the fiend's favourite scent.

The captain also, a sour-faced mariner with a squint, known in Dunwich, whence he hailed, as Miser Goody, because of his earnestness in pursuing wealth and his skill in hoarding it, seemed to feel the unhallowed influence of his Satanic Majesty. So far everything had gone wrong upon this voyage, which already had been delayed six weeks, that is, till the very worst period of the year, while he waited for certain mysterious letters and cargo which his owners said he must carry to Seville. Then he had sailed out of the river with a fair wind, only to be beaten back by fearful weather that nearly sank the ship.

Item: six of his best men had deserted because they feared a trip to Spain at that season, and he had been obliged to take others at hazard. Among them was a broad-shouldered, black-bearded fellow clad in a leather jerkin, with spurs upon his heels—bloody spurs—that he seemed to have found no time to take off. This hard rider came aboard in a skiff after the anchor was up, and, having cast the skiff adrift, offered good money for a passage to Spain or any other foreign port, and paid it down upon the nail. He, Goody, had taken the money, though with a doubtful heart, and given a receipt to the name of Charles Smith, asking no questions, since for this gold he need not account to the owners. Afterwards also the man, having put off his spurs and soldier's jerkin, set himself to work among the crew, some of whom seemed to know him, and in the storm that followed showed that he was stout-hearted and useful, though not a skilled sailor.

Still, he mistrusted him of Charles Smith, and his bloody spurs, and had he not been so short-handed and taken the knave's broad pieces would have liked to set him ashore again when they were driven back into the river, especially as he heard that there had been man-slaying about Blossholme, and that Sir John Foterell lay slaughtered in the forest. Perhaps this Charles Smith had murdered him. Well, if so, it was no affair of his, and he could not spare a hand.

Now, when at length the weather had moderated, just as he was hauling up his anchor, comes the Abbot of Blossholme, on whose will he had been bidden to wait, with a lean-faced monk and another passenger, said to be a sick religious, wrapped up in blankets and to all appearance dead.

Why, wondered that astute mariner Goody, should a sick monk wear harness, for he felt it through the blankets as he helped him up the ladder, although monk's shoes were stuck upon his feet. And why, as he saw when the covering slipped aside for a moment, was his crown bound up with bloody cloths?

Indeed, he ventured to question the Abbot as to this mysterious matter while his Lordship was paying the passage money in his cabin, only to get a very sharp answer.

"Were you not commanded to obey me in all things, Captain Goody, and does obedience lie in prying out my business? Another word and I will report you to those in Spain who know how to deal with mischief-makers. If you would see Dunwich again, hold your peace."

"Your pardon, my Lord Abbot," said Goody; "but things go so upon this ship that I grow afraid. That is an ill voyage upon which one lifts anchor twice in the same port."

"You will not make them go better, captain, by seeking to nose out my affairs and those of the Church. Do you desire that I should lay its curse upon you?"

"Nay, your Reverence, I desire that you should take the curse off," answered Goody, who was very superstitious. "Do that and I'll carry a dozen sick priests to Spain, even though they choose to wear chain shirts—for penance."

The Abbot smiled, then, lifting his hand, pronounced some words in Latin, which, as he did not understand them, Goody found very comforting. As they passed his lips the *Great Yarmouth* began to move, for the sailors were hoisting up her anchor.

"As I do not accompany you on this voyage, fare you well," he said. "The saints go with you, as shall my prayers. Since you will not pass the Gibraltar Straits, where I hear many infidel pirates lurk, given good weather your voyage should be safe and easy. Again farewell. I commend Brother Martin and our sick friend to your keeping, and shall ask account of them when we meet again."

I pray it may not be this side of hell, for I do not like that Spanish Abbot and his passengers, dead or living, thought Goody to himself, as he bowed him from the cabin.

A minute later the Abbot, after a few earnest, hurried words with Martin, began to descend the ladder to the boat, that, manned by his own people, was already being drawn slowly through the water. As he did so he glanced back, and, in the clinging mist of dawn, which was almost as dense as wool, caught sight of the face of a man who had been ordered to hold the ladder, and knew it for that of Jeffrey

Stokes, who had escaped from the slaying of Sir John—escaped with the damning papers that had cost his master's life. Yes, Jeffrey Stokes, no other. His lips shaped themselves to call out something, but before ever a syllable had passed them an accident happened.

To the Abbot it seemed as though the whole ship had struck him violently behind—so violently that he was propelled headfirst among the rowers in the boat, and lay there hurt and breathless.

"What is it?" called the captain, who heard the noise.

"The Abbot slipped, or the ladder slipped, I know not which," answered Jeffrey gruffly, staring at the toe of his sea-boot. "At least he is safe enough in the boat now," and, turning, he vanished aft into the mist, muttering to himself—

"A very good kick, though a little high. Yet I wish it had been off another kind of ladder. That murdering rogue would look well with a rope round his neck. Still I dared do no more and it served to stop his lying mouth before he betrayed me. Oh, my poor master, my poor old master!"

****

Bruised and sore as he was—and he was very sore—within little over an hour Abbot Maldon was back at the ruin of Cranwell Towers. It seemed strange that he should go there, but in truth his uneasy heart would not let him rest. His plans had succeeded only far too well. Sir John Foterell was dead—a crime, no doubt, but necessary, for had the knight lived to reach London with that evidence in his pocket, his own life and those of many others might have paid the price of it, since who knows what truths may be twisted from a victim on the rack? Maldon had always feared the rack; it was a nightmare that haunted his sleep, although the ambitious cunning of his nature and the cause he served with heart and soul prompted him to put himself in continual danger of that fate.

In an unguarded moment, when his tongue was loosed with wine, he had placed himself in the power of Sir John Foterell, hoping to win him to the side of Spain, and afterwards, forgetting it, made of him a dreadful enemy. Therefore this enemy must die, for had he lived, not only might he himself have died in place of him, but all his plans for the rebellion of the Church against the Crown must have come to nothing. Yes, yes, that deed was lawful, and pardon for it assured should the truth become known. Till this morning he had hoped that it never would be known, but now Jeffrey Stokes had escaped upon the ship *Great Yarmouth*.

Oh, if only he had seen him a minute earlier; if only something—could it have been that impious knave, Jeffrey? he wondered—had not struck him so violently in the back and hurled him to the boat, where he lay almost senseless till the vessel had glided from them down the river! Well, she was gone, and Jeffrey in her. He was but a common serving-man, after all, who, if he knew anything, would never have the wit to use his knowledge, although it was true he had been wise enough to fly from England.

No papers had been discovered upon Sir John's body, and no money. Without doubt the old knight had found time to pass them on to Jeffrey, who now fled the kingdom disguised as a sailor. Oh! what ill chance had put him on board the same vessel with Sir Christopher Harflete?

Well, Sir Christopher would probably die; were Brother Martin a little less of a fool he would certainly die, but the fact remained that this monk, though able, in such matters *was* a fool, with a conscience that would not suit itself to circumstances. If Christopher could be saved, Martin would save him, as he had already saved him in the shed, even if he handed him over to the Inquisition afterwards. Still, he might slip through his fingers or the vessel might be lost, as was devoutly to be prayed, and seemed not unlikely at this season of the year. Also, the first opportunity must be taken to send certain messages to Spain that might result in hampering the activities of Brother Martin, and of Sir Christopher Harflete, if he lived to reach that land.

Meanwhile, reflected Maldon, other things had gone wrong. He had wished to proclaim his wardship over Cicely and to immure her in a nunnery because of her great possessions, which he needed for the cause, but he had not wished her death. Indeed, he was fond of the girl, whom he had known from a child, and her innocent blood was a weight that he ill could bear, he who at heart always shrank from the shedding of blood. Still, Heaven had killed her, not he, and the matter could not now be mended. Also, as she was dead, her inheritance would, he thought, fall into his hands without further trouble, for he—a mitred Abbot with a seat among the Lords of the realm—had friends in London, who, for a fee, could stifle inquiry into all this far-off business.

No, no, he must not be faint-hearted, who, after all, had much for which to be thankful. Meanwhile the cause went on—that great cause of the threatened Church to which he had devoted his life. Henry the heretic would fall; the Spanish Emperor, whose spy he was and who loved him well, would invade and take England. He would yet live to see the Holy Inquisition at work at Westminster, and himself—yes, himself; had it not been hinted to him?—enthroned at Canterbury, the Cardinal's red hat he coveted upon his head, and—oh, glorious thought!—perhaps afterwards wearing the triple crown at Rome.

****

Rain was falling heavily when the Abbot, with his escort of two monks and half-a-dozen men-at-arms, rode up to Cranwell. The house was now but a smoking heap of ashes, mingled with charred beams and burnt clay, in the midst of which, scarcely visible through the clouds of steam caused by the falling rain, rose the grim old Norman tower, for on its stonework the flames had beat vainly.

"Why have we come here?" asked one of the monks, surveying the dismal scene with a shudder.

"To seek the bodies of the Lady Cicely and her woman, and give them Christian burial," answered the Abbot.

"After bringing them to a most unchristian death," muttered the monk to himself, then added aloud, "You were ever charitable, my Lord Abbot, and though she defied you, such is that noble lady's due. As for the nurse Emlyn, she was a witch, and did but come to the end that she deserved, if she be really dead."

"What mean you?" asked the Abbot sharply.

"I mean that, being a witch, the fire may have turned from her."

"Pray God, then, that it turned from her mistress also! But it cannot be. Only a fiend could have lived in the heat of that furnace; look, even the tower is gutted."

"No, it cannot be," answered the monk; "so, since we shall never find them, let us chant the Burial Office over this great grave of theirs and begone—the sooner the better, for yon place has a haunted look."

"Not till we have searched out their bones, which must be beneath the tower yonder, whereon we saw them last," replied the Abbot, adding in a low voice, "Remember, Brother, the Lady Cicely had jewels of great price, which, if they were wrapped in leather, the fire may have spared, and these are among our heritage. At Shefton they cannot be found; therefore they must be here, and the seeking of them is no task for common folk. That is why I hurried hither so fast. Do you understand?"

The monk nodded his head. Having dismounted, they gave their horses to the serving-men and began to make an examination of the ruin, the Abbot leaning on his inferior's arm, for he was in great pain from the blow in the back that Jeffrey had administered with his sea-boot, and the bruises which he had received in falling to the boat.

First they passed under the gatehouse, which still stood, only to find that the courtyard beyond was so choked with smouldering rubbish that they could make no entry—for it will be remembered that the house had fallen outwards. Here, however, lying by the carcass of a horse, they found the body of one of the men whom Christopher had killed in his last stand, and caused it to be borne out. Then, followed by their people, leaving the dead man in the gateway, they walked round the ruin, keeping on the inner side of the moat, till they came to the little *pleasaunce* garden at its back.

"Look," said the monk in a frightened voice, pointing to some scorched bushes that had been a bower.

The Abbot did so, but for a while could see nothing because of the wreaths of steam. Presently a puff of wind blew these aside, and there, standing hand in hand, he beheld the figures of two women. His men beheld them also, and called aloud that these were the ghosts of Cicely and Emlyn. As they spoke the figures, still hand in hand, began to walk towards them, and they saw that they were Cicely and Emlyn indeed, but in the flesh, quite unharmed.

For a moment there was deep silence; then the Abbot asked—

"Whence come you, Mistress Cicely?"

"Out of the fire," she answered in a small, cold voice.

"Out of the fire! How did you live through the fire?"

"God sent His angel to save us," she answered, again in that small voice.

"A miracle," muttered the monk; "a true miracle!"

"Or mayhap Emlyn Stower's witchcraft," exclaimed one of the men behind; and Maldon started at his words.

"Lead me to my husband, my Lord Abbot, lest, thinking me dead, his heart should break," said Cicely.

Now again there was silence so deep that they could hear the patter of every drop of falling rain. Twice the Abbot strove to speak, but could not, but at the third effort his words came.

"The man you call your husband, but who was not your husband, but your ravisher, was slain in the fray last night, Cicely Foterell."

She stood quite quiet for a while, as though considering his words, then said, in the same unnatural voice—

"You lie, my Lord Abbot. You were ever a liar, like your father the devil, for the angel told me so in the midst of the fire. Also he told me that, though I seemed to see him fall, Christopher is alive upon the earth—yes, and other things, many other things;" and she passed her hand before her eyes and held it there, as though to shut out the sight of her enemy's face.

Now the Abbot trembled in his terror, he who knew that he lied, though at that time none else there knew it. It was as though suddenly he had been haled before the Judgment-seat where all secrets must be bared.

"Some evil spirit has entered into you," he said huskily.

She dropped her hand, pointing at him.

"Nay, nay; I never knew but one evil spirit, and he stands before me."

"Cicely," he went on, "cease your blaspheming. Alas! that I must tell it you. Sir Christopher Harflete is dead and buried in yonder churchyard."

"What! So soon, and all uncoffined, he who was a noble knight? Then you buried him living, and, living, in a day to come he shall rise up against you. Hear my words, all. Christopher Harflete shall rise up living and give testimony against this devil in a monk's robe, and afterwards—afterwards—" and she laughed shrilly, then suddenly fell down and lay still.

Now Emlyn, the dark and handsome, as became her Spanish, or perhaps gypsy blood, who all this while had stood silent, her arms folded upon her high bosom, leaned down and looked at her. Then she straightened herself, and her face was like the face of a beautiful fiend.

"She is dead!" she screamed. "My dove is dead. She whom these breasts nursed, the greatest lady of all the wolds and all the vales, the Lady of Blossholme, of Cranwell and of Shefton, in whose veins ran the blood of mighty nobles, aye, and of old kings, is dead, murdered by a beggarly foreign monk, who not ten days gone butchered her father also yonder by King's Grave—yonder by the mere. Oh! the arrow in his throat! the arrow in his throat! I cursed the hand that shot it, and to-day that hand is blue beneath the mould. So, too, I curse you, Maldonado, evil-gifted one, Abbot consecrated by Satan, you and all your herd of butchers!" and she broke into the stream of Spanish imprecations whereof the Abbot knew the meaning well.

Presently Emlyn paused and looked behind her at the smouldering ruins.

"This house is burned," she cried; "well, mark Emlyn's words: even so shall your house burn, while your monks run squeaking like rats from a flaming rick. You have stolen the lands; they shall be taken from you, and yours also, every acre of them. Not enough shall be left to bury you in, for, priest, you'll need no burial. The fowls of the air shall bury you, and that's the nearest you will ever get to heaven—in their filthy crops. Murderer, if Christopher Harflete is dead, yet he shall live, as his lady swore, for his seed shall rise up against you. Oh! I forgot; how can it, how can it, seeing that she is dead with him, and their bridal coverlet has become a pall woven by the black monks? Yet it shall, it shall. Christopher Harflete's seed shall sit where the Abbots of Blossholme sat, and from father to son tell the tale of the last of them—the Spaniard who plotted against England's king and overshot himself."

Her rage veered like a hurricane wind. Forgetting the Abbot, she turned upon the monk at his side and cursed him. Then she cursed the hired men-at-arms, those present and those absent, many by name, and lastly—greatest crime of all—she cursed the Pope and the King of Spain, and called to God in heaven and Henry of England upon earth to avenge her Lady Cicely's wrongings, and the murder of Sir John Foterell, and the murder of Christopher Harflete, on each and all of them, individually and separately.

So fierce and fearful was her onslaught that all who heard her were reduced to utter silence. The Abbot and the monk leaned against each other, the soldiers crossed themselves and muttered prayers, while one of them, running up, fell upon his knees and assured her that he had had nothing to do with all this business, having only returned from a journey last night, and been called thither that morning.

Emlyn, who had paused from lack of breath, listened to him, and said—

"Then I take the curse off you and yours, John Athey. Now lift up my lady and bear her to the church, for there we will lay her out as becomes her rank; though not with her jewels, her great and priceless jewels, for which she was hunted like a doe. She must lie without her jewels; her pearls and coronet, and rings, her stomacher and necklets of bright gems, that were worth so much more than those beggarly acres—those that once a Sultan's woman wore. They are lost, though perhaps yonder Abbot has found them. Sir John Foterell bore them to London for safe keeping, and good Sir John is dead; footpads set on him in the forest, and an arrow shot from behind pierced his throat. Those who killed him have the jewels, and the dead bride must lie without them, adorned in the naked beauty that God gave to her. Lift her, John Athey, and you monks, set up your funeral chant; we'll to the church. The bride who knelt before the altar shall lie there before the altar—Clement Maldonado's last offering to God. First the father, then the husband, and now the wife—the sweet, new-made wife!"

So she raved on, while they stood before her dumb-founded, and the man lifted up Cicely. Then suddenly this same Cicely, whom all thought dead, opened her eyes and struggled from his arms to her feet.

"See," screamed Emlyn; "did I not tell you that Harflete's seed should live to be avenged upon all your tribe, and she stands there who will bear it? Now where shall we shelter till England hears this tale? Cranwell is down, though it shall rise again, and Shefton is stolen. Where shall we shelter?"

"Thrust away that woman," said the Abbot in a hoarse voice, "for her witchcrafts poison the air. Set the Lady Cicely on a horse and bear her to our Nunnery of Blossholme, where she shall be tended."

The men advanced to do his bidding, though very doubtfully. But Emlyn, hearing his words, ran to the Abbot and whispered something in his ear in a foreign tongue that caused him to cross himself and stagger back from her.

"I have changed my mind," he said to the servants. "Mistress Emlyn reminds me that between her and her lady there is the tie of foster-motherhood. They may not be separated as yet. Take them both to the Nunnery, where they shall dwell, and as for this woman's words, forget them, for she was mad with fear and grief, and knew not what she said. May God and His saints forgive her, as I do."

Chapter 7

The Abbot's Offer

The Nunnery at Blossholme was a peaceful place, a long, grey-gabled house set under the shelter of a hill and surrounded by a high wall. Within this wall lay also the great garden—neglected enough—and the chapel, a building that still was beautiful in its decay.

Once, indeed, Blossholme Priory, which was older than the Abbey, had been rich and famous. Its foundress in the time of the first Edward, a certain Lady Matilda, one of the Plantagenets, who retired from the world after her husband had been killed in the Crusade, being childless, endowed it with all her lands. Other noble ladies who accompanied her there, or sought its refuge in after days, had done likewise, so that it grew in power and in wealth, till at its most prosperous time over twenty nuns told their beads within its walls. Then the proud Abbey rose upon the opposing hill, and obtained some royal charter that the Pope confirmed, under which the Priory of Blossholme was affiliated to the Abbey of Blossholme, and the Abbot of Blossholme became the spiritual lord of its religious. From that day forward its fortunes began to decline, since under this pretext and that the abbots filched away its lands to swell their own estates.

So it came about that at the date of our history the total revenue of this Nunnery was but £130 a year of the money of the day, and even of this sum the Abbot took tithe and toll. Now in all the great house, that once had been so full, there dwelt but six nuns, one of whom was, in fact, a servant, while an aged monk from the Abbey celebrated Mass in the fair chapel where lay the bones of so many who had gone before. Also on certain feasts the Abbot himself attended, confessed the nuns, and granted them absolution and his holy blessing. On these days, too, he would examine their accounts, and if there were money in hand take a share of it to serve his necessities, for which reason the Prioress looked forward to his coming with little joy.

It was to this ancient home of peace that the distraught Cicely and her servant Emlyn were conveyed upon the morrow of the great burning. Indeed, Cicely knew it well enough already, since as a child during three years or more she had gone there daily to be taught by the Prioress Matilda, for every head of the Priory took this name in turn to the honour of their foundress and in accordance with the provisions of her will. Happy years they were, as these old nuns loved her in her youth and innocence, and she, too, loved them every one. Now, by the workings of fate, she was borne back to the same quiet room where she had played and studied—a new-made wife, a new-made widow.

But of all this poor Cicely knew nothing till three weeks or more had gone by, when at length her wandering brain cleared and she opened her eyes to the world again. At the moment she was alone, and lay looking about her. The place was familiar. She recognized the deep windows, the faded tapestries of Abraham cutting Isaac's throat with a butcher's knife, and Jonah being shot into the very gateway of a castle where his family awaited him, from the mouth of a gigantic carp with goggle eyes, for the simple artist had found his whale's model in a stewpond. Well she remembered those delightful pictures, and how often she had wondered whether Isaac could escape bleeding to death, or Jonah's wife, with the outspread arms, withstand the sudden shock of her husband's unexpected arrival out of the interior of the whale. There also was the splendid fireplace of wrought stone, and above it, cunningly carved in gilded oak, gleamed many coats-of-arms without crests, for they were those of sundry noble prioresses.

Yes, this was certainly the great guest-chamber of the Blossholme Priory, which, since the nuns had now few guests and many places in which to put them, had been given up to her, Sir John Foterell's heiress, as her schoolroom. There she lay, thinking that she was a child again, a happy, careless child, or that she dreamed, till presently the door opened and Mother Matilda appeared, followed by Emlyn, who bore a tray, on which stood a silver bowl that smoked. There was no mistaking Mother Matilda in her black Benedictine robe and her white wimple, wearing the great silver crucifix which was her badge of office, and the golden ring with an emerald bezel whereon was cut St. Catherine being broken on the wheel—the ancient ring which every Prioress of Blossholme had worn from the beginning. Moreover, who that had ever seen it could forget her sweet, old, high-bred face, with the fine lips, the arched nose, and the quick, kind grey eyes!

Cicely strove to rise and to do her reverence, as had been her custom during those childish years, only to find that she could not, for lo! she fell back heavily upon her pillow. Thereon Emlyn, setting down the tray with a clatter upon a table, ran to her, and putting her arms about her, began to scold, as was her fashion, but in a very gentle voice; and Mother Matilda, kneeling by her bed, gave thanks to Jesus and His blessed saints—though why she thanked Him at first Cicely did not understand.

"Am I ill, reverend Mother?" she asked.

"Not now, daughter, but you were very ill," answered the Prioress in her sweet, low voice. "Now we think that God has healed you."

"How long have I been here?" she asked.

The Mother began to reckon, counting her beads, one for every day—for in such places time slips by—but long before she had finished Emlyn replied quickly—

"Cranwell Towers was burned three weeks yesternight."

Then Cicely remembered, and with a bitter groan turned her face to the wall, while the Mother reproached Emlyn, saying she had killed her.

"I think not," answered the nurse in a low voice. "I think she has that which will not let her die"—a saying that puzzled the Prioress at this time.

Emlyn was right. Cicely did not die. On the contrary, she grew strong and well in her body, though it was long before her mind recovered. Indeed, she glided about the place like a ghost in her black mourning robe, for now she no longer doubted that Christopher was dead, and she, the wife of a week, widowed as well as orphaned.

Then in her utter desolation came comfort; a light broke on the darkness of her soul like the moon above a tortured midnight sea. She was no longer quite alone; the murdered Christopher had left his image with her. If she lived a child would be born to him, and therefore she would surely live. One evening, on her knees, she whispered her secret to the Prioress Matilda, whereat the old nun blushed like a girl, yet, after a moment's silent prayer, laid a thin hand upon her head in blessing.

"The Lord Abbot declares that your marriage was no true marriage, my daughter, though why I do not understand, since the man was he whom your heart chose, and you were wed to him by an ordained priest before God's altar and in presence of the congregation."

"I care not what he says," answered Cicely in a stubborn voice. "If I am not a true wife, then no woman ever was."

"Dear daughter," answered Mother Matilda, "it is not for us unlearned women to question the wisdom of a holy Abbot who doubtless is inspired from on high."

"If he is inspired it is not from on high, Mother. Would God or His saints teach him to murder my father and my husband, to seize my heritage, or to hold my person in this gentle prison? Such inspirations do not come from above, Mother."

"Hush! hush!" said the Prioress, glancing round her nervously; "your woes have crazed you. Besides, you have no proof. In this world there are so many things that we cannot understand. Being an abbot, how could he do wrong, although to us his acts seem wrong? But let us not talk of these matters, of which, indeed, I only know from that rough-tongued Emlyn of yours, who, I am told, was not afraid to curse him terribly. I was about to say that whatever may be the law of it, I hold your marriage good and true, and its issue, should such come to you, pure and holy, and night by night I will pray that it shall be crowned with Heaven's richest blessings."

"I thank you, dear Mother," answered Cicely, as she rose and left her.

When she had gone the Prioress rose also, and, with a troubled face, began to walk up and down the refectory, for it was here that they had spoken together. Truly she could not understand, for unless all these tales were false—and how could they be false?—this Abbot, whom her high-bred English nature had always mistrusted, this dark, able Spanish monk was no saint, but a wicked villain? There must be some explanation. It was only that *she* did not understand.

Soon the news spread throughout the Nunnery, and if the sisters had loved Cicely before, now they loved her twice as well. Of the doubts as to the validity to her marriage, like their Prioress, they took no heed, for had it not been celebrated in a church? But that a child was to be born among them—ah! that was a joyful thing, a thing that had not happened for quite two hundred years, when, alas!—so said tradition and their records—there had been a dreadful scandal which to this day was spoken of with bated breath. For be it known at once this Nunnery, whatever may or may not have been the case with some others, was one of which no evil could be said.

Beneath their black robes, however, these old nuns were still as much women as the mothers who bore them, and this news of a child stirred them to the marrow. Among themselves in their hours of recreation they talked of little else, and even their prayers were largely occupied with this same matter. Indeed, poor, weak-witted, old Sister Bridget, who hitherto had been secretly looked down upon because she was the only one of the seven who was not of gentle birth, now became very popular. For Sister Bridget in her youth had been married and borne two children, both of whom had been carried off by the smallpox after she was widowed, whereon, as her face was seamed by this same disease, so that she had no hope of another husband, as her neighbours said, or because her heart was broken, as she said, she entered into religion.

Now she constituted herself Cicely's chief attendant, and although that lady was quite well and strong, persecuted her with advice and with noxious mixtures which she brewed, till Emlyn, descending on her like a storm, hunted her from the room and cast her medicines through the window.

That these sisters should be thus interested in so small a matter was not, indeed, wonderful, seeing that if their lives had been secluded before, since the Lady Cicely came amongst them they were ten times more so. Soon they discovered that she and her servant, Emlyn Stower, were, in fact, prisoners, which meant that they, her hostesses, were prisoners also. None were allowed to enter the Nunnery save the silent old monk who confessed them and celebrated the Mass, nor, by an order of the Abbot, were they suffered to go abroad upon any business whatsoever.

For the rest, as their only means of communication with those who dwelt beyond was the surly gardener, who was deaf and set there to spy on them, little news ever reached them. They were almost dead to the world, which, had they known it, was busy enough just then with matters that concerned them and all other religious houses.

At length one day, when Cicely and Emlyn were seated in the garden beneath a flowering hawthorn-tree—for now June had come and with it warm weather—of a sudden Sister Bridget hurried up saying that the Abbot of Blossholme desired their presence. At this tidings Cicely turned faint, and Emlyn rated Bridget, asking if her few wits had left her, or if she thought that name was so pleasant to her mistress that she should suddenly bawl it in her ear.

Thereon the poor old soul, who was not too strong-brained and much afraid of Emlyn since she had thrown her medicines out of the window, began to weep, protesting that she had meant no harm, till Cicely, recovering, soothed her and sent her back to say that she would wait upon his lordship.

"Are you afraid of him, Mistress?" asked Emlyn, as they prepared to follow.

"A little, Nurse. He has shown himself a man to be afraid of, has he not? My father and my husband are in his net, and will he spare the last fish in the pool—a very narrow pool?" and she glanced at the high walls about her. "I fear lest he should take you from me, and wonder why he has not done so already."

"Because my father was a Spaniard, and through him I know that which would ruin him with his friends, the Pope and the Emperor. Also, he believes that I have the evil eye, and dreads my curse. Still, one day he may try to murder me; who knows? Only then the secret of the jewels will go with me, for that is mine alone; not yours even, for if you had it they would squeeze it out of you. Meanwhile he will try to profess you a nun, but push him off with soft words. Say that you will think of it after your child is born. Till then he can do nothing, and, if Mother Matilda's fresh tidings are true, by that time perchance there will be no more nuns in England."

Now very quietly and by the side door they were entering the old reception-hall, that was only used for the entertainment of visitors and on other great occasions, and close to them saw the Abbot seated in his chair, while the Prioress stood before him, rendering her accounts.

"Whether you can spare it or no," they heard him say sharply, "I must have the half-year's rent. The times are evil; we servants of the Lord are threatened by that adulterous king and his proud ministers, who swear they will strip us to the shirt and turn us out to starve. I'm but just from London, and, although our enemy Anne Boleyn has lost her wanton head, I tell you the danger is great. Money must be had to stir up rebellion, for who can arm without it, and but little comes from Spain. I am in treaty to sell the Foterell lands for what they will fetch, but as yet can give no title. Either that stiff-necked girl must sign a release, or she must profess, for otherwise, while she lives, some lawyer or relative might upset the sale. Is she yet prepared to take her first vows? If not, I shall hold you much to blame."

"Nay," answered the Prioress; "there are reasons. You have been away, and have not heard"—she hesitated and looked about her nervously, to see Cicely and Emlyn standing behind them. "What do you there, daughter?" she asked, with as much asperity as she ever showed.

"In truth I know not, Mother," answered Cicely. "Sister Bridget told us that the Lord Abbot desired our presence."

"I bid her say that you were to wait him in my chamber," said the Prioress in a vexed voice.

"Well," broke in the Abbot, "it would seem that you have a fool for a messenger; if it is that pockmarked hag, her brain has been gone for years. Ward Cicely, I greet you, though after the sorrows that have fallen on you, whereof by your leave we will not speak, since there is no use in stirring up such memories, I grieve to see you in that worldly garb, who thought you would have changed it for a better. But ere you entered the holy Mother here spoke of some obstacle that

415

stood between you and God. What is it? Perchance my counsel may be of service. Not this woman, as I trust," and he frowned at Emlyn, who at once answered, in her steady voice—

"Nay, my Lord Abbot, I stand not between her and God and His holiness, but between her and man and his iniquity. Still I can tell you of that obstacle—which comes from God—if you so need."

Now the old Prioress, blushing to her white hair, bent forward and whispered in the Abbot's ear words at which he sprang up as though a wasp had stung him.

"Pest on it! it cannot be," he said. "Well, well, there it is, and must be swallowed with the rest. Pity, though," he added, with a sneer on his dark face, "since many a year has gone by since these walls have seen a bastard, and, as things are, that may pull them down about your ears."

"I know such brats are dangerous," interrupted Emlyn, looking Maldon full in the eyes; "my father told me of a young monk in Spain—I forget his name—who brought certain ladies to the torture in some such matter. But who talks of bastards in the case of Dame Cicely Harflete, widow of Sir Christopher Harflete, slain by the Abbot of Blossholme?"

"Silence, woman. Where there is no lawful marriage there can be no lawful child—"

"To take that lawful inheritance that it lawfully inherits. Say, my Lord Abbot, did Sir Christopher make you his heir also?"

Then, before he could answer, Cicely, who had been silent all this while, broke in—

"Heap what insults you will on me, my Lord Abbot, and having robbed me of my father, my husband, and my heart, rob me of my goods also, if you can. In my case it matters little. But slander not my child, if one should be born to me, nor dare to touch its rights. Think not that you can break the mother as you broke the girl, for there you will find that you have a she-wolf by the ear."

He looked at her, they all looked at her, for in her eyes was something that compelled theirs. Clement Maldon, who knew the world and how a she-wolf can fight for its cub, read in them a warning which caused him to change his tone.

"Tut, tut, daughter," he said; "what is the good of vapouring of a child that is not and may never be? When it comes I will christen it, and we will talk."

"When it comes you will not lay a finger on it. I'd rather that it went unbaptized to its grave than marked with your cross of blood."

He waved his hand.

"There is another matter, or rather two, of which I must speak to you, my daughter. When do you take your first vows?"

"We will talk of it after my child is born. 'Tis a child of sin, you say, and I am unrepentant, a wicked woman not fit to take a holy vow, to which, moreover, you cannot force me," she replied, with bitter sarcasm.

Again he waved his hand, for the she-wolf showed her teeth.

"The second matter is," he went on, "that I need your signature to a writing. It is nothing but a form, and one I fear you cannot read, nor in faith can I," and with a somewhat doubtful smile he drew out a crabbed indenture and spread it before her on the table.

"What?" she laughed, brushing aside the parchment. "Have you remembered that yesterday I came of age, and am, therefore, no more your ward, if such I ever was? You should have sold my inheritance more swiftly, for now the title you can give is rotten as last year's apples, and I'll sign nothing. Bear witness, Mother Matilda, and you, Emlyn Stower, that I have signed and will sign nothing. Clement Maldon, Abbot of Blossholme, I am a free woman of full age, even though, as you say, I am a wanton. Where is your right to chain up a wanton who is no religious? Unlock these gates and let me go."

Now he felt the wolf's fangs, and they were sharp.

"Whither would you go?" he asked.

"Whither but to the King, to lay my cause before him, as my father would have done last Christmas-time."

It was a bold speech, but foolish. The she-wolf had loosed her hold to growl—to growl at a hunter with a bloody sword.

"I think your father never reached his Grace with his sack of falsehoods; nor might you, Cicely Foterell. The times are rough, rebellion is in the air, and many wild men hunt the woods and roads. No, no; for your own sake you bide here in safety till—"

"Till you murder me. Oh! it is in your mind. Do you remember the angel who spoke with me in the fire and told me my husband was not dead?"

"A lying spirit, then; no angel."

"I am not so sure," and again she passed her hand across her eyes, as she had done in that dreadful dawn at Cranwell. "Well, I prayed to God to help me, and last night that angel came again and spoke in my sleep. He told me to fear you not at all, my Lord Abbot; however sore my case and however near my death might seem, since God had shaped a stone to drop upon your head. He showed it me; it was like an axe."

417

Now the old Prioress held up her hands and gasped in horror, but the Abbot leapt from his seat in rage—or was it fear?

"Wanton, you named yourself," he exclaimed; "but I name you witch also, who, if you had your deserts, should die the death of a witch by fire. Mother Matilda, I command you, on your oath, keep this witch fast and make report to me of all her sorceries. It is not fitting that such a one should walk abroad to bring evil on the innocent. Witch and wanton, begone to your chamber!"

Cicely listened, then, without another word, broke into a little scornful laugh, and, turning, left the room, followed by the Prioress.

But Emlyn did not go; she stayed behind, a smile on her dark, handsome face.

"You've lost the throw, though all your dice were loaded," she said boldly.

The Abbot turned on her and reviled her.

"Woman," he said, "if she is a witch, you're the familiar, and certainly you shall burn even though she escape. It is you who taught her how to call up the devil."

"Then you had best keep me living, my Lord Abbot, that I may teach her how to lay him. Nay, threaten not. Why, the rack might make me speak, and the birds of the air carry the matter!"

His face paled; then suddenly he asked—

"Where are those jewels? I need them. Give me the jewels and you shall go free, and perchance your accursed mistress with you."

"I told you," she answered. "Sir John took them to London, and if they were not found upon his body, then either he threw them away or Jeffrey Stokes carried them to wherever he has gone. Drag the mere, search the forest, find Jeffrey and ask him."

"You lie, woman. When you and your mistress fled from Shefton a servant there saw you with the box that held those jewels in your hand."

"True, my Lord Abbot, but it no longer held them; only my mistress's love-letters, which she would not leave behind."

"Then where is the box, and where are those letters?"

"We grew short of fuel in the siege, and burned both. When a woman has her man she doesn't want his letters. Surely, Maldonado," she added, with meaning, "you should know that it is not always wise to keep old letters. What, I wonder, would you give for some that I have seen and that are *not* burned?"

"Accursed spawn of Satan," hissed the Abbot, "how dare you flaunt me thus? When Cicely was wed to Christopher she wore those very

418

gems; I have it from those who saw her decked in them—the necklace on her bosom, the priceless rosebud pearls hanging from her ears."

"Oho! oho!" said Emlyn; "so you own that she was wed, the pure soul whom but now you called a wanton. Look you, Sir Abbot, we will fence no more. She wore the jewels. Jeffrey took nothing hence save your death-warrant."

"Then where are they?" he asked, striking his fist upon the table.

"Where? Why, where you'll never follow them—gone up to heaven in the fire. Thinking we might be robbed, I hid them behind a secret panel in her chamber, purposing to return for them later. Go, rake out the ashes; you might find a cracked diamond or two, but not the pearls; they fly in fire. There, that's the truth at last, and much good may it do to you."

The Abbot groaned. Like most Spaniards he was emotional, and could not help it; his bitterness burst from his heart.

Emlyn laughed at him.

"See how the wise and mighty of this world overshoot themselves," she said. "Clement Maldonado, I have known you for some twenty years, and when I was called the Beauty of Blossholme, and the Abbot who went before you made me the Church's ward, though I ever hated you, who hunted down my father, you had softer words for me than those you name me by to-day. Well, I have watched you rise and I shall watch you fall, and I know your heart and its desires. Money is what you lust for and must have, for otherwise how will you gain your end? It was the jewels that you needed, not the Shefton lands, which are worth little now-a-days, and will soon be worth less. Why, one of those pink pearls placed among the Jews would buy three parishes, with their halls thrown in. For the sake of those jewels you have brought death on some and misery on some, and on your own soul damnation without end, though had you but been wise and consulted me—why, they, or some of them, might have been yours. Sir John was no fool; he would have parted with a pearl or two, of which he did not know the value, to end a feud against the Church and safeguard his title and his daughter. And now, in your madness, you've burnt them—burnt a king's ransom, or what might have pulled down a king. Oh! had you but guessed it, you'd have hacked off the hand that put a torch to Cranwell Towers, for now the gold you need is lacking to you, and therefore all your grand schemes will fail, and you'll be buried in their ruin, as you thought we were in Cranwell."

The Abbot, who had listened to this long and bitter speech in patience, groaned again.

"You are a clever woman," he said; "we understand each other, coming from the same blood. You know the case; what is your counsel to me now?"

"That which you will not take, being foredoomed for your sins. Still I'll give it honestly. Set the Lady Cicely free, restore her lands, confess your evil doings. Fly the kingdom before Cromwell turns on you and Henry finds you out, taking with you all the gold that you can gather, and bribe the Emperor Charles to give you a bishopric in Granada or elsewhere—not near Seville, for reasons that you know. So shall you live honoured, and one day, after you have been dead a long while and many things are forgotten, perchance be beatified as Saint Clement of Blossholme."

The Abbot looked at her reflectively.

"If I sought safety only and old age comforts your counsel might be good, but I play for higher stakes."

"You set your head against them," broke in Emlyn.

"Not so, woman, for in any case that head must win. If it stays upon my shoulders it will wear an archbishop's mitre, or a cardinal's hat, or perhaps something nobler yet; and if it parts from them, why, then a heavenly crown of glory."

"Your head? *Your* head?" exclaimed Emlyn, with a contemptuous laugh.

"Why not?" he answered gravely. "You chance to know of some errors of my youth, but they are long ago repented of, and for such there is plentiful forgiveness," and he crossed himself. "Were it not so, who would escape?"

Emlyn, who had been standing all this while, sat herself down, set her elbows on the table and rested her chin upon her clenched hands.

"True," she said, looking him in the eyes; "none of us would escape. But, Clement Maldon, how about the unrepented errors of your age? Sir John Foterell, for instance; Sir Christopher Harflete, for instance; my Lady Cicely, for instance; to say nothing of black treason and a few other matters?"

"Even were all these charges true, which I deny, they are no sins, seeing that they would have been done, every one of them, not for my own sake, but for that of the Church, to overset her enemies, to rebuild her tottering walls, to secure her eternally in this realm."

"And to lift you, Clement Maldon, to the topmost pinnacle of her temple, whence Satan shows you all the kingdoms of the world, swearing that they shall be yours."

Apparently the Abbot did not resent this bold speech; indeed,

Emlyn's apt illustration seemed to please him. Only he corrected her gently, saying—

"Not Satan, but Satan's Lord." Then he paused a while, looked round the chamber to see that the doors were shut and make sure that they were alone, and went on, "Emlyn Stower, you have great wits and courage—more than any woman that I know. Also you have knowledge both of the world and of what lies beyond it, being what superstitious fools call a witch, but I, a prophetess or a seer. These things come to you with your blood, I suppose, seeing that your mother was of a gypsy tribe and your father a high-bred Spanish gentleman, very learned and clever, though a pestilent heretic, for which cause he fled for his life from Spain."

"To find his dark death in England. The Holy Inquisition is patent and has a long arm. If I remember right, also it was this business of the heresy of my father that first brought you to Blossholme, where, after his vanishing and the public burning of that book of his, you so greatly prospered."

"You are always right, Emlyn, and therefore I need not tell you further that we had been old enemies in Spain, which is why I was chosen to hunt him down and how you come to know certain things."

She nodded, and he went on—

"So much for the heretic father—now for the gypsy mother. She died, by her own hand it is said, to escape the punishment of the law."

"No need to beat about the bush, Abbot; let's have truth between old friends. You mean, to escape being burnt by you as a witch, because she had the letters which were not burned and threatened to use them—as I do."

"Why rake up such tales, Emlyn?" he interposed blandly. "At least she died, but not until she had taught you all she knew. The rest of the history is short. You fell in love with old yeoman Bolle's son, or said you did—that same great, silly Thomas who is now a lay-brother at the Abbey—"

"Or said I did," she repeated. "At least he fell in love with me, and perhaps I wished an honest man to protect me, who in those days was young and fair. Moreover, he was not silly then. That came upon him after he fell into *your* hands. Oh! have done with it," she went on, in a voice of suppressed passion. "The witch's fair daughter was the Church's ward, and you ruled the Abbot of that time, and he forced me into marriage with old Peter Stower, as his third wife. I cursed him, and he died, as I warned him that he would, and I bore a child, and it died. Then with what was left to me I took refuge with Sir John

Foterell, who ever was my friend, and became foster-mother to his daughter, the only creature, save one, that I have loved in this wide, wicked world. That's all the story; and now what more do you want of me, Clement Maldonado—evil-gifted one?"

"Emlyn, I want what I always wanted and you always refused—your help, your partnership. I mean the partnership of that brain of yours—the help of the knowledge that you have—no more. At Cranwell Towers you called down evil on me. Take off that ban, for I'll speak truth, it weighs heavy on my mind. Let us bury the past; let us clasp hands and be friends. You have the true vision. Do you remember that when you thought Cicely dead, you said that her seed should rise up against me, and now it seems that it will be so."

"What would you give me?" asked Emlyn curiously.

"I will give you wealth; I will give you what you love more—power, and rank too, if you wish it. The whole Church shall listen to you. What you desire shall be done in this realm—yes, and across the world. I speak no lie; I pledge my soul on it, and the honour of those I serve, which I have authority to do. In return all I ask of you is your wisdom—that you should read the future for me, that you should show me which way to walk."

"Nothing more?"

"Yes, two things—that you should find me those burned jewels and with them the old letters that were not burned, and that this child of the Lady Cicely shall not chance to live to take what you promised to it. Her life I give you, for a nun more or less can matter little."

"A noble offer, and in this case I am sure you will pay what *you* promise—should you live. But what if I refuse?"

"Then," answered the Abbot, dropping his fist upon the table, "then death for both of you—the witch's death, for I dare not let you go to work my ruin. Remember, I am master here, you are my prisoners. Few know that you live in this place, except a handful of weak-brained women who will fear to speak—puppets that must dance when I pull the string—and I'll see that no soul shall come near these walls. Choose, then, between death and all its terrors or life and all its hopes."

On the table there stood a wooden bowl filled with roses. Emlyn drew it to her, and taking the roses into her hands, threw them to the floor. Then she waited for the water to steady, saying—

"The riddle is hard; perhaps, if in truth I have such power, I shall find its answer here." Presently, as he gazed at her, fascinated, she breathed upon the water and stared into it for a long while. At length she looked up, and said—

"Death or Life; that was the choice you gave me. Well, Clement Maldonado, on behalf of myself and the Lady Cicely, and her husband Sir Christopher, and the child that shall be born, and of God who directs all these things, I choose—death."

There was a solemn silence. Then the Abbot rose, and said—

"Good! On your own head be it."

Again there was a silence, and, as she made no answer, he turned and walked towards the door, leaving her still staring into the bowl.

"Good!" she repeated, as he laid his hand upon the latch. "I have told you that I choose death, but I have not told you whose death it is I choose. Play your game, my Lord Abbot, and I'll play mine, remembering that God holds the stakes. Meanwhile I confirm the words I spoke in my rage at Cranwell. Expect evil, for I see now that it shall fall on you and all with which you have to do."

Then with a sudden movement she upset the bowl upon the table and watched him go.

CHAPTER 8

Emlyn Calls Her Man

One by one the weeks passed over the heads of Cicely and Emlyn in their prison, and brought them neither hope nor tidings. Indeed, although they could not see its cords, they felt that the evil net which held them was drawing ever tighter. There were fear and pity as well as love in the eyes of Mother Matilda when she looked at Cicely, which she did only if she thought that no one observed her. The nuns also were afraid, though it was clear that they knew not of what. One evening Emlyn, finding the Prioress alone, sprang questions on her, asking what was in the wind, and why her lady, a free woman of full age, was detained there against her will.

The old nun's face grew secret. She answered that she did not know of anything unusual, and that, as regarded the detention, she must obey the commands of her spiritual superior.

"Then," burst out Emlyn, "I tell you that you do so at your peril. I tell you that whether my lady lives or dies, there are those who will call you to a strict account, aye, and those who will listen to the prayer of the helpless. Mother Matilda, England is not the land it was when as a girl they buried you in these mouldy walls. Where does God say that you have the right to hold free women like felons in a jail? Tell me."

"I cannot," moaned Mother Matilda, wringing her thin hands. "The right is very hard to find, this place is strictly guarded, and whatever I may think, I must do what I am bid, lest my soul should suffer."

"Your soul! You cloistered women think always of your miserable souls, but of those of other folk, aye, and of their bodies too, nothing. Then you'll not help me?"

"I cannot, I cannot, who am myself in bonds," she replied again.

"So be it, Mother; then I'll help myself, and when I do, God help *you* all," and with a contemptuous shrug of her broad shoulders she walked away, leaving the poor old Prioress almost in tears.

Emlyn's threats were bold as her own heart, but how could she execute even a tenth of them? The right was on their side, indeed, but, as many a captive has found in those and other days, right is no Joshua's trumpet to cause high walls to fall. Moreover, Cicely would not aid her. Now that her husband was dead she took interest in one thing only—his child who was to be.

For the rest she seemed to care nothing. Since she had no friends with whom she could communicate, and her wealth, as she understood, had been taken from her, what better place, she asked, could there be for that child to see the light than in this quiet Nunnery? When it was born and she was well again she would consider other matters. Meanwhile she was languid, and why was Emlyn always prating to her of freedom? If she were free, what should she do and whither should she go? The nuns were very kind to her; they loved her as she did them.

So she talked on, and Emlyn, listening, did not dare to tell her the truth: that here she feared for the life of her child, dreading lest that news might bring about the death of both of them. So she let her be, and fell back on her own wits.

First she thought of escape, only to abandon the idea, for her mistress was in no state to face its perils. Moreover, whither should they go? Then rescue came into her mind, but, alas! who would rescue them? The great men in London, perhaps, as a matter of policy, but great men are hard to come at, even for the free. If she were free she might find means to make them listen, but she was not, nor could she leave her lady at such a time. What remained, then? So to contrive that they should be set free.

Perhaps it might be done at a price—that of Cicely's jewels, of which she alone knew the hiding-place, and with them a deed of indemnity against her persecutors. Emlyn was not minded to give either. Moreover, she guessed that it might be in vain. Once outside those walls, they knew too much to be allowed to live. And yet within those walls Cicely's child would not be allowed to live—the child that was heir to all. What, then, could loose them and make them safe?

Terror, perhaps—such terror as that through which the Israelites escaped from bondage. Oh! if she could but find a Moses to call down the plagues of Egypt upon this Pharaoh of an Abbot—those plagues with which she had threatened him—but although she believed that they would fall (why did she believe it? she wondered), she was as yet impotent to fulfil.

Now Thomas Bolle! If only she could have words with that faithful Thomas Bolle, the fierce and cunning man whom they thought foolish!

This idea of Thomas Bolle took possession of Emlyn's mind—Thomas Bolle, who had loved her all his life, who would die to serve her. She strove in vain to get in touch with him. The old gardener was so deaf that he could not, or would not, understand. The silly Bridget gave the letter that she wrote to him to the Prioress by mistake, who burnt it before her eyes and said nothing. The monks who brought provisions to the Nunnery were always received by three of the sisters, set to spy on each other and on them, so that she could not come near to them alone. The priest who celebrated Mass was an old enemy of hers; with him she could do nothing, and no one else was allowed to approach the place except once or twice the Abbot, who was closeted for hours with the Prioress, but spoke to her no more.

Why, wondered Emlyn, should less than half-a-mile of space be such a barrier between her and Thomas Bolle? If he stood within twenty yards of her she could make him understand; why not, then, when he stood within five hundred? This idea possessed her; these limitations of nature made her mad. She refused to accept them. Night by night, lying brooding in her bed, while Cicely slept in peace at her side, she threw out her strong soul towards the soul of her old lover, Thomas Bolle, commanding him to listen, to obey, to come.

At first nothing happened. Afterwards she had a vague sense of being answered; although she could not see or hear him, she felt his presence. Then one afternoon, looking from an upper dormer window, she saw a scuffle going on outside the gateway, and heard angry voices. Thomas Bolle was trying to force his way in at the door, whence he was repelled by the Abbot's men who always watched there.

In the evening she gathered the truth from the nuns, who did not know that she was listening to what they said. It seemed that Thomas, whom they spoke of as a madman or as drunk, had tried to break into the Nunnery. When he was asked what he wanted, he answered that he did not know, but he must speak with Emlyn Stower. At this tidings she smiled to herself, for now she knew that he had heard her, and that in this way or in that he would obey her summons and come.

Two days later Thomas came—thus.

The September evening was fading into night, and Emlyn, leaving Cicely resting on her bed, which now she often did for a while before the supper-hour, had gone into the garden to enjoy the pleasant air. There she walked until she wearied of its sameness, then entered the old chapel by a side door and sat herself down to think in the chancel, not far from a life-sized statue of the Virgin, in painted oak, which stood here because of its peculiarities, for the back half of it seemed to be built into the masonry. Also the eye-sockets were empty, which suggested to the observant Emlyn either that they had once held jewels or that this was no likeness of the holy Mother, but rather one of the blind St. Lucy.

While Emlyn mused there quite alone—for at this hour none entered the place, nor would until the next morning—she thought that she heard strange noises, as of some one stirring, which came from the neighbourhood of the statue. Now many would have been scared and departed; but not so Emlyn, who only sat still and listened. Presently, without moving her head, she looked also. As it happened, the light of the setting sun, pouring through the west window, fell almost full upon the figure, and by it she saw, or thought she saw, that the eye-sockets were no longer empty; there were eyes in them which moved and flashed.

Now for a moment even Emlyn was frightened. Then she reasoned with herself, reflecting that a priest or one of the nuns was watching her from behind the statue, which they might do for as long as they pleased. Or perhaps this was a miracle, such as she had heard so much of but never seen. Well, why should she fear spies or miracles? She would sit where she was and see what happened. Nor had she long to wait, for presently a voice, a hoarse, manly voice, whispered—

"Emlyn! Emlyn Stower!"

"Yes," she answered, also in a whisper. "Who speaks?"

"Who do you think?" asked the voice, with a chuckle. "A devil, perhaps."

"Well, if it be a friendly devil I don't know that I mind, who need company in this lone place. So appear, man or devil," answered Emlyn stoutly. But in secret she crossed herself beneath her cape, for in those days folk believed in the appearance of devils for no good purposes.

The statue began to creak, then opened like a door, though very unwillingly, as though its hinges had been fixed for a long, long time and rusted in the damp, which was indeed the case. Inside of it, like a corpse in an upright coffin, appeared a figure, a square, strong figure, clad in a tattered monk's robe, surmounted by a large head with fiery red hair and beetling brows, beneath which shone two wild grey eyes. Emlyn, whose heart had stood still—for, after all, Satan is awkward company for a mortal woman—waited till it gave a jump in her breast and went on again as usual. Then she said quietly—

"What are you doing here, Thomas Bolle?"

"That is what I want to know, Emlyn. Night and day for weeks you have been calling me, and so I came."

"Yes, I have been calling you; but how did you come?"

"By the old monk's road. They have forgotten it long ago, but my grandfather told me of it when I was a boy, and at last a fox showed me where it ran. It's a dark road, and when first I tried it I thought I should be poisoned, but now the air is none so bad. It ran to the Abbey once, and may still, but my door and Mrs. Fox's is in the copse by the park wall, where none would ever look for it. If you would like a cub to play with, I will bring you one. Or perhaps you want something more than cubs," he added, with his cunning laugh.

"Aye, Thomas, I want much more. Man," she said fiercely, "will you do what I tell you?"

"That depends, Mistress Emlyn. Have I not done what you told me all my life, and for no reward?"

She moved across the chancel and sat herself down against him, pushing the image door almost to and speaking to him through the crack.

"If you have had no reward, Thomas," she said in a gentle voice, "whose fault was it? Not mine, I think. I loved you once when we were young, did I not? I would have given myself to you, body and soul, would I not? Well, who came between us and spoiled our lives?"

"The monks," groaned Thomas; "the accursed monks, who married you to Stower because he paid them."

"Yes, the accursed monks. And now our youth has gone, and love—of that sort—is behind us. I have been another man's wife, Thomas, who might have been yours. Think of it—your loving wife, the mother of your children. And you—they have tamed you and made you their servant, their cattle-herd, the strong fellow to fetch and carry, the half-wit, as they call you, who can still be trusted to run an errand and hold his tongue, the Abbey mule that does not dare to kick, the grieve of your own stolen lands—you, whose father was almost a gentleman. That's what they have done for you, Thomas; and for me, the Church's ward—well, I will not speak of it. Now, if you had your will, what would you do for them?"

"Do for them? Do for them?" gasped Thomas, worked up to fury by this recital of his wrongs. "Why, if I dared I'd cut their throats, every one, and grallock them like deer," and he ground his strong white teeth. "But I am afraid. They have my soul, and month by month I must confess. You remember, Emlyn, I warned you when you and the lady would have ridden to London before the siege. Well, afterward—I must confess it—the Abbot heard it himself, and oh! sore, sore was my penance. Before I had done with it my ribs showed through my skin and my back was like a red osier basket. There's only one thing I didn't tell them, because, after all, it is no sin to grub the earth off the face of a corpse."

"Ah!" said Emlyn, looking at him. "You're not to be trusted. Well, I thought as much. Good-bye, Thomas Bolle, you coward. I'll find me a man for a friend, not a whimpering, priest-ridden hound who sets a Latin blessing which he does not understand above his honour. God in heaven! to think I should ever have loved such a thing. Oh! I am shamed, I am shamed. I'll go wash my hands. Shut your trap and get you gone down your rat-run, Thomas Bolle, and, living or dead, never dare to speak to me again. Also forget not to tell your monks how I called you to my side—for that's witchcraft, you know, and I shall burn for it, and your soul gain benefit. God in heaven! to think that once you were Thomas Bolle," and she made as though to go away.

He stretched out his great arm and caught her by the robe, exclaiming—

"What would you have me do, Emlyn? I can't bear your scorn. Take it off me or I go kill myself."

"That's what you had best do. You'll find the devil a better master than a foreign abbot. Farewell for ever."

"Nay, nay; what's your will? Soul or no soul, I'll work it."

"Will you? Will you indeed? If so, stay a moment," and she ran down the chapel, bolting the doors; then returned to him, saying—

"Now come forth, Thomas, and since you are once more a man, kiss me as you used to do twenty years ago and more. You'll not confess to that, will you? There. Now, kneel before the altar here and swear an oath. Nay, listen to it before you swear, for it is wide."

Emlyn said the oath to him. It was a great and terrible oath. Under it he bound himself to be her slave and join himself with her in working woe to the monks of Blossholme, and especially to their Abbot, Clement Maldon, in payment of the wrongs that these had done to them both; in payment for the murder of Sir John Foterell and of Christopher Harflete, and of the imprisonment and robbery of Cicely Harflete, the daughter of the one and the wife of the other. He bound himself to do those things which she should tell him. He bound himself neither in the confessional nor, should it come to that, on the bed of torture or the scaffold to breathe a word of all their counsel. He prayed that if he did so his soul might pay the price in everlasting torment, and of all these things he took Heaven to be his witness.

"Now," said Emlyn, when she had finished setting out this fearful vow, "will you be a man and swear and thereby avenge the dead and save the innocent from death; or will you who have my secret be a crawling monk and go back to Blossholme Abbey and betray me?"

He thought a moment, rubbing his red head, for the thing frightened him, as well it might. The scales of the balance of his mind hung evenly, and Emlyn knew not which way they would turn. She saw, and put out all her woman's strength. Resting her hand upon his shoulder, she leaned forward and whispered into his ear.

"Do you remember, Thomas, how first we told our young love that spring day down in the copse by the water, and how sweet the daffodils bloomed about our feet—the daffodils and the wood-lilies? Do you remember how we swore ourselves each to each for all our lives, aye, and all the lives that were to come, and how for us two the earth was turned to heaven? And then—do you remember how that monk walked by—it was this Clement Maldon—and froze us with his cruel eyes, and said, 'What do you with the witch's daughter? She is not for you.' And—oh! Thomas, I can no more of it," and she broke down and sobbed, then added, "Swear nothing; get you gone and betray me, if you will. I'll bear you no malice, even when I die for it, for after more than twenty years of monk-craft, how could I hope that you would still remain a man? Come, get you gone swiftly, ere they take us together, and your fair fame is besmirched. Quick, now, and leave me and my lady and her unborn child to the doom Maldon brews for us. Alas! for the copse by the river; alas! for the withered lilies!"

Thomas heard; the big blue veins stood out upon his forehead, his great breast heaved, his utterance choked. At length the words came in a thick torrent.

"I'll not go, dearie; I'll swear what you will, by your eyes and by your lips, by the flowers on which we trod, by all the empty years of aching woe and shame, by God upon His throne in heaven, and by the devil in his fires in hell. Come, come," and he ran to the altar and clasped the crucifix that stood there. "Say the words again, or any others that you will, and I'll repeat them and take the oath, and may fiery worms eat me living for ever and ever if I break a letter of it."

With a little smile of triumph in her dark eyes Emlyn bent over the kneeling man and whispered—whispered through the gathering bloom, while he whispered after her, and kissed the Rood in token.

It was done, and they drew away from the altar back to the painted saint.

"So you are a man after all," she said, laughing aloud. "Now, man— my man—who, if we live through this, shall be my husband if you will—yes, my husband, for I'll pay, and be proud of it—listen to my commands. See you, I am Moses, and yonder in the Abbey sits Pharaoh with a hardened heart, and you are the angel—the destroying angel with the sword of the plagues of Egypt. To-night there will be fire in the Abbey—such fire as fell on Cranwell Towers. Nay, nay, I know; the church will not burn, nor all the great stone halls. But the dormitories, and the storehouses, and the hayricks, and the cattle-byres, they'll flame bravely after this time of drought, and if the wains are ashes, how will they draw in their harvest? Will you do it, my man?"

"Surely. Have I not sworn?"

"Then away to the work, and afterwards—to-morrow or next day—come back and make report. Just now I am much moved to solitary prayer, so wait till you see me here alone upon my knees. Stay! Wrap yourself in grave-clothes, for then if you are seen they will think you are a ghost, such as they say haunt this place. Fear not, by then I will have more work for you. Have you mastered it?"

He nodded his head. "All. All, especially your promise. Oh! I'll not die now; I'll live to claim it."

"Good. There's on account," and again she kissed him. "Go."

He reeled in the intoxication of his joy; then said—

"One word; my head swims; I forgot. Sir Christopher is not dead, or wasn't—"

"What do you mean?" she almost hissed at him. "In Christ's name be quick; I hear voices without."

"They buried another man for Christopher. I scraped him up and saw. Christopher was sent foreign, sore wounded, on the ship—pest! I have forgotten its name—the same ship that took Jeffrey Stokes."

"Blessings on your head for that tidings," exclaimed Emlyn, in a strange, low voice. "Away; they are coming to the door!"

The wooden figure creaked to and stared at her blandly, as it had stared for generations. For a moment Emlyn stood still, her hand upon her heart. Then she walked swiftly down the chapel, unlocked the door, and in the porch, just entering it, met the Prioress Matilda, another nun, and old Bridget, who was chattering.

"Oh! it is you, Mistress Stower," said Mother Matilda, with evident relief. "Sister Bridget here swore that she heard a man talking in the chapel when she came to shut the outer window at sunset."

"Did she?" answered Emlyn indifferently. "Then her luck's better than my own, who long for the sound of a man's voice in this home of babbling women. Nay, be not shocked, good Mother; I am no nun, and God did not create the world all female, or we should none of us be here. But, now you speak of it, I think there's something strange

431

about that chapel. It is a place where some might fear to be alone, for twice when I knelt there at my prayers I have heard odd sounds, and once, when there was no sun, a cold shadow fell upon me. Some ghost of the dead, I suppose, of whom so many lie about. Well, ghosts I never feared; and now I must away to fetch my lady's supper, for she eats in her room to-night."

When she had gone the Prioress shook her head and remarked in her gentle fashion—

"A strange woman and a rough, but, my sisters, we must not judge her harshly, for she is of a different world to ours, and I fear has met with sorrows there, such as we are protected from by our holy office."

"Yes," answered the sister, "but I think also that she has met with the ghost that haunts the chapel, of which there are many records, and that once I saw myself when I was a novice. The Prioress Matilda—I mean the fourth of that name, she who was mixed up with Edward the Lame, the monk, and died suddenly after the—"

"Peace, sister; let us have no scandal about that departed—woman, who left the earth two hundred years ago. Also, if her unquiet spirit still haunts the place, as many say, I know not why it should speak with the voice of a man."

"Perhaps it was the monk Edward's voice that Bridget heard," replied the sister, "for no doubt he still hangs about her skirts as he did in life, if all tales are true. Well, Mistress Emlyn says that she does not mind ghosts, and I can well believe it, for she is a witch's daughter, and has a strange look in her eyes. Did you ever see such bold eyes, Mother? However it may be, I hate ghosts, and rather would I pass a month on bread and water than be alone in that chapel at or after sundown. My back creeps to think of it, for they say that the unhallowed babe walks too, and gibbers round the font seeking baptism—ugh!" and she shuddered.

"Peace, sister, peace to your goblin talk," said Mother Matilda again. "Let us think of holier things lest the foul fiend draw near to us."

****

That night, about one in the morning, the foul fiend drew very near to Blossholme, and he came in the shape of fire. Suddenly the nuns were aroused from their beds by the sound of bells tolling wildly. Running to the window-places, they saw great sheets of flame leaping from the Abbey roofs. They threw open the casements and stared out terrified. Sister Bridget was sent even to wake the deaf gardener and his wife, who lived in the gateway, and command them to go forth and learn what passed, and the meaning of the shouts they heard, for they feared that Blossholme was attacked by some army.

A long while went by, and Bridget returned with a confused tale, which, as it had been gathered by an imbecile from a deaf gardener, was not easy to understand. Meanwhile the shoutings went on and the fire at the Abbey burnt ever more fiercely, so that the nuns thought that their last hour had come, and knelt down to pray at the casement.

Just then Cicely and Emlyn appeared among them, and stared at the great fire.

Suddenly Cicely turned round, and, fixing her large blue eyes on Emlyn, said, in the hearing of them all—

"The Abbey burns. Why, Nurse, they told me that you said it would be so, yonder amid the ashes of Cranwell Towers. Surely you are foresighted."

"Fire calls for fire," answered Emlyn grimly, and the nuns around looked at her with doubtful eyes.

It was a very fierce fire, which appeared to have begun in the dormitories, whence, even at that distance, they saw half-clad monks escaping through the windows, some by means of bed-coverings tied together and some by jumping, notwithstanding the height. Presently the roof of the building fell in, sending up showers of glowing embers, which lit upon the thatch of the farm byres and sheds, and upon the ricks built and building in the stackyard, so that all these caught also, and before dawn were utterly consumed.

One by one the watchers in the Nunnery wearied of the lamentable sight, and muttering prayers, departed terrified to their beds. But Emlyn sat on at the open casement till the rim of the splendid September sun showed above the hills. There she sat, her head resting on her hand, her strong face set like that of a statue. Only her dark eyes, in which the flames were reflected, seemed to smile hardly.

"Thomas is a great tool," she muttered to herself at length, "and the first cut has bitten to the bone. Well, there shall be worse to come. You will live to beg Emlyn's mercy yet, Clement Maldonado."

CHAPTER 9

The Blossholme Witchings

On the afternoon of that day the Abbot came again to visit the Nunnery, and sent for Cicely and Emlyn. They found him alone in the guest-hall, walking up and down its length with a troubled face.

"Cicely Foterell," he said, without any form of greeting, "when last we met you refused to sign the deed which I brought with me. Well, it matters nothing, for that purchaser has gone back upon his bargain."

"Saying that he liked not the title?" suggested Cicely.

"Aye; though who taught you of titles and the ins and outs of law? But what need to ask—?" and he glowered at Emlyn. "Well, let it pass, for now I have a paper with me that you *must* sign. Read it if you will. It is harmless—only an instruction to the tenants of the lands your father held to pay their rents to me this Michaelmas, as warden of that property."

"Do they refuse, then, seeing that you hold it all, my Lord Abbot?"

"Aye, some one has been at work among them, and the stubborn churls will not without instruction under your hand and seal. The farms your father worked himself I have reaped, but last night every grain of corn and every fleece of wool were burned in the fire."

"Then I pray you keep account of them, my Lord, that you may pay me their value when we come to settle our score, seeing that I never gave you leave to shear my sheep and harvest my corn."

"You are pleased to be saucy, girl," he replied, biting his lip. "I have no time to bandy words—sign, and do you witness, Emlyn Stower."

Cicely took the document, glanced at it, then slowly tore it into four pieces and threw it to the floor.

"Rob me and my unborn child if you can and will, at least I'll be no thief's partner," she said quietly. "Now, if you want my name, go forge it, for I sign nothing."

The Abbot's face grew very evil.

"Do you remember, woman," he asked, "that here you are in my power? Do you not know that rebellious sinners such as you are can be shut in a dark dungeon and fed on the bread and water of affliction and beaten with the rods of penance? Will you do my bidding, or shall these things fall on you?"

Cicely's beautiful face flushed up, and for a moment her blue eyes filled with the tears of shame and terror. Then they cleared again, and she looked at him boldly and answered—

"I know that a murderer can be a torturer also. Why should not he who butchered the father scourge the daughter too? But I know also that there is a God who protects the innocent, though sometimes He is slow to lift His hand, and to Him I appeal, my Lord Abbot. I know, moreover, that I am Foterell and Carfax, and that no man or woman of my blood has ever yet yielded to fear or pain. I sign nothing," and, turning, she left the room.

Now the Abbot and Emlyn were alone. Suddenly, before she could speak, for her tongue was tied with rage, he began to rate and curse her and to threaten horrible things against her and her mistress, such things as only a cruel Spaniard could imagine. At length he paused for breath, and she broke in—

"Peace, wicked man, lest the roof fall on you, for I am sure that every cruel word you speak shall become a snake to strike you. Will you not take warning by what befell you last night, or must there be more such lessons?"

"Oho!" he answered; "so you know of that, do you? As I thought, your witchcraft was at work there."

"How can I help knowing what the whole sky blazoned? The fat monks of Blossholme must draw their girdles tight this winter. Those stolen lands bring no luck, it seems, and John Foterell's blood has turned to fire. Be warned, I say, be warned. Nay, I'll hear no more of your foul tongue. Lay a finger on that poor lady if you dare, and pay the price," and she too turned and went.

Ere he left the Nunnery the Abbot had an interview with Mother Matilda.

Cicely must be disciplined, he said; gently at first, afterwards with roughness, even to scourging, if need were—for her soul's sake. Also her servant Emlyn must be kept away from her—for her soul's sake, since without doubt she was a dangerous witch. Also, when the time of the birth of the child came on, he would send a wise woman to wait upon her, one who was accustomed to such cases—for her body's sake and that of her child. In the midst of the great trouble that had fallen upon them through the terrible fire at the Abbey, which had cost them such fearful loss, to say nothing of the lives of two of the servants and others burned and maimed, he had not much time to talk of such small things; but did she understand?

Then it was that Mother Matilda, the meek and gentle, brought pain and astonishment to the heart of the Lord Abbot, her spiritual superior.

She did not understand in the least. Such discipline as he suggested, whatever might be her faults and frailty, was, she declared with vigour, entirely unsuited to the case of the Lady Cicely, who, in her opinion, had suffered much for a small cause, and who, moreover, was about to become a mother, and therefore should be treated with every gentleness. For her part, she washed her hands of the whole business, and rather than enforce such commands would lay the case before the Vicar-General in London, who, she understood, was ready to look into such matters. Or at least she would set the Lady Harflete and her servant outside the gates and call upon the charitable to assist them. Of course, however, if his Lordship chose to send a skilled woman to wait upon her in her trouble, she could have no objection, provided that this woman were a person of good repute. But in the circumstances it was idle to talk to her of bread and water and dark cells and scourgings. Such things should never happen while she was Prioress. Before they did, she and her sisters would walk out of the Nunnery and leave the King's Courts to judge of the matter.

Now the state of the Abbot was very like to that of a terrier dog which, being accustomed to worry and torment a certain ewe-sheep, comes upon the same after it has lambed and finds a new creature—one that, instead of running in affright, turns upon it and, with head and hood and all its weight of mutton, butts, and leaps, and tramples. Then what chance has that dog against the terrible and unsuspected fury of the sheep, born, as it thought, for it to tear? Then what can it do but run, panting and discomfited, to its kennel? So it was with the Abbot at the onslaught of Mother Matilda in the defence of her lamb—Cicely. With Emlyn he had been prepared to exchange bite for bite—but Mother Matilda! his own pet quarry. It was too much. He could only go away, cursing all women and their infinite variety, on which no man might build. Who would have thought it of Mother Matilda, of all people on the earth!

So it came to pass that at the Nunnery, notwithstanding these terrible threats, things went on much as they had done before, since the times were such that even an all-powerful and remote Lord Abbot, with "right of gallows," could not drive matters to an extremity.

Cicely was not shut into the dungeon and fed on bread and water, much less was she scourged. Nor was she separated from her nurse Emlyn, although it is true that the Prioress reproved her for her resistance to established authority, and when she had finished her lecture, kissed and blessed her, and called her "her sweet child, her dove and joy."

But if there was sameness at the Nunnery, at the Abbey there was constant change and excitement. Only three days after the fire the great flock of eight hundred lambs rushed one night over the Red Cliff on the fell, where, as all shepherds in that country know, there is a sheer drop of forty feet. Never was lamb's flesh so cheap in Blossholme and the country round as on the morrow of that night, while every hind within ten miles could have a winter coat for the skinning. Moreover, it was said and sworn to by the shepherds that the devil himself, with horns and hoofs, and mounted on a jackass, had been seen driving the same lambs.

Next the ghost of Sir John Foterell appeared, clad in armour, sometimes mounted and sometimes afoot, but always at night-time. First this dreadful spirit was perceived walking in the gardens of Shefton Hall, where it met the Abbot's caretaker—for the place was now shut up—as he went to set a springe for hares. He was a man advanced in years, yet few horses ever covered the distance between Shefton and Blossholme Abbey more quickly than he did that night.

Nor would he or any other return to his charge, so that henceforth Shefton was left as a dwelling for the ghost, which, as all might see from time to time, shone in the window-places like a candle. Moreover, the said ghost travelled far and wide, for on dark, windy nights it knocked upon the doors of those that in its lifetime had been its tenants, and in a hollow voice declared that it had been murdered by the Abbot of Blossholme and his underlings, who held its daughter in durance, and, under threats of unearthly vengeance, commanded all men to bring him to justice, and to pay him neither fees nor homage.

So much terror did this ghost cause that Thomas Bolle, the swift of foot, was set to watch for it, and returned announcing that he had seen it and that it called him by his name, whereon he, being a bold fellow and believing that it was but a man, sent an arrow straight through it, at which it laughed and forthwith vanished away. More; in proof of these things he led the Abbot and his monks to the very place, and showed them where he had stood and where the ghost stood—yes, and the arrow, of which all the feathers had been mysteriously burnt

off and the wood seared as though by fire, sunk deep into a tree beyond. Then, as this thing had become a scandal and a dread, the Abbot, in his robes, solemnly laid the ghost, Thomas Bolle showing him
exactly where it had passed.

This spirit being well and truly laid (like a foundation-stone), the
Abbot and his monks returned homeward through the wood, but as
they went a dreadful voice, which all recognized as that of Sir John
Foterell, called these words from the shadows of an impenetrable
thicket—for now the night was falling—

"Clement Maldonado, Abbot of Blossholme, I, whom thou didst murder, summon thee to meet me within a year before the throne of God."

Thereon all fled; yes, even the Abbot fled, or rather, as he said, his
horse did, Thomas Bolle, who had lagged behind, outrunning them
every one and getting home the first, saying *Aves* as he went.

After this, although the whole countryside hunted for it, Sir
John's ghost was seen no more. Doubtless its work was done; but the
Abbot explained matters differently. Other and worse things were
seen, however.

One moonlight night a disturbance was heard among the cows,
that bellowed and rushed about the field into which they had been
turned after milking. Thinking that dogs had got amongst them, the
herd and a watchman—for now no man would stir alone after sunset
at Blossholme—went to see what was happening, and presently fell
down half dead with fright. For there, leaning over the gate and laughing at them, was the foul fiend himself—the fiend with horns and tail,
and in his hand an instrument like a pitchfork.

How the pair got home again, they never knew, but this is certain,
that after that night no one could milk those cows; moreover, some
of them slipped their calves, and became so wild that they must be
slaughtered.

Next came rumours that even the Nunnery itself was haunted, especially the chapel. Here voices were heard talking, and Emlyn Stower, who was praying there, came out vowing that she had seen a ball of
fire which rolled up and down the aisle, and in the centre of it a man's
head, that seemed to try to talk to her, but could not.

Into this matter inquiry was held by the Abbot himself, who asked
Emlyn if she knew the face that was in the ball of fire. She answered
that she thought so. It seemed very like to one of his own guards,
named Andrew Woods, or more commonly Drunken Andrew, a
Scotchman whom Sir Christopher Harflete was said to have killed on
the night of the great burning. At least his Lordship would remember

that this Andrew had a broken nose, and so had the head in the fire, but, as it appeared to have changed a great deal since death, she could not be quite certain. All she was sure of was that it seemed to be trying to give her some message.

Now, recalling the trick that had been played with the said Andrew's body, the Abbot was silent. Only he asked shrewdly, if Emlyn had seen so terrible a thing there, how it came about that she was not afraid to be alone in the chapel, which he was informed she frequented much. She answered, with a laugh, that it was men she dreaded, not spirits, good or ill.

"No," he exclaimed, with a burst of rage, "you do not dread them, woman, because you are a witch, and summon them; nor shall we be free from these wizardries until the fire has you and your company."

"If so," replied Emlyn coolly, "I will ask dead Andrew for his message to you next time we meet, unless he chooses to deliver it to you himself."

So they parted, but that very night there happened the worst thing of all. It was about one in the morning when the Abbot, whose window was set open, was wakened by a voice that spoke with a Scotch accent and repeatedly called him by his name, summoning him to look out and see. He and others rose and looked, but could see nothing, for the night was very dark and rain fell. When the dawn came, however, their search was rewarded, for there, set upon a pinnacle of the Abbey church, and staring straight into the window of his Lordship's sleeping-room, from which it was but a few yards distant, was the dreadful head of Andrew Woods!

Furiously the Abbot asked who had done this horrible thing, but the monks, who were sure that it was the same being that had bewitched the cows, only shrugged their shoulders, and suggested that the grave of Andrew should be opened to see if he had lost his head. This was done at length, although, for his own reasons, the Abbot forbade it, talking of the violation of the dead.

Well, the grave was opened when Maldon was away on one of his mysterious journeys, and lo! no Andrew was there, but only a beam of oakwood stuffed out with straw to the shape of a man and sewn up in a blanket. For the real Andrew, or rather what was left of him, lay, it may be remembered, in another grave that was supposed to be filled by Sir Christopher Harflete.

From this day forward the whole countryside for fifty miles round rang with the tales of what were known as the Blossholme witchings, of which a proof was still to be seen by all men in the withered head of Andrew perched upon its pinnacle, whence none could be found to remove it for love or money. Only it was noted that the Abbot changed his sleeping-chamber, after which, except for a sickness which struck the monks—it was thought from the drinking of sour beer—these bedevilments were abated.

Indeed, at that time men had other things to think of, since the air was thick with rumours of impending change. The King threatened the Church, and the Church prepared to resist the King. There was talk of the suppression of the monasteries—some, in fact, had already been suppressed—and more talk of a rising of the faithful in the shires of York and Lincoln; high matters which called Abbot Maldon much away from home.

One day he returned weary, but satisfied, from a long journey, and amongst the news that awaited him found a message from the Prioress, over which he pondered while he ate his food. Also there was a letter from Spain, which he studied eagerly.

Some nine months had passed since the ship *Great Yarmouth* sailed, and during this time all that had been heard of her was that she had never reached Seville, so that, like every one else, the Abbot believed she had foundered in the deep seas. This was a sad event which he had borne with resignation, seeing that, although it meant the loss of his letters, which were of importance, she had aboard of her several persons whom he wished to see no more, especially Sir Christopher Harflete and Sir John Foterell's serving-man, Jeffrey Stokes, who was said to carry with him certain inconvenient documents. Even his secretary and chaplain, Brother Martin, could be spared, being, Maldon felt, a character better suited to heaven than to an earth where the best of men must be prepared sometimes to compromise with conscience.

In short, the vanishing of the *Great Yarmouth* was the wise decree of a far-seeing Providence, that had removed certain stumbling-blocks from his feet, which of late had been forced to travel over a rough and thorny road. For the dead tell no tales, although it was true that the ghost of Sir John Foterell and the grinning head of Drunken Andrew on his pinnacle seemed to be instances to the contrary. Christopher Harflete and Jeffrey Stokes at the bottom of the Bay of Biscay could bring no awkward charges, and left him none to deal with save an imprisoned and forgotten girl and an unborn child.

Now things were changed again, however, for the Spanish letter in his hand told him that the *Great Yarmouth* had not sunk, since two members of her crew who escaped—how, it was not said—declared that she had been captured by Turkish or other infidel pirates and taken away through the Straits of Gibraltar to some place unknown. Therefore, if he had survived the voyage, Christopher Harflete might still be living, and so might Jeffrey Stokes and Brother Martin. Yet this was not likely, for probably they would have perished in the fight, being hot-headed Englishmen, all three of them, or at the best have been committed to the Turkish galleys, whence not one man in a thousand ever returned.

On the whole, then, he had little cause to fear them, who were dead, or as good as dead, especially in the midst of so many more pressing dangers. All he had to fear, all that stood between him, or rather the Church, and a very rich inheritance was the girl in the Nunnery and an unborn child, and—yes, Emlyn Stower. Well, he was sure that the child would not live, and probably the mother would not live. As for Emlyn, as she deserved, she would be burned for a witch, ere long too, now that he had time to see to it, and, if she survived her sickness, although he grieved for her, Cicely, her accomplice, should justly accompany her to the stake. Meanwhile, as Mother Matilda's message told him, this matter of the child was urgent.

The Abbot called a monk who was waiting on him and bade him send word to a woman known as Goody Megges, bidding her come at once. Within ten minutes she entered, having, as she explained, been warned to be close at hand.

This Goody Megges, who had some local repute as a "wise woman," was a person of about fifty years of age, remarkable for her enormous size, a flat face with small oblong eyes and a little, twisted mouth, which had caused her to be nicknamed "the Flounder." She greeted the Abbot with much reverence, curtseying till he thought she would fall backwards, and having received his fatherly blessing, sank into a chair, that seemed to vanish beneath her bulk.

"You will wonder why I summon you here, friend, since this is no place for the services of those of your trade," began the Abbot, with a smile.

"Oh, no, my Lord," answered the woman; "I've heard it is to wait upon Sir Christopher Harflete's wife in her trouble."

"I wish that I could call her by the honoured name of wife," said the Abbot, with a sigh. "But a mock-marriage does not make a wife, Mistress Megges, and, alas! the poor babe, if ever it should be born, will be but a bastard, marked from its birth with the brand of shame."

Now, the Flounder, who was no fool, began to take her cue.

"It is sad, very sad, your Holiness—no, that's wrong; but never mind, it will be right before all's done, and a good omen, I say, coming so sudden and chancy—your Lordship, I mean—not but what there's lots of the sort about here, as is generally the case round a—I mean everywhere. Moreover, they generally grow up bad and ungrateful, as I know well from my own three—not but what, of course, I was married fast enough. Well, what I was going to say was, that when things is so, sometimes it is a true blessing if the little innocents should go off at the first, and so be spared the finger of shame and the sniff of scorn," and she paused.

"Yes, Mistress Megges, or at least in such a case it is not for us to rail at the decree of Heaven—provided, of course, that the infant has lived long enough to be baptized," he added hastily.

"No, your Eminence, no. That's just what I said to that Smith girl last spring, when, being a heavy sleeper, I happened to overlie her brat and woke up to find it flat and blue. When she saw it she took on, bellowing like a heifer that has lost its first calf, and I said to her, 'Mary, this isn't me; it's Heaven. Mary, you should be very thankful, since my burden has rid you of your burden, and you can bury such a tiny one for next to nothing. Mary, cry a little if you like, for that's natural with the first, but don't come here flying in the face of Heaven with your railings, and gates, and posts—especially the rails, for Heaven hates 'em.'"

"Ah!" asked the Abbot, with mild interest, "and pray what did Mary do then?"

"Do, the graceless wench? Why, she said, 'Is it rails you're talking of, you pig-smothering old sow? Then here's a rail for you,' and she pulled the top bar off my own fence—for we were talking by the door—oak it was, and three by two—and knocked me flat—here's the scar of it on my head—singing out, 'Is that enough, or will you have the gate and the posts too?' Oh! If there's one thing I hate, it is railing, 'specially if made of hard oak and held edgeways."

So the wicked old hag babbled on, after her hideous fashion, while the Abbot stared at the ceiling.

"Enough of these sad stories of vice and violence. Such mischances will happen, and of course you were not to blame. Now, good Mistress Megges, will you undertake this case, which cannot be left to ignorant nuns? Though times are hard here, since of late many losses have fallen on our house, your skill shall be well paid."

The woman shuffled her big feet and stared at the floor, then looked up suddenly with a glance that seemed to bore to his heart like a bradawl, and asked—

"And if perchance the blessed babe should fly to heaven through my fingers, as in my time I have known dozens of them do, should I still get that pay?"

"Then," the Abbot answered, with a smile—a somewhat sickly smile—"then I think, mistress, you should have double pay, to console you for your sorrow and for any doubts that might be thrown upon your skill."

"Now that's noble trading," she replied, with an evil leer, "such as one might hope for from an Abbot. But, my Lord, they say the Nunnery is haunted, and I can't face ghosts. Man or woman, with rails or without 'em, Mother Flounder doesn't mind, but ghosts—no! Also Mistress Stower is a witch, and might lay a curse on me; and those nuns are full of crinks and cranks, and can pray an honest soul to death."

"Come, come, my time is short. What is it you want, woman? Out with it."

"The inn there at the ford—your Lordship, will need a tenant next month. It's a good paying house for those who know how to keep their mouths shut and to look the other way, and through vile scandal and evil slanderers, such as the Smith girl, my business isn't what it was. Now if I could have it without rent for the first two years, till I had time to work up the trade—"

The Abbot, who could bear no more of the creature, rose from his chair and said sharply—

"I will remember. Yes, I will promise. Go now; the reverent Mother is advised of your coming. And report to me night and morning of the progress of the case. Why, woman, what are you doing?" for she had suddenly slid to her knees and grasped his robes with her thick, filthy hands.

"Absolution, holy Lordship; I ask absolution and blessing—*pax Meggiscum*, and the rest of it."

"Absolution? There is nothing to absolve."

"Oh! yes, my Lord, there is plenty, though I am wondering who will absolve *you* for your half. Also there are rows of little angels that sometimes won't let me sleep, and that's why I can't stomach ghosts. I'd rather sup in winter on cold small ale and half-cooked pork than face even a still-born ghost."

"Begone!" said the Abbot, in such a voice that she scrambled to her feet and went, unblessed and unabsolved.

When the door had closed behind her he went to the window and flung it wide, although the night was foul.

"By all the saints!" he muttered, "that beastly murderess poisons the air. Why, I wonder, does God allow such filthy things to live? Cannot

443

she ply her hell-trade less grossly? Oh! Clement Maldonado, how low are you sunk that you must use tools like these, and on such a business. And yet there is no other way. Not for myself, but for the Church, O Lord! The great plot thickens, and all men clamour to me, its head and spring, for money. Give me money, and within six months Yorkshire and the North will be up, and without a year Henry the Anti-Christ will be dead and the Princess Mary fast upon the throne, with the Emperor and the Pope for watchdogs. That stiff-necked Cicely must die and her babe must die, and then I'll twist the secret of the jewels out of the witch, Emlyn—on the rack, if need be. Those jewels—I've seen them so often; why, they would feed an army; but while Cicely or her brat lives where is my claim to them? So, alas! they must die, but oh! the hag is right. Who shall give me absolution for a deed I hate? Not for me, not for me, O my Patron, but for the Church!" and flinging himself to the floor before the holy image of his chosen Saint, he rested his head upon its feet and wept.

CHAPTER 10

Mother Megges and the Ghost

Flounder Megges, with all the paraphernalia of her trade, was established as nurse to Cicely at the Nunnery. This establishment, it is true, had not been easy since Emlyn, who knew something of the woman's repute, and suspected more, resisted it with all her strength, but here the Prioress intervened in her gentle way. She herself, she explained, did not like this person, who looked so odd, drank so much beer and talked so fast. Yet she had made inquiries and found that she was extraordinarily skilled in matters of that nature. Indeed, it was said that she had succeeded in cases that were wonderfully difficult which the leech had abandoned as hopeless, though of course there had been other cases where she had not succeeded. But these, she was informed, were generally those of poor people who did not pay her well. Now in this instance her pay would be ample, for she, Mother Matilda, had promised her a splendid fee out of her private store, and for the rest, since no man doctor might enter there, who else was competent? Not she or the other nuns, for none of them had been married save old Bridget, who was silly and had long ago forgotten all such things. Not Emlyn even, who was but a girl when her own child was born, and since then had been otherwise employed. Therefore there was no choice.

To this reasoning Emlyn agreed perforce, though she mistrusted her of the fat wretch, whose appearance poor Cicely also disliked. Still, for very fear Emlyn was humble and civil to her, for if she were not, who could know if she would put out all her skill upon behalf of her mistress? Therefore she did her bidding like a slave, and spiced her beer and made her bed and even listened to her foul jests and talk unmurmuringly.

****

The business was over at length, and the child, a noble boy, born into the world. Had not the Flounder produced it in triumph laid upon a little basket covered with a lamb-skin, and had not Emlyn and Mother Matilda and all the nuns kissed and blessed it? Had it not also, for fear of accident (such was the fatherly forethought of the Abbot), been baptized at once by a priest who was waiting, under the names of John Christopher Foterell, John after its grandfather and Christopher after its father, with Foterell for a surname, since the Abbot would not allow that it should be called Harflete, being, as he averred, base-born?

So this child was born, and Mother Megges swore that of all the two hundred and three that she had issued into the world it was the finest, nine and a half pounds in weight at the very least. Also, as its voice and movements testified, it was lusty and like to live, for did not the Flounder, in sight of all the wondering nuns, hold it up hanging by its hands to her two fat forefingers, and afterwards drink a whole quart of spiced ale to its health and long life?

But if the babe was like to live, Cicely was like to die. Indeed, she was very, very ill, and perhaps would have passed away had it not been for a device of Emlyn's. For when she was at her worst and the Flounder, shaking her head and saying that she could do no more, had departed to her eternal ale and a nap, Emlyn crept up and took her mistress's cold hand.

"Darling," she said, "hear me," but Cicely did not stir. "Darling," she repeated, "hear me, I have news for you of your husband."

Cicely's white face turned a little on the pillow and her blue eyes opened.

"Of my husband?" she whispered. "Why, he is gone, as I soon shall be. What news of him?"

"That he is not gone, that he lives, or so I believe, though heretofore I have hid it from you."

The head was lifted for a moment, and the eyes stared at her with wondering joy.

"Do you trick me, Nurse? Nay, you would never do that. Give me the milk, I want it now. I'll listen. I promise you I'll not die till you have told me. If Christopher lives why should I die who only hoped to find him?"

So Emlyn whispered all she knew. It was not much, only that Christopher had not been buried in the grave where he was said to be buried, and that he had been taken wounded aboard the ship *Great Yarmouth*, of the fate of which ship fortunately she had heard nothing. Still, slight as they might be, to Cicely these tidings were a magic medicine, for did they not mean the rebirth of hope, hope that for nine long months had been dead and buried with Christopher? From that moment she began to mend.

When the Flounder, having slept off her drink, returned to the sickbed, she stared at her amazed and muttered something about witchcraft, she who had been sure that she would die, as in those days so many women did who fell into hands like hers. Indeed, she was bitterly disappointed, knowing that this death was desired by her employer, who now after all might let the Ford Inn to another. Moreover, the child was no waster, but one who was set for life. Well, that at least she could mend, and if it were done quickly the shock might kill the mother. Yet the thing was not so easy as it looked, for there were many loving eyes upon that babe.

When she wished to take it to her bed at night Emlyn forbade her fiercely, and on being appealed to, the Prioress, who knew the creature's drunken habits and had heard rumours of the fate of the Smith infant and others, gave orders that it was not to be. So, since the mother was too weak to have it with her, the boy was laid in a little cot at her side. And always day and night one or more of the sweet-faced nuns stood at the head of that cot watching as might a guardian angel. Also it took only Nature's food since from the first Cicely would nurse it, so that she could not mix any drug with its milk that would cause it to sleep itself away.

So the days went on, bringing black wrath, despair almost, to the heart of Mother Megges, till at length there came the chance she sought. One fine evening, when the nuns were gathered at vespers, but as it happened not in the chapel, because since the tale of the hauntings they shunned the place after high noon, Cicely, whose strength was returning to her, asked Emlyn to change her garments and remake her bed. Meanwhile, the babe was given to Sister Bridget, who doted on it, with instructions to take it to walk in the garden for a time, since the rain had passed off and the afternoon was now very soft and pleasant. So she went, and there presently was met by the Flounder, who was supposed to be asleep, but had followed her, a person of whom the half-witted Bridget was much afraid.

"What are you doing with my babe, old fool?" she screeched at her, thrusting her fat face to within an inch of the nun's. "You'll let it fall and I shall be blamed. Give me the angel or I will twist your nose for you. Give it me, I say, and get you gone."

In her fear and flurry old Bridget obeyed and departed at a run. Then, recovering herself a little, or drawn by some instinct, she returned, hid herself in a clump of lilac bushes and watched.

Presently she saw the Flounder, after glancing about to make sure that she was alone, enter the chapel, carrying the child, and heard her bolt the door after her. Now Bridget, as she said afterwards, grew very frightened, she knew not why, and, acting on impulse, ran to the chancel window and, climbing on to a wheelbarrow that stood there, looked through it. This is what she saw.

Mother Megges was kneeling in the chancel, as she thought at first, to say her prayers, till she perceived, for a ray from the setting sun showed it all, that on the paving before her lay the infant and that this she-devil was thrusting her thick forefinger down its throat, for already it grew black in the face, and as she thrust muttering savagely. So horror-struck was Bridget that she could neither move nor cry.

Then, while she stood petrified, suddenly there appeared the figure of a man in rusty armour. The Flounder looked up, saw him and, withdrawing her finger from the mouth of the child, let out yell after yell. The man, who said nothing, drew a sword and lifted it, whereon the murderess screamed—

"The ghost! The ghost! Spare me, Sir John, I am poor and he paid me. Spare me for Christ's sake!" and so saying, she rolled on to the floor in a fit, and there turned and twisted until she lay still.

Then the man, or the ghost of a man, having looked at her, sheathed his sword and lifting up the babe, which now drew its breath again and cried, marched with it down the aisle. The next thing of which Bridget became aware was that he stood before her, the infant in his arms, holding it out to her. His face she could not see, for the visor was down, but he spoke in a hollow voice, saying—

"This gift from Heaven to the Lady Harflete. Bid her fear nothing, for one devil I have garnered and the others are ripe for reaping."

Bridget took the child and sank down on to the ground, and at that moment the nuns, alarmed by the awful yells, rushed through the side door, headed by Mother Matilda. They too saw the figure, and knew the Foterell cognizance upon its helm and shield. But it waited not to speak to them, only passed behind some trees and vanished.

Their first care was for the infant, which they thought the man was stealing; then, after they were sure that it had taken no real hurt, they questioned old Bridget, but could get nothing from her, for all she did was to gibber and point first to the barrow and next to the chancel window. At length Mother Matilda understood and, climbing on to the barrow, looked through the window as Bridget had done. She looked, she saw, and fell back fainting.

****

An hour had gone by. The child, unhurt save for a little bruising of its tender mouth, was asleep upon its mother's breast. Bridget, having recovered, at length had told all her tale to every one of them save Cicely, who as yet knew nothing, for she and Emlyn did not hear the screams, their rooms being on the other side of the building. The Abbot had been sent for, and, accompanied by monks, arrived in the midst of a thunder-storm and pouring rain. He, too, had heard the tale, heard it with a pale face while his monks crossed themselves. At length he asked of the woman Megges. They replied that living or dead she was, as they supposed, still in the chapel, which none of them had dared to enter.

"Come, let us see," said the Abbot, and they went there to find the door locked as Bridget had said.

Smiths were sent for and broke it in while all stood in the pouring rain and watched. It was open at last, and they entered with torches and tapers, for now the darkness was dense, the Abbot leading them. They came to the chancel, where something lay upon the floor, and held down the torches to look. Then they saw that which caused them all to turn and fly, calling on the saints to protect them. In her life Mother Megges had not been lovely, but in the death that had overtaken her—!

****

It was morning. The Lord Abbot and his monks were assembled in the guest-chamber, and opposite to them were the Lady Prioress and her nuns, and with them Emlyn.

"Witchcraft!" shouted the Abbot, smiting his fist upon the table, "black witchcraft! Satan himself and his foulest demons walk the countryside and have their home in this Nunnery. Last night they manifested themselves—"

"By saving a babe from a cruel death and bringing a hateful murderess to doom," broke in Emlyn.

"Silence, Sorceress," shouted the Abbot. "Get thee behind me, Satan. I know you and your familiars," and he glared at the Prioress.

"What may you mean, my Lord Abbot?" asked Mother Matilda, bridling up. "My sisters and I do not understand. Emlyn Stower is right. Do you call that witchcraft which works so good an end? The ghost of Sir John Foterell appeared here—we admit it who saw that ghost. But what did the spirit do? It slew the hellish woman whom you sent among us and it rescued the blessed babe when her finger was down its throat to choke out its pure life. If that be witchcraft I

449

stand by it. Tell us what did the wretch mean when she cried out to the spirit to spare her because she was poor and had been bribed for her iniquity? Who bribed her, my Lord Abbot? None in this house, I'll swear. And who changed Sir John Foterell from flesh to spirit? Why is he a ghost to-day?"

"Am I here to answer riddles, woman, and who are you that you dare put such questions to me? I depose you, I set your house under ban. The judgment of the Church shall be pronounced against you all. Dare not to leave your doors until the Court is composed to try you. Think not you shall escape. Your English land is sick and heresy stalks abroad; but," he added slowly, "fire can still bite and there is store of faggots in the woods. Prepare your souls for judgment. Now I go."

"Do as it pleases you," answered the enraged Mother Matilda. "When you set out your case we will answer it; but, meanwhile, we pray that you take what is left of your dead hireling with you, for we find her ill company and here she shall have no burial. My Lord Abbot, the charter of this Nunnery is from the monarch of England, whatever authority you and those that went before you have usurped. It was granted by the first Edward, and the appointment of every prioress since his day has been signed by the sovereign and no other. I hold mine under the manual of the eighth Henry. You cannot depose me, for I appeal from the Abbot to the King. Fare you well, my Lord," and, followed by her little train of aged nuns, she swept from the room like an offended queen.

After the terrible death of the child-murderess and the restoration of her babe to her unharmed, Cicely's recovery was swift. Within a week she was up and walking, and within ten days as strong, or stronger, than ever she had been. Nothing more had been heard of the Abbot, and though all knew that danger threatened them from this quarter they were content to enjoy the present hour of peace and wait till it was at hand.

But in Cicely's awakened mind there arose a keen desire to learn more of what her nurse had hinted to her when she lay upon the very edge of death. Day by day she plied Emlyn with questions till at length she knew all; namely, that the tidings came from Thomas Bolle, and that he, dressed in her father's armour, was the ghost who had saved her boy from death. Now nothing would serve her but that she must see Thomas herself, as she said, to thank him, though truly, as Emlyn knew well, to draw from his own lips every detail and circumstance that she could gather concerning Christopher.

For a while Emlyn held out against her, for she knew the dangers of such a meeting; but in the end, being able to refuse her lady nothing, she gave way.

At length at the appointed hour of sunset Emlyn and Cicely stood in the chapel, whither the latter told the nuns she wished to go to return thanks for her deliverance from many dangers. They knelt before the altar, and while they made pretence to pray there heard knocks, which were the signal of the presence of Thomas Bolle. Emlyn answered them with other knocks, which told that all was safe, whereon the wooden image turned and Thomas appeared, dressed as before in Sir John Foterell's armour. So like did he seem to her dead father in this familiar mail that for a moment Cicely thought it must be he, and her knees trembled until he knelt before her, kissing her hand, asking after her health and that of the infant and whether she were satisfied with his service.

"Indeed and indeed yes," she answered; "and oh, friend! all that I have henceforth is yours should I ever have anything again, who am but a prisoned beggar. Meanwhile, my blessing and that of Heaven rest upon you, you gallant man."

"Thank me not, Lady," answered the honest Thomas. "To speak truth it was Emlyn whom I served, for though monks parted us we have been friends for many a year. As for the matter of the child and that spawn of hell, the Flounder, be grateful to God, not to me, for it was by mere chance that I came here that evening, which I had not intended to do. I was going about my business with the cattle when something seemed to tell me to arm and come. It was as though a hand pushed me, and the rest you know, and so I think by now does Mother Megges," he added grimly.

"Yes, yes, Thomas; and in truth I do thank God, Whose finger I see in all this business, as I thank you, His instrument. But there are other things whereof Emlyn has spoken to me. She said—ah! she said my husband, whom I thought slain and buried, in truth was only wounded and not buried, but shipped over-sea. Tell me that story, friend, omitting nothing, but swiftly for our time is short. I thirst to hear it from your own lips."

So in his slow, wandering way he told her, word by word, all that he had seen, all that he had learned, and the sum of it was that Sir Christopher had been shipped abroad upon the *Great Yarmouth*, sorely wounded but not dead, and that with him had sailed Jeffrey Stokes and the monk Martin.

"That's ten months gone," said Cicely. "Has naught been heard of this ship? By now she should be home again."

Thomas hesitated, then answered—

"No tidings came of her from Spain. Then, although I said nothing of it even to Emlyn, she was reported lost with all hands at sea. Then came another story—"

"Ah! that other story?"

"Lady, two of her crew reached the Wash. I did not see them, and they have shipped again for Marseilles in France. But I spoke with a shepherd who is half-brother to one of them, and he told me that from him he learned that the *Great Yarmouth* was set upon by two Turkish pirates and captured after a brave fight in which the captain Goody and others were killed. This man and his comrade escaped in a boat and drifted to and fro till they were picked up by a homeward-bound caravel which landed them at Hull. That's all I know—save one thing."

"One thing! Oh, what thing, Thomas? That my husband is dead?"

"Nay, nay, the very opposite, that he is alive, or was, for these men saw him and Jeffrey Stokes and Martin the priest, no craven as I know, fighting like devils till the Turks overwhelmed them by numbers, and, having bound their hands, carried them all three unwounded on board one of their ships, wishing doubtless to make slaves of such brave fellows."

Now, although Emlyn would have stopped her, still Cicely plied him with questions, which he answered as best he could, till suddenly a sound caught his ear.

"Look at the window!" he exclaimed.

They looked, and saw a sight that froze their blood, for there staring at them through the glass was the dark face of the Abbot, and with it other faces.

"Betray me not, or I shall burn," he whispered. "Say only that I came to haunt you," and silently as a shadow he glided to his niche and was gone.

"What now, Emlyn?"

"One thing only—Thomas must be saved. A bold face and stand to it. Is it our fault if your father's ghost should haunt this chapel? Remember, your father's ghost, no other. Ah! here they come."

As she spoke the door was thrown wide, and through it came the Abbot and his rout of attendants. Within two paces of the women they halted, hanging together like bees, for they were afraid, while a voice cried, "Seize the witches!"

Cicely's terror passed from her and she faced them boldly.

"What would you with us, my Lord Abbot?" she asked.

"We would know, Sorceress, what shape was that which spoke with you but now, and whither has it gone?"

"The same that saved my child and called the Sword of God down upon the murderess. It wore my father's armour, but its face I did not see. It has gone whence it came, but where that is I know not. Discover if you can."

"Woman, you trifle with us. What said the Thing?"

"It spoke of the slaughter of Sir John Foterell by King's Grave Mount and of those who wrought it," and she looked at him steadily until his eyes fell before hers.

"What else?"

"It told me that my husband is not dead. Neither did you bury him as you put about, but shipped him hence to Spain, whence it prophesied he will return again to be revenged upon you. It told me that he was captured by the infidel Moors, and with him Jeffrey Stokes, my father's servant, and the priest Martin, your secretary. Then it looked up and vanished, or seemed to vanish, though perhaps it is among us now."

"Aye," answered the Abbot, "Satan, with whom you hold converse, is always among us. Cicely Foterell and Emlyn Stower, you are foul witches, self-confessed. The world has borne your sorceries too long, and you shall answer for them before God and man, as I, the Lord Abbot of Blossholme, have right and authority to make you do. Seize these witches and let them be kept fast in their chamber till I constitute the Court Ecclesiastic for their trial."

So they took hold of Cicely and Emlyn and led them to the Nunnery. As they crossed the garden they were met by Mother Matilda and the nuns, who, for a second time within a month, ran out to see what was the tumult in the chapel.

"What is it now, Cicely?" asked the Prioress.

"Now we are witches, Mother," she answered, with a sad smile.

"Aye," broke in Emlyn, "and the charge is that the ghost of the murdered Sir John Foterell was seen speaking to us."

"Why, why?" exclaimed the Prioress. "If the spirit of a woman's father appears to her is she therefore to be declared a witch? Then is poor Sister Bridget a witch also, for this same spirit brought the child to her?"

"Aye," said the Abbot, "I had forgotten her. She is another of the crew, let her be seized and shut up also. Greatly do I hope, when it comes to the hour of trial, that there may not be found to be more of them," and he glanced at the poor nuns with menace in his eye.

So Cicely and Emlyn were shut within their room and strictly guarded by monks, but otherwise not ill-treated. Indeed, save for their confinement, there was little change in their condition. The child was allowed to be with Cicely, the nuns were allowed to visit her.

Only over both of them hung the shadow of great trouble. They were aware, and it seemed to them purposely suffered to be aware, that they were about to be tried for their lives upon monstrous and obscene charges; namely, that they had consorted with a dim and awful creature called the Enemy of Mankind, whom, it was supposed, human beings had power to call to their counsel and assistance. To them who knew well that this being was Thomas Bolle, the thing seemed absurd. Yet it could not be denied that the said Thomas at Emlyn's instigation had worked much evil on the monks of Blossholme, paying them, or rather their Abbot, back in his own coin.

Yet what was to be done? To tell the facts would be to condemn Thomas to some fearful fate which even then they would be called upon to share, although possibly they might be cleared of the charge of witchcraft.

Emlyn set the matter before Cicely, urging neither one side nor the other, and waited her judgment. It was swift and decisive.

"This is a coil that we cannot untangle," said Cicely. "Let us betray no one, but put our trust in God. I am sure," she added, "that God will help us as He did when Mother Megges would have murdered my boy. I shall not attempt to defend myself by wronging others. I leave everything to Him."

"Strange things have happened to many who trusted in God; to that the whole evil world bears witness," said Emlyn doubtfully.

"May be," answered Cicely in her quiet fashion, "perhaps because they did not trust enough or rightly. At least there lies my path and I will walk in it—to the fire if need be."

"There is some seed of greatness in you; to what will it grow, I wonder?" replied Emlyn, with a shrug of her shoulders.

On the morrow this faith of Cicely's was put to a sharp test. The Abbot came and spoke with Emlyn apart. This was the burden of his song—

"Give me those jewels and all may yet be well with you and your mistress, vile witches though you are. If not, you burn."

As before she denied all knowledge of them.

"Find me the jewels or you burn," he answered. "Would you pay your lives for a few miserable gems?"

Now Emlyn weakened, not for her own sake, and said she would speak with her mistress.

He bade her do so.

"I thought that those jewels were burned, Emlyn, do you then know where they are?" asked Cicely.

"Aye, I have said nothing of it to you, but I know. Speak the word and I give them up to save you."

Cicely thought a while and kissed her child, which she held in her arms, then laughed aloud and answered—

"Not so. That Abbot shall never be richer for any gem of mine. I have told you in what I trust, and it is not jewels. Whether I burn or whether I am saved, he shall not have them."

"Good," said Emlyn, "that is my mind also, I only spoke for your sake," and she went out and told the Abbot.

He came into Cicely's chamber and raged at them. He said that they should be excommunicated, then tortured and then burned; but Cicely, whom he had thought to frighten, never winced.

"If so, so let it be," she replied, "and I will bear all as best I can. I know nothing of these jewels, but if they still exist they are mine, not yours, and I am innocent of any witchcraft. Do your work, for I am sure that the end shall be far other than you think."

"What!" said the Abbot, "has the foul fiend been with you again that you talk thus certainly? Well, Sorceress, soon you will sing another tune," and he went to the door and summoned the Prioress.

"Put these women upon bread and water," he said, "and prepare them for the rack, that they may discover their accomplices."

Mother Matilda set her gentle face, and answered—

"It shall not be done in this Nunnery, my Lord Abbot. I know the law, and you have no such power. Moreover, if you move them hence, who are my guests, I appeal to the King, and meanwhile raise the country on you."

"Said I not that they had accomplices?" sneered the Abbot, and went his way.

But of the torture no more was heard, for that appeal to the King had an ill sound in his ears.

CHAPTER 11

Doomed

It was the day of trial. From dawn Cicely and Emlyn had seen people hurrying in and out of the gates of the Nunnery, and heard workmen making preparation in the guest-hall below their chamber. About eight one of the nuns brought them their breakfast. Her face was scared and white; she only spoke in whispers, looking behind her continually as though she knew she was being watched.

Emlyn asked who their judges were, and she answered—

"The Abbot, a strange, black-faced Prior, and the Old Bishop. Oh! God help you, my sisters; God help us all!" and she fled away.

Now for a moment Emlyn's heart failed her, since before such a tribunal what chance had they? The Abbot was their bitter enemy and accuser; the strange Prior, no doubt, one of his friends and kindred; while the ecclesiastic spoken of as the "Old Bishop" was well known as perhaps the cruellest man in England, a scourge of heretics—that is, before heresy became the fashion—a hunter-out of witches and wizards, and a time-server to boot. But to Cicely she said nothing, for what was the use, seeing that soon she would learn all?

They ate their food, knowing both of them that they would need strength. Then Cicely nursed her child, and, placing it in Emlyn's arms, knelt down to pray. While she was still praying the door opened and a procession appeared. First came two monks, then six armed men of the Abbot's guard, then the Prioress and three of her nuns. At the sight of the beautiful young woman kneeling at her prayers the guards, rough men though they were, stopped, as if unwilling to disturb her, but one of the monks cried brutally—

"Seize the accursed hypocrite, and if she will not come, drag her with you," at the same time stretching out his hand as though to grasp her arm.

But Cicely rose and faced him, saying—

"Do not touch me; I follow. Emlyn, give me the child, and let us go."

So they went in the midst of the armed men, the monks preceding, the nuns, with bowed heads, following after. Presently they entered the large hall, but on its threshold were ordered to pause while way was made for them. Cicely never forgot the sight of it as it appeared that day. The lofty, arched roof of rich chestnut-wood, set there hundreds of years before by hands that spared neither work nor timber, amongst the beams of which the bright light of morning played so clearly that she could see the spiders' webs, and in one of them a sleepy autumn wasp caught fast. The mob of people gathered to watch her public trial—faces, many of them, that she had known from childhood.

How they stared at her as she stood there by the head of the steps, her sleeping child held in her arms! They were a packed audience and had been prepared to condemn her—that she could see and hear, for did not some of them point and frown, and set up a cry of "Witch!" as they had been told to do? But it died away. The sight of her, the daughter of one of their great men and the widow of another, standing in her innocent beauty, the slumbering babe upon her breast, seemed to quell them, till the hardest faces grew pitiful—full of resentment, too, some of them, but not against her.

Then the three judges on the bench behind the table, at which sat the monkish secretaries; the hard-faced, hook-nosed "Old Bishop" in his gorgeous robes and mitre, his crosier resting against the panelling behind him, peering about him with beady eyes. The sullen, heavy-jawed Prior, from some distant county, on his left, clad in a simple black gown with a girdle about his waist. And on the right Clement Maldon, Abbot of Blossholme and enemy of her house, suave, olive-faced, foreign-looking, his black, uneasy eyes observing all, his keen ears catching every word and murmur as he whispered something to the Bishop that caused him to smile grimly. Lastly, placed already in the roped space and guarded by a soldier, poor old Bridget, the half-witted, who was gabbling words to which no one paid any heed.

The path was clear now, and they were ordered to walk on. Half-way up the hall something red attracted Cicely's attention, and, glancing round, she saw that it was the beard of Thomas Bolle. Their eyes met, and his were full of fear. In an instant she understood that he dreaded lest he should be betrayed and given over to some awful doom.

"Fear nothing," she whispered as she passed, and he heard her, or perhaps Emlyn's glance told him that he was safe. At least, a sign of relief broke from him.

Now they had entered the roped space, and stood there.

"Your name?" asked one of the secretaries, pointing to Cicely with the feather of his quill.

"All know it, it is Cicely Harflete," she answered gently, whereon the clerk said roughly that she lied, and the old wrangle began again as to the validity of her marriage, the Abbot maintaining that she was still Cicely Foterell, the mother of a base-born child.

Into this argument the Bishop entered with some zest, asking many questions, and seeming more or less to take her side, since, where matters of religion were not concerned, he was a keen lawyer, and just enough. At length, however, he swept the thing away, remarking brutally that if half he had heard were true, soon the name by which she had last been called in life would not concern her, and bade the clerks write her down as Cicely Harflete or Foterell.

Then Emlyn gave her name, and Sister Bridget's was written without question. Next the charge against them was read. It was long and technical, mixed up with Latin words and phrases, and all that Cicely made out of it was that they were accused of many horrible crimes, and of having called up the devil and consorted with him in the shape of a monster with horns and hoofs, and of her father's ghost. When it was finished they were commanded to answer, and pleaded Not Guilty, or rather Cicely and Emlyn did, for Bridget broke into a long tale that could not be followed. She was ordered to be silent, after which no one took any more heed of what she said.

Now the Bishop asked whether these women had been put to the question, and when he was told No, said that it seemed a pity, as evidently they were stubborn witches, and some discipline of the sort might have saved trouble. Again he asked if the witch's marks had been found on them—that is, the spot where the devil had sealed their bodies, on which, as was well known, his chosen could feel no pain. He even suggested that the trial should be adjourned until they had been pricked all over with a nail to find this spot, but ultimately gave up the point to save time.

A last question was raised by the beetle-browed Prior, who submitted that the infant ought also to be accused, since he, too, was said to have consorted with the devil, having, according to the story, been rescued from death by him and afterwards been carried in his arms and given to the nun Bridget, which was the only evidence against the said Bridget. If she was guilty, why, then, was the infant innocent? Ought not they to burn together, since a babe that had been nursed by the Evil One was obviously damned?

The legal-minded Bishop found this argument interesting, but ultimately decided that it was safer to overrule it on account of the tender age of the criminal. He added that it did not matter, since doubtless the foul fiend would claim his own ere long.

Lastly, before the witnesses were called, Emlyn asked for an advocate to defend them, but the Bishop replied, with a chuckle, that it was quite unnecessary, since already they had the best of all advocates—Satan himself.

"True, my Lord," said Cicely, looking up, "we have the best of all advocates, only you have mis-named him. The God of the innocent is our advocate, and in Him I trust."

"Blaspheme not, Sorceress," shouted the old man; and the evidence commenced.

To follow it in detail is not necessary, and, indeed, would be long, for it took many hours. First of all Emlyn's early life was set out, much being made of the fact that her mother was a gypsy who had committed suicide and that her father had fallen under the ban of the Inquisition, an heretical work of his having been publicly burned. Then the Abbot himself gave evidence, since, where the charge was sorcery, no one seemed to think it strange that the same man should both act as judge and be the principal witness for the prosecution. He told of Cicely's wild words after the burning of Cranwell Towers, from which burning she and her familiar, Emlyn, had evidently escaped by magic, without the aid of which it was plain they could not have lived. He told of Emlyn's threats to him after she had looked into the bowl of water; of all the dreadful things that had been seen and done at Blossholme, which no doubt these witches had brought about—here he was right—though how he knew not. He told of the death of the midwife and of the appearance which she presented afterwards—a tale that caused his audience to shudder; and, lastly, he told of the vision of the ghost of Sir John Foterell holding converse with the two accused in the chapel of the Nunnery, and its vanishing away.

When at length he had finished Emlyn asked leave to cross-examine him, but this was refused on the ground that persons accused of such crimes had no right to cross-examine.

Then the Court adjourned for a while to eat, some food being brought for the prisoners, who were forced to take it where they stood. Worse still, Cicely was driven to nurse her child in the presence of all that audience, who stared and gibed at her rudely, and were angry because Emlyn and some of the nuns stood round her to form a living screen.

When the judges returned the evidence went on. Though most

of it was entirely irrelevant, its volume was so great that at length the Old Bishop grew weary, and said he would hear no more. Then the judges went on to put, first to Cicely and afterwards to Emlyn, a series of questions of a nature so abominable that after denying the first of them indignantly, they stood silent, refusing to answer—proof positive of their guilt, as the black-browed Prior remarked in triumph. Lastly, these hideous queries being exhausted, Cicely was asked if she had anything to say.

"Somewhat," she answered; "but I am weary, and must be brief. I am no witch; I do not know what it means. The Abbot of Blossholme, who sits as my judge, is my grievous enemy. He claimed my father's lands—which lands I believe he now holds—and cruelly murdered my said father by King's Grave Mount in the forest as he was riding to London to make complaint of him and reveal his treachery to his Grace the King and his Council—"

"It is a lie, witch," broke in the Abbot, but, taking no heed, Cicely went on—

"Afterwards he and his hired soldiers attacked the house of my husband, Sir Christopher Harflete, and burnt it, slaying, or striving to slay—I know not which—my said husband, who has vanished away. Then he imprisoned me and my servant, Emlyn Stower, in this Nunnery, and strove to force me to sign papers conveying all my own and my child's property to him. This I refused to do, and therefore it is that he puts me on my trial, because, as I am told, those who are found guilty of witchcraft are stripped of all their possessions, which those take who are strong enough to keep them. Lastly, I deny the authority of this Court, and appeal to the King, who soon or late will hear my cry and avenge my wrongs, and maybe my murder, upon those who wrought them. Good people all, hear my words. I appeal to the King, and to him under God above I entrust my cause, and, should I die, the guardianship of my orphan son, whom the Abbot sent his creature to murder—his vile creature, upon whose head fell the Almighty's justice, as it will fall on yours, you slaughterers of the innocent."

So spoke Cicely, and, having spoken, worn out with fatigue and misery, sank to the floor—for all these hours there had been no stool for her to sit on—and crouched there, still holding her child in her arms—a piteous sight indeed, which touched even the superstitious hearts of the crowd who watched her.

Now this appeal of hers to the King seemed to scare the fierce Old Bishop, who turned and began to argue with the Abbot. Cicely, listening, caught some of his words, such as—

"On your head be it, then. I judge only of the cause ecclesiastic, and shall direct it to be so entered upon the records. Of the execution of the sentence or the disposal of the property I wash my hands. See you to it."

"So spoke Pilate," broke in Cicely, lifting her head and looking him in the eyes. Then she let it fall again, and was silent.

Now Emlyn opened her lips, and from them burst a fierce torrent of words.

"Do you know," she began, "who and what is this Spanish priest who sits to judge us of witchcraft? Well, I will tell you. Years ago he fled from Spain because of hideous crimes that he had committed there. Ask him of Isabella the nun, who was my father's cousin, and her end and that of her companions. Ask him of—"

At this point a monk, to whom the Abbot had whispered something, slipped behind Emlyn and threw a cloth over her face. She tore it away with her strong hands, and screamed out—

"He is a murderer, he is a traitor. He plots to kill the King. I can prove it, and that's why Foterell died—because he knew—"

The Abbot shouted something, and again the monk, a stout fellow named Ambrose, got the cloth over her mouth. Once more she wrenched herself loose, and, turning towards the people, called—

"Have I never a friend, who have befriended so many? Is there no man in Blossholme who will avenge me of this brute Ambrose? Aye, I see some."

Then this Ambrose, and others aiding him, fell upon her, striking her on the head and choking her, till at length she sank, half stunned and gasping, to the ground.

Now, after a hurried word or two with his colleagues, the Bishop sprang up, and as darkness gathered in the hall—for the sun had set—pronounced the sentence of the Court.

First he declared the prisoners guilty of the foulest witchcraft. Next he excommunicated them with much ceremony, delivering their souls to their master, Satan. Then, incidentally, he condemned their bodies to be burnt, without specifying when, how, or by whom. Out of the gloom a clear voice spoke, saying—

"You exceed your powers, Priest, and usurp those of the King. Beware!"

A tumult followed, in which some cried "Aye" and some "Nay," and when at length it died down the Bishop, or it may have been the Abbot—for none could see who spoke—exclaimed—

"The Church guards her own rights; let the King see to his."

461

"He will, he will," answered the same voice. "The Pope is in his bag. Monks, your day is done."

Again there was tumult, a very great tumult. In truth the scene, or rather the sounds, were strange. The Bishop shrieking with rage upon the bench, like a hen that has been caught upon her perch at night, the black-browed Prior bellowing like a bull, the populace surging and shouting this and that, the secretary calling for candles, and when at length one was brought, making a little star of light in that huge gloom, putting his hand to his mouth and roaring—

"What of this Bridget? Does she go free?"

The Bishop made no answer; it seemed as though he were frightened at the forces which he had let loose; but the Abbot hallooed back—

"Burn the hag with the others," and the secretary wrote it down upon his brief.

Then the guards seized the three of them to lead them away, and the frightened babe set up a thin, piercing wail, while the Bishop and his companions, preceded by one of the monks bearing the candle—it was that Ambrose who had choked Emlyn—marched in procession down the hall to gain the great door.

Ere ever they reached it the candle was dashed from the hand of Ambrose, and a fearful tumult arose in the dense darkness, for now all light had vanished. There were screams, and sounds of fighting, and cries for help. These died away; the hall emptied by degrees, for it seemed that none wished to stay there. Torches were lit, and showed a strange scene.

The Bishop, the Abbot, and the foreign Prior lay here and there, buffeted, bleeding, their robes torn off them, so that they were almost naked, while by the Bishop was his crosier, broken in two, apparently across his own head. Worse of all, the monk Ambrose leaned against a pillar; his feet seemed to go forward but his face looked backward, for his neck was twisted like that of a Michaelmas goose.

The Bishop looked about him and felt his hurts; then he called to his people—

"Bring me my cloak and a horse, for I have had enough of Blossholme and its wizardries. Settle your own matters henceforth, Abbot Maldon, for in them I find no luck," and he glanced at his broken staff.

Thus ended the great trial of the Blossholme witches.

****

Cicely had sunk to sleep at last, and Emlyn watched her, for, since there was nowhere else to put them, they were back in their own room, but guarded by armed men, lest they should escape. Of this, as Emlyn knew well, there was little chance, for even if they were once outside the Priory walls, how could they get away without friends to help, or food to eat, or horses to carry them? They would be run down within a mile. Moreover, there was the child, which Cicely would never leave, and, after all she had undergone, she herself was not fit to travel. Therefore it was that Emlyn sat sleepless, full of bitter wrath and fear, for she could see no hope. All was black as the night about them.

The door opened, and was shut and locked again. Then, from behind the curtain, appeared the tall figure of the Prioress, carrying a candle that made a star of light upon the shadows. As she stood there holding it up and looking about her, something came into Emlyn's mind. Perhaps she would help, she who loved Cicely. Did she not look like a figure of hope, with her sweet face and her taper in the gloom? Emlyn advanced to meet her, her finger on her lips.

"She sleeps; wake her not," she said. "Have you come to tell us that we burn to-morrow?"

"Nay, Emlyn; the Old Bishop has commanded that it shall not be for a week. He would have time to get across England first. Indeed, had it not been for the beating of him in the dark and the twisting of the neck of Brother Ambrose, I believe that he would not have suffered it at all, for fear of trouble afterwards. But now he is full of rage, and swears that he was set upon by evil spirits in the hall, and that those who loosed them shall not live. Emlyn, *who* killed Father Ambrose? Was it men or—?"

"Men, I think, Mother. The devil does not twist necks except in monkish dreams. Is it wonderful that my lady—the greatest lady of all these parts and the most foully treated—should have friends left to her? Why, if they were not curs, ere now her people would have pulled that Abbey stone from stone and cut the throat of every man within its walls."

"Emlyn," said the Prioress again, "in the name of Jesus and on your soul, tell me true, is there witchcraft in all this business? And if not, what is its meaning?"

"As much witchcraft as dwells in your gentle heart; no more. A man did these things; I'll not give you his name, lest it should be wrung from you. A man wore Foterell's armour, and came here by a secret hole to take counsel with us in the chapel. A man burnt the Abbey dormers and the stacks, and harried the beasts with a goatskin on his head, and dragged the skull of drunken Andrew from his grave. Doubtless it was his hand also that twisted Ambrose's neck because he struck me."

The two women looked each other in the eyes.

"Ah!" said the Prioress. "I think I can guess now; but, Emlyn, you choose rough tools. Well, fear not; your secret is safe with me." She paused a moment; then went on, "Oh! I am glad, who feared lest the Fiend's finger was in it all, as, in truth, they believe. Now I see my path clear, and will follow it to the death. Yes, yes; I will save you all or die."

"What path, Mother?"

"Emlyn, you have heard no tidings for these many months, but I have. Listen; there is much afoot. The King, or the Lord Cromwell, or both, make war upon the lesser Houses, dissolving them, seizing their goods, turning the religious out of them upon the world to starve. His Grace sends Royal Commissioners to visit them, and be judge and jury both. They were coming here, but I have friends and some fortune of my own, who was not born meanly or ill-dowered, and I found a way to buy them off. One of these Commissioners, Thomas Legh, as I heard only to-day, makes inquisition at the monastery of Bayfleet, in Yorkshire, some eighty miles away, of which my cousin, Alfred Stukley, whose letter reached me this morning, is the Prior. Emlyn, I'll go to this rough man—for rough he is, they say. Old and feeble as I am, I'll seek him out and offer up the ancient House I rule to save your life and Cicely's—yes, and Bridget's also."

"You will go, Mother! Oh! God's blessing be on you. But how will you go? They will never suffer it."

The old nun drew herself up, and answered—

"Who has the right to say to the Prioress of Blossholme that she shall not travel whither she will? No Spanish Abbot, I think. Why, but now that proud priest's servants would have forbidden me to enter your chamber in my own House, but I read them a lesson they will not forget. Also I have horses at my command, but it is true I need an escort, who am not too strong and little versed in the ways of the outside world, where I have scarcely strayed for many years. Now I have bethought me of that red-haired lay-brother, Thomas Bolle. I am told that though foolish, he is a valiant man whom few care to face; moreover, that he understands horses and knows all roads. Do you think, Emlyn Stower, that Thomas Bolle will be my companion on this journey, with leave from the Abbot, or without it?" and again she looked her in the eyes.

"He might, he might; he is a venturous man, or so I remember him in my youth," answered Emlyn. "Moreover, his forefathers have served the Harfletes and the Foterells for generations in peace and war, and doubtless, therefore, he loves my lady yonder. But the trouble is to get at him."

"No trouble at all, Emlyn; he is one of the watch outside the gate. But, woman, what token?"

Emlyn thought for a moment, then drew a ring off her finger in which was set a cornelian heart.

"Give him this," she said, "and say that the wearer bade him follow the bearer to the death, for the sake of that wearer's life and another's. He is a simple soul, and if the Abbot does not catch him first I believe that he will go."

Mother Matilda took the ring and set it on her own finger. Then she walked to where Cicely lay sleeping, looked at her and the boy upon her breast. Stretching out her thin hands, she called down the blessing and protection of Almighty God upon them both, then turned to depart.

Emlyn caught her by the robe.

"Stay," she said. "You think I do not understand; but I do. You are giving up everything for us. Even if you live through it, this House, which has been your charge for many years, will be dissolved; your sheep will be scattered to starve in their toothless age; the fold that has sheltered them for four hundred years will become a home of wolves. I understand full well, and she"—pointing to the sleeping Cicely— "will understand also."

"Say nothing to her," murmured Mother Matilda; "I may fail."

"You may fail, or you may succeed. If you fail and we burn, God shall reward you. If you succeed and we are saved, on her behalf I swear that you shall not suffer. There is wealth hidden away—wealth worth many priories; you and yours shall have your share of it, and that Commissioner shall not go lacking. Tell him that there is some small store to pay him for his trouble, and that the Abbot of Bloss-holme would rob him of it. Now, my Lady Margaret—for that, I think, used to be your name, and will be again when you have done with priests and nuns—bless me also and begone, and know that, living or dead, I hold you great and holy."

So the Prioress blessed her ere she glided thence in her stately fashion, and the oaken door opened and shut behind her.

****

Three days later the Abbot visited them alone.

"Foul and accursed witches," he said, "I come to tell you that next Monday at noon you burn upon the green in front of the Abbey gate, who, were it not for the mercy of the Church, should have been tortured also till you discovered your accomplices, of whom I think that you have many."

"Show me the King's warrant for this slaughter," said Cicely.

"I will show you nothing save the stake, witch. Repent, repent, ere it be too late. Hell and its eternal fires yawn for you."

"Do they yawn for my child also, my Lord Abbot?"

"Your brat will be taken from you ere you enter the flames and laid upon the ground, since it is baptized and too young to burn. If any have pity on it, good; if not, where it lies, there it will be buried."

"So be it," answered Cicely. "God gave it; God save it. In God I put my trust. Murderer, leave me to make my peace with Him," and she turned and walked away.

Now the Abbot and Emlyn were face to face.

"Do we really burn on Monday?" she asked.

"Without doubt, unless faggots will not take fire. Yet," he added slowly, "if certain jewels should chance to be found and handed over, the case might be remitted to another Court."

"And the torment prolonged. My Lord Abbot, I fear that those jewels will never be found."

"Well, then you burn—slowly, perhaps, for much rain has fallen of late and the wood is green. They say the death is dreadful."

"Doubtless one day you will find it so, Clement Maldonado, here or hereafter. But of that we will talk together when all is done—of that and many other things. I mean before the Judgment-seat of God. Nay, nay, I do not threaten after your fashion—it shall be so. Meanwhile I ask the boon of a dying woman. There are two whom I would see—the Prioress Matilda, in whose charge I desire to leave a certain secret, and Thomas Bolle, a lay-brother in your Abbey, a man who once engaged himself to me in marriage. For your own sake, deny me not these favours."

"They should be granted readily enough were it in my power, but it is not," answered the Abbot, looking at her curiously, for he thought that to them she might tell what she had refused to him—the hiding-place of the jewels, which afterwards he could wring out.

"Why not, my Lord Abbot?"

"Because the Prioress has gone hence, secretly, upon some journey of her own, and Thomas Bolle has vanished away I knew not where. If they, or either of them, return ere Monday you shall see them."

"And if they do not return I shall see them afterwards," replied Emlyn, with a shrug of her shoulders. "What does it matter? Fare you well till we meet at the fire, my Lord Abbot."

****

466

On the Sunday—that is, the day before the burning—the Abbot came again.

"Three days ago," he said, addressing them both, "I offered you a chance of life upon certain conditions, but, obstinate witches that you are, you refused to listen. Now I offer you the last boon in my power—not life, indeed; it is too late for that—but a merciful death. If you will give me what I seek, the executioner shall dispatch you both before the fire bites—never mind how. If not—well, as I have told you, there has been much rain, and they say the faggots are somewhat green."

Cicely paled a little—who would not, even in those cruel days?—then asked—

"And what is it that you seek, or that we can give? A confession of our guilt, to cover up your crime in the eyes of the world? If so, you shall never have it, though we burn by inches."

"Yes, I seek that, but for your own sakes, not for mine, since those who confess and repent may receive absolution. Also I seek more—the rich jewels which you have in hiding, that they may be used for the purposes of the Church."

Then it was that Cicely showed the courage of her blood.

"Never, never!" she cried, turning on him with eyes ablaze. "Torture and slay me if you will, but my wealth you shall not thieve. I know not where these jewels are, but wherever they may be, there let them lie till my heirs find them, or they rot."

The Abbot's face grew very evil.

"Is that your last word, Cicely Foterell?" he asked.

She bowed her head, and he repeated the question to Emlyn, who answered—

"What my mistress says, I say."

"So be it!" he exclaimed. "Doubtless you sorceresses put your trust in the devil. Well, we shall see if he will help you to-morrow."

"God will help us," replied Cicely in a quiet voice. "Remember my words when the time comes."

Then he went.

CHAPTER 12

The Stake

It was an awful night. Let those who have followed this history
think of the state of these two women, one of them still but a girl, who
on the morrow, amidst the jeers and curses of superstitious men, were
to suffer the cruellest of deaths for no crime at all, unless the trafficks-
ings of Emlyn with Thomas Bolle, in which Cicely had small share,
could be held a crime. Well, thousands quite as blameless were called
on to undergo that, and even worse fates in the days which some
name good and old, the days of chivalry and gallant knights, when
even little children were tormented and burned by holy and learned
folk who feared a visible or at least a tangible devil and his works.

Doubtless their cruelty was that of terror. Doubtless, although he
had other ends to gain which to him were sacred, the Abbot Maldon
did believe that Cicely and Emlyn had practised horrible witchcraft;
that they had conversed with Satan in order to revenge themselves
upon him, and therefore were too foul to live. The "Old Bishop" believed it also, and so did the black-browed Prior and the most of the
ignorant people who lived around and knew of the terrible things
which had happened in Blossholme. Had not some of them actu-
ally seen the fiend with horns and hoofs and tail driving the Abbey
cattle, and had not others met the ghost of Sir John Foterell, which
doubtless was but that fiend in another shape? Oh, these women were
guilty, without doubt they were guilty and deserved the stake! What
did it matter if the husband and father of one of them had been
murdered and the other had suffered grievous but forgotten wrongs?
Compared to witchcraft murder was but a light and homely crime,
one that would happen when men's passions and needs were involved,
quite a familiar thing.

It was an awful night. Sometimes Cicely slept a little, but the most of
it she spent in prayer. The fierce Emlyn neither slept nor prayed, except

once or twice that vengeance might fall upon the Abbot's head, for her whole soul was up in arms and it galled her to think that she and her beloved mistress must die shamefully while their enemy lived on triumphant and in honour. Even the infant seemed nervous and disturbed, as though some instinct warned it of terror at hand, for although it was well enough, against its custom it woke continually and wailed.

"Emlyn," said Cicely towards morning, but before the light had come, after at length she had soothed it to rest, "do you think that Mother Matilda will be able to help us?"

"No, no; put it from your mind, dearie. She is weak and old, the road is rough and long, and mayhap she has never reached the place. It was a great venture for her to try such a journey, and if she came there, why, perhaps the Commissioner man had gone, or perhaps he will not listen, or perhaps he cannot come. What would he care about the burning of two witches a hundred miles away, this leech who is sucking himself full upon the carcass of some fat monastery? No, no, never count on her."

"At least she is brave and true, Emlyn, and has done her best, for which may Heaven's blessing rest upon her always. Now, what of Thomas Bolle?"

"Nothing, except that he is a red-headed jackass that can bray but daren't kick," answered Emlyn viciously. "Never speak to me of Thomas Bolle. Had he been a man long ago he'd have broken the neck of that rogue Abbot instead of dressing himself up like a he-goat and hunting his cows."

"If what they say is true he did break the neck of Father Ambrose," replied Cicely, with a faint smile. "Perhaps he made a mistake in the dark."

"If so it is like Thomas Bolle, who ever wished the right thing and did the wrong. Talk no more of him, since I would not meet my end in a bad spirit. Thomas Bolle, who lets us die for his elfish pranks! A pest on the half-witted cur, say I. And after I had kissed him too!"

Cicely wondered vaguely to what she referred, then, thinking it well not to inquire, said—

"Not so, a blessing on him, say I, who saved my child from that hateful hag."

Then there was silence for a while, the matter of poor Thomas Bolle and his conduct being exhausted between them, who indeed were in no mood for argument about people whom they would never see again. At last Cicely spoke once more through the darkness—

"Emlyn, I will try to be brave; but once, do you remember, I burnt my hand as a child when I stole the sweetmeats from the cooling pot, and ah! it hurt me. I will try to die as those who went before me would have died, but if I should break down think not the less of me, for the spirit is willing though the flesh be weak."

Emlyn ground her teeth in silence, and Cicely went on—

"But that is not the worst of it, Emlyn. A few minutes and it will be over and I shall sleep, as I think, to awake elsewhere. Only if Christopher should really live, how he will mourn when he learns—"

"I pray that he does," broke in Emlyn, "for then ere long there will be a Spanish priest the less on earth and one the more in hell."

"And the child, Emlyn, the child!" she went on in a trembling voice, not heeding the interruption. "What will become of my son, the heir to so much if he had his rights, and yet so friendless? They'll murder him also, Emlyn, or let him die, which is the same thing, since how otherwise will they get title to his lands and goods?"

"If so, his troubles will be done and he will be better with you in heaven," Emlyn answered, with a dry sob. "The boy and you in heaven midst the blessed saints, and the Abbot and I in hell settling our score there with the devil for company, that's all I ask. There, there, I blaspheme, for injustice makes me mad; it clogs my heart and I throw it up in bitter words, for your sake, dear, and his, not my own. Child, you are good and gentle, to such as you the Ear of God is open. Call to him; ask for light, He will not refuse. Do you remember in the fire at the Towers, when we crouched in that vault and the walls crumbled overhead, you said you saw His angel bending over us and heard his speech. Call to Him, Cicely, and if He will not listen, hear me. I have a means of death about me. Ask not what it is, but if at the end I turn on you and strike, blame me not here or hereafter, for it will be love's blow, my last service."

It seemed as though Cicely did not understand those heavy words, at the least she took no heed of them.

"I'll pray again," she whispered, "though I fear that heaven's doors are closed to me; no light comes through," and she knelt down.

For long, long she prayed, till at length weariness overcame her, and Emlyn heard her breathing softly like one asleep.

"Let her sleep," she murmured to herself. "Oh! if I were sure—she should never wake again to see the dawn. I have half a mind to do it, but there it is, I am not sure. If there is a God He will never suffer such a thing. I'd have paid the jewels, but what's the use? They would have killed her all the same, for else where's their title? No, my heart bids me wait."

Cicely awoke.

"Emlyn," she said in a low, thrilling voice, "do you hear me, Emlyn? That angel has been with me again. He spoke to me," and she paused.

"Well, well, what did he say?"

"I don't know, Emlyn," she answered, confused; "it has gone from me. But, Emlyn, have no fear, all is well with us, and not only with us but with Christopher and the babe also. Oh, yes, with Christopher and the babe also," and she let her fair head fall upon the couch and burst into a flood of happy tears. Then, rising, she took up the child and kissed it, laid herself down and slept sweetly.

Just then the dawn broke, a glorious dawn, and Emlyn held out her arms to it in an ecstasy of gratitude. For with that light her terror passed away as the darkness passed. She believed that God had spoken to Cicely and for a while her heart was at peace.

****

When about eight o'clock that morning the door was opened to allow a nun to bring them their food, she saw a sight which filled her with amazement. Her own eyes, poor woman, were red with tears, for, like all in the Priory, she loved Cicely, whom as a child she had nursed on her knee, and with the other sisters had spent a sleepless night in prayer for her, for Emlyn, and for Bridget, who was to be burned with them. She had expected to find the victims prostrate and perhaps senseless with fear, but behold! there they sat together in the window-place, dressed in their best garments and talking quietly. Indeed, as she entered one of them—it was Cicely—laughed a little at something that the other had said.

"Good-morning to you, Sister Mary," said Cicely. "Tell me now, has the Prioress returned?"

"Nay, nay, we know not where she is; no word has come from her. Well, at least she will be spared a dreadful sight. Have you any message for her ear? If so, give it swiftly ere the guard call me."

"I thank you," said Cicely; "but I think that I shall be the bearer of my own messages."

"What? Do you, then, mean that our Mother is dead? Must we suffer woe upon woe? Oh! who could have told you these sorrowful tidings?"

"No, sister, I think that she is alive and that I, yet living, shall talk with her again."

Sister Mary looked bewildered, for how, she wondered, could close prisoners know these things? Staring round to see that she was not observed, she thrust two little packets into Cicely's hand.

"Wear these at the last, both of you," she whispered. "Whatever they say we believe you innocent, and for your sake we have done a great crime. Yes, we have opened the reliquary and taken from it our most precious treasure, a fragment of the cord that bound St. Catherine to the wheel, and divided it into three, one strand for each of you. Perhaps, if you are really guiltless, it will work a miracle. Perhaps the fire will not burn or the rain will extinguish it, or the Abbot may relent."

"That last would be the greatest miracle of all," broke in Emlyn, with grim humour. "Still we thank you from our hearts and will wear the relics if they do not take them from us. Hark! they are calling you. Farewell, and all blessings be on your gentle heads."

Again the loud voices of the guards called, and Sister Mary turned and fled, wondering if these women were not witches, how it came about that they could be so brave, so different from poor Bridget, who wailed and moaned in her cell below.

Cicely and Emlyn ate their food with good appetite, knowing that they would need support that day, and when it was done sat themselves again by the window-place, through which they could see hundreds of people, mounted and on foot, passing up the slope that led to the green in front of the Abbey, though this green they could not see because of a belt of trees.

"Listen," said Emlyn presently. "It is hard to say, but it may be that your vision of the night was but a merciful dream, and, if so, within a few hours we shall be dead. Now I have the secret of the hiding-place of those jewels, which, without me, none can ever find; shall I pass it on, if I get the chance, to one whom I can trust? Some good soul—the nuns, perhaps—will surely shelter your boy, and he might need them in days to come."

Cicely thought a while, then answered—

"Not so, Emlyn. I believe that God has spoken to me by His angel, as He spoke to Peter in the prison. To do this would be to tempt God, showing that we have no trust in Him. Let that secret lie where it is, in your breast."

"Great is your faith," said Emlyn, looking at her with admiration. "Well, I will stand or fall by it, for I think there is enough for two."

The Convent bell chimed ten, and they heard a sound of feet and voices below.

"They come for us," said Emlyn; "the burning is set for eleven, that after the sight folk may get away in comfort to their dinners. Now summon that great Faith of yours and hold him fast for both our sakes, since mine grows faint."

The door opened and through it came monks followed by guards, the officer of whom bade them rise and follow. They obeyed without speaking, Cicely throwing her cloak about her shoulders.

"You'll be warm enough without that, Witch," said the man, with a hideous chuckle.

"Sir," she answered, "I shall need it to wrap my child in when we are parted. Give me the babe, Emlyn. There, now we are ready; nay, no need to lead us, we cannot escape and shall not vex you."

"God's truth, the girl has spirit!" muttered the officer to his companions, but one of the priests shook his head and answered—

"Witchcraft! Satan will leave them presently."

A few more minutes and, for the first time during all those weary months, they passed the gate of the Priory. Here the third victim was waiting to join them, poor, old, half-witted Bridget, clad in a kind of sheet, for her habit had been stripped off. She was wild-eyed and her grey locks hung loose about her shoulders, as she shook her ancient head and screamed prayers for mercy. Cicely shivered at the sight of her, which indeed was dreadful.

"Peace, good Bridget," she said as they passed, "being innocent, what have you to fear?"

"The fire, the fire!" cried the poor creature. "I dread the fire."

Then they were led to their place in the procession and saw no more of Bridget for a while, although they could not escape the sound of her lamentations behind them.

It was a great procession. First went the monks and choristers, singing a melancholy Latin dirge. Then came the victims in the midst of a guard of twelve armed men, and after these the nuns who were forced to be present, while behind and about were all the folk for twenty miles round, a crowd without number. They crossed the footbridge, where stood the Ford Inn for which the Flounder had bargained as the price of murder. They walked up the rise by the right of way, muddy now with the autumn rains, and through the belt of trees where Thomas Bolle's secret passage had its exit, and so came at last to the green in front of the towering Abbey portal.

Here a dreadful sight awaited them, for on this green were planted three fourteen-inch posts of new-felled oak six feet or more in height, such as no fire would easily burn through, and around each of them a kind of bower of faggots open to the front. Moreover, to the posts hung new wagon chains, and near by stood the village blacksmith and his apprentice, who carried a hand anvil and a sledge hammer for the cold welding of those chains.

At a distance from these stakes the procession was halted. Then out from the gate of the Abbey came the Abbot in his robes and mitre, preceded by acolytes and followed by more monks. He advanced to where the condemned women stood and halted, while a friar stepped forward and read their sentence to them, of which, being in Latin or in crabbed, legal words, they understood nothing at all. Then in sonorous tones he adjured them for the sake of their sinful souls to make full confession of their guilt, that they might receive pardon before they suffered in the flesh for their hideous crime of sorcery.

To this invitation Cicely and Emlyn shook their heads, saying that being innocent of any sorceries they had nothing to confess. But old Bridget gave another answer. She declared in a high, screaming voice that she was a witch, as her mother and grandmother had been before her. She described, while the crowd listened with intense interest, how Emlyn Stower had introduced her to the devil, who was clad in red hose and looked like a black boy with a hump on his back and a tuft of red hair hanging from his nose, also many unedifying details of her interviews with this same fiend.

Asked what he said to her, she answered that he told her to bewitch the Abbot of Blossholme because he was such a holy man that God had need of him and he did too much good upon the earth. Also he prevented Emlyn Stower and Cicely Foterell from working his, the devil's, will, and enabled them to keep alive the baby who would be a great wizard. He told her moreover that midwife Megges was an angel (here the crowd laughed) sent to kill the said infant, who really was his own child, as might be seen by its black eyebrows and cleft tongue, also its webbed feet, and that he would appear in the shape of the ghost of Sir John Foterell to save it and give it to her, which he did, saying the Lord's Prayer backwards, and that she must bring it up "in the faith of the Pentagon."

Thus the poor crazed thing raved on, while sentence by sentence a scribe wrote down her gibberish, causing her at last to make her mark to it, all of which took a very long time. At the end she begged that she might be pardoned and not burnt, but this, she was informed, was impossible. Thereon she became enraged and asked why then had she been led to tell so many lies if after all she must burn, a question at which the crowd roared with laughter. On hearing this the priest, who was about to absolve her, changed his mind and ordered her to be fastened to her stake, which was done by the blacksmith with the help of his apprentice and his portable anvil.

Still, her "confession" was solemnly read over to Cicely and Emlyn, who were asked whether, after hearing it, they still persisted in a denial of their guilt. By way of answer Cicely lifted the hood from her boy's face and showed that his eyebrows were not black, but light-coloured. Also she bared his feet, passing her little finger between his toes, and asking them if they were webbed. Some of them answered, "No," but a monk roared, "What of that? Cannot Satan web and unweb?" Then he snatched the infant from Cicely's arms and laid it down upon the stump of an oak that had been placed there to receive it, crying out—

"Let this child live or die as God pleases."

Some brute who stood by aimed a blow at it with a stick, yelling, "Death to the witch's brat!" but a big man, whom Emlyn recognized as one of old Sir John's tenants, caught the falling stick from his hand and dealt him such a clout with it that he fell like a stone, and went for the rest of his life with but one eye and the nose flattened on the side of his face. Thenceforward no one tried to harm the babe, who, as all know, because of what befell him on this day, went in after life by the nickname of Christopher Oak-stump.

The Abbot's men stepped forward to tie Cicely to her stake, but ere they laid hands on her she took off her wool-lined cloak and threw it to the yeoman who had struck down the fellow with his own stick, saying—

"Friend, wrap my boy in this and guard him till I ask him from you again."

"Aye, Lady," answered the great man, bending his knee; "I have served the grandsire and the sire, and so I'll serve the son," and throwing aside the stick he drew a sword and set himself in front of the oak boll where the infant lay. Nor did any venture to meddle with him, for they saw other men of a like sort ranging themselves about him.

Now slowly enough the smith began to rivet the chain round Cicely.

"Man," she said to him, "I have seen you shoe many of my father's nags. Who could have thought that you would live to use your honest skill upon his daughter!"

On hearing these words the fellow burst into tears, cast down his tools and fled away, cursing the Abbot. His apprentice would have followed, but him they caught and forced to complete the task. Then Emlyn was chained up also, so that at length all was ready for the last terrible act of the drama.

Now the head executioner—he was the Abbey cook—placed some pine splinters to light in a brazier that stood near by, and while waiting for the word of command, remarked audibly to his mate that there was a good wind and that the witches would burn briskly.

The spectators were ordered back out of earshot, and went at last, some of them muttering sullenly to each other. For here the company could not be picked as it had been at the trial, and the Abbot noted anxiously that among them the victims had many friends. It was time the deed was done ere their smouldering love and pity flowed out into bloody tumult, he thought to himself. So, advancing quickly, he stood in front of Emlyn and asked her in a low voice if she still refused to give up the secret of the jewels, seeing that there was yet time for him to command that they should die mercifully and not by the fire.

"Let the mistress judge, not the maid," answered Emlyn in a steady voice.

He turned and repeated the question to Cicely, who replied—

"Have I not told you—never. Get you behind me, O evil man, and go, repent your sins ere it be too late."

The Abbot stared at her, feeling that such constancy and courage were almost superhuman. He had an acute, imaginative mind which could fancy himself in like case and what his state would be. Though he was in such haste a great curiosity entered into him to know whence she drew her strength, which even then he tried to satisfy.

"Are you mad or drugged, Cicely Foterell?" he asked. "Do you not know how fire will feel when it eats up that delicate flesh of yours?"

"I do not know and I shall never know," she answered quietly.

"Do you mean that you will die before it touches you, building on some promise of your master, Satan?"

"Yes, I shall die before the fire touches me; but not here and now, and I build upon a promise from the Master of us all in heaven."

He laughed, a shrill, nervous laugh, and called out loud to the people around—

"This witch says that she will not burn, for Heaven has promised it to her. Do you not, Witch?"

"Yes, I say so; bear witness to my words, good people all," replied Cicely in clear and ringing tones.

"Well, we'll see," shouted the Abbot. "Man, bring flame, and let Heaven—or hell—help her if it can!"

The cook-executioner blew at his brands, but he was nervous, or clumsy, and a minute or more went by before they flamed. At length one was fit for the task, and unwillingly enough he stooped to lift it up.

Then it was that in the midst of the intense silence, for of all that multitude none seemed even to breathe, and old Bridget, who had fainted, cried no more, a bull's voice was heard beyond the brow of the hill, roaring—

"In the King's name, stay! In the King's name, stay!"

All turned to look, and there between the trees appeared a white horse, its sides streaked with blood, that staggered rather than galloped towards them, and on the horse a huge, red-bearded man, clad in mail and holding in his hand a woodman's axe.

"Fire the faggots!" shouted the Abbot, but the cook, who was not by nature brave, had already let fall his torch, which went out on the damp ground.

By now the horse was rushing through them, treading them under foot. With great, convulsive bounds it reached the ring and, as the rider leapt from its back, rolled over and lay there panting, for its strength was done.

"It is Thomas Bolle!" exclaimed a voice, while the Abbot cried again—

"Fire the faggots! Fire the faggots!" and a soldier ran to fetch another brand.

But Thomas was before him. Snatching up the brazier by its legs he smote downwards with it so that the burning charcoal fell all about the soldier and the iron cage remained fixed upon his head, shouting as he smote—

"You sought fire—take it!"

The man rolled upon the ground screaming in pain and terror till some one dragged the cage off his head, leaving his face barred like a grilled herring. None took further heed of what became of him, for now Thomas Bolle stood in front of the stakes waving his great axe, and repeating, "In the King's name, stay! In the King's name, stay!"

"What mean you, knave?" exclaimed the furious Abbot.

"What I say, Priest. One step nearer and I'll split your crown."

The Abbot fell back and Thomas went on—

"A Foterell! A Foterell! A Harflete! A Harflete! O ye who have eaten their bread, come, scatter these faggots and save their flesh. Who'll stand with me against Maldon and his butchers?"

"I," answered voices, "and I, and I, and I!"

"And I too," hallooed the yeoman by the oak stump, "only I watch the child. Nay, by God I'll bring it with me!" and, snatching up the screaming babe under his left arm, he ran to him.

On came the others also, hurling the faggots this way and that.

"Break the chains," roared Bolle again, and somehow those strong hands did it; indeed, the only hurt that Cicely took that day was from their hacking at these chains. They were loose. Cicely snatched the child from the yeoman, who was glad enough to be rid of it, having other work to do, for now the Abbot's men-at-arms were coming on.

"Ring the women round," roared Bolle, "and strike home for Foterell, strike home for Harflete! Ah, priest's dog, in the King's name—this!" and the axe sank up to the haft into the breast of the captain who had told Cicely that she would be warm enough that day without her cloak.

Then there began a great fight. The party of Foterell, of whom there may have been a score, captained by Bolle, made a circle round the three green oak stakes, within which stood Cicely and Emlyn and old Bridget, still tied to her post, for no one had thought or found time to cut her loose. These were attacked by the Abbot's guard, thirty or more of them, urged on by Maldon himself, who was maddened by the rescue of his victims and full of fear lest Cicely's words should be fulfilled and she herself set down henceforth, not as a witch, but as a prophetess favoured by God.

On came the soldiers and were beaten back. Thrice they came on and thrice they were beaten back with loss, for Bolle's axe was terrible to face and, now that they had found a leader and their courage, the yeoman lads who stood with him were sturdy fighters. Also tumult broke out among the hundreds who watched, some of them taking one side and some the other, so that they fell upon each other with sticks and stones and fists, even the women joining in the fray, biting and tearing like bagged cats. The scene was hideous and the sounds those of a sacked city, for many were hurt and all gave tongue, while shrill and clear above this hateful music rose the yells of Bridget, who had awakened from her faint and imagined all was over and that she fathomed hell.

Thrice the attackers were rolled back, but of those who defended a third were down, and now the Abbot took another counsel.

"Bring bows," he cried, "and shoot them, for they have none!" and men ran off to do his bidding.

Then it was that Emlyn's wit came to their aid, for when Bolle shook his red head and gasped out that he feared they were lost, since how could they fight against arrows, she answered—

"If so, why stand here to be spitted, fool? Come, let us cut our way through ere the shafts begin to fly, and take refuge among the trees or in the Nunnery."

"Women's counsel is good sometimes," said Bolle. "Form up, Foterells, and march."

"Nay," broke in Cicely, "loose Bridget first, lest they should burn her after all; I'll not stir else."

So Bridget was hacked free, and together with the wounded men, of whom there were several, dragged and supported thence. Then began a running fight, but one in which they still held their own. Yet they would have been overwhelmed at last, for the women and the wounded hampered them, had not help come. For as they hewed their path towards the belt of trees with the Abbot's fierce fellows, some of whom were French or Spanish, hanging on their flanks, suddenly, in the gap where the roadway ran, appeared a horse galloping and on it a woman, who clung to its mane with both hands, and after her many armed men.

"Look, Emlyn, look!" exclaimed Cicely. "Who is that?" for she could not believe her eyes.

"Who but Mother Matilda," answered Emlyn; "and by the saints, she is a strange sight!"

A strange sight she was indeed, for her hood was gone, her hair, that was ever so neat, flew loose, her robe was ruckled up about her knees, the rosary and crucifix she wore streamed on the air behind her and beat against her back, and her garb had burst open at the front; in short, never was holy, aged Prioress seen in such a state before. Down she came on them like a whirlwind, for her frightened horse scented its Blossholme stable, clinging grimly to her unaccustomed seat, and crying as she sped—

"For God's love, stop this mad beast!"

Bolle caught it by the bridle and threw it to its haunches so that, its rider speeding on, flew over its head on to the broad breast of the yeoman who had watched the child, and there rested thankfully. For, as Mother Matilda said afterwards with her gentle smile, never before did she know what comfort there was to be found in man.

When at length she loosed her arms from about his neck the yeoman stood her on her feet, saying that this was worse than the baby, and her wandering eyes fell upon Cicely.

"So I am in time! Oh! never more will I revile that horse," she exclaimed, and sinking to her knees then and there she gasped out some prayer of thankfulness. Meanwhile, those who followed her had reined up in front, and the Abbot's soldiers with the accompanying crowd had halted behind, not knowing what to make of these strangers, so that Bolle and his party with the women were now between the two.

From among the new-comers rode out a fat, coarse man, with a pompous air as of one who is accustomed to be obeyed, who inquired in a laboured voice, for he was breathless from hard riding, what all this turmoil meant.

"Ask the Abbot of Blossholme," said some one, "for it is his work."

"Abbot of Blossholme? That's the man I want," puffed the fat stranger. "Appear, Abbot of Blossholme, and give account of these do-ings. And you fellows," he added to his escort, "range up and be ready, lest this said priest should prove contumacious."

Now the Abbot stepped forward with some of his monks and, looking the horseman up and down, said—

"Who may it be that demands account so roughly of a consecrated Abbot?"

"A consecrated Abbot? A consecrated peacock, a tumultuous, tur-bulent, traitorous priest, a Spanish rogue ruffler who, I am told, keeps about him a band of bloody mercenaries to break the King's peace and slay loyal English folk. Well, consecrated Abbot, I'll tell you who I am. I am Thomas Legh, his Grace's Visitor and Royal Commissioner to inspect the Houses called religious, and I am come hither upon complaint made by yonder Prioress of Blossholme Nunnery, as to your dealings with certain of his Highness's subjects whom, she says, you have accused of witchcraft for purposes of revenge and unlawful gain. That is who I am, my fine fowl of an Abbot."

Now when he heard this pompous speech the rage in Maldon's face was replaced by fear, for he knew of this Doctor Legh and his mission, and understood what Thomas Bolle had meant by his cry of, "In the King's name!"

CHAPTER 13

The Messenger

"Who makes all this tumult?" shouted the Commissioner. "Why do I see blood and wounds and dead men? And how were you about to handle these women, one of whom by her mien is of no low degree?" and he stared at Cicely.

"The tumult," answered the Abbot, "was caused by yonder fool, Thomas Bolle, a lay-brother of my monastery, who rushed among us armed and shouting 'In the King's name, stay.'"

"Then why did you not stay, Sir Abbot? Is the King's name one to be mocked at? Know that I sent on the man."

"He had no warrant, Sir Commissioner, unless his bull's voice and great axe are a warrant, and I did not stay because we were doing justice upon the three foulest witches in the realm."

"Doing justice? Whose justice and what justice? Say, had you a warrant for your justice? If so, show it me."

"These witches have been condemned by a Court Ecclesiastic, the judges being a bishop, a prior and myself, and in pursuance of that judgment were about to suffer for their sins by fire," replied Maldon.

"A Court Ecclesiastic!" roared Dr. Legh. "Can Courts Ecclesiastic, then, toast free English folk to death? If you would not stand your trial for attempted murder, show me your warrant signed by his Grace the King, or by his Justices of Assize. What! You do not answer. Have you none? I thought as much. Oho, Clement Maldon, you hang-faced Spanish dog, learn that eyes have been on you for long, and now it seems that you would usurp the King's prerogative besides—" and he checked himself, then went on, "Seize that priest, and keep him fast while I make inquiry of this business."

Now some of the Commissioner's guard surrounded Maldon, nor did his own men venture to interfere with them, for they had enough of fighting and were frightened by this talk about the King's warrant.

Then the Commissioner turned to Cicely, and said—

"You are Sir John Foterell's only child, are you not, who allege yourself to be wife to Sir Christopher Harflete, or so says yonder Prioress? Now, what was about to happen to you, and why?"

"Sir," answered Cicely, "I and my waiting-woman and the old sister, Bridget, were condemned to die by fire at those stakes upon a charge of sorcery. Although it is true," she added, "that I knew we should not perish thus."

"How did you know that, Lady? By all tokens your bodies and hot flame were near enough together," and he glanced towards the stakes and the scattered faggots.

"Sir, I knew it because of a vision that God sent to me in my sleep last night."

"Aye, she swore that at the stake," exclaimed a voice, "and we thought her mad."

"Now can you deny that she is a witch?" broke in Maldon. "If she were not one of Satan's own, how could she see visions and prophecy her own deliverance?"

"If visions and prophecies are proof of witchcraft, then, Priest, all Holy Writ is but a seething pot of sorcery," answered Legh. "Then the Blessed Virgin and St. Elizabeth were witches, and Paul and John should have been burnt as wizards. Continue, Lady, leaving out your dreams until a more convenient time."

"Sir," went on Cicely, "we have worked no sorcery, and my crime is that I will not name my child a bastard and sign away my lands and goods to yonder Abbot, the murderer of my father and perhaps of my husband. Oh! listen, listen, you and all folk here, and briefly as I may I will tell my tale. Have I your leave to speak?"

The Commissioner nodded, and she set out her story from the beginning, so sweetly, so simply and with such truth and earnestness, that the concourse of people packed close about her, hung upon her every word, and even Dr. Legh's coarse face softened as he heard. For the half of an hour or more she spoke, telling of her father's death, of her flight and marriage, of the burning of Cranwell Towers, and her widowing, if such it were; of her imprisonment in the Priory and the Abbot's dealings with her and Emlyn; of the birth of her child and its attempted murder by the midwife, his creature; of their trial and condemnation, they being innocent, and of all they had endured that day.

"If you are innocent," shouted a priest as she paused for breath, "what was that Thing dressed in the livery of Satan which worked evil at Blossholme? Did we not see it with our eyes?"

Just then some one uttered an exclamation and pointed to the shadow of the trees where a strange form was moving. Another moment and it came out into the light. One more and all that multitude scattered like frightened sheep, rushing this way and that; yes, even the horses took the bits between their teeth and bolted. For there, visible to all, Satan himself strolled towards them. On his head were horns, behind his back hung down a tail, his body was shaggy like a beast's, and his face hideous and of many colours, while in his hand he held a pronged fork with a long handle. This way and that rushed the throng, only the Commissioner, who had dismounted, stood still, perhaps because he was too afraid to stir, and with him the women and some of the nuns, including the Prioress, who fell upon their knees and began to utter prayers.

On came the dreadful thing till it reached the King's Visitor, bowing to him and bellowing like a bull, then very deliberately untied some strings and let its horrid garb fall off, revealing the person of Thomas Bolle!

"What means this mummery, knave?" gasped Dr. Legh.

"Mummery do you call it, sir?" answered Thomas with a grin. "Well, if so, 'tis on the faith of such mummery that priests burn women in merry England. Come, good people, come," he roared in his great voice, "come, see Satan in the flesh. Here are his horns," and he held them up, "once they grew upon the head of Widow Johnson's billy-goat. Here's his tail, many a fly has it flicked off the belly of an Abbey cow. Here's his ugly mug, begotten of parchment and the paint-box. Here's his dreadful fork that drives the damned to some hotter corner; it has been death to whole stones of eels down in the marsh-fleet yonder. I have some hell-fire too among the bag of tricks; you'll make the best of brimstone and a little oil dried out upon the hearth. Come, see the devil all complete and naught to pay."

Back trooped the crowd a little fearfully, taking the properties which he held, and handling them, till first one and then all of them began to laugh.

"Laugh not," shouted Bolle. "Is it a matter of laughter that noble ladies and others whose lives are as dear to some," and he glanced at Emlyn, "should grill like herrings because a poor fool walks about clad in skins to keep out the cold and frighten villains? Hark you, I played this trick. I am Beelzebub, also the ghost of Sir John Foterell. I entered the Priory chapel by a passage that I know, and saved yonder babe from murder and scared the murderess down to hell; yes, from the sham devil to the true. Why did I do it? Well, to protect the innocent and scourge the wicked in his pride. But the wicked seized the innocent and the innocent said nothing, fearing lest I should suffer with them, and—O God, you know the rest!

"It was a near thing, a very near thing, but I'm not the half-wit I've feigned to be for years. Moreover, I had a good horse and a heavy axe, and there are still true hearts round Blossholme; the dead men that lie yonder show it. Heaven has still its angels on the earth, though they wear strange shapes. There stands one of them, and there another," and he pointed first to the fat and pompous Visitor, and next to the dishevelled Prioress, adding: "And now, Sir Commissioner, for all that I have done in the cause of justice I ask pardon of you who wear the King's grace and majesty as I wore old Nick's horns and hoofs, since otherwise the Abbot and his hired butchers, who hold themselves masters of King and people, will murder me for this as they have done by better men. Therefore pardon, your Mightiness, pardon," and he kneeled down before him.

"You have it, Bolle; in the King's name you have it," replied Legh, who was more flattered by the titles and attributes poured upon him by the cunning Thomas than a closer consideration might have warranted. "For all that you have done, or left undone, I, the Commissioner of his Grace, declare that you shall go scot free and that no action criminal or civil shall lie against you, and this my secretary shall give to you in writing. Now, good fellow, rise, but steal Satan's plumes no more lest you should feel his claws and beak, for he is an ill fowl to mock. Bring hither that Spaniard Maldon. I have somewhat to say to him."

Now they looked this way and that, but no Abbot could they see. The guards swore that they had never taken eye off him, even when they all ran before the devil, yet certainly he was gone.

"The knave has given us the slip," bellowed the Commissioner, who was purple with rage. "Search for him! Seize him, for which my command shall be your warrant. Draw the wood. I'll to the Abbey, where perchance the fox has gone to earth. Five golden crowns to the man who nets the slimy traitor."

Now every one, burning with zeal to show their loyalty and to win the crowns, scattered on the search, so that presently the three "witches," Thomas Bolle, Mother Matilda, and the nuns, were left standing almost alone and staring at each other and the dead and wounded men who lay about.

"Let us to the Priory," said Mother Matilda, "for by the sun I judge that it is time for evening prayer, and there seem to be none to hinder us."

Thomas went to her horse, which grazed close at hand, and led it up. "Nay, good friend," she exclaimed, with energy, "while I live no more of that evil beast for me. Henceforth I'll walk till I am carried. Keep it, Thomas, as a gift; it is bought and paid for. Sister, your arm."

"Have I done well, Emlyn?" Bolle asked, as he tightened the girths.

"I don't know," she answered, looking at him sideways. "You played the cur at first, leaving us to burn for your sins, but afterwards, well, you found the wits you say you never lost. Also your manners mended, and yonder captain knave learned that you can handle an axe, so we'll say no more about it, lad, for doubtless that Abbot and his spies were sore task-masters and broke your spirit with their penances and talk of hell to come. Here, lift my lady on to this horse, for she is spent, and let me lean upon your shoulder, Thomas. It's weary work standing at a stake."

****

Cicely's recollections of the remainder of that day were always shadowy and tangled. She remembered a prayer of thanksgiving in which she took small part with her lips, she whose heart was one great thanksgiving. She remembered the good sister who had given them the relics of St. Catherine assuring her, as she received them back with care, that these and these alone had worked the miracle and saved their lives. She remembered eating food and straining her boy to her breast, and then she remembered no more till she woke to see the morning sun streaming into that same room whence on the previous day they had been led out to suffer the most horrible of deaths.

Yes, she woke, and see, near by was Emlyn making ready her garments, as she had done these many years, and at her side lay the boy crowing in the sunlight and waving his little arms, the blessed boy who knew not the terrors he had passed. At first she thought that she had dreamed a very evil dream, till by degrees all the truth came back to her, and she shivered at its memory, yes, even as the weight of it rolled off her heart she shivered and whitened like an aspen in the wind. Then she rose and thanked God for His mercies, which were great.

Oh, if the strength of that horse of Thomas Bolle's had failed one short five minutes sooner, she, in whom the red blood still ran so healthily, would have been but a handful of charred bones. Or if her faith had left her so that she had yielded to the Abbot and shortened all his talk at the place of burning, then Bolle would have come too late. But it proved sufficient to her need, and for this also truly she should be thankful to its Giver.

After they had eaten, a message came to them from the Prioress, who desired to see them in her chamber. Thither they went, rejoiced to find that they were no longer prisoners but had liberty to come and go, and found her seated in a tall chair, for she was too stiff to walk. Cicely ran to her, knelt down and kissed her, and she laid her left hand upon her head in blessing, for the right was cut with the chafing of the reins.

"Surely, Cicely," she said, smiling, "it is I who should kneel to you, were I in any state to do so. For now I have heard all the tale, and it seems that we have a prophetess among us, one favoured with visions from on high, which visions have been most marvellously fulfilled."

"That is so, Mother," she answered briefly, for this was a matter of which she would never talk at length, either then or thereafter, "but the fulfilment came through you."

"My daughter, I was but the minister, you were the chosen seer, still let the holy business lie a while. Perhaps you will tell me of it afterwards, and meantime the world and its affairs press us hard. Your deliverance has been bought at no small cost, my daughter, for know that yonder coarse and ungodly man, the King's Visitor, told me as we rode that this Nunnery must be dissolved, its house and revenues seized, and I and my sisters turned out to starve in our old age. Indeed, to bring him here at all I was forced to petition that it might be so in a writing that I signed. See, then, how great is my love for you, dear Cicely."

"Mother," she answered, "it cannot be, it shall not be."

"Alas! child, how will you prevent it? These Visitors, and those who commission them, are hungry folk. I hear they take the lands and goods of poor religious such as we are, and if these are fortunate, give one or two of them a little pittance to get bread. Once I had moneys of my own, but I spent them to buy back the Valley Farm which the Abbot had seized, and of late to satisfy his extortions," and she wept a little.

"Mother, listen. I have wealth hidden away, I know not where exactly, but Emlyn knows. It is my very own, the Carfax jewels that came to me from my mother. It was because of these that we were brought to the stake, since the Abbot offered us life in return for them, and when it was too late to save us, a more merciful death than that by fire. But I forbade Emlyn to yield the secret; something in my heart told me to do so, now I know why. Mother, the price of those gems shall buy back your lands, and mayhap buy also permission from his Grace the King for the continuance of your house, where you and yours shall worship as those who went before you have done for many generations. I swear it in my own name and in that of my child and of my husband also—if he lives."

"Your husband if he lives might need this wealth, sweet Cicely."

"Then, Mother, except to save his life, or liberty or honour, I tell you I will refuse it to him, who, when he learns what you have done for me and our son, would give it you and all else he has besides—nay, would pay it as an honourable debt."

"Well, Cicely, in God's name and my own I thank you, and we'll see, we'll see! Only be advised, lest Dr. Legh should learn of this treasure. But where is it, Emlyn? Fear not to tell me who can be secret, for it is well that more than one should know, and I think that your danger is past."

"Yes, speak, Emlyn," said Cicely, "for though I never asked before, fearing my own weakness, I am curious. None can hear us here."

"Then, Mistress, I will tell you. You remember that on the day of the burning of Cranwell we sought refuge on the central tower, whence I carried you senseless to the vault. Now in that vault we lay all night, and while you swooned I searched with my fingers till I found a stone that time and damp had loosened, behind which was a hollow. In that hollow I hid the jewels that I carried wrapt in silk in the bosom of my robe. Then I filled up the hole with dust scraped from the floor, and replaced the stone, wedging it tight with bits of mortar. It is the third stone counting from the eastern angle in the second course above the floor line. There I set them, and there doubtless they lie to this day, for unless the tower is pulled down to its foundations none will ever find them in that masonry."

At this moment there came a knocking on the door. When it was opened by Emlyn a nun entered, saying that the King's Visitor demanded to speak with the Prioress.

"Show him here since I cannot come to him," said Mother Matilda, "and you, Cicely and Emlyn, bide with me, for in such company it is well to have witnesses."

A minute later Dr. Legh appeared accompanied by his secretaries, gorgeously attired and puffing from the stairs.

"To business, to business," he said, scarcely stopping to acknowledge the greetings of the Prioress. "Your convent is sequestrated upon your own petition, Madam, therefore I need not stop to make the usual inquiries, and indeed I will admit that from all I hear it has a good repute, for none allege scandal against you, perhaps because you are all too old for such follies. Produce now your deeds, your terrier of lands and your rent-rolls, that I may take them over in due form and dissolve the sisterhood."

"I will send for them, Sir," answered the Prioress humbly; "but, meanwhile, tell us what we poor religious are to do? I am turned sixty years of age, and have dwelt in this house for forty of them; none of my sisters are young, and some of them are older than myself. Whither shall we go?"

"Into the world, Madam, which you will find a fine, large place. Cease snuffling prayers and from all vulgar superstitions—by the way, forget not to hand over any reliquaries of value, or any papistical emblems in precious metals that you may possess, including images, of which my secretaries will take account—and go out into the world. Marry there if you can find husbands, follow useful trades there. Do what you will there, and thank the King who frees you from the encumbrance of silly vows and from the circle of a convent's walls."

"To give us liberty to starve outside of them. Sir, do you understand your work? For hundreds of years we have sat at Blossholme, and during all those generations have prayed to God for the souls of men and ministered to their bodies. We have done no harm to any creature, and what wealth came to us from the earth or from the benefactions of the pious we have dispensed with a liberal hand, taking nothing for ourselves. The poor by multitudes have fed at our gates, their sick we have nursed, their children we have taught; often we have gone hungry that they might be full. Now you drive us forth in our age to perish. If that is the will of God, so be it, but what must chance to England's poor?"

"That is England's business, Madam, and the poor's. Meanwhile I have told you that I have no time to waste, since I must away to London to make report concerning this Abbot of yours, a veritable rogue, of whose villainous plots I have discovered many things. I pray you send a messenger to bid them hurry with the deeds."

Just then a nun entered bearing a tray, on which were cakes and wine. Emlyn took it from her, and pouring the wine into cups offered them to the Visitor and his secretaries.

"Good wine," he said, after he had drunk, "a very generous wine. You nuns know the best in liquor; be careful, I pray you, to include it in your inventory. Why, woman, are you not one of those whom that Abbot would have burnt? Yes, and there is your mistress, Dame Foterell, or Dame Harflete, with whom I desire a word."

"I am at your service, Sir," said Cicely.

"Well, Madam, you and your servant have escaped the stake to which, as near as I can judge, you were sentenced upon no evidence at all. Still, you were condemned by a competent ecclesiastical Court, and under that condemnation you must therefore remain until or unless the King pardons you. My judgment is, then, that you stay here awaiting his command."

"But, Sir," said Cicely, "if the good nuns who have befriended me are to be driven forth, how can I dwell on in their house alone? Yet you say I must not leave it, and indeed if I could, whither should I go? My husband's hall is burnt, my own the Abbot holds. Moreover, if I bide here, in this way or in that he will have my life."

"The knave has fled away," said Dr. Legh, rubbing his fat chin.

"Aye, but he will come back again, or his people will, and, Sir, you know these Spaniards are good haters, and I have defied him long. Oh, Sir, I crave the protection of the King for my child's sake and my own, and for Emlyn Stower also."

The Commissioner went on rubbing his chin.

"You can give much evidence against this Maldon, can you not?" he asked at length.

"Aye," broke in Emlyn, "enough to hang him ten times over, and so can I."

"And you have large estates which he has seized, have you not?"

"I have, Sir, who am of no mean birth and station."

"Lady," he said, with more deference in his voice, "step aside with me, I would speak with you privately," and he walked to the window, where she followed him. "Now tell me, what was the value of these properties of yours?"

"I know not rightly, Sir, but I have heard my father say about £300 a year."

His manner became more deferential still, since for those days such wealth was great.

"Indeed, my Lady. A large sum, a very comfortable fortune if you can get it back. Now I will be frank with you. The King's Commissioners are not well paid and their costs are great. If I so arrange your matters that you come to your own again and that the judgment of witchcraft pronounced against you and your servant is annulled, will you promise to pay me one year's rent of these estates to meet the various expenses I must incur on your behalf?"

Now it was Cicely's turn to think.

"Surely," she answered at length, "if you will add a condition—that these good sisters shall be left undisturbed in their Nunnery."

He shook his fat head.

"It is not possible now. The thing is too public. Why, the Lord Cromwell would say I had been bribed, and I might lose my office."

"Well, then," went on Cicely, "if you will promise that one year of grace shall be given to them to make arrangements for their future."

"That I can do," he answered, nodding, "on the ground that they are of blameless life, and have protected you from the King's enemy. But this is an uncertain world; I must ask you to sign an indenture, and its form will be that you acknowledge to have received from me a loan of £300 to be repaid with interest when you recover your estates."

"Draw it up and I will sign, Sir."

"Good, Madam; and now that we may get this business through, you will accompany me to London, where you will be safe from harm. We'll not ride to-day, but to-morrow morning at the light."

"Then my servant Emlyn must come also, Sir, to help me with the babe, and Thomas Bolle too, for he can prove that the witchcraft upon which we were condemned was but his trickery."

"Yes, yes; but the costs of travel for so many will be great. Have you, perchance, any money?"

"Yes, Sir, about £50 in gold that is sewn up in one of Emlyn's robes."

"Ah! A sufficient sum. Too much indeed to be risked upon your persons in these rough times. You will let me take charge of half of it for you?"

"With pleasure, Sir, trusting you as I do. Keep to your bargain and I will keep to mine."

"Good. When Thomas Legh is fairly dealt with, Thomas Legh deals fairly, no man can say otherwise. This afternoon I will bring the deed, and you'll give me that £25 in charge."

Then, followed by Cicely, he returned to where the Prioress sat, and said—

"Mother Matilda, for so I understand you are called in religion, the Lady Harflete has been pleading with me for you, and because you have dealt so well by her I have promised in the King's name that you and your nuns shall live on here undisturbed for one year from this day, after which you must yield up peaceable possession to his Majesty, whom I will beg that you shall be pensioned."

"I thank you, Sir," the Prioress answered. "When one is old a year of grace is much, and in a year many things may happen—for instance, my death."

"Thank me not—a plain man who but follows after justice and duty. The documents for your signature shall be ready this afternoon, and by the way, the Lady Harflete and her servant, also that stout, shrewd fellow, Thomas Bolle, ride with me to London to-morrow. She will explain all. At three of the clock I wait upon you."

The Visitor and his secretaries bustled out of the room as pompously as they had entered, and when they had gone Cicely explained to Mother Matilda and Emlyn what had passed.

"I think that you have done wisely," said the Prioress, when she had listened. "That man is a shark, but better give him your little finger than your whole body. Certainly, you have bargained well for us, for what may not happen in a year? Also, dear Cicely, you will be safer in London than at Blossholme, since with the great sum of £300 to gain that Commissioner will watch you like the apple of his eye and push your cause."

"Unless some one promises him the greater sum of £1000 to scotch it," interrupted Emlyn. "Well, there was but one road to take, and paper promises are little, though I grudge the good £25 in gold. Meanwhile, Mother, we have much to make ready. I pray you send some one to find Thomas Bolle, who will not be far away, for since we are no longer prisoners I wish to go out walking with him on an errand of my own that perchance you can guess. Wealth may be useful in London town for all our sakes. Also horses and a pack beast must be got, and other things."

****

In due course Thomas Bolle was found fast asleep in a neighbour's house, for after his adventures and triumph he had drunk hard and rested long. When she discovered the truth Emlyn rated him well, calling him a beer-tub and not a man, and many other hard names, till at last she provoked him to answer, that had it not been for the said beer-tub she would be but ash-dust this day. Thereon she turned the talk and told them their needs, and that he must ride with them to London. To this he replied that good horses should be saddled by the dawn, for he knew where to lay hands on them, since some were left in the Abbot's stables that wanted exercise; further, that he would be glad to leave Blossholme for a while, where he had made enemies on the yesterday, whose friends yet lay wounded or unburied. After this Emlyn whispered something in his ear, to which he nodded assent, saying that he would bustle round and be ready.

That afternoon Emlyn went out riding with Thomas Bolle, who was fully armed, as she said, to try two of the horses that should carry them on the morrow, and it was late when she returned out of the dark night.

"Have you got them?" asked Cicely, when they were together in their room.

"Aye," she answered, "every one; but some stones have fallen, and it was hard to win an entrance to that vault. Indeed, had it not been for Thomas Bolle, who has the strength of a bull, I could never have done it. Moreover, the Abbot has been there before us and dug over every inch of the floor. But the fool never thought of the wall, so all's well. I'll sew half of them into my petticoat and half into yours, to share the risk. In case of thieves, the money that hungry Visitor has left to us, for I paid him over half when you signed the deeds, we will carry openly in pouches upon our girdles. They'll not search further. Oh, I forgot, I've something more besides the jewels, here it is," and she produced a packet from her bosom and laid it on the table.

"What's this?" asked Cicely, looking suspiciously at the worn sail-cloth in which it was wrapped.

"How can I tell? Cut it and see. All I know is that when I stood at the Nunnery door as Thomas led away the horses, a man crept on me out of the rain swathed in a great cloak and asked if I were not Emlyn Stower. I said Yea, whereon he thrust this into my hand, bidding me not fail to give it to the Lady Harflete, and was gone."

"It has an over-seas look about it," murmured Cicely, as with eager, trembling fingers she cut the stitches. At length they were undone and a sealed inner wrapping also, revealing, amongst other documents, a little packet of parchments covered with crabbed, unreadable writing, on the back of which, however, they could decipher the names of Shefton and Blossholme by reason of the larger letters in which they were engrossed. Also there was a writing in the scrawling hand of Sir John Foterell, and at the foot of it his name and, amongst others, those of Father Necton and of Jeffrey Stokes. Cicely stared at the deeds, then said—

"Emlyn, I know these parchments. They are those that my father took with him when he rode for London to disprove the Abbot's claim, and with them the evidence of the traitorous words he spoke last year at Shefton. Yes, this inner wrapping is my own; I took it from the store of worn linen in the passage-cupboard. But how come they here?"

Emlyn made no answer, only lifted the wrappings and shook them, whereon a strip of paper that they had not seen fell to the table.

"This may tell us," she said. "Read, if you can; it has words on its inner side."

Cicely snatched at it, and as the writing was clear and clerkly, read with ease save for the chokings of her throat. It ran—

"My Lady Harflete,

"These are the papers that Jeffrey Stokes saved when your father fell. They were given for safekeeping to the writer of these words, far away across the sea, and he hands them on unopened. Your husband lives and is well again, also Jeffrey Stokes, and though they have been hindered on their journey, doubtless he will find his way back to England, whither, believing you to be dead, as I did, he has not hurried. There are reasons why I, his friend and yours, cannot see you or write more, since my duty calls me hence. When it is finished I will seek you out if I still live. If not, wait in peace until your joy finds you, as I think it will.

"One who loves your lord well, and for his sake you also."

Cicely laid down the paper and burst into a flood of weeping.

"Oh, cruel, cruel!" she sobbed, "to tell so much and yet so little. Nay, what an ungrateful wretch am I, since Christopher truly lives, and I also live to learn it, I, whom he deems dead."

"By my soul," said Emlyn, when she had calmed her, "that cloaked man is a prince of messengers. Oh, had I but known what he bore I'd have had all the story, if I must cling to him like Potiphar's wife to Joseph. Well, well, Joseph got away and half a herring is better than no fish, also this is good herring. Moreover, you have got the deeds when you most wanted them and what is better, a written testimony that will bring the traitor Maldon to the scaffold."

CHAPTER 14

Jacob and the Jewels

Cicely's journey to London was strange enough to her, who never before had travelled farther than fifty miles from her home, and but once as a child spent a month in a town when visiting an aunt at Lincoln. She went in ease, it is true, for Commissioner Legh did not love hard travelling, and for this reason they started late and halted early, either at some good inn, if in those days any such places could be called good, or perhaps in a monastery where he claimed of the best that the frightened monks had to offer. Indeed, as she observed, his treatment of these poor folk was cruel, for he blustered and threatened and inquired, accusing them of crimes that they had not committed, and finally, although he had no mission to them at the time, extracted great gifts, saying that if these were not forthcoming he would make a note and return later. Also he got hold of tale-bearers, and wrote down all their scandalous and lying stories told against those whose bread they ate.

Thus, long before they saw Charing Cross, Cicely came to hate this proud, avaricious and overbearing man, who hid a savage nature under a cloak of virtue, and whilst serving his own ends, mouthed great words about God and the King. Still, she who was schooled in adversity, learned to hide her heart, fearing to make an enemy of one who could ruin her, and forced Emlyn, much against her will, to do the same. Moreover, there were worse things than that since, being beautiful, some of his companions talked to her in a way she could not misunderstand, till at length Thomas Bolle, coming on one of them, thrashed him as he had never been thrashed before, after which there was trouble that was only appeased by a gift.

Yet on the whole things went well. No one molested the King's Visitor or those with him, the autumn weather held fine, the baby boy kept his health, and the country through which they passed was new to her and full of interest.

At last one evening they rode from Barnet into the great city, which she thought a most marvellous place, who had never seen such a multitude of houses or of men running to and fro about their business up and down the narrow streets that at night were lit with lamps. Now there had been a great discussion where they were to lodge, Dr. Legh saying that he knew of a house suitable to them. But Emlyn would not hear of this place, where she was sure they would be robbed, for the wealth that they carried secretly in jewels bore heavily on her mind. Remembering a cousin of her mother's of the name of Smith, a goldsmith, who till within a year or two before was alive and dwelling in Cheapside, she said that they would seek him out.

Thither then they rode, guided by one of the Visitor's clerks, not he whom Bolle had beaten, but another, and at last, after some search, found a dingy house in a court and over it a sign on which were painted three balls and the name of Jacob Smith. Emlyn dismounted and, the door being open, entered, to be greeted by an old, white-bearded man with horn spectacles thrust up over his forehead and dark eyes like her own, since the same gypsy blood ran strong in both of them.

What passed between them Cicely did not hear, but presently the old man came out with Emlyn, and looked her and Bolle up and down sharply for a long while as though to take their measures. At length he said that he understood from his cousin, whom he now saw for the first time for over thirty years, that the two of them and their man desired lodgings, which, as he had empty rooms, he would be pleased to give them if they would pay the price.

Cicely asked how much this might be, and on his naming a sum, ten silver shillings a week for the three of them and their horses, that would be stabled close by, told Emlyn to pay him a pound on account. This he took, biting the gold to see that it was good, but bidding them in to inspect the rooms before he pouched it. They did so, and finding them clean and commodious if somewhat dark, closed the bargain with him, after which they dismissed the clerk to take their address to Dr. Legh, who had promised to advise them so soon as he could put their business forward.

When he was gone and Thomas Bolle, conducted by Smith's apprentice, had led off the three horses and the pack beast, the old man changed his manner, and conducting them into a parlour at the back of his shop, sent his housekeeper, a middle-aged woman with a pleasant face, to make ready food for them while he produced cordials from squat Dutch bottles which he made them drink. Indeed he was all kindness to them, being, as he explained, rejoiced to see one of his own blood, for he had no relations living, his wife and their two children having died in one of the London sicknesses. Also he was Blossholme born, though he had left that place fifty years before, and had known Cicely's grandfather and played with her father when he was a boy. So he plied them with question after question, some of which they thought it was not to answer, for he was a merry and talkative old man.

"Aha!" he said, "you would prove me before you trust me, and who can blame you in this naughty world? But perhaps I know more about you all than you think, since in this trade my business is to learn many things. For instance, I have heard that there was a great trying of witches down at Blossholme lately, whereat a certain Abbot came off worst, also that the famous Carfax jewels had been lost, which vexed the said holy Abbot. They were jewels indeed, or so I have heard, for among them were two pink pearls worth a king's ransom—or so I have heard. Great pity that they should be lost, since my Lady there would own them otherwise, and much should I have liked, who am a little man in that trade, to set my old eyes upon them. Well, well, perhaps I shall, perhaps I shall yet, for that which is lost is sometimes found again. Now here comes your dinner; eat, eat, we'll talk afterwards."

This was the first of many pleasant meals which they shared with their host, Jacob Smith. Soon Emlyn found from inquiries that she made among his neighbours without seeming to do so, that this cousin of hers bore an excellent name and was trusted by all.

"Then why should we not trust him also?" asked Cicely, "who must find friends and put faith in some one."

"Even with the jewels, Mistress?"

"Even with the jewels, for such things are his business, and they would be safer in his strong chest than tacked into our garments, where the thought of them haunts me night and day."

"Let us wait a while," said Emlyn, "for once they were in that box how do we know if we should get them out again?"

On the morrow of this talk the Visitor Legh came to see them, and had no cheerful tale to tell. According to him the Lord Cromwell declared that as the Abbot of Blossholme claimed these Shefton estates, the King stood, or would soon stand, in the shoes of the said Abbot of Blossholme, and therefore the King claimed them and could not surrender them. Moreover, money was so wanted at Court just then, and here Legh looked hard at them, "that there could be no talk of parting with anything of value except in return for a consideration," and he looked at them harder still.

"And how can my Lady give that," broke in Emlyn sharply, for she feared lest Cicely should commit herself. "To-day she is but a home-less pauper, save for a few pounds in gold, and even if she should come to her own again, as your Worship knows, her first year's profits are all promised."

"Ah!" said the Doctor sadly, "doubtless the case is hard. Only," he added, with cunning emphasis, "a tale has just reached me that the Lady Harflete has wealth hidden away which came to her from her mother; trinkets of value and such things."

Now Cicely coloured, for the man's little eyes pierced her like gintlets, and her powers of deceit were very small. But this was not so with Emlyn, who, as she said, could play thief to catch a thief.

"Listen, Sir," she said, with a secret air, "you have heard true. There were some things of value—why should we hide it from you, our good friend? But, alas! that greedy rogue, the Abbot of Blossholme, has them. He has stripped my poor Lady as bare as a fowl for roasting. Get them back from him, Sir, and on her behalf I say she'll give you half of them, will you not, my Lady?"

"Surely," said Cicely. "The Doctor, to whom we owe so much, will be most welcome to the half of any movables of mine that he can re-cover from the Abbot Maldon," and she paused, for the fib stuck in her throat. Moreover, she knew herself to be the colour of a peony.

Happily the Commissioner did not notice her blushes, or if he did, he put them down to grief and anger.

"The Abbot Maldon," he grumbled, "always the Abbot Maldon. Oh! what a wicked thief must be that high-stomached Spaniard who does not scruple first to make orphans and then to rob them? A black-hearted traitor, too. Do you know that at this moment he stirs up re-bellion in the north? Well, I'll see him on the rack before I have done. Have you a list of those movables, Madam?"

Cicely said no, and Emlyn added that one should be made from memory.

"Good; I'll see you again to-morrow or the next day, and mean-while fear not, I'll be as active in your business as a cat after a sparrow. Oh, my rat of a Spanish Abbot, you wait till I get my claws into your fat back. Farewell, my Lady Harflete, farewell. Mistress Stower, I must away to deal with other priests almost as wicked," and he departed, still muttering objurgations on the Abbot.

"Now, I think the time has come to trust Jacob Smith," said Emlyn, when the door closed behind him, "for he may be honest, whereas this Doctor is certainly a villain; also, the man has heard something and suspects us. Ah! there you are, Cousin Smith, come in, if you please, since we desire to talk with you for a minute. Come in, and be so good as to lock the door behind you."

Five minutes later all the jewels, whereof not one was wanting, lay on the table before old Jacob, who stared at them with round eyes.

"The Carfax gems," he muttered, "the Carfax gems of which I have so often heard; those that the old Crusader brought from the East, having sacked them from a Sultan; from the East, where they talk of them still. A sultan's wealth, unless, indeed, they came straight from the New Jerusalem and were an angel's gauds. And do you say that you two women have carried these priceless things tacked in your cloaks, which, as I have seen, you throw down here and there and leave behind you? Oh, fools, fools, even among women incomparable fools! Fellow-travellers with Dr. Legh also, who would rob a baby of its bauble."

"Fools or no," exclaimed Emlyn tartly, "we have got them safe enough after they have run some risks, as I pray that you may keep them, Cousin Smith."

Old Jacob threw a cloth over the gems, and slowly transferred them to his pocket.

"This is an upper floor," he explained, "and the door is locked, yet some one might put a ladder up to the window. Were I in the street I should know by the glitter in the light that there were precious things here. Stay, they are not safe in my pocket even for an hour," and going to the wall he did something to a panel in the wainscot causing it to open and reveal a space behind it where lay sundry wrapped-up parcels, among which he placed, not all, but a portion of the gems. Then he went to other panels that opened likewise, showing more parcels, and in the holes behind these he distributed the rest of the treasure.

"There, foolish women," he said, "since you have trusted me, I will trust you. You have seen my big strong-boxes in my office, and doubtless thought I keep all my little wares there. Well, so does every thief in London, for they have searched them twice and gained some store of pewter; I remember that some of it was discovered again in the King's household. But behind these panels all is safe, though no woman would ever have thought of a device so simple and so sure."

For a moment Emlyn could find no answer, perhaps because of her indignation, but Cicely asked sweetly—

"Do you ever have fires in London, Master Smith? It seems to me that I have heard of such things, and then—in a hurry, you know—"

Smith thrust up his horned spectacles and looked at her in mild astonishment.

"To think," he said, "that I should live to learn wisdom out of the mouth of babes and sucklers—"

"Sucklings," suggested Cicely.

"Sucklers or sucklings, it means the same thing—women," he replied testily; then added, with a chuckle, "Well, well, my Lady, you are right. You have caught out Jacob at his own game. I never thought of fire, though it is true we had one next door last year, when I ran out with my bed and forgot all about the gold and stones. I'll have new hiding-places made in the masonry of the cellar, where no fire would hurt. Ah! you women would never have thought of that, who carry treasure sewn up in a nightshift."

Now Emlyn could bear it no longer.

"And how would you have us carry it, Cousin Smith?" she asked indignantly. "Tied about our necks, or hanging from our heels? Well do I remember my mother telling me that you were always a simple youth, and that your saint must have been a very strong one who brought you safe to London and showed you how to earn a living there, or else that you had married a woman of excellent intelligence—though it is plain now she has long been dead. Well, well," she added, with a laugh, "cling to your man's vanities, you son of a woman, and since you are so clever, give us of your wisdom, for we need it. But first let me tell you that I have rescued those very jewels from a fire, and by hiding them in masonry in a vault."

"It is the fashion of the female to wrangle when she has the worst of the case," said Jacob, with a twinkle in his eye. "So, daughter of man, set out your trouble. Perchance the wisdom that I have inherited from my mothers straight back to Eve may help that which your mothers lacked. Now, have you done with jests. I listen, if it pleases you to tell me."

So, having first invoked the curse of Heaven on him if ever he should breathe a word, Emlyn, with the help of Cicely, repeated the whole matter from the beginning, and the candles were lighted ere ever her tale was done. All this while Jacob Smith sat opposite to them, saying little, save now and again to ask a shrewd question. At length, when they had finished, he exclaimed—

"Truly women are fools!"

"We have heard that before, Master Smith," replied Cicely; "but this time—why?"

"Not to have unbosomed to me before, which would have saved you a week of time, although, as it happens, I knew more of your story than you chose to tell, and therefore the days have not been altogether wasted. Well, to be brief, this Dr. Legh is a ravenous rogue."

"O Solomon, to have discovered that!" exclaimed Emlyn.

"One whose only aim is to line his nest with your feathers, some of which you have promised him, as, indeed, you were right to do. Now he has got wind of these jewels, which is not wonderful, seeing that such things cannot be hid. If you buried them in a coffin, six foot underground, still they would shine through the solid earth and declare themselves. This is his plan—to strip you of everything ere his master, Cromwell, gets a hold of you; and if you go to him empty-handed, what chance has your suit with Vicar-General Cromwell, the hungriest shark of all—save one?"

"We understand," said Emlyn; "but what is your plan, Cousin Smith?"

"Mine? I don't know that I have one. Still, here is that which might do. Though I seem so small and humble, I am remembered at Court—when money is wanted, and just now much money is wanted, for soon they will be in arms in Yorkshire—and therefore I am much remembered. Now, if you care to give Dr. Legh the go-by and leave your cause to me, perhaps I might serve you as cheaply as another."

"At what charge?" blurted out Emlyn.

The old man turned on her indignantly, asking—

"Cousin, how have I defrauded you or your mistress, that you should insult me to my face? Go to! you do not trust me. Go to, with your jewels, and seek some other helper!" and he went to the panelling as though to collect them again.

"Nay, nay, Master Smith," said Cicely, catching him by the arm; "be not angry with Emlyn. Remember that of late we have learned in a hard school, with Abbot Maldon and Dr. Legh for masters. At least I trust you, so forsake me not, who have no other to whom to turn in all my troubles, which are many," and as she spoke the great tears that had gathered in her blue eyes fell upon the child's face, and woke him, so that she must turn aside to quiet him, which she was glad to do.

"Grieve not," said the kind-hearted old man, in distress; "'tis I should grieve, whose brutal words have made you weep. Moreover, Emlyn is right; even foolish women should not trust the first Jack with whom they take a lodging. Still, since you swear that you do in your kindness, I'll try to show myself not all unworthy, my Lady Harflete. Now, what is it you want from the King? Justice on the Abbot? That you'll get for nothing, if his Grace can give it, for this same Abbot stirs up rebellion against him. No need, therefore, to set out his past misdeeds. A clean title to your large inheritance, which the Abbot claims? That will be more difficult, since the King claims through him. At

500

best, money must be paid for it. A declaration that your marriage is good and your boy born in lawful wedlock? Not so hard, but will cost something. The annulment of the sentence of witchcraft on you both? Easy, for the Abbot passed it. Is there aught more?"

"Yes, Master Smith; the good nuns who befriended me—I would save their house and lands to them. Those jewels are pledged to do it, if it can be done."

"A matter of money, Lady—a mere matter of money. You will have to buy the property, that is all. Now, let us see what it will cost, if fortune goes with me," and he took pen and paper and began to write down figures.

Finally he rose, sighing and shaking his head. "Two thousand pounds," he groaned; "a vast sum, but I can't lessen it by a shilling—there are so many to be bought. Yes; £1000 in gifts and £1000 as loan to his Majesty, who does not repay."

"Two thousand pounds!" exclaimed Cicely in dismay; "oh! how shall I find so much, whose first year's rents are already pledged?"

"Know you the worth of those jewels?" asked Jacob, looking at her.

"Nay; the half of that, perhaps."

"Let us say double that, and then right cheap."

"Well, if so," replied Cicely, with a gasp, "where shall we sell them? Who has so much money?"

"I'll try to find it, or what is needful. Now, Cousin Emlyn," he added sarcastically, "you see where my profit lies. I buy the gems at half their value, and the rest I keep."

"In your own words: go to!" said Emlyn, "and keep your gibes until we have more leisure."

The old man thought a while, and said—

"It grows late, but the evening is pleasant, and I think I need some air. That crack-brained, red-haired fellow of yours will watch you while I am gone, and for mercy's sake be careful with those candles. Nay, nay; you must have no fire, you must go cold. After what you said to me, I can think of naught but fire. It is for this night only. By to-morrow evening I'll prepare a place where Abbot Maldon himself might sit unscorched in the midst of hell. But till then make out with clothes. I have some furs in pledge that I will send up to you. It is your own fault, and in my youth we did not need a fire on an autumn day. No more, no more," and he was gone, nor did they see him again that night.

On the following morning, as they sat at their breakfast, Jacob Smith appeared, and began to talk of many things, such as the badness of the weather—for it rained—the toughness of the ham, which he said was not to be compared to those they cured at Blossholme in his youth, and the likeness of the baby boy to his mother.

"Indeed, no," broke in Cicely, who felt that he was playing with them; "he is his father's self; there is no look of me in him."

"Oh!" answered Jacob; "well, I'll give my judgment when I see the father. By the way, let me read that note again which the cloaked man brought to Emlyn."

Cicely gave it to him, and he studied it carefully; then said, in an indifferent voice—

"The other day I saw a list of Christian captives said to have been recovered from the Turks by the Emperor Charles at Tunis, and among them was one 'Huflit,' described as an English *señor*, and his servant. I wonder now—"

Cicely sprang upon him.

"Oh! cruel wretch," she said, "to have known this so long and not to have told me!"

"Peace, Lady," he said, retreating before her; "I only learned it at eleven of the clock last night, when you were fast asleep. Yesterday is not this same day, and therefore 'tis the other day, is it not?"

"Surely you might have woke me. But, swift, where is he now?"

"How can I know? Not here, at least. But the writing said—"

"Well, what did the writing say?"

"I am trying to think—my memory fails me at times; perhaps you will find the same thing when you have my years, should it please Heaven—"

"Oh! that it might please Heaven to make you speak! What said the writing?"

"Ah! I have it now. It said, in a note appended amidst other news, for—did I tell you this was a letter from his Grace's ambassador in Spain? and, oh! his is the vilest scrawl to read. Nay, hurry me not—it said that this 'Sir Huflit'—the ambassador has put a query against his name—and his servant—yes, yes, I am sure it said his servant too—well, that they both of them, being angry at the treatment they had met with from the infidel Turks—no, I forgot to add there were three of them, one a priest, who did otherwise. Well, as I said, being angry, they stopped there to serve with the Spaniards against the Turks till the end of that campaign. There, that is all."

"How little is your all!" exclaimed Cicely. "Yet, 'tis something. Oh! why should a married man stop across the seas to be revenged on poor ignorant Turks?"

"Why should he not?" interrupted Emlyn, "when he deems himself a widower, as does your lord?"

"Yes, I forgot; he thinks me dead, who doubtless himself will be dead, if he is not so already, seeing that those wicked, murderous Turks will kill him," and she began to weep.

"I should have added," said Jacob hastily, "that in a second letter, of later date, the ambassador declares that the Emperor's war against the Turks is finished for this season, and that the Englishmen who were with him fought with great honour and were all escaped unharmed, though this time he gives no names."

"All escaped! If my husband were dead, who could not die meanly or without fame, how could he say that they were all escaped? Nay, nay; he lives, though who knows if he will return? Perchance he will wander off elsewhere, or stay and wed again."

"Impossible," said old Jacob, bowing to her; "having called you wife—impossible."

"Impossible," echoed Emlyn, "having such a score to settle with yonder Maldon! A man may forget his love, especially if he deems her buried. But as he stayed foreign to fight the Turk, who wronged him, so he'll come home to fight the Abbot, who ruined him and slew his bride."

There followed a silence, which the goldsmith, who felt it somewhat painful, hastened to break, saying—

"Yes, doubtless he will come home; for aught we know he may be here already. But meanwhile we also have our score against this Abbot, a bad one, though think not for his sake that all Abbots are bad, for I have known some who might be counted angels upon earth, and, having gone to martyrdom, doubtless to-day are angels in heaven. Now, my Lady, I will tell you what I have done, hoping that it will please you better than it does me. Last night I saw the Lord Cromwell, with whom I have many dealings, at his house in Austin Friars, and told him the case, of which, as I thought, that false villain Legh had said nothing to him, purposing to pick the plums out of the pudding ere he handed on the suet to his master. He read your deeds and hunted up some petition from the Abbot, with which he compared them; then made a note of my demands and asked straight out—How much?

"I told him £1000 on loan to the King, which would not be asked for back again, the said loan to be discharged by the grant to me—that is, to you—of all the Abbey lands, in addition to your own, when the said Abbey lands are sequestered, as they will be shortly. To this he agreed, on behalf of his Grace, who needs money much, but inquired as to himself. I replied £500 for him and his jackals, including Dr. Legh, of which no account would be asked. He told me it was not enough, for after the jackals had their pickings nothing would be left for him but the bones; I, who asked so much, must offer more, and he made as though to dismiss me. At the door I turned and said I had a wonderful pink pearl that he, who loved jewels, might like to see—a pink pearl worth many abbeys. He said, 'Show it;' and, oh! he gloated over it like a maid over her first love-letter. 'If there were two of these, now!' he whispered.

"'Two, my Lord!' I answered; 'there's no fellow to that pearl in the whole world,' though it is true that as I said the words, the setting of its twin, that was pinned to my inner shirt, pricked me sorely, as if in anger. Then I took it up again, and for the second time began to bow myself out.

"'Jacob,' he said, 'you are an old friend, and I'll stretch my duty for you. Leave the pearl—his Grace needs that £1000 so sorely that I must keep it against my will,' and he put out his hand to take it, only to find that I had covered it with my own.

"'First the writing, then its price, my Lord. Here is a memorandum of it set out fair, to save you trouble, if it pleases you to sign.'

"He read it through, then, taking a pen, scored out the clause as regards acquittal of the witchcraft, which, he said, must be looked into by the King in person or by his officers, but all the rest he signed, undertaking to hand over the proper deeds under the great seal and royal hand upon payment of £1000. Being able to do no better, I said that would serve, and left him your pearl, he promising, on his part, to move his Majesty to receive you, which I doubt not he will do quickly for the sake of the £1000. Have I done well?"

"Indeed, yes," exclaimed Cicely. "Who else could have done half so well—?"

As the words left her lips there came a loud knocking at the door of the house, and Jacob ran down to open it. Presently he returned with a messenger in a splendid coat, who bowed to Cicely and asked if she were the Lady Harflete. On her replying that such was her name, he said that he bore to her the command of his Grace the King to attend upon him at three o'clock of that afternoon at his Palace of Whitehall, together with Emlyn Stower and Thomas Bolle, there to make answer to his Majesty concerning a certain charge of witchcraft that had been laid against her and them, which summons she would neglect at her peril.

"Sir, I will be there," answered Cicely; "but tell me, do I come as a prisoner?"

"Nay," replied the herald, "since Master Jacob Smith, in whom his Grace has trust, has consented to be answerable for you."

"And for the £1000," muttered Jacob, as, with many salutations, he showed the royal messenger to the door, not neglecting to thrust a gold piece into his hand that he waved behind him in farewell.

CHAPTER 15

The Devil at Court

It was half-past two of the clock when Cicely, who carried her boy in her arms, accompanied by Emlyn, Thomas Bolle and Jacob Smith, found herself in the great courtyard of the Palace of Whitehall. The place was full of people waiting there upon one business or another, through whom messengers and armed men thrust their way continually, crying, "Way! In the King's name, way!" So great was the press, indeed, that for some time even Jacob could command no attention, till at length he caught sight of the herald who had visited his house in the morning, and beckoned to him.

"I was looking for you, Master Smith, and for the Lady Harflete," the man said, bowing to her. "You have an appointment with his Grace, have you not? but God knows if it can be kept. The ante-chambers are full of folk bringing news about the rebellion in the north, and of great lords and councillors who wait for commands or money, most of them for money. In short the King has given order that all appointments are cancelled; he can see no one to-day. The Lord Cromwell told me so himself."

Jacob took a golden angel from his pouch and began to play with it between his fingers.

"I understand, noble herald," he said. "Still, do you think that you could find me a messenger to the Lord Cromwell? If so, this trifle—"

"I'll try, Master Smith," he answered, stretching out his hand for the piece of money. "But what is the message?"

"Oh, say that Pink Pearl would learn from his Lordship where he can lay hands upon £1000 without interest."

"A strange message, to which I will hazard an answer—nowhere," said the herald, "yet I'll find some one to deliver it. Step within this archway and wait out of the rain. Fear not, I will be back presently."

They did as he bid them, gladly enough, for it had begun to drizzle and Cicely was afraid lest her boy, with whom London did not agree too well, should take cold. Here, then, they stood amusing themselves in watching the motley throng that came and went. Bolle, to whom the scene was strange, gaped at them with his mouth open; Emlyn took note of every one with her quick eyes, while old Jacob Smith whispered tales concerning individuals as they passed, most of which were little to their credit.

As for Cicely, soon her thoughts were far away. She knew that she was at a crisis of her fortune; that if things went well with her this day she might look to be avenged upon her enemies, and to spend the rest of her life in wealth and honour. But it was not of such matters that she dreamed, whose heart was set on Christopher, without whom naught availed. Where was he, she wondered. If Jacob's tale were true, after passing many dangers, but a little while ago he lived and had his health. Yet in those times death came quickly, leaping like the lightning from unexpected clouds or even out of a clear sky, and who could say? Besides, he believed her gone, and that being so would be careless of himself, or perchance, worst thought of all, would take some other wife, as was but right and natural. Oh! then indeed—

At this moment a sound of altercation woke her to the world again, and she looked up to see that Thomas Bolle was bringing trouble on them. A coarse fat lout with a fiery and a knotted nose, being somewhat in liquor, had amused himself by making mock of his country looks and red hair, and asking whether they used him for a scarecrow in his native fields.

Thomas bore it for a while, only answering with another question: whether he, the fat fellow, hired out his nose to London housewives to light their fires. The man, feeling that the laugh was against him, and noticing the child in Cicely's arms pointed it out to his friends, inquiring whether they did not think it was exactly like its dad. Then Thomas's rage burnt up, although the jest was silly and aimless enough.

"You low, London gutter-hound!" he exclaimed; "I'll learn you to insult the Lady Harflete with your ribald japes," and stretching out his big fist he seized his enemy's purple nose in a grip of iron and began to twist it till the sot roared with pain. Thereon guards ran up and would have arrested Bolle for breaking the peace in the King's palace. Indeed, arrested he must have been, notwithstanding all Jacob Smith could do to save him, had not at that moment a man appeared at whose coming the crowd that had gathered, separated, bowing; a man of middle age with a quick, clever face, who wore rich clothes and a fur-trimmed velvet cap and gown.

Cicely knew him at once for Cromwell, the greatest man in England after the King, and marked him well, knowing that he held her fate and that of her child in the hollow of his hand. She noted the thin-lipped mouth, small as a woman's, the sharp nose, the little brownish eyes set close together and surrounded by wrinkled skin that gave them a cunning look, and noting was afraid. Before her stood a man who, though at present he seemed to be her friend, if he chanced to become her enemy, as once he had been bribed to be her father's, would show her no more pity than the spider shows a fly.

Indeed she was right, for many were the flies that had been snared and sucked in the web of Cromwell, who, in his full tide of power and pomp, forgot the fate of his master, Wolsey, in his day a greater spider still.

"What passes here?" Cromwell said in a sharp voice. "Men, is this the place to brawl beneath his Grace's very windows? Ah! Master Smith, is it you? Explain."

"My Lord," answered Jacob, bowing, "this is Lady Harflete's servant and he is not to blame. That fat knave insulted her and, being quick-tempered, her man, Bolle, wrang his nose."

"I see that he wrang it. Look, he is wringing it still. Friend Bolle, leave go, or presently you will have in your hand that which is of no value to you. Guard, take this beer-tub and hold his head beneath the pump for five minutes by the clock to wash him, and if he comes back again set him in the stocks. Nay, no words, fellow, you are well served. Master Smith, follow me with your party."

Again the crowd parted as they walked after Cromwell to a side door that was near at hand, to find themselves alone with him in a small chamber. Here he stopped and, turning, surveyed them all narrowly, especially Cicely.

"I suppose, Master Smith," he said, pointing to Bolle, who was wiping his hands clean with the rushes from the floor, "this is the man that you told me played the devil yonder at Blossholme. Well, he can play the fool also. In another minute there would have been a tumult and you would have lost your chance of seeing his Grace, for months perhaps, since he has determined to ride from London to-morrow morning northwards, though it is true he may change his mind ere then. This rebellion troubles him much, and were it not for the loan you promise, when loans are needed, small hope would you have had of audience. Now come quickly and be careful that you do not cross the King's temper, for it is tetchy to-day. Indeed, had it not been for the Queen, who is with him and minded to see this Lady Harflete, that they would have burnt as a witch, you must have waited till a more convenient season which may never come. Stay, what is in that great sack you carry, Bolle?"

"The devil's livery, may it please your Lordship."

"The devil's livery, many wear that in London. Still, bring the gear, it may make his Grace laugh, and if so I'll give you a gold piece, who have had enough of oaths and scoldings, aye," he added, with a sour grin, "and of blows too. Now follow me into the Presence, and speak only when you are spoken to, nor dare to answer if he rates you."

They went from the room down a passage and through another door, where the guards on duty looked suspiciously at Bolle and his sack, but at a word from Cromwell let them through into a large room in which a fire burned upon the hearth. At the end of this room stood a huge, proud-looking man with a flat and cruel face, broad as an ox's skull, as Thomas Bolle said afterwards, who was dressed in some rich, sombre stuff and wore a velvet cap upon his head. He held a parchment in his hand, and before him on the other side of an oak table sat an officer of state in a black robe, who wrote upon another parchment, whereof there were many scattered about on the table and the floor.

"Knave," shouted the King, for they guessed that it was he, "you have cast up these figures wrong. Oh, that it should be my lot to be served by none but fools!"

"Pardon, your Grace," said the secretary in a trembling voice, "thrice have I checked them."

"Would you gainsay me, you lying lawyer," bellowed the King again. "I tell you they must be wrong, since otherwise the sum is short by £1100 of that which I was promised. Where are the £1100? You must have stolen them, thief."

"I steal, oh, your Grace, I steal!"

"Aye, why not, since your betters do. Only you are clumsy, you lack skill. Ask my Lord Cromwell there to give you lessons. He learned under the best of masters, and is a merchant by trade to boot. Oh, get you gone and take your scribblings with you."

The poor officer hastened to avail himself of this invitation. Hurriedly collecting his parchments he bowed himself from the presence of his irate Sovereign. At the door, about twelve feet away, however, he turned.

"My gracious Liege," he began, "the casting of the count is right. Upon my honour as a Christian soul I can look your Majesty in the face with truth in my eye—"

Now on the table there was a massive inkstand made from the horn of a ram mounted with silver feet. This Henry seized and hurled with all his strength. The aim was good, for the heavy horn struck the wretched scribe upon the nose so that the ink squirted all over his face, and felled him to the floor.

"Now there is more in your eye than truth," shouted the King. "Be off, ere the stool follows the inkpot."

Two ladies who stood by the fire talking together and taking no heed, for to such rude scenes they seemed to be accustomed, looked up and laughed a little, then went on talking, while Cromwell smiled and shrugged his shoulders. Then in the midst of the silence which followed Thomas Bolle, who had been watching open-mouthed, ejaculated in his great voice—

"A bull's eye! A noble bull! Myself cannot throw straighter."

"Silence, fool," hissed Emlyn.

"Who spoke?" asked the king, looking towards them sharply.

"Please, my Liege, it was I, Thomas Bolle."

"Thomas Bolle! Can you sling a stone, Thomas Bolle, whoever you may be?"

"Aye, Sire, but not better than you, I think. That was a gallant shot."

"Thomas Bolle, you are right. Seeing the hurry and the unhandiness of the missile, it was excellent. Let the knave stand up again and I'll bet you a gold noble to a brass nail that you'll not do as well within an inch. Why, the fellow's gone! Will you try on my Lord Cromwell? Nay, this is no time for fooling. What's your business, Thomas Bolle, and who are those women with you?"

Now Cromwell stepped forward, and with cringing gestures began to explain something to the King in a low voice. Meanwhile, the two ladies became suddenly interested in Cicely, and one of them, a pale but pretty woman, splendidly dressed, stepped forward to her, saying—

"Are you the Lady Harflete of whom we have heard, she who was to have been burnt as a witch? Yes? And is that your child? Oh! what a beautiful child. A boy, I'll swear. Come to me, sweet, and in after years you can tell that a queen has nursed you," and she stretched out her arms.

As good fortune would have it the child was awake, and attracted by the Queen's pleasant voice, or perhaps by the necklace of bright gems that she wore, he held out his little hands towards her and went quite contentedly to her breast. Jane Seymour, for it was she, began to fondle him with delight, then, followed by her lady, ran to the King, saying—

"See, Harry, see what a beautiful boy, and how he loves me. God send us such a son as this!"

The King glanced at the child, then answered—

"Aye, he would do well enow. Well, it rests with you, Jane. Nurse him, nurse him, perhaps the sex is catching. I and all England would see you brought to bed of that sickness, Sweet. What said you, Cromwell?"

The great minister went on with his explanations, till the King, wearying of him, called out—

"Come here, Master Smith."

Jacob advanced, bowing, and stood still.

"Now, Master Smith, the Lord Cromwell tells me that if I sign these papers, you, on behalf of the Lady Harflete, will loan me £1000 without interest, which as it chances I need. Where, then, is this £1000?— for I will have no promises, not even from you, who are known to keep them, Master Smith."

Jacob thrust his hand beneath his robe, and from various inner pockets drew out bags of gold, which he set in a row upon the table.

"Here they are, your Grace," he said quietly. "If you should wish for them they can be weighed and counted."

"God's truth! I think I had better keep them, lest some accident should happen to you on the way home, Master Smith. You might fall into the Thames and sink."

"Your Grace is right, the parchments will be lighter to carry, even," he added meaningly, "with your Highness's name added."

"I can't sign," said the King doubtfully, "all the ink is spilt."

Jacob produced a small ink-horn, which like most merchants of the day he carried hung to his girdle, drew out the stopper and with a bow set it on the table.

"In truth you are a good man of business, Master Smith, too good for a mere king. Such readiness makes me pause. Perhaps we had better meet again at a more leisured season."

Jacob bowed once more, and stretching out his hand slowly lifted the first of the bags of gold as though to replace it in his pocket.

"Cromwell, come hither," said the King, whereon Jacob, as though in forgetfulness, laid the bag back upon the table.

"Repeat the heads of this matter, Cromwell."

"My Liege, the Lady Harflete seeks justice on the Spaniard Maldon, Abbot of Blossholme, who is said to have murdered her father, Sir John Foterell, and her husband, Sir Christopher Harflete, though rumour has it that the latter escaped his clutches and is now in Spain. Item: the said Abbot has seized the lands which this Dame Cicely should have inherited from her father, and demands their restitution."

"By God's wounds! justice she shall have and for nothing if we can give it her," answered the King, letting his heavy fist fall upon the table. "No need to waste time in setting out her wrongs. Why, 'tis the same Spanish knave Maldon who stirs up all this hell's broth in the north. Well, he shall boil in his own pot, for against him our score is long. What more?"

"A declaration, Sire, of the validity of the marriage between Christopher Harflete and Cicely Foterell, which without doubt is good and lawful although the Abbot disputes it for his own ends; and an indemnity for the deaths of certain men who fell when the said Abbot attacked and burnt the house of the said Christopher Harflete."

"It should have been granted the more readily if Maldon had fallen also, but let that pass. What more?"

"The promise, your Grace, of the lands of the Abbey of Blossholme and of the Priory of Blossholme in consideration of the loan of £1000 advanced to your Grace by the agent of Cicely Harflete, Jacob Smith."

"A large demand, my Lord. Have these lands been valued?"

"Aye, Sire, by your Commissioner, who reports it doubtful if with all their tenements and timber they would fetch £1000 in gold."

"Our Commissioner? A fig for his valuing, doubtless he has been bribed. Still, if we repay the money we can hold the land, and since this Dame Harflete and her husband have suffered sorely at the hands of Maldon and his armed ruffians, why, let it pass also. Now, is that all? I weary of so much talk."

"But one thing more, your Grace," put in Cromwell hastily, for Henry was already rising from his chair. "Dame Cicely Harflete, her servant, Emlyn Stower, and a certain crazed old nun were condemned of sorcery by a Court Ecclesiastic whereof the Abbot Maldon was a member, the said Abbot alleging that they had bewitched him and his goods."

"Then he was pleader and judge in one?"

"That is so, your Grace. Already without the royal warrant they were bound to the stake for burning, the said Maldon having usurped the prerogative of the Crown, when your Commissioner, Legh, arrived and loosed them, but not without fighting, for certain men were killed and wounded. Now they humbly crave your Majesty's royal pardon for their share in this man-slaying, if any, as also does Thomas Bolle yonder, who seems to have done the slaying—"

"Well can I believe it," muttered the King.

"And a declaration of the invalidity of their trial and condemning, and of their innocence of the foul charge laid against them."

"Innocence!" exclaimed Henry, growing impatient and fixing on the last point. "How do we know they were innocent, though it is true that if Dame Harflete is a witch she is the prettiest that ever we have heard of or seen. You ask too much, after your fashion, Cromwell."

"I crave your Grace's patience for one short minute. There is a man here who can prove that they were innocent; yonder red-haired Bolle."

"What? He who praised our shooting? Well, Bolle, since you are so good a sportsman, we will listen to you. Prove and be brief."

"Now all is finished," murmured Emlyn to Cicely, "for assuredly fool Thomas will land us in the mire."

"Your Grace," said Bolle in his big voice, "I obey in four words—I was the devil."

"The devil you were, Thomas Bolle. Now, your meaning?"

"Your Grace, Blossholme was haunted, I haunted it."

"How could you do otherwise if you lived there?"

"I'll show your Grace," and without more ado, to the horror of Cicely, Thomas tumbled from his sack all his hellish garb and set to work to clothe himself. In a minute, for he was practised at the game, the hideous mask was on his head, and with it the horns and skin of the widow's billy-goat; the tail and painted hides were tied about him, and in his hand he waved the eel spear, short-handled now. Thus arrayed he capered before the astonished King and Queen, shaking the tail that had a wire in it and clattering his hoofs upon the floor.

"Oh, good devil! Most excellent devil!" exclaimed his Majesty, clapping his hands. "If I had met thee I'd have run like a hare. Stay, Jane, peep you through yonder door and tell me who are gathered there."

The Queen obeyed and, returned, said—

"There be a bishop and a priest, I cannot see which, for it grows dark, with chaplains and sundry of the lords of Council waiting audience."

"Good. Then we'll try the devil on these devil-tamers. Friend Satan, go you to that door, slip through it softly and rush upon them roaring, driving them through this chamber so that we may see which of them will be bold enough to try to lay you. Dost understand, Beelzebub?"

Thomas nodded his horns and departed silently as a cat.

"Now open the door and stand on one side," said the King.

Cromwell obeyed, nor had they long to wait. Presently from the hall beyond there rose a most fearful clamour. Then through the door shot the bishop panting, after him came lords, chaplains, and secretaries, and last of all the priest, who, being very fat and hampered by his gown, could not run so fast, although at his back Satan leapt and bellowed. No heed did they take of the King's Majesty or of aught else, whose only thought was flight as they tore down the chamber to the farther door.

"Oh, noble, noble!" hallooed the King, who was shaking with laughter. "Give him your fork, devil, give him your fork," and having the royal command Bolle obeyed with zeal.

In thirty seconds it was all over; the rout had come and gone, only Thomas in his hideous attire stood bowing before the King, who exclaimed—

"I thank thee, Thomas Bolle, thou hast made me laugh as I have not laughed for years. Little wonder that thy mistress was condemned for witchcraft. Now," he added, changing his tone, "off with that mummery, and, Cromwell, go, catch one of those fools and tell them the truth ere tales fly round the palace. Jane, cease from merriment, there is a time for all things. Come hither, Lady Harflete, I would speak with you."

Cicely approached and curtseyed, leaving her boy in the Queen's arms, where he had gone to sleep, for she did not seem minded to part with him.

"You are asking much of us," he said suddenly, searching her with a shrewd glance, "relying, doubtless, on your wrongs, which are deep, or your face, which is sweet, or both. Well, these things move Kings mayhap more than others, also I knew old Sir John, your father, a loyal man and a brave, he fought well at Flodden; and young Harflete, your husband, if he still lives, had a good name like his forebears. Moreover your enemy, Maldon, is ours, a treacherous foreign snake such as England hates, for he would set her beneath the heel of Spain.

"Now, Dame Harflete, doubtless when you go hence you will bear away strange stories of King Harry and his doings. You will say he plays the fool, pelting his servants with inkpots when he is wrath, as God knows he has often cause to be, and scaring his bishops with sham Satans, as after all why should he not since it is a dull world? You'll say, too, that he takes his teaching from his ministers, and signs what these lay before him with small search as to the truth or falsity. Well, that's the lot of monarchs who have but one man's brain and one man's time; who needs must trust their slaves until these become their masters, and there is naught left," here his face grew fierce, "save to kill them, and find more and worse. New servants, new wives," and he glanced at Jane, who was not listening, "new friends, false, false, all three of them, new foes, and at the last old Death to round it off. Such has been the lot of kings from David down, and such I think it shall always be."

He paused a while, brooding heavily, then looked up and went on, "I know not why I should speak thus to a chit like you, except it be, that young though you are, you also have known trouble and the feel of a sick heart. Well, well, I have heard more of you and your affairs than you might think, and I forget nothing—that's my gift. Dame Harflete, you are richer than you have been advised to say, and I repeat you ask much of me. Justice is your due from your Sovereign, and you shall have it; but these wide Abbey lands, this Priory of Blossholme, whose nuns have befriended you and whom you desire to save, this embracing pardon for others who had shed blood, this cancelling outside of the form of law of a sentence passed by a Court duly constituted, if unjust, all in return for a loan of a pitiful £1000? You huckster well, Lady Harflete, one would think that your father had been a chapman, not rough John Foterell, you who can drive so shrewd a bargain with your King's necessities."

"Sire, Sire," broke in Cicely in confusion, "I have no more, my lands are wasted by Abbot Maldon, my husband's hall is burnt by his soldiers, my first year's rents, if ever I should receive them, are promised—"

"To whom?"

She hesitated.

"To whom?" he thundered. "Answer, Madam."

"To your Royal Commissioner, Dr. Legh."

"Ah! I thought as much, though when he spoke of you he did not tell it, the snuffling rogue."

"The jewels that came to me from my mother are in pawn for that £1000, and I have no more."

"A palpable lie, Dame Harflete, for if so, how have you paid Cromwell? He did not bring you here for nothing."

"Oh, my Liege, my Liege," said Cicely, sinking to her knees, "ask not a helpless woman to betray those who have befriended her in her most sore and honest need. I said I have nothing, unless those gems are worth more than I know."

"And I believe you, Dame Harflete. We have plucked you bare between us, have we not? Still, perchance, you will be no loser in the end. Now, Master Smith, there, does not work for love alone."

"Sire," said Jacob, "that is true, I copy my masters. I have this lady's jewels in pledge, and I hope to make a profit on them. Still, Sire, there is among them a pink pearl of great beauty that it might please the Queen to wear. Here it is," and he laid it upon the table.

"Oh, what a lovely thing," said Jane; "never have I seen its like."

"Then study it well, Wife, for you look your last upon it. When we cannot pay our soldiers to keep our crown upon our head, and preserve the liberties of England against the Spaniard and the Pope of Rome, it is no time to give you gems that I have not bought. Take that gaud and sell it, Master Smith, for whatever it will fetch among the Jews, and add the price to the £1000, lessened by one tenth for your trouble. Now, Dame Harflete, you have bought the favour of your King, for whoever else may, I'll not lie. Ah! here comes Cromwell. My Lord, you have been long."

515

"Your Grace, yonder priest is in a fit from fright, and thinks himself in hell. I had to tarry with him till the doctor came."

"Doubtless he'll get better now that you are gone. Poor man, if a sham devil frights him so, what will he do at last? Now, Cromwell, I have made examination of this business and I will sign your papers, all of them. Dame Harflete here tells me how hard you have worked for her, all for nothing, Cromwell, and that pleases me, who at times have wondered how you grew so rich, as your learner, Wolsey, did before you. *He* took bribes, Cromwell!"

"My Liege," he answered in a low voice, "this case was cruel, it moved my pity—"

"As it has ours, leaving us the richer by £1000 and the price of a pearl. There, five, are they all signed? Take them, Master Smith, as the Lady Harflete is your client, and study them to-night. If aught be wrong or omitted, you have our royal word that we will set it straight. This is our command—note it, Cromwell—that all things be done quickly as occasion shall arise to give effect to these precepts, pardons and patents which you, Cromwell, shall countersign ere they leave this room. Also, that no further fee, secret or declared, shall be taken from the Lady Harflete, whom henceforth, in token of our special favour, we create and name the Lady of Blossholme, from her husband or her child, as to any of these matters, and that Commissioner Legh, on receipt thereof, shall pay into our treasury any sum or sums that Dame Harflete may have promised to him. Write it down, my Lord Cromwell, and see that our words are carried out, lest it be the worse for you."

The Vicar-General hastened to obey, for there was something in the King's eye that frightened him. Meanwhile the Queen, after she had seen the coveted pearl disappear into Jacob's pocket, thrust back the child into Cicely's arms, and without any word of adieu or reverence to the King, followed by her lady, departed from the room, slamming the door behind her.

"Her Grace is cross because that gem—your gem, Lady Harflete—was refused to her," said Henry, then added in an angry growl, "'Fore God! does she dare to play off her tempers upon me, and so soon, when I am troubled about big matters? Oho! Jane Seymour is the Queen to-day, and she'd let the world know it. Well, what makes a queen? A king's fancy and a crown of gold, which the hand that set it on can take off again, head and all, if it stick too tight. And then where's your queen? Pest upon women and the whims that make us seek their company! Dame Harflete, you'd not treat your lord so, would you? You have never been to Court, I think, or I should have known your eyes again. Well, perhaps it is well for you, and that's why you are gentle and loving."

"If I am gentle, Sire, it is trouble that has gentled me, who have suffered so much, and know not even now whether after one week of marriage I am wife or widow."

"Widow? Should that be so, come to me and I will find you another and a nobler spouse. With your face and possessions it will not be difficult. Nay, do not weep, for your sake I trust that this lucky man may live to comfort you and serve his King. At least he'll be no Spaniard's tool and Pope's plotter."

"Well will he serve your Grace if God gives him the chance, as my murdered father did."

"We know it, Lady. Cromwell, will you never have finished with those writings? The Council waits us, and so does supper, and a word or two with her Grace ere bedtime. You, Thomas Bolle, you are no fool and can hold a sword; tell me, shall I go up north to fight the rebels, or bide here and let others do it?"

"Bide here, your Grace," answered Thomas promptly. "'Twixt Wash and Humber is a wild land in winter and arrows fly about there like ducks at night, none knowing whence they come. Also your Grace is over-heavy for a horse on forest roads and moorland, and if aught should chance, why, they'd laugh in Spain and Rome, or nearer, and who would rule England with a girl child on its throne?" and he stared hard at Cromwell's back.

"Truth at last, and out of the lips of a red-haired bumpkin," muttered the King, also staring at the unconscious Cromwell, who was engaged on his writing and either feigned deafness or did not hear. "Thomas Bolle, I said that you were no fool, although some may have thought you so, is there aught you would have in payment for your counsel—save money, for that we have none?"

"Aye, Sire, freedom from my oath as a lay-brother of the Abbey of Blossholme, and leave to marry."

"To marry whom?"

"Her, Sire," and he pointed to Emlyn.

"What! The other handsome witch? See you not that she has a temper? Nay, woman, be silent, it is written in your face. Well, take your freedom and her with it, but, Thomas Bolle, why did you not ask otherwise when the chance came your way? I thought better of you. Like the rest of us, you are but a fool after all. Farewell to you, Fool Thomas, and to you also, my fair Lady of Blossholme."

CHAPTER 16

The Voice in the Forest

The four were back safe in their lodging in Cheapside, whither, after the deeds had been sealed, three soldiers escorted them by command.

"Have we done well, have we done well?" asked Jacob, rubbing his hands.

"It would seem so, Master Smith," replied Cicely, "thanks to you; that is, if all the King said is really in those writings."

"It is there sure enough," said Jacob; "for know, that with the aid of a lawyer and three scriveners, I drafted them myself in the Lord Cromwell's office this morning, and oh, I drew them wide. Hard, hard we worked with no time for dinner, and that was why I was ten minutes late by the clock, for which Emlyn here chided me so sharply. Still, I'll read them through again, and if aught is left out we will have it righted, though these are the same parchments, for I set a secret mark upon them."

"Nay, nay," said Cicely, "leave well alone. His Grace's mood may change, or the Queen—that matter of the pearl."

"Ah, the pearl, it grieved me to part with that beautiful pearl. But there was no way out, it must be sold and the money handed over, our honour is on it. Had I refused, who knows? Yes, we may thank God, for if the most of your jewels are gone, the wide Abbey lands have come and other things. Nothing is forgot. Bolle is unfrocked and may wed; Cousin Stower has got a husband—"

Then Emlyn, who until now had been strangely silent, burst out in wrath—

"Am I, then, a beast that I should be given to this man like a heriot at yonder King's bidding?" she exclaimed, pointing with her finger at Bolle, who stood in the corner. "Who gave you the right, Thomas, to demand me in marriage?"

"Well, since you ask me, Emlyn, it was you yourself; once, many years ago, down in the mead by the water, and more lately in the chapel of Blossholme Priory before I began to play the devil."

"Play the devil! Aye, you have played the devil with me. There in the King's presence I must stand for an hour or more while all talked and never let a word slip between my lips, and at last hear myself called by his Grace a woman of temper and you a fool for wishing to marry me. Oh, if ever we do marry, I'll prove his words."

"Then perhaps, Emlyn, we who have got on a long while apart, had best stay so," answered Thomas calmly. "Yet, why you should fret because you must keep your tongue in its case for an hour, or because I asked leave to marry you in all honour, I do not know. I have worked my best for you and your mistress at some hazard, and things have not gone so ill, seeing that now we are quit of blame and in a fair way to peace and comfort. If you are not content, why then, the King was right, and I'm a fool, and so good-bye, I'll trouble you no more in fair weather or in foul. I have leave to marry, and there are other women in the world should I need one."

"Tread on their tails and even worms will turn," soliloquized Jacob, while Emlyn burst into tears.

Cicely ran to console her, and Bolle made as though he would leave the room.

Just then there came a great knocking on the street door, and the sound of a voice crying—

"In the King's name! In the King's name, open!"

"That's Commissioner Legh," said Thomas. "I learned the cry from him, and it is a good one at a pinch, as some of you may remember."

Emlyn dried her tears with her sleeve; Cicely sat down and Jacob shovelled the parchments into his big pockets. Then in burst the Commissioner, to whom some one had opened.

"What's this I hear?" he cried, addressing Cicely, his face as red as a turkey cock's. "That you have been working behind my back; that you have told falsehoods of me to his Grace, who called me knave and thief; that I am commanded to pay my fees into the Treasury? Oh, ungrateful wench, would to God that I had let you burn ere you disgraced me thus."

"If you bring so much heat into my poor house, learned Doctor, surely all of us will soon burn," said Jacob suavely. "The Lady Harflete said nothing that his Highness did not force her to say, as I know who was present, and among so many pickings cannot you spare a single dole? Come, come, drink a cup of wine and be calm."

But Dr. Legh, who had already drunk several cups of wine, would not be calm. He reviled first one of them and then the other, but especially Emlyn, whom he conceived to be the cause of all his woes, till at length he called her by a very ill name. Then came forward Thomas Bolle, who all this while had been standing in the corner, and took him by the neck.

"In the King's name!" he said, "nay, complain not, 'tis your own cry and I have warrant for it," and he knocked Legh's head against the door-post. "In the King's name, get out of this," and he gave him such a kick as never Royal Commissioner had felt before, shooting him down the passage. "For the third time in the King's name!" and he hurled him out in a heap into the courtyard. "Begone, and know if ever I see your pudding face again, in the King's name, I'll break your neck!"

Thus did Visitor Legh depart out of the life of Cicely, though in due course she paid him her first year's rent, nor ever asked who took the benefit.

"Thomas," said Emlyn, when he returned smiling at the memory of that farewell kick, "the King was right, I am quick-tempered at times, no ill thing for it has helped me more than once. Forget, and so will I," and she gave him her hand, which he kissed, then went to see about the supper.

While they ate, which they did heartily who needed food, there came another knock.

"Go, Thomas," said Jacob, "and say we see none to-night."

So Thomas went and they heard talk. Then he re-entered followed by a cloaked man, saying—

"Here is a visitor whom I dare not deny," whereon they all rose, thinking in their folly that it was the King himself, and not one almost as mighty in England for a while—the Lord Cromwell.

"Pardon me," said Cromwell, bowing in his courteous manner, "and if you will, let me be seated with you, and give me a bite and a sup, for I need them, who have been hard-worked to-day."

So he sat down among them, and ate and drank, talking pleasantly of many things, and telling them that the King had changed his mind at the Council, as he thought, because of the words of Thomas Bolle, which he believed had stuck there, and would not go north to fight the rebels after all, but would send the Duke of Norfolk and other lords. Then when he had done he pushed away his cup and platter, looked at his hosts and said—

"Now to business. My Lady Harflete, fortune has been your friend this day, for all you asked has been granted to you, which, as his Grace's temper has been of late, is a wondrous thing. Moreover, I thank you that you did not answer a certain question as to myself which I learn he put to you urgently."

"My Lord," said Cicely, "you have befriended me. Still, had he pressed me further, God knows. Commissioner Legh did not thank me to-night," and she told him of the visit they had just received, and of its ending.

"A rough man and a greedy, who doubtless henceforth will be your enemy," replied Cromwell. "Still you were not to blame, for who can reason with a bull in his own yard? Well, while I have power I'll not forget your faithfulness, though in truth, my Lady of Blossholme, I sit upon a slippery height, and beneath waits a gulf that has swallowed some as great, and greater. Therefore I will not deny it, I lay by while I may, not knowing who will gather."

He brooded a while, then went on, with a sigh—

"The times are uncertain; thus, you who have the promise of wealth may yet die a beggar. The lands of Blossholme Abbey, on which you hold a bond that will never be redeemed, are not yet in the King's hands to give. A black storm is bursting in the north and, I say this in secret, the fury of it may sweep Henry from the throne. If it should be so, away with you to any land where you are not known, for then after this day's work here a rope will be your only heritage. More, this Queen, unlike Anne who is gone, is a friend to the party of the Church, and though she affects to care little for such things, is bitter about that pearl, and therefore against you, its owner. Have you no jewel left that you could spare which I might take to her? As for the pearl itself, which Master Smith here swore to me was not to be found in the whole world when he showed me its fellow, it must be sold as the King commanded," and he looked at Jacob somewhat sourly.

Now Cicely spoke with Jacob, who went away and returned presently with a brooch in which was set a large white diamond surrounded by five small rubies.

"Take her this with my duty, my Lord," said Cicely.

"I will, I will. Oh! fear not, it shall reach her for my own sake as well as yours. You are a wise giver, Lady Harflete, who know when and where to cast your bread upon the waters. And now I have a gift for you that perchance will please you more than gems. Your husband, Christopher Harflete, accompanied by a servant, has landed in the north safe and well."

"Oh, my Lord," she cried, "then where is he now?"

"Alas! the rest of the tale is not so pleasing, for as he journeyed, from Hull I think, he was taken prisoner by the rebels, who have him fast at Lincoln, wishing to make him, whose name is of account, one of their company. But he being a wise and loyal man, contrived to send a letter to the King's captain in those parts, which has reached me this night. Here it is, do you know the writing?"

"Aye, aye," gasped Cicely, staring at the scrawl that was ill writ and worse spelt, for Christopher was no scholar.

"Then I'll read it to you, and afterwards certify a copy to multiply the evidence."

"To the Captain of the King's Forces outside Lincoln.

"This to give notice to you, his Grace, and his ministers and all others, that we, Christopher Harflete, Knight, and Jeffrey Stokes, his servant, when journeying from the seaport whither we had come from Spain, were taken by rebels in arms against the King and brought here to Lincoln. These men would win me to their party because the name of Harflete is still strong and known. So violent were they that we have taken some kind of oath. Yet this writing advises you that so I only did to save my life, having no heart that way who am a loyal man and understand little of their quarrel. Life, in sooth, is of small value to me who have lost wife, lands and all. Yet ere I die I would be avenged upon the murderous Abbot of Blossholme, and therefore I seek to keep my breath in me and to escape.

"I learn that the said Abbot is afoot with a great following within fifty miles of here. Pray God he does not get his claws in me again, but if so, say to the King, that Harflete died faithful.

"Christopher Harflete.

"Jeffrey Stokes, X his mark."

"My Lord," said Cicely, "what shall I do, my Lord?"

"There is naught to be done, save trust in God and hope for the best. Doubtless he will escape, and at least his Grace shall see this letter to-morrow morning and send orders to help him if may be. Copy it, Master Smith."

Jacob took the letter and began to write swiftly, while Cromwell thought.

"Listen," he said presently. "Round Blossholme there are no rebels, all of that colour have drawn off north. Now Foterell and Harflete are good names yonder, cannot you journey thither and raise a company?"

"Aye, aye, that I can do," broke in Bolle. "In a week I will have a hundred men at my back. Give commission and money to my Lady there and name me captain and you'll see."

"The commission and the captaincy under the privy signet shall be at this house by nine of the clock to-morrow," answered

Cromwell. "The money you must find, for there is none outside the coffers of Jacob Smith. Yet pause, Lady Harflete, there is risk and here you are safe."

"I know the risk," she answered, "but what do I care for risks who have taken so many, when my husband is yonder and I may serve him?"

"An excellent spirit, let us trust that it comes from on high," remarked Cromwell; but old Jacob, as he wrote *vera copia* for his Lordship's signature at the foot of the transcript of Christopher's letter, shook his head sadly.

In another minute Cromwell had signed without troubling to compare the two, and with some gentle words of farewell was gone, having bigger matters waiting his attention.

Cicely never saw him again, indeed with the exception of Jacob Smith she never saw any of those folk again, including the King, who had been concerned in this crisis of her life. Yet, notwithstanding his cunning and his extortion, she grieved for Cromwell when some four years later the Duke of Suffolk and the Earl of Southampton rudely tore the Garter and his other decorations off his person and he was haled from the Council to the Tower, and thence after abject supplications for mercy, to perish a criminal upon the block. At least he had served her well, for he kept all his promises to the letter. One of his last acts also was to send her back the pink pearl which he had received as a bribe from Jacob Smith, with a message to the effect that he was sure it would become her more than it had him, and that he hoped it would bring her a better fortune.

****

When Cromwell had gone Jacob turned to Cicely and inquired if she were leaving his house upon the morrow.

"Have I not said so?" she asked, with impatience. "Knowing what I know how could I stay in London? Why do you ask?"

"Because I must balance our account. I think you owe me a matter of twenty *marks* for rent and board. Also it is probable that we shall need money for our journey, and this day has left me somewhat bare of coin."

"Our journey?" said Cicely. "Do you, then, accompany us, Master Smith?"

"With your leave I think so, Lady. Times are bad here, I have no shilling left to lend, yet if I do not lend I shall never be forgiven. Also I need a holiday, and ere I die would once again see Blossholme, where I was born, should we live to reach it. But if we start to-morrow I have much to do this night. For instance, your jewels which I hold in pawn must be set in a place of safety; also these deeds, whereof copies should be made, and that pearl must be left in trusty hands for sale. So at what hour do we ride on this mad errand?"

"At eleven of the clock," answered Cicely, "if the King's safe-conduct and commission have come by then."

"So be it. Then I bid you good-night. Come with me, worthy Bolle, for there'll be no sleep for us. I go to call my clerks and you must go to the stable. Lady Harflete and you, Cousin Emlyn, get you to bed."

On the following morning Cicely rose with the dawn, nor was she sorry to do so, who had spent but a troubled night. For long sleep would not come to her, and when it did at length, she was tossed upon a sea of dreams, dreams of the King, who threatened her with his great voice; of Cromwell, who took everything she had down to her cloak; of Commissioner Legh, who dragged her back to the stake because he had lost his bribe.

But most of all she dreamed of Christopher, her beloved husband, who was so near and yet as far away as he had ever been, a prisoner in the hands of the rebels; her husband who deemed her dead.

From all these fantasies she awoke weeping and oppressed by fears. Could it be that when at length the cup of joy was so near her lips fate waited to dash it down again? She knew not, who had naught but faith to lean on, that faith which in the past had served her well. Meanwhile, she was sure that if Christopher lived he would make his way to Cranwell or to Blossholme, and, whatever the risk, thither she would go also as fast as horses could carry her.

Hurry as they would, midday was an hour gone ere they rode out of Cheapside. There was so much to do, and even then things were left undone. The four of them travelled humbly clad, giving out that they were a party of merchant folk returning to Cambridge after a visit to London as to an inheritance in which they were interested, especially Cicely, who posed as a widow named Johnson. This was their story, which they varied from time to time according to circumstances. In some ways their minds were more at ease than when they travelled to the great city, for now at least they were clear of the horrid company of Commissioner Legh and his people, nor were they haunted by the knowledge that they had about them jewels of great price. All these jewels were left behind in safe keeping, as were also the writings under the King's hand and seal, of which they only took attested copies, and with them the commission that Cromwell had duly sent to Cicely addressed to her husband and herself, and

Bolle's certificate of captaincy. These they hid in their boots or the linings of their vests, together with such money as was necessary for the costs of travel.

Thus riding hard, for their horses were good and fresh, they came unmolested to Cambridge on the night of the second day and slept there. Beyond Cambridge, they were told, the country was so disturbed that it would not be safe for them to journey. But just when they were in despair, for even Bolle said that they must not go on, a troop of the King's horse arrived on their way to join the Duke of Norfolk wherever he might lie in Lincolnshire.

To their captain, one Jeffreys, Jacob showed the King's commission, revealing who they were. Seeing that it commanded all his Grace's officers and servants to do them service, this Captain Jeffreys said that he would give them escort until their roads separated. So next day they went on again. The company was not pleasant, for the men, of whom there were about a hundred, proved rough fellows, still, having been warned that he who insulted or laid a finger on them should be hanged, they did them no harm. It was well, indeed, that they had their protection, for they found the country through which they passed up in arms, and were more than once threatened by mobs of peasants, led by priests, who would have attacked them had they dared.

For two days they travelled thus with Captain Jeffreys, coming on the evening of the second to Peterborough, where they found lodgings at an inn. When they rose the next morning, however, it was to discover that Jeffreys and his men had already gone, leaving a message to say that he had received urgent orders to push on to Lincoln.

Now once more they told their old tale, declaring that they were citizens of Boston, and having learned that the Fens were peaceful, perhaps because so few people lived in them, started forward by themselves under the guidance of Bolle, who had often journeyed through that country, buying or selling cattle for the monks. An ill land was it to travel in also in that wet autumn, seeing that in many places the floods were out and the tracks were like a quagmire. The first night they spent in a marshman's hut, listening to the pouring rain and fearing fever and ague, especially for the boy. The next day, by good fortune, they reached higher land and slept at a tavern.

Here they were visited by rude men, who, being of the party of rebellion, sought to know their business. For a while things were dangerous, but Bolle, who could talk their own dialect, showed that they were scarcely to be feared who travelled with two women and a babe, adding that he was a lay-brother of Blossholme Abbey disguised as a serving-man for dread of the King's party. Jacob Smith also called for ale and drank with them to the success of the Pilgrimage of Grace, as their revolt was named.

In this way they disarmed suspicion with one tale and another. Moreover, they heard that as yet the country round Blossholme remained undisturbed, although it was said that the Abbot had fortified the Abbey and stored it with provisions. He himself was with the leaders of the revolt in the neighbourhood of Lincoln, but he had done this that he might have a strong place to fall back on.

So in the end the men went away full of strong beer, and that danger passed by.

Next morning they started forward early, hoping to reach Blossholme by sunset though the days were shortening much. This, however, was not to be, for as it chanced they were badly bogged in a quagmire that lay about two miles off their inn, and when at length they scrambled out had to ride many miles round to escape the swamp. So it happened that it was already well on in the afternoon when they came to that stretch of forest in which the Abbot had murdered Sir John Foterell. Following the woodland road, towards sunset they passed the mere where he had fallen. Weary as she was, Cicely looked at the spot and found it familiar.

"I know this place," she said. "Where have I seen it? Oh, in the ill dream I had on that day I lost my father."

"That is not wonderful," answered Emlyn, who rode beside her carrying the child, "seeing that Thomas says it was just here they butchered him. Look, yonder lie the bones of Meg, his mare; I know them by her black mane."

"Aye, Lady," broke in Bolle, "and there he lies also where he fell; they buried him with never a Christian prayer," and he pointed to a little careless mound between two willows.

"Jesus, have mercy on his soul!" said Cicely, crossing herself. "Now, if I live, I swear that I will move his bones to the chancel of Blossholme church and build a fair monument to his memory."

This, as all visitors to the place know, she did, for that monument remains to this day, representing the old knight lying in the snow, with the arrow in his throat, between the two murderers whom he slew, while round the corner of the tomb Jeffrey Stokes gallops away.

While Cicely stared back at this desolate grave, muttering a prayer for the departed, Thomas Bolle heard something which caused him to prick his ears.

"What is it?" asked Jacob Smith, who saw the change in his face.

"Horses galloping—many horses, master," he answered; "yes, and riders on them. Listen."

They did so, and now they also heard the thud of horse's hoofs and the shouts of men.

"Quick, quick," said Bolle, "follow me. I know where we may hide," and he led them off to a dense thicket of thorn and beech scrub which grew about two hundred yards away under a group of oaks at a place where four tracks crossed. Owing to the beech leaves, which, when the trees are young, as every gardener knows, cling to the twigs through autumn and winter, this place was very close, and hid them completely.

Scarcely had they taken up their stand there, when, in the red light of the sunset, they saw a strange sight. Along, not that road they had followed, but another, which led round the farther side of King's Grave Mount, now seen and now hidden by the forest trees, a tall man in armour mounted on a grey horse, accompanied by another man in a leathern jerkin mounted on a black horse, galloped towards them, whilst, at a distance of not more than a hundred yards behind them, appeared a motley mob of pursuers.

"Escaped prisoners being run down," muttered Bolle, but Cicely took no heed. There was something about the appearance of the rider of the grey horse that seemed to draw her heart out of her.

She leaned forward on her beast's neck, staring with all her eyes. Now the two men were almost opposite the thicket, and the man in mail turned his face to his companion and called cheerily—

"We gain! We'll slip them yet, Jeffrey."

Cicely saw the face.

"Christopher!" she cried; *"Christopher!"*

Another moment and they had swept past, but Christopher—for it was he—had caught the sound of that remembered voice. With eyes made quick by love and fear she saw him pulling on his rein. She heard him shout to Jeffrey, and Jeffrey shout back to him in tones of remonstrance. They halted confusedly in the open space beyond. He tried to turn, then perceived his pursuers drawing nearer, and, when they were already at his heels, with an exclamation, pulled round again to gallop away. Too late! Up the slope they sped for another hundred yards or so. Now they were surrounded, and now, at the crest of it, they fought, for swords flashed in the red light. The pursuers closed in on them like hounds on an outrun fox. They went down—they vanished.

Cicely strove to gallop after them, for she was crazed, but the others held her back.

At length there was silence, and Thomas Bolle, dismounting, crept out to look. Ten minutes later he returned.

"All have gone," he said.

"Oh! he is dead!" wailed Cicely. "This fatal place has robbed me of father and of husband."

"I think not," answered Bolle. "I see no bloodstains, nor any signs of a man being carried. He went living on his horse. Still, would to Heaven that women could learn when to keep silent!"

CHAPTER 17

Between Doom and Honour

The day was about to break when at last, utterly worn out in body and mind, Cicely and her party rode their stumbling horses up to the gates of Blossholme Priory.

"Pray God the nuns are still here," said Emlyn, who held the child, "for if they have been driven out and my mistress must go farther, I think that she will die. Knock hard, Thomas, that old gardener is deaf as a wall."

Bolle obeyed with good will, till presently the grille in the door was opened and a trembling woman's voice asked who was there.

"That's Mother Matilda," said Emlyn, and slipping from her horse, she ran to the bars and began to talk to her through them. Then other nuns came, and between them they opened one of the large gates, for the gardener either could not or would not be aroused, and passed through it into the courtyard where, when it was understood that Cicely had really come again, there was a great welcoming. But now she could hardly speak, so they made her swallow a bowl of milk and took her to her old room, where sleep of some kind overcame her. When she awoke it was nine of the clock. Emlyn, looking little the worse, was already up and stood talking with Mother Matilda.

"Oh!" cried Cicely, as memory came back to her, "has aught been heard of my husband?"

They shook their heads, and the Prioress said—

"First you must eat, Sweet, and then we will tell you all we know, which is little."

So she ate who needed food sadly, and while Emlyn helped her to dress herself, hearkened to the news. It was of no great account, only confirming that which they had learnt from the Fenmen; that the Abbey was fortified and guarded by strange soldiers, rebellious men from the north or foreigners, and the Abbot supposed to be away.

Bolle, who had been out, reported also that a man he met declared that he had heard a troop of horsemen pass through the village in the night, but of this no proof was forthcoming, since if they had done so the heavy rain that was still falling had washed out all traces of them. Moreover, in those times people were always moving to and fro in the dark, and none could know if this troop had anything to do with the band they had seen in the forest, which might have gone some other way.

When Cicely was ready they went downstairs, and in Mother Matilda's private room found Jacob Smith and Thomas Bolle awaiting them.

"Lady Harflete," said Jacob, with the air of a man who has no time to lose, "things stand thus. As yet none know that you are here, for we have the gardener and his wife under ward. But as soon as they learn it at the Abbey there will be risk of an attack, and this place is not defensible. Now at your hall of Shefton it is otherwise, for there it seems is a deep moat with a drawbridge and the rest. To Shefton, therefore, you must go at once, unobserved if may be. Indeed, Thomas has been there already, and spoken to certain of your tenants whom he can trust, who are now hard at work preparing and victualling the place, and passing on the word to others. By nightfall he hopes to have thirty strong men to defend it, and within three days a hundred, when your commission and his captaincy are made known. Come, then, for there is no time to tarry and the horses are saddled."

So Cicely kissed Mother Matilda, who blessed and thanked her for all she had done, or tried to do on behalf of the sisterhood, and within five minutes once more they were on the backs of their weary beasts and riding through the rain to Shefton, which happily was but three miles away. Keeping under the lee of the woods they left the Priory unobserved, for in that wet few were stirring, and the sentinels at the Abbey, if there were any, had taken shelter in the guard-house. So thankfully enough they came unmolested to walled and wooded Shefton, which Cicely had last seen when she fled thence to Cranwell on the day of her marriage, oh, years and years ago, or so it seemed to her tormented heart.

It was a strange and a sad home-coming, she thought, as they rode over the drawbridge and through the sodden and weed-smothered *pleasaunce* to the familiar door. Yet it might have been worse, for the tenants whom Bolle had warned had not been idle. For two hours past and more a dozen willing women had swept and cleaned; the fires had been lit, and there was plenteous food of a sort in the kitchen and the store-room.

Moreover, in all the big hall were gathered about a score of her people, who welcomed her by raising their bonnets and even tried to cheer. To these at once Jacob read the King's commission, showing them the signet and the seal, and that other commission which named Thomas Bolle a captain with wide powers, the sight and hearing of which writings seemed to put a great heart into them who so long had lacked a leader and the support of authority. One and all they swore to stand by the King and their lady, Cicely Harflete, and her lord, Sir Christopher, or if he were dead, his child. Then about half of them took horse and rode off, this way and that, to gather men in the King's name, while the rest stayed to guard the Hall and work at its defences.

By sunset men were riding up from all sides, some of them driving carts loaded with provisions, arms and fodder, or sheep and beasts that could be killed for sustenance, while as they came Jacob enrolled their names upon a paper and by virtue of his commission Thomas Bolle swore them in. Indeed that night they had forty men quartered there, and the promise of many more.

By now, however, the secret was out, for the story had gone round and the smoke from the Shefton chimneys told its own tale. First a single spy appeared on the opposite rise, watching. Then he galloped away, to return an hour later with ten armed and mounted men, one of whom carried a banner on which were embroidered the emblems of the Pilgrimage of Grace. These men rode to within a hundred paces of Shefton Hall, apparently with the object of attacking it, then seeing that the drawbridge was up and that archers with bent bows stood on either side, halted and sent forward one of their number with a white flag to parley.

"Who holds Shefton," shouted this man, "and for what cause?"

"The Lady Harflete, its owner, and Captain Thomas Bolle, for the cause of the King," called old Jacob Smith back to him.

"By what warrant?" asked the man. "The Abbot of Blossholme is lord of Shefton, and Thomas Bolle is but a lay-brother of his monastery."

"By warrant of the King's Grace," said Jacob, and then and there at the top of his voice he read to him the Royal Commission, which when the envoy had heard, he went back to consult with his companions. For a while they hesitated, apparently still meditating attack, but in the end rode away and were seen no more.

Bolle wished to follow and fall on them with such men as he had, but the cautious Jacob Smith forbade it, fearing lest he should tumble into some ambush and be killed or captured with his people, leaving the place defenceless.

So the afternoon went by, and ere evening closed in they had so much strength that there was no more cause for fear of an attack from the Abbey, whose garrison they learned amounted to not over fifty men and a few monks, for most of these had fled.

That night Cicely with Emlyn and old Jacob were seated in the long upper room where her father, Sir John Foterell, had once surprised Christopher paying his court to her, when Bolle entered, followed by a man with a hang-dog look who was wrapped in a sheepskin coat which seemed to become him very ill.

"Who is this, friend?" asked Jacob.

"An old companion of mine, your worship, a monk of Blossholme who is weary of Grace and its pilgrimages, and seeks the King's comfort and pardon, which I have made bold to promise to him."

"Good," said Jacob, "I'll enter his name, and if he remains faithful your promise shall be kept. But why do you bring him here?"

"Because he bears tidings."

Now something in Bolle's voice caused Cicely, who was brooding apart, to look up sharply and say—

"Speak, and be swift."

"My Lady," began the man in a slow voice, "I, who am named Basil in religion, have fled the Abbey because, although a monk, I am true to the King, and moreover have suffered much from the Abbot, who has just returned raging, having met with some reverse out Lincoln way, I know not what. My news is that your lord, Sir Christopher Harflete, and his servant Jeffrey Stokes are prisoners in the Abbey dungeons, whither they were brought last night by a company of the rebels who had captured them and afterwards rode on."

"Prisoners!" exclaimed Cicely. "Then he is not dead or wounded? At least he is whole and safe?"

"Aye, my Lady, whole and safe as a mouse in the paws of a cat before it is eaten."

The blood left Cicely's cheeks. In her mind's eye she saw Abbot Maldon turned into a great cat with a monk's head and patting Christopher with his claws.

"My fault, my fault!" she said in a heavy voice. "Oh, if I had not called him he would have escaped. Would that I had been stricken dumb!"

"I don't think so," answered Brother Basil. "There were others watching for him ahead who, when he was taken, went away and that is how you came to get through so neatly. At least there he lies, and if you would save him, you had best gather what strength you can and strike at once."

"Does he know that I live?" asked Cicely.

"How can I tell, Lady? The Abbey dungeons are no good place for news. Yet the monk who took him his food this morning said that Sir Christopher told him that he had been undone by some ghost which called to him with the voice of his dead wife as he rode near King's Grave Mount."

Now when Cicely heard this she rose and left the room accompanied by Emlyn, for she could bear no more.

But Jacob Smith and Bolle remained questioning the man closely upon many matters, and, having learned all he could tell them, sent him away under guard and sat there till midnight consulting and making up their plans with the farmers and yeomen whom they called to them from time to time.

Next morning early they sought out Cicely and told her that to them it seemed wise that the Abbey should be attacked without delay.

"But my husband lies there," she answered in distress, "and then they will kill him."

"So I fear they may if we do not attack," replied Jacob. "Moreover, Lady, to tell the truth, there are other things to be thought of. For instance, the King's cause and honour, which we are bound to forward, and the lives and goods of all those who through us have declared themselves for him. If we lie idle Abbot Maldon will send messengers to the north and within a few days bring down thousands upon us, against whom we cannot hope to stand. Indeed, it is probable that he has already sent. But if they hear that the Abbey has fallen the rebels will scarcely come for revenge alone. Lastly, if we sit with folded hands, our own people may grow cold with doubts and fears and melt away, who now are hot as fire."

"If it must be, so let it be. In God's hands I leave his life," said Cicely in a heavy voice.

****

That day the King's men, under the captaincy of Bolle, advanced and invested the Abbey, setting their camp in Blossholme village. Cicely, who would not be left behind, came with them and once more took up her quarters in the Priory, which on a formal summons opened its gates to her, its only guard, the deaf gardener, surrendering at discretion. He was set to work as a camp servant, and never in his life did he labour so hard before, since Emlyn, who owed him many a grudge, saw to it that he did not lack for tasks that were mean and heavy.

Now that day Thomas and others spied out the Abbey and returned shaking their heads, for without cannon—and as yet they had none—the great building of hewn stone seemed almost impregnable. At but one spot indeed was attack possible, from the back where once stood the dormers and farm steadings which Emlyn had egged on Thomas to burn. These had been built up to the inner edge of the moat, making, as it were, part of the Abbey wall, but the fierce fire had so cracked and crumbled their masonry that several rods of it had fallen forward into the water.

For purposes of defence the gap this formed was now closed by a double palisade of stout stakes, filled in with faggots, the charred beams of the old buildings and other rubbish. Yet to carry this palisade, protected as it was by the broad and deep moat and commanded from the windows and the corner tower, was more than they dared try, since if it could be done at all it would certainly cost them very many lives. One thing they had learned, however, from the monk Basil and others, that in the Abbey there was but small store of food to feed so many: three days' supply, said Basil, and none put it at over four.

That evening, then, they held another council, at which it was determined to starve the place out and only attempt an onslaught if their spies reported to them that the rebels were marching to its relief.

"But," urged Cicely, "then my lord and Jeffrey Stokes will starve also," whereon they went away sadly, saying there was no choice, seeing that they were but two men and the lives of many lay at stake.

The siege began, just such a siege as Cicely had suffered at Cranwell Towers. The first day the garrison of the Abbey scoffed at them from the walls. The second day they scoffed no longer, noting that the force of the besiegers increased, which it did hourly. The third day suddenly they let down the drawbridge and poured out on to it as though for a sortie, but when they perceived the scores of Bolle's men waiting bow in hand and arrow on string, changed their minds and drew the bridge up again.

"They grow hungry and desperate," said the shrewd Jacob. "Soon we shall have some message from them."

He was right, since just before sunset a postern gate was opened and a man, holding a white flag above his head, was seen swimming across the moat. He scrambled out on the farther side, shook himself like a dog, and advanced slowly to where Bolle and the women stood upon the Abbey green out of arrow-shot from the walls. Indeed, Cicely, who was weak with dread and wretchedness, leaned against the oaken stake that had never been removed, to which once she was tied to be burned for witchcraft.

"Who is that man?" said Emlyn to her.

Cicely scanned the gaunt, bearded figure who walked haltingly like one that is sick.

"I know not—yes, yes, he puts me in mind of Jeffrey Stokes!"

"Jeffrey it is and no other," said Emlyn, nodding her head. "Now what news does he bear, I wonder?"

Cicely made no reply, only clung to her stake and waited, with just such a heart as once she had waited there while the Abbey cook blew up his brands to fire her faggots. Jeffrey was opposite to her now; his sunken eyes fell upon her, and at the sight his bearded chin dropped, making his face look even more long and hollow than it had before.

"Ah!" he said, speaking to himself, "many wars and journeyings, months in an infidel galley, three days with not enough food to feed a rat and a bath in November water! Well, such things, to say nothing of a worse, turn men's brains. Yet to think that I should live to see a daylight ghost in homely Blossholme, who never met with one before."

Still staring he shook the water from his beard, then added, "Laybrother or Captain Thomas Bolle, whichever you may be now-a-days, if you're not a ghost also, give me a quart of strong ale and a loaf of bread, for I'm empty as a gutted herring, and floating heavenward, so to speak, who would stick upon this scurvy earth."

"Jeffrey, Jeffrey," broke in Cicely, "what news of your master? Emlyn, tell him that we still live. He does not understand."

"Oh, you still live, do you?" he added slowly. "So the fire could not burn you after all, or Emlyn either. Well, then, there's hope for every one, and perhaps hunger and Abbot Maldon's knives cannot kill Christopher Harflete."

"He lives, then, and is well?"

"He lives and is as well as a man may be after a three days' fast in a black dungeon that is somewhat damp. Here's a writing on the matter for the captain of this company," and, taking a letter from the folds of the white flag in which it had been fastened, he handed it to Bolle, who, as he could not read, passed it on to Jacob Smith. Just then a lad brought the ale for which Jeffrey had asked, and with it a platter of cold meat and bread, on which he fell like a famished hound, drinking in great gulps and devouring the food almost without chewing it.

"By the saints, you are starved, Jeffrey," said a yeoman who stood by. "Come with me and shift those wet clothes of yours, or you will take harm," and he led him off, still eating, to a tent that stood near by.

Meanwhile, Jacob, having studied the letter with bent and anxious brows, read it aloud. It ran thus—

535

"To the Captain of the King's men, from Clement, Abbot of Blossholme.

"By what warrant I know not you besiege us here, threatening this Abbey and its Religious with fire and sword. I am told that Cicely Foterell is your leader. Say, then, to that escaped witch that I hold the man she calls her husband, and who is the father of her base-born child, a prisoner. Unless this night she disperses her troop and sends me a writing signed and witnessed, promising indemnity on behalf of the King for me and those with me for all that we may have done against him and his laws, or privately against her, and freedom to go where we will without pursuit or hindrance or loss of land or chattels, know that to-morrow at the dawn we put to death Christopher Harflete, Knight, in punishment of the murders and other crimes that he has committed against us, and in proof thereof his body shall be hung from the Abbey tower. If otherwise we will leave him unharmed here where you shall find him after we have gone. For the rest, ask his servant, Jeffrey Stokes, whom we send to you with this letter.

"Clement, Abbot."

Jacob finished reading and a silence fell upon all who listened.

"Let us go to some private place and consider this matter," said Emlyn.

"Nay," broke in Cicely, "it is I, who in my lord's absence, hold the King's commission and I will be heard. Thomas Bolle, first send a man under flag to the Abbot, saying, that if aught of harm befalls Sir Christopher Harflete I'll put every living soul within the Abbey walls to death by sword or rope, and stand answerable for it to the King. Set it in writing, Master Smith, and send with it copy of the King's commission for my warrant. At once, let it be done at once."

So they went to a cottage near by, which Bolle used as a guardhouse, where this stern message was written down, copied out fair, signed by Cicely and by Bolle, as captain, with Jacob Smith for witness. This paper, together with a copy of the King's commissions, Cicely with her own hand gave to a bold and trusty man, charged to ask an answer, who departed, carrying the white flag and wearing a steel shirt beneath his doublet, for fear of treachery.

When he had gone they sent for Jeffrey, who arrived clad in dry garments and still eating, for his hunger was that of a wolf.

"Tell us all," said Cicely.

"It will be a long story if I begin at the beginning, Lady. When your worshipful father, Sir John, and I rode away from Shefton on the day of his murder—"

"Nay, nay," interrupted Cicely, "that may stand, we have no time. My lord and you escaped from Lincoln, did you not, and, as we saw, were taken in the forest?"

"Aye, Lady. Some tricksy spirit called out with your voice and he heard and pulled rein, and so they came on to us and overwhelmed us, though without hurt as it chanced. Then they brought us to the Abbey and thrust us into that accursed dungeon, where, save for a little bread and water, we have starved for three days in the dark. That is all the tale."

"How, then, did you come out, Jeffrey?"

"Thus, my Lady. Something over an hour ago a monk and three guards unlocked the dungeon door. While we blinked at his lantern, like owls in the sunlight, the monk said that the Abbot purposed to send me to the camp of the King's party to offer Christopher Harflete's life against the lives of all of them. He told him, Harflete, also, that he had brought ink and paper and that if he wished to save himself he would do well to write a letter praying that this offer might be accepted, since otherwise he would certainly die at dawn."

"And what said my husband?" asked Cicely, leaning forward.

"What said he? Why, he laughed in their faces and told them that first he would cut off his hand. On this they haled me out of the dungeon roughly enough, for I would have stayed there with him to the end. But as the door closed he shouted after me, 'Tell the King's officers to burn this rats' nest and take no heed of Christopher Harflete, who desires to die!'"

"Why does he desire to die?" asked Cicely again.

"Because he thinks his wife dead, Mistress, as I did, and believes that in the forest he heard her voice calling him to join her."

"Oh God! oh God!" moaned Cicely; "I shall be his death."

"Not so," answered Jeffrey. "Do you know so little of Christopher Harflete that you think he would sell the King's cause to gain his own life? Why, if you yourself came and pleaded with him he would thrust you away, saying, 'Get thee behind me, Satan!'"

"I believe it, and I am proud," muttered Cicely. "If need be, let Harflete die, we'll keep his honour and our own lest he should live to curse us. Go on."

"Well, they led me to the Abbot, who gave me that letter which you have, and bade me take it and tell the case to whoever commanded here. Then he lifted up his hand and, laying it on the crucifix about his neck, swore that this was no idle threat, but that unless his terms were taken, Harflete should hang from the tower top at to-morrow's dawn, adding, though I knew not what he meant, 'I think you'll find one yonder who will listen to that reasoning.' Now he was dismissing me when a soldier said—

"'Is it wise to free this Stokes? You forget, my Lord Abbot, that he is alleged to have witnessed a certain slaying yonder in the forest and will bear evidence.' 'Aye,' answered Maldon, 'I had forgotten who in this press remembered only that no other man would be believed. Still, perhaps it would be best to choose a different messenger and to silence this fellow at once. Write down that Jeffrey Stokes, a prisoner, strove to escape and was killed by the guards in self-defence. Take him hence and let me hear no more.'

"Now my blood went cold, although I strove to look as careless as a man may on an empty stomach after three days in the dark, and cursed him prettily in Spanish to his face. Then, as they were haling me off, Brother Martin—do you remember him? he was our companion in some troubles over-seas—stepped forward out of the shadow and said, 'Of what use is it, Abbot, to stain your soul with so foul a murder? Since John Foterell died the King has many things to lay to your account, and any one of them will hang you. Should you fall into his hands, he'll not hark back to Foterell's death, if, indeed, you were to blame in that matter.'

"'You speak roughly, Brother,' answered the Abbot; 'and acts of war are not murder, though perchance afterwards you might say they were, to save your own skin, or others might. Well, if so, there's wisdom in your words. Touch not the man. Give him the letter and thrust him into the moat to swim it. His lies can make no odds in the count against us.'

"Well, they did so, and I came here, as you saw, to find you living, and now I understand why Maldon thought that Harflete's life is worth so much," and, having done his tale, once more Jeffrey began to eat.

Cicely looked at him, they all looked at him—this gaunt, fierce man who, after many other sorrows and strivings, had spent three days in a black dungeon with the rats, fed upon water and a few fingers of black bread. Yes; with the crawling rats and another man so dear to one of them, who still sat in that horrid hole, waiting to be hung like a felon at the dawn. The silence, with only Jeffrey's munching to break it, grew painful, so that all were glad when the door opened and the messenger whom they had sent to the Abbey appeared. He was breathless, having run fast, and somewhat disturbed, perhaps because two arrows were sticking in his back, or rather in his jerkin, for the mail beneath had stopped them.

"Speak," said old Jacob Smith; "what is your answer?"

"Look behind me, master, and you will find it," replied the man. "They set a ladder across the moat and a board on that, over which a priest tripped to take my writing. I waited a while, till presently I heard a voice hail me from the gateway tower, and, looking up, saw Abbot Maldon standing there, with a face like that of a black devil.

"'Hark you, knave,' he said to me, 'get you gone to the witch, Cicely Foterell, and to the recreant monk, Bolle, whom I curse and excommunicate from the fellowship of Holy Church, and tell them to watch for the first light of dawn, for by it, somewhat high up, they'll see Christopher Harflete hanging black against the morning sky!'

"On hearing this I lost my caution, and hallooed back—

"'If so, ere to-morrow's nightfall you shall keep him company, every one of you, black against the evening sky, except those who go to be quartered at Tower Hill and Tyburn.' Then I ran and they shot at me, hitting once or twice, but, though old, the mail was good, and here am I, unhurt except for bruises."

****

A while later Cicely, Jacob Smith, Thomas Bolle, Jeffrey Stokes, and Emlyn Stower sat together taking counsel—very earnest counsel, for the case was desperate. Plan after plan was brought forward and set aside for this reason or for that, till at length they stared at each other emptily.

"Emlyn," exclaimed Cicely at last, "in past days you were wont to be full of comfortable words; have you never a one in this extreme?" for all the while Emlyn had sat silent.

"Thomas," said Emlyn, looking up, "do you remember when we were children where we used to catch the big carp in the Abbey moat?"

"Aye, woman," he answered; "but what time is this for fishing stories of many years ago? As I was saying, of that tunnel underground there is no hope. Beyond the grove it is utterly caved in and blocked—I've tried it. If we had a week, perhaps—"

"Let her be," broke in Jacob; "she has something to tell us."

"And do you remember," went on Emlyn, "that you told me that there the carp were so big and fat because just at this place 'neath the drawbridge the Abbey sewer—the big Abbey sewer down which all foul things are poured—empties itself into the moat, and that therefore I would eat none of those fish, even in Lent?"

"Aye, I remember. What of it?"

"Thomas, did I hear you say that the powder you sent for had come?"

"Yes, an hour ago; six kegs, by the carrier's van, of a hundredweight each. Not so much as we hoped for, but something, though, as the cannon has not come—for the King's folk had none—it is of no use."

"A dark night, a ladder with a plank on it, a brick arched drain, two hundredweight, or better still, four of powder set beneath the gate, a slow-match and a brave man to fire it—taken together with God's blessing, these things might do much," mused Emlyn, as though to herself.

Now at length they took her point.

"They'd be listening like a cat for a mouse," said Bolle.

"I think the wind rises," she answered; "I hear it in the trees. I think presently it will blow a gale. Also, lanterns might be shown at the back where the breach is, and men might shout there, as though preparing to attack. That would draw them off. Meanwhile Jeffrey Stokes and I would try our luck with the ladder and the kegs of powder—he to roll and I to fire when the time came, for being, as you have heard, a witch, I understand how to humour brimstone."

****

Ten minutes later, and their plans were fixed. Two hours later, and, in the midst of a raving gale, hidden by the pitchy darkness and the towering screen of the lifted drawbridge, Emlyn and the strong Jeffrey rolled the kegs of powder over planks laid across the moat, into the mouth of the big drain and twenty feet down it, till they lay under the gateway towers! Then, lying there in the stinking filth, they drew the spigots out of holes that they had made in them, and in their place set the slow-matches. Jeffrey struck a flint, blew the tinder to a glow, and handed it to Emlyn.

"Now get you gone," she said; "I follow. At this job one is better than two."

A minute later she joined him on the farther bank of the moat. "Run!" she said. "Run for your life; there's death behind!"

He obeyed, but Emlyn turned and screamed, till, hearing her through the gale, all the guard hurried up the towers, flashing lanterns, to see what passed.

"*Storm! Storm!*" she cried. "*Up with the ladders! For the kind and harflete! Storm! Storm!*"

Then she too turned and fled.

CHAPTER 18

Out of the Shadows

Through the black night sudden and red there shot a sheet of fire illumining all things as lightning does. Above the roaring of the gale there echoed a dull and heavy noise like to that of muffled thunder. Then after a moment's pause and silence the sky rained stones, and with them the limbs of men.

"The gateway's gone," shouted a great voice, it was that of Bolle. "Out with the ladders!"

Men who were waiting ran up with them and thrust them, four in all, athwart the moat. By the planks that were lashed along their staves they scrambled across and over the piles of shattered masonry into the courtyard beyond where none waited them, for all who watched here were dead or maimed.

"Light the lanterns," shouted Bolle again, "for it will be dark in yonder," and a man who followed with a torch obeyed him.

Then they rushed across the courtyard to the door of the refectory, which stood open. Here in the wide, high-roofed hall they met the mass of Maldon's people pouring back from the faggoted breach, where they had been gathered, expecting attack, some of them also bearing lanterns. For a moment the two parties stood staring at each other; then followed a wild and savage scene. With shouts and oaths and battle-cries they fought furiously. The massive, oaken tables were overthrown, by the red flicker of the pole-borne lanterns men grappled and fell and slew each other upon the floor. A priest struck down a yeoman with a brazen crucifix, and next moment himself was brained with its broken shaft.

"For God and Grace!" shouted some; "For the King and Harflete!" answered others.

"Keep line! Keep line!" roared Bolle, "and sweep them out."

The lanterns were dashed down and extinguished till but one remained, a red and wavering star. Hoarse voices shouted for light, for none knew friend from foe. It came; some one had fired the tapestries and the blaze ran up them to the roof. Then fearing lest they should be roasted, the Abbot's folk gave way and fled to the farther door, followed by their foes. Here it was that most of them fell, for they jammed in the doorway and were cut down there are on the stair beyond.

While Bolle still plied his axe fiercely, some one caught his arm and screamed into his ear—

"Let be! Let be! The wretch is sped."

In his red wrath he turned to strike the speaker, and saw by the flare that it was Cicely.

"What do you here?" he cried. "Get gone."

"Fool," she answered in a low, fierce voice, "I seek my husband. Show me the path ere it be too late, you know it alone. Come, Jeffrey Stokes, a lantern, a lantern!"

Jeffrey appeared, sword in one hand and lantern in the other, and with him Emlyn, who also held a sword which she had plucked from a fallen man, Emlyn still foul with the filth of the sewer and the mud of the moat.

"I may not leave," muttered Thomas Bolle. "I seek Maldon."

"On to the dungeons," shrieked Emlyn, "or I will stab you. I heard them give word to kill Harflete."

Then he snatched the light from Jeffrey's hand, and crying "Follow me," rushed along a passage till they came to an open door and beyond it to stairs. They descended the stairs and passed other passages which ran underground, till a sudden turn to the right brought them to a little walled-in place with a vaulted roof. Two torches flared in iron holders in the masonry, and by the light of them they saw a strange and fearful sight.

At the end of the open place a heavy, nail-studded door stood wide, revealing a cell, or rather a little cave beyond—those who are curious can see it to this day. Fastened by a chain to the wall of this dungeon was a man, who held in his hand a three-legged stool and tugged at his chain like a maddened beast. In front of him, holding the doorway, stood a tall, lank priest, his robe tucked up into his girdle. He was wounded, for blood poured from his shaven crown and he plied a great sword with both hands, striking savagely at four men who tried to cut him down. As Bolle and his party appeared, one of these men fell beneath the priest's blows, and another took his place, shouting—

"Out of the way, traitor. We would kill Harflete, not you."

"We die or live together, murderers," answered the priest in a thick, gasping voice.

At this moment one of them, it was he who had spoken, heard the sound of the rescuers' footsteps and glanced back. In an instant he turned and was running past them like a hare. As he went the light from the lantern fell upon his face, and Emlyn knew it for that of the Abbot. She struck at him with the sword she held, but the steel glanced from his mail. He also struck, but at the lantern, dashing it to the ground.

"Seize him," screamed Emlyn. "Seize Maldon, Jeffrey," and at the words Stokes bounded away, only to return presently, having lost him in the dark passages. Then with a roar Bolle leaped upon the two remaining men-at-arms as they faced about, and very soon between his axe and the sword of the priest behind, they sank to the ground and died still fighting, who knew they had no hope of quarter.

It was over and done and dreadful silence fell upon the place, the silence of the dead broken only by the heavy breathing of those who remained alive. There the wounded monk leaned against the door-post, his red sword drooping to the floor. There Harflete, the stool still lifted, rested his weight against the chain and peered forward in amazement, swaying as though from weakness. And lastly there lay the three slain men, one of whom still moved a little.

Cicely crept forward; over the dead she went and past the priest till she stood face to face with the prisoner.

"Come nearer and I will dash out your brains," he said in a hoarse voice, for such light as there was came from behind her whom he thought to be but another of the murderers.

Then at length she found her voice.

"Christopher!" she cried, "Christopher!"

He hearkened, and the stool fell from his hand.

"The Voice again," he muttered. "Well, 'tis time. Tarry a while, Wife, I come, I come!" and he fell back against the wall shutting his eyes.

She leapt to him, and throwing her arms about him kissed his lips, his poor, bloodless lips. The shut eyes opened.

"Death might be worse," he said, "but so I knew that we would meet."

Now Emlyn, seeing some change in his face, snatched one of the torches from its iron and ran forward, holding it so that the light fell full on Cicely.

"Oh, Christopher," she cried, "I am no ghost, but your living wife."

He heard, he stared, he stared again, then lifted his thin hand and stroked her hair.

543

"Oh God," he exclaimed, "the dead live!" and down he fell in a heap at her feet.

They thrust Cicely aside, Cicely who stood there shivering, she who thought he had gone again and this time for ever. With difficulty they broke the chain whereby he had been held like a kennelled hound, and bore him, still senseless, up the long passages, Bolle going ahead as guard and Jeffrey Stokes following after. Behind them came Emlyn supporting the wounded monk Martin, for it was he and no other who had saved the life of Christopher.

As they went up towards the stairs they heard a roaring noise.

"Fire!" said Cicely, who knew that sound well, and next instant the light of it burst upon them and its smoke wrapped them round. The Abbey was ablaze, and its wide hall in front looked like the mouth of hell.

"Did I not prophesy that it would be so—yonder at Cranwell burning?" asked Emlyn, with a fierce laugh.

"Follow me!" shouted Bolle. "Be swift now ere the roof falls and traps us."

On they went desperately, leaving the hall on their left, and well for them was it that Thomas knew the way. One little chamber through which they passed had already caught, for flakes of fire fell among them from above and here the smoke was very thick. They were through it, who even a minute later could never have walked that path and lived. They were through it and out into the open air by the cloister door, which those who fled before them had left wide. They reached the moat just where the breach had been mended with faggots, and mounting on them Bolle shouted till one of his own men heard him and dropped the bow that he had raised to shoot him as a rebel. Then planks and ladders were brought, and at last they escaped from danger and the intolerable heat.

******

Thus it was that Cicely who lost her love in fire, in fire found him once again.

For Christopher was not dead as at first they feared. They carried him to the Priory, and there Emlyn, having felt his heart and found that it still beat, though faintly, sent Mother Matilda to fetch some of that Portugal wine of hers which Commissioner Legh had praised. Spoonful by spoonful she poured it down his throat, till at length he opened his eyes, though only to shut them again in natural sleep, for the wine had taken a hold of his starved body and weakened brain. For hour after hour Cicely sat by him, only rising from time to time to watch the burning of the great Abbey church, as once she had watched that of its dormers and farmsteading.

About three in the morning the lead ceased to pour down in a silvery molten shower, its roofs fell in, and by dawn it was nothing but a fire-blackened shell much as it remains to-day. Just before daybreak Emlyn came to her, saying—

"There is one who would speak with you."

"I cannot see him," she answered, "I bide by my husband."

"Yet you should," said Emlyn, "since but for him you would now have no husband. The monk Martin, who held off the murderers, is dying and desires to bid you farewell."

Then Cicely went to find the man still conscious, but fading away with the flow of his own blood, which could not be stayed by any skill they had.

"I have come to thank you," she murmured, who knew not what else to say.

"Thank me not," he answered faintly, pausing often between his words, "who did but strive to repay part of a great debt. Last winter I shared in awful sin, in obedience, not to my heart, but to my vows. I who was set to watch the body of your husband found that he lived, and by my help he was borne away upon a ship. That ship was taken by the Infidels, and afterwards he and I and Jeffrey served together upon their galleys. There I fell sick, and your husband nursed me back to life. It was I who brought you the deeds and wrote the letter which I gave to Emlyn Stower. My vows still held me fast, and I did no more. This night I broke their bonds, for when I heard the order given that he should be slain I ran down before the murderers and fought my best, forgetting that I was a priest, till at length you came. Let this atone my crimes against my Country, my King and you that I died for my friend at last, as I am glad to do who find this world—too difficult."

"I will tell him if he lives," sobbed Cicely.

He opened his eyes, which had shut, and answered—

"Oh, he'll live, he'll live. You have had many troubles, but, save for the creep of age and death, they are over. I can see and know."

Again he shut his eyes and the watchers thought that all was done, till of a sudden once more he opened them and added in broken tones—

"The Abbot—show him mercy—if you can. He is wicked and cruel, but I have been his confessor and know his heart. He strove for a good end—by an evil road. Queen Catherine was the King's lawful wife. To seize the monasteries is shameless theft. Also his blood is not English; he sees otherwise, and serves the Pope as I do, and Spain, as

I do not. As I have helped you, help him. Judge not, that ye be not judged. Promise!" and he raised himself a little on the bed and looked at her earnestly.

"I promise," answered Cicely, and as she spoke Martin smiled. Then his face turned quite grey, all the light went out of his eyes and a moment later Emlyn threw a linen cloth over his head. It was finished.

Cicely returned to Christopher to find him sitting up in bed drinking a bowl of broth.

"Oh, my husband, my husband," she said, casting her arms about him. Then she took her son and laid him upon his father's breast.

Three days had gone by and Christopher and Cicely were walking in the shrubbery of Shefton Hall. By now, although still weak, he was almost recovered, whose only sickness had been grief and famine, for which joy and plenty are wonderful medicines. It was evening, a pleasant and beautiful early winter evening just fading into night. Seated on a bench he had been telling her his adventures, and they were a moving tale worthy, as Cicely wrote afterwards in a letter to old Jacob Smith that is still extant in her fine, quaint handwriting, to be recorded in a book, though this it would seem was never done.

He told her of the great fight on the ship *Great Yarmouth*, when they were taken by the two Turkish pirates, and of how bravely Father Martin bore himself. Afterwards when they came to the galleys, by good fortune Martin, Jeffrey and he served on the same bench. Then Martin fell sick of some Southern fever, and being in port at Tunis at the time, where they could get fruit, they nursed him back to life and strength. Four months later the Emperor Charles attacked Tunis, and when it fell, through God's mercy, they were rescued with the other Christian slaves, after which Martin returned to England taking old Sir John's writings to be delivered to his next heir, for they all believed Cicely to be dead.

But Christopher and Jeffrey, having nothing to seek at home, stayed to fight with the Spaniards against the Turks, who had oppressed them so sorely. When that war was over they made their way back to England, not knowing where else to go and having a score to settle against the Spanish Abbot of Blossholme, and—well, she knew the rest.

Aye, answered Cicely, she knew it and never would forget it, but it was chill for him sitting on that bench, he must come in. Christopher laughed at her, and answered—

"Sweetheart, if you could have seen the bench on which it was my lot to sit yonder off the coast of Africa, but new recovered from the wound which I had of Maldon's men at Cranwell Towers, you

546

would not be anxious for me here. There for six long months chained to Jeffrey and to Father Martin, for it pleased those heathen devils to keep the three of us together, perhaps that they might watch us better, through the hot days that scorched us, and the chill, wet nights, we laboured at our oars, while infidel overseers ran up and down the boards and thrashed us with their whips of hide. Yes," he added slowly, "they thrashed us as though we were oxen in a yoke. You have seen the scars upon my back."

"Oh, God! to think of it," she murmured; "you, a noble Englishman, beaten by those savage wretches like a brute? How did you bear it, Christopher?"

"I know not, Wife. I think that had it not been for that angel in man's form, the priest Martin—peace be to his noble soul—that angel who thrice at least has saved my life, I should have dashed out my brains against the thwarts, or starved myself to death, or provoked the Moors to kill me; I, who, thinking you dead, had no hope to live for. But Martin taught me otherwise; he preached patience and submission, saying that I did not suffer for nothing—of his own miseries he never spoke—and that he was sure that fearful as was my lot, all things worked together for good to me."

"And therefore it was that you lived on, Husband? Oh! I'll build a shrine to that saint Martin."

"Not altogether, dear. I'll tell you true; I lived for vengeance—vengeance on Clement Maldon, the man, or the devil, who wrought me all this ill, and, being yet young, made me old with grief and pain," and he pointed to his scarred forehead and the hair above, that was now grizzled with white, "and vengeance, too, upon those worshippers of Mohammed, my masters. Yes; though Martin reproved me when I made confession to him, I think it was for that I lived, and the saints know," he added grimly, "afterwards at the sack, and elsewhere, I took it on the Turks. Oh! you should have seen the last meeting of Jeffrey and myself with the captain of that galley and his officers who had so often beaten us. No, I am glad you did not see it, for it was fierce and bloody; even the hard-hearted Spaniards stared."

He paused, and perhaps to change the current of his mind—for during all his after-life, when Christopher brooded on these things he grew gloomy for hours, and even days—Cicely said hurriedly—

"I wonder what has chanced to our enemy, the Abbot. The search has been close, the roads are watched, and we know that he had none with him, for all his foreign soldiers are slain or taken. I think he must be dead in the fire, Christopher."

He shook his head.

"A devil does not die in fire. He is away somewhere, to plot fresh murders—perhaps our own and our boy's. Oh!" he added savagely, "till my hands are about his throat and my dagger is in his heart there's no peace for me, who have a score to pay and you both to guard."

Cicely knew not what to answer; indeed, when this mood was on him it was hard to reason with Christopher, who had suffered so fearfully, and, like herself, been saved but by a miracle or the mandate of Heaven.

Of a sudden a hush fell upon the place. The blackbirds ceased their winter chatter in the laurels; it grew so still that they heard a dead leaf drop to the ground. The night was at hand. One last red ray from the set sun struck across the frosty sky and was reflected to the earth. In the light of that ray Christopher's trained eyes caught the gleam of something white that moved in the shadow of the beech tree where they sat. Like a tiger he sprang at it, and the next moment haled out a man.

"Look," he said, twisting the head of his captive so that the glow fell on it. "Look; I have the snake. Ah! Wife, you saw nothing, but I saw him, and here he is at last—at last!"

"The Abbot!" gasped Cicely.

The Abbot it was indeed, but oh! how changed. His plump, olive-coloured countenance had shrunk to that of a skeleton still covered by yellow skin, in which the dark eyes rolled bloodshot and unnaturally large. His tonsure and jaws showed a growth of stubbly grey hair, his frame had become weak and small, his soft and delicate hands resembled those of a woman dead of some wasting disease, and, like his garments, were clogged with dirt. The mail shirt he wore hung loose upon him; one of his shoes was gone, and the toes peeped through his stockinged foot. He was but a living misery.

"Deliver your arms," growled Christopher, shaking him as a terrier shakes a rat, "or you die. Do you yield? Answer!"

"How can he," broke in Cicely, "when you have him by the throat?"

Christopher loosed his grip of the man's windpipe, and instead seized his wrists, whereon the Abbot drew a great breath, for he was almost choked, and fell to his knees, in weakness, not in supplication.

"I came to you for mercy," he said presently, "but, having overheard your talk, know that I can hope for none. Indeed, why should I, who showed none, and whose great cause seems dead, that cause for which I fought and lived? Let me die with it. I ask no more. Still, you are a gentleman, and therefore I beg a favour of you. Do not hand me over to be drawn, hanged and quartered by your brute-king. Kill me now. You can say that I attacked you, and that you did it in self-defence. I have no arms, but you may set a dagger in my hand."

Christopher looked down at the poor creature huddled at his feet and laughed.

"Who would believe me?" he asked; "though, indeed, who would question, seeing that your life is forfeit to me or any who can take it? Yet that is a matter of which the King's Justices shall judge."

Maldon shivered. "Drawn, hanged and quartered," he repeated beneath his breath. "Drawn, hanged and quartered as a traitor to one I never served!"

"Why not?" asked Christopher. "You have played a cruel game, and lost."

He made no answer; indeed, it was Cicely who spoke, saying—

"How came you in such a case? We thought you fled."

"Lady," he answered, "I've starved for three days and nights in a hole in the ground like an earthed-up fox; a culvert in your garden hid me. At last I crept out to see the light and die, and heard you talking, and thought that I would ask for mercy, since mortal extremity has no honour."

"Mercy!" said Cicely. "Of your treasons I say nothing, for you are not English, and serve your own king, who years ago sent you here to plot against England. But look on this man, my husband. Did he not starve for three days and nights in your strong dungeon ere you came thither to massacre him? Did you not strive to burn him in his Hall, and ship him wounded across the seas to doom? Did you not send your assassin to kill my babe, who stood between you and the wealth you needed for your plots, and bind me, the mother, to the stake—a food for fire? Did you not shoot down my father in the wood, fearing lest he should prove you traitor, and after rob me of my heritage? Did you not compel your monks to work evil and bring some of them to their deaths? Oh! have done! Worm dressed up as God's priest, how can you writhe there and ask for mercy?"

"I said I *came* to seek for mercy because the agony of sleepless hunger drove me, who *now* seek only death. Insult not the fallen, Cicely Foterell, but take the vengeance that is your due, and kill," replied the Abbot, looking up at her with his hollow eyes, adding, with a laugh that sounded like a groan, "Come, Sir Christopher; you have got a sword, and it is time you went to supper. The air is cold; your wife—if such she be—said it but now."

"Cicely," said Christopher, "go to the Hall and summon Jeffrey Stokes. Emlyn will know where to find him."

"Emlyn!" groaned the Abbot. "Give me not over to Emlyn. She'd torture me."

"Nay," said Christopher, "this is not Blossholme Abbey; though what may chance in London I know not. Go now, Wife."

But Cicely did not stir; she only stared at the wretched creature at her feet.

"I bid you go," repeated Christopher.

"And I'll not obey," she answered. "Do you remember what I promised Martin ere he died?"

"Martin dead! Is Martin, who saved your husband, dead?" exclaimed the Abbot, lifting his face and letting it fall again. "Happy Martin, to be dead."

"I was not there, and I am not bound by your promises, Cicely."

"But I am, and you and I are one. I vowed mercy to this man if he should fall into our power, and mercy he shall have."

"Then you spare him to destroy us. The wheels go round quick in England, Wife."

"So be it. What I vowed, I vowed. With God be the rest. He has watched us well heretofore, and I think," she added, with one of her bursts of triumphant faith, "will do so to the end. Abbot Maldon, sinful, fallen Abbot Maldon, you are as you were made, and Martin, the saint, said that there is good in your heart, though you have shown none of it to me or mine. Now, look you; yonder is a wooden summer-house, thatched and warm. Get you there, and I'll send you food and wine and new clothing by one who will not talk; also a pass to Lincoln. By to-morrow's dawn you will be refreshed, and then you will find a good horse tied to yonder tree, and so away to sanctuary at Lincoln, and, if aught of ill befalls you afterwards, know it is not our doing, but that of some other enemy, or of God, with Whom I pray you make your peace. May He forgive you, as I do, Who knows all hearts, which I do not. Now, farewell. Nay, say nothing. There is nothing to be said. Come, Christopher, for this once you obey me, not I you."

So they went, and the wretched man raised himself upon his hands and looked after them, but what passed in his heart at that moment none will ever learn.

****

Some months had gone by and Blossholme, with all the country round, was once more at peace. The tide of trouble had rolled away northward, whence came rumours of renewed rebellion. Abbot Maldon had been seen no more, and for a while it was believed that al-

550

though he never took sanctuary at Lincoln, he had done a wiser thing and fled to Spain. Then Emlyn, who heard everything, got news that this was not so, but that he was foremost among those who stirred up sedition and war along the Scottish border.

"I can well believe it," said Cicely. "The sow must to its wallowing in the mire. Nature made him a plotter, and he will follow his heart to the end."

"Ere long he may find it hard to follow his head," answered Emlyn grimly. "Oh, to think that you had that wolf caged and turned him loose again to prey on England and on us!"

"I did but show mercy to the fallen, Nurse."

"Mercy? I call it madness. Why, when Jeffrey and Thomas heard of it I thought they would burst with rage, especially Jeffrey, who loved your father well and loved not the infidel galleys," answered the fierce Emlyn.

"Vengeance is mine, I will repay, saith the Lord," murmured Cicely in a gentle voice.

"The Lord also said that whoso sheddeth man's blood by man shall his blood be shed. Why, I've heard this Maldon quote it to your husband at Cranwell Towers."

"So will it be, Emlyn, if so it is to be, only let others shed that cruel blood. I would not have it on my hands or on those of any of my house, for after all he is an ordained priest of my own faith. Moreover, I had promised. Still, talk not of the matter lest it should bring trouble on us all, who had no right to loose him. Also these are ill thoughts for your wedding day. Go, deck yourself in those fine clothes which Jacob Smith has sent from London, since the clergyman will be at Blossholme church by four, and I think that Thomas has waited long enough for you."

Emlyn smiled a little, and shrugged her broad shoulders, muttering something that would have angered Thomas if he could have heard it, as Cicely went off to join Christopher, who called to her from another room.

She found him adding up figures on paper, a very different Christopher to the broken man they had rescued from the dungeon, though still much aged by the terrors of the past year and just now looking rueful.

"See, Sweet," he said, "we should give a marriage portion to Emlyn, who has earned it if ever woman did, but where it is to come from I know not. Those Abbey lands Jacob Smith bought from the King are not yours yet, nor Henry's either, though doubtless he will have them soon. Neither have any rents been paid to you from your own estates, and when they come they are promised up in London, while the Abbot's razor has shaved my own poor parsimony bare as a churchyard skull. Also Mother Matilda and her nuns must be kept till we can endow them with their lands again. One day we, or our boy yonder, may be rich, but till it comes there are hard times for all of us."

"Not so hard as some we have known, Husband," she answered, laughing, "for at least we are free and have food to eat, and for the rest we will borrow from Jacob Smith on the jewels that remain over. Indeed, I have written to him and he will not refuse."

"Aye, but how about Thomas and Emlyn?"

"They must do as their betters do. Though there is little stock on it, Thomas has the Manor Farm at low rent, which he may pay when he can, while Jacob put a present in the pocket of Emlyn's wedding dress. What's more, I think he will make her his heir, and if so she will be rich indeed, so rich that I shall have to curtsey to her. Now, go make ready for this marriage, and as you have no fine doublet, bid Jeffrey put on your mail, for you look best in that, or so at least I think, who to my mind look best in anything you chance to wear."

Then while he demurred, saying that there was now no need to bear arms in Blossholme, also that Jeffrey was away settling himself as landlord of the Ford Inn, the same that the Abbot had once promised to Flounder Megges, she kissed him, and seizing her boy, who lay crowing in the sunlight, danced with him from the room. For oh, Cicely's heart was merry.

****

There were many folk at the marriage of Emlyn Stower and Thomas Bolle, for of late Blossholme had been but a sorry place, and this wedding came to it like the breath of spring to the woods and meads around, a hint of happiness after the miseries of winter. The story of the pair had got about also. How they had been pledged in youth and separated by scheming men for their own purposes. How Emlyn had been married off against her will to an aged partner whom she hated, and Thomas, who was set down as a fool, forced to serve the monastery as a lay-brother, a strong hind skilled in the management of cattle and such matters, but half crazy, as indeed it had suited him to feign himself to be.

People knew the end of the thing also; that Emlyn had cursed the Abbot, and that her curse had been fulfilled. That Thomas Bolle had shaken off his superstitious fears and risen up against him and at last been given the commission of the King, and, as his Grace's officer, shown himself no fool but a man of mettle who had taken the Abbey by storm and rescued Sir Christopher Harflete from its dungeons. Emlyn also, like her mistress, had been bound to the stake as a witch, and saved from burning by this same Thomas, who with her had been concerned in many remarkable events whereof the countryside was full of tales, true or false. Now at last after all these adventures they came together to be wed, and who was there for ten miles round that would not see it done?

The monks being gone Father Roger Necton, the old vicar of Cranwell, he who had united Christopher and his wife Cicely in strange circumstances, and for that deed been obliged to fly for his life when the last Abbot of Blossholme burned Cranwell Towers, came to tie the knot before his great congregation. Notwithstanding that they were both of middle age, Emlyn in her grand gown and the brawny, red-haired Thomas in his yeoman's garb of green, such as he had worn when he wooed her many years before he put on the monk's russet robe, made a fine and handsome pair at the altar. Or so folk thought, though some friend of the monks, remembering Bolle's devil's livery and Emlyn's repute as a sorceress, cried out from the shadow that Satan was marrying a witch, and for his pains got his head broken by Jeffrey Stokes.

So the white-haired and gentle Father Necton, having first read the King's order releasing Thomas from his vows, tied them fast according to the ancient rites and blessed them both. At length it was finished, and the pair walked from the old church to the Manor Farm, where they were to dwell, followed, as was the custom, by a company of their friends and well-wishers. As they went they passed through a little stretch of woodland by the stream, where on this spring day the wild daffodils and lilies of the valley were abloom making sweet the air. Here Emlyn paused a moment and said to her husband, Captain Bolle—

"Do you remember this place?"

"Aye, Wife," he answered, "it was here that we plighted our troth in youth, and looked up to see Maldon passing us just beyond that same oak, and felt the shadow of him strike cold to our hearts. You spoke of it yonder in the Priory chapel when I came up by the secret way, and its memory made me mad."

"Yes, Thomas, I spoke of it," answered Emlyn in a rich and gentle voice, a new voice to him. "Well, now let its memory make you happy, as, notwithstanding all my faults, I will if I can," and swiftly she bent towards him and kissed him, adding, "Come on, Husband, they press behind us and I hope that we have done with perils and plottings."

"Amen," answered Bolle, and as he spoke certain strange men who wore the King's colours and carried a long ladder went by them at a distance. Wondering what was their business at Blossholme, the pair passed through the last of the woodland and reached the rise whence they could see the gaunt skeleton of the burnt-out Abbey that appeared within fifty paces of them. At this they paused to look, and presently were joined there by Christopher and Cicely, Mother Matilda and her good nuns, Jeffrey Stokes, and others. The place seemed grim and desolate in the evening light, and all of them stood staring at it filled with their separate thoughts.

"What is that?" said Cicely, with a start, pointing to a round black object new set over the ruin of the gateway tower.

Just then a red ray from the sunset struck upon the thing.

It was the severed head of Clement Maldon the Spaniard.

CPSIA information can be obtained
at www.ICGtesting.com
Printed in the USA
BVHW042124220522
637755BV00001B/1

9 781846 779978